SO-FES-163

Sarah's Holy Mountain

D.W. HOFFMAN

DISCARDED

ADAMS PRESS
CHICAGO, IL

Dillsburg Area Public Library

204 Mumper Lane
Dillsburg, PA 17019

Copyright © 1995
by D.W. HOFFMAN

LIBRARY OF CONGRESS
CATALOG CARD #95-94424

ISBN: 0-9650656-5-0

PRINTED IN THE
UNITED STATES OF AMERICA

SARAH'S HOLY MOUNTAIN

A Novel By

D. W. Hoffman

1

A MEETING OF MINDS?

I must confess at the outset, and with not a little regret, that I never had a personal acquaintance with the young girl whose story I am about to relate to you. That is to say, I never actually had the pleasure of meeting her face to face, or even of speaking with her on the telephone or of corresponding with her by post. As a matter of fact, most of the events I am about to describe took place some years before my own rather unremarkable existence in this world commenced. In order to tell this story, therefore, I have had to rely solely on the testimony of others. If I am unable to reveal the identity of these "others," it is not because I wish to protect them, or feel that they are even in need of protecting: it is because they have chosen not to reveal themselves to me. They came to me unseen, most often during those early hours of the morning just before night gives way to day, within that mysterious portal between darkness and light which seems to belong to neither day nor night, to neither waking nor sleeping. It may be suggested by some that these "others" did not exist at all, that the story came entirely from my own imagination, from out of my own mind, and I would not wish to spend an undue amount of time arguing the point. I would only ask, do any of us fully understand what "imagination" is? what "mind" is? I only know that I awoke one morning and the story was there. It came unsolicited and unexpected. I had the "sense" that it was *given* to me, that it came not so much *from* my mind as *through* my mind, but this "sense," not being one of the five through which we are accustomed to perceiving the world, is not a clear one, and I cannot with any certainty confirm its intimations. Whatever the source—or sources—I found the story to be an intriguing one, and I felt absolutely compelled from the very first to commit it to paper. Had I known at the beginning what I know now—that the story would continue to unfold over a period of weeks and months and even years—I would never have had the patience or courage to begin. But the task is now completed, and I hereby give the story to you as it was given to me—or as I conceived it out of my own imagination, as the case may be.

It is the story of a young girl who grew up in the mountains of western North Carolina in the 1930s and -40s. She was, by all accounts, a very unusual girl, but beyond that, not all accounts agree. Some believed her to be an angel sent from Heaven; others, a practitioner of witchcraft, a maidservant of the Devil. Whether she was good or evil—on the side of the angels or in the service of darker powers—the reader will have to judge for him-or herself. But whether one judges her favorably or unfavorably—indeed, whether one even finds her to be a credible character at all, or a total fiction, the product of unrestrained imagination—will depend, as in all things, as much on one's own understanding of reality as on the facts themselves.

There is a temptation to begin this story on that warm, end-of-summer afternoon in September of 1932, when Sarah first came to Rushing Creek. She was just a child then, bright and energetic, not quite six years of age. But to better understand Sarah, it is necessary to first say something about her parents, Daniel Wicker and Elizabeth Ashby Wicker, and about those earlier years lived in Massachusetts. In order to do that, we must go back another twelve years, to the spring of 1920.

When Daniel Wicker left his home in the Blue Ridge Mountains of western North Carolina in the spring of 1920, he did not expect that he would ever again set foot in the small town of Rushing Creek or drop his fishing line into the swift-flowing stream which had given the town its name. The youngest of five children, he had seen no future for himself on the family farm. During the labor-short war years his services on the farm had been absolutely indispensable, but when his two older brothers, Isaac and Jacob, returned home from the war late in 1918, young Daniel's role was again reduced to that of mere lackey. Then in the fall of 1919, his sister Hester, to whom he had been especially close, had, at the age of twenty-six, finally gotten married. Having found no one in Rushing Creek or in the neighboring hills and hollows who would have her—or whom she considered worthy of having—she had given herself to an "outlander," to a big, congenial fellow of Swedish stock named Nathan Andersson, who had moved down from Ohio and had bought the John R. Hyatt farm just outside of Rushing Creek. John R. Hyatt was one of those less fortunate ones who had not returned from the war.

Besides his two brothers, Isaac and Jacob, and his sister Hester, there had been another sibling, a sister named Ruth, who had been Hester's twin, but as Ruth had died in childhood when Daniel was only four, he had no memory of her. The four older children—Isaac, Jacob, and the twins—had all been born within three years of one another, but Daniel had come along seven years later, at a time when his mother had thought that her days of "lookin' after babes" was long since past. Consequently, the main burden of raising young Daniel had fallen upon his sister Hester, who was all of seven years old when he was born—"plenny old enough," in the words of their mother, "to be lookin' after young'uns." As a result of this circumstance, there had developed a close bond between Daniel and Hester, one that had only strengthened as the two children grew older. But when Hester moved out of the house in the fall of 1919 to make a home with her new husband, the bond that had held Daniel to the home place had begun to come undone, and with the death of his father three months later, it had loosened even more.

When Daniel left Rushing Creek in the spring of 1920 he had no clear idea as to where he was going, except north. Why he stepped off the train in Springfield, Massachusetts, rather than in any of the scores of other cities and towns in the industrial Northeast, he could not have told you precisely. Perhaps it was the name. Both "spring" and "field" were words that conjured up familiar and agreeable images in his mind, and to a young man of twenty, such as himself, embarking on his first adventure into the world beyond the friendly confines of his native mountains, anything that looked or sounded familiar—anything that reminded him of home—was especially welcome. Moreover, Springfield had all the appearance of being a bustling town, a place where an ambitious young man such as himself could find work. His hunch proved to be right. On the very day of his arrival, within hours of stepping off the train, he was hired by the J. M. Stanton Machine and Tool Company. By evening of the same day he had found himself a place to stay and the next morning he reported for his first day of work. He had never worked as a machinist before, but as he had been raised on a farm, where a man had to learn to do just about everything with his hands, he learned quickly and soon became adept at his new job. His life in the north had begun.

But it was not until he met Elizabeth Ashby three years later that he knew for certain that it was Providence that had steered him to Springfield. He met her in Forest Park on a Sunday afternoon in the spring of 1923. He had just received a letter from his sister Hester in which she had described spring bursting forth in all its glory in the Carolina hills—it was always in the spring of the year that he felt the most homesick—and he had walked down along the Connecticut River to the park after church that Sunday afternoon, hoping to breathe in some fresh spring air and, perchance, to find some nourishment for his soul.

As he strolled down the wooded path toward the pond, he noticed a bicycle leaning against a clump of white birch trees. It was not unusual to see bicycles in the park—they were a common sight on Sunday afternoons during the spring and summer months—but as this one was a woman's bike, and as it was standing alone, Daniel's curiosity was aroused. He saw no one at first, but as he drew nearer, he was able to make out, through the trunks of white birch, the form of a female figure seated on the ground on the other side. He had meant only to steal a quick glimpse of her as he passed by, but when he saw that her attention was completely absorbed in the sketchpad on her lap and in the subjects of her sketch—several small children feeding the ducks in the pond—he allowed his eyes to linger for a moment. She was a young, well-dressed woman—he judged her to be in her late teens or early twenties—and as he passed, she looked up at him and smiled. Daniel nodded respectfully, but did not speak.

He would not have known how to begin to address such an elegant-looking young lady—even had he still had the breath to do so.

When he reached the edge of the pond, he squatted down on his haunches, closed his eyes, and allowed the warm rays of the sun to soak into his winter-bleached, machine-shop face. Peaceful moments passed as he listened, with eyes closed, to the laughter of the children, to the quacking of the ducks, to the singing of the birds, and to the humming of bees and other insects. All the creatures of wood and pond, as well as the human creatures only visiting from the town, seemed to have joined voices to celebrate the return of spring and the end of the long period of inactivity or exile that winter had imposed upon them.

Even though he was no more than an easy stone's throw from the clump of white birches, under which sat the young lady with the sketchpad, he might never have met her at all if it had not been for a chance gust of wind. A distressed cry of "Oh dear!" caused him to wake from his reverie and look around. Upon doing so, he saw the young lady of the birches in pursuit of half a dozen sheets of paper—presumably her drawings—which the playful breeze had rendered airborne. As the fugitive foils of paper were on a course that would carry them directly into the pond, Daniel sprang to his feet in an attempt to head them off. He gathered two of them quickly, chased down a third, and arrived at a fourth at exactly the same moment as the young woman herself. He picked it up and handed it to her, along with the other three.

"What wonderful hands you have," she said, smiling, as she took the drawings and placed them on top of the two which she herself had retrieved.

Her words fell on deaf ears. All of Daniel's senses were concentrated into the single sense of sight at the moment. He had never seen such a divinely beautiful creature in all his life. The gusting breeze had partially undone her long, dark brown hair, allowing loose curls of it to spill into her face and down over her shoulders. While clutching the drawings in one hand, she reached with the other to her face and pushed aside the stray locks of hair which had fallen over her eyes. When her eyes met his he felt all the strength go out of his body. She had the softest, brownest, most fetchingly beautiful eyes he had ever seen. Again she smiled at him.

"You're welcome, ma'am," he mumbled incoherently.

Tickled at his response, she laughed a quiet, gentle laugh. "I *do* thank you for saving my drawings, but what I said was, you have wonderful hands."

Uncomprehending, Daniel lifted his hands to belt level and stared at them, rotating them backs to palms as he did so. "They're just hands, ma'am."

"They're *working* hands."

"Yes, ma'am," he replied apologetically, looking at his rough, soiled hands, "I reckon they are that. I was raised on a farm. An' for the past three years I been a-workin' at Mr. J. M. Stanton's machine shop here in Springfield."

She smiled, but whether to register her approval or her sympathy, Daniel could not be sure.

"That farm on which you were raised," she asked, still smiling congenially, "would that by any chance have been in the South?" There was no doubt in her mind that it was.

"Yes,ma'am, hit would. I'm from . . . "

"No, let me guess! . . . Virginia!"

"No, ma'am, I'm from, . . . "

"North Carolina!"

"That's right, ma'am. Rushin' Creek, North Carolina."

"Russian Creek? That's a curious name for a town in North Carolina. Was it settled by Russians?"

"No, ma'am, at least not so far as I know. The town was named after the creek."

"But why was the creek called Russian Creek?"

"I reckon 'cause it runs so fast. By all rights hit should be called a river, but the folks who first settled thar called it Rushin' *Creek,* an' the name stuck."

"Oh!" exclaimed the young woman, feeling a little foolish, "*Rushing* Creek!"

"Yes, ma'am, Rushin' Creek."

"Rushing Creek," she repeated to herself, "I like the sound of that! It sounds romantic!"

Daniel gave her a quizzical look. "Romantic, ma'am? Rushin' Creek?"

She pushed the hair out of her eyes again. "By the way, you don't have to call me 'ma'am.' My name is Elizabeth. Elizabeth Ashby."

"Dan'l Wicker, ma'am . . . I mean, Miss 'Lizbeth. I'm mighty pleased t' meet yuh." He thought of offering his hand, but decided it wouldn't be proper to shake hands with a young woman–certainly not with a young woman as proper and elegant as the one standing before him now–and certainly not with his rough hands. But what *was* he expected to do? Was he expected to *kiss* her hand? He had never kissed anyone's hand before in his life. She did not seem to be expecting him to do anything. She was not holding out her hand for him to kiss *or* shake. She was simply standing there, completely at ease, smiling benignly at him. But though *she* appeared to be perfectly comfortable with the awkward silence that followed the exchanging of their names, he found *himself* becoming increasingly uneasy. He could not understand why she kept looking at him. He was not, however, about to ask her to leave.

"Could I ask a favor of you?" she said at last.

"I'll do anythang I can t' be of help, ma'am."

"Elizabeth," she reminded him.

"Miss 'Lizbeth . . . ma'am."

"Would you allow me to draw you?"

"You want t' *drar* me?" he asked, surprised and a little embarrassed.

"Yes, I'd like to draw your face. Would you be so kind as to allow that?"

Daniel blushed. "Well, I reckon that would be all right by me, ma'am . . . Miss 'Lizbeth. . . but why anyone would want t' drar this homely face, I'm sure I cain't imagine."

But Elizabeth Ashby had seen something in Daniel Wicker's face. It was not a particularly handsome face, but it was a pleasant face—open and honest—and in it could be seen, at one and the same time, both an inner strength and a childlike innocence. It was not the kind of face Elizabeth had been accustomed to seeing. She had been born into an upper middle-class family. Her father, Horace Ashby, had risen from humble beginnings and had accumulated a small fortune over the years as a result of his various business ventures and investments. He had become a self-proclaimed master of the art of "buying low and selling high," but what all it was exactly that he "bought low" and "sold high," Elizabeth had never had a very clear idea—nor sufficient interest to want to find out. Her father had always maintained that he had discovered one Great Truth in life, and it was a truth he had tried to communicate to Elizabeth over the dinner table ever since she was about six years of age: "Remember, Elizabeth, it *takes* money to *make* money. Borrow it if you have to, steal it if you must, but get it! Once you've got *some*, the rest will come easy. Money *makes* money!" Not a religious man, he nonetheless sometimes cited a passage in the Bible to support the Great Truth he had discovered: "To those who have, more will be given; from those who have not, even that which they have will be taken away."

Elizabeth was able to forgive her father in part for his obsession with money. She supposed that if she had been born as poor as he had been, she might have been more interested in money as well. But as it was, all her father's talk about money usually left her depressed. She found the subject deathly uninspiring. She was more interested in the arts herself—in music, painting, poetry, and literature—which she considered far more noble pursuits of the human spirit than the pursuit of material wealth. She had come to see her father as a sort of blind mole, who spent all his life's energy burrowing underground in search of insects and grubs. By contrast, she saw herself as a bird soaring freely through the air, who touched down to earth only rarely, and then only to take a sip of poetry or to consume a few crumbs of philosophy before taking flight again.

Elizabeth had spent three years at Wellesley College, but had not returned for her final year because she had come to find the structure and routine of formal schooling unsuitable to her free-soaring creative spirit. Horace Ashby had wanted his daughter to finish school, not because he had any particular use for art and poetry and the other subjects she had been studying—"It takes money to make money" was as close as he ever came to reciting a line of poetry himself—but because of the status that a college diploma automatically bestowed upon its recipient, and because a diploma was often a prerequisite to entering many of the more lucrative professions. He had wanted his only child to have all the advantages that he had never had when he was a young man scratching to make his fortune. Undoubtedly he would have preferred that his only child had been a son, and it is questionable whether he would have been willing to pay to have a daughter educated had she not been his only child, but, in the absence of a son, he had not hesitated to make a heavy investment in his daughter's future. It was, in large part, because of this substantial monetary investment that he had been quite furious at her when she announced at dinner one evening, soon after she had finished her third year at Wellesley, that she would not be returning for her final year to get her degree.

But Horace Ashby was not a man to suffer losses lightly. He was determined, if at all possible, to find some other means to turn his investment to good profit. If his foolish daughter could not be trusted to secure her own future, he had no choice but to take matters into his own hands. Having concluded that the only way she would ever succeed in attaining to a level of wealth which he considered adequate, was if she married into it, he had determined to make the best possible match for her. It should not, he had thought, be difficult to find her a husband of means. She was not, after all, an unattractive girl. Foolish, yes. A dreamer, yes. But not unattractive. And she *was* educated. Accordingly, he and his wife had gone to some trouble to see that their daughter met all the eligible young men in the community, and from communities as far away as Boston, who, in their opinion, had "good breeding" or "good connections." But Elizabeth found them, to a man, uninspiring, and after nearly two years of being forced into the company of one such insipid creature after another, she decided that she would as soon stay home in her room with Keats or Shelley or Lord Byron as to have to spend yet another evening with someone with "good breeding" or "good connections."

The problem with all these worthies, in Elizabeth's opinion, was that they were not authentic human beings: they were merely expensive imitations. Behind the well-groomed, finely-tailored facades, there was little or nothing of interest to be found. They were as hollow and disingenuous as the store-front manikins they so closely resembled. They deliberately avoided contact with the real world. They would never have condescended to setting foot in the fields, factories, foundries, and workshops where the real work of the world was being conducted, where the real drama of life was being played out. To Elizabeth's way of thinking, they were little more than parasites who lived off the labor of others. They depended on others to feed them, clothe them, and maintain their dwellings for them. They had learned from others of their ilk how to ride on the backs of the working poor and to pick their pockets at the same time. When they chose to play an active role in the world at all, they invariably chose to go into one of the prestigious white-color professions—into banking or "financial management," into law or politics—which would allow them to continue to grow rich and fat on the blood and sweat of others.

If any of these gentlemen of "good breeding" were to be suddenly deprived of the social and economic structure which allowed their kind to exist—if any of them were to be somehow shipwrecked and left stranded on a desert island like Robinson Crusoe—he would, in Elizabeth's opinion, perish within a week. Because they had always had the money to buy everything they had ever needed or wanted, they had never learned to do anything for themselves. As a species they were totally unfit for survival. If, by some ironic twist of fate, Elizabeth mused, the whole worthless lot of them were stranded on a desert island together, they would perish in *less* than a week, as they would certainly bore one another to death. There were plenty of young women, who, out of desire for security or status, were only too willing and anxious to marry such men, but Elizabeth did not count herself among them.

The problem with such men, in Elizabeth's opinion, and with all others who aspired to be like them, was that they failed to appreciate the singular opportunity that life presented. Elizabeth had come to see life as a great adventure, frought with struggle, yes, with hardship, yes, with disappointment and insecurity, yes; but also rich with possibilities: possibilities for triumph, growth, and joy. But these young men of means did not seem to see it that way. Instead they seemed to see life as something to be got through as easily, as comfortably, and with as little effort as possible. Their highest goal in life seemed to be the acquisition of ever more wealth, and the enjoyment of the comfort, leisure, and status that wealth provided. To Elizabeth's mind such lives were without value or meaning, and those who lived such lives would, in the end, leave this world empty-handed, all of their accumulated wealth notwithstanding. They would leave this life without ever having experienced it.

For Elizabeth's part, she wanted to experience all of life: all of its richness, all of its fullness, all of its joys, all of its sorrows. Life was too precious and too fleeting to settle for anything less. What was the point of being alive, of being human, if one was not going to be part of life, not going to participate in the human experience? In her father and mother's circle of friends she had seen too many gentlemen and gentlewomen who had failed to participate, who had held themselves aloof from life, who had not only avoided the struggle, but who held those engaged in it in a kind of contempt. As a result, she thought, they lacked substance, character, the inner strength that comes from struggle, the inner confidence that comes from success in that struggle. In Daniel Wicker's face–and in his hands–she saw that substance, that character, that strength, that confidence–all those things she had not seen heretofore.

There was something else Elizabeth Ashby saw in Daniel Wicker. In addition to the many fine intrinsic qualities she saw in him–his natural, unaffected manner; his total openness and honesty; his cheerful acceptance of his humble lot in life; his warmth, his gentleness, his self-effacing sense of humor–she saw in him also a means to an end. Elizabeth's mind was an engine racing, fueled by the songs of poets and the visions of philosophers. But she had no means of engaging that mind in the world. She feared that if she did not, she might spend the rest of her life skittering all over the place, a bird unable to land. Or worse, she might end up in an institution for the mentally insane. The specter of mental insanity was one that had haunted her all her young life. Her mother's family had a history of mental illness. Her mother herself suffered from chronic depression. For her mother life was little more than a seemingly endless series of days and nights–each day like the day before, each night like the night before–which had to be patiently endured, until merciful Death finally intervened and cut the thread.

Elizabeth's mother, while hardly a model of sound mental health, was, nevertheless, not insane, and no psychiatrist would have pronounced her so. She had not slipped over the edge. Elizabeth's Aunt Katherine, however–her mother's younger sister–apparently *had* slipped over the edge. Katherine had, by all accounts, left little doubt concerning the question of her sanity, or lack thereof. From an early age Katherine had heard voices inside her head. It was as a result of following the promptings of these "voices" that Katherine's behavior had often been bizarre, and, at times, extremely dangerous. At the age of ten she had inflicted a serious, though not fatal, wound in her mother's neck with a kitchen knife. At the age of eleven, she had tried, unsuccessfully, to set fire to the house. Considered too dangerous to be allowed to run free after this latter incident, she had been moved into a small cottage on the grounds behind the house. At the age of sixteen, she attempted to burn this down as well. This time she succeeded, and as she was locked inside at the time, she had perished in the fire. At least this was the story as Elizabeth had heard it from her mother, as all this had taken place some years before Elizabeth was born.

It might be thought that a skeleton such as Katherine might be kept locked securely in the family closet and not be allowed to see the light of day, but Elizabeth could remember hearing about Katherine from a very early age. Whenever Elizabeth had misbehaved as a child–whenever she had become over-emotional, as she had occasionally been wont to do–her mother had often brought up Katherine as a warning: "Behave yourself," she would say, "or the same thing will happen to you that happened to your Aunt Katherine."

Elizabeth saw no reason to tell Daniel about the mental instability on her mother's side of the family. After all, she was *not* her mother, she was *not* Katherine. She felt that she herself had a perfectly sound mind. All she needed was a way to engage that mind–that racing engine–into the machinery of the world. She saw in Daniel the transmission for which she had been looking, the means that would allow her to translate her idealism into reality.

The one and only time that Elizabeth invited Daniel to her home to meet her parents was not a happy occasion. Elizabeth had not expected it would be. It was simply something that had to be done. The Ashbys were coldly polite throughout dinner, but they made no effort to conceal the fact that they did not share their daughter's enthusiasm for this rustic young man. When Daniel left, they expressed their concerns to Elizabeth. It was Elizabeth's mother who spoke first.

"I suppose he's a nice enough young man," she whined, "but, for God's sake, Elizabeth, he's from the working class."

Her father was even less tactful. "I'm sorry to say, that young fellow has no prospects whatsoever." In his opinion there was nothing more to be said.

"But, Daddy," objected Elizabeth, "he's a good, honest, hard-working man."

"Don't be a fool, Elizabeth. Nobody ever made any money by working."

Elizabeth made no further verbal protestation, but in the quiet rage that burned within her at that moment, any lingering doubts that she might have had about marrying Daniel Wicker were consumed.

From the moment he had met Elizabeth Ashby, Daniel Wicker's life had taken on the quality of a dream, and any morning he expected to wake up to find himself back on the cold doorstep of the real world. He could not begin to comprehend what this beautiful and educated young woman, who could have had any man her heart desired, had seen in a simple country boy like himself. In May of 1924, a little more than a year after that first meeting in Forest Park, over the strong objections of Elizabeth's parents, Daniel and Elizabeth were married. He was twenty-four, she was twenty-two. The Ashbys did not attend the wedding.

Daniel gave up his room at the boarding house where he had lived for four years and rented a small house on the outskirts of town. It was a small, unpretentious house, with a white picket fence around it, a few shade trees, and enough space in the back for a garden. Daniel continued to work at the machine shop, though now he had to walk two miles to get to work. But he enjoyed the walk and wondered why he had ever decided to live so close to the shop in the first place. Elizabeth spent most of her days at home, looking after the house and tending the garden she had planted. Her artistic touch could soon be seen in both house and garden. She took up needlework, and before the summer was over, there was not a towel or pillowcase in the house that was not embroidered with one of her own designs. Her garden was a jumble of colors and textures, with flowers and vegetables all mixed together. When she wasn't at home, she could usually be found riding her bicycle, either along the river, or through the park, or along the roads outside of town, and always she carried her sketchpad with her. She especially liked to draw simple people at work. Ever since she was a schoolgirl, one of her favorite paintings had been "The Gleaners" by French painter Jean Francois Millet. Millet had often used simple peasants as subject matter for his paintings, and Elizabeth too found simple working people the most interesting to draw. Among her own drawings, one of her favorites was of an elderly woman in bonnet and long dress to the ground, hoeing her beans. Another was of two small children with woven wooden baskets picking raspberries along a country road. Before long there was not a wall in the house that wanted for one of Elizabeth's drawings.

Elizabeth was happy. She had wanted her life to be a poem, a song, a work of art. Had her mother or father ever come to visit her–which they did not–they would not have found anything very poetic or romantic about their daughter's life. But Elizabeth's heart was full. Then, on November 12, 1926, Sarah was born.

If Elizabeth's heart was full before, now it was overflowing. As contented as she had been before Sarah's arrival, now she wondered how she had ever lived without her. Elizabeth had taken up knitting when she had first learned that she was with child, so even before Sarah was born she had a drawer full of sweaters and booties waiting for her. Daniel was a proud father, albeit a little apprehensive in the beginning. He was reluctant at first to pick the baby up for fear that his rough, soiled hands, which handled hard metal all day, might injure a creature so small and clean and fragile-seeming. But with experience, along with Elizabeth's repeated assurances that the baby actually preferred his bigger, rougher hands to her own, Daniel soon overcame his trepidation. And indeed little Sarah did seem quite happy to be held by her father.

During the next several years Elizabeth's life was the poem she had always dreamed for herself. She took great delight in watching Sarah grow into a beautiful little girl. The two were inseparable. Elizabeth never did anything or went anywhere without her–Daniel had even made a seat for Sarah on the back of Elizabeth's bicycle–yet she never seemed to tire of being with her. When Sarah learned to walk, she wanted to go everywhere and see and touch everything. When she learned to talk, she asked every question a child had ever asked, and even asked some which Elizabeth was sure had never been asked before. Elizabeth did her best to answer Sarah's questions, trying to explain the world in terms the child could understand, but she was not always successful. Occasionally she would find it necessary to tell Sarah, "Honey, you will understand better when you're older," but would then wonder to herself if Sarah was able to grasp the concept of "older," or whether any concept of time other than the present moment made any sense in Sarah's seemingly timeless world.

There were many wonderful moments during those early years that Elizabeth would have loved to have preserved into eternity, moments with Daniel, moments with Sarah, when Elizabeth would utter a silent prayer, "Please don't let this moment pass away." But the passing of time was not something she dreaded. The prospect that this child would be with her for many years to come—years in which they would continue to learn and grow together—was a pleasing one to Elizabeth—even if the child did at times ask the most vexing questions.

When these questions first started, Elizabeth felt it to be her duty as a mother to come up with answers, no matter how unsatisfactory the answers might be, even to herself. An exchange that took place one evening in the spring of 1930 as Elizabeth was getting Sarah ready for bed was not untypical. Sarah was three and a half at the time.

"Mommy, do I *have* to go to bed?"

"Yes, Sarah, you *have* to go to bed."

"But why?"

"Because you need your sleep."

"But why do I need my sleep?"

"All children need to sleep, Sarah. Mommies and Daddies too."

"But why?"

"Because if we didn't sleep, we'd all be very tired. You'd be too tired to play, your Daddy would be too tired to go to work . . . "

"Why does Daddy have to go to work? Why doesn't he stay home and play with me?"

"Your Daddy has to go to work to earn money."

"But why does he have to earn money?"

"So he can pay the rent, for one thing. If he didn't pay the rent, we wouldn't have a house to live in . . . So he can buy us food to eat, for another . . . "

"But why couldn't we just live outside like the squirrels in the park and eat acorns?"

"I think we would get very cold if we lived outside in the winter. And I think we would find that acorns are not very tasty."

"If I didn't like them, I wouldn't eat them."

"Yes, I'm quite sure of *that*. But you'd have to eat *something*."

"Why?"

"We *have* to eat, Sarah. If we didn't eat, we'd get weak and . . ." She had been about to say, "we'd get weak and die," but had caught herself in time. She was having enough trouble explaining why it was necessary to eat and sleep without going into a detailed exposition of complex physiological processes of which she herself had only a passing understanding. She did not wish to further complicate her life by introducing the subject of dying. Besides, she reasoned, a child of three and a half had a right to be spared *some* things. Knowledge of death would come soon enough.

Sarah paused for a moment to ponder her mother's answers. Elizabeth seized the opportunity to help Sarah out of her dress and into her nightgown. As she tucked Sarah under the covers and kissed her on the forehead, she could see by the pained expression on her daughter's face that there was at least one more question struggling to be born.

"Mommy, where do I go when I sleep?"

"You don't go anywhere, Honey. You stay right here in your bed all night."

"*All* night?"

"Yes, *all* night."

"Not *all* night. Sometimes I get up to go to the bathroom."

"Well, yes, sometimes you get up to go to the bathroom."

"But sometimes I wet my bed," she said meekly, apologetically. It was evident from the plaintive tone of her voice that this was a habit that caused her some embarrassment.

Elizabeth had been so sure that Sarah was going to ask, "Why do we have to go to the bathroom?" that she now found it necessary to shift gears in mid-thought. She had temporarily to abandon her roll as teacher and assume another role that fell to all mothers, that of comforter.

"Yes, sometimes you wet the bed. But that's all right, Honey. Sometimes we can't help if we wet the bed."

"Do *you* wet *your* bed too, Mommy?"

Elizabeth smiled. "No, Sarah. I meant that little children can't help if they sometimes wet their beds."

"I only wet my bed when I don't get back in time."

"When you don't get back in time from where?"

"From wherever it is that I go when I'm asleep."

"Good night, Sarah."

"Good night, Mommy."

Elizabeth turned off the light and left the room, closing the door behind her. But if she thought that by putting Sarah to bed and closing the door would give her respite from the questions, she was mistaken. Two hours later, as she lay in bed herself, she found herself still thinking about some of Sarah's questions and wondering whether she had answered them as well as she could have. "Why can't we live outside like the squirrels in the park?" Sarah had asked. The question had struck Elizabeth as amusing at the time. It was the kind of innocent question that one might expect to come from a child's mind. After all, everyone lived in a house, didn't they? But now, upon further reflection, she realized that not everyone *did* live in a house. In all parts of the world and in all periods of history there have been whole bands and tribes of people who have lived, and who are still living, without permanent shelter. In the early history of the human race, before the discovery of agriculture, nomadism was probably more the rule than the exception. And even after the discovery of agriculture, some peoples, either out of preference or necessity, continued to live a simple, nomadic style of life. She knew, for example, that as recently as the last century, the American Indians of the Great Plains did not live in permanent towns and villages as did some of their Eastern counterparts, but were constantly on the move, following the buffalo herds, which provided them their sustenance. Even in this century, even to this day, the Laplanders of northern Scandinavia do not live in one place year round, but migrate with the reindeer herds, which are as necessary to their survival as the buffalo had been to the Plains Indians. Even now, all around the world, from the Bedouins of the Arabian desert to the aboriginal tribes of Africa, Australia, and South America, there are whole tribes of people who live with only temporary shelter at best, as their ancestors before them have done for millennia. So, while Elizabeth felt that some sort of permanent abode was probably necessary to her *own* happiness and sense of well-being, she realized now that the idea that she had tried to communicate to Sarah, namely, that a house—a permanent shelter—is necessary for survival, was certainly a fallacious one. She would have to correct this misimpression at the first available opportunity. She knew that the question would come up again in any case. Sarah's questions always had a way of coming up again and again.

Another question of Sarah's had caused her to ponder even more deeply. Why do we have to sleep? Why wasn't simple rest sufficient for the body to carry out its restorative activities? Why was it necessary for us to lose consciousness? Did anyone have the answer to that one? And what about Sarah's other question, "Where do I go when I sleep?" Elizabeth had understood that to mean, "When I wake up in the morning, why do I have no memory of those hours that have passed since I went to bed?" But is that what *Sarah* had meant by it?

Sometimes Elizabeth would refer Sarah's questions to Daniel, but he would usually beg off, insisting that he was just a poor country boy who could barely read and write, and he was sure that he had no idea where we go when we sleep, or why we have to go to sleep in the first place; or why the sky was blue and the grass was green; or why there were colors like blue and green in the first place; or why there was sky and grass, or even a world, in the first place, for that matter; or why spiders don't get caught in their own webs; or what caterpillars dream about when they're inside their cocoons, or if they know when they go to sleep that they are going to be moths and butterflies when they wake up.

Daniel was exaggerating when he said that he could hardly read or write. He had had only seven years of formal schooling, but his reading and writing skills were certainly adequate. He continued to exchange letters with his sister Hester on a regular basis. But there was something in his answers to Sarah's questions—or, rather, in his non-answers—that caused Elizabeth to re-evaluate her own attempts to answer Sarah's questions. It occurred to her that it might be a mistake to give Sarah the impression that grown-ups have all the answers. Elizabeth herself had always found existence to be a complete mystery, totally beyond the power of her mind to comprehend. To her the world was a beautiful but totally strange and mysterious place, and no one had ever—nor *could* anyone have ever—explained it to her satisfaction. She also understood that whether one found one's *own* existence, one's *own* life, to be a joyous experience or a heavy burden, depended as much on one's attitude *toward* life as on one's cicumstances *in* it. She decided, therefore, that it might be better to cultivate Sarah's own natural sense of wonder, rather than impose on her that grown-up view of the world that explains everything and leaves no room for wonder.

It was a poor bargain, Elizabeth mused. As we grow from childhood to adulthood we yield up our sense of wonder in exchange for the illusion that we *understand* this world in which we find ourselves, when, in fact, we never really understand it at all: we merely become *more familiar* with it. We give names to things and deceive ourselves into thinking that by so doing we have somehow made the world more comprehensible. Consider the rose. It may very well be the case, as young Juliet philosophized from the balcony, that that which we call a rose by any other name would smell as sweet. But it was also the case that that which we call a rose by any other name would be just as unknowable. We can smell its sweetness, we can see its redness, we can feel its delicate softness—but what *is* this thing we call a rose? And more importantly, what is this thing that is doing the smelling and the seeing and the feeling? What, pray tell, are *we*?

What, pray tell, is consciousness? We accept the fact of consciousness because it is always with us. It is who we are. But who *are* we?–who and what *are* we?–and how is consciousness even possible? How can one collection of atoms and molecules possibly be aware of another? The great secret to life, Elizabeth had decided when she was in college, was to never take consciousness for granted. The moment you take consciousness for granted–the moment you accept it as a given–the moment you cease to be astonished by your own existence in the world–from that moment does the sense of wonder begin to ebb from your life; and once the sense of wonder is extinguished from your life, from that moment do you begin to die. Nothing saddened her more than to think how many enthusiastic little children, innocent and trusting and filled with delight, are transformed over the years into distrustful, cynical, uncaring adults, arrogant in their ignorance and contemptuous of life. It was as though the blood is slowly bled from their veins and replaced with embalming fluid.

Elizabeth took some satisfaction in the knowledge that she had not allowed this to happen to her, not entirely at any rate, and she was determined that she would not allow it to happen to Sarah. She decided that in the weeks and months to come, she would not be Sarah's teacher so much as her fellow-explorer. She wanted to see the world as Sarah saw it. She wanted to be able to look at a rose as though she were seeing that utterly unknowable thing that we have chosen to call a "rose" for the very first time. Sarah, on the other hand, wanted to see the world as her mother saw it. She wanted to know the names of *everything*. In this sometimes-frustrating but always-stimulating interchange between mother and daughter, Elizabeth found that her own sense of wonder–which, it can be truly said, she had never really lost–was being nurtured by her efforts to see the world through Sarah's eyes–a world fresh and new and waiting to be discovered.

Elizabeth considered herself blessed–blessed with a happy marriage, blessed with a beautiful and healthy child, blessed with a modest but comfortable home. Even the news of her father's death early in 1930 did not cause her to change her opinion. She and her father had never been very close. In fact, since the day of her marriage to Daniel, she had not been in communication with either parent. They had made it clear that they no longer considered her their daughter. Consequently, she learned of her father's death not through her mother, but through an old friend of the family, and only then as a result of a chance meeting, and only then two weeks after the fact. It seemed that her father's health had declined almost in direct relation to his financial fortunes, which had suffered a severe setback as a result of the stock market crash in the fall of 1929. Her mother, she learned, was being looked after by friends.

Several months later a letter from Daniel's sister Hester brought news of another death, that of Daniel's mother. Suddenly it seemed to Elizabeth that events in the world outside were conspiring to disrupt their perfect happiness, to invade the little island of blessedness they had created for themselves. Elizabeth had been surprised by how little she had been moved upon learning of her father's death, as she had never thought of herself as an unsympathetic person. She wondered if she had become so obsessed with preserving her own personal happiness—with having it endure, with having it continue—that she was refusing to allow herself to be affected by events in the world outside. But when she found herself sharing deeply in the sorrow that Daniel felt at the loss of his mother, she realized that it was not her capacity for sympathy that had been diminished, but only her ability to feel anything at all for her father. But what Elizabeth could not have known in the spring of 1930 was that any perceived threat to her little island of blessedness posed by these and other outside events would soon be overshadowed by an even greater one, one that would originate not from without, but from within. Even before the year was out the first symptoms of this darker and more insidious threat would begin to manifest themselves.

In order to place this, what to Elizabeth's mind would be an ominous development, in its proper context, it is necessary at this point to say a few words about a certain rag doll that Elizabeth made for Sarah, because it was, in retrospect, just about the time that Sarah was given the rag doll that the first symptoms began to appear. There was nothing very extraordinary about the rag doll itself. It was not a work of art; in fact it was rather commonplace. It was something that Elizabeth quickly pieced together from scraps of cloth one afternoon early in December of 1930. About the only respect in which it differed from the myriad of other objects which flowed out of her reservoir of creative energy, was that the idea for it came not from her own imagination but from one of Daniel's stories.

Over the years, almost from their first meeting that day in Forest Park, Daniel had told Elizabeth stories about his boyhood days in the hills of North Carolina. He might never have spoken of those early years at all if left to himself, but Elizabeth never tired of hearing his stories and always encouraged him to tell more. It all sounded so romantic to her. Even the name "Rushing Creek" had, to her ears, a wild and romantic ring to it. It was during one of these stories that Elizabeth first heard of a rag doll that Daniel's sister Hester had had when she was a child. In those early years, it seems, when Daniel was a "young 'un" and his sister Hester had looked after him, Hester would often carry Daniel in one arm and her doll in the other. Whenever she had needed a free hand to remove a kettle from the stove or to carry a pail of water—or for any other purpose for which a child of seven or eight might require a free hand—she would simply shove the doll into Daniel's small hands and instruct him not to drop it. More often than not, he *would* drop it, which would result in a mock scolding. Daniel himself did not actually remember any of this, but years later, when both children were older, Hester had seemed to take great delight in teasing him about the time when she had been his "Ma" and had had to dress him, feed him, and wipe his nose and bottom. There had seemed to be no end to the number of stories she could recall, and after a time, Daniel had begun to suspect that she was making some of them up. Consequently many of the stories that Daniel related to Elizabeth over the years were not *his* stories at all, but *Hester's* stories, and as many of his sister's stories were quite embarrassing to him, he considered it to be a sign of his great love and affection for Elizabeth that he was willing to tell them at all.

One evening after supper early in December of 1930 Elizabeth asked Daniel to describe his sister Hester's old rag doll, as nearly as he could remember it.

"I can prob'bly drar it better'n I can tell it," he said, and proceeded to make a rough sketch.

When Daniel came home from work the next day, Sarah greeted him at the door. "Look, Daddy! Mommy made me a doll!" She was four at the time. And this was about the time that the aforementioned symptoms began to manifest themselves.

When Sarah was first born, Elizabeth could not bear to be parted from her, not even at night. Consequently, during her first year, infant Sarah had slept most nights in the same bed as her parents. Daniel had not seemed to mind. He too had seemed to enjoy the smell and the warmth of her. If he and Elizabeth had wanted the bed to themselves, Elizabeth had simply picked the baby up and laid it in the cradle that stood by the side of the bed at night. During the day Elizabeth had moved the cradle from room to room and even outside into the garden, so as to keep Sarah near her while she worked. It had been a handsome cradle that Daniel had made of white pinewood just before Sarah was born. At Elizabeth's request he had later added a handle, to make it easier to carry from place to place.

During her second year Sarah had spent the better part of each night in a crib next to her parents' bed, but when she was about three she had started sleeping in her own little bed in her own room. That is to say, she had been laid down to sleep in her own room, but come morning Daniel and Elizabeth would usually find her once again in their room, tucked under the covers with them. Usually she would toddle over, fully awake, around four o'clock in the morning. This had become such a habit that if she hadn't arrived by half past four, Elizabeth would get up and go to Sarah's room, just to make sure that she was all right.

This stopped in the winter of 1930-31, when Sarah was four, and about the time she was given the rag doll. For the first time she began spending the entire night in her own bed, even if not all of those hours in bed were spent sleeping. Elizabeth knew that Sarah was still waking up at an early hour, usually an hour or two before the first light of day, because she could sometimes hear her talking to herself through the door. As the winter passed, Sarah's early-morning talks to herself became more and more frequent and of greater and greater duration. Whenever Elizabeth chanced to wake in the night to hear Sarah talking she would always smile, pleased to know that her child was alive and well–and becoming more and more adept in the use of language. If she stayed awake long enough, she would marvel at the length of some of Sarah's talks to herself. How, she wondered, could a child of four find so many things to talk about?

Finally, one morning in late January, Elizabeth's curiosity got the better of her. Slipping out of bed before daybreak, she tiptoed quietly across the hall to Sarah's room. There she stopped and listened. Once again the sound of animated conversation could be heard through the door. After listening for a while, Elizabeth pushed open the door and peered into the darkened room. "Sarah?"

"Is that you, Mommy?"

"Yes. I thought I heard you talking."

"Yes, I was talking to Kati."

"To whom?" It had sounded like she had said "Kot-tee."

"To Kati."

Yes, she had said "Kot-tee." Elizabeth turned on the light and saw the rag doll tucked under Sarah's arm. "Is that Kati?" she asked, smiling.

Sarah nodded. "I was telling her about all the fun we had in the snow yesterday."

"Did you tell her about the snowman we made in the yard?"

"Yes."

"Did you tell her about our walk in the park?"

"Yes."

"How about all the animal tracks we saw in the snow?"

"Yes."

"Did you tell her that we saw a fox?"

"Not yet, Mommy. I was just getting to that."

Elizabeth smiled. "Well then, I guess I'd better go back to bed and let you and Kati finish your conversation."

Sarah returned her smile. "Good night, Mommy."

"Good night, Honey." Elizabeth turned out the light and left the room, closing the door behind her. As she climbed back into bed, Daniel rolled over to face her. "She's talking to her doll," she explained, anticipating his question. He smiled and both went back to sleep.

Sarah continued to talk to her new-found friend almost every morning thereafter. Occasionally, in the early hours of the morning, Elizabeth would hear her call, "Kati, where are you?" or "Kati, I can't see you." Elizabeth would smile, as she imagined to herself the scene in the other room, Sarah searching through the bed covers for the misplaced doll. She was pleased that something she had made with her own hands had assumed such a pre-eminent place in her child's life. Then, through the door across the hall, she would hear, "Oh, there you are, Kati."

It was over a year later, in the spring of 1932, when Sarah was about five and a half, that she made an unusual request. As she was helping her mother wash the breakfast dishes, she asked, "Mommy, can we set a place at the table for Kati tonight?"

Elizabeth smiled. "Of course we can."

Late that afternoon, while Sarah was outside playing, Elizabeth went to Sarah's room to find the rag doll. She found it in Sarah's bed neatly tucked up to its chin under the covers as always. She picked it up and examined her handiwork. It was holding up pretty well, probably because Sarah almost always kept it in her bed and was not in the habit of dragging it around with her everywhere she went as Daniel's sister Hester had apparently been in the habit of doing with hers.

Elizabeth carried the doll into the kitchen and placed it on the seat of the one chair that always stood at the table unoccupied, except on those rare occasions when they had a guest over for dinner. For the most part, the three of them lived in a world of their own. Daniel and Elizabeth were both amicable enough when they found themselves in the company of others, but they did not go out of their way to seek company or to make friends, and so seldom invited anyone to dinner. Sarah too seemed not to be very interested in making close friends with any of the other children in the neighborhood, though she did sometimes play with them.

Elizabeth looked at the doll in the seat of the chair and realized that it just wasn't going to do. "I'm just going to have to make you higher, aren't I, Kati?" she said to the doll, and then laughed at herself for talking to stuffed cloth. She went to the living room and removed several pillows from the sofa. Upon returning to the kitchen, she stacked the pillows on the seat of the chair, then placed the rag doll securely on top, so as to give it an unimpeded view of the top of the table and of the three humans who would be joining it for dinner.

When Daniel came home from work, he found Sarah waiting for him at the gate. He could always expect her to be waiting for him at the gate during the spring and summer months when the days were long. He picked her up and they came into the house together. Elizabeth greeted them at the door. "Get cleaned up, you two. Supper is almost ready."

Daniel put Sarah down. "You use the bathroom, Sweetheart. I'll use the kitchen sink."

Sarah ran for the bathroom. "You'd better put on a clean dress, Sarah," Elizabeth called after her. "I see you've been crawling in the dirt again."

The two doting parents smiled at each other, both glad to have such an active child. Elizabeth considered the extra laundry a small price to pay.

Sarah hurriedly washed up, then went to her room to change her dress. "Mommy, have you seen my dolly?"

"She's already in the kitchen, Honey. Remember, you wanted me to set a place at the table for her tonight."

Sarah came into the kitchen, a puzzled look on her face. She saw the rag doll sitting atop the pillows. "No, Mommy, not my dolly . . . Kati!"

Elizabeth was confused. "Sarah, if this isn't Kati," she asked, her hands resting on the back of the rag doll's chair, "then who's Kati?"

"Kati is my friend who comes to visit me in the night when you and Daddy are asleep."

Elizabeth, stunned and speechless, looked at Daniel. He was not sure what to make of this revelation either. He crouched down on his haunches directly in front of Sarah, so that his eyes were at the same level as hers. He took her hands in his. "You say that your friend . . . What's that name again?"

"Kati."

"Is that a him or a her?"

"It's a her, Daddy. Kati's a girl."

"You say that she comes t' visit you durin' the night?"

Sarah nodded.

"For how long has she been a-comin' t' visit you? When did you first meet her?"

"I don't remember exactly when, Daddy. It was a long time ago. One morning I woke up, and there she was, standing next to my bed."

Confused, Daniel looked up at Elizabeth, then back at Sarah. "Well, what does she look like? Can you describe her to me?"

"She's not like us, Daddy. She's a white person."

Elizabeth, whose attention was now riveted to Sarah's every word, interjected. "But we're white people, Honey."

"No, I mean she's a white-light person, Mommy. She's made out of white light. She's very beautiful."

"How old is your friend Kati, Sarah?" asked Daniel.

"How old?"

"Yes. How big is she? Is she a little girl like yourself?"

"No, Daddy, she's bigger than me."

"Is she as big as your Mommy?"

Sarah laughed. "No, Daddy, she's not *that* big."

Under other circumstances Elizabeth might have laughed at Sarah's remark about her size. The remark had, however, struck her as a bit odd. At five-feet-seven-inches, one hundred twenty pounds, Elizabeth had never thought of herself as an especially large woman, a little taller perhaps than most, but not nearly as stout as some of the other women in the neighborhood. She realized now, however, that from Sarah's point of view, she must appear gargantuan, gigantic, as great in size as Gulliver appeared to the Lilliputians. Elizabeth quickly deduced that if Sarah's mysterious friend was neither child nor full-grown woman, she must be something in between.

"Sarah, is your friend Kati as big as Pauline Nissel?" Pauline was the fifteen-year-old daughter of Paul and Elaine Nissel who lived next door.

Sarah's eyes lit up. "Yes, Mommy," she exclaimed, "that's how big she is. She's as big as Pauline."

Elizabeth exchanged puzzled glances with her husband. Apparently they had succeeded in establishing the approximate age and size of Sarah's friend Kati, but still they had little idea as to who or what she was.

"When you talk to Kati," asked Elizabeth, "what do you talk about?"

"I tell her about all the things I see during the day and about all the things I do. And she tells me about her world."

"*Her* world?"

"Yes, the White Light World. She says the White Light World is a beautiful place, more beautiful than the Earth even. She says I can't go there yet, but someday when I'm older, she's going to take me there. She promised."

Elizabeth did not sleep well that night. Neither did Daniel. They lay in bed in the dark talking in whispers. Elizabeth, who thought she knew her daughter as well as she knew the thoughts in her own mind, was the more distraught. "My God, Daniel, what's going on?"

In the hours that had passed since supper, Daniel had pondered over and over again what Sarah had said about her friend "Kati" and the White Light World, but had been unable to decide what to make of it. Now he saw it as his first duty to comfort his wife. "Hit could be she's just a-'maginin' the whole thang."

"Yes, I'm sure she's just imagining it, but why? Do you realize that she's been talking to her friend Kati every morning for over a year now? The whole time I thought she was talking to her rag doll, she's been talking to–to what? To nobody. To nothing. . . And she says that her friend Kati talks to *her*."

Elizabeth all but gasped aloud as a terrifying thought suddenly entered her mind. She remembered that her Aunt Katherine had heard voices when *she* was a child. In fact, Katherine had heard voices all her life–until she had died so tragically in a fire at the age of sixteen.

"Do you reckon it's harmful for children to have 'maginary playmates?" asked Daniel.

"No, no, I don't suppose so," replied Elizabeth distractedly. "Most of them seem to outgrow it. But why should Sarah need to fantasize an imaginary friend? She can't be lonely. I'm with her all the time. And why wouldn't she fantasize someone her own age? Why someone who's so much older than herself? And what if she doesn't outgrow it? What if she continues to see imaginary people and to hear imaginary voices? In the end she may not be able to distinguish between fantasy and reality. In the end . . . "

Daniel waited for Elizabeth to finish her thought, but she broke off and fell silent, unable to say aloud the painful but logical conclusion of what she had said up to this point: in the end Sarah could go mad. Daniel listened but did not say anything. A minute passed, then two, then three. The change in Elizabeth's breathing told him that she was calming down. He waited, staring in the direction of the ceiling, which he knew was somewhere in the darkness above him. Finally she laughed softly–that was a good sign–and continued.

"Listen to me! After all my noble resolutions, here I am trying to impose my adult view of the world on my child again. Instead of trying to see the world as Sarah sees it, I am making the judgement that Sarah can't possibly be seeing the world the way in which she says she's seeing it. I am saying, in effect, that there is something wrong, something defective, about the way my child sees the world. My God, I'm no better than all the other adults in the world. For all I know, Sarah may actually *be* seeing white people or ghosts or whatever Kati is."

Again she fell into silence, apparently thinking about what she had just said and the ramifications thereof. Daniel *thought* he understood what Elizabeth was saying, but when she talked like this, he could never be sure. She had become increasingly animated, but when she continued, she was more subdued.

"But even if she is seeing and hearing things that other people can't see or hear, how will she ever be able to talk about it? Who will believe her? I'm her own mother, and I'm not sure *I* believe her. It may be harmless enough now, but what if it continues? What happens when she goes to school and starts telling other children about her 'white people' and her 'voices?' She *will* be going to school soon, you know. We can't keep her sheltered here forever."

Daniel thought he had anticipated Elizabeth's next thought. "Do you reckon we should try t' get her t' stop?"

She hesitated a moment before responding. She was clearly struggling inside. "Oh, Daniel, if only you could have seen how radiant she looked that morning I went into her room. I wouldn't want to do anything to hurt that child."

They talked late into the night until, exhausted, they fell asleep. Early the next morning, before dawn, Elizabeth was awakened by a sound coming from the next room. It was Sarah, talking to Kati.

In the days and weeks that followed, both Daniel and Elizabeth encouraged Sarah to spend more time playing with other children. Sarah was willing enough to comply with this request, but she had so much frenetic energy that other children her age were often overwhelmed by her. This had always been a problem. One little boy, in fact, had already been injured in his attempt to keep pace with her. The previous fall–Sarah was not quite five at the time–she had gone up the street to play with little Billy Malesic. The two children had been raking leaves in Billy's backyard for the purpose of jumping into the pile afterwards, when Sarah had decided to climb to the top of a young maple tree in order to shake down the last of the leaves. She had seemed to be having such a good time swaying back and forth in the top of the tree that Billy had decided to join her. He had climbed about halfway up when his mother had come out of the house. Upon seeing five-year-old Sarah in the top of the tree, twenty feet above the ground, and her own son struggling to reach her, she had become alarmed and had yelled for both of them to come down at once. Sarah had scrambled down safely, but Billy had fallen and broken his arm. Since then, Mrs. Malesic had refused to allow her son to play with the "crazy girl" down the street.

Sarah was mature for her years, both in terms of her physical coordination and her mental development, if not her size, and clearly she needed older children to play with. The older children would soon be out of school for the summer, but whether any would condescend to play with a five-year-old, a mere pre-schooler, remained to be seen. Elizabeth was not hopeful. It appeared to her, from her own observations of the children in the neighborhood, that children who had been to school tended to look down upon pre-school-aged children with the same contempt that her father had looked down upon people with less money than himself. Elizabeth hoped that once Sarah started to school herself, she would meet so many new friends that she would no longer have a need to fantasize them. But so far, other children did not seem to be the answer. Sarah could spend a whole day playing with another little boy or girl up the street. The next morning she would tell Kati all about it.

The problem of Sarah's imaginary friend—or whatever "Kati" was—was not the only thing that threatened to destroy Elizabeth's poem-life that spring and summer. The year was 1932, and for the past two years the economy of the country had been fast collapsing around them. A number of banks had closed, and every day, it seemed, another shop-keeper was hanging an "out of business" sign in the window. When the banks began to close,

Daniel was glad that he had followed his father's advice. "Don't trust banks, my boy," he remembered his father telling him. "Keep your money in your pocket. If you got too much for your pocket, put some of it in your shoe." Over the years Daniel had managed to save up a small sum of money, and while he had not kept it in his pocket or in his shoe, neither had he put it in the bank. In the event that he lost his job, as he feared he might, they would at least have something to fall back on. Then, late in the summer, came the bad news they had been expecting: the J. M. Stanton Machine and Tool Company, which had been in business since 1882, closed its doors for good.

Even before Daniel lost his job, the decision had been made. He and Elizabeth had discussed it all through the summer, and they had decided that if the machine shop closed, which had seemed all but inevitable, they would pack up and go to Daniel's home in North Carolina. It would make no sense to stay in the north and look for another job: there simply were none to be had. Daniel had not made up his mind by himself. Elizabeth in fact had been the first to suggest the idea of going to North Carolina. She had long entertained wonderfully romantic notions about the place of Daniel's boyhood, and she had looked forward to the opportunity of seeing it for herself. She thought also that the move might be good for Sarah, that in the excitement of beginning a new life in a new place, Sarah might forget about "Kati." Perhaps they could leave Kati behind in Springfield.

But before they could begin their new life, they would have to make an end to their old one, and that would not be easy. It was with a heavy heart that Elizabeth began the painful task of packing. She wished that she could just pack up the whole house, white picket fence and all, and take it with her. But even had that been practical, she could not have done so. The house did not belong to them. They had only rented it.

When they had finished packing everything they wanted to take with them, and the trunks were being carried out, Elizabeth took one last walk through the house, pausing for a moment in each room, trying to coax one last memory out of each–for she had been packing away memories that last week even as she had been packing clothing, books, drawings, and other keepsakes. When she had finished her farewell tour of the house, she walked out into the backyard. It was the end of summer and her little garden was in all its glory. It made her too sad to look at it. She stepped outside the white picket fence for the last time and closed the gate. Daniel and Sarah were already at the curb, helping to load the two big trunks and the smaller suitcases and bags into the taxi. Elizabeth stared at the white picket fence, which for eight wonderful years had contained all her hopes and joys and dreams. Now she was outside it, never to set foot inside it again.

And so it was that after twelve years in the land of the Yankee, Daniel Wicker was finally going home.

2

RUSHING CREEK

Daniel had sent a telegram to his sister Hester telling her what day they'd be arriving, but when the train pulled into the station in Asheville, neither Nathan nor Hester were anywhere to be seen. While Elizabeth and Sarah went into the station to find a washroom, Daniel waited on the platform to claim their luggage. He had been standing there about five minutes when a voice greeted him from behind.

"Well, I'll be danged. The prodigal son has returned."

Daniel turned around to find his brother Isaac grinning from ear to ear and holding out his hand. Daniel smiled and reached out for the hand offered him. For just a moment the two brothers stood at arm's length and shook hands as they studied each other's smiling face, until Isaac, apparently satisfied that this was indeed his long lost brother, threw his arms around Daniel and vigorously embraced him, clapping him on the back repeatedly as he did so.

They were still locked in each other's arms when Elizabeth found them. Daniel, seeing her over Isaac's shoulder, wrestled free from his brother's bear-like hug. "Isaac, I'd like you t' meet my wife Elizabeth. Elizabeth, this is my oldest brother Isaac."

During the brief half-minute that Elizabeth had stood there watching them before Daniel noticed her, she had been struck by the two brothers' contrasting personalities. She realized at once that not all the menfolk of Rushing Creek, North Carolina were as backward and shy as Daniel. She could tell by his manner and speech that this demonstrative stranger who was cheerfully squeezing the breath out of her husband—who she had at first assumed was Hester's husband Nathan—was quite clearly a self-assured and outgoing sort of fellow, and so she was not a little surprised when Isaac turned around to greet her. She fully expected him to say something ridiculous like "So you're the little lady!"–then proceed to lift her off the floor and swing her about.

She had even braced herself for this eventuality. Instead he neither spoke nor moved. He just stared at her with a look of adulation on his face, as though he had just seen the Blessed Virgin herself.

"Hello, Isaac," said Elizabeth finally, "Daniel has told me so much about you." It was only partly true—Daniel had mentioned Isaac on occasion, but he talked mostly about Hester when he talked about his family—but she felt that she had to say something to break the embarrassing silence.

"I'm very pleased t' meet yuh, ma'am," stammered Isaac finally, almost reverently.

Elizabeth was reminded of that spring day in Forest Park almost ten years before when she had first met Daniel and how uncomfortable she had made *him*. Now here she was doing the same thing to his brother Isaac. She wondered what it was about herself that so unnerved these simple salt-of-the-earth farmers from the hills of North Carolina.

Isaac, for his part, had never seen a woman so stunningly beautiful in all his life. But there was something else about her, something besides her dark good looks and trim figure that set her apart. There was a dignity, an elegance about her, that manifested itself in the expression on her face, in the graceful manner in which she carried herself, in the quiet, deliberate manner in which she spoke. How his little brother Daniel had ever persuaded a fine lady like this to marry him, Isaac was sure he had no idea. He had heard, back in 1924, by way of Hester, that Daniel had taken a wife up north, but he hadn't remembered Hester saying that he had married into money. Yet Isaac would have been willing to bet his last dollar that this elegant-looking lady that Daniel had just introduced as his wife, had aristocratic, if not royal, blood flowing in her veins. It was the sudden shock of learning that a woman of such aristocratic bearing was his brother's wife, combined with the stunning presence of Elizabeth herself, that had left Isaac temporarily paralyzed and speechless. He was delivered from his state of embarrassing discomfort when Sarah came running up.

"Are you my Uncle Nathan?" she asked.

"Heck no," he said, as he picked her up and swung her around, "I'm your Uncle Isaac. And who might you be?"

"I'm Sarah. I'm almost six."

"Well, hello, Sarah-Almost-Six," said Isaac, grinning from ear to ear. "I'm just as happy as a pig in a mud puddle t' meet yuh."

Sarah laughed at her uncle's colorful metaphor. He then pulled the child to his chest and commenced to squeeze the breath out of her.

Their baggage claimed, they began loading the trunks and suitcases onto the back of Isaac's truck. Even before the first trunk was loaded Sarah had jumped aboard.

"May I ride in the back, Uncle Isaac?" she pleaded.

"I don't think that would be such a good idea, Sarah-Almost-Six," he replied. "The road 'twixt here an' Rushin' Creek, she goes up an' down like one of them rolly-coasters, an' has more twists an' turns than a rattlesnake with rheumatism. If you was t' fly out a-gwine over one of the mountains, we might never find you ag'in. An' we wouldn't wanna lose you on your very first day in North Carolina now, would we?"

"Asheville's grown a lot taller since I was last here," observed Daniel as they drove through downtown. "I don't think thar were any buildin's over two stories high back in 1920."

"She's growed a lot, that's for sure," agreed Isaac, "both up *and* out. She was really boomin' thar for a while–til the Depression hit."

"Look, Mommy," cried Sarah, "streetcars!"

They drove out of town on a road heading west with Isaac driving, Daniel sitting next to the passenger door with Sarah on his lap, and Elizabeth tucked in the middle between the two brothers. For the next forty miles Isaac talked almost continuously. He began by explaining how it was that he, and not Nathan and Hester, had met them at the station.

"Believe it or not, Dan'l, hit was Hester who axed me t' come fetch yuh in the truck—Hester, mind you, who ain't had a kind word t' say about this truck since the day I bought it . . . I guess I better explain that for Miss 'Lizbeth. Nathan an' Hester, they're good hard-workin' folks all right, but they're just a little backwards in their thinkin'. They ain't got no use for such 'newfangled thangs' like trucks an' tractors. I told Nathan last Thanksgivin' that one day he was a-gwine t' wake up an' find that the world has left him behind."

"Wha'd he say to that?" asked Daniel.

"He just laughed an' said that if the world was so all fired up t' go to Hell, he'd just as soon be left behind . . . 'Course, Hester's just as bad. She takes after our Ma. Our Ma didn't believe in usin' nuthin' that wasn't mentioned in the Bible. She had Pa a-plowin' with mules right up until the day he died. An' she had *me* a-plowin' with mules right up until the day *she* died. No sir, Ma would never a-allowed a tractor on the place. To her way of thinkin', anythang that roared an' spit smoke just had t' be the Devil's own invention. Thar was just no two ways about it.

"Hester, she's almost as cantankerous as Ma was. But when she got Dan'l's telegram sayin' you all was a-comin', she weren't ag'in' axin' me t' come fetch yuh in the truck. I think she has the notion that Dan'l might a-growed a little soft livin' up north. An' besides, she figgered that you an' the young 'un would be more comfortable a-ridin' in my dandy new Hawkeye truck here than in Nathan's bumpety old wagon. Can you imagine, ridin' forty miles over roads like this in a wagon!"

He shifted into a lower gear and as the truck strained upward toward a gap between the mountains, Sarah watched intently out the passenger-side window. Up to this point she had been craning her neck to look *up*—she had never seen mountains so high back in Massachusetts—but now as they climbed ever higher, she found herself looking *down*. Through openings in the trees she had been catching glimpses of the ever-receding valley through which they had just come. When they reached the top, the view that opened up to them was nothing short of spectacular. Elizabeth gasped.

Like Sarah, she had never seen anything like this before, and she made no effort to conceal her astonishment.

Isaac, who from the outset of the journey had considered it an honor to be sitting next to this fine lady, felt tickled that he was in some small way responsible for bringing her this pleasure. After all, *he* was driving, and it was *his* truck she was riding in.

It had been over twelve years since Daniel himself had traveled this road, but he had to admit that he had seen nothing in the intervening years that compared to the sheer power of these vistas to take one's breath away, to make every nerve in one's body tingle with excitement. Sarah was tingling too. She could not believe her eyes. She had never imagined that it was possible to see so much of the world at one time.

"You ain't seen nuthin' yet," Isaac assured them. "This is only the beginnin'."

It was evident to Elizabeth from the pride in Isaac's voice and from the broad grin on his face that he derived a great deal of satisfaction out of being able to call these mountains home. He could scarcely have exuded more satisfaction, she thought, if he had made them with his own hands.

As the travelers crested the top and headed down the other side, Sarah leaned her head out the window and allowed the wind to rush against her face and to blow through her hair. She was ecstatic. Yes, she thought, she was going to like this new world they had come to explore.

Isaac continued to talk—about the poorness of that summer's crops, about the need for rain, about the Depression. "Even when we can grow a decent crop, nobody's got any money to buy what we grow . . . 'Course, we ain't as bad off as folks in the cities. As long as a man has a piece of land an' can scrape up enough money t' pay his taxes, he can survive."

Elizabeth smiled to herself. Isaac's home-spun wisdom was a confirmation of her own view that simple farmers and peasant folk who knew how to provide for themselves with their own hands were better equipped for survival than even the most successful of their brethren in the cities and towns who depended on complex social and economic structures to support them. She felt secure sitting between these two men of the earth.

"How's Martha an' the kids?" inquired Daniel.

"Martha, she's still strong as an ox," replied Isaac, "an' just as good-lookin'. . ." He deliberately paused just long enough to allow Elizabeth to conjure up in her mind a picture of a woman resembling an ox, then added, "as she was on the day we was married." Another pause. "Which ain't sayin' a whole lot, I reckon."

"Benjamin, he's hardly a kid no more. He's nineteen now. He's a-workin' for the gov'ment, a-buildin' roads in the Smokies. I guess you heared they're a-makin' the Smokies into a national park. The fed'ral gov'ment's been a-buyin' up all the land. They're a-lettin' the old-timers stay on—if'n they want—t' live out the rest of their days in their own homes—but most folks is glad t' be a-sellin' out. Hit's mighty poor land for farmin'—too poor t' raise a fight, as they say—an' the gov'ment's a-payin' a good price—considerin' thar's a Depression gwine on. If I had a piece of worthless land up in the mountains, an' the gov'ment offered me more money than I ever seed in my life, I reckon I'd be glad t' sell too . . . 'Course, hit was the big lumber comp'nies that owned most of the land. Lots of men who once worked for the lumber comp'nies is a-workin' for the gov'ment now, a-buildin' roads . . .

"Lucy, she's seventeen now. She's still a-livin' at home, but I don't know how long she's a-gwine t' be with us either. She's got herself a feller, name of Charles Fox. He's a decent enough feller, I reckon—a little too citified for my taste though—no offense, ma'am. At least he's got a job. That counts for somethin' these days."

"How are Jacob and Emily?" asked Daniel.

"Jacob, he ain't changed much. He was purty upset when Ma died two years ago, but he's gettin' over that now—as much as Jacob ever does get over thangs like that . . . Emily? Well, you know, Dan'l, she's always been a sickly thang. She spent most of last winter in bed. But she's holdin' her own now."

Nathan, Hester, Isaac, Martha, Benjamin, Lucy, Jacob, Emily . . . Elizabeth had heard all these names before, of course—from

Daniel—but she always had trouble remembering who was who. Hester was Daniel's sister. That was easy enough to remember because Daniel talked about her all the time. He had even allowed her to read Hester's letters. Isaac and Jacob were his two older brothers. That was easy enough to remember too because of the Bible story. But after that, when it came to spouses and offspring, it got more complicated. But even though she could never keep all the names straight, Elizabeth never tired of hearing about the Wickers. She had been an only child herself. Not only had she never had a brother or sister with whom to share her early childhood experiences, but, except in a strictly biological sense, she had never even had a mother or father. Her parents had never seemed to have much time for her, or be much interested in the kinds of things in which she was interested. She had, since meeting Daniel, been able to relive her childhood—a much happier childhood—vicariously through his stories. She found herself warmed and affected by the warmth and affection with which he talked about his family. She often wondered how it was that he had ever left his home in the mountains in the first place. And now here was his brother Isaac talking about the same family, and while it was clear that he did not always agree with all members of his family, or approve of their tastes in boyfriends, they were his family nonetheless. Elizabeth almost envied Daniel and Isaac these bonds. Clearly, she thought, she had missed an important part of the human experience.

"Well, little brother," asked Isaac, as he shifted gears to begin another climb, "now that you're back home, what do yuh plan t' do with yourself? You can stay with me an' Martha, yuh know."

All the while Isaac had been talking—which was almost from the moment they had left Asheville—he had been in the habit of alternately looking at the road, then over at Daniel, continuously back and forth, so that his eyes were never on the road for more than a few seconds at a time—a habit which made Elizabeth a little nervous, especially on the hairpin turns and on the blind bends in the road. He did not seem to mind that he could not actually *see* Daniel, and if truth be known, he was more interested in catching glimpses of Elizabeth who was sitting between them.

No, he thought, the prospect of having Daniel and his lovely wife and daughter living under the same roof with him and his family was not an unpleasant one, not at all.

Whenever Daniel spoke, which wasn't often, he did not look at Isaac, but continued to look straight through the windshield at the road ahead, and now was no exception. "I was wond'rin' if the old Puckett place was still for sale."

A look of consternation came over Isaac's face. "You don't mean the old Jeremiah Puckett place?"

"That would be the one," replied Daniel, still looking straight ahead.

"I'd be willin' t' bet my last dollar on it," said Isaac, making a mighty effort to suppress his most immediate reaction, which was one of total incredulity. Normally he was in the habit of saying the first thing that came to mind, but just this once he decided that a little diplomacy might be in order. "The only problem would be findin' someone t' buy it *from*. The whole family has either died off or moved away. I guess you'd haf t' go over to the courthouse in Haynesville to find out who holds the title now."

Elizabeth had detected the uneasiness in Isaac's voice, and wondered what there was about the old Puckett place that had caused it. She had not heard Daniel mention the old Puckett place before, and her curiosity was aroused. But nothing more was said on the subject, because as they neared the bottom of another steep grade, the road flattened out and a settlement came into view.

"This is it," announced Isaac, "Rushin' Creek the creek an' Rushin' Creek the town–such as it is."

Elizabeth peered intently through the windshield, excited but at the same time a little apprehensive that the place whose name had become so familiar to her might not live up to her romantic expectations.

"That's Bryson's mill," said Isaac, pointing to a building on the left as they approached the creek. "That's whar ever'body in these parts takes their corn t' be ground up."

As they pulled up onto the bridge, Sarah leaned her head out the window as far as she dared without falling out, so as to get the best possible look at the water below. She saw at once why it was called Rushing Creek. The stream was not nearly as wide as the Connecticut River that flowed through Springfield, but the water in it was moving much faster. It was rushing madly, smashing into rocks, and throwing sprays of white foam in all directions. It jumped and rushed and roared–yes, Sarah could hear it roaring–like a wild beast as it charged under the bridge and disappeared into the forest of trees downstream. It was water gone crazy, thought Sarah. It was exciting just to watch it!

Just beyond the bridge Isaac pointed to a well-traveled footpath leading up along the creek. "Just 'round the bend up thar is the dam an' the swimmin' hole . . . "

"Can we go back and see it, Uncle Isaac?"

"Not now, Sarah-Almost-Six. You can see it another time. You *are* plannin' to' stay for a while, aren't you?"

"Oh yes! I'm going to stay *forever!*"

A short distance beyond the bridge they came to a crossroads, and Isaac brought the truck to a stop.

"You don't have to stop, Uncle Isaac," said Sarah. "There's no stop sign."

"I know thar's no stop sign, Sarah-Almost-Six, but I thought you might like t' see the town."

Sarah looked around. "Don't be silly, Uncle Isaac. This isn't a town."

"Oh, no? Well, whatta yuh call that?" asked Isaac, pointing again to a building on his side of the road.

Sarah climbed over Elizabeth and leaned across Isaac to get a better view. "That's not a town. That's just a store."

"That's not *just* a store," huffed Isaac, pretending to take offense. "That's Walter Lehman's *General Store*. See that sign out front? Hit says, 'If we ain't got it, you don't need it!' Walter's got ever'thang from coffee an' sugar an' tobacca to hats an' shoes an' long underwear . . . Are you wearin' your long underwear, Sarah-Almost-Six?" Unable to resist the temptation presented to him by her unguarded torso, he grabbed her and tickled her ribs.

"Of course I'm not," she replied without a giggle. "It's too hot for long underwear."

"Well, hit won't be too hot this winter."

"What else does Mr. Lehman sell in his store?" asked Sarah, her attention still fixed on the two-story building across the street.

"Well, let's see, he's got all kinds of tools—axes an' hammers an saws, shovels an' hoes an' pitchforks... An' he's got peppermint candy. I'll bet you'd like some peppermint candy."

"I'd like to have a hoe!" She turned to her father. "Daddy, can I have a hoe?"

Daniel smiled. "I'm sure we can manage that when the time comes."

"Well now, Sarah," said Isaac, craning his neck about in all directions, "I seem to a-got us lost. Mebbe I'd better let you drive."

"I don't know, Uncle Isaac," replied Sarah, assuming a very serious expression, "I never drove a truck before."

"Shucks, thar's nuthin' to it. Just set down here on my lap."

"Promise me that you won't tickle me."

"I promise."

She sat down on his lap and placed both hands on the steering wheel.

"Can you see?"

"Yes."

"All right. You steer, I'll work the pedals. Ready?"

"Yes."

As Isaac released the clutch and stepped on the throttle, Sarah turned the wheel sharply to the left.

"Well, I'll be danged," declared Isaac. "You sure you ain't a-been here before, Sarah-Almost-Six?" Then, turning to Elizabeth, he explained. "She's a-takin' us to Nathan an' Hester's—exackly whar I was a-plannin' t' go. If we'd a-gone straight, we'd a-ended up in Haynesville. If we'd a-turned right, we'd a-gone down along the creek to my place—to Dan'l's old home."

The direction that Sarah had chosen took them down the main street of "town." There were a dozen or so houses in addition to the other commercial enterprises.

"That's Lloyd Stanley's shop," said Isaac, pointing to what appeared to Elizabeth to be a junkyard on the right side of the street. "Lloyd's a blacksmith an' a welder–also the best mechanic in the holler. His Daddy used t' be a wainwright–built wagons–but Lloyd couldn't see no future in wagons. He's a-learnin' t' work on cars instead. Smart man."

Outside of town, the road began to climb again and to bend somewhat north, away from the creek.

"Back thar," said Isaac, pointing to a grove of trees set back off the road to the right, "is the Rushin' Creek Baptist Church. The Baptists built it away off in the woods thar about a hunnert years ago. I reckon they wanted t' be away from the noise an' clamor of the town."

Daniel had to smile at this. No one who had lived in Springfield for twelve years, or had passed through cities like Hartford, New York, Philadelphia, or Baltimore, would ever have thought to call Rushing Creek a noisy, clamorous town. "I reckon they figgered hit was a-gwine t' grow a li'l more than it did," he mused in a relaxed drawl, reverting effortlessly to his native mountain dialect.

"I reckon that's whar you'll be a-gwine to school, Sarah-Almost-Six," said Isaac, nodding in the direction of the church.

Since assuming her duties as assistant driver, Sarah had hardly looked at the road once. She was much too busy looking out the side windows, taking in all the sights as rapidly as her brain could process them. Elizabeth did not feel their lives to be in any jeopardy, however–at least, in *no more* jeopardy–as she saw that Isaac had his left hand firmly placed on the bottom of the steering wheel.

"Don't be silly, Uncle Isaac," laughed Sarah, "I wouldn't go to school in a *church*."

"Well, hit's only a church on Sundays, yuh know. The rest of the week hit's a *school*."

Sarah looked at her mother as if to ask, "Is he teasing me?" Elizabeth *thought* Isaac was telling her the truth, though she herself had difficulty imagining children sitting in church pews doing their school lessons. "Well," she said, "I guess we'll find out soon enough, won't we?"

Another mile and a half up the valley, Isaac eased up on the throttle as they approached a narrow lane forking off to the left.

"Well, Sarah hit looks like we're a-gwine t' haf t' decide which way t' go ag'in. You wanna keep to the main road, or you wanna go down this old bear track here?"

"I like the bear track," decided Sarah without so much as a moment's hesitation and immediately turned the wheel to the left.

Though the lane running down through the woods was badly rutted, Isaac did not slow down at all. As they bounced along, throwing up a great cloud of dust behind them, Sarah was almost glad that she wasn't riding in the back. Another quarter mile brought them out of the woods again and into a clearing. They drove through a small apple orchard, and suddenly, there before them stood a cluster of buildings. As Elizabeth's eyes focused on the two-story farmhouse approaching them from the front left, Sarah's eye was caught by the much larger weather-stained barn passing by them on the right. When Sarah caught a glimpse of two sleek black horses go blurring by barn side, she abandoned her driving altogether and hurried back across Elizabeth to Daniel's lap so as to get a better look. Daniel's eyes, meanwhile, had sought out things green and growing, resting for a moment on the extensive garden that lay between the orchard and the house, before moving on to the fields of corn, hay, and sorghum that stretched down over the hill behind the barn to the creek, and settling finally on the blue-green mountains that loomed up all around them.

Even before they had come to a complete stop, a plainly-dressed woman with her hair pulled back in a tight bun came running out of the house. Daniel jumped out of the truck to greet her, dumping Sarah on the seat he had just vacated.

"My baby! My baby!" cried the woman as she ran down the porch-steps and threw her arms around Daniel.

Most days of the year Hester was a practical, no-nonsense woman, not given to displays of emotion—and certainly not to levity—but she had always had a soft spot in her heart for her baby brother which made her act a little foolish at times. It had been twelve long years, however, since she had last had occasion to exercise the lighter, more foolish side of her nature. She continued to hold him tightly to her, swaying back and forth in a rocking motion. She would have given anything to have been able to pick him up.

"This is my daughter Sarah and my wife Elizabeth," said Daniel, as the other occupants of the truck emerged. Isaac was already out, checking on the luggage in the back.

Hester did not have the same temporary loss of speech and motor function that had afflicted Isaac earlier in the day upon first seeing Elizabeth, for which Elizabeth was grateful.

"Well, you're just as purty as Dan'l said you was," she said with the greatest of ease as she took Elizabeth's hands and kissed her on the cheek.

Isaac, who was observing all this from his vantage point on the back of the truck, could have kicked himself. "Tarnation!" he grumbled under his breath, "why didn't I have the presence of mind t' do that?"

Hester bent over to get a closer look at Sarah, and she was apparently satisfied by what she saw. "Oh, Dan'l," she said with delight, "this young'un of yourn, she's a reg'lar beam of sunshine, she is."

"I'm Sarah," proclaimed the beam of sunshine.

"She's almost six," added Isaac.

Elizabeth had been studying Hester ever since she had seen her come running out onto the porch. She had heard so much about her–this time it was true–and Daniel had always shared Hester's letters with her, so it seemed like she had known her for years, and was having some difficulty absorbing the fact that she had never really met her until now. As she was busily but pleasantly engaged in the mental exercise of comparing the Hester that stood before her now with the Hester she had created in her imagination, out of the corner of her eye she caught sight of another new face. A tall, blond, sturdily-built man with wide-brimmed straw hat and chin whiskers had just come around the corner of the barn and was approaching the group gathered around the truck.

"Welcome home, Dan'l," he said, extending a sun-browned arm and hand.

"Thanks, Nathan," replied Daniel, warmly shaking the offered hand, "hit's good t' be back."

Isaac waited until all the introductions were properly made, then spoke up. "We got three strong men here. Let's see if'n we cain't get this stuff unloaded afore dark."

Nathan peered over the side of the truck and ran his right index finger through the dust on one of the trunks. "I can see now that I should a-taken the horses an' wagon after all," he quipped dryly to Isaac. "At least that way we could a-saved some of the cargo." He turned his head, smiled, and winked an eye at the others. "Better bring a broom, Hester."

"Well, I reckon you could a-done that all right," retorted Isaac, feigning indignation, "but why a man would wanna use up a whole day just t' do a coupla hours work is beyond me. Hell, by the time you got all the way from here to Asheville in that dad-blamed old wagon of yourn, you'd a-done forgot why it was that you went thar in the first place. An' if'n you did just happen t' remember—which I doubt that you woulda—by the time you got these here folks picked up an' fetched back here, poor little Sarah-Almost-Six thar would a-been a-gwine on seven."

Elizabeth, who was thoroughly enjoying watching and listening to the easy and affectionate manner in which the various members of the Wicker and Andersson clans related to one another, found this good-natured banter between Isaac and Nathan especially entertaining. She surmised at once that the two had a sort of friendly running feud going.

Hester brought the broom and Nathan climbed up into the bed of the truck and began to sweep off the trunks with more vigor than was probably necessary, but the cloud of dust he raised produced the desired result, as Isaac was forced to jump down to keep from being engulfed. When Nathan was satisfied that the trunks and bags were sufficiently clean—and that he had made his point—the three men carried the luggage into the house. As the

48

others milled around the kitchen, Isaac walked out onto the porch and Hester followed him out.

"Won't you stay to supper, Isaac?" she asked. "Hit's almost ready."

"No, thanks just the same, Sis. I'd better be a-runnin' along. Martha will be expectin' me."

Returning to his truck, he cranked the engine, then swung himself into the driver's seat and shut the door. Leaning out the window he motioned for Hester to come near.

"By the way," he said in a low voice, so as not to be overheard by the others in the kitchen, "you'd better talk some sense into that little brother of yourn. He's think' about buyin' the old Puckett place."

"Not the old Jeremiah Puckett place?"

"That be the one." Shifting into reverse, he turned around, then roared off out the lane, throwing up another cloud of dust in his wake.

"Ma was right," mumbled Hester to herself as she watched the dust settle over her garden, "them infernal combustion machines was the Devil's own invention."

As Hester turned to go back into the house, she met Nathan and Daniel coming down the porch steps.

"I'm gonna show Dan'l around a bit," said Nathan.

"Well, don't be too long. Supper'll be ready in a few minutes."

She went back into the house where she found Elizabeth in the kitchen stirring the contents of one of the kettles that was simmering away on top of the stove.

"Oh my goodness!" cried Hester, "in all the excitement, I plum' forgot about supper. I sure do thank you for lookin' after it."

Elizabeth had never in her life been in a kitchen like Hester's before. From the exposed joists in the ceiling hung pots and pans of every size and shape. On the wall above the sink-board hung dozens of utensils, many of which Elizabeth could not identify. Another two walls were lined with shelves and cupboards, all crammed full of jars and tins of home-canned and home-dried produce. In the very center of the room stood a massive oak table, which served as both dining table and work table. The scores of knife nicks and stains on the table's surface testified to its heavy use. That this kitchen was, day in and day out, a beehive of industry, Elizabeth could see at a glance. She felt a little overwhelmed just standing in it.

Sarah, who had been running from room to room, now came flying into the kitchen and nearly collided with Hester.

"Slow down, child, or you'll knock me over," exclaimed Hester in her best mock-scolding tone of voice.

"I'm sorry, Aunt Hester. But Aunt Hester . . . "

"Yes, child, what is it?"

"Aunt Hester, where's Otis?"

"He's s'posed t' be doin' his chores, but he's prob'bly down at the creek fishin'. Tell yuh what. Why don't you run down thar an' fetch him? Tell him I said for him t' come up an' finish his chores."

"Good idea!" exclaimed Sarah and like a bolt she was out the door. Almost as suddenly she was back in again. "Aunt Hester?"

"Yes, child?"

"Where's the creek?"

Hester and Elizabeth both laughed.

"C'mon, Sunshine, I'll show yuh."

Hester led Sarah out the door and around to the back of the house, then pointed down the hill to a row of trees at the far end of the fields. "If'n yuh foller that path thar betwixt the hayfield an' the cornfield til yuh come to them trees, you'll find the creek. Otis should be along thar somewhar."

Again Sarah was off like a bolt.

"Slow down, child," Hester called after her, "or you'll fall in the creek!"

As Sarah ran down the path between the hayfield and the cornfield, she pondered for a second or two her Aunt Hester's warning to slow down. Her mother and father had told her that she must be mindful of her Aunt Hester as there was a good possibility that she might be living at Nathan and Hester's for a while. So she had resolved to be on her best behavior. But she could not believe that her Aunt Hester had really meant for her to slow down—even though she had said it twice now. She wasn't sure she would even know how to go about it. Was she expected to *walk* instead of run? Sarah dismissed the idea from her mind as too silly to even contemplate. No, surely no one could *really* expect her to slow down. To prove to her Aunt Hester that her fears were unfounded, Sarah resolved to try extra hard not to fall in the creek.

Having so resolved, when she reached the end of the fields, she came to an abrupt stop, and began to proceed into the woods on tiptoe, moving only one foot at a time and keeping one hand on a tree whenever possible. From the moment she entered the woods she could hear the rushing water. As she descended a steep bank, the larger trees–the sycamores, slippery elms, and black willows–gave way to smaller trees–to silverbells and witch-hazels–and finally to rhododendron bushes, to which Sarah was able to cling with both hands. Through the foliage she could see the churning water. She felt her whole body tremble with excitement. Surely, she thought, this must be the same Rushing Creek she had seen under the bridge back at town. She found the roaring and rushing of the water both terrifying and thrilling at the same time.

She looked upstream and down, but couldn't see much of anything through the thick tangle of rhododendron, in the midst of which she now found herself. She decided to look for Otis upstream, since that was more in the direction that her Aunt Hester had pointed, and began making her way carefully through the all but impenetrable forest of rhododendron, crawling on her hands and knees wherever necessary. When she emerged from the bushes she had an unobstructed view of the creek, and her eyes fixed immediately on a fishing line drifting in a quiet pool of water along the bank just ahead. She could see one end of the pole hanging out over the water's edge, but the other end, and whoever might be attached to it, were hidden from her view by the trunk of a giant sycamore tree that stood on the bank and leaned out over the water.

Sarah tiptoed to the large trunk and peered around. There, lying on the mossy bank, with his head propped up against a log, was a boy, only slightly bigger than herself, with the blondest head of hair she had ever seen. His hair was so blond it was almost white. His eyes were closed, and by the peaceful expression on his face, Sarah thought he must be daydreaming. Next to him, sound asleep, lay a big brown-and-white floppy-eared dog. Sarah stepped out carefully from behind the tree.

"Otis?" she whispered.

Suddenly the dog let out a tremendous bark, causing the boy with the almost-white hair to nearly jump out of his skin. He dropped his pole and before he could scramble to his feet, it went scooting into the creek.

"I'll get it!" cried Sarah, and immediately jumped into the water to retrieve the pole.

"Be careful!" shouted the boy with the almost-white hair. He hesitated for just a moment, then jumped in after her.

The water along the bank where Otis had been fishing was comparatively calm and not very deep, but Otis wanted to make sure that this forest sprite or whatever it was that had just scared the living Jesus out of him, did not chase his fishing pole out into the middle of the creek where the water was much deeper and the current was too strong for even a grown man to swim against. His father had told him more than once that if a small boy like himself ever got out in the middle of the creek, he'd be all the way down to the dam at Bryson's mill before anyone would even know he was missing.

But Sarah had reacted so quickly that she had caught up with the pole almost as soon as she had jumped into the water, and by the time Otis had reached her side, she was already scrambling back up onto the bank. Otis followed her out. As the two children stood on the bank, their clothes dripping wet, they looked at each other and burst out laughing.

"Are you Otis?!" asked Sarah.

"Uh-huh," replied the white-haired boy, "an' this here's Pokey."

While the children had been in the creek chasing down the fishing pole, Pokey had continued to bark, but now he was quietly absorbed in the very serious business of giving Sarah a thorough inspection with his nose.

"I'm your cousin Sarah from Mass-a-chu-setts," said Sarah. She always had to say that word "Massachusetts" very slowly so as not to trip over the letters. She had dropped to her knees to pet the inquisitive dog, but she was looking up at Otis and staring at him in fascination. She thought he was just about the funniest-looking little boy she had ever seen. On the top of his head toward the back, a tuft of white-blond hair stood straight up like a clump of Indian feathers. And the face! The comical expression on his freckled face seemed to suggest that he was more or less in a permanent state of confusion. It was all Sarah could do to keep from laughing, and she would have done so, if she hadn't thought it impolite. Besides, she liked her cousin's face, especially his freckles and the color of his eyes. His eyes were the color of robins' eggs.

Sarah's senses were overwhelmed, as they had been ever since this day began. Everything was so exciting! She wanted to take it all in at once. She couldn't decide which was the more fascinating—her freckle-faced cousin, the floppy-eared dog, or the torrent of water rushing past them. "Is that Rushing Creek?" she asked.

"*Rushin'* Creek," articulated Otis, correcting her pronunciation.

"Oh, I almost forgot!" exclaimed Sarah. "Aunt Hester—I mean your mother—sent me to find you—no, *fetch* you. She said you're supposed to come up to the house and finish your . . . something or other . . . I forget."

"My supper?" he asked tentatively, hopefully, doubtfully.

"No, that wasn't it. It was something you're supposed to be doing."

"Oh," he groaned, "my chores."

"Yes," cried Sarah, "that was it . . . What's chores?"

"You don't know what chores is?" asked Otis incredulously.

She shook her head.

"You must never a-lived on a farm."

She shook her head again.

"You're lucky. Chores is *work*. On a farm the grown-ups make the kids do all the work."

53

He wrapped his fishing line around his pole and wedged the pole into a clump of river birches, which Sarah surmised was where he kept it.

"Do you ever catch any fish?" she asked.

"'Course I do! Zillions of 'em. But my Ma makes me clean everthang I bring home, so I mostly just look at 'em an' throw em' back."

They walked up through the woods together with Pokey following close behind. When they reached the fields an idea suddenly flashed into Otis' mind. "C'mon," he said, "I'll race you up to the house!"

Even before all the words were out of his mouth, he was off and running up the hill. Sarah was right behind him.

"That young'un of yours sure is a ball of fire!" declared Hester, still shaking her head, as she came back into the kitchen.

"Sarah has been looking forward to meeting Otis," explained Elizabeth. "On the long train ride down here, Sarah wanted to know all about this new place we were coming to. When Daniel mentioned that you had a little boy about her age, she could talk about nothing else the rest of the way. Daniel wasn't quite sure how old Otis was, but he figured he must be about eight now, since he remembered him being born soon after we were married."

"He just turned eight the first week in September."

"He's your only child, isn't he?" Elizabeth knew that he was.

"Yes, an' I reckon he's as precious to me as yourn is to you. He's the only one I got an' the only one I'll ever have. I lost two others afore he come along, an', Lord knows, I almost lost him. An' now I cain't have no more . . . But God's will be done."

It was evident to Elizabeth from the sadness in Hester's voice and in her eyes that this stoic woman's inability to have any more children was the great sorrow of her life, the cross she had to bear.

"Hit's a wonder *you* never had any more, Miss 'Lizbeth," said Hester, trying to direct the conversation away from herself.

"Well, the thought *has* crossed my mind," said Elizabeth. Yes, it was true, the thought had crossed her mind, but only because many thoughts crossed her mind in the course of an average day. It was a thought she never entertained for long. She had decided, for the time being at least, that she did not want a second child. In fact, she had never even *wanted* Sarah. She had been perfectly content living alone with Daniel those first two and half years of their marriage before Sarah was born, and she had never subscribed to the view that it was a woman's *duty* to bear children. But of course now she could not imagine her life without Sarah, and it was because she had such a special relationship with her daughter that Elizabeth did not want to take a chance on altering that relationship, or possibly even destroying it, by bringing a second child into the home. But rather than trying to communicate all these thoughts to Hester, Elizabeth simply said, "I find that Sarah is about as much as one mother can handle. I can't imagine where I'd find the time or the energy to look after a second one."

"Shucks," replied Hester, "thar wouldn't be no need for *you* t' look after a second one. Sarah could mind the second one, same as I minded Dan'l when he was a babe . . . Did he ever tell you how I looked after him when he was a young 'un?"

Elizabeth smiled. "Yes, he *has* told me something about that." In truth, Daniel had told her quite a lot about his childhood years, mainly because Elizabeth had badgered it out of him. She was now recalling some of Hester's stories of those early years as Daniel remembered them, and was looking forward to hearing them from Hester herself. But at the moment Elizabeth had something more pressing on her mind. "Speaking of Daniel," she said, "today on the way out here, he asked Isaac if something called the old Puckett place was still for sale. Do you know anything about a place by that name?"

Hester furrowed her brow, much the same as Isaac had done when Daniel had brought up the same subject. Elizabeth wasn't sure if she was just trying to remember, or whether she was trying to decide on the most diplomatic way to phrase her answer.

"I was never up thar myself," she began slowly, "so's I can only tell you what I've heared. What folks say, Miss 'Lizbeth, is that at one time the old Puckett place must a-been the most beautiful farm on God's green earth . . . "

Hester paused. Elizabeth guessed that she had heard the good news and now was waiting for the bad.

"But not a soul has lived up thar for the past twenny years or more," Hester continued, "an' the reason for that is that hit's so darn far back in the mountains that hit takes the better part of a day just t' get up thar. Thar ain't never been no real road up thar. Isaac could never get his danged old truck up–'course, that might be as good a reason as any for a body t' move up thar–an' I doubt if Nathan could get up thar with a wagon either. 'Bout the only way up is on foot or on the back of a horse or a mule. If'n a man had a mind t' farm the old place ag'in, he'd sure 'nuff haf t' have hisself a mule. The fields are just too steep for a horse t' work in. They's almost too steep for a mule. I don't know if'n hit's true or not, but thar's a story told in these parts 'bout how old Jeremiah Puckett–way back in the 1850s or thar'bouts–was out a-plowin' in his cornfield with his mule one day, when he an' the mule both just up an' fell off the mountain, an' neither one of them was ever heared from ag'in. Leastwise, that's the way the story goes, an' like I said, I don't know if'n hit's true or not. As for the rest of the Pucketts, well, most of Jeremiah's children an' gran'children who was unfortunate enough to a-been borned up thar, they didn't wait around t' fall of the mountain. Most of them just left as quick as they could get away an' went t' live in the towns. The ones that stayed up thar eventually just died off from the awful lonesomeness of the place. An' like I said, ain't no one been fool enough to even try a-livin' up thar these past twenny years."

Elizabeth had been listening intently to Hester's every word. It was not only because she was interested in hearing what Hester had to say about the old Puckett place–she was, very much so–but she had to listen carefully to make out Hester's words. Elizabeth had been able to make out most of what Hester had said, but she had found the dialect a little difficult at times and she had missed an occasional word. The problem had been compounded by the activity the two women had been engaged in the whole time they were talking. Hester had been moving about continuously, removing kettles from the stove, taking biscuits out of the oven, damping down the fire. She had handed Elizabeth a stack of plates for setting the table and had showed her where to find the silverware. So, amidst all the bustle and clatter and clanging, it was not surprising that Elizabeth had missed an occasional word. She was about to ask Hester another question when Nathan and Daniel walked in.

"Smells good, Ma," teased Daniel, giving her another hug.

"Where are the children?" asked Nathan.

"Down at the creek," replied Hester. "They should be here any minute now."

No sooner had Hester finished her sentence than Sarah hit the porch and came flying through the screendoor.

"Bless my soul, child, you're soakin' wet!" exclaimed Hester.

Before she could say another word, another body came flying through the door. "Good Heavens, Otis, you're wet too!"

"I didn't *fall* in, Aunt Hester," beamed Sarah, "I *jumped* in!"

"So did I!" declared Otis just as emphatically. Otis had been told more times than he cared to remember that he was never, never to go into the creek unless his Daddy or another grown-up was with him—and Sarah didn't exactly qualify as a grown-up—so he fully expected to get a good scolding. He never got a licking, so he wasn't afraid of that, but he would just as soon have avoided the scolding as well if at all possible. He thought his cousin's tactic of making a direct and enthusiastic confession a little unusual, but he figured if it worked for her, it just might work for him as well.

"Well, get some dry clothes on," said Hester, "then bring them wet ones down here t' hang by the stove. We're about t' set down to supper."

Elizabeth went upstairs with Sarah to help her find a dry dress amongst the as-yet-unpacked luggage. "What do you think of Otis?" Elizabeth asked her daughter when they were alone.

"I like him, Mommy," replied Sarah. "I like him a lot!"

The two families sat down around the big oak table and held hands as Nathan said grace. As they consumed a sumptuous meal of ham, sweet potatoes, green beans, and biscuits, Elizabeth found herself drifting into a peaceful reverie. She felt wonderfully warm inside, rapturously happy, as if she had just drunk a whole bottle of wine, when in fact she had drunk nothing headier than a glass of spring water. She could not remember another time in her life, unless it was that time many years ago when, as a child of nine or ten, she had tagged along with a group of carolers on Christmas Eve, that she had felt so joyously happy–peaceful and secure–in the company of other people. She had always been a solitary person–had always felt out of place in groups of people–but now the hard protective covering around her soul seemed to be dissolving and she felt herself melting, warmly, lovingly, into the soul of the group.

Several times during the course of the meal she found herself looking around the table at the others seated there. At Daniel. At Nathan. At Hester. At the two children. Their faces all glowed in the soft light of the kerosene lamp that hung from the ceiling joist above the table. In the soft glow of the lamp they looked like faces that Rembrandt might have painted. She especially studied the faces of Nathan and Hester. They were good faces, real faces–sun-browned and strong, yet gentle and loving. How good it felt to be sitting here in this rustic farm kitchen surrounded by such faces; sitting here at this heavy oak table which over the years had been the hub of so many hours of patient labor and love; sitting here eating this food that these good people had grown with their own hands. How she enjoyed partaking of this food from the earth, partaking of its rich colors, flavors, and aromas. The simple act of eating supper had become for her a visual and sensual feast. She drank it all in until she was quite intoxicated.

Thoroughly enraptured she listened dreamily to every conversation, no matter how mundane, and cherished the words as though they were rare gems. She watched Daniel's face as he talked to Nathan, then Nathan's as he replied. They were still talking about things of which she had little knowledge or understanding, but she could not have cared less: she treasured every word. She watched Nathan's face again as he asked Otis about his day in school, then Otis' as he wrinkled up his little brow in deep thought as he tried to remember, but without much success. Her gaze then drifted dreamily over to Hester's face as she asked Otis how it was that both children had ended up in the creek.

It was then that Elizabeth woke from her reverie, because she too was curious to know what had happened at the creek—as were Nathan and Daniel.

Sarah told her version of it first, making sure to emphasize once again that she had not *fallen* in the creek, but had *jumped* in, so that her Aunt Hester would not make her stop running. Otis, finding himself in the embarrassing predicament of having to explain how it was that Sarah had caused him to drop his pole, squirmed in his seat. Nathan, seeing his son's discomfort, decided to have a little good-natured fun and press Otis on this point. Ordinarily he would have resisted the temptation to do so—Hester did not like him to tease Otis, not even in fun—but Hester had just gotten up from the table to get the apple pie from the oven. Nathan seized the opportunity.

"What I don't understand, Son," he said, leaning over the table in Otis' direction, "is how a big boy like you could let a little girl like this scare you so bad that you dropped your fishin' pole in the creek."

"Well, she jumped out from behind the tree!" Otis lied.

"I *did not jump!*" shouted Sarah most emphatically, amazed that Otis could tell such a fib.

"So you *did* fall in!" exclaimed Hester, returning to the table with the warm apple pie.

Sarah, confused and flustered, tried to explain, but by this time everyone was laughing so hard, she was forced to give up in frustration. She wasn't sure that she understood what was so funny, but the laughter was so infectious, that she started laughing herself. She wasn't about to miss out on a good time.

Elizabeth was laughing so hard that tears came to her eyes. This was one of those moments, she thought, one of those moments she'd like to bottle up and preserve into eternity. The whole evening had been wonderful. She thought she would be content to spend the rest of her life right here.

By the time supper was over, a couple of things had been decided. Sarah would go to school with Otis the next morning—and yes, the Baptist Church was doubling as a schoolhouse since the real schoolhouse had burned down in 1928—and Daniel would be going down to Isaac and Jacob's.

"Nathan tells me that Jacob still keeps a coupla mules on the place," explained Daniel, rising from the table. "He don't use them much, mostly just keeps them around t' remember Ma by. I think I'll go down thar tomorruh an' see if'n I cain't borruh one of them. *I'd* kinda like somethin' t' remember Ma by too."

Elizabeth and Hester exchanged glances. Yes, it certainly sounded like Daniel was thinking about buying the old Puckett place.

3

THE OLD PUCKETT PLACE

Daniel had *not* decided to buy the old Puckett place, not yet, at any rate. But he did want to go up into the mountains and take a look at it. For all he knew the place might have fallen down since he had last seen it, which was back in the autumn of 1919, almost thirteen years ago, just a few months before he had left Rushing Creek to look for work in the north. He had gone up then to satisfy his curiosity. Ever since he was a boy he had heard strange stories about the old place, how the fields were so steep that old Jeremiah Puckett had fallen out of one while plowing and was never seen again, how the place was so wild and isolated that some of Jeremiah's descendants had been eaten by bears—usually at night on the path that led from the house to the outdoor privy—and how the rest of the Pucketts had either fled to the towns in the nearby valleys or had just stayed up there on that lonely mountain and gone crazy from staring at all the trees. He had heard that the place was for sale then—as far as he knew, no one had lived up there since about 1910—and had even considered for the better part of a day the idea of buying it himself. He was a young man of nineteen at the time, the youngest of three brothers, trying to find his own way in the world, looking for a way to prove himself as a man. The challenge of trying to farm the old Puckett place again tempted him sorely. It would certainly have caused folks all over the nearby hills and hollows to sit up and take notice. Why, anyone who even tried to live up there again, let alone farm the place, would become part of the legend almost overnight. But the challenge, though tempting, was also a daunting one, and since he had no money anyway, in the end he decided to leave the mountains altogether and seek his fortune and reknown elsewhere.

But during all those years in the north, something about the old place continued to haunt him—its wild, isolated beauty, the cathedral-like stillness of the surrounding forest, its romantic legends—and he promised himself that if he ever returned to North Carolina, one of the first things he would do, would be to go back up into the mountains and take another look at it.

He had made the journey on foot that first time, back in 1919, but he decided he would ask his brother Jacob for the use of one of his mules for his proposed return trip. The long trek would be no faster by mule—it would still require about eight hours of slow and steady trudging up and over mountains to get there—but at least he could save on shoe leather, not to mention the wear on his legs, if he could ride instead of walk. Besides, he wanted to see Jacob.

Early the next morning Daniel said good-by to Elizabeth and Hester and climbed up onto the seat of the wagon beside Nathan. Otis and Sarah were already in the back. It was customary for Otis to walk the mile and a half to school, except when the weather was bad, in which case Nathan drove him in the wagon, or, in the event of snow, in the sleigh. But since Nathan had agreed to drive Daniel over to Isaac and Jacob's this morning in exchange for half a day's labor—a good bargain from Nathan's point of view as the round trip would take only about an hour of his time—he had offered to give the children a ride as well, as he would be passing right by the school, that is, the church, on the way. Besides, it would be Sarah's first day of school and Nathan wasn't sure if his little niece was up to such a long walk. Hester had no such concern about Sarah's ability to get herself to school. If she had any apprehensions at all, it was for the teacher, Susan Kinney, who would have the unenviable task of controlling this child for the duration of the school day. Sarah, for her part, was delighted at the prospect of finally getting a chance to ride in the back of *something*.

When they reached the end of the lane, Nathan pulled on the right rein and the horse trotted out onto the clay road. The horse's hooves clopped loudly on the hard sun-baked surface as they headed toward the town. The morning air was warm and damp, the dew lay heavy on the leaves of the trees and on the multifarious roadside vegetation. The mountains that rose up in the distance on all sides of them were shrouded in the gauze of morning mist. Neither man spoke as they clattered and rumbled along. Both were content to sit quietly and drink in the tranquility of the morning.

When they reached the lane leading back to the church, Nathan brought the wagon to a stop and the two children jumped out. Daniel jumped down as well and embraced his daughter.

"Now you behave yourself in school today, hear?"

"I will, Daddy."

"And you mind the teacher."

"I will, Daddy."

"I'll miss you."

"I'll miss you too."

"I'll see you in a coupla days."

"Okay, Daddy."

No sooner had the two children started down the lane than Sarah turned to Otis and began talking. The two fathers watched as the two children receded in the distance, becoming smaller and smaller. The last view they had of them, just before they disappeared around a bend in the lane, Sarah was still talking, and Otis, with his white-blond head cocked to the side toward her, was still dutifully listening.

"They're gonna be about an hour early," said Nathan, smiling his wry smile, "but I expect they'll be able t' keep themselves occupied til school starts."

"I expect so," laughed Daniel. "I just hope that they don't get themselves so occupied that they don't hear the bell when it rings."

Nathan shook the reins and the two travelers proceeded on into the town.

"Mornin', Walter," shouted Nathan as they passed the General Store.

A short, robust man with spectacles and a bushy white mustache, who was sweeping the porch, looked up. "Mornin', Nathan. Who's that you got with yuh? Is that Daniel?"

Again Nathan reined in the horse, and Walter stepped off the porch to greet them.

"Good mornin', Walter," said Daniel, reaching down from his perch on the wagon seat and clasping the storekeeper's extended hand. "Hit's a real pleasure t' see you ag'in. How yuh been?"

"Can't complain too much," replied the storekeeper, smiling broadly through his bushy mustache. "Hay fever's been actin' up, like it always does this time of year, but I'll survive it. Always do." He released Daniel's hand, pulled a large red polka-dot handkerchief out of his hip pocket, and blew his already red and swollen nose. He returned the handkerchief to his pocket and smiled again at Daniel, his blue eyes still twinkling through films of moisture. "How *you* been keepin'?"

"Right well enough, I reckon."

"I reckon Hester she was right glad t' see yuh?"

"You might say that," interjected Nathan. "I've known Hester for nigh onto fourteen years now, an' I ain't never seen her carry on like this before. If she's this excited now, what's she gonna be like when Jesus comes back?"

"I hear you got yourself married up north," continued the storekeeper.

Daniel nodded. "You heard right."

"And you got yourself a little girl."

"Uh-huh. Her name's Sarah. We just dropped her off at the school."

"And I hear you're think about buyin' the old Jeremiah Puckett place."

"Now who in tarnation told you that?"

"Isaac. He stopped in last night after he drove you all over to Nathan an' Hester's."

"I might a-known. What else did Isaac tell you?"

"Not much. Only that your wife is some sort of Duchess or somethin' an' you're rich as the Vanderbilts now. Which is why he can't understand why you want t' buy the old Puckett place."

Daniel shook his head in disbelief. "Walter, you should know better than t' believe anythang Isaac tells yuh. First of all, my wife is not a Duchess. Hit's true, her family had some money, but *she* never saw any of it an' neither did I. Second of all, I *do* have some money saved up, but it's money I earned honestly with my own two hands. Third of all, I never said I was a-gwine t' buy the old Puckett place. I just want t' go up an' take a look at it."

Walter scratched his head. "Well now, you got me wond'rin' about somethin' else Isaac said."

"What's that?"

"He said this wife of yours is as purty as she is rich. But if you say she ain't rich . . ."

"She's purty enough," volunteered Nathan, "I'll vouch for that."

"I reckon you'll get t' meet her soon enough," added Daniel, "then you can judge for yourself."

"I'll be lookin' forward to it. I'd kinda like t' meet that young'un of yours too."

"My daughter Sarah. I s'pose Isaac's told you all about her as well."

Walter nodded. "An' it was all good. Except for one thang."

"Oh? What's that?"

"He said she's the worst driver he's ever seen."

All three men laughed.

"Well," said Daniel, "we'd better be gettin' a move on. I wanna see my brother Jacob, an' then I hope t' get up to the old Puckett place yet today."

Nathan shook the reins and the horse again began to move forward.

"You be sure an' stop by sometime," called the storekeeper after the moving wagon.

"I'll do that," replied Daniel, raising his voice so as to be heard over the sound of the horse's hooves and the creaking wagon wheels. "I expect you'll be a-seein' a lot of me from now on."

"It's good t' have yuh back," said the storekeeper, fairly shouting.

"Thanks, Walter," shouted Daniel in return. "Hit's good t' *be* back."

"I don't know where this town would be without Walter Lehman," confided Nathan as they headed out of town in an easterly direction. "Lots of folks around these parts have been real short on money these past couple years, so Walter's been lettin' folks barter for things they need. An', hell, if you've got nothin' of value to barter, he'll still let you have the stuff, on credit. I don't like buyin' things on credit myself, but for some folks it's the only way. Times are bound to get better. Lord knows, they couldn't get much worse."

"Isaac seems t' be doin' all right," said Daniel. "He's got himself a new tractor and a new truck."

"Well, appearances can be deceivin' sometimes. He had to borrow money to buy the truck an' now he's got no way of payin' it back. An' what's more, he don't even have the money for gasoline. The truck mostly just sits. He had to borrow a dollar from me so he could buy enough gasoline to go pick you up yesterday.

"I'll admit, he does get some use out of the tractor. It runs on kerosene. It only takes a little bit of gasoline to get it started. But when it breaks down, he doesn't have the first idea about how to go about fixin' it. An' he doesn't have the money to pay someone else to fix it for him.

"Isaac keeps tellin' me *I* should get a tractor. I tell him, well, maybe one day I will: when they make one that runs on apple cider or somethin' else I can grow myself; when they make one that doesn't break down, or if it *does* break down, will fix itself if you just give it a couple days rest; when they make one that will breed an' reproduce itself; when they make one that runs so quiet that I can hear the birds singin' while I'm plowin' . . . I mean, what's the point of man bein' a farmer in the first place if he can't hear the birds singin' while he's doin' his spring plowin'? He might as well go to work at the paper mill."

Daniel laughed. "You don't haf t' convince *me*, Nathan. I'm the one who's gwine t' borruh the mule, remember?"

When they reached the lane leading back to Isaac and Jacob's, Daniel asked to be let off. "No need t' take me to the door," he said. I'd kinda like t' walk this last part if'n yuh don't mind."

"You wouldn't be tryin' to weasel your way out of our bargain now, would you, Dan'l?"

"Don't worry, Nathan," laughed Daniel as he climbed down, "you'll get your half-day's work. I'll consider myself as good as delivered to the parlor."

Nathan laughed. He turned the wagon around, waved good-by, and headed back up the road. As he watched the mist rise off the mountains to the west, he smiled. Yes, he thought to himself, it was certainly good to have Daniel back home again. Over the years he had heard as much about Hester's youngest brother from Hester as Elizabeth had heard about Hester from Daniel, the only difference being that Nathan had already met Daniel. He had made his acquaintance back in 1918, when he had first started courting Hester. He had always liked him.

The feeling was mutual. Hester could not have found herself a better man, thought Daniel to himself as he started to walk down the long lane that led back to the Wicker homestead, even if he is an "outlander." Daniel laughed at the irony of it. Even though Nathan had lived in Rushing Creek for the past fourteen years, he would always be considered an outlander by some of the local folks because he hadn't been born here, but had come down from Ohio. He himself, on the other hand, was "home-grown," and even though he had spent the last twelve years in Massachusetts, in the very heart of Yankee country, he would always be accepted by folks in these parts as one of their own.

The day was already starting to heat up, he thought, or was it just that he was now walking instead of riding?

But these idle, disconnected thoughts that jangled in his head like loose change in his pocket were soon hushed as long-dormant memories began to waken within him. How many times had he walked this lane as a boy growing up on this farm? In all the years he was away he had not given so much as a passing thought to this dusty winding lane. But here were the same black walnut trees under which he had gathered nuts as a boy. Here were the same wild cherry trees, whose black bitter fruits he had tasted years before. There, on either side of the lane, were the rows of piled stones, encrusted with lichen, overgrown with honeysuckle and poison ivy—stones that had been hauled from the fields and piled there over the past century by four generations of Wickers—rows of stones to which he himself had contributed his small share. No, he had not thought about this lane at all, but now it seemed as though he had walked it only yesterday. He seemed to remember every bend in the road, every tree, every bush, every lichen-covered stone. The same flies hummed around his head, the same smell of new-mown hay wafted to his nostrils. He could easily imagine that he was still a boy of seven and that the twenty-five years that had passed since then were only a dream. He could easily imagine that when he got to the farm he would find his Pa in the barn hitching up the mules and his Ma in the kitchen mixing up a batch of biscuits for dinner. Nothing had changed, except that the fields on either side of him were longer and wider now. Where there had been fence-rows and woodlots, there were now continuous fields of pasture grass, corn, tobacco, and hay. But if he kept his eyes focused on the lane ahead, he could easily imagine that the year was 1907 and he was seven years old again.

From time to time he glanced down at his hands and legs and feet, just to make sure he was still full-grown. It gave him an eerie feeling. Daniel was not one to bother his head much with deep philosophizing—he was not one to try to comprehend the incomprehensible, as Elizabeth was always trying to do—but he did come to one conclusion as he walked down the lane to the old Wicker farm: there was something very eerie, spooky even, about the passing of time, and if a man were to think about it too long, he could go queer in the head.

When the farmhouse and barn came into view, Daniel's fantasy of seeing his mother and father again evaporated almost instantly. The house had not changed all that much—there were screens in the windows now where there had been none before, but that was the only immediately perceptible difference—but there were several new outbuildings which had not been there at all when his father was alive.

The sound of a human voice issuing from one of the new buildings caused Daniel to set his course in that direction. He recognized the voice as Isaac's but even had he not recognized it, the bellicosity of the tone and the profanity of the language would have told him that it could only belong to his irascible eldest brother. But as he approached the low open-ended shed from which the voice had emanated, the first person he saw was Jacob.

"All right, crank it ag'in," came the impatient voice from somewhere within the shed.

As Jacob's back was toward him, Daniel was able to approach quite near without being detected. He stopped just around the corner of the shed to watch as Jacob, standing nose to nose with the recalcitrant tractor, gave the starting crank another quick, sharp turn. Still the tractor did not respond.

"What could be wrong with the dad-blamed thang?" came the angry disembodied voice again.

Jacob shrugged his shoulders but made no vocal response.

"I don't remember the mules ever bein' that hard t' start," said Daniel, announcing himself, as he stepped forward.

"Dan'l!" cried Jacob, turning suddenly around. Reaching for his brother's outstretched hand, he grasped it and embraced him.

Jacob was not as ostentatious in his display of affection as Isaac had been, but Daniel knew it to be just as genuine, perhaps more so.

"What seems t' be the problem here?" inquired Daniel, turning his attention to the tractor.

Jacob shrugged. "Won't start," he replied calmly, quietly.

"Good thang Nathan ain't here t' see this," said Daniel, smiling, as he walked around to the side of the tractor where Isaac had been standing solemnly, waiting for his two brothers to finish exchanging their greetings. "Mind if I take a look at it?"

"Be my guest," muttered Isaac.

Daniel stood for a moment studying the arrangement of the various engine parts, then reached for the fuel cap.

"No need t' look," shot Isaac, "I just filled both tanks."

"Well, then, let me ask you this," said Daniel. "The last time you used it, when you shut it off, did you close the fuel valve first, or did you cut the engine first?"

"I did both."

"Yes, but which did you do first?"

"Hell, I don't know. Cut the engine, I guess. How do you expect me t' remember somethin' like that?"

Selecting a small open-ended wrench from the tool box, Daniel moved to the other side of the tractor. He was shadowed by Isaac.

"Hey, careful!" exclaimed Isaac excitedly, "you're spillin' fuel all over the ground."

"Just a trickle." replied Daniel, unperturbed. "Thar, hit's stopped now." He stepped away from the tractor. "Okay, Jacob, crank it ag'in."

Jacob gave the crank another quick, sharp turn and suddenly the tractor roared to life.

"How'd you do that?" shouted a startled Isaac over the noise of the engine.

"All I did was bleed some fuel out," explained Daniel, also fairly shouting to make himself heard. "Hit was just flooded, that's all."

Isaac shook his head, partly in gratitude, partly in disgust, and mounted the tractor. "Did you come t' see *me*?"

"No, I came t' see Jacob."

"Good. Then I'll be gettin' t' work. I got a field t' plow."

Pulling on the shift stick, Isaac threw the tractor into gear. Daniel stepped back so as to be well clear of the heavy cleated iron wheels. He watched for a moment as Isaac clawed his way toward the field, throwing up dirt and sod in his wake, then turned to Jacob.

"Nathan tells me you still keep a coupla mules," he said as the two men stepped out from the shadow of the shed and into the sunshine.

"Sure do," replied Jacob. "You wanna see 'em?"

"Yeah, I do."

"C'mon then, I'll show 'em to you. They're right over in the pasture here."

As they approached the fence Daniel spotted the two mules grazing quite contentedly and quite anonymously amongst a herd of about two dozen cows.

Jacob leaned over the fence. "Here, Jack. Here, Jesse."

Raising their heads almost in unison, the two mules left off their feeding and ambled over to the fence. Jacob rubbed their ears and noses.

"You remember old Jack here. He was here afore you left. He's gettin' on in years now . . . " He caressed the mule's head and neck with affectionate strokes. "But Jesse here, he's the young one. Just a li'l over two years old. Two years an' three months to be exact. I remember 'cause he was born right around the time that Ma died, just a coupla days after. His ma birthed him the same day that ours was laid to rest."

These last words were uttered only with difficulty, in a voice heavy and sad. Daniel remembered this about Jacob, that of all the Wicker children, Jacob was the most sentimental. When Hester had written back in June of 1930 with the news that their mother had died, she had also mentioned that Jacob was taking it the hardest. This had come as no surprise to Daniel, because he remembered how long and how intensely Jacob had grieved when their father had died eleven years before. And one always had to be careful not to mention sister Ruth around Jacob, as the sound of her name never failed to bring tears to her eyes, even though sister Ruth had died back in 1904! Daniel had no memory at all of his sister Ruth. He was only four years old when she died, so all he knew about her was what he had been told. The few facts, as he knew them, were essentially these: Ruth had been Hester's twin sister, and she had died at the age of eleven during one of the smallpox epidemics that had swept through the mountain communities every few years back then. It was feared at the time that both of the twins might be lost, as Hester too had been stricken. But in the end Hester had recovered; Ruth, being the frailer of the two, had not. That was about all that Daniel knew about Ruth–that and the fact that nobody seemed to like to talk about her, especially Jacob. Apparently Jacob and Ruth had been very close. He was only thirteen himself at the time of her death. From all accounts, his grief had been, and was still, inconsolable.

Isaac, on the other hand, was chiseled from harder rock. When their father died back in 1919, Isaac couldn't wait to take over the farm. He was aggressive, ambitious, and eager to plunge into the task that lay ahead. He had no time for grieving. When their mother died, even as he was helping to lower her coffin into the ground, he was laying plans to get rid of the mules and buy himself a tractor. Jacob had been shocked by his elder brother's flagrant disregard for their mother's long-held religious convictions, and when the tractor was delivered only six weeks after their mother's death, Jacob feared that she just might be looking down on them from Heaven—as she had promised them she would be—and be horrified by what she saw. It was right then and there that Jacob had vowed that he would not allow Isaac to get rid of the mules. Even if they weren't going to be used to work the fields anymore, Jacob would at least keep them on the farm in remembrance of, and perhaps in an attempt to keep peace with, their mother in Heaven.

"I was wond'rin' if'n I might borruh one of them for a coupla days," said Daniel, after a half minute or so had passed and Jacob had had some time to recollect himself.

Jacob's eyes lit up. "Take Jesse! He's young. He needs the exercise . . . You figger on gwine up to the old Puckett place?"

"Yeah, I am."

"Isaac says you're a-fixin' t' buy the old place."

"Isaac knows about as much about my plans as he knows about tractors, which is next to nuthin'. I'm just gwine up t' take a look at it today, Jacob. What I do after that will depend on what I see today."

Jacob walked over to the gate in the fence and opened it. "C'mon, Jesse, you're gwine for a ride today, up in the mountains." He led the mule to the barn and slipped a bridle over his head.

"You know, Dan'l," continued Jacob, turning again to his brother, "You can always stay with me an' Emily in the new house. Thar's plenny of room."

"Thanks, Jacob, that's mighty kind. But I haven't decided what I'm a-gwine t' do just yet."

"Course, if you *was* t' buy the old Puckett place," said Jacob, considering another possibility, "you could keep Jesse. I know Ma would be pleased t' see one of her mules bein' put to good use ag'in. An' I'm sure Pa would want you t' have the old harness an' plow an' anythang else yuh might need."

"That's mighty generous of you, Jacob, but, like I say, I haven't decided yet. I'm a-gwine t' haf t' look the place over first."

Before leaving, Daniel walked over to the old farmhouse to pay his respects to Isaac's wife Martha and their daughter Lucy.

Jacob's wife Emily was there as well. He found all three women assembled in the kitchen, preparing to can the last of the summer's sweet corn. They could easily have kept him there talking the rest of the day, but he made the visit a brief one, explaining that he had a long journey ahead of him and promising that he would come back soon for a longer visit.

"I expect t' be back tomorruh night," he told Martha as he left the house, "but if I'm not, don't wait supper on me."

He swung himself up onto the mule's back, waved to Jacob and set off out the lane. Halfway to the hard road he abandoned the lane and cut across the field of fresh-cut hay in order to reach the field beyond, where Isaac was plowing. When Isaac saw him coming, he stopped his tractor, dismounted, and walked over to meet him.

"Let me guess," said Isaac with a broad grin, "you're on your way up to the old Puckett place."

"Yeah, I am," replied Daniel.

"You know, Dan'l," said Isaac, his tone more serious now, "you're always welcome t' throw in with me an' Jacob. You'd be a mighty handy feller t' have around, an' we'd be glad t' have yuh. Hell, this is your home too."

"Thanks, Isaac," replied Daniel, equally serious now, "I appreciate the offer. And in the end, who knows? I just might do that. But I've got some other sticks in the fire right now that I haf t' tend to. Could be one of 'em just might catch."

"Well, suit yourself."

Daniel nudged his heels into the mule's ribs. "C'mon, Jesse, git! . . . I'll see you tomorruh night, Isaac."

"Oh, Dan'l," Isaac called after him, "if'n you decide t' go a-traipsin' around in them old cornfields up thar, you'd best tie that mule to a tree first. I've heared a mule can fall right out of them fields up thar. A man too, 'specially if'n he's a li'l off balance in the haid t' start with."

Daniel coaxed the mule up onto the hard road and headed west. The first five miles of the journey would be the easiest as they would be entirely over "improved" road, a simple re-tracing of the course that he and Nathan had traveled earlier in the morning. But after that, the road–if one could call it that–would deteriorate rather quickly. As he passed the church he saw no children running about outside and assumed that school was now in session for the day, as well over an hour had passed since he and Nathan had dropped Otis and Sarah off. His little girl. Almost six years old. Already in school. He could scarcely believe it.

As he passed the lane leading back to Nathan's he wondered how Elizabeth was getting along on this, her first day of living with her in-laws. He wondered if Hester had put her to work yet. It seemed so strange to be leaving his small family so alone and so scattered in surroundings which to them must seem very unfamiliar, amongst people whom they had only just met–and in Sarah's case, amongst people whom she was only just meeting for the first time this morning. But Daniel knew that there was very little he could do to make the transition any easier for them. Only time could make the unfamiliar familiar. Only time could make this strange new place to which they had come seem like home.

Once beyond Nathan's lane he was no longer retracing his earlier course. Approximately three-quarters of a mile up the road he passed another lane leading off into the woods to the left. Local folks called this the Whiskey Run Road, on account of all the bootleg whiskey that had been transported along it at one time. Like the lane leading into Nathan's, Whiskey Run Road also led back to the creek.

At one time the Hyatt family had owned most of the land between the hard road and the creek–at least most of the land along that mile-long stretch of creek that lay between Nathan's and Whiskey Run Road. The land that Nathan was now farming had once belonged to John R. Hyatt. Nathan had bought the place from John's widow after John was killed in the Great War in Europe. John's father, also named John–the son's name being John R. Hyatt, the father's John W. Hyatt–had farmed a small parcel of land at the place where Whiskey Run Road forded the creek. As far as anybody knew, none of the Hyatts themselves had ever been guilty of trafficking in illegal whiskey. The fact that the elder Hyatt lived on Whiskey Run Road was not in itself proof of his guilt. It was suspected that most of the whiskey was coming not from the Hyatt place, but from stills up in the mountain on the other side of the creek. In any case, within a year after losing his son in the war, the elder Hyatt had also died, and most of the land once owned by the family was sold at public auction. The elder Hyatt's place back along Whiskey Run Road was bought by a man named Wesley Hicks, an extremely unpleasant man, about whom more will be said in due course.

From the outset of his journey the road on which Daniel had been traveling had been taking him mostly west, but somewhat north. As his ultimate destination was mostly west but somewhat *south*, he understood that there would come a point beyond which it would no longer be profitable to follow the road, no matter how good the road, no matter how easy the travel. A road, after all, is good only to the extent that it takes you where you want to go. A half mile beyond Whiskey Run Road he reached that point. Here the road was forced to bend suddenly and sharply to the north in order to skirt the formidable mountain that rose up directly to the west, effectively blocking any further progress in that direction. Daniel bade farewell to the road and made directly for the mountain. He would skirt it also, but through a gap to the south. For the rest of the journey there would be no "improved" road, hardly a road of any kind, only a trail, and in some places only the barest rudiments of even a trail.

As he rode through the woods Daniel thought about what Isaac had said about throwing in with him and Jacob. The night before Nathan had made him the same offer. Of the two, Nathan's offer was the more tempting. Isaac and Jacob worked well together because their personalities complemented each other so well. Isaac was loud, aggressive, argumentative. Jacob was quiet, passive, disinclined to argue. Isaac made the decisions, Jacob went along with him. It might be difficult to assimilate a third party, especially someone of Daniel's temperament, into this harmonious arrangement without causing serious disruption. Daniel had in his head some very firmly-rooted notions about the way some things should be done, and he wasn't sure he could be comfortable following Isaac's lead all the time. After all, that was one of the reasons he had left home in the first place. He would always be the youngest of the three brothers—and therefore the least deserving of respect—and no amount of time would ever change that.

At least with Nathan he might be accorded more respect. He might have been Hester's younger brother, but he was not Nathan's younger brother. But more importantly, he and Nathan seemed to see eye to eye on a good many things, not the least of which was their approach to farming. And, of course, one of the strongest incentives for staying at Nathan's was Hester. Of the surviving members of his family it was Hester for whom he felt the most affection, and who felt the most affection for him. Also, if he stayed at Nathan and Hester's, Sarah would have Otis for a friend. The two children had only just met, but it seemed as though they had already become stuck to each other like a pair of cockleburs, which was quite unexpected, given Sarah's past history of making friends.

On the negative side was the fact that Nathan's farm was comparatively small—only a little over forty acres, including woodlots—and the house, while it might have been quite comfortable for three or four occupants, would be a bit crowded with six—even though, as Daniel well knew, many houses in the surrounding hills and hollows, no larger than Nathan's, housed as many as a dozen or more under one roof, mostly children. Isaac and Jacob's farm, on the other hand, was much larger—about seventy-five acres—and at Isaac and Jacob's there were two houses. There was the original farmhouse, in which he himself had grown up, which Isaac and Martha now occupied; but there was also the "new" house which Jacob had built for himself and Emily when they were first married back in 1912. It was a spacious two-story farmhouse—every bit as large as the "old" house—and as Jacob and Emily had no children, there was ample room to spare. And, like Nathan and Isaac before him, Jacob had also invited Daniel and his family to move in with him.

Whatever he decided to do in the short term, Daniel knew that in the long term he would need to find a place of his own. He figured that Elizabeth, even though she could probably get along well enough with any one of her three sisters-in-law–Hester or Martha or Emily–would eventually want a place of her own as well. He had already decided that, for the winter at least, Elizabeth and Sarah would stay at Nathan and Hester's. What they did in the spring depended on a number of things, one of which was what he found at the old Puckett place.

Daniel would never even have considered the possibility of living in so remote a place had he thought that either Elizabeth or Sarah needed to be near people. But back in Springfield, where there were people aplenty, the three of them had, for all practical purposes, shut themselves off from the world. The white picket fence around their house might just as well have been a wall or a moat or a strip of burning sand–or a formidable expanse of mountain wilderness that took a man on a mule eight hours to ride through.

As the crow flew, it was probably not more than five or six miles from the town of Rushing Creek to the old Puckett place, but to the more earth-bound traveler, the winding, contorted trek up, over, and around the mountains was easily twice that. Whereas a crow could simply fly in a straight line from one peak to the next, a man–or a mule, for that matter–attempting the same journey, was obliged to descend all the way down the side of one mountain before even beginning to ascend the next.

The day was definitely warmer now, thought Daniel, as he coaxed Jesse higher and higher into the mountains. Down in the valley the foliage on the trees had still been summer-green, but here at the higher elevations signs of fall were already beginning to appear. It was nearly five o'clock in the afternoon as Daniel urged his tired mule up the last stretch of trail leading up to the old farmstead. He held his breath in anticipation as he neared his destination. When the house came into view he breathed a sigh of relief: the house was still standing. He had been half afraid that it might have burned down or simply fallen down after so many years of neglect, but no. If nothing else, the house was still standing.

He dismounted and led Jesse to a clump of young poplar saplings that had grown up in what once had been the Pucketts' garden. He knew that mules could be unpredictable and he didn't want to take a chance on Jesse suddenly taking a notion to bolt and run back down the mountain without him. As he tied the reins around one of the trees, he smiled to himself, remembering Isaac's admonition to tie the mule to a tree lest it fall off the mountain. He rubbed Jesse's sweat-lathered neck to show his gratitude and gave him a handful of oats and two ears of corn from the two-days' supply of feed that Jacob had sent along.

Slowly Daniel walked over to the house. He could not help but feel a kind of reverence for the early mountain settlers who had built houses like this. Like many another mountain cabin, the Puckett house had been built of matched chestnut logs. Great chestnut trees had once grown in abundance in these woods, before the blight began killing them off, and the early builders had preferred them because chestnut, quite simply, lasted forever—or, if not forever, for well over a hundred years.

The Jeremiah Puckett house was one of the finest examples of a matched-log house that Daniel had ever seen. Only the straightest chestnut trees had been used in its construction—the almost total absence of stubs and knots testified to that. After these trees had been felled and cut to length, the round logs had then been squared up. Old Jeremiah had done this by first scoring them with a felling ax—Daniel could still see the nicks—and then by hewing them with a broad ax. Each squared log had then been split in half, thereby producing two "matched" logs. The purpose in using matched logs, besides saving on trees, had been that by using the two matched logs in opposite walls—one of them in the west wall, say; the other in the east—all four walls could be made to rise more uniformly. Before being set into place, the logs had first been notched at each end, both top and bottom, so as to lock together at the corners. Any cracks between the logs had then been chinked with clay mud.

Daniel walked around the house, running his fingers along the chestnut logs, and found that though there had been some deterioration, due to nearly a hundred years of constant exposure to the elements, it was superficial. Just beneath the crumbly surface, the logs were still solid. Much of the mud chinking between the logs, however, had fallen out. Daniel pulled off some of the wild grape and Virginia creeper vines that all but covered one corner of the house, dislodging even more of the chinking. The walls would have to be re-chinked, he thought to himself, but otherwise, they were practically as good as new. The massive stone fireplace and chimney that towered up on the east end of the house was also still standing–Daniel had had no doubt that it would be–but it also would have to be re-chinked.

He gingerly walked up the steps to the porch, testing each step–which was nothing more than a chestnut log split in half and turned flat side up–as he did so. Even if these had to be replaced, that could be easily done. He had seen enough dead chestnut on the ride up to make all the porch steps he would ever need. The door to the house was lying on the porch. The leather hinges had become brittle with age and had given way. Daniel wondered how many years the door had banged open and shut in the wind before finally yielding.

As he stepped inside the cabin he remembered the feeling of awe that had come over him the first time he had come up here– and the same feeling came over him again. To him the most remarkable feature of these early mountain cabins was the floor. He had never seen floors like them anywhere else. The boards–if one could call them that–were hand-hewn, not sawn, out of yellow poplar, and were commonly three to four inches thick and three feet or more wide! On his previous visit to the Puckett house he had made a rough measurement of an especially wide floor plank using the span between his thumb and forefinger, and had found it to be approximately forty-five inches across! The Pucketts may have had to worry about falling off the mountain, Daniel thought, but it was not likely that they ever worried about falling through the floor!

Daniel kicked aside some of the debris that all but covered the thick, broad puncheon planks. Despite the leaking roof the floor was not too badly stained. The floor of the loft above had sustained the greater part of the rain damage, so much so that most of it had rotted away and fallen through the ceiling joists. It was the rotting remains of the inch-thick floorboards above that now accounted for most of the debris under Daniel's feet—that and the bushels of black walnuts that lay scattered everywhere. Apparently squirrels had used the loft of the abandoned house as a storehouse for their winter food supply. When the floor had collapsed, their food supply had gone with it. It may even have been the weight of all those walnuts, Daniel reckoned, that had caused the floor to collapse in the first place.

Daniel looked up at the shafts of sunlight filtering through the roof. As long as the sun shone, he mused, everything would be just fine—in fact, the additional light helped to illuminate the normally dark interior of the cabin—but in the event of a heavy downpour, he would be obliged to flee the house and seek shelter under the nearest pine tree! One of the first things he had noticed when he had first approached the house was that the roof was in desperate need of repair. The oak shingles had all but decomposed into rich black humus. He expected that when he examined the north side of the roof he might even find moss growing on it. Doubtlessly the roof had already been replaced one or two times during the seven decades that the Pucketts had occupied the house. Replacing it again would take time, and would require a few tools: a good cross-cut saw for sawing the pin oak logs into proper lengths, a maul and a couple of wedges for splitting and quartering them, and a froe and a mallet for riving the quartered chunks into shingles. He'd also need a hammer for nailing the shingles onto the batons—but he already had a hammer. Daniel figured that if a man *did* have a mind to restore the old place, about the only things he'd have to buy—assuming he could borrow whatever tools he might need—would be some nails and some glass panes for the windows, and these he could get at Walter Lehman's store. All the other materials he could get right out of the surrounding forest, just as old Jeremiah Puckett and all the other early mountain men had done before him.

Having decided that the house with a little bit of work—well, more than a little bit, a considerable amount of work actually—was salvageable, Daniel walked back outside and around the corner of the house to the barn. The barn, like the house, had been built of chestnut logs, but not as much care had been taken in its construction. The logs had not been fitted as closely together and the spaces between the logs had never been chinked. However, this had not been due to any laziness or carelessness on the part of the builder. A barn, after all, was not a house. There had simply been no need to make the barn as impervious to wind and cold and blowing rain as the house. Upon closer inspection Daniel found that the logs here were also in good condition.

But the roof, like the roof of the house, was in a state of advanced disintegration and would have to be replaced, and as the barn roof was about twice the size of the house roof, any would-be renovator would have to be prepared to split thousands of shingles. But given enough time and patience it could be done. After all, it had been done before, and almost certainly more than once, probably once every generation.

The only other structure still standing was the spring house. This had been the source of water for the farmstead, as well as the place where milk and butter and other perishables had been kept cool. Daniel peered inside the open doorway. The door was gone and part of the roof had fallen in, but as the stone-walled structure was small, he figured that one or two days work could restore it to its original condition. Clearing away some of the debris, Daniel took a handful of water and brought it to his lips. In addition to replacing the roof and the door, he would also want to hollow out a new buckeye log to catch the water. For some reason unbeknownst to him, buckeye had always been used for this purpose. Perhaps it was because the early mountain folk had believed that buckeye helped to purify the water, or perhaps they had felt that it gave the water a more "interesting" flavor. The handful of water that Daniel had just tasted had certainly had an interesting flavor–perhaps a little too interesting–but whether that was due to the buckeye log itself, which, though still capable of holding water, was in a state of decay, or to the great quantity of leaves and roof debris which had fallen into it and now lay rotting on the bottom, he had no way of knowing. At any rate, a fresh buckeye log would be one of the first orders of business.

Thinking Jesse might also appreciate a drink, Daniel walked back to where he had left the mule, untied him, and led him to the water. Daniel watched as the mule drank long and deep, then treated himself to another handful. They had stopped at a number of springs and small streams on their journey through the mountains, but as the last part of the trek had been the most arduous, both man and beast were glad for the cool water, whatever the flavor.

Having re-tied the mule, Daniel's next point of business was to survey the fields, or rather, those parts of the forest above the house and barn which had once been the fields. Daniel found exactly what he had expected to find: the fields had all reverted to forest and would have to be re-cleared. He was thankful for at least one thing: there were no three-and four-foot wide yellow poplars growing in the old Puckett fields. But there were quite a few smaller trees that had been growing for from ten to twenty years and it would take a lot of time and muscle to remove them—that is, if anyone had any reason to do so. If anyone *should* one day decide to reclaim the old Puckett fields, Daniel reasoned, it would not all have to be done at once. He could clear just enough land the first year for a garden and a small cornfield, and then a little more each succeeding year as time and the enthusiasm for the job permitted—just as the early Pucketts had probably done originally.

He ambled slowly through the fields of scrub pines and poplar saplings until he came to what he thought must have been the legendary cornfield from which old Jeremiah and his mule had made their celebrated departure from this life. Daniel had no doubt that the plot must have been cleared at one time, as there were no trees standing in it more than four or five inches in diameter, but the steep slope of the "field" made him shake his head in disbelief—and admiration, for anyone who had the courage to try to grow corn on a hillside this steep. He judged the angle of the rise to be better than fifty degrees, perhaps closer to sixty. Holding onto the trees he cautiously moved down the slope to what he believed must have been the lower boundary of this cornfield-for-the-fearless, and, indeed, he discovered upon looking down over the edge that this "field" did pretty much just drop right off the mountain. He paused to wonder whether the old story about Jeremiah and his mule might not be true after all.

Lifting his eyes, he directed his gaze out across the treetops below. He understood why the early Pucketts had cleared this slope: it had given them an unobstructed view deep into the hollow below and out across to the mountains beyond–an extraordinary view even for these mountains, where spectacular views were commonplace. And of course once a piece of land had been cleared, someone sooner or later–and usually sooner–would just naturally take a notion to try growing corn on it. Not that they had much choice. Flat land was hard to come by in the mountains, except on the grassy balds. Up here any field with a pitch of less than thirty degrees was considered flat. If a man could find a truly flat piece of ground big enough to build his house on, he counted himself fortunate. You had to make your farm where the water was, and the water always seemed to come bubbling out of the mountainsides.

Daniel walked back toward the house, but instead of going directly to it, he walked around it, giving it a wide berth, so as to get a better view. He then climbed up onto some rocks in the woods overlooking the old farmstead, and sat quietly for the next hour, lost in thought. He realized that ever since he had arrived and found the house still standing, he had been thinking about what would need to be done to restore it. Did he really want to live up here? He searched his soul and found the answer forthcoming: he really did. Not at Nathan's. Not at Isaac's. Not at Jacob's. But here. Here on this isolated mountain farm where men fell out of cornfields and bears ate children on their way to the privy at night. Here in his own world, where that other world–that mad, rushing world of bankers and businessmen, wars and depressions–could not reach him. Here in his own world, where a simple man like himself could have some control over his own life, and not be the victim of forces which he did not even understand. Yes, here where people had been known to die from the awful loneliness of the place, and where *his* heart too had been made to ache, but not from the loneliness, but by the awesome beauty of the place.

It was getting dark. Daniel got up and walked back toward the house. He had brought no food with him, but he wasn't hungry. He was much too excited to think about eating. But he *had* brought a heavy coat along and this he now put on as the night air was becoming cool. For the next two hours he sat on the top porch step looking into the rapidly darkening forest and listening to the whippoorwills. It had been years since he had heard a whippoorwill. It was late in the season for them, he thought, and they would soon be gone. Soon be gone, he repeated to himself, in time with the whippoorwill's piercing cry, soon be gone. His mood suddenly turned somber. That strange sensation that he had experienced earlier in the day as he walked down the lane to Isaac and Jacob's welled up in him again. He thought of all the old Pucketts who must have sat on this same porch step in years gone by and listened to the whippoorwills at night. They were all gone now, all buried up on the wooded hillside in a small neglected cemetery, their graves overgrown with brambles, vines, and scrub pines. They were all gone now, all crumbled into dust, as he too one day would be.

He thought of Elizabeth and Sarah. Somewhere far off in the valley below Elizabeth was probably putting Sarah to bed about now, perhaps reading her a story by the light of the kerosene lamp. The thought lifted his spirits. He stood up, stretched his legs, and walked inside the cabin. Seeking out the forty-five-inch-wide floorboard, he cleared it of debris and lay down upon it. He moved his head from side to side until his eyes fixed upon that for which he was looking: a star shining through a hole in the roof. He had only one wish to make and he made it. If there was any way in the world, even if it meant moving Heaven and Earth to do it, he wished to buy the old Puckett place.

The morning that Daniel left to go to Isaac and Jacob's, Hester, like her sisters-in-law Martha and Emily, was also getting ready to do some late-season canning. The night before, after supper, Elizabeth had offered to help with anything that needed to be done, so as soon as Nathan and Daniel and the two children had left, Hester handed her a basket, "C'mon, Miss 'Lizbeth, we got us some limer beans t' pick."

Elizabeth followed Hester into the labyrinthine garden. After passing rows of lettuce, cabbage, carrots, beets, turnips, and several kinds of dark leafy things which Elizabeth could not identify, they came to what appeared to Elizabeth to be two long rows of Indian teepees. Each "teepee" consisted of three poles, each about eight feet in length, spaced about three and a half feet apart at the base and meeting at a point about six feet above the ground. How they were fastened together at the top Elizabeth could only guess, as the point at which the three poles met, as well as the entire length of each pole, was completely covered by thick leafy bean vines. There were two long rows of these lima bean teepees, with about fifteen teepees in each row.

"You go down that side," instructed Hester, as they set their baskets down at the first teepee in the first row, "an I'll go down this'un."

Elizabeth assumed her position on the inside of the row and commenced picking. It was not the first time she had picked beans–she had grown snap beans in her little garden back in Springfield–but she soon found that she could not keep up with Hester, try as she may. After the first teepee she was already behind, even though Hester had picked two of the three poles and she had only picked one. Moving on to the second teepee, she discovered that two of the three poles were now on *her* side, only one on Hester's, and looking down the row she saw that this was the pattern: on the odd-numbered teepees two of the three poles would be on Hester's side; on the even-numbered teepees two of the three poles would be on *her* side. By the time Elizabeth had finished the second teepee, Hester had already finished the third and was moving on to the fourth.

Before she had filled her first basket, Elizabeth's back and knees were aching. She looked up to see how near she was to the end of the row. She was distressed to find that she still had about two-thirds of the row yet to pick. And after that there would be the whole other row! She had just finished her first basket and was starting her second when she saw Hester coming around the corner at the far end of the row. Hester, it appeared, had already finished her side of the row and was now going to help her finish hers. By the time the two women met, they had picked nearly five full baskets between them. Hester had picked three by herself and had helped Elizabeth finish her second.

"How do you *do* it?" marveled Elizabeth.

" 'Tain't nuthin' once you get the hang of it," replied Hester modestly, disclaiming any super-human power. There was still the other row of teepees to pick. "Might as well start right here," said Hester, turning to face the other row. "I'll go this way an' you go that, an' we'll meet somewhars on the other side."

When they had finished picking the second row of teepees, the two women carried the ten baskets of beans into the kitchen. Elizabeth was glad to discover she could still walk. She had begun to fear, as she struggled through that last row of beans, that she might never be able to stand without assistance, let alone walk, again.

The morning had already become quite warm and humid, and the cool of the kitchen was a welcome relief to Elizabeth. Hester offered her a glass of cold spring water and she gladly accepted. She was hot and tired and she was sure her back and knees would never function properly again. As she sipped the cold water she wondered what she had gotten herself into. Hester worked like this every day of her life, she reflected, and here I am ready to die after only two hours!

"Now we gotta shell 'em," announced Hester as she bustled about the kitchen gathering together the necessary paraphernalia: two chairs, two washtubs, and a large iron kettle. She quickly placed the two chairs about five feet apart and facing each other, and then placed a washtub in front of each chair. Between the two washtubs she set the kettle. She sat down on one of the chairs to demonstrate the procedure to Elizabeth, but this was unnecessary as Elizabeth had figured it out at a glance. The beans would go in the kettle; the discarded pods would go in the washtubs.

"You'll find thar's not near as much here as it looks," Hester reassured her. "The darned thangs are mostly shuck. Sometimes I wonder why I bother t' grow 'em–'ceptin' they taste so darned good."

For the rest of the morning the two women shelled beans and talked. Elizabeth wanted to know more about the old Puckett place, but Hester didn't know much more than she had already told the day before.

"But I could tell you some tales 'bout when Dan'l was a young'un an' I looked after him," volunteered Hester.

"Oh yes!" exclaimed Elizabeth, "please do. I'd love to hear them."

As Daniel's sister related one amusing anecdote after another, Elizabeth soon forgot about her aching knees and back and her earlier agony amongst the bean poles. And Daniel was right: some of Hester's stories were quite outrageous.

"I 'member one time when he was about three years old," chuckled Hester, recalling another story, "I had just give him a bath an' put nice clean clothes on him—nice clean clothes fresh off the laundry line. I mean, if thar ever was a clean child on this earth, he was it that day. He was so clean that if yuh rubbed his haid, he'd squeak.

"I told him, Dan'l, whatever you do, you stay clean now, you hear? . . . Well, lookin' back on it, I can see now that that was the worst thang I could a-said, 'cause soon as my back was turned, he was outside a-throwin' dirt all over hisself. I was so mad I picked him up an' carried him straight to the hog pen an' stuck him in–stuck him right in the waller. Ever' time he'd try t' crawl out, I'd pick him up an' stick him right back in. He was a-bawlin' somethin' awful but I paid him no mind. Ever' time he crawled out, I stuck him right back in. When I finally let him out, he was covered haid to foot in hog's waller. He looked like a little mud baby . . . Next time I told him t' stay clean," concluded Hester, smiling with satisfaction, "he stayed clean."

Again Elizabeth laughed with delight. She could have listened to Hester tell stories all day. When, after several minutes however, another story was not forthcoming, Elizabeth decided to do a little prompting. "Daniel said you used to have a rag doll."

"Sure did. I used t' carry Dan'l in one arm an' my rag doll in the other. An' would you believe it? Dan'l was so jealous of that doll! He was all the time a-tryin' t' hide it. Once he even throwed it in the root cellar."

Now that was an interesting detail that Elizabeth had not heard before: Daniel had been *jealous* of Hester's rag doll.

"Did Daniel ever tell you that I made Sarah a doll just like the one you used to have?" asked Elizabeth.

"I believe he did mention it in a letter once."

"Apparently we left it on the train because we can't seem to find it. But Sarah used to love that doll. She'd sleep with it every night and when she'd wake up in the morning, the first thing she'd do would be talk to that doll, sometimes for *hours*."

Curious I should say that, Elizabeth thought to herself. She realized that she was still holding on to her earlier misconception that Sarah had been talking to her rag doll in those early morning hours during the last year they had lived in Springfield. She really did not want to believe that all those animated conversations were not with the doll but with–"Kati."

Hester, still laughing over how angry and indignant she had been as a child when she found her rag doll in the bin of squash in the root cellar after a frantic week of searching, would not have anticipated Elizabeth's next question in a hundred years.

"Did Otis ever have an imaginary friend?"

"A 'maginary friend?" repeated Hester, taken aback by this sudden turn in the conversation and wishing to confirm that Elizabeth had asked what she thought she had asked.

"Yes, like an imaginary playmate. I mean, he is an only child and there are no other children who live close by. Sometimes children in that situation invent imaginary friends to play with."

"Well, if'n he ever had one, he never said a word to me about it. I ain't so sure I woulda approved if'n he had. I don't hold much with makin' believe somethin' is real when it ain't. A body can go quare in the haid gwine on like that. No, Otis is about as normal as they come, praise the Lord. Besides, he's got a playmate. He's got Pokey."

Elizabeth was half afraid that Hester was going to ask what had possessed her to ask such a strange question in the first place, and given Hester's views on the matter, Elizabeth was not so sure that she wanted to tell her about Sarah's friend "Kati." Fortunately Nathan came in just about then for dinner. He had returned from Isaac and Jacob's while the women were picking beans and had been out in the barn sharpening the knives of his mowing blade. Hester showed him the large kettle of beans she and Elizabeth had shelled.

"Like it says in the Good Book," said Nathan with a playful twinkle in his eye, "many hands make light work."

"You won't find that in the Lord's Word an' you know it, Nathan Andersson," retorted Hester, "but it happens t' be true all the same."

Elizabeth too was surprised to see how many beans they had done. She had so enjoyed herself listening to Hester's stories that it hardly seemed like they had been working at all.

After dinner Nathan allowed that, as much as he'd like to spend the rest of the day in the nice cool kitchen, he'd be going out to mow hay for the rest of the afternoon.

"Once we start cannin' these beans," Hester assured him, "hit'll be hotter in here than it is out thar. But neither place will be half as hot as the place you'll be a-gwine if'n you don't stop pokin' fun at the Lord's Word."

"Now don't get your hackles up," laughed Nathan. "I was sure I remembered readin' that in the Good Book somewhere. Maybe in the Book of Nathan ... "

Hester shooed him out the door and went back to her beans.

About half past three in the afternoon Sarah and Otis came walking in the lane. Sarah was still talking and Otis, head bent to the side, was still listening as hard as he knew how. Suddenly

Sarah stopped dead in her tracks and put a hand over Otis' mouth.

"Shhh," she said.

Otis, who hadn't said but two or three words since the two had left school, lurched to a stop and remained obediently silent. Sarah listened intently. There was a curious clackety-clacking sound coming from behind the barn. She released her grip on Otis and ran to investigate. Otis, thrown off balance by Sarah's sudden departure, dropped his books, picked them up again, and ran after her. Pokey, sprawled on the porch, barked as first Sarah, then Otis, ran by, but did not bother to get up.

In the hayfield behind the barn Sarah found her Uncle Nathan sitting atop the strangest-looking contraption she had ever seen. Two horses were pulling it and as it moved through the field, the hay in its path kept falling down. Curious to see what it was that was making the hay fall down, Sarah ran closer. Nathan had seen her coming and reined in the team.

"What makes the high grass fall down, Uncle Nathan?" she asked.

Nathan pointed to the cutting bar. "See all those sharp knives down there? Well, when the wheels go 'round, those knives move back an' forth real fast. You've gotta be real careful around mowers, Sarah. They can cut your toes off faster'n you can snap your fingers."

Sarah immediately jumped two steps back.

"What are the horses' names, Uncle Nathan?"

"Well, the one nearest you there is Blackie. We call the other one Old Blue."

"Old Blue? Why do you call him that? He's not blue, he's black, the same as Blackie."

Nathan smiled. "That's true. We call him Blue 'cause he always looks so sad. When he was born, he was the saddest lookin' little colt you'd ever wanna see . . . Go 'round an' look at his eyes. See how sad he looks."

Sarah walked around to the front of the horses and studied the face of the one, then the other, in order to compare the two.

"See how sad he looks?" inquired Nathan.

"Yes," replied Sarah, "he does look a little sad. But I still don't understand why you call him 'Old Blue'."

" 'Blue' means 'sad.' "

"No, it doesn't, Uncle Nathan. Blue is a color. It's the color of the sky."

"It also means 'sad.' If you don't believe me, you can ask your mother."

"I will. And she'll *know* too. She knows what *all* words mean."

Just then Otis came running up. "Pa, after I finish my chores, can we go down to the creek?"

"All right, *after* you finish your chores. But I don't want either one of you fallin' in. *Or* jumpin' in."

He shook the reins, and the horses, which had been eating the hay as they waited, moved forward. Sarah watched in fascination as the wheels turned, the knives went clackety-clack back and forth, and the hay fell. When she was satisfied that she understood more or less how it all worked, she turned to Otis. "Come on, I'll help you with your chores."

At supper that night Elizabeth was interested in hearing how Sarah had enjoyed her first day of school.

"It was awful!" declared Sarah without hesitation. "She made us sit still all day and only let us go outside two times."

"Three times," Otis corrected her.

"Three times." She stood corrected. "If you count the end of the day."

"Who is 'she?' " asked Elizabeth.

"Mean old Miss Kinney," replied Sarah.

"Miss Kinney is the school teacher," explained Nathan. "She teaches the first three grades." Then with an impish twinkle in his eye he turned to Otis. "Is that true, Son? Is Miss Kinney mean and old?"

"Oh yeah, Pa," confirmed Otis, "she's *real* mean an' *real* old ... She gave Frank Hicks another lickin' today."

"He prob'bly had it comin'," interjected Hester. "None of them Hicks children is any good. 'Course hit's their pa's t' blame. Anyone who would chop off a young'un's fingers with an ax just for touchin' somethin' he weren't supposed t' touch, cain't be in his right mind."

Sarah, who had been reaching for a biscuit, quickly withdrew her hand.

Elizabeth shuddered. "He really did that?"

"He sure 'nuff did. He's terrible mean to them kids. Always has been. Hit's no wonder they've turned out as bad as they have. The oldest, Wesley Jr., is already in prison, servin' a life sentence for murder. An' mark my words, the other six will end up in jail too—if'n their Pa don't manage t' kill them first."

Nathan looked at Otis. "Which one did you say got the lickin' today?"

"Frank. He's the one who always gets the lickin'."

"He's the youngest, isn't he?"

"Yeah, Pa, he's even younger'n me."

"He ain't the youngest," Hester corrected him. "Thar's another one still at home."

A moment of grave silence fell over the table.

"You sure gotta feel sorry for those kids," said Nathan at last.

"Yes," agreed Elizabeth, "and for their mother too."

Later that night as Elizabeth was helping Sarah get ready for bed, she could not help but notice that her daughter was not her usual high-spirited self. Elizabeth had been aware since supper that something was troubling her. "What is it, Honey?" she asked sympathetically. She knelt down and Sarah put her arms around her neck.

"Mommy, do I have to go back to school? Please don't make me."

Sarah's plaintive cry pierced straight through to Elizabeth's heart. Elizabeth hugged her closely as she tried to think of a way to make it easier for her.

"Sarah," she began hesitantly, "you know how you like to explore new places?" She could feel Sarah's head nodding against her neck. "Well, there are whole new worlds in books that you haven't even begun to explore yet. Once you learn how to read, you can explore wonderful new places that you can't even imagine now. Learning can be a great adventure. Can't you think of it as a great adventure? Every day you can discover new words. Believe me, Sarah, it may seem hard now, but once you learn to read and write, you'll never regret it."

Elizabeth paused to allow Sarah's mind to absorb the import of her words, then continued. "I know this is an exciting time for you. We've come to a new place and I know you'd rather be outside playing than sitting in a schoolroom all day. But we're going to be here for a very long time, and the mountains and the woods and the fields and that rushing creek out there will always be here. You can spend the rest of your life exploring them if you want to. But as long as we're living here at your Aunt Hester's I think you should go to school. Once your Daddy finds us our own place to live, you may not be able to go to school."

Sarah released herself from her mother's embrace and looked into her face. "What do you mean, Mommy?"

"I mean, as long as we're living this close to a school I think you should go. When we move to our own place, there may not be a school close enough for you to go to." If Daniel buys the old Puckett place, Elizabeth thought to herself, there *certainly* wouldn't be a school close enough for Sarah to go to, even if only half of what Hester had said was true. "But you will still have to learn to read and write. If you don't go to school, I will have to teach you myself."

Sarah seemed more at ease now. Her eyes grew brighter and she smiled. How Elizabeth loved that smile. She was glad that something she had said had helped to ease her daughter's anxiety, but whether it had been her eloquent speech about learning being a great adventure or her statement that there might not be a school close enough to go to once they moved to a place of their own, she could not be sure.

"Now, how about a bedtime story?" suggested Elizabeth, hoping that the enthusiasm in her voice might ignite something in Sarah.

"Good idea!" exclaimed Sarah as she jumped into bed.

Soon after Sarah had fallen asleep, Elizabeth blew out the kerosene lamp and crawled under the covers herself. She had had an exhausting day and was ready for sleep. As there was only the one double bed in the spare upstairs room at Hester's, she and Sarah would share it. The night before, Sarah had slept downstairs on the sofa in the parlor, and she and Daniel had shared the double bed. Elizabeth wondered where Daniel was at that very moment. Was he at Isaac and Jacob's? Or was he far back in the mountains, up at the old Puckett place?

She missed him, but she was glad for the opportunity to spend some time alone with Sarah. It had been a long time since Sarah had slept with her and Daniel in their bed, and Elizabeth was glad for the opportunity to renew the closer physical contact. She had always enjoyed cuddling Sarah close to her and stroking her long soft hair. She had never realized how much until Sarah had stopped coming over to their bed in the mornings, which was about the time that Sarah had started sleeping with her rag doll and talking to—"Kati."

That was another reason Elizabeth welcomed the opportunity to sleep with Sarah again. Perhaps she could come to a better understanding about what, only a few months ago, had been the one great concern in her life—that is, before it was overwhelmed by greater and more urgent concerns. Would Sarah talk to her friend "Kati" with her mother lying in the same bed next to her? Elizabeth was a light sleeper. She knew that if Sarah moved or spoke at any time during the night she would be aware of it.

It was normally between four and five o'clock in the morning that Sarah and "Kati" had their conversations, but four o'clock, then five o'clock passed without any sound or movement out of Sarah. Then, around six o'clock, just as the first light of dawn was beginning to illuminate the room, Elizabeth was awakened. Sarah had begun to move restlessly. Her arms and legs were twitching and her head was tossing back and forth on the pillow. Suddenly she began screaming. "No, no, no, no . . . !"

Immediately Elizabeth began shaking her. "Sarah, wake up! Wake up!"

Sarah's eyes popped open. Elizabeth had never seen such a frightened look on her child's face. Her small body rigid as a board, Sarah looked around the room, only her eyes moving, rolling nervously in their sockets.

"It's all right, Honey, it's all right."

"Where are we, Mommy?" asked Sarah, terrified, still looking around.

Elizabeth stroked her hair to comfort her. "We're at your Aunt Hester's, Sweetie. You just had a bad dream, that's all." And Elizabeth was almost certain she knew what that bad dream was about.

"Mommy?" said Sarah. She was somewhat calmer now.

"Yes, Sarah?" In her mind Elizabeth could already hear Sarah asking the question, "Mommy, do I really *have* to go to school?"

"Mommy, where did we live before we lived in our house with the white fence?"

The question had come so unexpected that Elizabeth, who had been preparing in her mind another speech on the importance of going to school, now had to start all over again. What had Sarah asked? Where had they lived before the little house in Springfield?

"Well," she answered, as coherently as it is possible to answer a question at six o'clock in the morning when one is suddenly awakened from sleep, "I lived in a big house on a hill in another part of Springfield, and your Daddy lived in a rooming house near where he worked. And before that, he lived on a farm right here in North Carolina about five miles from where we are now. But *you* didn't live anywhere before the little house in Springfield. That's where you were born."

The puzzled look on Sarah's face told Elizabeth that Sarah was not at all satisfied with the answer.

"But then where did I live before I came to live with you and Daddy?"

"You didn't live *anywhere*, Sweetheart. You were *born* in Springfield." Clearly, Sarah was having trouble grasping the concept of being born. This was ground they had tried to cover before, but without much success. Elizabeth decided to try again.

"Sarah, do you understand what it means to be born?"

No, she did not. Anyone looking into the child's face could see that.

"Do you remember when we planted our little garden back in Springfield?"

Sarah nodded.

"Do you remember how we'd bury those tiny little seeds in the ground in the spring, and in the summer our little garden would be filled with all different kinds of flowers and vegetables . . . ?"

"I liked the sunflowers best. They were the biggest."

"Yes, they were tall, weren't they? . . . Well, all those wonderful flowers and vegetables came out of those tiny seeds . . . And do you remember in the park when we gathered acorns and I told you that those giant oak trees had all grown out of little acorns just like the ones you were holding in your hand?"

Sarah nodded again. So far she was following it, but then she always followed it this far. But after this it always got more difficult. Part of the problem was that Elizabeth herself had no idea how any of this happened. She knew that it *did* happen—marigolds and cabbages *did* grow from tiny seeds, acorns *did* grow into oak trees—but *how* it happened, how it was even possible that it *could* happen, she didn't have a clue in the world. It all seemed utterly miraculous to her, too incredible to be believed.

Sarah couldn't believe it either. "Mommy, are you trying to tell me that I came from a seed?"

"Yes, Honey . . . well, sort of. A seed that your Daddy and I planted."

Sarah laughed. "That's the silliest thing I ever heard."

Elizabeth had to agree.

"Mommy, are we going to have a garden next year?"

"Well, if your Daddy finds us our own place to live, I'm sure we'll have our own garden."

"That's good. I want to plant sunflowers. Aunt Hester doesn't have any sunflowers in her garden . . . Mommy?"

"Yes, Sarah?"

"Do you think Otis is up yet?"

"I don't know. I haven't heard him. Your Uncle Nathan and Aunt Hester are up though. They've been up for over an hour."

"Otis said we don't have to go to school on Saturday and Sunday."

"That's right."

"That's good. I wouldn't want to go to school *every* day... Can we get up now?"

Elizabeth laughed at her daughter's impatience to be up and moving. She had wondered how long Sarah was going to be content to lie in bed and chatter idly. Normally she did her "conversing" earlier in the morning, so as to be ready for action by the first light of dawn. Elizabeth herself was normally an early riser, but her body felt unusually stiff and sore this morning, the bed unusually comfortable. "I certainly hope so," she replied in answer to Sarah's question, as she struggled to force her reluctant body into motion.

As Elizabeth supervised Sarah's dressing of herself, she marveled at the moment-to-moment vicissitudes in the normal course of a child's mental life. Only a few minutes before, Sarah had been in the throes of a terrifying nightmare. Now she seemed to have forgotten all about it, her mind having moved on to other things. Perhaps that was also the reason she had not had her pre-dawn conversation with "Kati:" perhaps her mind had now moved on to other things. There were certainly enough other things in Sarah's life at the moment to occupy even *her* active mind, from the totally new and exciting physical environment in which she found herself, to all the new people she was meeting (not the least of whom was her cousin Otis), and, yes, even to school. Whatever Sarah's bad dream had been about, apparently it had not been about school. Sarah seemed to have resigned herself, for the time being at least, to the idea of going to school. If all of this new and stimulating activity had no other effect than to crowd "Kati" out of Sarah's mind—to drive out that "voice" in the night—then Elizabeth would have considered the move from Springfield to Rushing Creek an unqualified success. More than anything else in the world, she wished Sarah to be a normal, healthy, and happy child. Granted this, she could endure almost any amount of pain to her own body that this change in the course of their lives might entail.

It was on Thursday evening, the evening of their fourth full day at Nathan and Hester's, that Isaac's truck came in the lane. Hester, who was weeding in her garden, frowned when she saw it coming until it stopped in the driveway and Daniel stepped out. Rushing to the truck Hester threw her arms around him and hugged him as though another twelve years had just passed since their last meeting. When Elizabeth and Sarah came rushing out of the house, Daniel wheeled to meet them with open arms, causing Hester to be spun off at a tangent. Hester, feeling as though she had just been thrown from a horse, watched as Daniel embraced first Sarah, then Elizabeth, then both together, holding them warmly and tightly in his arms and kissing each repeatedly.

"Well, how do yuh like that?" remarked Hester playfully. "He's got more affection for these purty young Yankee women than he does for his own sister."

They all laughed and Daniel hugged Hester again, this time picking her up and swinging her around.

"We've already et supper, but I can heat somethin' up for yuh," offered Hester, when she had been returned to earth.

"No need t' do that, Sis. I already had supper over at Isaac and Martha's, but I'll take a piece of pie if you have some around." Daniel knew that Hester always had pie around.

"Sure do," replied Hester as they all moved up the steps and into the house.

"I didn't know you knew how to drive," said Elizabeth, flushed with emotion. She was surprised at the strange giddy feeling that had come over her upon seeing Daniel again.

"Didn't til yesterday," replied Daniel. "Isaac learned me." No sooner had the words left his mouth than he realized his error.

He had forgotten for the moment to whom it was he was speaking. "What I mean is, I learned from Isaac. Isaac *taught* me." Being bilingual did not come easy to a simple farmboy from the hills of North Carolina.

"I didn't know Isaac knew how to drive," drawled Nathan sarcastically. Nathan had been sitting in the kitchen cleaning his rifle when they came in.

Hester put a plateful of apple pie on the table and Daniel sat down.

"You got a gleam in your eye," observed Hester. "You got some news t' tell."

"Yes, I do," said Daniel, digging into his pie, "I've bought the old Puckett place."

The others all looked at Daniel, then at one another.

"Well, that *is* news," said Nathan.

"Hit took me two days of drivin' all over three counties an' part of Tennessee, but I finally did it. Yesterday mornin' I went over to the courthouse in Haynesville to find out who owned the place an' learned that the present owner was a Mr. Clarence Puckett who lived in Bryson City. So I drove down to Bryson City only t' learn that Mr. Clarence had died an' left the place to his sister over in Newport, Tennessee. So I drove on over to Newport to find this sister, a widow lady named Miss Lillian Crum. Hit seems like the lumber comp'nies had been after Mr. Clarence to sell the place for years, but his old gran'daddy had made all the children in the family promise never t' let the lumber comp'nies have it. Neither Mr. Clarence nor Miss Lillian had ever been up to the old place themselves, an' Miss Lillian had no plans to go up. She didn't have no use for the place herself, but, like her brother Clarence, she didn't want t' break her promise to her old gran'daddy. When I told her I was int'rested in buyin' the old place, the first thang she asked me was, Are you a lumber man? When I swore to her I wasn't she was so grateful, she would like to a-give me the old place just for takin' it off her hands. But with a little bit of persuadin' I was able t' get her to agree on a fair price."

"That was yesterday. Then today, Miss Lillian and I met at the courthouse in Haynesville an' signed all the papers nice an' proper an' legal-like. An' here," he concluded, pulling a long envelope out of his coat pocket, "is the deed."

He removed the folded piece of paper from the envelope and opened it up and laid it on the table for all to see.

"Now, I'm a-gwine t' haf t' do a lotta work on the old place before we can move in, so what I was a-hopin', if'n it's all right with you" —he looked at Nathan, then at Hester—"is that Elizabeth an' Sarah can stay here with you through the winter. By spring I should have the place in good enough shape t' move in."

"Sure, Dan'l," said Nathan, "that's fine by me."

"They can stay for as long as they like an' be mighty welcome," agreed Hester.

Secretly Hester had been hoping they'd *all* stay, Daniel included, and for more than just a few months. But whatever misgivings she had about Daniel's buying the old Puckett place, she kept them to herself. She didn't want to say anything that might put a damper on his enthusiasm.

Later that night, after Sarah had been put to bed, Daniel enticed Elizabeth outside. It was a warm moonlit night, and as they strolled hand in hand through the apple orchard and along the field of fresh-cut hay, they were reminded of their courting days—their "spoonin' " days, as Daniel had called them. And in many ways they *were* beginning all over again. Elizabeth realized that she would not be seeing much of her husband during the next six months and she knew there would be times when she would miss him desperately. During the eight and a half years they had been married—all the years they had lived in Massachusetts—not a day had gone by when they had not sat down to breakfast and supper together. Every night for eight and a half years they had shared the same bed. Now all that was changing.

Daniel assured her that whatever she might have heard about the old Puckett place, she would fall in love with it once she saw it. But he didn't want her to see it until he had had a chance to fix it up. Then he wanted to surprise her. He was afraid that if she saw it now, in its present condition, it might be too great a surprise, and probably not a very pleasant one. He wasn't sure that Elizabeth had his capacity for seeing the potential in the old place. There was no sense taking the chance of scaring her off by taking her up too soon.

"I'm going to miss you," said Elizabeth sadly. "You know that, don't you?"

"'Course I know that," replied Daniel, seeking now to cheer and comfort his wife, "but, hey, listen, hit's a-gwine t' be twice as hard for me, yuh know. I've got two of you t' miss. At least you'll have Sarah. I won't have nobody, 'ceptin' them old dead Pucketts buried up on the hillside—an' they ain't much comp'ny. But hit's only gwine t' be for a few months. When spring comes, an' all the trees start t' bud out, an' all the flowers are a-bustin' into bloom, an' the birds are a-singin' ag'in, I'll be a-comin' t' fetch yuh. An' once we get settled into our new home, I'll never leave yuh ag'in. I won't even haf t' go off to work ever' day like I did back in Springfield. Oh, I expect I'll haf t' come down here from time t' time t'. do a little work for Nathan or for Isaac an' Jacob—in exchange for some thangs we cain't raise or make ourselves—but most days I'll be home with you an' Sarah, a-working' right thar on our own place. You'll prob'bly get so tired of havin' me underfoot, that after a while you'll be a-wishin' that I go away an' give you some peace."

"Daniel," said Elizabeth after a moment's silence, "have you given any thought as to what we're going to do for money?"

"A little. We won't be a-needin' much money, but we *will* need *some*. I have an idea, but before I tell you what it is, I'd kinda like t' discuss it with Walter Lehman first. He's the feller who runs the general store."

"Yes, I've met him. Nathan and Hester took me into the store yesterday. What an incredible place!"

"Like the sign out front says, if Walter ain't got it, you don't need it. Hit's been over twelve years since I been in thar, but I'll be a-gwine in tomorruh. Thar's a coupla thangs I need t' pick up. Mebbe I'll talk to Walter about my idea then."

The next morning Daniel gave Sarah and Otis a ride to school in the back of the truck, then proceeded on to Isaac and Jacob's.

There he re-traded the truck for the mule and borrowed a number of tools. Returning to Nathan and Hester's around noon with pack mule in tow, he relieved Jesse of his burden, then spent the rest of the day helping Nathan gather the season's last cutting of hay into the barn. The following morning he re-packed the mule, said good-by to his wife, daughter, sister, brother-in-law, and nephew and set off for the mountains to the west. It would be two months before any of them would see Daniel again.

4

SETTLING IN

Even before she had stepped off the train in Asheville, Elizabeth had understood that there was a very good possibility that she and Daniel and Sarah would be staying, for a while at least, with some member of Daniel's family, either with his sister Hester or with one of his two brothers. That was one of the things they had discussed during the long train ride down from Massachusetts. But Elizabeth had assumed that Daniel would be staying with them. She had not imagined that Daniel might leave her and Sarah in the company of strangers to fend for themselves. But now that it had been decided that she and Sarah—she and Sarah *alone*—would be staying with Nathan and Hester through the fall and winter, Elizabeth proceeded to unpack the rest of their things and prepare herself mentally to settle in. The only home she had ever known was now a thousand miles away. The man she had married, the man who had brought her here, was not going to be with her, to protect her, to act as a buffer against the sharp edges of this unfamiliar environment. She was determined to succeed at this new life upon which she had embarked, and determined to begin by making the most of the circumstances in which she now found herself, but she was under no illusion that the adjustments that she and Sarah would have to make would be easy.

Nathan and Hester had welcomed them with open arms and open hearts. Both seemed genuinely glad to be able to share their modest home with their kinfolk from the north. If Elizabeth had sensed the least hesitancy or resistance on the part of either of them, the situation would have been intolerable. Still, Elizabeth knew that she was being welcomed, not because of who *she* was, but because she was Daniel's wife. As of yet her gracious hosts had very little idea about who Daniel's wife was and how different she was from them. On first meeting they had no way of knowing the kinds of thoughts that ran through the deepest channels of her mind, or the kinds of ideals and values which she had come to hold most dear.

Not that Elizabeth felt that her ideals and values were all that different from Nathan and Hester's. Even though she had come from a very different background, had been brought up with very different values, she had discarded many of the values of her parents and come to appreciate a very different set of values—a set of values much nearer to those of Nathan and Hester, she believed, than to those of her father and mother. It had been largely through the writings of the Romantic poets and philosophers that she had come to have an admiration for simple peasant folk, for people who lived close to nature, who were honest, hard-working, frugal, and self-sufficient. That was one of the reasons, perhaps the main reason, she had been so attracted to Daniel. He was a living embodiment of all those qualities and virtues she had come to admire, and it was through Daniel's stories of his sister Hester and other members of his family that she had come to have a deep respect and admiration for these people amongst whom he had grown up. Now that she too would be living among them, she would have the opportunity to put into practice, in a meaningful way, the values and ideals to which she had intellectually committed herself.

But the fact remained that she was different from them: different from Nathan and Hester, different from Isaac, different even from Daniel—and it would never be otherwise. Even though she now shared many of the same values, she had not been bred to those values. She had come by them by a very different route, and, as a consequence, she had acquired a number of other beliefs and attitudes along the way—beliefs and attitudes which she knew her husband and his family did *not* share, and which would prevent her from ever feeling completely at home among them. Even if she lived out the rest of her days amongst these mountains and hollows, she would always be an "outlander." It would be nothing new to her. All her life she had felt like an "outlander," even back in Massachusetts, and never more so than in her own family home. The closest friends she had ever had were in college, and even they, she felt, had never really understood her. She had seldom felt totally comfortable among groups of people. She was ever the outsider looking in. The closest she had ever come to feeling that she was actually *part* of a group, that she actually *belonged*, was the first night here at Nathan and Hester's, that wonderfully heady evening around the supper table. Her life among her husband's people could not have had a more auspicious beginning, but Elizabeth was not so unrealistic as to believe that that kind of rapport could be sustained. She knew that their respective differences would manifest themselves soon enough. It was on a Saturday morning that Daniel left to begin work on the old Puckett place. Elizabeth expected that the first confrontation with Nathan and Hester would come the following morning. She was right.

"Ain't a-gwine to church?" exclaimed Hester in surprise. "Ain't a-gwine to church? Nathan, she says she ain't a-gwine to church!"

Nathan, still adjusting his tie, walked into the kitchen, where the scene between Hester and Elizabeth was being played out, but said nothing.

Hester turned back to Elizabeth. "You mean t' tell me, that you an' Dan'l didn't go to church when you lived up north?"

"Daniel sometimes went," replied Elizabeth, "but I never did. I respected his right to worship in his way; he respected my right to do likewise."

"What about your young'un? Surely you're a-gwine t' 'low Sarah t' go to Sunday school with Otis."

"No, Hester, I'm sorry. I'm afraid I can't allow that."

" 'Train up a child in the way he should go, an' when he is old he will not depart from it.' Proverbs, twenty-two, six."

Elizabeth looked at Otis, all dressed up in his Sunday finery. "I have no doubt that Otis will grow up to be a fine young man," she said.

"Hit's not mine I'm a-worryin' about," declared Hester, becoming a little exasperated, "hit's yourn."

"I'm not worried about either of them," replied Elizabeth quietly, as though she had taken no notice whatever of Hester's perturbation, "and I don't want you to worry either. I can assure you that I *am* training up Sarah in the way I think she should go. She and I will continue to worship in our own way."

Hester continued to fret. To Elizabeth's surprise it was Nathan who came to her defense.

"You've got to remember, Hester, not everyone believes the same as you. You've got to let people worship God in the way they see fit. God isn't just t' be found inside of churches, you know. He's t' be found wherever folks look for Him."

Hester listened but was not convinced. There might be other ways to worship God, she fumed to herself, but there was only one right way, and that was inside of a church. She promised herself that she'd say nothing more about it, but she was not happy about this unexpected development. She knew when she got to church that everyone would want to know why Daniel's wife and daughter had not come, as by now everyone for miles around had heard that Daniel Wicker had returned home and had brought his wife and daughter with him. What would she tell them? The truth? That Daniel's wife was a heathen and was raising her daughter to be the same? She couldn't do that. Already she could hear the mumbling and the gossip, the hushed whispers behind her back. Perhaps she could explain her sister-in-law's aberrant behavior by reminding everyone that Elizabeth had, after all, through no fault of her own, been born and raised in the north, and as everyone knew, people from up north were a little peculiar and therefore some allowances had to be made for them. Hester realized that she'd have to say *something* in her sister-in-law's defense. Elizabeth was, after all, family. Besides, Hester genuinely liked her educated sister-in-law from the north. Who knows? She might have liked her even if she *hadn't* been Daniel's wife.

Elizabeth would have given anything to have avoided distressing Hester—anything short of sending Sarah to Sunday School. She was not about to do that. She was just as strong in her conviction regarding the matter as Hester was in hers. She simply did not want Sarah's young mind absorbing the dogmatic teachings of the Christian Church, Baptist or any other, before she was even old enough to understand what she was absorbing.

The verse from Proverbs that Hester had quoted was, in Elizabeth's opinion, little more than a call to indoctrination: teach a child what to believe before he is old enough to understand it, and he will never believe otherwise. Elizabeth had known too many people, even people of advanced years, who had accepted without question everything taught them in early childhood, and who had remained intellectually crippled for life, unable even to *consider* other points of view. She had also known, in college, young people—fellow students—who had rebelled in anger *against* the religious indoctrination of their childhood, had rejected it in its entirety, and were left with a prejudice against, almost with a passionate hatred of, anything religious. They had recoiled from blind faith only to embrace blind prejudice. Many of these same young people, driven by this prejudice, by this emotion, had rushed then to embrace, just as fervently, just as blindly, another faith: that of anti-religion, of scientific materialism. No doubt many of these converts to materialism were now raising children of their own, training them up in the way *they* think they should go, teaching them the doctrine of materialism.

If at all possible, and for as long as possible, Elizabeth wanted to keep Sarah's mind open to all possibilities and free from "absolute truth"—be it the "absolute truth" of religion or the "absolute truth" of science. Then perhaps when Sarah was old enough to *think*, rather than simply absorb, she could sort it all out for herself. A child's mind was such an impressionable thing, like a sponge ready to soak up indiscriminately anything with which it came in contact. If a mother had a duty, besides loving her child and caring for its physical needs, it was to protect that precious mind. Even if Elizabeth had felt herself to be in possession of the "absolute truth"—which she did not—she would have still felt bound by duty to protect Sarah from it. She was training Sarah up to be a wonder-filled seeker after truth. She was training up Sarah to find her own way.

Of course Elizabeth expounded none of this to Hester. She knew that if she had, Hester would have complained that she had misunderstood the intent of the Biblical injunction to "train up a child." To Hester's way of thinking, it was not a matter of teaching a child *what to believe*— it would never have occurred to her that there was any question about that—but of teaching a child *how to behave*. If this interpretation of the verse did not immediately occur to Elizabeth it was because, in her limited child-raising experience, behavior was not something that was taught. She had never taught Sarah *how* to behave: Sarah had always *known* how to behave. It might be argued that she had learned good behavior by imitating the good behavior of her parents, but it was Elizabeth's considered opinion that Sarah's behavior, like her personality, was something innate to her: it was something she had brought into the world with her. Sarah had always known *naturally* how to behave. It was Elizabeth's hope that one day she would know naturally what to believe as well.

In the days that followed, Elizabeth continued to work side by side with Hester in the kitchen and in the garden. After the lima beans came a succession of other crops. Hester had already canned over two hundred quarts of tomatoes that summer, but the plants kept producing, so Hester, hating to see anything go to waste, made sure that the ripe red fruits were picked regularly, and every tomato that could not be eaten fresh found its way into a canning jar. The last planting of sweet corn was beginning to ripen as well, and though Elizabeth at first had difficulty determining which of the ears were ripe enough to pick, under Hester's patient tutelage, and after a brief period of trial and error, she soon learned, and though she realized that she was not now, or ever would be, as fast a corn-picker as Hester, she was glad to have acquired yet another skill.

As the two women sat on the porch step husking the corn, Hester related how every time a new crop of corn came in, she and Nathan and Otis made a heroic effort to eat as much as possible of the corn fresh—stuffing themselves with "roastin' ears" dinner and supper—but since they were such a small family, they were never quite up to the task of eating it all. Consequently, during corn season, she often worked late into the night canning the surplus. Nathan had repeatedly assured her that there was no need to can it all. Nature, he reminded her, was bountiful and never intended for its creatures to consume everything it produced. Besides, he said, the hogs would be grateful for any of the surplus. But Hester was as stubborn as she was frugal, and as a result, the hogs had to be satisfied with husks and cobs. The hogs could have all the field corn Nathan could grow, but they were not about to get her sweet corn.

Less urgent, though equally important to the winter food supply, were the onions, the squashes, and the root crops. The two women pulled up long rows of onions, braided the tops together, and carried them up to the attic where they hung them up to dry. Here Elizabeth found strings of beans–"leather britches" Hester called them–and red pepper pods already hung and drying in the warm attic air. When thoroughly dried, sometime before winter set in, these would be removed from the attic and stored in the kitchen.

They dug bushels of beets, carrots, and turnips, harvested more bushels of pumpkins and winter squash, and stored these in the root cellar. The first time Elizabeth followed Hester down through the trap door in the kitchen floor to the root cellar beneath, she could scarcely believe her eyes. When she had walked into Hester's kitchen for the first time, she had marveled at how well-stocked with foodstuffs the shelves and cupboards were, but the kitchen cupboards were bare compared to the root cellar. Here hundreds of jars lined the shelves, neat rows of jars filled with colorful garden and orchard produce: green peas, red tomatoes, yellow peaches, on and on, row after row. One whole wall of shelves was filled with jams–red jams, yellow jams, purple jams–jams made from every fruit and berry, cultivated or wild, that grew in the garden and surrounding countryside. Now, to this multi-colored underground treasury they were adding bushels of orange pumpkins, red beets, brown-skinned potatoes. The root crops, with the dirt still clinging to them, were carefully placed in wooden bins and baskets in the center of the cellar. The squashes and pumpkins were spread out on boards that covered the damp earthen floor. Elizabeth looked around the cellar in wonder. Let the seven years of famine begin, she thought to herself: Hester is ready for them.

Nathan and the two children helped to dig the potatoes. Elizabeth's back no longer ached as it did on that first day of lima-bean picking, but still she liked to stand up and stretch from time to time, partly to keep her back from tightening up, and partly just to watch the others working. It was a wonderful scene, she thought, these simple, gentle people toiling humbly, yet joyfully, in the earth. It reminded her of the quiet pastoral scenes of the French countryside that Millet and Van Gogh had so lovingly painted. Yet, if possible, this scene was even more beautiful, enhanced by the awesome blue-green mountains that rose dramatically all around them. Hester looked up at her.

"What're you smilin' about, Miss 'Lizbeth?"

Elizabeth wasn't sure she could explain it. "I guess I'm just happy to be here," she said simply. Happy to be here digging these potatoes, she mused to herself, finishing her thought–happy to be in the world, happy to be alive.

Sarah was happy to be there too. She loved digging potatoes. The two children worked right alongside Hester and Elizabeth, as they all followed Nathan down the row, gathering up the nests of potatoes he uncovered as he turned the earth with his horse and plow. Sarah exclaimed with glee every time a new cluster came popping out of the ground. It was like finding buried treasure!

"I'm going to be a potato-hunter when I grow up," she declared before they had gone thirty feet down the first row.

As a result of Sarah's enthusiasm for potatoes, Otis, who had never cared much for this particular chore in the past, now took a renewed interest in it. Elizabeth marveled at how nimbly Sarah gathered up the potatoes and threw them into the baskets. If Sarah was experiencing any problems with *her* back, she gave no indication of it.

Apart from their difference of opinion over the necessity of going to church, Hester and Elizabeth got along well together, and considering that the two women had come from such different backgrounds, it could very easily have been otherwise. Elizabeth had come from a wealthy family, had been to an elite New

England women's college, and had probably read more books than most of the people who lived in Rushing Creek had ever seen. Hester, like Daniel, had grown up poor, had had very little schooling, and the only book she had ever read—or ever considered worth reading—was the Bible. Yet the two women had a great deal of respect for each other. In fact, Elizabeth thought at times that Hester showed her too much respect, respect she did not deserve. Ever since the first day, Hester had fallen into the habit of calling her "Miss 'Lizbeth," and though Elizabeth had insisted on more than one occasion that there was no need to call her "Miss," Hester always seemed to forget. "Hit just ain't right that a proper lady like yourself be called just plain "Lizbeth,' " Hester had protested.

Hester admired Elizabeth for her "book-learnin' " and "educated ways." She had never met anyone who knew so much about so many things. True, Hester considered many of Elizabeth's ideas to be peculiar, and probably would have characterized much of what her sister-in-law had learned from books as useless and foolish, yet at the same time she had to admit that Elizabeth possessed a goodly measure of common sense and practical wisdom as well. But quite apart from her acquired attributes, Elizabeth possessed two inner virtues which, in Hester's opinion, were essential to good character. The first of these was perseverance. If there was one single thing about Elizabeth that won Hester over it was Elizabeth's iron-willed determination to see a job through to its completion no matter how much pain and physical exhaustion she had to endure in the process. She simply *made* herself do it. Hester knew that it was not easy for Elizabeth, coming as she did from a city in the north to a subsistence farm in the Appalachians. She knew that this well-bred sister-in-law of hers had never done any real work before, and to tell the truth, when Hester had first laid eyes on her, she had had no expectation that Elizabeth would be of much use around the farm. But Elizabeth had proved her wrong. Despite the blisters on her hands, despite the soreness in her muscles and the ache in her back, Elizabeth had persevered. Nathan had been right of course—many hands did make the work lighter—and Hester appreciated Elizabeth's help. But she soon became concerned that Elizabeth was pushing herself too hard. She encouraged her to rest more, to take a day off now and then. But even though there was many a night during those first two weeks when Elizabeth had barely enough strength left at the end of the day to make it up the stairs and fall into bed, she was always up early the next morning ready to begin again. Day by day Hester's respect for her deepened.

The other virtue that Elizabeth possessed which helped endear her to Hester was the virtue of humility. Despite her high breeding and education, Elizabeth had never been one to put on airs, and in her relationship with Hester, she never tried to lord her superior learning over her less educated sister-in-law or make her feel ignorant. On the contrary, Elizabeth always made Hester feel that she, a simple farm woman, was the possessor of the greater knowledge. And indeed that is exactly how Elizabeth felt. She was glad she knew what she knew, and would not have given up her book-learning for anything in the world. But what she wanted to know *now*, what she needed to know *now*, were things that Hester could teach her. Elizabeth felt that Hester's whole life had been more "real" than hers had been. Hester's whole life had been lived close to the earth, close to the source of life. She had always dealt directly with the necessities. When Elizabeth contemplated her own early life, she felt that hers had been vain and superficial by comparison. She had spent her formative years not dealing with necessities, but preoccupied with concerns and pursuits of the most frivolous nature. Time and again, during those first few weeks that Elizabeth spent at Nathan and Hester's, she marveled at the ingenuity and resourcefulness with which these simple farming people—"ignorant farmers" her father would have called them—provided for themselves and their families. It was a great education for her and she was an eager learner.

Sarah became an eager learner too. Once she had reconciled herself to the idea of going to school, she went without protest and soon was coming home in the afternoons excited about something or other she had learned during the day. She was smiling again, laughing again, and, most importantly, running again. Elizabeth knew that as long as Sarah was running, all was well with her child. The only time Sarah slowed to a walk was when she was upset or unhappy about something.

It was pleasing to Elizabeth, and to Nathan and Hester as well, to see how well Sarah and Otis got along together. The two children had taken to each other immediately and were fast becoming all but inseparable. Almost from the day she arrived, Sarah had been helping Otis with his chores. If Otis brought in firewood, *she* brought in firewood. If Otis was sent to the spring house to fetch milk and butter, he carried the milk, she carried the butter. They worked in the garden together and occasionally they helped Nathan in the fields, in the orchard, or in the barn. But just as soon as their chores were completed–and to Otis' great delight they were now being completed in less than half the time as before–they were off and running. More often than not they went down to the creek, but sometimes they played in the run, that is, in the much smaller stream that flowed from the spring house down to the creek. At least they were allowed to play *in* the run. There were no prohibitions against falling in or jumping in. In the run they could do just as they pleased. As the water only came up to their ankles, there was little danger of their drowning. Here they turned over rocks looking for crayfish and salamanders. At last Sarah had found an explorer after her own heart.

When they were not at the creek or in the run, they usually could be found in the woods that lay all around the farm, just beyond the boundaries of the fields and orchards. As the leaves were beginning to turn color now, from the various shades of summer green to the multifarious shades of autumn gold and red and purple, the woods were an exciting place to be. Sometimes they played hide-and-seek in the woods. Sometimes they simply climbed trees. At other times they pretended to be explorers Lewis and Clark. For his part, Otis was glad to have finally found someone to whom to show his "secret place"–a tree fort he had built in the crotch of a tree out of discarded lumber, bent nails, and tarpaper. For her part, Sarah was glad to have finally found someone who could climb trees almost as well as she could.

On the occasional rainy days the two children were able to keep themselves happily occupied in the loft of the barn, where all three cuttings of that summer's hay had been stored. The great mountain of sweet-smelling alfalfa and timothy seemed to beckon to them irresistably, and they could spend many breathless hours climbing and re-climbing the great mountain, then jumping and sliding down the slippery slopes.

Whether indoors or out, Sarah enjoyed most of the games that she and Otis played. There was one game, however, that she did not enjoy as much as the others. That was Otis' "soldier" game.

"I got an idea," said Otis one day after chores, "let's play soldier."

"I don't know how to play soldier," confessed Sarah.

"Hit's easy. I'll learn yuh. You wait here. I'll get us some muskets."

Otis climbed over the fence into his mother's garden. Removing his pocketknife from his pocket, he opened it, then dropping to his knees between the rows of corn, began sawing away at the bottom of one of the yellowed and withered stalks, from which the ears had already been picked. When, after some effort, he had finally succeeded in cutting through the tough, fibrous stalk, he pulled off the dried tassle and leaves, and raising the stalk to a horizontal position, he tucked the thicker end into his shoulder and sighted down along the smooth, clean "barrel."

"That'll do just fine," he said with some satisfaction. He then dropped down and began cutting a second "musket" for Sarah.

When he had finished, he folded his pocketknife and returned it to his pocket. He then carried the two "muskets" to the fence, handed them over to Sarah, and climbed over himself.

"I never used a musket before," said Sarah, examining her cornstalk.

"Hit's easy, but first you gotta learn how t' be a soldier. Just do what I do, okay?"

"Okay."

"First you gotta stand up real straight."

Following Otis' example Sarah threw her shoulders back and her chest out, assuming a stiff, erect posture.

"Then you take your musket in one hand an' rest it on your shoulder like this."

"That's easy," she said, again imitating his example.

"Now, whenever I say 'attention,' you gotta stand like that, okay?"

"Okay."

"Ready?"

"Ready."

"At-ten-*shun!*"

"At-ten-*shun!*"

"No, no, no, *you* don't say 'at-ten-shun.' *I* say 'at-ten-shun.'"

"You said to do what you do."

"You're only s'posed t' *do* what I *do*. You ain't s'posed t' *say* what I *say*."

"But I want to say 'attention' too."

"You cain't."

"Why not?"

" 'Cause I'm a general. You're just a private. I give the orders, you follow them."

"Why can't I be a general too?"

"You never even been a soldier before this minute. You gotta be a private before you can be a general. Now let's try it again. Ready?"

"Ready."

"At-ten-*shun!*"

"I don't understand."

"What now?"

"Why do you keep yelling at me to pay attention when I'm already paying attention?"

"C'mon, Sarah," complained Otis, "you're ruinin' the game."

"Well, I think it's a silly game."

"How would you know? We haven't even started playin' yet."

"You mean there's more?"

" 'Course thar's more."

"Well then, what's next?"

"Next you gotta learn how t' march. I'll show yuh."

"Otis, I already know how to march. I've seen parades, you know."

To demonstrate she marched half a dozen paces along the garden fence, turned, and marched back, being careful to keep her cornstalk perched securely on her shoulder.

"That's purty good, but you're s'posed t' wait til I *say* 'march.'"

Sarah sighed. "If we ever play this silly game again, *I'm* going to be the general."

"Ready?"

"Ready."

"At-ten-*shun*!" Sarah snapped to attention. "Forward . . . march!"

With their cornstalks gleaming in the late afternoon sun, the two barefooted soldiers commenced to march, with the little general in the lead and the little private following behind at a respectful distance. They marched westward along the garden fence, then around the corner of the house.

"Don't go too far," called Hester from the porch. "Supper'll be ready before too long."

"We won't, Ma," returned Otis without losing cadence.

They marched down the hill along the edge of the woods in the direction of the creek. Three-quarters of the way down the hill Otis came to an abrupt stop. "Company . . . halt!"

He looked over his shoulder, and seeing that Sarah had obeyed his order, smiled. "Right . . . face!"

Otis pivoted ninety degrees to face the woods. Casting a glance to his side, he discovered that Sarah had turned in the opposite direction and was now facing the hayfield. "I said '*right.*' "

"I *did* turn right."

Otis stared at her through squinted eyes, his face contorted in painful thought. As annoyed as he had been at her for not obeying orders, he was even more annoyed at her when he realized that she had indeed turned right and it was *he* who had turned in the wrong direction.

"Well, I meant 'left,' " he muttered in a tone of voice which was not only not apologetic, but which left little doubt that he still felt that it was *she*, not *he*, who was to blame for the order not being properly executed. "You're s'posed t' do what *I* do, remember?"

Sarah turned one hundred eighty degrees to face the woods.

"At ease," commanded the general.

"What does that mean?"

"It means you don't gotta stand at attention no more."

Sarah relaxed her posture. "Do I still have to follow orders?"

"You *always* haf t' follow orders. If you don't follow orders, you'll be a traitor. You know what happens to traitors, don't yuh?"

"No."

"They get shot. You don't wanna get shot, do yuh?"

She shook her head.

"All right then . . . Now," said Otis, lowering his voice to a whisper, "we gotta be real quiet. The enemy is right in these here woods."

Wide-eyed, Sarah peered into the woods.

"C'mon, follow me," whispered Otis, "an' don't make any noise."

On tip-toe the two soldiers entered the woods, cornstalks in hand, eyes and ears alert.

"I don't see anyone," whispered Sarah.

"Shhh, they'll hear you."

Stealthily they moved deeper into the woods. Suddenly, head down, Otis made a dash for a fallen tree. Sarah, mimicking his every movement, followed him. When she reached the fallen tree, she crouched down beside him.

"We'll hide behind this here log," whispered Otis, "then when the bluecoats come along, we'll ambush 'em."

Together the two children peered over the top of the log and waited.

"Otis," whispered Sarah.

"What?" asked Otis, without daring to take his eyes off the trees ahead lest the bluecoats should take them by surprise.

"Who are the bluecoats?"

"The dirty Yankees, of course."

"Who are the dirty Yankees?"

"You know, Yankees, from up north. Once I kilt over a hunnert of 'em in a single battle."

"You *killed* them?"

"Yup. I prob'bly done kilt close to a zillion of 'em in all."

"That's a lot."

There was a moment's silence as the two children continued to watch the trees ahead for any sign of movement.

"Otis?"

"Shh."

"Otis?"

"Call me General Lee."

"General Lee?"

"What *is* it?"

"I think I'm a dirty Yankee."

General Lee jumped to his feet, his eyes wide with startled disbelief, and nearly fell over backwards trying to distance himself from her. "What?"

"I said, I think *I'm* a dirty Yankee. *I'm* from up north."

"You cain't be."

"Why not?"

"You just cain't be, that's all. If you was a Yankee, I'd haf t' shoot yuh . . . Are you sure you're a Yankee?"

"I'm not sure, but I think so. I was born in Mass-a-chu-setts."

"Is that up north?"

"Yes."

"How far up north?"

"I don't know exactly. Pretty far. It was a long train ride."

Suddenly oblivious to the danger lurking in the woods, Otis began to pace fitfully back and forth, thumping the cornstalk against the side of his head. This was a most unexpected turn of events. Yankees were the enemy. Yankees were for shooting. That's why God had put Yankees on the earth in the first place:

to shoot. By his own estimation he had shot close to a zillion himself. But never before had he ever confronted one live and face to face.

"I s'pose I wouldn't *haf* t' shoot yuh. I s'pose I could just take yuh pris'ner an' lock yuh in the smokehouse . . . But that wouldn't be no fun."

He was thinking only that, with Sarah locked in the smokehouse, there would be no fun in it for *him*, as then he would have no one with whom to play, and, more to the point, no one to whom to issue orders. He hadn't troubled himself to think that being locked in the smokehouse might not be much fun for Sarah either.

He paced and thumped some more. Suddenly he had an idea. "I know what! We'll pretend hit's the Revolutionary War—you know, the War for Dependence. That way we can both be 'mericans an' we can fight the redcoats. . . An' I'll be General George Washington."

"Who will I be?"

"You'll be a private."

"But I was a private in the last war."

"Well, you'll be a private in this war too."

"If I was a Yankee, I could be a general."

"If you was a Yankee general, I'd haf t' shoot yuh. Which would yuh rather be, a dead general or a live private?"

"I'll be a private," sighed Sarah, resigning herself once again to her lower rank.

That settled, Otis rejoined his cousin behind the fallen tree, and with the barrels of their cornstalks-turned-muskets resting on the top of the log, the two soldiers resumed their vigil.

"I think I hear them comin'," whispered Otis excitedly, after a full ten seconds of steady vigilance. "Sure 'nuff, here they come!"

He jumped up and, aiming his cornstalk, opened fire. "Pow . . . pow . . . pow . . . pow . . . "

Taking cover once again behind the fallen tree, he found Sarah staring at him with a look of incomprehension on her face. "What are you shooting at?" she whispered.

"The redcoats! They got us surrounded!"

Sarah looked around. "I don't see anyone."

"They're hidin' behind the trees!"

She looked again. "I still don't see them."

"You gotta *pretend* . . . Look, thar's one a-comin' at yuh now! Shoot 'im."

"I don't want to shoot. This is a silly game. I don't think I want to play anymore."

"You *gotta* play. That's an order. If you don't wanna shoot, you load the muskets an' *I'll* shoot."

"How do I do that?"

"First you take the powder horn here"–he grasped the imaginary powder horn in his hand–"an' you dump some powder down the muzzle of the musket . . . "

"Which end is the muzzle?"

"Hit don't matter . . . Next you take a musketball out of your sack of musketballs here an' push hit into the end of the barrel with your thumb . . . Then you take your rammin' rod"–he held up the imaginary ramrod for her to see–"an you ram the musketball down the barrel like this. Then hit's ready t' shoot . . . Okay?"

"Okay, I guess."

"Okay, you give me your musket an' you reload the one I just fired."

Sarah surrendered her unfired musket as ordered. Otis watched as she loaded the other musket, the one he had just fired. Satisfied that she was doing it correctly, he turned his attention back to the advancing enemy. "Here they come ag'in!"

Now the battle commenced in earnest. Fast as her hands could be made to move, Sarah reloaded the muskets and handed them to her cousin the general, but it was not fast enough. The redcoats apparently had them greatly outnumbered, as Otis sometimes found it necessary to fire up to half a dozen shots per musket before handing it back to Sarah for reloading.

"We're runnin' outa powder!" shouted Otis.

"No, we have lots."

"No, we're runnin' out!"

"No, we have lots. Lots of musketballs too."

"*Pretend* we're runnin' out!"

"I'm pretending we have lots."
"Pretend we're runnin' out! That's an order!"
"Otis!"
"Call me General Washington!"
"General Washington!"
"What is it, Private?"
"We're running out of powder! But we have *lots* of musketballs!"
"Musketballs is no good without powder! We'll haf t' fight it out hand t' hand!"

Sarah was about to suggest that they *throw* the musketballs, but before she had a chance to do so, Otis had jumped over the log and was charging at the trees. Wielding his cornstalk like a baseball bat, he began wailing at the trees like one possessed. "Take that!" he shouted, "an' that!"

Sarah watched in amazement as bits of cornstalk flew in all directions. When he had smote his cornstalk down to a bare stub, Otis ran back to the log. "Quick, Private, hand me the other musket!"

Sarah did as ordered and Otis returned to his battle with the trees. Though he fought valiantly, dashing from tree to tree, thrashing furiously, it soon became apparent–at least to him–that the situation was hopeless. "Thar's too many of them! They got us surrounded! . . . Agh, they got me!"

With those words he dropped what was left of his cornstalk, clutched his stomach, moaned pitifully, reeled around several times in melodramatic fashion, then, with arms outstretched, made a spectacular face-first fall onto the ground.

From her position of relative safety behind the log, from which she had not moved throughout the battle, Sarah watched and waited for her cousin to get up again. She preferred that he not get up immediately, however, as the calm which had settled over the forest upon the general's heroic demise was a welcome respite after the furious antics which had preceded it. But when Otis had still not moved after a full minute and a half, she became concerned that, in his wild flailing about, or, more likely, in his dramatic fall, he actually *had* hurt himself. Climbing over the

121

log, she walked cautiously over to the place where his inert body lay and knelt down beside him. "Otis are you all right?"

He did not respond. He remained absolutely motionless, his eyes closed. He did not even appear to be breathing.

"Otis, are you all right?" she asked again, this time shaking his shoulder.

Still he did not move. His body felt limp. Convinced now that he really *had* hurt himself–struck his head on a rock or something–she began to sob. "Please, Otis, please get up."

Suddenly Otis jumped to his feet. "Ha ha, made yuh cry, made yuh cry."

Sarah stared at him for a moment, not knowing whether to cry or laugh or be angry, then turned and walked away.

"Hey, whar yuh gwine?"

"I'm going back to the house. This is a silly game."

"No, it's not. Hit's a fun game."

"It's a silly game."

"You come back here this minute, you hear me? That's an order!"

She continued to walk away.

"Traitor! Traitor! Traitors get shot, remember?"

"You *can't* shoot me. We're out of powder, *remember*? We're out of muskets too."

"C'mon, Sarah. Please come back . . . You can be the general."

Suddenly she stopped. Slowly she turned around. "I can be the general?"

"Yeah," he conceded begrudgingly, "you can be the general. You can be General Lucy S. Grant."

"And you'll be the private?"

"No, I'll be General Robert E. Lee."

"But if we're both generals, who will give the orders?"

"Nobody."

Sarah paused for a moment to consider this new arrangement. "I think I like that. That's the way it should be." Just then they heard Hester calling them.

"We better get to the house quick," advised Otis. "If we're late for supper ag'in, Ma will lock us *both* in the smokehouse . . .

122

'Magine that," he laughed, "General Grant an' General Lee locked in the smokehouse together. Wouldn't that be somethin'?"

They hurried out of the darkening woods and emerged into the hayfield in time to see the sun balanced like a big red ball on the rim of the mountains to the west. Sarah paused just a moment to marvel at the spectacle. It was all Otis needed.

"Last one to the house is a dirty Yankee," he shouted back at her as he sprinted up the hill.

She took off in pursuit. Now this was *her* idea of fun! It would have been even more fun if Otis had been a faster runner. As it was, he was scarcely any faster than Pokey the dog. The outcome was never in doubt. By the time Otis had reached the top of the hill, she had already caught up to him, and, in another two strides, had passed him and was pulling away. She made sure to slap the corner of the house as she ran by, lest Otis should try to cheat her out of her victory as he had done once before. She had been the first one *inside* the house on that occasion, but as she had not been the first one to *touch* the house, Otis had declared himself the winner. Now, as she turned the second and final corner of the house before the porch, she slapped it also, just for good measure. When she reached the porch, she found her passage to the screen door blocked by her Uncle Nathan, whose rather prodigious form was occupying most of the top step. Desperately she tried to squeeze by.

"Hey, what's your hurry, Sunshine?" asked Nathan, tackling her about the waist.

"Please, Uncle Nathan, let me go. I've got to get into the house quick. Otis said the last one to the house was a dirty Yankee."

Nathan laughed but did not release her. "You're already *at* the house. You've won fair an' square. Why don't you sit here with me for a spell? We can watch the sun go down."

Sarah felt she had no choice but to sit down with her Uncle Nathan. She began to reconcile herself to another defeat. She just knew that Otis was going to come rushing up the steps past the both of them and claim victory.

"Uncle Nathan, promise me that you won't let Otis into the house before me."

Nathan smiled. "All right, if it'll put your mind at ease, I promise . . . In fact, I'll do more than that. I will personally declare you the winner."

Reassured, Sarah now turned her attention to the sunset.

"Hester said she saw you an' Otis playin' soldier," continued Nathan, apparently deciding that a little conversation would go well with the sunset. "How'd he manage t' talk you into that?"

"He said it was a fun game. But it wasn't. At least not the way we played it today. He was the general and I was the private person. He got to give all the orders and I had to follow them. If I didn't, he said he'd shoot me . . . We're both generals now though. I'm General Lucy S. Grant and he's General Robert E. Lee."

"Speakin' of General Lee, where is he anyway? Shouldn't he be here by now?"

A terrible thought caused Sarah to jump quickly to her feet. "I'll bet he's sneaking in the back window right this minute!"

Just then a very tired, out-of-breath Otis came dragging himself around the corner of the house. Sarah looked at her Uncle Nathan and smiled. "Remember what you promised, Uncle Nathan."

Nathan waited for Otis to reach the porch, then stood up, and taking Sarah by the wrist, raised her arm above her head. "I hereby declare that the official winner of today's Race to the House is . . . General Lucy S. Grant. And you, General Robert E. Lee, I'm sorry to say, are a dirty Yankee."

Nathan and Sarah laughed, but Otis was too tired and too dejected to be amused.

"Come on, Son," said Nathan, putting an arm around Otis' shoulders, "you look a little spent. Let me help you into the house. A soldier always feels better after a good hot meal."

True to his word Nathan allowed Sarah to enter the house first. Otis would not steal her victory from her this day.

It was a gray and damp day in late September, just when Elizabeth was beginning to think that she and Sarah were adjusting fairly well to their new environment and new routine, that an incident happened which caused her to re-evaluate their progress. It had been drizzling off and on since early morning and she and Hester had spent the better part of the day in the kitchen making and canning apple butter. They had just ladled the last of the scalding hot butter into jars and sealed them and were beginning to prepare supper when Sarah burst into the kitchen crying. She ran straight to Elizabeth and buried her face in her mother's apron. Sarah did not often cry, but she was crying now, convulsively. Elizabeth wiped her hands on her apron and gently cradled Sarah's head against her stomach.

"What happened, Honey? Did you get hurt?" She knew that Sarah and Otis had been playing in the barn loft.

With difficulty Sarah lifted her tear-streaked face and shook her head. She tried to speak but the words would not come. She was sobbing uncontrollably. Again she buried her face in her mother's apron.

Elizabeth stroked her daughter's hair and rocked her gently back and forth to comfort her. Hester, as bewildered as Elizabeth, looked on, waiting for Sarah to become composed enough to speak. The poor child was crying so pitifully, Hester could not help but feel sorry for her. She could not imagine what had happened to her. She did not appear to be injured in any way. Just then Otis came through the kitchen door from outside.

"Come on, Sarah," he pleaded, "let's go play. Hit was only a rabbit."

"Otis," interrupted Hester, "what's this all about? What happened to Sarah? Did you hurt her?"

"No, Ma," protested Otis, emphatically declaring his innocence, "she's cryin' 'cause Pa shot a rabbit."

A momentary silence fell over the kitchen as Hester and Elizabeth absorbed this unexpected revelation. Sarah continued to sob into her mother's apron. Hester was the first to break the stillness. She began bustling again, resuming the interrupted business of the moment, that of getting supper cooked.

"For Heaven's sake, child," she complained, "is that what all this fuss is about? A silly old rabbit? Why, Nathan must a-shot half a hunnert rabbits this year. If you don't shoot the varmints, they'll eat ever' thang in sight. They'll eat the food right off our table."

Before Hester had said two words, Elizabeth had guessed the gist of what she was about to say and had taken the precaution of covering one of Sarah's ears with her hand and pressing the other against her stomach, in the hope that Sarah would not be able to hear Hester's reaction. As soon as Otis had explained the reason for Sarah's distress, Elizabeth remembered that she had heard the shot, but had thought nothing of it at the time, as she had become accustomed to hearing shots. Nathan seemed to be forever shooting rabbits in the garden. He may have very well shot fifty that year: he had shot at least half a dozen in the two and a half weeks that she had been there. She herself had helped to skin them and prepare them for dinner. But now she realized that on all those previous occasions Nathan had shot the troublesome rodents during the day when the children were at school. This was the first time since she and Sarah had been there that he had shot one while the children were home. And it was the first time in Sarah's life that she had seen a rabbit killed before her very eyes. Elizabeth remembered how many pleasant hours she and Sarah had spent watching rabbits hopping about in their yard and in their neighbors' yards back in Springfield. Sarah had delighted especially in watching the young ones in the spring. Elizabeth could easily understand how the killing of one of these gentle, timid creatures had caused Sarah so much grief.

But she could also understand Hester's point of view. If something weren't done about the "varmints," they could eat a garden bare, and here in the country, where a family's very survival depended on the food they raised themselves, that could not be allowed to happen. Understandably, farmers took whatever measures they considered necessary to protect their crops against intruders: they put up fences, they kept dogs, and if all else failed, they resorted quite readily to shotgun and rifle. Inevitably, any rabbit or woodchuck that managed to sneak by the dogs and squeeze through or burrow under the fence, found itself on the dinner table, usually within hours.

As Elizabeth pondered how best to make Sarah understand why it was that Nathan had shot the rabbit, Nathan himself came into the house. Elizabeth was glad to see that he had neither his gun nor the rabbit with him. Meekly he approached Elizabeth.

"Elizabeth," he said, the tone of his voice bespeaking his genuine sympathy, "I'm sorry. I should have known . . . "

"It's all right, Nathan, she'll be fine. She'll be just fine." Elizabeth continued to stroke Sarah's hair. "Just let me have some time alone with her."

Elizabeth took Sarah upstairs to their room. When she returned half an hour later she found that Hester had supper ready and on the table. The others had already taken their places at the table, but had not commenced eating. They had been waiting for her. As Elizabeth took her seat, Nathan looked up at her, an anxious expression on his face.

"Is she all right?" he asked.

"She'll be fine," replied Elizabeth. "I'm sure she'll have forgotten all about it by morning."

"Ain't she a-comin' down to supper?" asked Hester.

"No, she doesn't feel much like eating right now."

"The child has got t' eat somethin'," protested Hester.

"If she feels like eating later on, I'll get her something."

Elizabeth could tell that this assurance on her part did little to relieve Hester's anxiety, and as she looked around the table she found the concerned faces of Nathan and Otis staring at her as well.

"Believe me, all of you," she re-iterated quietly but firmly, "she'll be fine."

Otis, looking a little confused, turned to his father. "I don't understand, Pa. Hit was just a silly rabbit."

Nathan looked at Otis solemnly. "Did you ever stop t' think, Son, that rabbits might not be silly to Sarah? Did you ever stop t' think that rabbits are creatures made by God the same as you an' me? You haf t' remember that Sarah isn't used t' seein' animals killed the way we are. I'm sorry she had t' see it. I could a-kicked myself for not thinkin' first. But in a way, I'm glad it happened. 'Cause seein' the shock an' the grief on that little girl's face, an' seein' her eyes fill up with tears, made me remember somethin' I had plum' forgot. It made me remember the first time *I* saw a rabbit killed when I was a boy back in Ohio. I choked up just the same as she did this afternoon. And I remember the first time I saw a hog butchered. I was sick for a week. But somehow, over the years, I guess I just sort of got used t' seein' it. A body can get used to anything if he sees it often enough . . . But I'm glad for that little girl. She made me remember how we *ought* t' feel when one of God's creatures dies. *Her* reaction was the natural one, it's *ours* that's tainted. Maybe I ain't done right by you, Son. You seen killin' an' butcherin' all your life. I ain't sayin' it's wrong t' kill animals—the Good Lord knows we got to eat—but maybe it's wrong to get so used to it that you got no feelin's for the creature what's dyin'. . . "

Otis bowed his head. Elizabeth, sensing that the mood at the supper table was becoming much too solemn, decided that something had to be done to lift the spirits of all those assembled, including herself. And since it was *her* daughter who had been the cause of all this gravity, she knew that the burden of altering the course of everyone's thoughts was one that she had to bear.

"I don't know about the rest of you," she said with as much cheer as she could muster, "but I'm getting hungry." She removed the lid from the kettle in front of her and ladled some of its contents onto her plate. She then reached for Otis' plate, studying his face as she did so. "How about you, Otis? Would you like some silly rabbit stew?"

Elizabeth could see that Otis was tickled by her unexpected question, but before he allowed his face to break into a smile, he glanced up at his father as if to ask permission. When he saw that his father was already smiling, he allowed himself a grin from ear to ear. "Yes, Ma'am," he responded with enthusiasm, "I'm hongry too!"

After supper Elizabeth drew Nathan aside. "Nathan, I want to thank you for what you said to Otis . . . about killing animals, I mean. I hope you were not offended by my flippant remark afterwards."

"Not at all," he grinned. "The air was gettin' purty heavy in here. It was just what we needed t' clear it out."

After she had helped Hester clean up the dishes, Elizabeth went to her room. She had left Sarah lying on the bed, but now she found her under the covers and a small pile of dusty clothes crumpled up on the floor. Sarah was still awake but no longer crying. Elizabeth sat down on the edge of the bed and leaned over and kissed her daughter's still-moist cheek. Sarah responded with a feeble smile, but continued staring at the wall, her eyes dull and blank.

"You didn't wash up, did you?" asked Elizabeth as she pulled a strand of hay out of Sarah's hair.

Sarah shook her head slightly, almost imperceptibly.

"Do you want anything to eat?"

Sarah indicated that she did not by another all but imperceptible movement of the head.

Elizabeth continued to study her daughter's face, waiting for some sign of life to return to her eyes. As she watched, Sarah's eyes once again began to fill with tears. So intense was Elizabeth's empathy with this child of her womb and of her heart, that now as she watched Sarah courageously but unsuccessfully struggle to fight back the tears, she felt her own eyes beginning to moisten, her own heart beginning to tear.

"Mommy," she heard her child saying in a voice so plaintive that she had to bite her lip to keep from crying herself, "I want to go home. I don't want to live here anymore."

Elizabeth remained silent for a moment, as she tried to collect herself and to think of something to say to comfort her child.

"You know, Sarah," she said at last, "I wanted to go home too– or thought I did–the very first day after we came here." Sarah did not turn to face her mother, but Elizabeth could tell that she was trying to listen. "I was helping your Aunt Hester pick lima beans, and by the middle of the morning my back was hurting so badly that I didn't think I would ever be able to stand up straight again. I asked myself, what have I gotten myself into? Why did I ever want to come here? . . . But do you know what? I'm glad we did come. Because I really do like it here. I think it's a good place to be. And do you want to know something else? That pain in my back is almost all gone now—not quite, but almost."

She paused a moment, then continued. "I know that you saw something today that caused you to hurt too. I know that you're feeling a pain inside that you think will never go away. But it will, Sarah, believe me, it will. I know how much you like animals, and it's only natural that you should feel sad when you see one get killed. I think it's important for you to understand why your Uncle Nathan shot the rabbit. You know, back in Springfield, whenever we needed food, we walked up the street to the market and bought it. Of course we had our little garden in the back yard—and a fine little garden it was, with lots of bright flowers planted in amongst the vegetables—but it only provided us with enough food for a few meals in the summertime. The rest of the year all our food came from the market. It's different here. Almost all the food that Nathan and Hester and Otis eat, they raise right here on their own farm. That's why their garden is so important to them. And that's why they can't let rabbits run loose in their garden. Do you understand that? The rabbits would eat all their food.

"I like the way Nathan and Hester live. It's the way we're going to live too once we get settled into our own home. It's a good way, an honest way. I don't know, somehow it seems more real, more natural, than buying everything at the store. I think it's probably the way we were meant to live.

"And you mustn't imagine that animals aren't killed back in Springfield and in the other cities and towns up north, because they are. It's just that it's done in places outside of town where little girls can't see it." She remembered the graphic descriptions of the slaughterhouses of Chicago in Upton Sinclair's novel *The Jungle* and shuddered. Sarah would eventually come to learn of such places, but now was certainly not the time to tell her.

All the while Elizabeth had been talking, Sarah had been struggling to control her sobs. Now that Sarah had become calm again, Elizabeth tried once again to reach her.

"What do you say, Honey? How about a hug?"

For the first time since Elizabeth entered the room, Sarah turned her head to face her mother. For the first time Sarah saw the tears in her mother's eyes. She sat up in bed and fell into Elizabeth's waiting arms. Tenderly Elizabeth held her wounded child close to her. Not quite a minute had gone by when there came a gentle knocking on the door. Mother and daughter looked at each other, each wondering who it might be.

"Come in," said Elizabeth, wiping the tears from her eyes.

The door opened and Nathan stepped tentatively into the room. Immediately Sarah threw herself back down into the bed and pulled the covers over her head. Elizabeth could see the hurt in Nathan's eyes.

"I was just wond'rin' how she was," he said, uncomfortably.

"She'll be fine, Nathan, really she will. Thank you for asking."

It was not until Nathan had left the room and closed the door behind him that Sarah emerged from the covers.

"Mommy, I miss my Daddy," she said plaintively. "I don't like Uncle Nathan."

Elizabeth pushed the hair away from Sarah's face and smiled. "Do you want to know something? Your Uncle Nathan likes *you*. He thinks you're a very special little girl. He said so at supper . . . And do you want to know something else?" Sarah raised her eyes to meet her mother's. "I think your Uncle Nathan is a very special man. I think if you give him a chance, you and he could become very good friends . . . What do you say? Will you give him a chance?"

For a long moment Sarah remained absorbed in thought, staring into the blankets. Then she looked up at her mother, smiled, and nodded her head.

"Today I need two volunteers under the age of ten to help me pick apples," announced Nathan at breakfast three days later. It was a Saturday morning, the first Saturday in October. "The Winesaps are startin' t' drop. What do you say? Do I have two volunteers?"

Even before Elizabeth had time to look in Sarah's direction, Sarah had volunteered. "I'll help, Uncle Nathan," she exclaimed, "I'm under ten."

"Me too, Pa," cried Otis, trying to match his cousin's enthusiasm.

"Okay, I'll take you two. That's all I need. All the rest of you can put your hands down."

Sarah and Otis looked at each other and laughed. Elizabeth smiled. Sarah had been true to her word: she was prepared to make an effort to be friends with her Uncle Nathan again; she was not going to let one dead rabbit stand between them.

After the breakfast dishes had been cleaned up and some other kitchen chores had been attended to, Elizabeth walked out into the orchard to see how the apple harvest was progressing. It was a glorious fall day–the sky could not have been any clearer or any bluer–and a slight breeze lifted wisps of her hair as she walked among the apple trees. The sudden sound of laughter caused her to redirect her course. When she finally came upon the tree from which the sound of merriment was emanating, the scene that presented itself to her eyes reminded her of a Currier and Ives lithograph. Nathan was up on a long straight ladder picking the apples at the top of the tree, Otis was picking the lower apples from a step-ladder, and Sarah was under the tree busily gathering up the apples that had fallen on the ground. The scene seemed to be one of perfect tranquility.

What Elizabeth did not know was that before her arrival Nathan and Sarah had had another altercation, albeit not a very serious one. Sarah had wanted to climb the tall ladder and pick the apples high in the tree, but Nathan had not allowed her. Instead, he had directed her to the apples on the ground. When she demurred, he had assured her that the apples on the ground were just as valuable as the apples on the tree because they would be used for cider. Sarah knew what cider was and she liked it—the sweet kind; she had never tasted hard cider—and so had set about her task of picking up the dropped apples with a sense of purpose and with her usual enthusiasm, but not until she had made Nathan promise that he would let her pick from the tall ladder when she was bigger.

Elizabeth had come upon them so quietly that she was able to stand and watch for a full two minutes before being discovered. Sarah was the first to see her.

"Mommy," she exclaimed excitedly, "I'm going to be an apple-picker when I'm big! Uncle Nathan said I could."

"I thought you were gonna be a 'tater-hunter," Nathan reminded her.

"I thought you was gwine t' be a great explorer," said Otis.

Elizabeth smiled, waiting for Sarah's rejoinder. She knew that she must be weighing all the possibilities in her head.

Nathan rescued her from her difficult dilemma. "Well, I don't see any reason why she can't be all those things an' more," he said. "Nobody said you had t' be just one thing now, did they? That sure wouldn't be much fun, would it, t' do just one thing for your whole life?"

The whole time he was talking Nathan kept picking apples and putting them in his sack. Elizabeth wondered that he was able to keep his balance, pick apples, and talk all at the same time without falling. Finally, his sack full, he came down the ladder and emptied the apples out through the bottom of the sack into a wooden basket. He then re-positioned his ladder and climbed back up. Before he was halfway to the top he was talking again.

"Would any of my volunteers like t' hear a story?"

"Yes!" shouted Otis and Sarah almost in unison.

"All right then, let me think, what story shall I tell?"

"Tell the story about Johnny Appleseed, Pa," suggested Otis.

"The story about Johnny Appleseed? Hmm, I'm not sure I know that one, Son."

"Sure you do, Pa. You must a-told it to me a hunnert times already."

"I have? Funny, I can't seem t' remember it. Was he the fella who planted watermelon seeds down in Mississippi?"

"No, Pa. Johnny *Appleseed,* the one who planted apple seeds in Ohio."

"Ohio, you say? Come t' think of it, that does sound vaguely familiar. What else can you tell me about him, Son?"

"He wore his cookin' pot on his haid for a hat, an' whenever he got hongry, he just took off his hat an' cooked his supper in it."

"That seems like a strange thing t' do. Do you suppose he ever put his hat on with his supper still in it?"

It was all Elizabeth could do to suppress her laughter. She knew that Hester would never have approved of Nathan's teasing Otis in this way, so she felt a little guilty that she found him so amusing. Unlike Hester, Elizabeth appreciated Nathan's sense of humor. In fact, she was probably his biggest fan. She often found him quite amusing, especially when playfully bantering with the children as he was now. Sarah found him amusing too. She nearly fell over with laughter at the thought of Johnny Appleseed wearing his supper on his head. But Otis was only becoming more flustered. He did not seem to have caught on that his father was only having fun with him.

"No, Pa," he groaned in frustration, "that weren't part of the story. Don't you remember? He was the one who never wore shoes. He walked all over the whole country barfoot, even in the winter when the snow was on the ground. An' he carried a Bible an' he . . . "

"He walked barefoot through the snow?"

"Yeah, Pa."

"What happened to his shoes?"

"I don't know, Pa. He didn't have any."

"Did he lose them in a poker game?"

Otis screwed up his face, trying to remember. "Yeah, Pa, I think that was it. He lost his shoes in a poker game."

Nathan came down the ladder with another sackful of apples. He looked at Elizabeth and smiled. She could see the mischief in his eyes. "What else did this hayseed character do, Son, besides plant hayseed an' play poker?"

"*Apple* seeds, Pa, he planted *apple* seeds . . . An' he always carried his Bible with him, an' he never got skeered, not even when he walked all alone by hisself through dark woods whar thar was lots of wild Injuns an' mean hongry bears just a-waitin' behind the trees t' jump on him. He was very brave, Pa. He didn't even have no gun."

"Brave, you say? He sounds a little crazy to me."

"No, Pa," Otis protested, "he weren't crazy."

"He *wasn't* crazy," Sarah corrected him.

"Oh, so you know this Appleseed fella too, do you, Sunshine?" teased Nathan, deliberately misinterpreting Sarah's correction of Otis' grammar as a statement of fact. "What can *you* tell us about him?"

Up to this point Sarah had said nothing, but Nathan knew that she had been listening, as he had heard the sweet notes of her musical laughter come pealing up periodically from under the tree. It gladdened his heart to hear her laughing again. But he really did not expect that she would know anything about Johnny Appleseed. Elizabeth knew that he was in for a surprise.

"I know that his real name was John Chapman," replied Sarah, "and that he was born in Mass-a-chu-setts. I was born in Mass-a-chu-setts too, you know."

"In fact," added Elizabeth, "he might even have been born in Springfield, though it is not known for certain where in Massachusetts he was born. A number of towns up there have laid claim to him."

"Well, bless my soul," exclaimed Nathan, "it seems like everybody know this story better than I do." Otis and Sarah looked at each other and laughed. "But maybe I can tell you somethin' you didn't know. It's true he was born in Massachusetts, but as the frontier moved west, so did he, first to Pennsylvania, then on to Ohio and Indiana. After he left Pennsylvania he never really had a home of his own. Wherever he went he stayed with friends, with the new settlers who were clearin' the wilderness. Sometimes he helped them build their cabins an' start their gardens—an' their orchards too, of course.

Well, one time when he was in Ohio, he stayed with a family named Andersson, who had just come over from Sweden . . . "

"Was that *you*, Pa?" asked Otis excitedly. "Did he stay with *you*?"

"Not with *me*, Son. This is a hundred years ago we're talkin' about. With great-ancestors of mine. The story has been passed down from generation to generation. I remember when I was a boy my grandmother showed me an old Bible that belonged to *her* grandfather an' grandmother. But it wasn't the Bible she wanted me t' see. It was somethin' *inside* the Bible, somethin' tucked inside near the back. What it was, was a page torn from a book, not from the Bible, from some other book. She wouldn't let me touch it, 'cause it was so old and brittle. She was afraid it would fall apart. It probably would've too. I asked her where it had come from. She said that it had been given to her grandfather an' grandmother by Johnny Appleseed himself."

"Wow!" exclaimed Otis.

Elizabeth too found Nathan's story astonishing, but it had left her with an eerie feeling, the kind of feeling she got whenever she heard a ghost story.

Nathan paused only long enough to allow his audience to settle their minds again and to empty another sack of apples, then continued. "I also remember when I was a boy there was an old apple tree in our back yard that was supposed to have been planted by Johnny Appleseed himself. I don't know if it really was or not. Makes no diff'rence now, 'cause it has since died an' been cut down for firewood . . . But this John Chapman was a remarkable fella, most remarkable . . . "

Now Nathan began telling the story of Johnny Appleseed in earnest, with no more teasing. To Elizabeth's surprise Nathan seemed to know quite a lot about the eccentric Mr. Chapman, certainly more than she did. She was listening with great interest when a car she had never seen before drove in the lane. It was unusual to see any cars come out this way, so it did not surprise Elizabeth that she did not recognize it. The car passed by the orchard and Elizabeth heard it stop at the house. She knew that Hester was either in the kitchen or just outside in the garden, so she felt no need to go to the house herself. But when she saw Hester and another woman walking toward the orchard, Elizabeth went to meet them.

"Miss 'Lizbeth," sputtered Hester, uncomfortable in the role that had befallen her, that of introducing the other two women to each other, "this is Miss Kinney, the schoolmarm. She says she'd like t' have a few words with you."

"Hello, I'm Susan Kinney, " said the visitor, re-introducing herself, "I'm Sarah's teacher."

"I'm Elizabeth Wicker, Sarah's mother." The two women shook hands. "You say you want to see me?"

"Yes," replied the schoolteacher. "Is there any place we could talk in private?"

"You can use the kitchen or the parlor," offered Hester, "I'll be out in the garden."

"That would be fine. Thank you, Mrs. Andersson."

As Elizabeth and Miss Kinney walked to the house, Elizabeth could not help but smile. So, this is Sarah's mean, old Miss Kinney, she thought to herself. *Real* mean and *real* old, Otis had said. Why, this woman was attractive and charming and was probably only in her mid-to late-twenties. Elizabeth's amusement did not go unnoticed. Miss Kinney smiled too. "What is it?" she asked.

"It's just that you're not at all what I expected."

"I'm not surprised. Parents who meet me for the first time are always telling me that. I'm afraid my students don't always portray me in the best light . . . I hope you don't mind my saying so, but in some ways you *are* what *I* expected."

"Oh, how so?"

"Your physical appearance, for one. I knew that Sarah had to have gotten her dark hair and dark eyes from someone, and it wouldn't have been from her father. All the Wickers are fair-haired and blue-eyed . . . But that's not all. Sarah is an exceptionally bright little girl, probably the brightest child I've had in the five years I've been teaching here. She already knows as much as most of my third-graders. My guess was that she had a mother who had spent a lot of time with her when she was younger and who had probably been to college. You have *been* to college, haven't you?"

"Three years at Wellesley," Elizabeth replied, trying not to blush.

"Yes, Sarah did tell us that you had moved here from Massachusetts."

Elizabeth decided they would have more privacy and be more comfortable in the parlor.

"Are you from Rushing Creek?" Elizabeth asked the young teacher when they were both seated.

"No, I'm from Durham. So I can appreciate what you must be going through."

"What do you mean?"

"I mean that moving into these hills from the outside world is like stepping back into the Middle Ages. Most people around here still believe that the Bible contains all the truth we'll ever need to know. It's sometimes difficult to teach anything new when you've got that attitude working against you."

"Yes, I see what you mean. I've had a little problem with that myself."

"I've noticed that you don't come to church. That takes a lot of courage. Around here church-going is sort of the test of respectability. All 'respectable' citizens of the community go to church. I'm the schoolteacher, so I have to go. If I didn't they'd consider me unfit to teach their children. But I try to be patient. I bide my time. I sow my seed and hope that some of it will fall on fertile soil. I have faith that, in the end, the truth will set them free."

"The truth?"

"Not the truth of the Bible. Scientific truth. Truth based on empirical evidence. Truth that can be tested."

"Do you think science has discovered 'the truth'?"

"A good part of it, yes. And every day it is discovering more. Science is the key to unlocking the mysteries of the universe, the only key we have. Surely you believe that."

"I believe the scientific method is a very useful tool for investigating the physical world. But as for unlocking all the mysteries of the universe, I'm not so sure about that... But that's a discussion for another time. You wanted to talk to me about Sarah?"

Elizabeth would have been content to talk with this educated young woman for the rest of the day, but she could not help but wonder what had brought her out here in the first place. Miss Kinney straightened herself in her chair and folded her hands. She had put on her schoolteacher look. Even her voice now sounded more professional.

"Yes," she began, "I'll get straight to the point. At the beginning of each school year, usually during the first or second week, I give each of my students a piece of drawing paper. I ask them to draw a 'happy' picture. By that I mean a picture of something that makes them feel good or happy. I ask them, if possible, to draw the first picture that comes into their minds. Then I give them a second piece of paper and ask them to draw an 'unhappy' picture, that is, a picture of something that makes them unhappy. Again, I ask them to draw the first picture that comes into their minds. I do this for two reasons. First, it helps me to determine if a child has any natural artistic talent, but more importantly, the pictures tell me something about what's going on inside the child's mind. I can even get a pretty good idea as to what kind of home a child comes from just by analyzing the pictures he or she draws. I'm not a trained psychologist, but I have had some courses in psychology.

"Sarah missed the first two weeks of school, so she was not present when the other students performed this exercise. I asked her to draw the pictures for me this past week. I didn't have the heart to ask her the first week she was in school. The poor little thing just looked sad and stared out the windows those first few days. She wanted so badly to be outside. I didn't think she was capable of drawing a happy picture that first week... I'd like you to take a look at the two pictures that Sarah drew."

She now pulled two drawings out of a folder she had been carrying with her and handed them to Elizabeth. "The one on top is her 'happy' picture."

Elizabeth studied the drawing. It was done in pencil and was unmistakably a child's drawing. In the picture were a man, a woman, and a child standing side by side with their hands linked, much like paper cut-out dolls. The child was in the middle. All were smiling. Behind them stood a small house, a tree, and some flowers. The human figures, the house, and the yard were all enclosed inside a fence of some sort. Above all of this a benevolent sun was smiling.

"This is our house in Springfield," explained Elizabeth. "It had a white picket fence around it."

"I thought as much," said Miss Kinney. "Children from happy homes will often draw pictures of their home and family. Notice that the child is standing between the father and the mother. That tells me that Sarah loves you both equally . . . But there is something unusual about this picture. Do you see it?"

Elizabeth looked again. "Oh yes," she said, "it's the heads of the three figures." She continued to ponder the picture.

"Yes, the three figures, who we assume to be you and your husband and Sarah, all have circles around their heads. As you know, we've been holding school in the church since the schoolhouse burned down, and though there are no stained-glass windows, religious pictures are in evidence. These circles that Sarah has drawn around the heads of the three human figures look very much like the haloes that medieval artists painted around the heads of the holy family and the saints. That may be where she got the idea, though in my five years of teaching, none of my other students has ever thought to do it."

"I guess I should be flattered," quipped Elizabeth, not knowing what else to say.

"But it's the other picture I really thought you should see," said Miss Kinney.

Elizabeth pulled out the bottom drawing and placed it on top. She went white. "Sarah drew this?" she asked incredulously.

"You see her name there at the bottom."

Elizabeth looked at the stiff, laboriously-made letters. Sarah had been practising writing her name since she was four and Elizabeth recognized the signature as being very much like hers, though she was not sure she would have been able to distinguish it from that of any other six-year-old named Sarah. She continued to stare at the picture in disbelief.

"When I ask the children to draw an 'unhappy' picture," explained Miss Kinney, "I ask them to try to remember a time when they were sad, or angry, or hurt, or frightened, something like that. As you can imagine I get some very disturbing pictures. I was hoping that you could help me understand this picture that Sarah drew."

"Is that blood?" asked Elizabeth in horror.

"Yes, apparently she pricked her finger. I have to admit, it was pretty ingenious."

The picture at which Elizabeth had been staring in disbelief was of a female figure—a woman, or perhaps a girl: the age was difficult to tell—who appeared to be bound to a post or stake. All around the lower part of the figure Sarah had dabbed streaks of blood, not to represent blood, but apparently to represent fire. There was evidence that she had first tried to *draw* fire with her pencil, but had not been satisfied with the result. Quite resourcefully, she had then taken some blood—probably from her finger as Miss Kinney had conjectured—and used it as finger paint. But the most shocking thing about the drawing was that the woman's—or girl's—head was not attached to her body, but was lying in the flames near her feet. At the stump of the neck there was more blood, a great blot of it, and this undoubtedly was meant to *be* blood.

"I have no idea what this means," said Elizabeth, nearly transfixed by shock, "I have no idea." She could not believe that the little girl who drew this picture was the same little girl she had just left in the orchard a few minutes before, the one who was taking such delight in scrambling around under the trees, picking up the apples that had fallen on the ground, and laughing at her Uncle Nathan's stories.

"To the best of your knowledge, has Sarah ever witnessed a scene like this?" asked the teacher.

"No, never."

"Has she ever heard the story of Joan of Arc?"

Elizabeth thought for a moment. "No, I'm almost certain she hasn't. I have even avoided reading her some of the traditional fairy tales because they're so frightening. "I'm sure I would not have told her about Joan of Arc."

"How about your husband? Would he have told her about Joan of Arc?"

"I don't think he even knows who Joan of Arc was . . . But even if Sarah *had* heard the story of Joan of Arc, how would that explain the head?"

The two women sat in silence for a moment, then the teacher spoke again. "Does Sarah seem to have an unusual fear of fire?"

"No, not that I've noticed. In fact, she seems to be fascinated by it."

"Fascinated by it?"

"Yes, you know what I mean. She's excited by it. She's curious about it. She's curious about lots of things."

"Yes, I *do* know what you mean. She *is* curious about lots of things. That's what makes her such a pleasure to teach."

"One of our neighbors back in Springfield had a brush fire this past summer. Sarah was excited about that. So were all the other children in the neighborhood. Fire *is* a very fascinating thing when you stop to think about it. Can you imagine what it must be like to be a child and to see fire for the first time?"

"Did anyone get burned in the fire?"

"No, it was just a small brush fire."

"Has Sarah ever *seen* anyone get burned in a fire?"

"No."

"Or *heard* of anyone being burned in a fire?"

"Not so far as I know."

"Perhaps from one of her playmates back in Springfield?"

"Well, possibly, but there's a lot more in this drawing than the fire. I'm more disturbed by the fact that the head appears to have been severed from the body."

"That could be symbolic."

"Symbolic?"

"Yes, I think the stake and the severed head could both be symbolic. I think the fire is the key to understanding the drawing . . . Does fire have any associations for *you*?"

"For *me*?"

"Yes, let's forget about Sarah for the moment. Does fire have any associations for *you*?"

Miss Kinney studied Elizabeth's face as Elizabeth continued to stare at Sarah's drawing. She was hoping that Elizabeth might recall some incident in the past that might provide a clue to unraveling the mystery.

"I had an Aunt Katherine," said Elizabeth at last, hesitantly, "who died in a fire . . . She was my mother's younger sister."

"How old were you when this happened?"

"I wasn't born yet. This happened before my mother was even married. I've always called her 'Aunt Katherine' because that's what my mother would always call her when she talked to me about her."

"Did your mother ever talk to you about the fire?"

"Yes, and so did my grandparents. That would be my maternal grandparents, my mother's and Katherine's parents. But they never seemed to be very comfortable talking about the fire. I can understand why. It must have been a great tragedy for all of them. Katherine was only sixteen when she died."

"Your Aunt Katherine," asked the schoolteacher cautiously, "was she by any chance . . . mentally disturbed?"

Elizabeth looked at the teacher, her eyes wide with astonishment. "Yes, by all accounts she was quite insane. How did you know?"

"It's in the drawing. I thought from the outset that the severed head might be a symbol for mental insanity. We speak of an insane person as someone who has 'lost his mind' or 'lost his senses.' Such expressions might very readily be rendered by the unconscious mind as 'lost his head.' The unconscious can be very literal at times . . . Was your Aunt Katherine restrained in any way?"

"She was never sent to an institution, but for the last four or five years of her life she was kept locked in a small cottage away from the main house because she was so dangerous, both to herself and to others. When she was younger–about eleven or twelve–she set fire to the main house, or so I've been told. Fortunately it was discovered in time and put out. After that she was kept locked in the cottage. When the cottage burned down, she was locked inside. My mother always told me that Katherine had started the fire herself . . ."

Miss Kinney thought she had detected a note of uncertainty in Elizabeth's voice. "Do you have any reason to believe otherwise?"

"Well, I don't know anything for certain, but I've always had the feeling that there was some dark family secret that my mother was keeping from me."

"Why did you think that?"

"Well, there were a number of little things. When I was growing up, my mother used to have a Slovakian woman named Helena come clean the house once a week. She had been a housekeeper for my mother's family for many years. In fact she had *lived* with my mother's family for many years. It was she who had looked after Katherine. Apparently it was clear from a very early age that Katherine was not a normal child, and once this was realized, my grandmother–Katherine's mother–would have nothing more to do with her. She gave her over to Helena to raise. I got the feeling that Helena had really loved Katherine despite her many problems, because whenever I asked her about Katherine, she would always shake her head and say, 'Some things are just too sad to talk about.' Only, she'd say it in her heavy Slovakian accent.

"Helena seemed to hold herself responsible for Katherine's death. She once told me that if she had been there it never would have happened. She was away visiting a friend who was ill. The only thing she'd ever say about the fire was, 'Don't believe everything you've been told.'

"There was something else too that made me think that I wasn't being told the whole truth about Katherine's death. When I was little, my mother sometimes locked *me* in *my* room, and threatened me by saying that if I didn't behave, the same thing would happen to me that happened to Aunt Katherine. At the time, I understood that to mean that I would be burned alive in my room. Years later, when I was in college, I reminded my mother of how she had threatened to burn me alive in my room when I was younger. She was shocked and surprised to hear that. She explained that she had meant nothing of the sort: she had only meant that if I didn't learn to control my emotions, I would *go insane* like Aunt Katherine. But I was never sure whether to believe her or not."

Miss Kinney had listened with fascination and horror to Elizabeth's absorbing story. It was a full minute before either of them was able to speak again.

"Well," said the schoolteacher sympathetically, "you seem to have survived your childhood in spite of your mother. We can be thankful that the human mind is as resilient as it is. I could show you some 'unhappy' pictures drawn by other children in my classes that would make you shudder. You would not care to hear about some of the fiendish crimes that are perpetrated against children even in this day and age."

"Yes," said Elizabeth, "I've been hearing about some of them."

"I'd like to keep those drawings for my files, if you don't mind."

"Yes, of course." Elizabeth was about to place the drawings in the teacher's hand when suddenly she retracted them. "But wait, I don't understand," she said, staring once again at Sarah's "unhappy" picture. "I can understand why *I*, or my mother, might have drawn a picture like this, but why Sarah? Why would Sarah draw a picture like this?"

"Obviously she's heard the story."

"No, she's never heard the story."

"Perhaps she overheard you and your husband talking about it."

"My husband has never heard the story. It was a decision I made before we were married. Rightly or wrongly, I decided never to tell him about Katherine."

"Perhaps your mother told Sarah about Katherine."

"My mother has never even seen Sarah. She and my father disowned me when I married Daniel."

"Well, you may not remember ever telling Sarah about your Aunt Katherine, but I'd be almost certain that Sarah has heard the story somewhere or other, perhaps even when she was very young, before you thought she was old enough to understand."

Elizabeth remained skeptical. "Have you asked Sarah about this drawing?"

"Yes, right after she drew it, but she wouldn't talk about it. She was physically unable to talk about it. I thought it was important for you to see it. Perhaps she'll talk to you."

Miss Kinney was getting up to leave. Elizabeth handed her the drawings.

"Well," said the teacher, "I'm very glad I had the chance to meet you."

The two women shook hands again. "Yes," said Elizabeth, still shaken, "I'm very glad you stopped by."

Elizabeth walked the schoolteacher to her car. When Miss Kinney opened the door, she found a basket of apples on the front seat.

"Nathan Andersson is a sweet man," she said, smiling.

"Yes, he is," agreed Elizabeth.

Elizabeth watched as the car started out the lane. She saw it stop at the orchard and watched as Nathan walked over and exchanged a few words with the teacher through the car window. Then, as the car started up again and disappeared into the woods, Elizabeth thought again of Sarah's "unhappy" picture. She was certain that Sarah had never heard the story of Katherine. She wondered if Sarah had somehow *inherited* the memory. Was that possible? Could memories be transmitted from parent to child through the genes, the same as physical characteristics? It was as clear as the nose on Sarah's face that Sarah had inherited a good many things from her mother—including the nose on her face. She had her mother's eyes, her mother's nose, her mother's cheekbones. Elizabeth would never have admitted that she herself was beautiful, but she could plainly see that Sarah was beautiful. In her opinion, Sarah was as beautiful a little girl as she had ever seen—and everyone said that Sarah looked just like her. Sarah even seemed to have inherited her mother's quickness of mind. What else of her mother's mind might she have inherited? Was it possible that she had also inherited some of its contents? Some mental conditions, like genius and insanity, seemed to run in families. Could mental phenomena, like thoughts and memories, run in families as well?

For better or worse, Elizabeth decided not to tell Daniel about Sarah's "unhappy" picture.

5

THE WINTER AT NATHAN AND HESTER'S

"Mommy, am I going to Hell?"

Elizabeth tried too late to suppress the burst of laughter that Sarah's question had evoked, but did manage to clap her hand over her mouth in time to prevent the full measure of it from resounding through the whole upstairs of the house. Embarrassed, she cast a quick glance at the door to their room to make sure it was closed. Elizabeth was not normally given to laughing out loud. It was not that she lacked a sense of humor. On the contrary. She often found humor in the most unexpected places, in places that others might have thought totally devoid of humor. She had a special gift for seeing the irony in things. Daniel was often unable to understand why she laughed when she did, and she was often unable to explain it to him. On many such occasions she simply found herself saying, "I guess I'm just a happy person," which was probably the best of all possible things to say under the circumstances, because, first of all, it was true–and she often wondered whether she would be so easily amused if she were not so happy–and, moreover, it gave Daniel pleasure to hear her say it, because more than anything else in the world, he wanted her to be happy.

But she was not often given to laughing out loud. She was one of those quiet laughers. She laughed inside. It was a habit of hers that some of her friends in college had found quite disconcerting. Whenever one of them told a funny story or made a humorous remark, they would find it necessary to look at her in order to gauge her reaction. The smile would be there on her face and in her eyes, but there would be no audible sound to accompany it. But Sarah's question had come so unexpectedly, had taken her so off guard–and struck her as so outrageously funny–that she laughed out loud. Not only had she found the question itself amusing, but equally amusing was the totally nonchalant manner in which Sarah had asked it. Sarah was getting ready for bed, and it was just as she was pulling the nightgown over her head that her inquiry concerning the ultimate destiny of her soul had found expression.

"No, Honey, you're not going to Hell. Where did you ever get such a silly idea?"

"Otis said I was going to Hell because I don't go to Sunday School."

Elizabeth laughed again and this time made no effort to contain it. She wanted Sarah to know that Otis' pronouncement did not warrant serious consideration. But her open demonstration of amusement was not affected; it was totally spontaneous. The idea that an all-loving, all-forgiving God would send little girls to Hell because they didn't go to Sunday School, she found delightfully absurd.

"Do you know what I think?" she asked.

"What?"

"I think Otis is a little confused. If I were you, I wouldn't worry about it. Besides, if anybody goes to Hell, it should be *me* for not *letting* you go to Sunday School."

"But why *don't* you let me go, Mommy?"

Suddenly Elizabeth turned serious. "Do you *want* to go?"

"Oh, no! But what I don't understand is, why you *make* me go to school all the other days, but on Sundays you make me stay home."

"Oh, I see. I guess that *is* a little confusing, isn't it? It's because Sunday School is different from other school. They teach things in Sunday School which I don't think little girls and boys should hear." Even as she was saying it, Elizabeth realized that the difference between Sunday School and public school might not be as great as she would like to have believed, as far as being purveyors of damaging and crippling ideas was concerned. Although she had the greatest respect for Susan Kinney, Elizabeth had no doubt that Sarah's mind had been absorbing all manner of subtle ideas and impressions at school, which, if not injurious, were of dubious value at best, and these came as much from other students as from the teacher.

"What kind of things?" Sarah wanted to know.

"Well, Hell, for example. Otis told you that you would go to Hell because you don't go to Sunday School?"

"Yes."

"Do you suppose he really believes that?"

"I don't know. He said it."

"Well, I'll tell you what I think. I think it's not good for a little boy–or a little girl–to believe that God sends children to Hell just because they don't go to Sunday School. What Otis said didn't hurt you, did it?"

"No."

"But it *does* hurt Otis to believe that –if he really *does* believe it. Think about it. What kind of God would send children to Hell?"

"A very *mean* God."

"Yes, a *very* mean God, and I don't want you–or Otis–to grow up thinking God is mean or that the world is a bad place. I want you to grow up believing that the world is an exciting and wonderful place. As for God, well, God is something you and I will have to talk about a lot in the years to come. God is not an easy idea for children–or grown-ups–to understand. We will have to do a lot of exploring, you and I."

Sarah's eyes lit up. "I like to do exploring," she said, thrilled at the prospect. "Maybe one day I will discover God."

Elizabeth smiled, quietly this time. "Yes, I dare say, maybe one day you will . . . Now, how about some more of *Heidi*?"

"Oh yes, more of *Heidi*!"

Sarah jumped into bed, and Elizabeth, picking up the book from the bedside table, opened it to the marker and began to read.

Heidi was only one of the books that Elizabeth had bought just before leaving Massachusetts. Once the decision had been made to move to Rushing Creek, she had visited all the used book shops in Springfield, looking specifically for children's classics, although she did acquire a number of additional volumes of poetry for her own collection as well. She had known that any books she bought would only add to the already sizeable number that would have to be packed for moving–the weight of her trunk of books would be about as much as two hefty men would care to handle—but she had not known how readily available books would be in the rural community to which they would be moving, and she didn't want to take a chance on being without. Elizabeth considered books to be among the necessities of life, as essential to nourishment and growth as food, water, and air. She did not think the money foolishly spent. If need be, she would go without food, but without nourishment for her mind—the kind she found only in books—she knew she would surely starve. It was through books that she maintained contact with other minds—original minds, creative minds, minds greater than her own, but minds with which she felt an empathy, a kinship. For Elizabeth, to become lost in a great book—be it a novel, a volume of poetry, or a philosophical discourse—was to take a journey through the labyrinthine mazes of another mind, and when she emerged, she always found her own mind the more enriched, her own consciousness the more expanded, for having made the journey. She was trying to instill the same love of reading in Sarah.

Sarah certainly enjoyed *being read to*. Elizabeth understood why Miss Kinney considered Sarah an exceptional child. Once Sarah became interested in something, she became absorbed in it. She could focus her mind and keep it focused for long periods of time. This same little girl who at times seemed so frenetic, running everywhere, never walking, could also squat in the garden for hours watching a butterfly emerge from its chrysalis. Elizabeth had never had close contact with other children, but she was sure that Sarah's power of concentration must be far greater than that of other children her age. When Sarah listened to a story, she was totally receptive, but in a very active way. She seemed to listen with her whole being. For Elizabeth it was a pleasure to read to a child who was putting so much energy into listening. If there was a word or passage she did not understand, Sarah would, without saying a word, turn her head in Elizabeth's direction, as a signal to her mother that something needed to be clarified, and she would not allow her mother to continue with the story until she understood exactly what the word or passage meant. When Sarah was only about four years old, she had explained to her mother, "I can't make the pictures in my head if I don't know what the words mean." Elizabeth had always wished she could see the pictures in Sarah's head. She wondered how they compared with her own.

As she read, Elizabeth smiled at the thought that she read in very much the same way that Isaac drove: she spent as much time looking at Sarah's face as she did at the words on the page. Watching the expression on Sarah's face as it changed according to the mood of the story, was, for her, the most rewarding part of these bedtime-story readings. It was not simply a coincidence that *Heidi* was the book being read at this particular time. It was soon after Daniel had announced that he had bought the old Puckett place that Elizabeth decided that this would be a good time to read to Sarah Johanna Spyri's classic story of the little Swiss girl who lived with her grandfather in a cottage on a mountainside. In the spring Sarah would be moving to a mountain of her own.

Thanksgiving was a special occasion. It was the annual custom for all the Wicker family to gather at the old homestead for Thanksgiving dinner—at least all those Wickers who weren't "stone-cold daid" or hadn't moved to a "furrin' country in the north," as Hester had so colorfully phrased it. The gathering had diminished in numbers in recent years, as parents had died, and Daniel had moved away, but this year there promised to be more Wickers gathered together under one roof than there had been in many a year. Everyone was looking forward to it, and no one more so than Elizabeth. Daniel had not said that he would be coming down from the mountains for the occasion, but Hester had managed to persuade Elizabeth that nothing could cause him to miss it. "He'll be thar for sure, Miss 'Lizabeth," she kept saying, "I can feel it in my bones." Although Elizabeth did not have the same confidence in Hester's "bones" as Hester herself seemed to have, Elizabeth had, nevertheless, looked forward to the day with nervous expectation. To her great delight, and to Sarah's as well, Hester's bones did not lie. Daniel arrived at Nathan and Hester's shortly after one o'clock in the afternoon of Thanksgiving Day, having been traveling since the first light of dawn, and just in time to ride with the others in the wagon down to Isaac and Martha's. It was the first time he had seen his wife and daughter, or they had seen him, in over two months.

They arrived at Isaac's just before two. Aside from a cheerful remark about having become a "shingle-splittin' fool," Daniel was reluctant to say much about his work on the old Puckett place, but he was in such high spirits that it was clear to everyone that the restoration was progressing smoothly and that he was enjoying himself immensely "up thar on that lonesome mountain"–as Hester despairingly referred to the far-off place to which Baby Brother had removed himself this time. Elizabeth could not remember ever seeing Daniel so happy. He had always been an easy-going and cheerful sort of fellow, but he was glowing now. His eyes were brighter, his cheeks were redder, and his grin seemed almost as wide as Isaac's. Clearly he was finding life in the mountains more agreeable to his nature than life in the town. She wondered if he might also be finding the life of the hermit more agreeable than the married life.

When they sat down to dinner, Elizabeth found herself once again studying faces. Isaac, despite whatever temporary loss of motor and speech function he might have experienced upon first meeting her, was easily the most boisterous member of the family. He was loud, assertive, self-assured. At the moment he was boasting how he had "bagged" the turkey that was to be the main course of the dinner. Jacob was the very opposite. He was quiet and very gentle of manner. It was not the first time Elizabeth had met Jacob. Isaac and Jacob and their wives had stopped in at Nathan and Hester's one Sunday afternoon in late September for the purpose of getting acquainted with their new kin–or, in Isaac's case, better acquainted. Elizabeth could not help but smile when she looked into Jacob's face. It was a kind face, a loving face, perhaps the tenderest, sweetest face she had ever seen on a man, at least on a man of Jacob's age. She had seen expressions as sweet on the faces of young boys, and even on occasion on the faces of very old men, but never on the face of a man in his middle years. In fact she found his countenance so pleasing to behold that she found it necessary to exert an act of will to turn her face away, and still it was difficult, as difficult as it would have been to turn away from the sun on a cold winter's morning.

The wives of the two elder brothers differed from each other in appearance every bit as much as their husbands differed from each other in personality. Isaac's wife Martha was a strong, robust, large-boned woman. She was not, Elizabeth thought, what would generally be considered an attractive woman. Jacob's wife Emily, by contrast, was thin and frail-looking, but the sweetness of her expression testified to the health of the soul within. Elizabeth guessed that the two brothers had had different objectives in mind when they had taken wives: Isaac had sought out a helpmeet, Jacob a companion for his soul.

During the course of the dinner, Elizabeth found herself playing a little mental game, the object of which was to determine the ages of all those assembled at the table. She was able to calculate most by simple arithmetic. Daniel's age was always easy to figure as he was born in 1900, and his age therefore was always the same as the current year, give or take a few months. As the year was now 1932, his age was, quite conveniently, thirty-two. Elizabeth knew that Hester was seven years older than Daniel, so that made her thirty-nine. Isaac and Jacob were ten and eight years older than Daniel respectively, so they would now be forty-two and forty. She could only guess at Nathan's age, but she imagined him to be somewhere between thirty-five and forty. She thought she remembered Daniel saying that Nathan was younger than Hester. Isaac's wife Martha appeared to be in her mid- to late-thirties as well, and Jacob's wife Emily she knew to be about the same age as Jacob, as the two had been childhood sweethearts. She remembered that from Daniel's stories. Elizabeth, at thirty, was the youngest of those gathered about the table with the exception of the children. Benjamin and Lucy, Isaac and Martha's two children, were both in their late teens and could hardly be called children anymore, except to describe their relationship to their parents. The two little ones, Otis and Sarah, were eight and six respectively, Sarah having celebrated her sixth birthday on the twelfth of November, less than two weeks before. It occurred to Elizabeth that this gathering was unusual as a farm family reunion with respect to the number of children present. She had always thought of farm families as consisting mainly of children, but here eight adults had produced only four children. She and Daniel had chosen to have only one child, or at least had thus far chosen not to have a second; Hester had been able to have only one; Isaac and Martha, for some reason unbeknownst to her, had only had two; and Jacob and Emily had had no children, due to the fact, according to Hester, that Emily was barren.

Daniel spent the next three days at Nathan and Hester's, helping Nathan to lay in a supply of firewood for the winter and getting re-acquainted with his wife and daughter. Throughout the three days Sarah followed him everywhere he went, telling him all about Heidi. It seemed that Daniel had never heard the story before, and Sarah gladly took it upon herself to acquaint him with it. "You really must hear about Heidi, Daddy," she insisted, and proceeded to tell him the story in great detail.

It was on Sunday night, the last night of Daniel's visit, that he brought up a subject that had been of great concern to both him and his wife a few months before. Although Sarah had expressed a desire to sleep behind the stove in the kitchen with Pokey, she had once again been shuttled to the sofa in the parlor. Daniel and Elizabeth had just gone to bed, but had not yet snuffed out the lamp.

"Does Sarah still talk to her 'maginary friend—what was her name?–Kati?"

Elizabeth had expected that her husband would get around to asking about Sarah's friend "Kati" sooner or later, and she had been looking forward to telling him the good news. "No, she hasn't mentioned Kati once since she's been here, nor has she been talking in the early mornings as she did back in Springfield. She *has* been having nightmares on occasion, but, other than that, nothing out of the ordinary."

Nothing out of the ordinary, that's what Daniel had wanted to hear. He had never been sure what to make of Sarah's imaginary friend, or whether it was something that was a cause for worry. But he knew that it worried Elizabeth, and that in itself was reason for him to be concerned. He was relieved to hear that the problem no longer existed.

"I reckon she's found a new friend now," he said, smiling.

"Yes, she and Otis get along very well."

"I didn't mean Otis. I meant Heidi."

They both laughed. Elizabeth knew how hard Sarah had been bending his ear the past three days. "She must a-memorized the whole danged book," he added, still laughing.

Elizabeth kept to her decision not to tell him about Sarah's "unhappy" picture.

Daniel returned at Christmas for an even longer visit, but, alas, that visit too ended and Elizabeth was left alone again. If anything, she missed him more now that winter had set in than she had back in the early fall when there had been so much work to do that she had hardly had time to think, and had been so exhausted at the end of each day that she had had no energy left over for thinking anyway. But now she had time on her hands. She had come to experience directly what she must have always known intellectually: that the natural life, life on the farm, was lived according to the rhythms of nature, and winter was nature's time for resting. Even Hester had slowed down, though she always seemed to find something to do. Elizabeth did as she had always done whenever she had the time or the need—and now she had both: she resorted to her books.

She was surprised one especially cold morning in early January when she returned to the house after walking the children to school, to find Nathan sitting next to the kitchen stove, smoking a pipe and reading. It did not fit her image of Nathan at all. Nathan was quick to notice her amusement.

"What's the matter? You never seen a man smoke a pipe before?"

Elizabeth laughed her quiet laugh. "No, it's not that."

"You never seen a man read a book before?"

Of course she had seen a man read a book before, but after a little reflection, she realized it was not a sight she had been accustomed to seeing in recent years. Her husband Daniel seldom read books. He always seemed to be busy doing something or other with his hands, but turning the pages of a book was generally not one of them. She had Nathan figured for another Daniel.

She did not answer, but continued smiling and shaking her head in feigned disbelief to let Nathan know that, while the sight of him so occupied had at first struck her as incongruous–she was much more accustomed to seeing this big bear of a man outside on wintry mornings splitting firewood in his shirtsleeves or pruning his apple trees–she at the same time found it a pleasing sight, one of which she approved.

"Hey, I sawed an' split all this firewood," he pleaded, in an attempt to justify his aberrant behavior, "I guess I'm entitled to a little of the heat."

Still smiling, Elizabeth left the room and went upstairs. She returned a moment later with her volume of Wordsworth, pulled up a chair, and joined Nathan beside the stove. The two read quietly for a few minutes, then Elizabeth laid her book in her lap, closed her eyes and smiled, as though savoring some lines of poetry she had just read. Nathan was watching her and when she opened her eyes again, he held up the book he was reading. "Have you ever read this?" he asked.

Elizabeth took the book from him and read the title, *The Travels Of William Bartram*. Her eyes lit up in recognition. "No, I haven't," she answered, "but I've heard of it. In fact,

Wordsworth here"—she picked up the book in her lap—"and a friend of his, another English poet, Samuel Taylor Coleridge, both read this book and were very much taken with it. But I must confess, I've never read it myself. How is it that you happen to have it?"

"This book," said Nathan, taking Bartram back from Elizabeth, "is the reason I'm in North Carolina today and not still back in Ohio."

He watched to see if Elizabeth would nibble at the bait he had just dangled in front of her, and when he saw that she was interested, he continued. "Let me tell you a little about William Bartram."

Elizabeth knew from past experience that Nathan's "little" could be quiet a lot, and so she made herself comfortable and prepared her mind to receive. It was seldom that she was on this end of a story, and she hoped that she could be as good a listener as Sarah.

"Before we can talk about William Bartram, we haf t' say somethin' about his father John. John Bartram was one of the first great plant collectors of the New World . . . What do you call those scientist fellas who study plants?"

"Botanists?"

"Right. Well, John Bartram was a botanist, one of the best. He lived just outside of Philadelphia, but he traveled to places as far north as the Great Lakes an' Canada, an' as far south as Florida, for the purpose of studyin' the plant and animal life an' collectin' specimens. This was back in the middle of the eighteenth century when North America was still purty much of a wilderness, and about the only way t' get around was by boat or on horseback. It was also before the American Revolution, so the United States of America didn't even exist yet. The individual states, like Pennsylvania where the Bartrams were from, were still colonies of England, an' most colonists still considered themselves to be English—at least those colonists who had come from England in the first place. John Bartram was a Fella of the Royal Society in England, and it was at the request of some important English gentlemen, including the king himself, that

John Bartram made his explorations into the North American wilderness: all the plant specimens he collected he sent to his wealthy patrons abroad. His son William, or Billy, as he was called, sometimes accompanied him on these trips an' made drawin's, mostly of those plants that were too delicate to ship back to England.

"Young Billy Bartram might never a-become a famous naturalist himself if it hadn't a-been for one of his father's English friends, a man named Fothergill. This fella Fothergill had seen some of the drawin's that Billy had done as a boy, an' some years later, when Billy was about thirty-five, Fothergill wrote to him and asked him if he'd like to explore Florida an' the western part of Carolina an' Georgia. Fothergill, bein' a London medical doctor and a man of means, offered to pay him, of course. William had been failin' at one thing after another–he doesn't seem to have had a real good head for business–so when Fothergill offered him the chance to go explorin'–his first true love–he jumped at it.

"So, in April of 1773, William Bartram set out on a four-year exploration of what is now the southeastern United States. He spent most of that time in Florida, travelin' up the rivers by small boat, often alone. He camped on the river banks at night, but doesn't seem to a-slept much. He had t' stay awake most nights tendin' his fire, so that the alligators wouldn't sneak up on him an' drag him into the river. On a couple of occasions he saw so many alligators in the river at one time that he said he could a-crossed the river by steppin' on their heads without ever gettin' wet–if the gators had been agreeable, that is. By his own accounts he seems to a-spent most of his time in Florida bein' chased by alligators an' mosquitoes. Florida must a-been a purty wild place in those days. Might still be that way for all I know. I wouldn't mind seein' those clear water springs that Bartram found there–purest, clearest water he ever saw, he says–or pickin' oranges off those orange trees that seemed to grow wild just about everywhere, but I ain't so sure I'd care for all those gators an' mosquitoes.

"Back in Bartram's day, there was hardly any white folks to be seen, at least not in the back woods where he was travelin'.

Florida was still mostly inhabited by Indians, an' the Indians were not always friendly. I guess we shouldn't be surprised at that. I mean, put yourself in their place. They were livin' on this continent for hundreds, maybe thousands, of years, then one day here come these white folks in their big boats from across the water. Nobody invited them. They just moved in an' made themselves at home. They just pushed the Indians aside. They stole their land, lied to them, cheated them . . . It's little wonder that the Indians weren't always friendly.

"But William Bartram was one of them Quaker fellas. He always treated the Indians like they were his own brothers. He had a lot of respect and admiration for them—and they, in turn, always treated *him* with respect. He sometimes stayed with them in their villages, and in his book he describes many of their customs. In Florida the Seminoles practically adopted him as one of their own. They called him 'Puc Puggy.' "

"Puc Puggy?" asked Elizabeth. Unfamiliar with the Seminole language, she found that she was unable to make the picture in her head.

Nathan smiled. "It means 'flower hunter.' . . . I read this book many years ago, when I was eighteen or nineteen, I think. I remember findin' Bartram's accounts of his travels in Florida *interestin'*, but I didn't get really excited until I got to the third part of the book. That's when he started up through Georgia on his way to the western Carolinas. It was in the spring of 1776."

"1776? The year the American Revolution began."

"Right, at least the year it began *officially*, the year the Declaration of Independence was signed. But the Revolution itself had been goin' on for over a year before Tom Jefferson and his friends got around to signin' the Declaration. If I'm not mistaken, it all started up there in that part of the country where you hail from."

"Yes, I suppose you could say the war really started when the Minutemen from Concord and Lexington fired on the British soldiers coming to seize their weapons in April of 1775."

"Right, the so-called 'shot heard 'round the world.' " Nathan laughed. "I don't reckon that shot was heard *quite* all the way 'round the world. Bartram makes no mention of hearin' it in his *Travels*. Either he didn't know there was a revolution goin' on up there in Massachusetts or he didn't think it was important enough to make a note of it. Besides, when he started up through Georgia an' the Carolinas in the spring of '76, he was more concerned about reports of some other skirmishes: between the Cherokee Indians an' the white settlers comin' down along the mountains from Virginia. The western Carolinas were all part of the Cherokee nation at that time: these were *their* mountains. In his book Bartram calls them the Cherokee Mountains. The land was supposed to a-been guaranteed to them by treaty, but if you know anything at all about the sorrowful history of the relations between the white man an' the red man in this country, then you know that treaties were not always strictly observed."

Elizabeth returned Nathan's wry smile. She was sure that she did not know as much about the history of relations between native Americans and their European antagonists as Nathan, who she surmised to be a sort of amateur authority on the subject, but she knew enough to understand the spirit of sarcasm in which he had rendered his monumental understatement.

"But Bartram, as always, found the Indians friendly an' hospitable. But he couldn't help but see why the Virginians envied the Cherokees their mountains. As he rode his horse through green meadows an' deep forests, along rushin' streams, over high mountains—with views of more mountains rollin' on like ocean waves as far as the eye could see—he was so overcome by the awesome beauty of the Cherokee land that he could scarce find the words to describe his delight. Anyone else in his place might never a-found the words at all, but Bartram was somethin' of a poet. Open up this book to just about any page an' you're most like to find a poetic description of some peaceful green meadow with deer grazin' an' wild turkeys struttin' about; or some cool refreshin' waterfall upon some deep-wooded mountainside; or some new flower he had never seen before; or even a thunderstorm. He was always singin' praises to the God of Creation. An' why shouldn't he be? He was seein' Creation the way God had created it. About the only time he wasn't givin' thanks or singin' praises was when he was bein' eaten up by mosquitoes down in those Florida swamps.

"Now, maybe it's just my imagination, but it seems to me that in all his travels, he was most excited an' most poetic when he rode into these Cherokee Mountains. It must a-been in May or June 'cause the wild strawberries were ripe. He describes ridin' through fields so thick with strawberries that his horse's feet and ankles were stained with the juice. One day, quite unexpectedly, in a clearin' on top of a mountain, he came upon a whole bunch of young Cherokee Indian girls—'young, innocent Cherokee virgins' is the way he describes them. Some of them were gatherin' strawberries into baskets, others were lyin' in the shade of the trees, still others were bathin' in the stream . . . He must a-thought he had just entered Paradise. He admits that seein' all those young girls in such an unspoiled wilderness made him a little excited . . . Makes *me* a little excited just thinkin' about it."

Nathan winked his eye. Elizabeth covered *her* eyes with her hand.

"But," Nathan hastened to add, "Bartram didn't take advantage of them. William Bartram was not that kind of fella. Also, he was no fool. He knew that the only way he could get out of Cherokee country alive was by maintainin' his friendship with the Indians, an' the old chiefs might not a-taken too kindly to his ravagin' their daughters.

"The reason I mention that scene is 'cause it gives you some idea of what this part of the country was like a hundred and sixty years ago. It was an unspoiled wilderness, a Garden of Eden. Here Bartram found the greatest diversity of plant life he had seen anywhere in his travels. He found specimens of trees common to Canada growin' on the same mountainsides as more southern species. He found oak an' poplar trees of tremendous size, some of them ten an' twelve feet in diameter. 'Course most of the big trees are gone now. The lumber comp'nies went in, cut them down, an' hauled them out. I'm glad William Bartram didn't live t' see it. The lumber comp'nies would a-cut them all down if the government hadn't stopped them—thirty years too late, in my opinion, but better late than not at all. So, things have changed some since Bartram's day. You're not likely t' stumble upon young Cherokee Indian girls pickin' strawberries up in the mountains these days, but still, this is mighty excitin' country, as excitin' as any I've ever laid eyes on. The *mountains* are still here. No one's figgered out a way t' get rid of *them* yet . . . But if you want t' know what it was like before–*before* the white settlers, *before* the lumber comp'nies–read this book."

Elizabeth took the book again and began leafing through it as Nathan puffed on his pipe. "Tell you what," he said, "why don't you read some of it out loud?–that is, if you don't mind."

Elizabeth did not mind and began to read. Hester, who had been upstairs in Otis' room tidying up, came downstairs into the kitchen with a handful of socks, a ball of yarn, and a darning needle. She pulled a chair up to the stove and began working on the socks.

Thus began a practice that was to be repeated many times throughout the remainder of the winter: Elizabeth reading aloud as Nathan and Hester listened. Hester did not always *sit* and listen. She sometimes stood at the kitchen table rolling dough or cutting apples for pies. And even when she did sit, she was never idle. She always found something to occupy her hands. If she wasn't sewing or darning, she was cracking walnuts or churning butter. Nathan, on the other hand, generally just sat in his chair and smoked his pipe.

All three enjoyed the readings and tried to schedule them as often as possible–as often as possible, that is, and still allow sufficient time to carry on the work of the farm. Even in winter a certain residual amount of work had to be done. Animals had to be fed, cows milked, eggs gathered, hogs butchered, cider pressed, trees pruned. Most days they found time for a one- or two-hour reading session immediately after the noon meal, and frequently they were able to squeeze in another hour or two in the morning as well. At this rate it took Elizabeth just over a week to read *The*

Travels Of William Bartram. When she finished, Hester had a special favor to ask of her.

"Miss 'Lizabeth . . ."

"Yes, Hester?"

"Would you read . . .? Would you read . . .?" Hester's face reddened, her hands fidgeted. "Oh, never mind," she said at last, unable to finish her sentence, "hit was a foolish idea anyway."

"Just tell me what it is, Hester. I'll read anything you want to hear."

Suddenly she blurted it out. "Would you read *Heidi*?"

"Oh yes, please do," seconded Nathan.

It was clear to Elizabeth that Nathan's enthusiastic endorsement of Hester's request was meant to assure his wife that there was no need to be embarrassed just because she wanted to hear a children's story. It was exactly the kind of thing Elizabeth had come to expect from Nathan. Besides being resident humorist he was also self-appointed protector of other people's feelings. Elizabeth was at first surprised by Hester's choice, but after a moment's reflection, she realized that she should not have been surprised at all. After all, if Daniel had never heard the story of Heidi, it was not likely that Hester had either. Elizabeth guessed that Hester had probably heard her reading to Sarah through the door at nights, and Elizabeth *knew* that Hester had heard bits and pieces of it during the three days that Sarah had assailed Daniel with it.

"I'd be happy to read *Heidi*," said Elizabeth, smiling warmly.

So it was that Elizabeth read *Heidi* twice that winter. At the end of the story, Hester cried just as Sarah had done.

Other books followed. The daily readings in the kitchen became such a central part of their lives that winter that Elizabeth wondered how Nathan and Hester had managed all those winters without her. The three of them would have been forced into each other's company in any case, due to the fact that the kitchen stove was the only source of heat in the house, and in the winter warm-blooded creatures just naturally tended to gravitate toward it. Pokey spent the better part of the winter sleeping behind it.

The readings had turned their forced companionship into a pleasant pastime. They all looked forward to the next chapter of a story, and in some subtle way, as their emotions rose and fell in unison through the course of a story's events—as they followed the adventures of Charles Dickens' David Copperfield or Louisa May Alcott's Little Women—they seemed to be drawn closer to each other. They were being bonded together by the sharing of common experiences, even though those experiences were, for all of them, vicarious. The fluidity with which Elizabeth read, and the feeling she put into all the readings, no doubt contributed to this effect in no small degree. In the course of time Hester came to realize that Elizabeth had really meant it when she said she'd read anything Hester wanted to hear. She had become so comfortable with Elizabeth that one morning when Nathan was outside splitting wood, she decided to ask her educated sister-in-law if she would read from the Bible.

"Of course," Elizabeth replied without hesitation. "Just tell me what parts of it you want to hear."

Half afraid that Hester was going to say, "All of it," Elizabeth was relieved when Hester handed her a Bible already opened to a page toward the back of the thick volume. "Read the Gospel of John," said Hester.

Elizabeth took the Bible and began to read with all the eloquence she could muster. As she read, she found herself watching Hester's face, just as she watched Sarah's face when she read bedtime stories to her. She knew that Hester must be thinking, how could a woman who doesn't go to church and won't even allow her child to go to Sunday School read the Scriptures with so much feeling? Halfway through Chapter Eleven, just as Jesus was saying, "I am the resurrection and the life," Nathan walked in with an armload of firewood. When he saw and heard what was transpiring around the stove, he could not help but appreciate its import. Could this be the healing of a wound? he wondered. He stood absolutely motionless, with the firewood still in his arms, while Jesus raised Lazarus from the dead.

When Elizabeth had finished the chapter, Hester turned to Nathan and beamed. "Don't she read good, Nathan? Don't she read good?"

"She does indeed," agreed Nathan, walking to the stove and unloading the wood.

"Bless my soul, Miss 'Lizabeth," declared Hester, continuing her praise, "I never in all my borned days heared anyone read the Good Book with so much feelin'–not even Reverend Eby!"

It would not be the last time that winter that Hester would ask Elizabeth to read from the Bible, and Elizabeth was always happy to oblige. Other books and poems continued to be read as well. Normally it was Elizabeth who decided what to read. "You're the one who knows the books," Hester always told her, "you pick one." Elizabeth always tried to "pick one" that all three of them would enjoy, but on one occasion late in the winter, she made a miscalculation. She had decided that Wordsworth's poem "Ruth" would be a very suitable selection as it tied in nicely with *The Travels Of William Bartram* which she had read earlier in the winter. In fact, it had been Bartram's book which had started them off on this reading spree in the first place. Apparently Wordsworth had written "Ruth" soon after reading Bartram, because Bartram's influence on the poem is unmistakable.

Written in 1800, "Ruth" tells the tragic story of a sad and lonely English maiden, a creature of the woods and fields, whose heart is stolen by a roguish young soldier who has just returned from "Georgia's shore." Bedecked with Indian feathers, he woos her with tales of the beautiful and savage land from which he has just come: tales of deep forests, of magnificent trees, of green savannas, of endless lakes, of wondrous flowers, of Indian girls who "gather strawberries all day long." He pleads with her to marry him and to return with him to this wild and enchanted land, to be his "helpmate in the woods," a "sylvan huntress" by his side. They marry, but, alas, as they are about to set sail, he deserts her, and she never sees him again.

As Elizabeth read the last few verses, those recounting poor Ruth's subsequent fate–her madness, her imprisonment, her lonely, homeless wanderings among the woods and hills of her childhood—she could see the expressions on Nathan's and Hester's faces becoming more and more heavy with sadness. Satisfied that she had succeeded in capturing her audience, she read the concluding verses with a flourish of passion, drawing every last ounce of pathos up from her soul. When she had finished, she noticed that Hester was visibly disturbed, so much so that she got up and left the room.

Elizabeth turned to Nathan. "I guess I overdid it there toward the end," she said, apologetically.

"It's not that," said Nathan, his voice low and solemn, "I don't know if Dan'l ever told you, but Hester had a twin sister named Ruth who died when she was very young. I think that last part got to her."

Elizabeth read the last verse again, this time to herself.

> "Farewell! and when thy days are told,
> Ill-fated Ruth, in hallowed mould
> Thy corpse shall buried be,
> For thee a funeral bell shall ring,
> And all the congregation sing
> A Christian psalm for thee."

As much as Elizabeth enjoyed the time spent alone with Nathan and Hester that winter, she always looked forward, in the afternoons, to the children's coming home from school. She could see that just as the three adults were being drawn together, so were the two children. More than once Sarah had told her that she liked Otis "a lot," and it was apparent that the feeling was reciprocated. Nathan confided to Elizabeth that Sarah was having a good influence on Otis. Not only was Otis much more willing to do his chores now, but he was also more interested in his school studies than he had ever been before. Why, now at supper when Nathan asked him what he had learned in school that day, Otis was sometimes actually able to remember.

Suppers were the best part of the day. Not only did Elizabeth have the satisfaction of knowing that she had had a hand in helping to harvest and put up much of the food they ate that winter, but it was also the time of day when all the family was together and relaxed. And while the magic of that first evening at Nathan and Hester's back in September was never quite repeated, there were some memorable moments nonetheless. As always, the children provided most of the entertainment.

One evening at supper Otis began doing a curious thing: he began "exploding." He did this by first closing his lips tightly, then allowing the air from his lungs to accumulate in his cheeks. When his cheeks looked like they were about to burst, he suddenly released the air, making a loud exploding sound as he did so. Hester had been trying to talk to Nathan about some things she would be needing from town, but after Otis' third explosion, she turned to him and said, "For Pete's sake, Otis, what's got into you? Are you havin' a fit?"

"He's making a big bang," explained Sarah, who had been watching her cousin with keen interest and fascination.

"Yeah, I'm makin' a big bang," Otis confirmed.

"If you ax me," retorted Hester, "you're makin' a big fool of yourself."

"That's how the world began!" said Sarah excitedly.

"Yeah, that's how the world began!" echoed Otis again.

"Billions of years ago," added Sarah.

"Yeah, mebbe even zillions of years ago," exclaimed Otis.

"Billions of years ago, my foot!" objected Hester. "Who told you that?"

"Miss Kinney," said Sarah.

"Yeah, Miss Kinney," echoed Otis.

"Do you mean *mean, old* Miss Kinney?" inquired Nathan, who, like Elizabeth, was following the conversation between Hester and the children with interest and amusement.

"Yeah, *mean, old* Miss Kinney," confirmed Otis.

"She's nice!" said Sarah emphatically, contradicting him.

Sarah's defense of Miss Kinney came as no surprise to Elizabeth, who knew that Sarah's opinion of her teacher had changed since the first day of school.

"She is not!" shouted Otis.

"She is too!" shouted Sarah back at him.

"Is not!"

"Is too!"

This might have gone on for the rest of the meal if Hester hadn't interrupted them. "Miss Kinney told you that the world began in a big bang?"

"Yes," replied Sarah, turning to face her aunt, "but she didn't say it was a fact, she said it was a the-o-ry." She made sure to enunciate the word "theory" very carefully as it was a new word for her.

"Yeah, a thee-ry," blurted Otis.

Hester bristled. "Hit ain't no fact, an' hit ain't no thee-ry neither. Hit's hogwash!"

"Yeah, it's hogwash! That's what I told her, Ma. I told her it was hogwash!" Otis sat up straight in his chair and beamed, waiting for his mother's praise.

"You told *that* to Miss Kinney?" asked Nathan, sounding a little incredulous. He knew his son was not in the habit of lying exactly, but sometimes Otis was known to stretch the truth to the breaking point.

"Yeah, that's what I told her, Pa."

"You did not!" Sarah shouted.

"Did too!" Otis shouted back.

"I didn't hear you."

"That's 'cause I said it real quiet-like."

"How quiet?" Sarah wanted to know.

Otis mouthed the word "hogwash" but no sound came out. Sarah groaned in disgust.

"I don't know what this world's a-comin' to," protested Hester. "Last year he comes home a-tellin' us that we all come from monkeys, an' now he's a-tellin' us the world come from a big bang. What's the matter with you, Otis? Why do you say thangs like that?" Otis shrugged. "You know very well how the world came t' be . . . You *do* know Who made the world, don't you, Otis?"

Otis wrinkled his brow and thought as hard as he knew how. "Did God make the world?" he asked tentatively.

"Of course God made the world," exclaimed Hester in exasperation.

"Maybe God made the big bang," suggested Sarah.

"The Bible tells us how God made the world," said Hester with finality, "and hit don't say nuthin' about no big bang." As far as she was concerned, there was nothing more to be said.

But try as she may, she could not put her mind to rest. "Miss Kinney's got no business puttin' such notions into the haids of young'uns," she began again, still fuming. "She's s'posed t' be teachin' readin' an' numbers, not how the world was made."

"She only told us how the world began because I asked her," explained Sarah, in defense of her teacher.

"If you went to Sunday School, you'd know how the world began," retorted Hester.

"Miss Kinney says no one knows for sure how the world began," rejoindered Sarah. "She says different people have different ideas. And she *did* read us the story of creation in the Bible before she told us about the big-bang the-o-ry."

Hester stared hard at Sarah for the next few seconds, then, shaking her head, resumed her meal.

After supper Nathan confided to Elizabeth that a similar incident had happened the year before. Otis had come home from school one day acting like a monkey, and when asked to explain his behavior, had said that Miss Kinney had told them that all human beings had descended from apes—again, she had presented it as a theory, not as a fact. Upon hearing this, Hester had become so upset that she had threatened to take Otis out of school. Elizabeth wondered if Hester might be considering doing the same thing now. If Hester *did* take Otis out of school, mused Elizabeth, it would make for a very interesting state of affairs. What they would then have would be two mothers living under the same roof, one who refuses to allow her son to go to public school, another who refuses to allow her daughter to go to Sunday School—both standing on principle. If the truancy officer came around, however, it would be Hester he'd be coming for. As far as Elizabeth knew, there was no penalty for not allowing a child to go to Sunday School—unless, of course, Otis happened to be right, in which case both she and Sarah could look forward to serving a very long sentence in Hell.

In January it finally snowed. It was a good thing too. Sarah had begun to think that it didn't snow in this land of high mountains and rushing streams to which they had come, though she had difficulty understanding how it was possible that a place which was otherwise so perfect, and which seemed to have everything, could not have snow. Back in December there had been a few flurries, but not enough to cover the ground. When it didn't snow on Christmas Eve, Sarah had begun to wonder whether they had not made a mistake in leaving Massachusetts. But in mid-January the heavy snows came and Sarah was jubilant. All winter long Otis had been telling her how his father took him to school in the sleigh when the snow was deep, but when December passed and there was still no snow, Sarah had begun to wonder if Otis weren't telling another of his stories. Otis never seemed to have much to say, but whenever he did say something, it seemed Sarah could never trust him to mean what she thought he meant. He always insisted that he didn't tell lies, but sometimes he did such violence to the truth that it seemed to Sarah that it would be more honest to tell an outright lie. But this time Otis had been telling the true truth. The snow fell thick and fast through the night, and the next morning Nathan hitched Old Blue to the sleigh and gave the two children a ride to school. In fact, all the rest of the week Otis and Sarah got a sleigh ride to and from school. Sarah had not missed a day of school since she started–though most days she could have thought of a dozen other things she'd rather be doing–but during that wintry week in mid-January she awoke every morning eager to go to school. She would not have missed a ride in her Uncle Nathan's sleigh for anything in the world. It almost made going to school something to look forward to.

Daniel too had been waiting for snow and was glad when it finally came. He had finished the roof on the house and had nearly half the new barn roof on–the work was going well–but there were some heavy items he needed from down in the valley and he had been counting on some snow to help him get them up the mountain. He had built a sledge back in the early part of the winter, so that he would be ready to make a supply run just as soon as the first good snow fell. He had not built the sledge only for this purpose. Nor had he built it only to run on snow. In the mountains, where the steep terrain made wagons impractical, the sled, or sledge, had always been the most common means of conveyance. With its lower center of gravity it was much less likely to tip over than a wagon. It was used in all seasons of the year, not just the wintertime, for such tasks as hauling corn out of the fields, or for transporting firewood from the woodlot to the house, or for any other purpose for which a wagon might be used on more level ground. Of course, it was much easier for a horse, an ox, or a mule to pull a wagon than a sledge, just as it was much easier for the same animal to pull a sledge over snow than over bare, rocky ground. Daniel did not have the luxury of choosing between a wagon and a sledge, but it was within his power at least to decide whether his sledge ran over bare ground or snow. It had snowed earlier in the winter—more in the mountains than it had down in the valleys—but he had been waiting for a heavy snow, one that would blanket the valleys as well as the peaks and last for several days.

When the heavy snow finally came in mid-January, he hitched Jesse up to the sledge and set off down the mountain for the village of Rushing Creek. He spent the night at Nathan and Hester's—it was to be his last visit that winter—and early the next morning he was off again. There were a number of items he needed from Lehman's store, among them glass for the windows. He had had the window openings temporarily boarded up for the winter, but now that he would be spending more time working on the interior of the house, and as he preferred not to work in the dark, he'd be needing to get some windows made. Also, he had decided to buy a small wood-burning cookstove. The Pucketts had used the fireplace for heating and cooking, as had Daniel himself since moving in, but he had found the fireplace to be not altogether satisfactory. Daniel was thrifty by nature; like Hester, it bothered him to see anything go to waste. The problem he had with the fireplace was that most of the heat went up the chimney. There was an abundance of firewood close at hand, more than he would ever be able to use in his lifetime. He wasn't worried about ever running out. That wasn't the problem. The problem was, he simply hated to see all that heat go to waste.

Another thing that bothered him about the fireplace was the smoke. While it was true that most of the smoke made its exit by way of the chimney, which he had cleaned and re-chinked, there always seemed to be some residual amount that ended up inside the house. When the wind blew, as it often did, it was far worse. On more than one wintry night, the wind had blown so much smoke back down the chimney that he had been forced to flee the house and sleep out in the unheated barn. He was just beginning to get accustomed to breathing clean mountain air again; he refused to breathe smoke. He wondered how the Pucketts and the other old mountain folk had ever put up with it. Did they all spend windy winter nights sleeping in their barns? Or did they simply breathe the smoke and go to early graves?

Daniel knew that Elizabeth would fall in love with the big old stone fireplace if she ever laid eyes on it–she was the sort who would gladly sacrifice a few years of life for a few romantic evenings in front of an open-hearth fireplace–so he knew he had to act quickly. He had to block up the mouth of the fireplace and have the wood stove installed before she had a chance to see it. He was doing it to protect his family, he told himself. Surely Elizabeth would understand that. Surely she wouldn't want little Sarah to get sick from breathing smoke. She might be willing to jeopardize her own health for the sake of open-hearth fires, but he knew she wouldn't jeopardize Sarah's. Besides, she would find it much easier to cook on the stove than in the fireplace.

There was no possibility of his transporting a stove the size of Hester's up the mountain, so he was looking for a smaller version of it, and Walter Lehman had just the model he wanted. So, with the stove, the window glass, a can of kerosene, and a few other supplies lashed securely to the sledge, Daniel set off once again for the mountains. It proved to be an exhausting ordeal. On the uphill portions of the trail, the workload was shared more or less evenly by man and beast as Jesse pulled and Daniel pushed, but on the down-hill portions, the greater part of the burden fell to Daniel, who found it necessary to provide a drag, to hold back on the sledge, to prevent it from over-running the mule. Hour after hour they struggled through the rugged snow-covered mountain terrain, and even though they had gotten an early start, they did not reach their destination until an hour after dark. Fortunately the white snow provided them with enough light to enable them to negotiate the last part of the trail.

The third week in February it snowed again, a heavy, wet snow, and once again Daniel and the mule set off down the mountain, this time bound for Isaac and Jacob's. Jacob had agreed to give Daniel their father's old plow and harrow, as well as some other old tools and implements which were no longer being used, and Daniel thought it prudent to move all these heavy items while the snow was on the ground. He knew that snow this late in winter could not last for long. Even as he and Jesse labored to move the sledge-load of farming implements up the mountainside, Daniel could feel the snow underfoot growing soft. The air was warmer. Snow was melting and dripping from the trees. In another day it would all be gone, and it would not snow again that winter. Spring was in the air. Daniel could smell it.

6

SPRING IN THE MOUNTAINS

Sarah had been running ahead of the others but suddenly she stopped to listen. She remained perfectly still, absorbing every sound in the forest, as her eyes searched the lacy green treetops above her head for the elusive bird that was making the flute-like music. She had seen and heard many new birds since leaving Nathan and Hester's that morning, wonderful strange birds that she had never seen nor heard before. It was early March and the woods were once again alive with the flutter of wings and the song and chatter of migrating birds. Sarah could not remember ever being so excited in all her life, unless it was that day last September when she rode in her Uncle Isaac's truck with her head out the window from the train station in Asheville to her Aunt Hester's house, when she had first seen these mountains. But now she was actually climbing up the side of one of them. All day long they had been following a trail through the forest, sometimes ascending steeply, sometimes descending, at other times forging between the mountains, following one of the many small streams that caught the rain that ran off the steep slopes. Earlier in the day they had crossed Rushing Creek, several miles upstream from her Uncle Nathan's farm, where the creek was not nearly as deep or the current as swift as further downstream. Sarah had started the journey riding on the mule with her mother, but once they had crossed the creek, she had asked her father to lift her down so she could run. They were going to their new home in the mountains, and the mule simply could not be made to go fast enough to suit her.

From time to time she thought of Otis. She could see him in the pictures in her head, sitting on his bench in school, his mind wandering far from his studies, not hearing a word Miss Kinney was saying. He was probably thinking of her, wishing he too could be outside running barefoot through the woods. She knew she would miss Otis, but if she had to choose between being in school with Otis and being out in the woods on a day like this, with the trees bursting into leaf and the birds singing their hearts out . . . well, no one with any sense, she thought, would *choose* to be in school.

Elizabeth too was excited, but unlike Sarah, her emotions were mixed. She had spent a lovely winter at Nathan and Hester's and had come to feel very close to her simple, hard-working sister-in-law and her big, gentle husband. The parting had been an emotional one. Elizabeth, more than anyone, knew how much Hester had hoped that Daniel would change his mind at the last hour and decide to stay there with them. Hester was not one to cry, but Elizabeth had seen the pain in her eyes when they left. Hester could, by force of will, turn the corners of her mouth into a smile, but she could not hide the pain in her eyes.

And what about the old Puckett place? Daniel had assured her that she would fall in love with it once she saw it, but what if she didn't? What if she found it horrid? What if it wasn't beautiful, but ugly and squalid? All during the course of the day such disquieting thoughts had been forcing themselves, uninvited, into her mind. They were not new thoughts—she had been beset by them throughout the winter, particularly in the latter stages of the winter, as the day for departing approached—but today she found them especially discordant. The day was a glorious one, and turn which way she may, she could find nothing to spoil the beauty of the wild mountain scenery that surrounded her. Even if the house were squalid, she thought, this magnificent forest would still be there to provide her solace. With a backyard as grand as this, one would not need a palace to live in.

Elizabeth rode the mule as long as she was able before asking Daniel to help her down. Unlike Sarah, it was not the mule's speed she objected to—she found Jesse's slow, steady pace to be to her satisfaction—but the hardness of the mule's back. The prolonged sitting had made her sore. She walked until the soreness in her feet made her forget the soreness in her buttocks, then asked Daniel to help her back onto the mule. Thus, alternately riding and walking, she was able to endure, with only a minimum of discomfort, the day-long trek through the mountains. Time and again she marveled at Sarah's ability to keep running on ahead. She could not remember ever having had that much energy herself, not even as a child.

As they slowly made their way up the last steep section of the trail, Elizabeth's anxiety was intense. The moment of truth was at hand. When the cabin came into view, she gasped. "Oh, Daniel!" she cried, but could say no more.

As Daniel led the mule slowly toward the house, Elizabeth continued to stare wide-eyed and speechless. Daniel tied the mule to a young poplar tree near the porch steps. He was smiling quietly to himself. He had known all along what his wife's reaction would be.

"What do yuh think?" he asked, knowing full well that Elizabeth was incapable of speech at the moment. He watched her face as her eyes grew moist and her open mouth transformed itself into a smile—not her usual smile, not the smile she put on in polite company, but a totally spontaneous, unguarded smile, like a child's smile, like Sarah's smile.

"It's like something out of a fairy tale," she said at last, gushing with delight. "It's absolutely beautiful! Absolutely beautiful!"

Daniel lifted her off the mule, but instead of putting her down, he kept her in his arms and carried her up the steps, across the porch, and through the door. Once inside, Elizabeth put her arms around his neck and kissed him. When he put her down, she looked around the interior of the house and again found herself unable to speak. She shook her head slowly back and forth in disbelief. It was a small house and she could see nearly everything at a glance. The main portion of the house, the ground floor, in which she now found herself, consisted of only two rooms. The larger of the two rooms was a combination kitchen, dining room, and parlor. In the middle of the end wall—the east wall—but somewhat out from it, stood a handsome new cookstove. Under the north window in the east wall stood a sinkboard and sink. Cupboards lined both walls in the northeast corner. On the other side of the stove, against the south wall and under the south window, stood a heavy oak table just like Hester's, only a little smaller, and newly built, not a mark or stain on it. Daniel had also made three oak-and-hickory ladder-back chairs, and these were neatly placed around the table, as though waiting for someone to come and sit down to dinner.

Elizabeth walked into the smaller back room in the west end of the house. Here she found a handsome four-poster bed, a chest, and a bureau, all smelling of new black cherry wood. Elizabeth was overwhelmed. She remembered her earlier anxiety. She had not known quite what to expect, but in her most fantastic dreams, she could never have imagined anything this beautiful.

Sarah, who had been exploring around the outside of the house, now came running through the door. She cast a quick glance around, then ran into the back room where she found her mother and father sitting on the edge of the bed. Her mother was crying and her father had his arm around her. Overcome by the sight of her mother's tears, Sarah climbed up onto her lap and hugged her.

"Don't cry, Mommy, don't cry," she pleaded, starting to cry herself. "It's nice, it really is."

Elizabeth pulled Sarah to her bosom and hugged her, harder, Sarah thought, than she had ever been hugged before, except maybe for that time in the train station when her Uncle Isaac had nearly crushed the life out of her. Elizabeth kissed her again and again on the forehead, temples, and cheeks.

"I'm not crying because I'm sad, Honey, I'm crying because I'm so happy."

Sarah looked into her mother's face. Her eyes and cheeks were wet, but there *was* a "happy" smile on her face. Sarah kissed her mother's wet cheeks, then tried to dry them with her own hair. It upset her to see her mother crying, even if it was happy crying.

"Daddy?" asked Sarah after several minutes, "where am *I* going to sleep? I don't see a bed for me."

"Come on, I'll show you," said Daniel, picking her up. He carried her out into the other room. "Your bed is up thar," he said, pointing to the loft above the kitchen.

Sarah looked up. Daniel put her down and nimbly as a squirrel she scampered up the ladder and into the loft. "Oh, Mommy, come see!" she shouted with glee. "It's just like Heidi's!"

Elizabeth looked at Daniel and smiled her approval. Very carefully she climbed up the ladder and peered into the loft. In the end wall of the loft and slightly south of center was a small window. Directly beneath the window was Sarah's bed.

"Look, Mommy," cried Sarah, throwing herself on the bed, "I can lie in bed and see the stars at night, just like Heidi!"

"I think we both have a lot to thank your Daddy for," said Elizabeth.

"Oh yes," agreed Sarah, jumping up from the bed and quickly traversing the loft. Elizabeth had just enough time to step off the ladder before Sarah came scrambling down.

"Thank you, Daddy, thank you," said Sarah, clutching Daniel about the waist.

"Yes, thank you," said Elizabeth, embracing him.

Daniel could not have been happier. This was the moment for which he had been waiting all his life. Every dream he had ever dreamed had been realized. With one arm around Elizabeth and the other hand gently cradling Sarah's head, he was now able to stand under his own roof–a roof he had re-built with his own hands–and embrace everything that was dear to him in the world. His family was all together at last in a home of their very own.

"No, no," he said softly, his voice filled with emotion, "*you* shouldn't be a-thankin' *me*. *I* should be a-thankin' *you*."

"Why should you be thanking me?" asked Elizabeth.

"For bein' in the park that day. For asking me t' pose for your pi'ture. For agreein' t' marry a backwoods farmboy like me."

Elizabeth laughed her soft laugh. "I believe it was *you* who agreed to marry *me*," she said, gently contradicting him. "If I remember correctly, it was *I* who suggested we get married."

"Well, mebbe so. In that case, thank you for suggestin'." He was silent for a moment, then, looking down at Sarah, added, "And thank you for the sunbeam."

Sarah looked up and smiled.

"I believe you had as much to do with that as I did," said Elizabeth. "Thank *you* for the sunbeam. And thank you for this beautiful house, for this wonderful home."

"Well, thar's still a lot of work t' do. Hit's gwine t' be real busy around here for a couple of years til we get settled in proper. But hit's not a bad place t' work. An' we'll all be together."

Yes, we'll all be together, Elizabeth thought to herself. She was remembering some of the anxieties she had had during the previous months. "I'm ashamed to think about some of the foolish ideas that ran through my head these past six months."

"Oh? What kind of ideas?"

"Well, I saw so little of you since you started working up here, and whenever you did come around, you seemed so happy, I thought perhaps you had found that the life of the hermit agreed with you more than family life."

Daniel laughed. "Well you were right about one thang."

"What's that?" Elizabeth asked with some trepidation.

"About that bein' a foolish idea. You were right about another thang too: about me bein' happy. But the reason I was happy was 'cause I knew from the beginnin'–I knew from the day I first bought this place back in September–that this day would come, the day when I would finally bring you an' Sarah up here. Hit was a-knowin' that this moment would come that kept me a-gwine all those days an' nights alone up here. If I hadn't a-had you, if I hadn't a-had Sarah, if I hadn't a-knowed that you were right down thar in the next holler, only a day's journey away, I'd a-been the loneliest, most wretchedest man alive. I'd prob'bly a-flung myself right off the mountain, just like all them crazy Pucketts."

Elizabeth hugged him even closer to her. She appreciated the reassuring words, even if Daniel had exaggerated a little.

But Daniel had not exaggerated about the amount of work that still had to be done. He was still in the process of putting new shingles on the barn roof, but before that could be completed, there were more urgent chores to be attended to. Ground would have to be cleared and plowed for a garden and cornfield. Daniel had made a start on clearing the trees during the winter, but there were still more to take down, and then there would be the prodigious task of removing the stumps. Elizabeth and Sarah helped with the clearing of the land as best they could, but the greater part of the burden fell to Daniel and Jesse. Daniel and Elizabeth used the cross-cut saw to fell the trees and to saw them into manageable lengths. Jesse and Sarah then pulled them to a pile out of the way. Later, when time permitted, they could be sawed into firewood. Sarah's job was to sit atop the mule and to make him go when she said "git" and to stop when she said "whoa." It was a job she enjoyed immensely. It was by far and away more fun than going to school.

When it came time to remove the stumps, Daniel first dug around the roots with a pick and shovel, with Elizabeth sometimes taking over the shovel while he worked with the pick. This was a slow job, one that took an hour or more on the larger stumps. Then, with Jesse pulling and he and Elizabeth pushing, they strained and sweated to coax the tenacious roots out of the ground. More often than not, Daniel had to resort to the ax and chop off those roots that refused to yield. It was an exhausting job, but it was not without its rewarding moments. Daniel had never seen Elizabeth work so hard, and though he repeatedly cautioned her not to strain herself, she insisted on working right by his side. He perhaps took more breaks than he would have done had he been working alone, to give her the needed rest. But he always took breaks from his work, no matter what he did. He always made it a point not to get so involved in the job at hand that he failed to appreciate the beauty of the day. And those early spring days in the mountains were days not to be missed. During the interludes, Daniel always found himself first drawing in a deep breath of air, then allowing his eyes to wander lazily through the sunlit treetops, which were becoming greener by the day, and to follow flocks of warblers as they flitted amongst the upper branches. But always during those breaks, his eyes finally came to rest on Elizabeth's face. How differently she looked now than she had that day in Forest Park ten years before when he had first seen her, sitting under the birch trees with the sketchpad in her lap. He remembered how elegant she had looked then: a real fine and proper lady, he had thought. Now her dark hair was disheveled and falling into her eyes, her face was sweaty and soiled, and, yes, he thought he saw lines in her face which hadn't been there ten years before. But, if anything, he found her even more beautiful now than he had then, and he found his heart all but bursting with love for her.

Though the job of clearing the land was an urgent one, they did not work at it every day. Daniel had always believed that work should be enjoyed if at all possible, and when it ceased being enjoyable, it should be laid aside for a while. He had always found that on a farm there were always so many jobs that needed doing at any one time, that a man with any ambition at all could usually find one to his liking—and, if not, he could always go hunting until the spirit moved him to commence working again. The woods around them teemed with game. He had shot half a dozen squirrels, a couple of turkeys, and a deer during the winter. In fact, he had practically subsisted on wild game during his months alone on the mountain. He had bought corn meal and flour and other staples whenever he went down to Rushing Creek for supplies, and Martha, Emily, and Hester had all forced hams, potatoes, onions, squash, and canned goods onto him, insisting he must eat a proper diet. He figured it was his lot in life to be the recipient of all this largesse as a result of his distinction of being the youngest in the family. But had he been allowed to follow his own natural inclinations, he might have maintained himself solely by living off the land, by eating only game he had shot with his own gun and skinned with his own knife.

But now that Elizabeth and Sarah were with him on the mountain, food became a more important consideration. Once they got settled they would be able to raise most of their own food, but for now most of their foodstuffs would have to be packed up from the valley. During the first three weeks they managed to exhaust most of the food supply they had brought up with them, and by the end of March Daniel found it necessary to make a trip down the mountain to replenish it. It was a trip he had known he would have to make in any event. In fact, he had known that he would have to make several trips down to Rushing Creek during those first couple of months. Not only would they be needing food, but also garden seed, feed for Jesse, and their extra clothing and other belongings which they had left at Nathan and Hester's. On the first trip up they had carried only the immediate essentials so that Elizabeth and Sarah could ride the mule. Had Daniel known before they started that Sarah was going to run all the way up the mountain, he would have thrown on another sack of flour.

During the days that Daniel was away, Elizabeth and Sarah took the opportunity to explore the woods around their house. Elizabeth had already come to understand why this mountainous country had so excited William Bartram. Never had she seen so many different kinds of trees; she could not begin to identify all of them. Some of them, some of the oaks and tulip poplars in particular, were of tremendous size, perhaps five feet in diameter, and must have already been hundreds of years old when Bartram traveled through these mountains over one hundred and fifty years before. In her imagination she could see Cherokee Indian children of an earlier time still running beneath these forest monarchs. Many of the birds too were as new to her as they were to Sarah. Daniel had helped her to identify the blue-gray gnatcatcher, the white-eyed vireo, the yellow-throated warbler and several other species with which she had been previously unfamiliar, but here in the deep woods, it was sometimes difficult to catch even a glimpse of some of the birds, though their songs could be heard quite clearly. They lived in a mysterious world of their own, high in the forest canopy above. But of all the wonderful natural forms with which this enchanted kingdom seemed to abound, it was the wildflowers that thrilled Elizabeth the most. It seemed to her that every time she stepped into the forest that spring there were a dozen new species of wildflowers to greet her. Some she already knew, either from firsthand acquaintance or from pictures–the trilliums, the bluetts, the violets, the lady slippers, the lilies of the valley–but most were totally unfamiliar to her. She remembered how, back in

Massachusetts, she had made an effort to look at a rose as though she were seeing it for the very first time. Here, she had to make no such effort, for here she *was* seeing many of these flowers for the very first time. She could not believe that any other forest in the world, outside of the tropics, could boast such a diversity of plant life. No wonder Bartram had waxed so poetic.

When they had finally removed the last tree stump from the garden plot, Daniel hitched Jesse to the plow and turned the soil. The soil was thin and rocky, not deep and rich like the earth in Hester's garden, but Daniel knew that with enough care it could be made to yield food for the table. He had bought a great variety of vegetable seeds and had been given others (more largesse). He would not know what would grow well up on the mountain until he tried everything, so he aimed to do just that. With Elizabeth's and Sarah's help he planted lettuce, cabbage, collards, tomatoes, okra, shell peas, snap beans, several kinds of squash, onions, carrots, beets, turnips, white potatoes, sweet potatoes, an assortment of herbs–and, of course, Sarah's sunflowers. Once the garden was planted he set about to clear an even larger piece of ground on the hillside above the house for corn. Once the corn was up, he could plant more beans–limas, pintos, black-eyed peas–and allow them to climb the cornstalks. Then, with a little rain and a little sun–and a lot of that other essential commodity, luck–he and his family would soon be eating food raised with their own hands, which, in Daniel's opinion, was the most nourishing kind. It might be no more nourishing to body than food bought at the market, but it was certainly more nourishing to soul.

Mules are known for their contrariness and Jesse was no exception. During the infrequent trips that Daniel and the mule had made up and down the mountain that first fall and winter, Jesse had been willing enough to go *down* the mountain, but sometimes balked at coming back up. This was easy enough for Daniel to understand: the uphill climb was far more strenuous for both man and beast, and especially for the latter, who was often forced to struggle under a heavy load. The mule's fits of stubbornness often delayed the return trips by as much as an hour or more, but Daniel always reasoned that whatever time was lost on the mule's account was more than made up for by the time saved him in the end. He would have much preferred to stand on the side of a mountain for half an hour waiting for the mule to make up its mind as to what it wanted to do next, to carrying all the supplies up the mountain on his own back.

Jesse's behavior was impeccable that day in early March when Daniel had brought Elizabeth and Sarah up the mountain for the first time, but for several weeks thereafter the mule's behavior had become increasingly erratic. The mule now balked at going *down* the mountain and seemed only too anxious to come back up, practically dragging Daniel with him. He had been remarkably cooperative when they had cleared the land of the trees and stumps, as he had been when they had plowed up the first plot of ground for the garden. But now when it came time to plow up the larger piece of ground on the hillside above the house for the cornfield, he balked again. Whether it was the steeper incline of the land or what, Daniel had no idea, but whatever the reason, the mule could not be made to pull the plow from one end of the field to the other without making repeated and lengthy stops en route. It was as though he had no interest at all in this particular chore. Finally he stopped in the middle of the field and could not be made to move at all.

Daniel's patience was wearing thin. He had tried coaxing the mule, had called him names and cursed him, had even threatened to starve him and beat him, but all to no avail. Now he squared up to the mule face to face to deliver his final ultimatum.

"All right, you worthless critter, you listen an' you listen good. If you don't move by the time I could ten, I'm a-gwine t' march down to the house an' get my rifle, then I'm a-comin' right back up here and I'm a-gwine t' shoot you right betwixt the ears. Do you ken that? ... One ... two ... three ... "

The mule flicked a fly with its left ear.

"Six . . . seven . . . eight . . . I'm a-warnin' you, this is your last chance." Daniel took hold of the mule's halter and once again tried to pull the animal forward. Jesse refused to be moved so much as an inch. "All right, that's it, nine, ten, I'm a-gwine for the gun."

Daniel stalked down the hill toward the house. It was a warm spring day in early May, but at the moment he was in no mood to be bothered by the beauty and tranquility all around him. He strode past the garden where Elizabeth was planting pumpkins and squash without so much as casting a glance in her direction.

Elizabeth, who had overheard some of the louder invective that her husband had leveled against the mule, had thought the whole thing amusing at first, but she could now see that Daniel was genuinely irritated and decided it would not be prudent to make light of his quarrel with the mule. When he passed, therefore, she kept herself busy and said nothing.

Sarah, who was practicing her letters at the kitchen table, looked up as her father came barging in. She watched him as he crossed the room and took his rifle down from its rack on the back wall. "Daddy, what are you going to do?" she asked in alarm.

"I'm a-gwine t' shoot that dad-blamed mule," he muttered as he hurried back out.

"No!" shouted Sarah. She jumped up from the table and ran outside after her father.

Elizabeth stood up from her planting at the sound of Sarah's voice, in time to see Daniel go by with his rifle. "Daniel . . ."

Daniel did not stop. "No need t' say nuthin'," he retorted sullenly, cutting her off. "He's had a fair chance."

Elizabeth watched anxiously as Daniel stormed up the hill. She wondered if she should try to stop him. She had never seen him so angry and unreasonable. Suddenly Sarah ran by.

"Sarah, wait!" shouted Elizabeth after her. But Sarah kept on running.

Halfway up the hill Sarah caught up with her father. "Daddy, you can't shoot Jesse, you just can't!"

Daniel paid her no mind. He continued to march in a straight line toward the mule, bent on his mission.

"Why, Daddy, why? Why are you going to shoot Jesse?"

"Why? 'Cause he refuses t' move, that's why," muttered Daniel through clenched teeth.

"Maybe he'll move for me," pleaded Sarah. "Lift me up on his back and let me try."

Daniel stopped and looked down into the tear-filled eyes of the terrified little girl tugging at his shirtsleeve. Suddenly his anger began to subside. "Okay, Sweetheart, hit's worth a try. Lord knows, I've tried ever'thang else."

He laid his rifle down and lifted Sarah onto the back of the mule.

"Git, Jesse," urged Sarah, gently nudging her heels into the animal's ribs. Obediently the mule moved forward.

"Well, I'll be damned," uttered Daniel under his breath. "Make him stop! Make him stop!"

"Whoa, Jesse," commanded Sarah. The mule came to an immediate halt.

"Just give me a minute t' get rid of this rifle." Daniel carried the rifle to the edge of the field and propped it against a tree. When he returned he assumed his position behind the plow, slipped his head and left arm through the reins, and gripped the handles. "Okay, Sweetheart, I'm ready whenever you are."

Again Sarah urged the mule forward and again Jesse responded without hesitation. As Daniel worked the plow back and forth the length of the field, he marveled at how readily Jesse responded to the commands of the little six-year-old girl on his back. He remembered how, when Sarah first saw Jesse, she had thought the mule to be just a funny-looking horse. Her initial objection to the beast was that his ears were too long. Later she had complained that he was too slow. But Sarah had since come to adore the mule, and Jesse seemed to know it.

So glad was Daniel to finally have the mule in motion, that he didn't even bother to stop for dinner. He had already wasted enough time on the mule's account; he did not care to waste more. For the rest of the day the motley trio crossed and re-crossed the field. It was almost dark when Daniel unhitched the plow and led the mule to the barn for oats and water. It was not until they were at the barn that he lifted Sarah down.

"Thank you, Sweetheart, I could never a-done that without you."

"Daddy?"

"Yes?"

"Would you really have shot Jesse?"

" 'Course not. Can you 'magine me tryin' t' plow that whole field without him. I was just plannin' t' part the hair betwixt his ears, just t' give him somethin' t' think about."

"But what if he still hadn't moved?"

"Well, thank goodness we didn't haf t' worry about that now, did we? C'mon, partner, we'd better get into the house. Your mother prob'bly had supper ready for us an hour ago . . . How 'bout I give you a ride?"

Daniel picked her up and swung her up onto his shoulders. "Git," Sarah commanded. Obediently Daniel moved toward the house.

A week later Molly came to live with them. Sarah liked Molly right off, right from the moment she first laid eyes on her. It was late in the afternoon when Sarah first heard the distant clanging of the bell. It was not a sound she had heard before in the mountains, so she immediately jumped off her swing and ran down the trail to investigate. A short distance down she met her father coming up, leading Jesse, who, as was always the case on these homeward treks, was laboring under a heavy load. Behind Jesse, attached by a rope to the mule's harness, was the source of the clanging. Immediately Sarah fell in beside the cow and began to study her closely, her eyes wide with fascination and delight. When the menagerie had finished its ascent of the mountain, Sarah ran to the house to tell her mother about the new addition to the family.

"Daddy brought us a cow, Mommy!" she exclaimed, scarcely able to contain her excitement. "He's brown and white and has a bell around his neck! And he's got big, round beautiful eyes!"

"I think the cow is probably a *she*, Honey."

"How do you know, Mommy?"

"Well, your Daddy has been talking about getting us a milk cow so we can have milk and butter. Only she-cows give milk."

"But Daddy said the cow's name was Hizzy."

"He probably said 'Izzy.' That's short for Isabel."

"I don't like 'Hizzy,' " declared Sarah. "I'm going to call her Molly."

"I'm sure that will be . . ." Elizabeth decided it would be really rather pointless to finish her sentence as Sarah was already out the door.

A few minutes later Daniel came in, himself now struggling under an armload of supplies. "Our daughter has certainly taken to that cow," he said, smiling. "She's already got a bucket out thar a-tryin' t' milk her."

Over the course of the next several days Daniel taught Sarah how to milk the cow, and though her hands were too small to work the teats in the most efficient manner, Molly was soon giving more milk for Sarah than she was for him. This was not an entirely new phenomenon for Daniel. He had spent all his growing-up years around animals and he knew that some folks could just naturally get on with them better than others. His brother Jacob, for instance, had always had a way with animals, just as surely as his other brother, Isaac, had not. On his brothers' farm it was always Jacob who milked the cows, because, according to their brother-in-law Nathan at least, the cows gave so little milk for Isaac that it hardly paid to milk them at all. Daniel knew that anything Nathan said about Isaac had to be taken with a grain of salt–and vice-versa. Nathan often poked fun at his oldest brother-in-law's cold, methodical, strictly-business-like approach to farming, but Daniel suspected there was some truth in what Nathan had said about Isaac and the cows. Daniel also suspected that one of the reasons, if not the main reason, that Isaac had bought the tractor was that he had never been able to get along with horses or mules. Isaac had always thought of animals as things to be used, not as creatures in their own right. Jacob, on the other hand, had always loved the animals for themselves and they somehow seemed to sense it. Whatever the reason, there was no denying that the animals responded more favorably to Jacob's kindness than to Isaac's cursing. Daniel wondered if he himself had become too much like Isaac, regarding Jesse as a beast of burden only, measuring the animal's worth by the amount of weight he could pull. He partially excused himself by rationalizing that there had been so much work to do that first spring, and Jesse was so invaluable to him in helping to get that work done, that perhaps he *had* come to think of the mule primarily as a beast of burden. Why, he had even come to think of *himself* primarily as a beast of burden. As for Molly, he had to admit to himself that he probably *did* look upon the cow primarily as a source of milk and butter. Sarah, on the other hand, like Jacob, loved the animals for themselves, so it came as no surprise to Daniel—once he had taken the time to reflect on it—that she had greater rapport with both the mule and the cow than he did.

"I got a riddle for you," said Daniel at breakfast one morning.
"Oh good!" exclaimed Sarah. "I like riddles."
"This one's for you an' your mother both, okay?"
"Okay."
"You ready?"
"Ready."
"Okay, here goes:

When the wind hit blows the windmill round,
Hit goes back an' forth or up an' down.
The more of them you make t' spin,
The faster comes the money in."

Both mother and daughter sat transfixed and mute for a moment, staring helplessly at one another. Elizabeth then turned back to Daniel. "Did you make that up yourself?" she asked, sounding a little surprised.

"Yup," replied Daniel, smiling with satisfaction. "Hit's purty good, huh? Do you know what it is?"

"Say it again," said Elizabeth.

Daniel repeated his riddle. Elizabeth ran the lines through her head several times. "I give up," she said at last.

"Me too," said Sarah.

"Hit's a whirligig," said Daniel.

Elizabeth and Sarah exchanged blank stares, then both looked at Daniel. "A whirligig?" asked Elizabeth.

"Yup, a whirligig."

"I don't understand," said Elizabeth.

"You can look it up in your word book, Mommy," suggested Sarah.

Elizabeth turned to Sarah. "I know what the word means, Honey. What I don't understand is how it's the answer to the riddle. How does a whirligig make the money come in?"

Daniel grinned a mischievous grin, apparently tickled with himself for the little mystery he had created.

"What is it, Mommy?" asked Sarah. "What is that thing that Daddy said?"

"A whirligig is a kind of children's toy," explained Elizabeth. "They were very popular in Colonial times. I saw a collection of them in a museum once. The most common type seems to have been a little wooden soldier with movable arms. The arms looked more like canoe paddles than real arms, but there was a reason for that. The children would hold these little wooden soldiers by the legs and run with them. If they ran fast enough, the arms would catch the wind and whirl about. That's why they were called 'whirligigs.' . . . Otis likes to play soldier, doesn't he? I'll bet he'd enjoy playing with one of those old soldier-type whirligigs."

"You never saw Otis play soldier," laughed Sarah. "When Otis plays soldier, he *is* a whirligig!"

Elizabeth laughed at the picture that Sarah's characterization of her cousin conjured up in her mind. "There are other types of whirligigs too," she continued. "They aren't all of the old soldier type."

"That's good," interjected Sarah. "I think the running part would be fun, but I don't think it would be much fun to watch a silly old soldier flap his arms around."

"No," said Elizabeth, laughing again, "I think I can agree with you there. But not all whirligigs are of the old soldier type, and they're not all made of wood, and they're not all designed to be run with." She didn't like to end sentences with a preposition, but she couldn't think of any other way to say it. "You often see whirligigs on the roofs of barns. They're used as weather vanes. Instead of wooden soldiers with whirling arms, they're usually metal ducks or geese with whirling wings. The wings only go around when the wind blows. By looking at the duck or goose on top of his barn, a farmer can tell how hard the wind is blowing and from which direction it's coming."

"Why can't he just *feel* the wind?" asked Sarah.

"Hmm, that's a good question. Well, I suppose he could feel it if he were outside, but if he were inside eating breakfast like we are now, he could just look out the window at his barn roof and . . ."

"Why couldn't he just look at the trees?"

"A lot of farms don't have trees, Sarah. Out in the Plains states there are hardly any trees at all—at least not compared with here."

Sarah's eyes popped open in disbelief. "How awful!"

"I agree," said Elizabeth.

"Me too," added Daniel.

A hush fell over the table as all three contemplated the horrors of a farm without trees. Daniel, who had followed the conversation between his wife and daughter with interest and amusement, decided to have a little more fun. "Windmill whirligigs," he uttered cryptically.

Sarah looked at Elizabeth. Elizabeth looked at Daniel. "Windmill whirligigs?" she asked.

"What's that, Mommy?" asked Sarah.

"I'm afraid he's got *me* stumped now, Honey."

Daniel laughed. "Windmill whirligigs is how I plan t' make us some money." He waited for Elizabeth to ask him to elaborate, but when she failed to do so—she simply continued to stare at him with a bewildered look on her face—he decided to explain himself anyway. "A windmill whirligig is a whirligig that's drove by a windmill. Hit's not exactly a toy. Hit's more of a . . . doodad."

"What's a doodad, Mommy?"

"You'll have to ask your father about that one, Honey."

"You don't know what a doodad is, Sweetheart?" asked Daniel, feigning surprise. "A doodad is somethin' your Daddy's a-gwine t' *do*: that's why hit's called a doodad. An' what your Daddy's a-gwine t' do is make doodads." He leaned back in his chair and smiled in satisfaction, as though he had just given an exhaustive exposition on the entire subject of "doodads."

"But what does a doodad do, Daddy?" asked Sarah, becoming more confused.

"Well, the doodads that I'm a-gwine t' make can do just about anythang: they can split wood, they can scrub clothes, they can milk cows, they can hoe corn . . ."

"I hope you're understanding this, Sarah," interjected Elizabeth, "because he's completely lost me."

Daniel laughed again. "Well, I reckon I'm just a-gwine t' haf t' show yuh. I just happen t' have one out in the barn. Y'all wait here." He got up from the table and hurried out of the house.

"What's he going to get, Mommy?" asked Sarah.

"I don't know, Honey. We'll just have to wait and see."

In less than a minute Daniel had returned with his "doodad." "Now this is what they call a windmill whirligig," he explained, placing same on the table.

"Oh, Daniel, it's wonderful!" cried Elizabeth. "You *made* this?"

" 'Course I made it. You don't think I just found it in the woods, do yuh?"

Daniel's "doodad," which had caused Elizabeth to marvel so, could best be described as a farm scene in miniature. Mounted on a board about twelve inches wide and eighteen inches long were a cow, a milkmaid, a milking stool and milk pail, all exquisitely carved or otherwise fashioned out of wood. Had the milkmaid been standing rather than sitting she would have been about eight inches tall. Her arms, which looked like real arms and not boat oars, were connected to her body by a single long thin metal rod, which ran all the way through both shoulders, then traversed about ten inches of empty space before ending at a miniature windmill mounted on one end of the board. The rod was not straight but had been bent in several strategic places.

"What does it do, Daddy?" asked Sarah.

"Well, why don't you turn the windmill with your finger an' find out."

Sarah did as her father suggested. Her eyes lit up with delight when the milkmaid's hands began to move up and down.

"Looks kind of like your Aunt Hester, don't it?" laughed Daniel.

"How did you ever think up something like this?" asked Elizabeth, still enthralled.

"Well, t' tell the truth, hit weren't my idea. I saw one of these windmill whirligigs back in Springfield. Hit was in the backyard of a house near the shop whar I worked. Only hit wasn't a woman a-milkin' a cow; hit was a man a-sawin' wood. Let me tell you, when the wind blowed, that little fella could sure saw up a storm . . .

"One day I saw a lady out weedin' in the yard whar this whirligig thang was, so I stopped an' talked to her. I asked her whar she had got it. She said that she an' her husband had bought it at a country store up in New Hampshire. Like me, they had growed up on a farm an' had wanted somethin' t' remind them of the 'good old days.'

"A lot of folks who growed up on farms are a-livin' in cities an' towns now. 'Course this Depression's got a lot of them a-runnin' back to the farm with their tails tucked 'tween their legs—like me—but as soon as times get better, mark my words, they'll all be a-headin' back to the cities an' towns ag'in . . . til the next Depression comes along."

"Are we going back to Springfield when times get better?" asked Sarah.

"No, I think we're a-gwine t' stay put now."

"Good! I like it here. Don't you, Mommy?"

"Yes, Sarah, I do, very much."

"But it kind of crossed my mind," continued Daniel, "that if *I* was a-missin' the farm when I lived in town, then mebbe some other folks a-livin' in town are a-doin' the same—like those folks with the whirligig that I talked to. Mebbe none of them would ever want t' go *back* to the farm, but mebbe from time t' time they might like t' be reminded about how it was, 'specially when they got older. Hit also crossed my mind that these whirligigs wouldn't be all that hard t' make, 'specially for an old country boy like myself who growed up with a whittlin' knife in his hand. An' you could make all differ'nt kinds. You could have your little farmer an' his wife doin' all kinds of chores: milkin' cows, sawin' wood, *choppin'* wood, hoein' corn, cuttin' hay, pickin' apples, scrubbin' clothes . . . almost anythang that takes a simple back-an'-forth or up-an'-down motion."

"I see," exclaimed Elizabeth, suddenly relating all this to Daniel's riddle, "when the wind it blows the windmill round"—she turned the windmill with her finger—"it goes back and forth or up and down."

"Right," said Daniel. "I talked to Walter Lehman about this idea of mine. He said I should go ahead an' give it a try. He said he'd even help me sell them. He said with the Smokies becomin' a national park, thar's a-gwine t' be more an' more people from the cities an' towns a-comin' out this way. Hit would just be a matter of me gettin' my whirligigs to the stores an' shops whar folks can see them. Hit's the folks from the cities an' towns that yuh got t' sell to, 'cause if anybody in this world is a-gwine t' have money, hit's a-gwine t' be the folks from the cities an' towns.

"Another nice thang about these here whirligigs is that they don't take up much room. I mean, hit wouldn't make much sense for me t' make chairs or cab'nets or tables. How would I ever get 'em down off the mountain? But with these here whirligigs I reckon I could strap a dozen or more to the mule at one time . . ."

"Daniel," exclaimed Elizabeth, "if you could get these things *to* the cities and towns, I'll bet you could sell *thousands* of them!"

"Hold on now," cautioned Daniel, "I know I said, the more of them you make t' spin, the faster comes the money in, but let's not get carried away here. We're only tryin' t' pay our taxes, remember? We ain't tryin' t' become Mr. an' Mrs. Vanderbilt."

Or Mr. and Mrs. Horace Ashby, thought Elizabeth, smiling in chagrin. She considered herself justly rebuked. After all, one of the reasons she had married Daniel in the first place was because he, unlike her father, was not preoccupied with the pursuit of material gain.

Sarah looked out the window. "Daddy, the wind's blowing! May I take Aunt Hester outside and play with her?"

Daniel laughed. "Okay, but don't break her."

"I won't."

Elizabeth held the door for her. Once outside Sarah sat the whirligig down on a tree stump and knelt down to watch. When a gust of wind sent the windmill whirring, she squealed with delight. Daniel and Elizabeth, watching from inside, were hardly less amused.

"I don't know if I ever seen anyone who could work as fast with their hands as my sister Hester," laughed Daniel, "but I never even saw *her* milk a cow *that* fast."

Sarah was awakened one morning in late May by the sound of scratching very close to her ear. She opened her eyes to find a squirrel on her window sill only inches from her face. The squirrel was nervously turning in circles, apparently unable to decide whether it wanted to come inside or go back out. Every time it turned away from her, she could feel the air from its bushy tail as it swept past her nose.

"Come here," she coaxed. "Don't be afraid. I won't hurt you."

Finally the animal summoned up enough courage to jump onto Sarah's bed, but just as suddenly lost its nerve and jumped back onto the window sill and disappeared out the open window. Sarah quickly rolled over and lifted herself onto her elbows. She watched through the window as the furry creature scurried across the ground to the nearby trees. With one graceful leap it bounded onto the trunk of a tall oak tree directly opposite Sarah's window and ran straight up the vertical trunk as effortlessly as it had traversed the horizontal ground. From the safety of the tree it stopped and looked back at Sarah and began chattering vociferously, apparently scolding her for being in a place where she had no business being. It then scampered into the upper branches of the tree, leaped to another tree and disappeared into the woods.

An hour later at breakfast, Sarah noticed that her mother was unusually quiet. She seemed to be absorbed in thought. Sarah had learned not to interrupt her mother when she was thinking, so she sat and ate her breakfast without saying a word, even though she had something exciting to tell her.

"Sarah," Elizabeth said finally, "did I hear you talking to someone earlier this morning?"

"That's what I wanted to tell you," said Sarah excitedly. "I was talking to a squirrel! A squirrel came right in my window and jumped onto my bed!"

"A squirrel?" cried Elizabeth, suddenly elated. "Oh, thank God!"

Sarah was a little startled by the sudden change in her mother's disposition. If she had known that the news of the squirrel was going to make her mother *this* happy, she would have told her as soon as she got up.

"Yes, a gray squirrel," she confirmed. "I think I made him nervous though. He didn't stay very long at all . . . Where's Daddy?"

"He's out in the woods. He should be back soon. He hasn't had his breakfast yet."

"Do I have to do my lessons today?"

"I think you'd better. You're getting behind."

"That's because I've been helping Daddy."

"I know. You've been a big help to Daddy, but your lessons are important too. After your Daddy's had his breakfast, we'll work on your arithmetic."

"Oh, not arithmetic," Sarah groaned. "I'd much rather practice reading."

"If you like, we can work on your reading *after* you've done your arithmetic."

Sarah's response to this enticement was not exactly enthusiastic. She turned away from her mother and looked forlornly out the window.

"I don't understand why you don't like arithmetic, Sarah. You're so good at it."

"Because it's boring, that's why. Don't *you* think it's boring?"

"Well, yes, but that's beside the point. You still have to learn it. I guess it's just one of those things in life we just have to do whether we like it or not . . . It's better than going to school, isn't it?"

"Anything's better than going to school."

Elizabeth knew there was no sense in arguing with Sarah about the need to learn arithmetic. She knew that when the time came to do it, Sarah would do it without complaining, and when she had finished, she would agree that it wasn't so bad after all. As was often the case in life, it required less energy to just get up and do an unpleasant but necessary task, than it did to spend a lot of time thinking about how unpleasant it was going to be. Moreover, whether one found a particular task pleasant or unpleasant depended as much or more on one's attitude toward it as it did on the nature of the task itself. "There is nothing either good or bad, but thinking makes it so." So said Hamlet, and quite correctly in Elizabeth's opinion. All that was required was for Sarah to change her attitude toward arithmetic, to think about it differently. But rather than addressing the problem head on, Elizabeth decided that what Sarah's mind needed at the moment was a diversion.

"Sarah, would you go up to the spring house and get me a bucket of water. We'll be needing some water to do dishes."

Instantly Sarah's demeanor changed. "I'll get *two* buckets!" she exclaimed, suddenly exhibiting the enthusiasm which had been lurking all the time just beneath the sullen surface. Quickly she picked up the two empty buckets and went out the door.

Elizabeth shook her head. Where had she gotten such a child, she wondered, who would rather carry water than do her arithmetic lessons? No sooner had Sarah gone out the door than Elizabeth heard a shot. The next sound she heard caused her to freeze with terror: the sound of two buckets crashing to the porch.

"Oh my God!" she cried, rushing to the door. Looking out she saw the two empty buckets lying on the porch but Sarah was nowhere to be seen. Elizabeth ran down the porch steps and around the corner of the house. There she found Sarah, standing rigid, her eyes riveted on the woods, whence the sound of the shot had come. Elizabeth walked up behind her and gently placed her hands on her shoulders. Both watched as Daniel emerged from the woods, his rifle in one hand, a dead squirrel in the other.

When he saw his wife and daughter, he held up the squirrel and smiled. "A little fresh game for supper tonight," he said proudly. His smile faded when he noticed the look of horror on Sarah's face. She was staring at the dead squirrel. "What is it, Sweetheart?"

Elizabeth, remembering Sarah's reaction to Nathan's killing of the rabbit, continued to hold Sarah by the shoulders, not to restrain her, but only to comfort her, to let her know that someone understood what she was feeling. "She'll be all right, Daniel," Elizabeth assured her husband. She had told Daniel about the incident at Nathan's, but he had chosen not to make too much of it. It was only natural for children to be upset when they saw an animal killed for the first time, he had said, but they soon get over it. But Daniel had not been there. He had not seen the terrible anguish that Sarah had suffered. Elizabeth had, and she was wondering now what was going through her daughter's mind. She was not crying. She had not run away. She was just standing there staring at the dead squirrel. Was she struggling in her mind to accept this killing of animals as part of the natural order of things?

"I'm famished," said Daniel. "Is breakfast ready?"

"Yes," stammered Elizabeth.

He headed for the house. Mechanically Sarah turned and followed him. Elizabeth followed them both. Daniel laid the dead squirrel on the porch and went into the kitchen. Elizabeth did not want to leave Sarah, but she knew she had to get her husband's breakfast. She tried once again to divert Sarah's attention, this time from the dead squirrel.

"Sarah, you were going to get me two buckets of water, remember?" Elizabeth hurried into the house and went to the stove. Daniel was already seated at the table. She dished him out a bowl of milk and mush.

"It will be good to have some fresh meat in the house ag'in," said Daniel, digging into the bowl of mush that had been set before him. "Smoked meat's all right, but after a time a body gets t' cravin' somethin' fresh-kilt."

Elizabeth enjoyed cooking for her husband. He worked hard and never failed to bring a hearty appetite to the dinner table with him.

"By the way," he asked, "did you find out who Sarah was talkin' to this mornin'? Was it her 'maginary friend ag'in?"

"You won't believe this, Daniel. She was talking to a squirrel."

Daniel's spoon stopped in mid-air halfway between his bowl and his mouth. "Oh no," he suddenly exclaimed, putting his spoon down and getting up from his chair, "I left that dead squirrel a-lyin' on the porch!" He opened the door and looked out. The squirrel was gone. So was Sarah. "Sarah!" he called. There was no answer. "We've got t' find her, Elizabeth. She's got the squirrel."

Daniel ran down the porch steps. "You look 'round by the garden," he shouted back to Elizabeth who was just coming through the door, "I'll go 'round by the barn."

Daniel rushed out to the barn, checked the stables and hayloft, then looked out into the semi-cleared area where he had staked the mule and the cow, but saw no sign of Sarah. He was on his way back to the house when he caught a glimpse of blue color in the woods just east of the house. He changed his course and made straight for the woods. As he drew nearer, that which he had glimpsed came into clear view. It was Sarah's blue dress. She was sitting cross-legged under an oak tree with her back toward him. When he walked around to face her, he saw that she was holding the dead squirrel in her lap and gently rubbing its fur.

"Give me the squirrel, Sarah."

Sarah shook her head vigorously and drew the squirrel closer to her bosom, as if to protect it. Daniel knew that he was going to need assistance.

"Elizabeth," he called, "I found her."

When Elizabeth arrived, he explained the problem.

"Sarah," Elizabeth pleaded gently, "give the squirrel to your Daddy."

For a long moment Elizabeth was not sure her entreaty was going to be any more effective than Daniel's, but finally Sarah relented and yielded up the dead squirrel.

"I tried to make it better," she sobbed, the tears now coming to her eyes, "but I couldn't, I couldn't."

"Come on, Sweetheart," Daniel coaxed her, "let's go to the spring house an' wash that blood off your hands."

He handed the squirrel to Elizabeth and helped Sarah to her feet. Holding her by the wrist, he led her to the spring house. As Daniel washed her hands, he scrutinized her face. She was not looking at him: she was staring at the blood on her hands. When he had rinsed the last of the blood off, he took her small delicate hands in his bigger, coarser ones and crouched down in front of her. He lifted her hands to his eye level so that she was forced to look into his eyes.

"Sarah, Sweetheart, the squirrel is dead. If I hadn't a-kilt it, somethin' else woulda–an owl, a fox, a bobcat–somethin'. You cain't go feelin' sorry for ever' squirrel an' rabbit that gets kilt an' eaten in these hills an' hollers or you'll be a-mournin' sun-up to sundown all the days of your life. Ever' critter that gets borned into this world is one day a-gwine t' die. We may not like it, but that's the way it is. The same is true for us human critters. All them old Pucketts who used t' live up on this mountain, they're all gone now, all dead an' buried in that hillside over yonder. An' one day all of us are a-gwine t' be dead too. *I'm* a-gwine t' die—hard as that may be for me t' believe right now—your Ma's a-gwine t' die, an' even you, my precious little Sarah, will one day leave this world behind. That's just the way it is, an' thar's nuthin' we can do about it.

"Look here." Cupping his hands together he dipped them into the hollowed-out buckeye log and withdrew them. "The life we're given when we come into this world is like the water we can hold in our hands. No matter how tight we hold onto it, sooner or later hit all slips through our fingers. You're the lucky one. You're young. You got all your life still ahead of you. Your hands are still full.

"But the important thang ain't how *long* we live. The important thang is t' be just as alive as we can be whilst we're here. So you drink as deep as you can for as long as you can, an' be sure t' taste ever' drop. An' don't ever make the mistake of thinkin' that you can save it by not drinkin' it, 'cause hit ain't the drinkin' that uses it up: only time can use it up. Sooner or later, whether we drink it or not, hit's all a-gwine t' slip through our fingers."

He opened his fingers, allowing the water to trickle through. Again he took hold of Sarah's hands.

"We can learn somethin' from that poor old squirrel, Sarah. An hour ago he was a-jumpin' from tree to tree, now he's dead. Hit's the same with us. We can go just like that." He clapped Sarah's hands together, causing her to blink. "The important thang is t' make the most of life whilst you can still hold it in your hands, 'cause once hit's gone, hit's gone forever . . . So don't you be a-grievin' over that old squirrel, you hear me? Life is too short for grievin'."

Sarah had been listening intently but she did not respond. Instead, when Daniel finished, she withdrew her hands from his and ran into the woods. Rising to his feet, Daniel watched her go.

He had washed the squirrel's blood from her hands, he thought to himself, but he had failed to salve the deeper wound inside. He walked back to the house where he found Elizabeth standing on the porch still holding the dead squirrel.

"I think I made a mess of it," he said dejectedly.

"I don't know if I could have done any better," said Elizabeth. "I've tried explaining to her what it means to be born with about as much success. I don't know which is the more difficult to grasp, the idea that something as improbable as life—*conscious* life no less—could ever come into being in the first place, or the idea that it will all one day end. Both are quite beyond my powers to comprehend."

Daniel took the squirrel from her and held it up to look at. "Our daughter's got me feelin' so bad about shootin' this poor critter that I don't know if I should skin it for you t' cook or take it out back an' give it a decent Christian burial."

"I think Hester would say, no sense letting a good squirrel go to waste," said Elizabeth, trying to cheer him. "You skin it for me and I'll make squirrel pot pie for supper."

Elizabeth had overheard most of Daniel's talk with Sarah and she could not help but wonder how much of it Sarah had understood. It almost seemed to her that Daniel had been soliloquizing on the transitoriness of life and Sarah had just happened to be there. Much of what he had said, she thought, had been unnecessarily morbid, too morbid for a six-year-old child to hear. She knew that if Sarah's mind had not been so agitated by the vivid images of the dead squirrel and the blood on her hands, she would have asked him so many questions that it would have been *he*, not she, that had gone fleeing into the woods. Elizabeth suspected that Sarah had simply waited for him to finish so that she could run off to be alone and try to come to some understanding on her own about what she had seen, and, if she could, to make some sense out of what her father had told her.

Elizabeth also knew that Sarah would eventually come to her with all her unanswered questions.

But there was something else about Daniel's talk with Sarah that had impressed itself upon Elizabeth. It had seemed to her as if he had been reciting a memorized speech, not struggling to articulate ideas with which his mind was grappling for the first time. As he spoke, it became apparent to Elizabeth that her husband had thought a great deal about life and death during his months alone on the mountain. She wondered if there was something about living up on this mountain far from other people, or whether it was just a coincidence, but she too, in the few weeks she had been up here, had found herself thinking more often that usual about the fleetingness of life. But it was not the old Pucketts in the graves on the hillside that had caused her thoughts to gravitate in that direction: it was the wildflowers.

So many of the flowers in the forest were so exquisitely beautiful, yet bloomed for such a very short time, some for only a day or two, before they were gone. It made Elizabeth sad to think that such uncommon beauty could come into existence and pass out again so quickly. It made her sad—and filled her almost with a sense of desperation—because she wanted to hold on to it and could not. What was the sense of it? she wondered. Why would God or Nature go to so much trouble to create such exquisite beauty, only to allow it to fade and perish in a matter of days? She had found that she had been genuinely distressed by the passing of the lady slippers, and again by the withering of the showy orchids, and it worried her that she could be so moved by the loss of simple wildflowers. She wondered about her capacity to deal with real tragedy. What if she lost something really dear to her? What if something happened to Daniel? Or to Sarah? Daniel was like an oak, she thought: he would be around for hundreds of years. But what about Sarah? Sarah was like a wildflower, a thing of exquisite beauty, so delicately constructed. She could not bear to even think about losing Sarah. Whenever that dark thought crept into her consciousness, she exorcised it by an act of will and forced herself to think of something else.

She wondered again if living in so isolated a place had caused first Daniel, then her, to think, more than they were ordinarily wont to do, about death. She knew that the religious ascetics of old had often taken themselves off to remote mountaintops and into the deserts for the express purpose of meditating on the impermanence of life in this world, but it had never occurred to her before this, that perhaps the remoteness of their hermitages and the solitariness of their lives had actually served to induce such thoughts. If that were the case, what then could be said of the great multitudes of people who, in all ages, have not sought out the solitary places of the earth, but have preferred instead to live in crowded cities, in close proximity to others of their kind? Did they, do they still, seek the companionship of their fellow humans out of fear? Out of fear that if left alone they would be forced to face the fact of their own mortality? Is this unwillingness to face the unknown the reason that humankind from time immemorial has gathered itself into societies? Is the primary function of society, of civilization, to *distract*, to keep ourselves so busy, so pre-occupied, so engaged, that we have no time to *think*, no time to think about life–its fragility, its uncertainty, its impermanence–no time to think about death?

Elizabeth thought about some of her acquaintances back in Massachusetts, in particular about some of the young men her parents had tried to foist upon her. They were products of their culture. They had accepted without question the values of the support group that had nurtured them–that had nurtured them and kept them safely insulated from any contact with reality. They had accepted their culture's dictum that the purpose of life was to achieve material success, and in return for their allegiance they had been guaranteed that they could live out their lives in banal comfort and idle amusement, without ever having to think about life and death–or anything else of any consequence.

Elizabeth had always had a passion for reality. This, she had always thought, had been her saving grace. She could never have explained what she meant by "reality," but she had always had an intuitive feeling–an inner sense–that there was something more to life than living in a fine house, wearing the latest fashion in clothing, and being able to converse intelligently at dinner parties. When she met Daniel, she felt that he was somehow more "real" than the other young men she had met. The past fall and winter at Nathan and Hester's she herself had felt more "real" than she had ever felt back in Springfield. And now, here in the mountains, "reality" came crashing down on her so hard as to sometimes cause her pain. But she would never in a million years have given up the life she had chosen for the comfortable life her parents had wanted for her. She felt more alive now than she ever had before in her life. The pulse of her life had quickened. Her awareness had reached a new level of intensity. Her senses seemed keener, her perceptions clearer, all of her day-to-day experiences fuller, richer, more fraught with meaning. And if, during those first few weeks in the mountains, she had known exhaustion and pain, she had also known deep, sweet peace—and a joy so excruciating it sometimes made her cry. She was in wholehearted agreement with something she had heard Daniel tell Sarah: the important thing was to be just as alive as we can be while we're here. We must take that handful of water that has been given us and drink deep and savor every drop—even, Elizabeth would have added, even if some of the drops are bitter.

7

CLOSE ENCOUNTERS

As Sarah ran back up the trail toward the house, she wondered about something her father had said. He had used another word she had never heard before. When she got back to the house she intended to ask her mother about it: her mother always knew what words meant. She would have asked her father, but she had not had the chance. He had said this strange word just as he waved good-by and disappeared down over the hill. He was going down to Rushing Creek to deliver his first dozen whirligigs to Mr. Lehman at the General Store and to do some work for her Uncle Nathan. He would be gone for several days.

Whenever Daniel made these trips down the mountain, Sarah often walked a short distance down the trail with him, to see him off, and she had done so this morning. Now as she headed back toward the house, she decided to walk instead of run. The day was warm and there was no need to hurry. It was the first week of August, the very middle of summer. Overhead she could hear bees humming amongst the blossoms of the sourwood trees. On both sides of the trail white snakeroot was in bloom. Something *always* seemed to be in bloom in these mountains. Curious to see what other new flowers might be in blossom, she decided to do a little exploring. Leaving the trail she cut up through the woods in order to follow the small rivulet of water that trickled down the mountainside from their spring house. She knew that it was along the narrow strip of soil moistened by this trickle of water that she had the best chance of finding wildflowers. This is where she and her mother had seen so many in the spring.

The first thing she discovered, to her delight, was that the small bed of bee balm, from which she and her mother sometimes gathered leaves for tea, now had a cluster of bright red fringed flowers hovering above it–happy flowers, Sarah thought–supported on stalks rising out of the bed of green leaves. As she squatted down to get a closer look, a butterfly fluttered lazily past her nose, lit briefly on one of the red flowers, then fluttered away. Sarah picked one of the leaves, put it into her mouth to suck on, then trying as best she could to imitate the carefree movement of the butterfly, she fluttered on up the hillside.

Her flight was arrested by the appearance of another plant in bloom, the dignified stiff gentian. The multitude of lilac-colored flowers standing proudly erect reminded her of Otis and of the silly soldier game he had sometimes made her play. She saluted the stiff gentian and moved on.

Further up the mountain, in a depression where the soil was especially wet, she found a more playful flower, the one her mother called jewelweed and her father called snapweed. She had noticed on a number of occasions that her mother and her father did not call things by the same name. For example, there was a tall straight tree very common in the forest which her father called "yaller poplar." Some of these trees were massive in breadth, up to five and six feet in diameter. Her father had told her that early pioneers had made canoes out of "yaller poplar" logs by simply hollowing them out. And, of course, the floor of their house had been made from slabs of "yaller poplar." Sarah had already figured out that when her father said "yaller," he meant "yellow," so she thought she was correct in calling these trees "yellow poplars"—until her mother told her they weren't poplar trees at all, but tulip trees.

Even more confusing was trying to figure out what laurel was. The bush that her mother called "laurel," her father called "ivy." To her father laurel was something else: it was a taller bush, the one that grew along the banks of Rushing Creek down at her Uncle Nathan's, the one that her mother called "rhododendron." Sarah did not know whom to believe. Her mother knew lots of words, and any word she didn't know in her head, she looked up in her word book. But her father seemed to know everything there was to know about the mountains. The only thing that Sarah knew for sure was that "rho-do-den-dron" was a hard word to say—almost as hard as "Mass-a-chu-setts."

With the muck oozing up between her toes, she gingerly approached the pale yellow flowers. She remembered jewelweed from Massachusetts and the fun she had had touching the seed pods and watching them explode. But these plants refused to play. Though she poked and prodded and jumped back each time in excited anticipation, there were no explosions. The seed pods were not yet mature. She would have to come back in a week or two and try again.

As she neared the house she found squirrels scurrying about on the ground, gathering up seeds which had parachuted down from the beech and maple trees. She hid behind a tree and watched them for a while, then ran around the house to the garden. Climbing up on the fence and leaning over, she found her mother picking beans.

"May I help?" she asked.

"What a silly question," Elizabeth replied. "Of course you may help."

Sarah jumped back down off the fence and entered the garden by the gate. "Mommy," she asked, as she joined her mother in the beans, "what's a coon?"

Elizabeth was shocked. "Sarah! Where did you hear that word?"

"Daddy said it."

"Well, he shouldn't have. It's not a very nice word to say."

"But what does it mean?"

"It's a name that some white people—some white people *who should know better*—call a dark-skinned person—you know, a member of the Negro race."

"You mean a nigger?"

"Sarah! That word is just as bad. Did you learn that from your father too?"

"No, from Otis."

"The correct word is 'Negro.' Can you say that?"

"Negro."

"Good."

"I don't understand, Mommy."

"What don't you understand?"

"Why Negroes would want to come during the night and eat all our corn."

"Sarah, what are you talking about?"

"That's what Daddy said. He said if he didn't shoot the Negroes, they would come during the night and eat all our corn. Only he didn't say 'Negroes.' He said that other word, the one I'm not supposed to say."

"Nigger?"

"No, the other one."

"Coon?"

"Yes."

"Your Daddy said if he didn't shoot the coons, they would come . . .?" Elizabeth did not finish her sentence. Instead she buried her face in her hands and burst out laughing.

"What's so funny, Mommy?"

"O-oh, I must have been in the sun too long. It's starting to affect my brain . . . When your Daddy said 'coons,' he meant *rac*coons."

"What's that?"

"Raccoons? You know what raccoons are, don't you?"

"I don't think so."

"A raccoon is an animal, a mammal, about the size of a woodchuck, only its fur is more gray than brown. And it's more agile than a woodchuck: it can climb trees. Also, its tail is bushier and has rings around it . . ."

"Rings?"

"Rings of different colored fur . . . But the most distinctive feature of the raccoon are the black patches of fur around its eyes. It looks like a masked bandit . . . Are you sure you've never seen a raccoon?"

"I don't think so."

"Not even in pictures?"

"Maybe in pictures, but pictures aren't real. I'd like to see a *real* raccoon."

"They are hard to see. They're nocturnal. Do you know what that means?"

"No."

"It means they're mostly active at night."

"What do they do during the daytime?"

"Sleep, I guess. In hollow trees, I think. But I'm not sure. When your father comes home, you should ask him about raccoons. I'm sure he knows more about them than I do."

Elizabeth stood up and stretched her back. As much as she had enjoyed working with Hester the previous fall, she was glad to have a garden of her own now, in which she could work at her own pace. The most exhausting thing about working with Hester had been trying to keep up with her.

Elizabeth was pleased with her first garden. It was not nearly as large as Hester's or as lush, but most of the vegetables they had planted had done fairly well. There were a few exceptions. The tomatoes were turning out to be a disappointment. The plants showed an unhappy tendency to wilt just before the fruit ripened. Daniel blamed it on the walnut trees. There was something about walnut trees, he said, that poisoned the soil for tomatoes. Apparently they had planted the tomatoes on or near a spot where some young walnut trees had stood the year before. Next spring they would plant the tomatoes in another part of the garden.

But for the most part, the garden had done well and she had already begun canning some of the surplus. To facilitate the canning, Daniel had constructed a makeshift fireplace outside near the garden, a simple structure consisting of a firepit lined with earth and stones and an iron plate on which to set the canning kettle. She sometimes cooked meals outside as well. As a result the house stayed cooler. It would have been cooler than Hester's house in any event due to the higher elevation and the almost constant movement of the air over the mountains. Elizabeth had feared that the summers this far south might be too warm for her New England blood, but she found to her relief that at this elevation summer temperatures were no more intolerable than they had been in Massachusetts.

But as proud as she was of her garden, she could not help but feel a twinge of envy when she looked out over Daniel's forest of corn. Daniel had planted to corn every inch of tillable ground outside the garden fence, right up to the edge of the woods. And next spring he planned to clear more land and plant even more, and perhaps a small hayfield as well. The crop was turning out better than even he had hoped, the thinness of the soil having been compensated for, in part, by the abundance of summer rain.

The corn was in tassle now and soon the ears would be forming. Elizabeth knew how long and hard Daniel had worked to raise the crop. She remembered how much trouble he had had in getting the ground plowed in the first place and how many hours he had spent patiently planting all the seed by hand. Then, throughout the spring and summer, he had worked a little each morning, whenever he was home, amongst the slowly unfurling plants, at first with his cultivator, then with his hoe, doing battle with encroaching weeds and breaking up the hard crust to keep the soil loose, so that the afternoon rain showers would be absorbed by the roots rather than simply run off the hillside. It would indeed be a shame, Elizabeth thought to herself, if raccoons did come during the night and eat all of this lovely corn, as Daniel feared they might.

But as unpleasant as this prospect was, Elizabeth could imagine one even more unpleasant. What if Daniel, in order to save his corn, was forced to shoot the raccoons and the bears and the deer and whatever else might be out there lurking in the woods. She didn't even want to think about what that might do to Sarah. After the incident with the squirrel back in the spring, Daniel too had come to realize that Sarah was an unusually sensitive little girl. He liked to hunt–he had always liked to hunt, even as a boy–but Elizabeth had persuaded him to forego his favorite pastime for the time being–at least until Sarah was a little older.

They did not need the game, it was true. They could survive without it. Nathan butchered half a dozen hogs every winter and smoked the pork. He had more than enough for his own family. He usually sold the surplus and he would just as soon sell to Daniel as anyone else. If Hester had her way, Daniel and his family would have eaten nothing but hog, as that would mean that she would see more of her brother. As Daniel always insisted on paying for everything with his labor, the more hams, bacons, shoulders, or other hog parts he "bought," the more time he would spend with them. It was during the late summer and early fall that Nathan needed the most help, getting in the hay, sorghum, apples, and corn. It was not the most convenient time for Daniel to be away from his own budding farm, but he was determined not to get behind in his debts. Therefore, it was Daniel's plan to work for Nathan a day or two here and there throughout the harvest season. Fortunately the days were long this time of year and a man could do a fair piece of work between the time the sun came up in the morning and the time it went down in the evening. Though it was an arrangement that was agreeable to all concerned—and to none more so than Hester—Daniel hoped to be more self-sufficient in the years to come. He hoped eventually to raise hogs of his own. He hoped also to supplement his meat supply by hunting. But he would be patient. He would wait until Sarah was older. Perhaps one day he would even teach her to hunt as well.

Elizabeth had had little trouble persuading him to temporarily give up hunting. He too had seen the look of horror on Sarah's face that day he had shot the squirrel. In his mind he could still see her pathetically rubbing the poor dead creature, trying to bring it back to life. He would gladly give up hunting for a year or two to spare the child that kind of hurt. But would he be willing to give up his corn crop, Elizabeth wondered, or would he defend it at all costs, even if it meant shooting the intruders?

"Daniel, wake up!"
"M-m-m... What is it?"
"Sarah went out over an hour ago and hasn't come back yet."
"She prob'bly just went to the outhouse."
"But she's been gone for over an hour."

Elizabeth had been awakened by the sound of Sarah opening the door and latching it behind her, and she had not been able to go back to sleep. Every time Sarah went out during the night, Elizabeth held her breath, remembering the stories she had heard about children being eaten by bears and panthers when they dared to venture outside after dark.

Daniel sat up on the edge of the bed and lit the bedside lamp. Pulling on his trousers, he picked up the lamp and walked out into the kitchen. Elizabeth, in her nightgown, followed close behind him.

"She must a-taken the lantern," he said, "I don't see it." He opened the door and stepped out onto the porch. "I'll check the outhouse, you wait here."

Elizabeth watched from the porch as the light moved down the hill toward the edge of the clearing where the outdoor privy stood. She folded her arms across her body to keep them warm. It was a cool night for the middle of August, considering how hot the day had been. She often found these summer nights in the mountains to be pleasantly cool, ideal for sleeping. She was wide awake now however.

While waiting for Daniel she stepped off the porch to see if the stars were out, then strolled leisurely around to the side of the house where the garden lay in order to get a better view of the night sky. As she studied the star-studded blackness above her, she thought again of Van Gogh's painting, "Starry Night." She could no longer look at the starry night sky without thinking of the Van Gogh painting. If she tried *not* to think of it, she was *aware* that she was trying not to think of it. She sometimes wondered whether her education in the arts had enriched her perception of the world or obstructed it. She always seemed to be referring the one to the other—the world she experienced with her senses to the world of ideas in her mind. She could not look at daffodils in the spring without thinking of Wordsworth, or watch autumn leaves blowing in the wind without thinking of Shelley—or look at a starry night sky without thinking of Van Gogh.

As she lowered her gaze she could see the tassling corn shimmering in the moon-and star-light. Suddenly she saw something that struck her as very odd. There seemed to be a faint glow coming from the upper part of the cornfield near the woods.

Where was Daniel? What was taking him so long? She walked back toward the house and looked toward the outhouse. The light was now coming toward her.

"She's not thar," he said, as he came into view.

"What took you so long?"

He grinned. "Well, I decided that as long as I was thar, I might as well use it. No sense wastin' all them steps."

"Daniel," Elizabeth said anxiously, impatient with her husband for not taking their child's disappearance more seriously, "come around to the garden. There's something I want you to see." Daniel followed her white nightgown through the darkness. "Do you see that glow up there on the hillside?"

Daniel held up the lamp. "All I can see is this danged light in my eyes . . . Here, wait til I put it out." He snuffed the lamp, leaving them in darkness. Again he looked in the direction Elizabeth had indicated. "Yeah, I see it. Hit's a-comin' from the cornfield."

"Do you think it's Sarah?"

"Don't know. Could be."

He was about to call out when Elizabeth stopped him. "No, wait. What would she be doing up there this time of night?" As concerned as she was about her daughter's safety, her curiosity was getting the better of her.

"You want for us to sneak on up thar an' find out? Just give me a minute t' put this here lamp back in the house."

When Daniel returned he took Elizabeth's hand and led her out around the garden, then up along the edge of the cornfield bordering the woods. Under other circumstances, Elizabeth thought as they climbed the hill, it would have been a very pleasant evening for a walk under the stars, but at the moment her mind could not be brought to bear on the beauty of the evening. When they had gone about three-quarters of the way up the hillside, Daniel turned and headed out between two rows of corn. Elizabeth followed him. By keeping their hands out to their sides and feeling for the stalks, they were able to steer a straight course. As the faint light toward which they were steadily progressing became increasingly brighter, they proceeded more stealthily. Finally the source of the mysterious glow came into view. Sitting on the ground, unattended, was the lantern from the kitchen. But there was no sign of Sarah. Their faces illuminated now by the light cast from the lantern, Daniel and Elizabeth exchanged puzzled glances. Daniel walked slowly around the lantern, causing, as he did so, a menacing moving shadow thirty feet high to be thrown up against the forest of trees that loomed just beyond the last rows of corn. Suddenly sounds of frantic rustling and scurrying caused Elizabeth to cry out. Immediately Daniel picked up the lantern and held it over his head. A half dozen rows above him he saw Sarah on her hands and knees. "Daddy," she said, looking back over her shoulder at him, "you scared them away."

She got to her feet and came toward her father, but before she could reach him Elizabeth rushed up and hugged her.

"Sarah, Honey, are you all right?"

"Mommy, I saw raccoons, real raccoons!"

"You did?" Elizabeth knelt down to get a better look at her. She had to be sure she was all right. "Sarah, what's that on your face?"

Daniel held the lantern up to Sarah's face and saw the patches of black around her eyes. "What *is* that?" he asked, touching the blackened area with his finger, "soot?"

Brimming with excitement, Sarah nodded. "I wanted to look like a raccoon," she explained, "so I wouldn't scare them away."

Elizabeth laughed. "You look more like a chimney sweep."

"Does a chimney sweep have a tail like this?" asked Sarah, turning the back of her head toward them and displaying her "tail." She had pulled her long dark hair into a pony tail and had tied half a dozen white ribbons to it, spacing them at regular intervals.

Daniel and Elizabeth laughed. "Well now," said Daniel, still contemplating with amusement the spectacle of his black-eyed, ribbon-tailed daughter, "are you ready t' go back down to the house with us, or should we leave you out here with the rest of the coons?"

Sarah laughed. "I'm ready to go back now," she said, casting one last glance back at the woods. "But I saw them! I really saw them!"

The three of them made their way single-file out through the rows of corn, with Sarah leading the way and Elizabeth right behind her. Daniel found himself bringing up the rear–with the lantern.

Sarah was still excited. "I like raccoons," she said, "I like raccoons a lot!"

Elizabeth sighed. Daniel groaned. There goes the corn crop, he thought to himself.

But Daniel's worst fears were not realized. Although he allowed the corn to stand until November before picking it, the amount of damage done by raccoons and other wildlife was minimal. The animals seemed to have confined their plundering to the outer perimeters of the field, to the rows nearest the woods. While Daniel would have preferred, of course, not to have lost any of his precious crop to the denizens of the forest, he considered the loss small enough to be acceptable. Even if he had waged war on the intruders he could not have saved every last ear of corn.

Indeed, as he stood and smiled with satisfaction upon his nearly full crib of corn, he reflected that he had every reason to be pleased. Only three months before he had feared that he might lose the entire crop, and now here was enough corn stored away to keep his livestock in feed and his family in corn meal for a year. And he had done it all without having fired a single shot. He had found himself on the horns of an impossible dilemma–either lose the crop to the animals, or shoot the animals and cause Sarah untold grief–and somehow he had managed to slip through like a greased pig, completely unscathed.

But Daniel's mind was not entirely at ease. He knew that Sarah's growing affection for the wild creatures of the forest did not bode well for the future. Not only would it make it more difficult for him to take up hunting again, but he knew that if he did not do something to deplete the wildlife population in the woods surrounding them, it would only be a matter of time before it would over-run the farm. He considered himself to have been lucky that first year: he might not be so lucky in the future. During the winter Daniel would see things that, while quite remarkable in themselves, did nothing to allay his anxieties.

That Sarah "had a way" with animals, Daniel would have readily acknowledged. Both the mule and the cow were more responsive to her than they were to either him or Elizabeth. He didn't understand it exactly, but he accepted it as a fact. Far more unusual, however, and far more unnerving to Daniel, was Sarah's growing rapport with the birds and the other wild animals that lived in the forest around them. It was during their first winter in the mountains as a family that Daniel began seeing things that he would not have believed if he hadn't seen them with his own eyes. By the time spring returned, bringing with it sun and warmth and new green life, both he and Elizabeth had seen enough to persuade them that Sarah "had a way" with even the wild creatures of the forest that was quite out of the ordinary.

It had started with the birds. As soon as the first snow had fallen, Sarah had taken to feeding the birds. With Daniel's help she had built a feeder, but before long she had chickadees and snowbirds eating sunflower seeds and cracked corn right out of her hand. By the time the woods had once again filled with birds in the early spring, she could get almost any bird to come to her by simply holding out her hand. Daniel had been astonished when he had first seen this, as he had never known anyone, not even his brother Jacob, who could call a wild bird right out of the air. Somehow the birds seemed to sense that she would not hurt them. The squirrels seemed to sense it too, as they seldom even bothered to move out of her path anymore as she ran by, and if she should perchance crouch down and hold out her hand, they too would almost invariably come to her. At first Elizabeth thought that the animals were unusually tame because they were unfamiliar with humans and therefore had no reason to fear them, though she knew that Daniel had shot squirrels that first winter that he had lived on the mountain alone. But try as she may, she never succeeded in getting a bird to eat out of *her* hand, or to coax a squirrel within eight or ten arm-lengths of her. On the contrary, as soon as the bushy-tailed rodents so much as caught sight of her, they would turn tail and run for the nearest tree. Daniel was so sure that he would have no such rapport with the wild creatures, they he didn't even try to get them to come to him. No, Elizabeth decided, it was not the creatures in this remote mountain wilderness that were unusual: it was Sarah.

Daniel worried that Sarah's befriending of the wild animals would prove their undoing. He knew that it was difficult enough to grow a garden in the mountains without having to contend with the birds, squirrels, raccoons, deer, bears, and any number of other creatures who just seemed to sit patiently in the woods year after year, waiting for some fool like himself to come along and plant them a garden and a nice field of corn. It was a problem that farmers had had to contend with ever since the earliest settlers had moved into these hills and hollows one hundred and fifty years before. A man broke his back to clear his land and plant his seed, and just as he was about to reap the rewards of his labor, along came some thieving varmint animals to eat off his greens or strip off his corn, as if these crops had been planted expressly for *them*, as if there was nothing else in all of creation for animals to eat. What, Daniel wondered, would all of these miserable creatures have eaten if poor fools like himself hadn't come along and cleared the land and planted the crops in the first place? They had no right, in his opinion, to come in uninvited and eat so freely, and with such voracious appetites, after others had labored so hard.

Fortunately they didn't have rabbits in the mountains–not yet anyway. Rabbits and woodchucks preferred the more open spaces where grasses and the more herbaceous vegetation flourished. But Daniel had no doubt that as he cleared more land, they too would find their way up the side of the mountain and under his garden gate. Then the war would begin in earnest. Daniel knew only too well how troublesome rabbits and woodchucks could be– and how persistent. No matter how many of the rodents fell before the guns of beleaguered farmers, there always seemed to be another and another. Though the population might decline for a year or two, they always came back. Daniel had never met a flatland farmer who had claimed to have shot the last rabbit or the last woodchuck.

As Daniel plowed his field that second spring, he could not help but wonder what the new season would bring. He had been lucky, in his opinion, to have suffered so little loss the first year. He wondered, as he planted the seed, what percentage of this year's crop he would be able to harvest. He knew that sooner or later, if he had any hope of growing enough food on this small mountain farm to feed his family and his livestock, he would have to take action against all and sundry who would try to divest him of that food—Sarah notwithstanding.

The need to take action came soon enough. No sooner had the tender green shoots of corn emerged from the earth than a flock of crows descended from out of the sky like a plague of locusts and began pulling up the young green blades to get at the seed beneath the ground. Alarmed that he would lose the entire crop before it even had a chance to get started, Daniel ran to the house for his shotgun and fired into the air. He could always tell Sarah that he was just shooting to scare them off, which was about the best he could hope for in any case, though he would not have minded in the least if he had hit one or two. As luck would have it, he did hit one, at least one, and as luck would also have it, it was Sarah who found it in the woods flopping around with an injured wing. When Sarah brought the wounded bird to him, Daniel, not wishing to reprise the traumatic scene of the previous spring, decided that the easiest course, and the only one he could think of on the spur of the moment, was to lie to her.

"I only shot t' skeer them out of the cornpatch, Sweetheart," he said, trying to sound as contrite as possible. "That one must a-injured itself a-tryin' t' get away."

"That's all right, Daddy," replied Sarah sympathetically, never suspecting that her father would tell her anything but the truth, "it's not hurt too badly. I think I can fix it."

Daniel felt like rot. Not only had he lied to this child who trusted him so completely, but now she was going to try to nurse this thieving bird back to health, so that, in all likelihood, he would have to shoot it again. Clearly, somehow he had to make Sarah understand that unless something was done about the crows and raccoons and all the other wild creatures just lying in wait in the woods, they would eat everything they tried to grow. Daniel was trying to discourage the intruders. If it had not been for Sarah, he would not have hesitated to resort to shotgun and rifle to keep them out of the garden and cornfield. Sarah, on the other hand, was befriending them, encouraging them, and now even nursing one he *had* shot. Clearly, Sarah, who had worked with him, had helped him, had been his partner, at plowing and planting time, was now working against him. She had turned traitor and was now collaborating with the enemy.

Or so it seemed to Daniel. But three weeks later a revelation was made to him that nearly shocked him out of his senses.

Much to Daniel's vexation, but true to her intention, Sarah had taken the injured crow under her care. In order to prevent it from trying to fly and possibly injuring itself further, she had taken an old sock with a hole in the toe and had pulled it over the bird, making sure to cut two more holes for its feet. She had kept it tethered for the first couple of days, but as soon as she was sure that it would not try to escape, she had removed the tether. Thereafter the crow had followed her everywhere, hopping about in its sock sweater. Now, after three weeks, she was ready to pronounce her feathered patient healed and to set it free. Daniel and Elizabeth had both interrupted their work to witness the send-off. They watched as Sarah removed the sock and listened as she gave the bird some parting words of advice.

"Now you fly away, Mr. Crow," Sarah lectured the bird, holding it only inches from her face, "and remember, you must never again eat corn from my Daddy's cornfield. If you ever get hungry, you come to me and I will give you something to eat, but you must not steal from my Daddy's field."

With that she kissed the bird on the back of the head and tossed it into the air. It flew away so quickly and so strongly that no one would ever have guessed that its wing had intercepted a shotgun blast only three weeks before.

"You'd make a wonderful nurse, Sweetheart," said Daniel, putting his arm around her, as they watched the bird fly away. Sarah smiled. "Do you reckon," Daniel continued, "that he'll mind what you said about not comin' back to the cornpatch?"

"Oh yes, Daddy, he'll mind. They all will. I've told all the crows they mustn't take corn out of our field."

Daniel smiled. Oh, if it could only be that easy, he thought to himself.

Elizabeth noticed the bemused look on his face. "Have you seen any crows in the cornfield these past three weeks?" she asked.

"Uh, no," admitted Daniel, taken somewhat aback by Elizabeth's question.

"And have you ever seen *any* animals inside our garden fence?" Daniel shook his head. "And didn't you say you were surprised at how little corn the raccoons ate last summer? . . . And last Thanksgiving didn't Nathan say that he didn't have a single rabbit in his garden last year, though there were plenty of them around?"

Daniel's mind was reaching, grasping, groping, as he tried to absorb the full meaning of Elizabeth's words. A look of incredulity swept over his face. "Are you sayin' . . . ?"

"Daniel, I don't know how it's possible, but she talks to them and they listen."

Sarah looked up at her father and smiled a knowing smile. Daniel just stared at her with his mouth agape, unable to speak.

Elizabeth did not pretend to understand Sarah's apparent ability to communicate with the birds and animals of the forest, but she had spent time alone in the woods with Sarah, much more than Daniel had, and she had slowly come to appreciate the fact that Sarah had an unusual gift. Daniel, for his part, was still not convinced that the birds and animals were staying away from their crops simply because Sarah had told them to do so. Who had ever heard of such a thing? It was true, he had never seen an animal inside the garden fence, but he had attributed this to the nearness of the garden to the house and to the tightness of the fence. It was also true that the raccoons, deer, and other animals had eaten very little of his corn, and while he couldn't understand it exactly, he thought perhaps that the wildlife population in the woods around them was not as dense as he had at first suspected, or that they had other sources of food which they found preferable to corn, though what that might be, he could not imagine. As for the crows, well, maybe the crows had left of their own accord. Crows were always on the move. But it was the rabbits at Nathan's that completely baffled him. Hester, of course, had given credit to the Lord, but Nathan didn't know how to explain it. He certainly gave no credit to his dog. Pokey might have been a good rabbit dog at one time, but he was getting slower every year. He could hardly see rabbits anymore, much less chase them. As for catching them, well, that was out of the question: he hadn't caught a rabbit in years. Nor was it the case that it was a lean year for rabbits. Nathan had said that there were plenty of rabbits around, and Daniel himself had seen them—in the fields, in the fencerows, in the woods—but for some mysterious reason they had stayed out of the garden. Now Elizabeth was suggesting that Sarah was that mysterious reason, that Sarah, just before leaving Nathan and Hester's the previous spring, had talked to the rabbits and persuaded them that it might be in their own best interest not to get into Hester's garden. That was preposterous!

Yet Daniel had to admit that maybe, just maybe, Sarah *could* talk to the wild creatures and make them understand. After all, he had seen her do some remarkable things with animals. As he pondered on this, he thought of something else. One day during the winter Sarah had told him that while she was out in the woods alone, a deer had come right up to her. Daniel knew that deer were among the shyest creatures that the Good Lord ever made, and at the time she told him, he thought surely she must be exaggerating. But now he wondered if it hadn't really happened.

He didn't have to wonder for long. One day later that spring he saw it with his own eyes. It had rained heavily during the night, so instead of working in the fields, he had spent the morning in his wood-working shop in the barn carving figures for his whirligigs. When he heard Elizabeth call him for dinner, he laid down his tools and headed for the house. As he was coming around the corner of the house, he saw something that made him stop short and take a step back. He tapped lightly on the kitchen window next to the chimney. Elizabeth, who was at the stove, looked up. Daniel, without saying a word, pointed in the direction of the clearing in front of the house. Elizabeth looked out the front window and there she saw what Daniel saw. Standing at the edge of the clearing, in the shade of the trees, was Sarah, and from out of the woods three deer—a doe and two fawns—were coming stealthily toward her. Elizabeth held her breath as the three deer came up to Sarah and began nuzzling her hand and rubbing their necks against her thigh. Daniel watched in amazement as Sarah rubbed their noses and necks each in turn. He watched for about five minutes, until he was absolutely certain that his eyes were not deceiving him, then he stepped out from behind the house. At the sight of him, the deer picked up their ears, then turned and melted slowly into the forest. Sarah came running up to him.

"Daddy, Daddy, did you see them? Did you see the deer?"

"I sure did, Sweetheart, I sure did."

"I told you I petted deer in the woods but you didn't believe me."

"I reckon that just goes t' show what a fool I can be sometimes." Together they went into the house.

"Did you see, Mommy, did you see?"

"Yes, I saw, Sarah, I saw it all."

Daniel looked at Elizabeth. He was shaking his head. "I was born an' raised at the foot of these here mountains," he said, "but in all my life I ain't never seen nor heard tell of anythang like that before."

Sarah beamed with satisfaction. It was not her encounter with the deer that pleased her so much—she saw nothing so very unusual in that—but that her father finally believed her story about the deer in the woods. She didn't want anyone to think that she told stories like her cousin Otis.

When Daniel saw that doe and her two fawns walk into the clearing in front of the house on that fine spring day in June of 1934 and rub their noses up against Sarah, he thought that if he lived to be a hundred, nothing he ever saw would surprise him again. But before another two months had passed, he saw something that again taxed the limits of his credulity, and again it was Sarah who was the agent of his discomfiture.

Sarah had spent the morning doing a variety of chores. She had milked the cow, carried water from the spring house, and ridden Jesse through the rows of four-foot-high corn as her father worked the cultivator behind. It was summer and Sarah was glad of it. Her mother didn't make her do her school lessons as often in the summer, which gave her more time to do the things which she considered really important, like helping her father and exploring. Immediately after dinner she disappeared into the woods, as she was often in the habit of doing. When she came back an hour and a half later, she found her mother working in the garden.

"Look, Mommy," she announced, "I found a kitty."

Elizabeth turned and looked at the ball of fur that Sarah was holding in her hands. Her first impulse was to smile, but as she looked more closely at Sarah's "kitty," a look of consternation came over her face. "I think we'd better show this to your Daddy," she said.

Together they walked around the house to the barn. "Daniel, I think you'd better take a look at this," said Elizabeth.

Proudly Sarah held up her "kitty" for her father to see. Daniel's reaction was the same as Elizabeth's had been. His smile too evaporated almost immediately. "Sarah, whar did you get this?" he asked.

"I found it in the woods. There were two of them, but I only took the one."

Elizabeth turned to Daniel. "Is it what I think it is?" she asked.

"Hit's a bobcat kitten, is what it is," replied Daniel, still scrutinizing the lively ball of fur.

"Sarah," said Elizabeth, "you've got to take your kitty back."

"You better take it back afore hits mother discovers hit's missin'," added Daniel, "but I expect hit's already too late for that ... I better go with you."

"You don't understand, Daddy," expostulated Sarah, "its mother was there when I took it. I promised her I'd bring it back just as soon as I showed it to you and Mommy."

If this had happened a year before, Daniel would not have believed any of it. It was difficult enough to believe even now. He had seen normally shy wild creatures let Sarah get close enough to touch them, and he even had reason to believe that just maybe she could talk to birds and animals in such a way that they could understand her. But now she was asking him to believe that she had walked into a bobcat's lair and had asked to borrow one of its kittens for a spell, and Mama Bobcat had said, "Sure, go right ahead." How could she ask him to believe that? Nobody could believe that. It just wasn't possible. Nature didn't work that way. On the other hand, the evidence was right there wriggling and squirming in her hands. He could see it with his own eyes. That little ball of fur was sure enough a young bobcat. And Sarah said she had taken it when the mother was there. He had heard her say it with his own ears. And Sarah did not lie, that was one thing he knew for sure. She could no more tell a lie than frogs could fly. Lying was against *her* nature. *She* didn't work that way. Daniel knew how exasperated Sarah got whenever folks even stretched the truth a little bit. She had no patience at all for made-up stories, unless, of course, they were presented as made-up stories. Whenever Sarah told you something, you knew she meant *exactly* what she said.

226

"What do we do now?" asked Elizabeth.

"I think I better go with her," replied Daniel. He did not sound at all sure of himself.

"So do I," agreed Elizabeth, but she too had her doubts about what might be the best way to get Sarah's "kitty" back to its mother. That it had to go back, there was no doubt. Sarah had promised to return it, and Elizabeth knew that there was no way Sarah could be made to break a promise. Elizabeth's only concern was for Sarah's safety. Would Sarah be safer if she went back to the bobcat's lair alone, or would she be safer if Daniel accompanied her? Elizabeth knew full well that the bobcat mother would never allow Daniel to get anywhere near it. His presence might even cause it to get nervous and attack both of them. On the other hand, if they sent Sarah off alone and something happened to her, how could they ever forgive themselves?

"I better take my gun, just in case," said Daniel, his voice very uneasy. He had been thinking the same thoughts that Elizabeth had been thinking.

"Please, Daddy, don't take your gun," pleaded Sarah, a look of horror in her eyes.

Daniel, who had started walking toward the house to get his rifle, stopped in his tracks. Elizabeth could see by the expression on his face as he turned back to Sarah that he was agonizing over whether to give in to his daughter's distraught plea or to follow what he considered to be the only prudent course.

"Okay, Sweetheart," he said at last, a look of resignation on his face, "I won't take the gun. You show us the way."

As Daniel and Elizabeth followed Sarah into the woods, Elizabeth felt again what she had felt so many times before over the course of the past seventeen months. Even though they lived in the mountains, even though the forest came almost up to the door of their cabin, always when she stepped outside the familiar boundary of her life, whenever she crossed that imaginary line that separated their "home" from the forest beyond, it seemed to her as though she were entering into another world, into a hauntingly beautiful but totally different other world. She understood why Sarah spent so much time in this world, and wondered why she herself did not spend more.

There was nothing in the tranquil setting that suggested that there might be any danger in the mission on which they had embarked, but Daniel knew that in the midst of all this raw untrammeled beauty, that life fed on life, and that swift and violent death was as commonplace as birth itself, and that both went on all the time, largely unseen by the human inhabitants of the mountains.

Daniel was surprised at how deep into the forest Sarah was leading them. He turned to Elizabeth. "Did you know she's been a-strayin' this far from the cabin?" he asked.

"She fancies herself an explorer, Daniel," replied Elizabeth, the pride in her voice tempered only slightly by an element of resignation. "It's very difficult to keep explorers close to home."

The forested terrain which they had been traversing, though uneven, had been comparatively free of difficulty—they had been following the contour of the mountain—but now they began ascending a very steep boulder-strewn hillside. It looked to Elizabeth as if some god or giant in mythical times had stood on top of the mountain and had emptied a great cauldron of rocks down over the side, perhaps to stop the advance of some enemy. Climbing over rocks and fighting their way through thickets of mountain laurel—or "ivy," as Daniel called it—they ascended ever higher until Sarah, who had been getting further and further ahead, suddenly stopped.

"You'd better wait here," she said, when her mother and father had caught up to her.

Nervously Daniel and Elizabeth watched as Sarah proceeded up the mountain alone. Daniel's eyes scanned the shelf of rocks above until he saw something that made his whole body stiffen. There, high above them, pacing back and forth on a rock ledge and looking straight at them, was a female bobcat. Daniel looked for Sarah. She was lost from sight now, hidden by rocks and trees and clumps of laurel. Suddenly she came into view again. She was almost up to the rock ledge on which the mother cat was nervously pacing. If the bobcat should decide to attack her now,

Daniel knew there was no way he could get to her in time to save her. He felt his forehead grow clammy with perspiration. He stopped breathing. Elizabeth at his side had clutched his hand. She too had stopped breathing. Both watched as Sarah climbed up onto the rock ledge and stood up. They watched in disbelief as Sarah moved even closer to the wary cat, then crouched down on both knees and released her "kitty." They watched, trembling, scarcely breathing, as the mother cat crossed the ledge toward Sarah.

Elizabeth fainted. Daniel tried to support her, but, in his own weakened condition, lost his balance and fell. With one arm around Elizabeth and the other flailing wildly, frantically reaching for something to grab onto, he began sliding on his back, headfirst, with Elizabeth on top of him, down the steep hillside. The last thing he remembered seeing was a blur of forest canopy and sky flashing by, then he felt his head strike a rock and everything went black.

Several minutes passed during which Daniel was aware of nothing at all, but as his mind slowly groped its way back toward consciousness, like a submerged buoy rising once again to the surface, he began to experience a vague sensation of falling. He seemed to be falling, endlessly falling, as if in a dream. Suddenly he remembered. He had fallen! He and Elizabeth had both fallen! He had to find Elizabeth! He had to get to Sarah! He opened his eyes to find Sarah standing over him.

"Daddy, Mommy, are you all right?" she asked anxiously.

Daniel tried to get up but he was stopped by a sharp pain in the back of his head. With effort he was able to force himself up onto one elbow and lean over toward Elizabeth. Anxiously he called to his wife, trying to rouse her. It was a full minute before she fluttered her eyes. "Are you all right?" he asked.

Her eyes darted about nervously as she tried to re-orient herself. "I don't know, I think so," she stammered. Suddenly she remembered. "Sarah! We've got to get to Sarah!"

"Sh, Sh, hit's all right. She's right here."

Elizabeth lifted her head and looked around until her eyes found the blurry image of her daughter's face. Sarah leaned down and kissed her on the forehead.

"Are you hurt, Mommy?"

Elizabeth tried to move. "I'm scraped and bruised," she concluded, once she had taken inventory of the damage, "but there doesn't seem to be anything broken."

"Good thang that rock was thar," said Daniel, rubbing his head and trying to laugh, "or we'd still be a-slidin' down this here mountain."

It was not until they had completely regained their senses and pulled themselves up into a sitting position that they noticed the furry object in Sarah's hands.

"Look," said the intrepid young explorer, holding out her prize, "I brought the other kitty for you to see!"

It was a chilly November day and the family had bundled up for the long trip down the mountain. Sarah could not have been more excited. She was looking forward to seeing Otis again. She knew that he would be at Uncle Isaac's for Thanksgiving dinner. Daniel and Elizabeth too had been looking forward to going down to Isaac and Martha's for the holiday. It was the main social event of the year for all of them, and this year Daniel had awaited the day with more than the usual anticipation. It wasn't just that he was anxious to see his family again–he had seen most of his kinfolk at one time or another during his regular trips down to Nathan's during the summer and early fall–but mainly because he had some extraordinary stories to tell which he had been saving up. He had deliberately said nothing about Sarah's remarkable encounters with animals on those previous trips down to the valley. He had wanted to save those stories until all the family was gathered together.

They arrived at Isaac's late in the afternoon and were immediately heralded into the parlor where they were met with a reception so warm and jubilant that they were made to feel as though they were the special guests of honor. Elizabeth and Sarah especially had become centers of attention at these annual Thanksgiving gatherings. Not only were they the two newest additions to the gatherings, but, with the single exception of Isaac's son Benjamin, they were the two members of the family who were most seldom seen by the others. It was extremely gratifying to Elizabeth to be so warmly greeted by her in-laws. She detected nothing at all disingenuous in the affection they lavished upon her. She remembered the first Thanksgiving at Isaac's two years before. This was Daniel's family then. Now it was her family as well.

Daniel, Elizabeth, and Sarah were the last to arrive, so it was not long after they had finished exchanging greetings with the others already gathered, that Isaac's wife Martha made the announcement that everyone had been waiting for: dinner was ready. When all the Wickers and related kin had taken their seats around the dining room table, it was Isaac as usual who offered the Thanksgiving prayer.

"Lord, I don't haf t' tell yuh, these are hard times, but we thank you for stickin' with us an' for seein' us through thick an' thin—mostly thin. We know a lot of folks in the cities have lost their jobs and are gwine hungry this Thanksgivin' Day. We thank you for seein' fit t' make us simple farmers. We may not have much, but we always seem t' have enough—or darn nigh to it. We have our land, we have the muscle in our backs, an' we have each other. For all these thangs we thank yuh . . . An' we thank you ag'in for givin' our baby brother Dan'l the good sense t' come back home . . . But we 'specially want t' thank you for this magnificent bird that you saw fit t' deliver into the hands of your humble servant, Isaac . . . Amen."

There followed a chorus of tentative "amens." It was the kind of Thanksgiving prayer that everyone had come to expect from Isaac. It had followed the same pattern as all his previous Thanksgiving prayers. He always began by enumerating, sometimes at great length, all the many things for which they all felt truly thankful, then at the very end he always added something that was entirely self-serving. Sometimes he did something even worse: he included a playful insult of Nathan. "Please, Lord," he had once prayed, "look after our brother-in-law Nathan, who, as you know, is a little short on common sense." Others seated at the table were then obliged to ratify his prayer, including the mischievous last part, by saying "amen." Nathan had been spared this year, but that did not prevent him from mumbling "Humble, my backside!" immediately following the "amens."

No sooner had the feasting begun than Isaac spoke up again. "I know you all been a-waitin' t' hear how it was I tracked down this handsome bird." Not deterred in the least by the all but total lack of response—no one save Otis expressing any desire to hear the story—Isaac began to relate in monotonous detail, as he did every year, how he had gone up into the mountains and stalked and shot the wild turkey. No one knew better than Isaac that his boastfulness was overbearing—that was half the fun of it—and he took great pleasure in being as offensive as possible in the hope that he might get a rise out of someone. Usually that someone was Nathan, but this year it was his own wife Martha who took up the gauntlet.

"The truth of it is," she began, looking around the table at the others, "ever' year about two days afore Thanksgivin', I lock my husband out of the house an' tell him not t' bother t' come back less'n he brings a turkey with him. I got t' give the old coot credit though: he usually manages t' skeer up somethin'. 'Course, by the looks of some of them birds he drags home, I'd haf t' say that either the dogs had chewed them up purty good, or they was already daid afore my husband shot them."

A burst of laughter reverberated around the table, with Nathan laughing the loudest and encouraging the others. Daniel, seeing an opportunity to further belittle Isaac's hunting prowess and to jump into his own stories at the same time, waited for the laughter to subside then seized the moment.

"Heck, Isaac," he began, "I don't see why yuh go to all that trouble in the first place. Why, whenever we want a turkey for dinner, we just open the door an' Sarah calls one in."

The others laughed at Daniel's rather tall tale. Nathan was clearly in a festive mood, and he took it upon himself to act as cheerleader. He pounded his fist on the table so hard that the silverware rattled.

"Is that true?" asked Otis, a look of wonderment on his face. He was addressing Sarah, who was seated next to him. As always, the two children had sought out seats next to each other.

"No, it's not true," answered Sarah, turning to him. She had been surprised by her father's story—and a little embarrassed. Turning back to her father she said, "Daddy, tell them it isn't true."

"All right, I admit it, that partic'lar story was not true. But hit wouldn't surprise me in the least if'n one day that li'l girl don't call wild turkeys right into the house. I seen her do some remarkable thangs, thangs I wouldn't a-believed if'n I hadn't a-seen them with my own eyes. Why, I seen her call wild birds right out of the air an' have them set in her hand. I seen her walk right up to chipmunks an' squirrels an' pick them up. I even seen deer come a-struttin' right out of the woods an' rub their noses up ag'in' her just like she was one of their own. Like I told my wife, in all my borned days, I ain't never seen or heard tell of anythang like that before . . . I thought *that* was somethin' special, but next thang I know she's a-bringin' home a bobcat kitten which she 'borrowed' from its mother.

"An' that ain't the half of it. What's more, she can *talk* to the wild critters an' they can understand her. She tells the coons not t' eat all our corn, an' they say, 'Okay, Miss Sarah, we'll just nibble a li'l bit around the edges.' She tells the crows not t' eat our seed, an' the crows say, 'Whatever you say, Miss Sarah; we'll just fly on down to Rushin' Creek an' eat Isaac's seed.' She even told the rabbits t' stay out of Nathan's garden. You can ask Nathan if he's seen any rabbits in his garden these past two years."

Daniel paused to allow his audience a chance to respond. The reaction was varied and confused. Some marveled aloud. Others, including Nathan, laughed at first, then fell into bewildered silence, not knowing whether to believe Daniel or not. The one person who did not doubt the veracity of Daniel's tales for a moment was Otis.

"Wow!" he exclaimed, staring wide-eyed at Sarah. He had never known that his little cousin was so remarkable, and his admiration for her was growing with each new revelation.

Elizabeth, who had been quietly studying the faces around the table in order to assess the impact that Daniel's recounting of their daughter's exploits was having, found herself, as was so often the case at these annual gatherings, staring, almost mesmerized, at Jacob. His gentle blue eyes were fixed on Sarah, and he was looking at her with the sweetest of expressions. Elizabeth thought she saw an unusual gleam in his eyes. Something that Daniel had said seemed to have aroused his interest, piqued his curiosity. Finally he turned to Daniel and began to speak. A hush fell over the table. Jacob spoke so seldom, and spoke so softly when he did speak, that it was not unusual for persons in his company to fall into almost reverent silence whenever he had something to say.

"I reckon you were too young to remember your sister Ruth," he said.

Daniel turned to his brother. "Yes, I'm afraid I don't remember her at all," he replied, his voice now almost as subdued as Jacob's. "I was only four when she . . . left this world." He did not want to say "died," not at Thanksgiving dinner, not in front of the children. He had talked about dying to Sarah once before, and had since come to believe that it had been a terrible mistake on his part to have done so. As for Ruth, about all he knew about her was that she had been Hester's twin sister, that she had died of the smallpox when she was only eleven, and that one must never mention her name around Jacob. If Jacob wanted to talk about her, that was fine, but Jacob had to be the one to broach the subject.

"Ruth had a way with animals," said Jacob, smiling serenely.

Daniel waited for his brother to continue, but apparently Jacob had said all that he cared to say for the moment about their long-departed sister. But it was clear from the distant look on

Jacob's face that for a long moment after his brief utterance he continued to cherish the memory of the sister he had adored.

All eyes at the table had fixed upon Jacob. Nathan, soon realizing that Jacob had said all that he had intended to say, and wishing to save him from the embarrassment that might result if everyone continued to stare at him, was the first to break the silence. He turned to Daniel.

"Dan'l, at first I thought you were pullin' our legs, but now I don't know whether to believe you or not."

"I swear to you, Nathan, hit's as true as I live. If you don't believe me, you can ask Sarah. You know *she* won't tell you any stories."

Nathan turned to Sarah. "How about it, Sarah? Is your Daddy tellin' us the truth?"

"Well," she said a little sheepishly, "*most* of what he said was true."

"Most?" queried Nathan. "You mean he said somethin' that wasn't true?"

"Yes, the part about the crows. It's true that I told the crows they mustn't eat the seed out of my Daddy's cornfield. But the crows didn't say they were going to go down to Uncle Isaac's and eat *his* seed. Crows don't talk. Neither do raccoons. You know that, Uncle Nathan."

Nathan laughed. "I'm not sure *what* I know anymore. I've heard stories about Johnny Appleseed that claim he could walk right up to wild critters in the woods, even play with their young, but I always figgered they were just stories. Now I ain't so sure . . . Did you really tell the rabbits to stay out of our garden?"

"Yes."

Nathan turned to his wife who was seated next to him. "You hear that, Hester? It wasn't your prayers after all: just this little mite of a girl who doesn't even go to Sunday School."

The dinner conversation that followed soon drifted to other subjects, but after dinner, when everyone had adjourned to the parlor and gathered around the fireplace, the conversation once again turned to Sarah and the animals. Daniel was asked to expound further on Sarah's remarkable encounters with the wild denizens of the forest. Questions were also asked of Elizabeth. Sarah, the object of all this attention, was off in another corner of the room with Otis. The two children had a lot of catching up of their own to do.

Otis too had some exciting news he had been waiting to tell, both bad and good. The bad news was that Pokey had died. The good news was that "mean old Miss Kinney," the schoolteacher who had taught grades one through three, had been fired and had left Rushing Creek. This "good news" had come two years too late to be of much help to Otis however. He was now in fifth grade and had another teacher, "Old Man McCarter." Otis was keeping his fingers crossed, hoping that Old Man McCarter would get fired too, because contrary to what he thought was possible, Old Man McCarter was even worse than Mean Old Miss Kinney.

Daniel and Elizabeth had planned to spend the night at Nathan and Hester's before heading back up the mountain the next day, but as they got up to leave, Jacob suggested that they spend the night with him and Emily instead. After all, he said, there was more room at their house than at Nathan's. It was true. Jacob had built the house with the expectation that he and Emily would be raising a large family, only to discover that they couldn't have any children at all. Elizabeth was in favor of the idea, so Daniel, after making an apology to his sister Hester and promising her that they'd stop in for breakfast on their way back up the mountain the following morning, accepted Jacob's offer.

Elizabeth guessed that it was partly, perhaps mainly, because of Sarah that Jacob had asked them to stay. He made no secret of the fact that he adored Sarah. He and Emily were such gentle souls, Elizabeth thought, it was a shame they had never had children of their own. They would have made wonderful parents.

Consequently, it came as no surprise to Elizabeth when, later that night, Jacob asked her if he might go into Sarah's room and say good-night to her. Elizabeth was happy to give her permission. "She's in bed, but she's still awake," Elizabeth told him. "She's practicing her reading."

Jacob opened the door and poked his head inside.

"Oh hello, Uncle Jacob," exclaimed Sarah, making no effort to conceal her surprise and delight.

"Hello, Sarah," he said in his characteristically gentle voice, "would it be all right with you if I came in an' visited with you for a few minutes?"

"I'd like that, Uncle Jacob," she replied, smiling warmly. "I was just reading a silly book."

Jacob pulled a chair up to the side of Sarah's bed and sat down. "Why do you say hit's a silly book?"

"Because it is. Mommy says I have to start with easy books, but all the easy books are silly books."

Jacob was listening intently to every word that Sarah spoke. He was completely absorbed in her. It gave him supreme pleasure to be this close to her, to behold the lovely vision of her lying in the bed before him. He could not take his eyes off her. He felt almost guilty for allowing himself to gaze so long upon her–upon the small, perfectly-shaped head resting so gently on the pillow; upon the long, soft, chestnut-colored hair that wreathed her face and reached to her shoulders and beyond; upon that exquisite face; upon those wonderfully expressive dark-brown eyes–her mother's eyes–that sparkled with excitement as she spoke; upon the small, perfectly-shaped nose; upon the mouth that moved so effortlessly from syllable to syllable as it formed the words. There was no denying that Jacob adored this child, not only for her physical beauty, but for the beauty of the soul he saw within.

Sarah had laid her book down and was now looking quietly into his eyes and smiling. For a long time neither of them moved or spoke; they just looked at each other and smiled. How Jacob wished he could touch her. Did he dare touch her? As if she had read his mind, Sarah lifted her hand from the bed and touched it to Jacob's left hand, the one resting on his knee nearest the bed. Jacob clasped the small hand in his, and for several more minutes they remained so engaged, looking and smiling at each other with their hands locked together.

"Well, I better say good-night an' let you get some sleep," said Jacob at last, releasing his grip on Sarah's hand.

"Don't go yet, Uncle Jacob," pleaded Sarah, grasping his hand more tightly. "I want to ask you something."

Jacob settled himself back in the chair, glad for the excuse to stay longer. "Okay," he said, still smiling sweetly, "ax me anythang you have a mind to. I only hope I know the answer."

"Did my Daddy's sister Ruth really like animals?"

Jacob smiled. "Yes, Sarah, she did."

"Uncle Jacob, could I ask you another question?"

He nodded.

Sarah hesitated for a moment, pondering how to connect the words together. Jacob could tell by the expression on her face that this was going to be a serious question. "At dinner," she began cautiously, as if feeling her way through a dark room, "when Daddy said that his sister Ruth left this world, did he mean that she died?"

"Yes, Sarah, he meant that Ruth died. She was *my* sister, too, you know, and Isaac's, an' Hester's. If she had lived, she would have been your Aunt Ruth. But she died when she was very young, when she was only 'leven years old . . . That was a long time ago . . . a very long time ago."

Sarah could see the sadness in Jacob's eyes. She was feeling sad herself. "But where did she go when she died, Uncle Jacob? Where is she now?"

"She went to Heaven, Sarah. She's with God in Heaven."

"Where *is* Heaven, Uncle Jacob? If I go there, can I see her?"

"I reckon hit's up thar somewhar," replied Jacob, rolling his eyes upward, "but you won't be able t' go thar til God calls you."

"You don't mean up in the attic, do you?" Sarah did not think so, but she had to be sure. It was not the first time she had tried to ascertain the whereabouts of Heaven. She had asked her mother once, but, as was so often the case, her mother had proved to be very difficult to pin down. But she had been left with the distinct impression that Heaven was not an easy place to find, so she doubted very much that it could be right upstairs in her Uncle Jacob's attic.

"No," said Jacob, smiling again, tickled at the thought that Heaven and all the heavenly host might be just beyond the ceiling in the attic above them, "I mean up in the sky, high above the clouds, higher than any bird can fly to."

"But how did Aunt Ruth get up there, Uncle Jacob?"

Jacob was beginning to realize that answering Sarah's questions was not going to be as easy as he had at first supposed. If she was interested in questions of this sort, he thought to himself, it was no wonder she finds the stories in her reading primer so silly. But Jacob was a patient man, and so made up his mind to persevere. "When we go to Heaven," he began, "we don't take our bodies with us. We leave our bodies here. Only our souls go to Heaven. Our souls weigh nothing at all–they're lighter than the air itself–so they have no trouble makin' the long journey up to Heaven."

"What do souls look like, Uncle Jacob?"

"You cain't see souls, Sarah. They're invisible like the air. You cain't see them or touch them."

Sarah was biting her lower lip. Jacob could see that something was troubling her. "But, Uncle Jacob, if we can't see souls or touch them, how do we know they're real?"

"Believe me, Sarah, they are. I don't know how to explain it to you. One day when you're older, mebbe you'll understand it. Souls are more real than bodies."

Sarah was silent for a moment. She was thinking about what her Uncle Jacob had said. One day when you're older, maybe you'll understand it. How many times had she heard that before? She was beginning to suspect that that was something grown-ups said when they didn't know an answer to a question. But there was something else that Jacob had said that she thought sounded very important: souls are more real than bodies. That was a very interesting idea. She would have to ask her mother about that.

"One more question, Uncle Jacob."

"Yes, Sarah?" said Jacob, not without some trepidation.

"Do you think my soul will go to Heaven when I die?"

"Yes," replied Jacob, relieved that this final question was such an easy one, "I'm sure of it."

"That's good, because Otis once told me that I was going to go to Hell."

"He did? Well, I'm sure your cousin Otis was quite mistaken."

"That's what my mother said. I'm glad you think so too. I don't want to go to Hell. I want to go to Heaven where Aunt Ruth is."

"Yes," said Jacob, releasing Sarah's hand and getting up to leave, "so do I, Sarah, so do I. Good night."

"Good night, Uncle Jacob."

8

EXPLORATION AND DISCOVERY

"Mommy?"

"Yes, Sarah?"

"Are souls more real than bodies?"

Elizabeth looked up from her book. Sarah was still standing at the window next to the chimney with her back toward her. She had been standing there quietly all morning, looking out the window at the cold, wet, and windy December day, watching the freezing rain pelt against the glass.

"Sarah, this is one of those questions which has no simple 'yes' or 'no' answer. At least *I* can't give you a simple 'yes' or 'no' answer. It's one of those questions we'll have to explore. Shall we go exploring?"

"Oh yes," exclaimed Sarah, spinning on her toes to face her mother, "let's go exploring!" It was the most enthusiasm she had shown all morning. She had wanted to go outside but Elizabeth had forbidden it.

"Well then, why don't you come over here by the stove and sit in your Daddy's rocker?"

As gracefully as a ballerina Sarah glided on her toes across the puncheon floor, twirled herself around her mother's chair, and fell lightly into the arms of the waiting rocker.

"All right then," began Elizabeth, "what's the first thing we have to do whenever we explore a question?"

Sarah began to rock. "We have to make sure that we understand what all the words mean," she replied without hesitation, reciting from memory the dictum that her mother had drilled into her.

"Right. Let's start with the easy word first. I think we understand what a body is, don't we?"

"Yes." Sarah slapped her legs.

"Well then, what about this word 'real'?"

"That's easy," said Sarah, continuing to rock.

"Can you tell me what it means?"

Sarah's face went blank and the rocking ceased.

Elizabeth smiled. "Sometimes the little words that we use every day are the most difficult to define. Generally when we say that something is real, we mean that it exists, it actually exists, it's not just imagined. The philosopher Plato, in one of his dialogues, gave a more precise definition. He said that something could be said to have real existence if it has the power to affect something else—or to be affected by something else—by any means whatever and to any degree whatever.

"That probably sounds a little more complicated than it actually is. Let me give you an example. I'll use the same example that my philosophy professor used when I was in college. Think of a gold mountain, a mountain made of pure gold. Can you picture that in your head?"

Sarah closed her eyes. "Does it have trees?"

"No. No trees. Just a great high mountain of gold gleaming in the sun . . . Gold is a metal, you know."

"Yes, I know. It's a sort of yellow color, right?"

"Right."

"Okay, I can see it."

"All right now, let me ask you this: is this gold mountain real?"

"My picture is real, but the gold mountain isn't real."

"Very good!" exclaimed Elizabeth. "Very good indeed!"

Sarah smiled with satisfaction and opened her eyes.

"All of us can imagine a gold mountain," continued Elizabeth. "We can have an *idea* of a gold mountain—we can make a picture in our minds—and that idea has the power to affect us in some way. It can give us pleasure—it can make us think, 'My, what a beautiful mountain'—or it can make us think how wealthy we would be if we owned such a mountain . . ."

"I didn't think it was beautiful," interjected Sarah, "and I wouldn't want to own it, not if it didn't have trees. Because if it didn't have trees, it wouldn't have birds or animals or anything. It would not be a very nice place to live."

"Well, there's not much chance of any of us owning it or ever living there," said Elizabeth, "because so far as we know, no such mountain exists. The *idea* of a gold mountain is real, but the gold mountain itself is not real. The gold mountain has no power to affect us in any way. Do you see the difference?"

"Yes."

"I think the same can be said of Hell. The *idea* of Hell is certainly real. It has the power to affect people in very profound ways. It makes them frightened and fearful. I suppose your Aunt Hester would say that it makes people behave better than they would otherwise behave, but I personally feel that belief in Hell is too high a price to pay for good behavior. Whether Hell itself exists is another question altogether. If your Aunt Hester is right, I expect I'll find out some day."

"What about God?" asked Sarah. "Is God real?"

Elizabeth sighed. "Sarah, I don't know if we want to get into that right now. That's a whole other exploration. But let me just say this for now. Whether God exists or not depends entirely on how you define 'God.' There are so many different ideas of God. If we think of God simply as creative force or creative energy, then the statement 'God exists' is almost true by definition. But when we begin ascribing personal attributes to God—when we begin to think of God as loving, caring, just and merciful, or as jealous, wrathful, and vengeful—then I think the existence of God becomes much less certain. But the point I'm trying to make here is that we can't even begin to answer the question, 'Does God exist?' or 'Is God real?' until we determine precisely which idea of God it is that we're talking about. And some of the smartest people who've ever lived have had very different ideas of God.

"What do you say we get back to your question, are souls more real than bodies? We were talking about the word 'real,' and we decided that something is real if it has the power to affect something else, or be affected by something else. I suppose it follows then that when we say something is 'more real,' we mean that it has *more* power to affect or be affected by something else. Are we agreed?"

"Yes."

"All right then, what about this word 'soul?' What does 'soul' mean? What is a soul? What do you think a soul is?"

"I don't know. Uncle Jacob said we can't see souls or touch them."

"Yes, I think most people would agree that a soul is not something physical, though there are a few people, to be sure, who would argue that a soul is simply a person. All of us sometimes use the word 'soul' to mean 'person,' as in the nursery rhyme, 'Old King Cole was a merry old soul . . .'"

"A merry old soul was he," interjected Sarah.

"Right. That's an example of the word 'soul' being used to mean 'person.' In the case of Old King Cole we'd probably say 'fellow.'"

"Old King Cole was a merry old fellow?"

"Yes."

"It doesn't rhyme," objected Sarah playfully.

"No, but you understand what I mean, don't you?"

"Yes. 'Soul' sometimes means 'person.' Or 'fellow.'"

"Here's another example. In the first book of the Bible, when God creates man, he kneels down and forms man from the dust of the earth, then blows into his nostrils the breath of life, and man becomes 'a living soul.'"

"Is that true?"

"I think it's probably just a myth."

"A what?"

"A myth. A story."

"I think so too."

"But the point I'm trying to make is that here is another case where the word 'soul' is used to mean the whole person. There are a few people, some Christians even, who would say that this is the way the word should be used. They believe that when people die, they just lie in their graves until Resurrection Day, then the whole person is raised up. But this is not what most people mean by the word 'soul.' Usually when people speak of the soul, they don't mean the whole person. They mean something inside us that can't be seen or touched. Can you think of something inside you that you can't see or touch?"

Sarah thought for a moment. "My heart?"

"Well, that's true. But your heart is something we *could* see if we took you apart–Heaven forbid! Can you think of something else, something inside your head, say, that we couldn't see even if we could get in there and look around?"

Sarah thought again. "A thought! I can think a thought, but I can't see it."

"Very good! We can't see thoughts or touch them, but I think everyone would agree that thoughts are real. Look at all the words that have been written in books. All those words were once invisible thoughts in someone's head . . . And what about feelings? When you fall and scrape your knee, it hurts, doesn't it?"

"It doesn't hurt much."

"No, not much, but it does hurt a little. Sometimes the skin is broken and we see a little blood. That's a kind of hurt we can see. But there are other hurts which can be much worse, which we can't see. Do you remember when your Uncle Nathan shot that rabbit?"

Sarah slowly nodded her head, recalling the unhappy incident.

"Do you remember how you felt inside? There were no scrapes, no bruises, no broken bones, no blood, but it hurt, didn't it? We can't see or touch feelings, but feelings can be very real. Of course, not all feelings are sad feelings. We have happy feelings too, and they're just as real.

"And what about memories? It was over two years ago that Nathan shot that rabbit, but you still remember it, don't you? Think of all the other things you can remember. Do you remember our little house back in Springfield?"

"Yes, it had a white fence around it."

For a brief instant the "happy" picture that Sarah drew for Miss Kinney two years before flashed into Elizabeth's mind. She still wondered about those curious drawings from time to time, and she hoped to one day ask Sarah about them, but this was not the time. "Do you remember the long train ride down here?"

"Yes, it was awful. It was fun at first, but I didn't think it was ever going to end. If I ever go back to Massachusetts, I'm going to run."

"Do you remember your Uncle Isaac meeting us at the train station?"

"He picked me up and swung me around, then he hugged me so tight I couldn't breathe."

"Do you remember when you first met Otis?"

Sarah laughed. "I scared him and he dropped his fishing pole in the creek. Then we both jumped in and got all wet. That made Aunt Hester upset."

"Already you have all those memories, and by the time you get to be my age, you will have many more. Think about what memories are. Can you see a memory?"

"I can see the pictures in my head."

"Can you show them to me?"

"No."

"Can you touch them?"

"No."

"But you have them, don't you?"

"Yes."

"The point I'm trying to make is that just because we can't see something or can't touch it or can't show it to someone else, it doesn't mean it's not real. Now, all of those things inside your head–your thoughts, your feelings, your memories–are what we call the mind. We have a body and we have a mind. The body is the part we can see and touch, the mind is the part we can't see or touch. I can see and touch your body"–Elizabeth reached over and touched Sarah's knee–"but the only person who knows what's going on inside your mind is you . . . Are you following me so far?"

"Yes."

"All right, now it gets a little more difficult. It's going to be like fighting our way through a thicket of mountain laurel . . . Let's get back to this word 'soul.' I think when most people use the word 'soul,' what they mean is the mind. For the most part they use the two words to mean the same thing–just like 'junco' and 'snowbird' are two different words for the same bird, and 'woodchuck' and 'groundhog' are two different words for the same animal..."

"And 'jewelweed' and 'snapweed' are two different words for the same flower."

"Right, the touch-me-not."

"What?"

" 'Jewelweed,' 'snapweed,' and 'touch-me-not' are *three* different names for the same flower. You knew that."

"I didn't know 'touch-me-not' was the name of the *flower*. I thought 'touch-me-not' was the name of the *game* it plays with us ... Why do things have so many different names?"

"And those are only the English names! People who speak other languages call all of these things by still other names."

"Do *we* speak English?"

"Yes, of course."

"What language does Daddy speak?"

Elizabeth laughed. "He speaks English too. It's just that here in the mountains where he grew up, they speak English a little differently than they do in Massachusetts where I grew up ... But we're getting a little off the path, aren't we? Do you still remember the question we're exploring?"

" 'Are souls more real than bodies?' "

"And what did we decide about the words 'soul' and 'mind?' "

"They're two different names for the same thing."

"Yes, in fact the word 'psychology,' which means 'study of the mind,' comes from the Greek word 'psyche,' which means 'soul.' "

"So psy...? What was that word you said?"

" 'Psy-cho-lo-gy.' "

"So 'psy-cho-lo-gy' also means 'study of the soul?' "

"Well, yes, I suppose you could say that, but most psychologists today do not like to use the word 'soul.' "

"Why is that?"

"We'll get to that, but for now let's just say that not everyone agrees that the mind and the soul are the same thing. But for the purposes of our exploration, we'll begin by assuming that they *are* the same thing. After all, we have to begin somewhere ... All right then, what kinds of things are we talking about when we use the words 'soul' or 'mind'?"

"Thoughts, feelings, and memories."

"And?"

Sarah knitted her brow.

"I think personality could be considered part of the soul—you know, all those subtle little things that make one person different from another—that make your Uncle Isaac different from your Uncle Jacob, for example.

"All right now . . . Some people believe the soul is immortal. That means it lives forever. If that is true, then I think we can safely say that souls are more real than bodies. Bodies, after all, don't live forever—not as bodies anyway. After we die, our bodies eventually decompose and go back into the earth, just like the old dead trees you see rotting on the ground in the woods. We come from the earth, to the earth we must return, as they say at funerals—dust to dust, ashes to ashes. You see, Nature is very resourceful. Nothing gets wasted. Everything that dies is used to nourish something else, some new life. So, in that sense, our bodies too live forever, but I doubt that we would recognize ourselves a thousand years from now.

"But people who believe in the immortality of the soul say that the soul does not die when the body dies. *It* does not decompose and go back into the earth. When the body dies, the soul *leaves* the body. Somehow this bundle of thoughts and feelings and memories separates itself from the body and goes to live somewhere else."

"You mean Heaven?"

"Well, different people have had different ideas about where the soul goes when it leaves the body. The ancient Greeks believed that all souls go down into the earth to a dark and gloomy place called the Underworld . . ."

"Sort of like a cave?"

"Yes, I suppose so, a very large cave . . . In the Underworld, souls exist only as ghostly shades. At least that's the way the Greek poet Homer described it. Not a very pleasant place at all.

"The Roman poet Virgil apparently decided that it wasn't fair that all souls, good and bad, should go to the same place, so in his story, the *Aeneid*, when souls arrive in the Underworld, they are judged. Only the bad souls are made to stay in the gloomy place. The good souls get to go to a beautiful place called the Elysian Fields–a sunny place with lovely green meadows and groves of fruit trees–a sort of Paradise. I think the early Egyptians believed very much the same thing. When they buried their Pharaohs they buried many of their earthly possessions with them, so that they would have them when they got to the Elysian Fields, or whatever they called the paradise they were going to. It seems to have been the custom in many early cultures to bury the dead person's possessions with him, though how they expected his soul to use physical things, I have no idea. Perhaps they too believed that the whole person would be resurrected.

"Curiously, the Bible–the Hebrew and Christian Bible–has very little to say about the afterlife, but the Christian Church teaches that a soul, once it leaves the body, will spend eternity in one of two places, either in Heaven or in Hell. According to one church teaching, however, the soul may not go *directly* to Heaven or Hell, but may go to Purgatory first."

"Purgatory? Where's that?"

"The Catholic Church teaches that good souls go to Heaven and wicked souls go to Hell, and those that are somewhere in between go to a place somewhere in between called Purgatory, but only temporarily. If they behave themselves in Purgatory, then they will eventually go to Heaven; if not, they'll go to Hell. It makes a lot of sense really–if you can believe any of this in the first place–because it seems to me that most people are not terribly good or terribly bad: they fall somewhere in between."

"Uncle Jacob must think I'm terribly good. He said I was going to go to Heaven. Aunt Ruth is there, you know."

Elizabeth smiled, but was not altogether comfortable with the kinds of ideas her daughter's mind had been absorbing. Sarah returned her smile, but then, remembering something else her mother had said, her smile gave way to a more troubled expression.

"What did you mean when you said, 'if you can believe any of this in the first place'?"

"I was about to get to that. So far we've talked about those people who believe in the immortality of the soul. But there are other people who would say that there is no such thing as a soul. They would say that the word 'soul' is meaningless, and that it only confuses people to talk about 'souls.' To them it makes no sense to talk about the soul or mind as though it were something that can exist apart from the body. They believe that thoughts and feelings and memories are nothing more than activities of the brain, and when the brain dies, all thoughts and feelings and memories stop. When the physical body dies, that is the end of everything. I think Miss Kinney probably believes that."

"What do *you* believe, Mommy?"

"That's a very good question. I believe that Miss Kinney could be right. I also believe your Uncle Jacob could be right. The truth is, I just don't know. As I see it, the real question is, can thoughts, feelings, memories, personality, and all those other subtle things that go to make up an individual person like Sarah or Daniel or Elizabeth exist outside a physical body? Can consciousness, or mind, exist apart from a physical brain? Most psychologists today would probably say 'no.' In fact, I'm sure they would say 'no.' They may be right. It would still be possible, I suppose, for some 'spirit' or 'essence' to survive the death of the body, but it seems to me that if it isn't conscious—if it can't think or feel or remember—then it makes little difference. It might as well evaporate into the air.

"But the psychologists could be wrong. I think it's instructive that most of the great philosophers of the past—those minds capable of the most complex thoughts—and most of the great poets and artists—those souls capable of the greatest depths of feeling—have believed in the immortality of the soul. Not all of them, it is true, but the great majority. Almost without exception, those who have manifested the greatest genius have sensed a reality beyond physical reality. Those who have reached the furthest with their minds, those who have plunged the deepest into their souls, seem to have experienced something that most of us never experience, at least not to the same degree. They seem to have glimpsed an Unseen Power at work in the world, at work in their own lives. I think most of them would have scoffed at the notion that man's most exalted achievements–the great works of literature, art, and music, as well as all the great philosophical and religious thought–have been produced by mere physical brains that somehow evolved out of dead matter. In their view, without the guidance of this Unseen Power, the Universe could never have produced a *Hamlet* or a *Mona Lisa* or a *Ninth Symphony*–all those billions of years of evolution notwithstanding.

"But it's not only the great intellects and artists who have believed in the immortality of the soul. I think it's interesting that virtually all primitive people have believed in it too–primitive people who never studied philosophy or theology–or psychology–whose minds were simple and uncluttered. They have believed in the immortality of the soul as if by instinct. I think the fact of consciousness itself predisposes one to believe in its continuity. The mind is such an extraordinary thing when you stop to think about it. I mean, how is it that we can *see* and *hear* and *think* and *feel*? How are these things possible? It's difficult to believe that the mind is nothing more than an activity of the physical brain. I don't see how it's possible that any configuration of atoms and molecules, no matter how complex, could produce something as exquisite as sight or hearing or even the simplest thought. In that sense, I would answer your original question in the affirmative: yes, souls *are* more real that bodies–even if they *don't* survive the death of the body. As to the question, *do* they survive?–does *anything* survive?–I think it's possible. I have often thought to myself: if consciousness is possible, anything is possible. I certainly don't pretend to have so completely solved all the mysteries of consciousness–all the mysteries of the mind–to say that survival is *not* possible."

"Mommy?"

"Yes, Sarah?"

"I think you've lost me in the thicket."

Elizabeth laughed. "I think maybe I've lost *myself* in the thicket."

Elizabeth enjoyed winters. She was not one of those people who dreaded winter, who regarded it only as something to be endured and could not wait for it to end. Winter had its own peculiar allurement for her. She found more time for reading in the winter, more time for thinking, more time for being inside her own head. Also, she was able to spend more time with Sarah. Or, more correctly, *Sarah* was able to spend more time with *her*.

Sarah, like her father, was an outdoors person. Elizabeth enjoyed being out of doors, working in the garden, walking in the woods, but she considered the cabin to be her home base of operations, from which she made excursions into the world outside its walls. But it was only during the winter months, with their short days and long cold nights, that Sarah spent more time inside than out. The rest of the year she practically lived out of doors, using the cabin only as a temporary shelter and as a place to take nourishment, and during the summer months, when a succession of small fruits and berries ripened in the forest, even much of her nourishment came from outside.

When Sarah was younger, Elizabeth had always accompanied her in her explorations of the natural world, but as Sarah had grown older, her need to be out of doors seemed to have increased, and Elizabeth had been unable or unwilling to spend as much time with her daughter as she had done previously. But on those occasions when Elizabeth did accompany Sarah, she found herself spending as much time watching her small companion as she did observing the flora and fauna of the forest. Sarah was a pleasure to watch! She moved as nimbly and as gracefully through the forest as the wild creatures themselves, sometimes cavorting exuberantly—running after butterflies, swinging around trees, leaping from rock to rock; at other times remaining perfectly still for long periods of time, absorbed in the sights and sounds of the forest.

Elizabeth had always enjoyed watching Sarah, and during the winters she had the opportunity to study her daughter at close range and for longer periods of time. She often found herself wondering what was going on inside Sarah's mind. It was true, what she had told Sarah that day they had explored the question of the soul: she could see and touch Sarah's body, but only Sarah herself knew what was going on inside her mind. That rainy day in December when Sarah had been standing at the window, lost in thought, Elizabeth had assumed that her restless child was merely bored and wishing she could be outside running in the rain–though Elizabeth knew well enough that in the past whenever she had tried to guess the contents of Sarah's mind, she had been, more often than not, not even close to being right.

Elizabeth was often surprised by the kinds of questions that Sarah asked. "Are souls more real than bodies?" Was that a question that other eight-year-olds asked? Elizabeth did not remember asking questions like that when she was a child. If she had, she certainly didn't remember getting any answers. But Sarah always seemed to be coming up with questions like that, and Elizabeth, in her attempts to answer them, often found her own thought processes stimulated to such a degree that she herself became absorbed in the exploration. In her attempt to answer Sarah's questions for *herself*, she often left her young petitioner "lost in the thicket."

Elizabeth was often amazed though at the kinds of things Sarah *could* understand. She had a very quick mind–as Miss Kinney had so astutely observed–and if she had the least interest in the subject matter, she was a very eager and able student. It was during the winter months that Elizabeth worked most intensively on Sarah's education. Teaching her daughter at home was an experience that Elizabeth found both challenging and gratifying. It had taken some persuading to convince Sarah of the importance of learning to read, but once Sarah had come to realize that her mother was right–that wonderful new worlds could be discovered in books–her progress was astonishing.

But Sarah still preferred *being read to*, and Elizabeth, who enjoyed reading aloud, was happy to accommodate her daughter.

The two of them spent many a winter afternoon together by the stove engrossed in a book. Elizabeth had always encouraged Sarah to ask questions about any words and passages she didn't understand, and, as a consequence, even some of the shorter readings were punctuated by long discussions and "explorations." It worked both ways: readings led to questions and explorations, and questions and explorations led to readings. After the exploration into the nature and destiny of the soul, Elizabeth decided that it would be good for Sarah to hear what non-Christian cultures had to say on the subject. She didn't want to tell Sarah that her Uncle Jacob was wrong–she didn't know that he was–but she thought that Sarah should be aware that the Christian concept was not the only one. Besides, Sarah herself had expressed a desire to hear more about this mysterious place called the Underworld.

Consequently, Elizabeth dusted off her volume of Greek mythology and read Sarah two of her favorite myths in which the Underworld is prominently featured: that of the beautiful young goddess Persephone, whose abduction by Pluto, Lord of the Underworld, brings winter to the earth; and the tragic tale of Orpheus and Eurydice, in which Orpheus, a mere mortal, but whose music has the power to charm even the gods, makes a journey to the Underworld, armed only with his sweet voice and lyre, to persuade the Lord of the Dead to release his bride, whom death has taken from him on his wedding day. Elizabeth had hesitated at first to read these stories to Sarah as both are terribly sad. Although both Persephone and Eurydice are released by the Lord of the Underworld, neither's release is unconditional. Persephone is permitted her freedom eight months of each year so that the earth might enjoy spring and summer, but the remaining four months she must dwell in the world of the dead as Pluto's queen. Orpheus secures Eurydice's release on the condition that, as she follows him up through the dark passages of the Underworld, he not look back at her until they have reached the world above. Needless to say, just as they are about to enter the sunlight, he *does* look back, and she is lost to him forever. Elizabeth also felt that the story of Persephone, in addition to being filled with the deepest pathos, might be extremely frightening to a child like Sarah, who spent so much time alone in the woods. Would Sarah ever be able to go outside again, Elizabeth wondered, without being afraid of being swallowed up by the earth? But Sarah listened to the stories with enthusiasm, even asked to hear them a second and third time—even though, as Elizabeth feared, they made her terribly sad.

"Every time I hear that story," she sighed after the third reading of Persephone, "I can feel my soul getting deeper."

Elizabeth, concerned that Sarah's soul might be getting a little *too* deep for an eight-year-old, suggested that they move on to happier stories, to stories more suited for children's ears. But Sarah wanted to know more about the soul. Reluctantly, Elizabeth removed the *Dialogues of Plato* from her bookcase.

Daniel seldom joined them for these afternoon readings. He preferred to spend the daylight hours outside sawing and splitting firewood or in his workshop working on his whirligigs. He always managed to find something to do. In the evenings after supper, he would have been content to just sit in his rocker by the stove with his family and enjoy the warmth and quiet, or to play on the harmonica that he had bought for a few pennies on one of his trips down to the general store. But he enjoyed listening to his wife read stories and poems, as she sometimes did in the evenings. Even if his mind did wander at times, he found the sound of her voice wonderfully soothing.

"Let's read Plato!" suggested Sarah, jumping up into Daniel's lap after supper one evening in early February.

"Sarah," said Elizabeth, coming to her husband's rescue, "I think we've read enough Plato for one day. Besides, I think your Daddy would fall asleep."

"Daddy *always* falls asleep when you read to us," stated Sarah matter-of-factly.

"That's not true," objected Daniel.

"It is too!" insisted Sarah.

It *was* true and Daniel knew it. He always excused himself to Elizabeth by saying, "I sleep much better when you read me to sleep." Elizabeth had never known Daniel to have any trouble sleeping whether she read to him or not, but she did know that he sometimes woke up in the morning with sore ribs as a result of his having fallen asleep during her readings. The reason for this was that Sarah too had her own regular place for the evening readings, and it was also in the rocker: on Daniel's lap. Whenever she would sense that her father was drifting off to sleep, she would poke him in the ribs with her elbow. After half a dozen pokes she would usually relent and allow her father to succumb—unless the story was especially exciting, in which case she would poke more vigorously, and as often as necessary, in order to get him through it.

"Sarah, I've got an idea," suggested Elizabeth, trying to divert her daughter's attention away from Greek philosophy. "Why don't *you* read to *us* tonight? Wouldn't you like to hear Sarah read, Daniel?"

"Why, that's the best idea I've heard all day!" exclaimed Daniel, seconding the motion. Then realizing he had unintentionally insulted Elizabeth, he quickly added, "I mean, I would be mighty pleased t' have either one of you fine ladies read me to sleep, but since we haven't heard Sarah read yet, why sure, I vote we let Sarah read."

"If I read, Daddy," said Sarah, "you're going to have to promise me that you won't fall asleep. Do you promise?"

"I promise, Sweetheart. Just keep it short, okay?"

"What would you like to read, Honey?" asked Elizabeth.

"*Hiawatha*! I'll go get it." Sarah jumped off Daniel's lap and ran up the ladder to her loft. Daniel jumped up too and hurried to the door. He stepped outside and took a deep breath of the cold air. When he came back in, he hurried to the sink and splashed some cold water from the bucket onto his face. He was back at his chair just as Sarah was coming down the ladder, but before he sat down in it, he moved it further away from the stove.

"I'm ready, Sweetheart," he said, once again seated comfortably in his rocker. He looked nervously at the book in Sarah's hands. "That's an awful big book."

"Don't worry, Daddy, I'm only going to read a little bit of it."

Elizabeth stood up. "Here, you sit in my chair under the lamp," she said. "I'll get another."

Sarah took the seat under the lamp and leafed through the pages until she found the verses she wanted. For a minute or two she sat quietly, going over the lines to herself to make sure she knew all the words. A couple of words puzzled her, but after a brief conference with her mother, she was ready. She glanced up to see if her father was still awake. He was, and he was looking at her with tears in his eyes and smiling. Daniel was thinking back over the years. How had his little girl, whom only yesterday, it seemed to him, he had been able to cradle in his hands–how had she grown up so fast? Where had all the time gone?

"*Hiawatha*, by Henry Wadsworth Longfellow," announced Sarah, enunciating very clearly and very carefully the title of the work from which she was about to read and the name of its author. Then, in the hushed stillness of the cabin, under the soft glow of the kerosene lamp, she began to read in a soft, musical, almost whispering voice:

> " 'Ye who love the haunts of Nature,
> Love the sunshine of the meadow,
> Love the shadow of the forest,
> Love the wind among the branches,
> And the rain-shower and the snowstorm,
> And the rushing of great rivers
> Through their palisades of pinetrees,
> And the thunder in the mountains,
> Whose innumerable echoes
> Flap like eagles in their eyries;–
> Listen to these wild traditions,
> To this song of Hiawatha!' "

The effect was mesmerizing. It was as if an Enchantress had cast a spell over the cabin. Daniel and Elizabeth sat rapt in wondrous silence. Flawlessly, fluently, like water running across polished glass, Sarah read on:

> " 'Ye, who sometimes in your rambles
> Through the green lanes of the country,
> Where the tangled barberry-bushes
> Hang their tufts of crimson berries
> Over stone walls gray with mosses,
> Pause by some neglected graveyard,
> For a while to muse, and ponder
> On a half-effaced inscription,
> Written with little skill of song-craft,
> Homely phrases, but each letter
> Full of hope, and yet of heart-break,
> Full of all the tender pathos
> Of the Here and the Hereafter;–
> Stay and read this rude inscription,
> Read this song of Hiawatha!' "

It was not until Sarah closed the book that the spell was broken. Elizabeth was effusive in her praise. "Sarah, that was beautiful!" she exuded. "Just beautiful!"

Sarah looked up at her mother and smiled. Then she looked at her father. His eyes were still open and now tears were rolling down his cheeks. He got up from his rocker and took two strides in her direction. Cupping her head gently in his rough hands, he kissed her on the forehead. "I'm so proud of you!" he said. "I cain't tell you how proud I am of you!"

"May I read a little bit more?" asked Sarah.

"You can read as much as you have a mind to," avowed Daniel, returning to his rocker. "I'll listen all night."

Elizabeth and Sarah both looked at him dubiously. Turning back to her book, Sarah leafed through the pages again. "This will be just a short one from further back in the book. It's a part I especially like.

" 'Then the little Hiawatha,
Learned of every bird its language,
Learned their names and all their secrets,
How they built their nests in Summer,
Where they hid themselves in Winter,
Talked with them whene'er he met them,
Called them "Hiawatha's Chickens."
   Of all beasts he learned the language,
Learned their names and all their secrets,
How the beavers built their lodges,
Where the squirrels hid their acorns,
How the reindeer ran so swiftly,
Why the rabbit was so timid,
Talked with them whene'er he met them,
Called them "Hiawatha's Brothers." ' "

Sarah closed the book and looked up. "Daddy!"
"Shh, Sarah," whispered Elizabeth, "let him sleep."

   The winter passed. Elizabeth would have been sad to see it end had it not been followed by another season which she loved just as much and perhaps more. Once the weather started getting warmer, Sarah once again became a creature of the forest. But Elizabeth was not about to begrudge the coming of spring on that account. Besides, as Sarah grew older, she was spending more and more time close to home, helping her mother more in the garden, helping her father more in the fields. But Sarah still needed her time in the woods, and there were days when Elizabeth would hardly see her daughter at all, days when Sarah would disappear immediately after breakfast and not return until suppertime, just before dark. Daniel and Elizabeth had always allowed Sarah free rein to do pretty much as she pleased. She had always been such a purposeful child: she needed no direction from them. If she were needed to help out around the farm, she was always glad to do so. But if she were not needed, she always had a plan of action of her own.

The reading sessions became more irregular as the days grew longer and there were more urgent and more exciting things to be done outside, but occasionally Sarah would still ask her mother to read something to her in the evenings after supper. One evening in late May, just after the supper dishes had been cleaned up, Sarah made such a request.

"Mommy, do you remember that story you read us from Isaac's book the winter before last?"

Elizabeth thought for a moment but could not remember reading anything from any of Isaac's books. She had never even had any of Isaac's books. "What story was that, Sarah?"

"The one about the holy mountain where all the animals live together in peace and a little child takes care of them."

"Oh, you mean the Book of Isaiah in the Bible?"

"Yes, that's the one. Will you read me that story again?"

"I think you can probably read it yourself now."

"I think so too, but I'd like to hear you read it."

Elizabeth removed the Bible from her case of books and turned to Isaiah, chapter eleven. Sarah sat down in her father's rocker and listened intently as her mother read.

" 'The wolf also shall dwell with the lamb, and the leopard shall lie down with the kid; and the calf and the young lion and the fatling together; and a little child shall lead them. And the cow and the bear shall feed; their young ones shall lie down together: and the lion shall eat straw like the ox. And the sucking child shall play on the hole of the asp, and the weaned child shall put his hand on the cockatrice' den. They shall not hurt nor destroy in all my holy mountain: for the earth shall be full of the knowledge of the Lord, as the waters cover the sea.' "

"Could I see that?" asked Sarah, reaching for the Bible. Elizabeth placed the heavy leather-bound tome in her lap. Sarah read the passage over again to herself.

"May I take the Bible up to my room with me?"

Elizabeth nodded her consent. Sarah jumped up from the rocker, and with the weighty volume tucked under her arm, climbed the ladder into her loft. Late into the evening, until long after her mother and father had gone to bed, she continued to read the passage over and over again and to make the pictures in her head. Finally she blew out her lamp and went to sleep.

The next morning Sarah was out of the house early. It was an electric day. The heavy, warm, muggy air that had hung over the mountains for the past several days had been pushed out during the night by a strong wind blowing from the northwest, and the clearer, cooler, drier air that had rushed in to fill the vacuum seemed to crackle with electricity. Sarah crackled too as she ran up the hillside behind the house.

She had made up her mind to find a holy mountain of her very own. For some time she had been intrigued by the higher mountain to the south, the top of which was clearly visible from the upper portion of the cleared area behind their house, and some irresistible unseen force seemed always to be pulling her in that direction. Now, as she stood among the upper rows of ten-inch-high corn, with her eyes fixed on that same peak to the south, she felt it again. How long it would take her to reach the top of that mountain, she had no idea, but in the sparkling clear morning air, it seemed almost close enough to touch.

Her body tingling with excitement, she ran back down the hill toward the house, but instead of stopping at the house she kept on going. With the words of the prophet Isaiah still ringing in her ears, she began her descent of Puckett Mountain. She could not have stopped running even if she had wanted to. The whole world was in motion. The canopy of foliage overhead was rocking wildly to and fro, heaving and swaying under the constant assault of the strong westerly breezes. In her reckless rush down the side of the mountain, she stumbled several times, but each time somersaulted to her feet again, and kept on running.

When she finally reached the bottom, she found a stream of water. It was just a small stream, not anything like Rushing Creek, but she took great delight in having discovered it all the same, and began to follow it upstream. She frolicked like a happy frog, leaping from stone to stone, occasionally missing and splashing in the icy water. On either side of the stream, growing in the shade of the white pine and hemlock trees, thick carpets of fern and skunk cabbage covered the ground. She crossed and re-crossed the stream as she followed its meandering course through the forest, forsaking it only briefly from time to time to follow narrow paths through the carpets of fern that animals had made, but never straying more than ten or fifteen feet from the water's edge. Whenever she came upon a dead tree that had fallen across the stream, she used it as a bridge to cross to the other side, only to cross back again on the next fallen tree.

In the course of her odyssey she moved alternately from darkness to light. Where the hemlocks grew especially thick, virtually all light from the sun was shut out, and the fern and skunk cabbage appeared to glow with an eerie green light in the gloom beneath. Wherever the swaying canopy opened, sunshine poured through and spilled onto the forest floor, dappling it with brilliant patterns of light.

Upon emerging into the sunlight after one particularly long dark passage through the hemlocks, Sarah was glad to feel the warmth of the sun again. The air was chilly for late May, especially in the shadows. It occurred to her that November was trying to sneak in early this year, which to her was not an unpleasant thought, because if she had a favorite month, November was it. Her birthday was in November; Thanksgiving, her favorite holiday, was in November; and after the long, hot steamy summer, the cooler, cracklier November air always exhilarated her. In November she felt like she could fly! In the summer the air was much too heavy for flying. In the summer she felt less like a bird, more like a salamander–like a salamander slithering through thick, warm mud.

But it was not November. It was May. One look around at the bright shimmering greenery told her that. She crouched down on a large flat rock in the middle of the stream to allow the warmth of the sun to soak into her face and arms. For the next few minutes she remained perfectly still as she allowed herself to be mesmerized by the dazzling display of light reflecting off the surface of the constantly moving water.

Reluctantly she left the stream and began making her way up the side of the mountain to the south. Now the hard part would begin, but she was not about to be deterred. The higher she ascended, the steeper the grade became. As she neared the top she found mountain laurel growing in tangled profusion and in glorious full bloom. How she loved these delicate white and pink flowers, clumped together in huge snowball clusters! Laurel grew in the woods above her house as well, but never had she seen a patch of it as thick and as extensive as this. She plunged headlong into the volley of snowballs and continued her ascent of the mountain. When she emerged again, she found herself standing on a huge boulder. After nearly three hours since leaving home, she had reached the crest of the great ridge.

Never had she seen so many huge rocks! How had they gotten there? she wondered. Had they been thrust up out of the earth, or had they been deposited there? By the shapes of some of them, she could have imagined that they were great stone ships with bows thrusting out into space. Perhaps, she mused, they were the petrified remains of an armada of great battleships that had sailed in some primordial flood and had become stranded or wrecked on the top of this mountain as the waters receded. As she climbed up and over the rocks, moving ever westward and ever higher among the wreckage of ships, she realized that she had to be very careful. One slip or one false step and she knew that she could end up badly bruised or broken. She paused on the bow of each ship to take in the view and to listen to the sound of the wind in the treetops below her. Every so often the rushing sound of the wind wrestling with the giants of the forest was interrupted by the rat-tat-tat of a woodpecker drumming on a hollow tree. Once, as her eyes searched the trees for a glimpse of the woodpecker, a yellow-and-black-striped tiger swallowtail butterfly wobbled past her. She watched it for a moment as it flitted about crazily, unable to control the course of its flight in the stiff breeze.

As she moved among the great rocks, she discovered numerous caves and crevices, peered into each and half-expected to find a fox or a bear peering back out at her. She was trying to imagine what it would be like to live in a cave herself when suddenly she stopped short. There in front of her, directly in her path, lay a timber rattlesnake, fully extended, sunning itself on the rocks. Sarah squatted down, and for a few seconds the two just stared at each other, neither moving, but when Sarah reached out her hand to touch it, the rattlesnake retreated into the rocks.

She continued to move westward out along the ridge, climbing ever higher. Suddenly she looked up in awe as a massive wall of rock appeared in front of her–the queen ship! Slowly she began to circumnavigate the base. Finding access, she began to climb very carefully up onto the great mass of boulders. The task of scaling the nearly vertical wall of rock proved to be a difficult one, one that required every one of her ten fingers and ten toes. As she neared the summit her excitement grew. Finally she pulled herself up onto the topmost rock and stood up. What she saw caused her to struggle for breath. Never had she seen anything like this before! She was standing on the very top of the world! Far below her to the south and east lay a deep forested valley, bounded on the far side by yet another mountain. To the west lay even more mountains, ridge after ridge of them as far as her eyes could see. Above her, clear open sky. She revelled in the thrill of discovery. There was no doubt in her mind. This was it! She had found her holy mountain!

Fearing she might be blown off balance by a sudden gust of wind, she sat down on the warm rock and contemplated the world around her. A moving shadow across the surface of the rock caused her to look up. She watched as a red-tailed hawk flapped its wings once, twice, then soared out across the valley, riding on the currents of wind. How she wished she could fly like that! As she sat there trying to imagine what it must feel like to be a hawk, she noticed that the large rock on which she was sitting continued to jut outwards and slightly upwards from the point at which she had lifted herself onto it. Realizing that she had not yet reached the furthest or the highest point, she resolved that she must do so at once. She was determined to see everything she could possibly see—a good explorer could not do otherwise—and she was very curious to know what lay just beyond the edge. She stood up, and carefully placing one foot in front of the other and holding her arms out from her sides to help her keep her balance, she made her way out toward the prow of the great stone ship. When she was within two feet of the edge, she was suddenly gripped by sheer terror. Instantly she dropped to her knees. Her heart was pounding; she felt faint. For several minutes she remained on her hands and knees, frozen to the spot, not daring to move a muscle. When she had regained some of her nerve, she inched forward again, this time on all fours. When she had reached the very edge, she stopped again. Did she dare to look out over the edge? She knew that if she did so, she might be more afraid than she had ever been before in her life. Did she want to be that frightened? Did she want to experience terror greater than she had ever known? Yes! Of course she did! A good explorer could not want otherwise. Not right at this very moment perhaps, but in a minute or two, just as soon as her heart stopped pounding so furiously in her breast.

When she felt she was ready, she craned her neck forward and peered over the edge. Instantly she drew back and flattened herself on the rock, gasping and trembling. There was absolutely *nothing* beyond the edge! Nothing but a great expanse of very empty space between the rock she was on and the boulders far below. For the next ten minutes she lay there clinging to the rock, trying to catch her breath and keep from fainting.

Finally, very, very carefully she inched her way back along the surface of the rock, slithering on her belly, to the wider part of it, where she felt it was safe to sit up again. She was not about to try to stand up, not for a while anyway. She just knew that if she tried to stand up now, she would faint dead away and fall right off the top of the world.

It was a full hour before she felt she was sufficiently recovered to try climbing back down. But ready or not, it was time for her to be heading home. She descended from her perch at the top of the high rocks even more carefully than she had climbed up. As she retraced her steps back along the trail of broken ships, climbing quickly and nimbly over the rocks, she was ecstatic. In all her years of exploring, surely this was her greatest discovery ever!– and she had made it all by herself! She resolved to tell no one about this place–not her mother, not her father, not anyone. This would be her secret place, and she would come here often. This beautiful and terrifying place at the top of the world would be her very own holy mountain!

Daniel leaned on his hoe and contemplated with satisfaction the idyllic scene that stretched out before him. From his vantage point high on the hillside above the house, his eyes could take in, in one easy sweep, the whole of the small mountain farm that had become his home and his kingdom. From where he stood he could see nearly a hundred rows of ten-inch-high corn rolling down over the hill to the garden fence, and just to the east a smaller field of hay and pasture grass covering the hillside above the barn. He could look with pride down upon the old weathered log house and barn which he had worked so patiently to restore. In the distance they appeared even smaller than they were. Nestled so comfortably in the cradle of surrounding forest greenery, they looked as if they were meant to be there, as if they had been heaved up out of the mountainside by natural forces and had grown up with the forest itself. Even the new wood shingles had begun to lose some of their fresh-split appearance.

Daniel raised his eyes and traced the frayed edge of the treetops from left to right across the skyline, lingering for a moment on the prominent peak to the south, the highest point on the near horizon, the one that the local folks called the Devil's Staircase. He looked up at the sun. It was mid-morning.

He was about to get back to his hoeing, when, amidst the constant stream of bird chatter and insect hum, he heard the door of the cabin open and close. He looked down toward the house and saw Elizabeth come around the corner of the porch and enter the garden. He watched her for a moment, then bent his back and returned to his work.

Daniel Wicker was a happy man, and never happier than when he had a hoe in his hands and a hillside of corn that needed hoeing. He had everything a man could ask for: a snug cabin with a roof that didn't leak, a loving wife and daughter, and an eyeful of mountains that seemed to go on forever. How had he ever managed to live all those years away from these mountains? This was home, this was the place for him, the place where God intended him to be. The mountain farmer, with his hoe in the earth and his soul only a stone's throw away from Heaven's door, lived in a kingdom that belonged neither to this world or the next, but, like the clouds that brought the summer rain, was constantly in transaction with both.

It was a good life, Daniel thought to himself, maybe the best there was. If there was a better way to live, he had never heard tell of it. He may not have been the richest man in the world, but he had everything he needed. What God didn't provide, with God's help he provided for himself. If he needed anything that he couldn't grow or make with his own hands, he bought it with money honestly earned or bartered for it with his own labor. He felt whole and complete and self-contained–almost. There was only one thing missing.

Daniel snuffed out the lamp and crawled into bed. In the dark he found his wife and pulled her gently toward him. For a few quiet moments they lay perfectly content in each other's embrace, each thinking his or her own private thoughts. Then

Elizabeth spoke in a voice barely above a whisper, so as not to waken Sarah.

"Daniel?"

"Hmm?"

"Do you ever think about having another child?"

Daniel did not answer immediately, but Elizabeth could tell by the change in his breathing that he was giving the question serious consideration. She decided to be more specific.

"Do you ever wish you had a son?"

"Well, I s'pose," he answered slowly, after another half-minute's deliberation, "if we had a second one, I'd hope hit was a boy... Are you...?"

"No, I'm not pregnant. It's just that if we're ever going to have another child, we're going to have to do it soon. I'm thirty-three years old and I don't have too many child-bearing years left."

"Do *you* want another one?" he asked.

"I've been asking myself that question, and I guess what I've decided is, it really doesn't make any difference to me. But I thought that you might be anxious to have a son to carry on the Wicker name. As it stands now, Isaac's son Benjamin is the only male offspring of your generation—except for Otis, of course, but he's an Andersson, not a Wicker."

"Hmm, I reckon I never gave much thought to that. 'Course, one is all it takes. My Pa was the only male child in his family—least-ways the only one t' survive to manhood—an' *he* fathered three sons. Besides," he chuckled, "if all the Wickers die out, I don't expect I'll be around t' worry about it."

"So it doesn't make that much difference to you?"

"No, I don't reckon it does. Besides, thar's no guarantee we'd have us a boy. We could have us another girl."

"And you wouldn't want another girl?"

Since the beginning of this conversation Daniel's mind had been slowly gravitating toward unconsciousness and sleep. Now suddenly he found it necessary to re-marshall his forces. "Hit ain't that," he countered in desperation, "hit's just that..." He felt like a trapped animal. Unaware that he was even being stalked, suddenly he found himself cornered.

"What, Daniel? What is it?"

"Hit's just that ..." There seemed to be no escape. "Now, don't get me wrong," he said defensively, "that little girl up thar in that loft is as dear to me as life itself..."

"She adores you. You know that, don't you?"

" 'Course I know that. An' I adore her. I remember one time last winter, she was helpin' me stack firewood, she asked me, 'Daddy, do you ever wish I was a boy?' Seems like Otis told her that boys were worth more than girls. Well, I can tell you, that purt-near brought tears to my eyes. I picked her up an' hugged her good an' I told her, 'Sweetheart, I wouldn't trade you for *ten* boys.' Hit's true too. Sometimes I think she can even do the work of ten boys. I never seen a kid who could stick to hoein' the way she does ... She loves it here, you know."

"Yes, she *does* love it here. So do I."

"An' 'course the way she has with animals is just plain unnatural. But..." Daniel paused.

"But?" Elizabeth, sensing her husband was troubled, wanted him to say what was on his mind.

"But I just wish she could get used to the idea of killin' animals. I mean, hit hardly makes sense for a man t' live in the mountains if he cain't go huntin'. By the time I was seven years old, my Pa was takin' me out in the woods huntin' with him. Sarah's gwine on nine. I think by this time she should be old enough..."

"I see. You're afraid that if we had another girl, it would start all over again. As soon as Sarah was old enough to understand and accept the killing of animals, little Emily or Rebekah would come along and..."

"Right. I'd haf t' wait another ten years."

Elizabeth sympathized with her husband. "I'm not so sure another little girl would react the same way. I think Sarah is very unusual in her feelings toward animals—at least in the *intensity* of her feelings. I think most children *like* animals—boys *and* girls—but most children don't have the opportunity to get as close to them as Sarah does . . . But who's to say, if we had a little boy, that he might not have the same feelings that Sarah has? Especially with Sarah there to teach him?"

Judging by the profound silence that ensued, that was a possibility that Daniel had not even considered.

"Don't worry, Daniel," Elizabeth assured him, "nobody is going to *make* us have another child." She had hoped that her rather light-hearted remark might lift her husband's spirits, but he did not respond.

"Daniel," she said, assuming a more serious tone, "have you ever talked to Sarah about hunting and how much it means to you?"

"No," he murmured.

"It might be worth a try. She's a very bright little girl. I think if you explained to her how important hunting is to you, she would understand. At least, I know that she loves you enough that she would *try* to understand."

"Hmm," he said wearily, giving his wife a good-night kiss, "that's not a bad idea. I just might do that. I'll sleep on it."

He rolled over, and before Elizabeth had returned to her side of the bed, he was asleep.

9

CHRISTMAS AND ITS CONSEQUENCES

Daniel did not talk to Sarah the next day, or the day after, but throughout the summer he thought from time to time about what he might say to her. Between keeping after his own farm and working at Nathan's he scarcely had time for hunting anyway, and as long as he was making frequent trips up and down the mountain, it was easy enough to bring smoked or salted meat up from Nathan's. It was during the late fall and winter, after the crops were all in, when the dried leaves crackled underfoot, or when the tracks of game could be seen in newly fallen snow, that Daniel most strongly felt the urge to be out in the woods with his rifle in hand, in pursuit of some elusive quarry. It was an urge he had had to suppress the past two winters. The single activity that provided the man of the mountains his greatest thrill, his deepest satisfaction, had been denied him. He *had* to make Sarah understand. He was determined not to let another winter go by without his once again taking up the hunt.

It was an afternoon late in November, soon after they had returned from the annual Thanksgiving gathering at Isaac's, that Daniel decided to broach the subject to Sarah. Sarah had spent the morning in the house, through no desire of her own, working on her school lessons, but after dinner she went out into the woods with Daniel to help him saw up a dead oak tree that he had felled that morning. She always liked helping her father gather firewood, and Daniel always enjoyed having her with him, not just for the sake of her company, but for the actual assistance she was able to render him. It was always helpful to have some weight and muscle on the other end of the two-man saw, no matter how slight, and her enthusiasm more than made up for any deficiency in size and strength. Her assistance was especially appreciated when he worked with bigger logs that required splitting, as she was able to pick up the split pieces and stack them on the sled as quickly as any man.

The oak that Daniel had felled was not one of the giants that grew in the forest around them, being little more than a foot in diameter at the base. Still, it would require the rest of the afternoon and perhaps part of the next day to render it into chunks of the proper length and width for burning in their small stove. Daniel was in no hurry. He had all afternoon, as well as all of the next day, and if it took longer than that, he had that too.

After they had been sawing for about an hour, he decided it was time for a break. "C'mon, Sweetheart," he called to his young helper, "let's set us down on this here log an' rest us a spell."

Sarah joined her father on the log. For a couple of minutes they sat quietly side by side on the fallen tree, drinking in the beauty and stillness of the forest.

"Hit sure is quiet, ain't it?"

"Hit sure is," replied Sarah, mimicking her father's speech.

"Sawdust sure smells good, don't it?"

"Hit sure do."

Another minute passed. Daniel knew that if he was ever going to talk to Sarah about what was on his mind, this was the time.

"Did you have a good time down at your Uncle Isaac's last week?"

"Oh yes! I like Thanksgiving. It's my favorite holiday."

"Did you like the turkey?"

"I liked the sweet potatoes best."

This was not the response Daniel had hoped for, but he decided to adhere to the speech he had planned anyway.

"I was thinkin' hit would be nice if we had a big Christmas dinner up here this year—just the three of us, I mean: mebbe some turkey, some sweet 'taters—you know, all sorts of good thangs. Don't that sound good?"

Sarah sat quietly for a moment, wondering why her father's proposition had sounded so much like an entreaty. "Daddy, are you saying you want me to call a turkey into the house?"

"No," he laughed, "but I was a-hopin' that I might go out in the woods an' shoot us one, the way your Uncle Isaac does ever' Thanksgivin'... How would you feel about that?"

Daniel looked down at his daughter and saw the worried expression that had come over her face. She did not look up at him, but continued to stare into the woods. He could see that she was too choked up to respond.

"Sarah," said Daniel sympathetically, "I know how much you like animals, but there are some thangs you haf t' understand. We haf t' kill animals in order t' live. That's just the way it is. Even animals kill other animals. That little bobcat kitten that you brung home last year is full-growed now, an' I'll bet right this minute hit's out lookin' for somethin' t' kill, a chipmunk mebbe or a squirrel. Hawks an' owls are always on the lookout for a mouse or a baby rabbit t' eat. Foxes too. Even those raccoons you like so much kill other animals. That's the way Nature works. That's the way God made it."

"It's not that way on the holy mountain."

"What holy mountain?"

"God's holy mountain in the Book of Isaiah."

The last thing Daniel had expected was for Sarah to confront him with the Bible. He had planned to use the Bible to help him make his own case.

"But that's not now, Sarah. That's in the kingdom t' come."

"But when will it come, Daddy?"

"I don't know, Sweetheart. Nobody knows that. Hit will be a wonderful day when it comes, but the world we live in now is not like that. If you put a wolf an' a lamb together now, the wolf would have that lamb et down to the bone afore it even has a chance t' say its prayers."

"But why do *we* have to kill animals and eat them?"

"Because that's the way the Good Lord intended it. He put the animals here for us to eat . . . Well, mebbe He didn't put them here for us to eat in the beginnin', but after the Great Flood, he told . . . "

"What great flood?"

"You know, the story of Noah an' the ark, when it rained for forty days an' forty nights."

"Oh yes, I remember. Mommy read that to me once. I think that's probably just a story, don't you?"

This was not going at all the way Daniel had intended. But he was determined to make his point—*and* to use the verses from the Bible he had memorized.

"Well, mebbe hit's just a story an' mebbe hit ain't. I can tell you for a fact that your Aunt Hester believes hit really happened. I think most folks in these parts believe hit happened just like the Bible says. Folks in them early days had become so wicked an' corrupted in the sight of the Lord that He was sorry He ever made man in the first place, so He sent the Great Flood to destroy ever' livin' thang on the face of the earth. Only Noah an' his family were saved."

"And the animals in the ark."

"Right, the animals in the ark. But what I want to tell you is what God said to Noah an' his sons after the Flood. He said to them, 'Be fruitful an' multiply, an' fill the earth. The fear of you an' the dread of you shall be upon ever' beast of the earth, an' upon ever' bird of the air, upon ever'thang that creeps on the ground an' all the fish of the sea: into your hands they are delivered. Ever' movin' thang that lives shall be food for you; an' as I gave you the green plants, I give you ever'thang.' ... That's what He said: 'Ever' movin' thang that lives shall be food for you ... I give you ever'thang!' "

"Daddy, do you suppose God really talked to Noah and to Isaiah and to those other old men in the Bible?"

"I reckon He did."

Sarah thought for a moment. "I suppose it *could* have really happened. I suppose God *could* have said those things. But I'm not altogether sure about God yet. I don't think I understand exactly what God is. Mommy says God is not easy to understand. She says that even some of the smartest people who've ever lived have had different ideas about God."

Daniel decided that there was nothing to be gained by going any further down this particular road. He was not about to argue with some of the smartest people who've ever lived. He decided it was time to back up and try another road altogether.

"Sarah, you know how much you like t' go explorin' in the woods?"

"Oh yes!"

"If for some reason or other you couldn't go explorin' anymore, you'd be sad, wouldn't you?"

"Do you mean like when I had to go to school?"

"Yes, like when you had t' go to school."

"Yes, I was very sad then."

"Well, that's sort of the way it is with me an' huntin'. I like t' go huntin', the same as you like t' go explorin'."

"You *like* to kill animals?"

"Yes . . . I mean, no . . . I mean, we need the meat, an' somebody's got t' kill the animals. If I don't do it, Nathan does it for us. I would rather do it myself, not just so's we can provide for ourselves–though that's important too–but 'cause I *like* t' hunt . . . From time t' time I like t' take my gun an' go out in the woods an' do me a little huntin'."

"Are you sad because you can't go hunting?"

"Well . . . yes." There, he had said it.

She bit her lower lip and stared into the woods for a moment. "I don't want you to be sad, Daddy."

"Then would it be all right with you if, mebbe the day before Christmas, I went out an' hunted us a turkey for Christmas dinner?"

She continued to stare into the woods. Finally she nodded her head. "I don't want you to be sad, Daddy."

He hugged her. "C'mon, Sweetheart, let's get back to work."

It was the morning before Christmas–a clear, cold December morning–and Daniel's blood was rushing as he sat down to breakfast.

"Yes sir, tomorruh we're a-gwine t' have us a Christmas dinner we won't soon forget," he exclaimed, as he dug into his plate of bacon and hot cakes.

"Are you going to shoot a turkey today, Daddy?" asked Sarah casually, her voice evincing not the least trace of alarm. Elizabeth looked at her daughter curiously.

"A turkey, or mebbe a grouse," replied Daniel, anticipating with excitement the day ahead. "I reckon I'd even settle for a quail if I had to . . . Yes sir, hit's gwine t' be a fine day t' be out in the woods."

"May I go with you, Daddy?"

Daniel and Elizabeth both looked at Sarah in surprise. Daniel smiled. This was even more than he had hoped for. " 'Course you can," he replied with enthusiasm. "Put on your long stockin's an' shoes. We'll get started right after breakfast."

Elizabeth packed them a lunch, then saw to it that Sarah was properly bundled. "Promise me you'll be careful out there," she instructed her daughter as she wrapped the scarf more tightly around Sarah's neck and buttoned the top button of her coat. "Don't you be running where your Daddy's shooting."

"I'll be careful, Mommy," she promised, kissing her mother on the cheek.

Elizabeth watched from the porch as her two hunters disappeared into the woods. She could not help but wonder what must be going through her daughter's mind. She knew that Sarah had done a lot of thinking since Daniel had talked to her back in late November. She knew that Sarah had been struggling to understand and accept her father's desire and need to go hunting. She knew because Sarah had talked to her about it. But Elizabeth had been just as surprised as Daniel when Sarah had asked to go along.

Around four o'clock in the afternoon Elizabeth heard the hunters returning. She looked out the window. She saw Daniel and Sarah coming toward the house, but she saw no turkey or grouse—not even a small quail. The look of disappointment on Daniel's face told the whole story. The door opened and they came in. Sarah ran directly to her mother. Daniel walked across the room.

"Didn't see a thang," he muttered solemnly as he returned his unfired shotgun to its rack. "I'm a-gwine out t' feed the animals."

"I'll go too," said Sarah, turning to follow him.

"Sarah," interceded Elizabeth, "why don't you stay here and help me string popcorn for the Christmas tree?"

"Okay," she said, taking off her coat and scarf. "May I eat some too?"

"You may eat *some*, but don't eat all of it."

Sarah took the bowl of popcorn and crouched down on her knees next to the stove. Elizabeth studied her daughter's face as Sarah deftly ran the needle and thread through the puffed kernels of corn.

"So, you didn't see anything in the woods today?"

"We saw lots of things."

"But you didn't see any turkeys?"

"No."

"Or grouse?"

"No."

"Or quail?"

"No."

"You know your Daddy's disappointed, don't you?"

Sarah didn't answer or look up. Elizabeth suspected there was something she wasn't telling. "Sarah, did you have anything to do with the fact that your Daddy didn't see any turkeys in the woods today? Did you warn them somehow?"

Now Elizabeth could see the tears coming into Sarah's eyes.

"I couldn't let him shoot them," she sobbed. "I wanted to, but I couldn't. Please don't tell Daddy."

Elizabeth knelt down beside her daughter and put her arm around her.

Daniel *was* disappointed, but as he fed the mule and the cow, he reflected on the events of the day and decided it had not been a total loss. He had never expected that Sarah would want to go hunting with him. He had asked only for her understanding and consent; it had never occurred to him that she might want to participate. She had been a wonderful companion in the woods. She was as light of foot and had as keen an eye as any Cherokee that had ever roamed this forest in days gone by. Perhaps he would make a hunter out of her yet. He hoped so. It was good for a woman living in these mountains to be able to handle a gun. You never knew when your life might depend on it. Perhaps in another year or so he would get Sarah a gun of her own and they would go hunting together, just as he and his father had done.

As Daniel came around the corner of the house, he saw something that made him stop in his tracks. He couldn't believe his eyes. Besides a few small birds he had seen nothing in the woods all day. But now, standing right at the edge of the clearing in front of the house, was a young deer buck, at almost the exact same spot where he had once seen the three deer come up to Sarah. Perhaps there could be a Christmas dinner after all. If only he could get into the house to get his rifle!

He retreated along the side of the house, turned the corner, and entered by the back door. As he stepped into the kitchen he glanced over at Elizabeth and Sarah to motion to them to make no sound or sudden movement, but they were crouched quietly over a bowl of popcorn on the floor by the stove with their backs toward him. Perfect! Quietly he lifted his rifle out of its rack, crossed the broad-slabbed puncheon floor, and slipped out the front door.

At the sound of the shot Sarah jumped to her feet and rushed to the window. The look of absolute horror on her face told Elizabeth that something dreadful had happened. Before Elizabeth could reach her, Sarah had bolted out the door.

The deer had fallen but had struggled to its feet again. Daniel was about to take a second shot when Sarah rushed past him.

"Sarah, come back here!" he called. But to no avail. She kept running toward the wounded deer.

Elizabeth ran out onto the porch. "Oh, Daniel," she cried, "not a deer!"

The deer, spurting blood from its neck, tried to run, but before it could reach the woods, it fell again. Dazed and panic-stricken it once again struggled to regain its feet. It was as if the sum-total of its remaining life-force was now concentrated and channeled into one all-consuming goal: escape. With one last supreme effort it lurched forward onto its feet, and on legs barely able to sustain its weight, ran crashing through the underbrush and disappeared into the woods.

"Sarah, come back here!" Daniel called again, but still she did not stop. Daniel ran after her. He hoped to catch her before she reached the deer, but he was too late. When he finally caught up to her, the sight that met his eyes was the most gruesome and pathetic he had ever seen. The deer had fallen, never to rise again, in a thicket of laurel. Sarah, sobbing and wailing as grievously as he had ever heard her, had thrown herself down on the dying creature and had put her arms around its neck. Daniel watched for a moment, shocked and unbelieving, unable to move, then reached down and put his hand gently on Sarah's shoulder.

"Come away now, Sweetheart, come away. Hit's gwine t' die."

The deer gave a sudden violent shudder causing Daniel to jump back, then laid its head down in the leaves and breathed its last. Crying pitifully, Sarah continued to hold the animal, pressing her face even more closely against its neck. After several minutes during which Daniel stood by dumbfounded and helpless, her crying suddenly stopped. She pushed herself away from the dead animal and slowly stood up. As she turned around, Daniel could see that her face and dress were soaked with the deer's blood. There was a strange, wild, frightened look in her eyes, a look he had never seen before. He made another attempt to reach for her, but she screamed and backed away.

"Sarah," he called, "hit's me, hit's Daddy." She continued to back away. Again he reached for her, but she screamed again, then quickly skirting around him, she took off running through the woods in the direction of the cabin.

Daniel's mind was churning madly. He didn't know what to do. He had never seen Sarah like this. Not even when he had shot the squirrel was it anything like this. It was like she had gone crazy. He knew there was nothing he could do with her now: it would be up to Elizabeth to calm her down. The only thing he could do now was to take care of the deer. There was still time to get it back to the cabin and strung up before dark.

When he reached the cabin he found Elizabeth waiting on the porch. "How is she?" he asked, shifting the weight of the deer on his shoulders.

"I was about to ask you the same thing," replied Elizabeth anxiously.

"You mean she didn't come back?"

"I haven't seen her."

"Well, she'll prob'bly be in soon," Daniel assured her, trying to conceal his own anxiety. "She's a little upset. You know how she is when she's upset. She just needs a little time to herself."

"I hope she doesn't stay out too long," said Elizabeth nervously, glancing around at the forest. "It's going to be dark soon, and she doesn't even have a coat on."

Sarah's heart was pounding furiously as she ran down the side of the mountain. She could not get the picture of the dead deer out of her head. Feelings were real all right. She had never hurt so badly in all her life. But she could no longer cry. She could no longer scream. All she could do now was run, run as long and as hard and as fast as she could, run until all the hurting stopped. Almost as soon as she had started running, she knew where she had to go. In the midst of all the confusion, all the pain, all the terrible anguish, one thought kept repeating itself over and over again in her mind, like a tree branch banging against a window pane in the wind. It was the line from Isaiah: "They shall not hurt nor destroy in all my holy mountain." Over and over again as she fled headlong from the unspeakable horror she had witnessed, those words beat against the window pane of her mind: "They shall not hurt . . . nor destroy . . . in all my holy mountain."

It was almost dark as she struggled up through the shadowy tangles of mountain laurel. By the time she reached the rocks it was too dark to see to climb. Gasping for breath after the long uphill run, she crawled under a great rock and, forcing herself back into the crevice as far as she could go, she lay down on her side and brought her knees up to her chest. She felt safe here, far from the guns and the killing, but she could not stop the pictures from coming, she could not stop the feelings. Still they rushed into her mind, kept coming and coming, like a river flooding its banks, rising ever higher. She could not run from them now.

For the next two hours she lay there in the darkness between the rocks like a small frightened animal, sobbing quietly. Suddenly her body began to tremble convulsively. She was shivering. She had completely forgotten her body. Now she felt her arms. They were cold, as cold as the rocks between which she lay. Vigorously she tried to rub some warmth into them. But the night air had become damp and cold and the temperature was dropping rapidly. It felt like snow. She knew that if she stayed outside all night, she would probably freeze to death. Somehow the idea of dying did not seem so unpleasant to her. Strangely, it filled her not with alarm, but with a kind of peace. Dying would be a release from the terrible hurt. Furthermore, it would be the perfect solution to her awful dilemma. If she died, she could go to Heaven and be with her Aunt Ruth. Her Aunt Ruth liked animals. Then her Daddy could go hunting and he wouldn't be sad anymore.

Elizabeth was nearly out of her mind with fear. As darkness approached both she and Daniel had called for Sarah and had searched the woods around the house until it became too dark to see. Then Daniel had gone out with the lantern to look for her, but that was over two hours ago and he had not returned. Again she went out onto the porch and called into the darkness, first for Sarah, then for Daniel. There was no answer. She went back inside, put another stick of wood in the stove, and looked at the supper no one had touched. She glanced at the still untrimmed Christmas tree in the corner, and for some strange reason the first lines of an old Christmas poem came into her head: " 'Twas the night before Christmas and all through the house, not a creature was stirring..."

She thought of the lifeless deer hanging out behind the cabin, its life's blood dripping from its severed jugular... She had to stop thinking. If she thought about what was happening, she would go mad. She had to keep busy. She knelt down by the stove and began working relentlessly on the string of popcorn Sarah had started.

She jumped to her feet at the sound of the door latch. It was Daniel. The look on his face gave her no reason to hope.

"Ran out of kerosene," he said despondently, holding up the dark lantern. "I been lost for the last hour. If it hadn't a-been for the light in the window, I'd never a-found my way back."

He set the lantern on the table and put his arms around his wife. " 'Bout the only thang we can do now is keep a lamp in the window an' pray she's close enough t' see it."

Elizabeth backed away from him, a look of disbelief and horror on her face. "No, Daniel, no! We have to find her!" She ran out onto the porch and screamed Sarah's name—again and again—each cry more desperate than the one before. Daniel went out onto the porch, put his arm around her and led her back in.

"Hit won't do no good," he said softly, trying to comfort her, but knowing there was no comfort in what he had to say. "I done yelled myself hoarse. I'd go back out thar myself if I thought it would do any good. But hit's like lookin' for a needle in a haystack—in the dark."

"But Daniel, we can't just give up and do nothing."

"We can *pray*, Elizabeth. We can keep a lamp in the window an' *pray*."

Elizabeth could not believe it. Daniel had given up hope. She could see the exhaustion in his eyes, the deep lines of despair etched into his face. He had given up hope. He never expected to see Sarah alive again.

Unable to bear the weight of this awful realization, she slumped into her chair. Daniel sat down in the chair next to her and began to pray. Elizabeth, too numbed by fear and grief to pray or cry, stared blankly at the reflection of the lamp in the window.

Late into the night she sat there as Daniel prayed, her mind frozen in some limbo state between waking and sleep. It all seemed so unreal, like a bad dream that refused to end. If only she could sleep and wake up, then maybe everything would be all right.

It was sometime after midnight that Elizabeth was suddenly wakened from her nightmare by what she thought was the sound of the door. Had she actually heard something or was it too part of the dream? When she saw Daniel jump to his feet and rush to the door, she knew it was not a dream. The door opened, and suddenly, miraculously, Sarah, her dress torn and stained with dirt and blood, was standing before them. She ran past Daniel and threw herself into her mother's waiting arms. Overwhelmed by the sight of her, Elizabeth hugged her desperately, passionately, joyously. "Oh, Sarah," she cried, her voice breaking with emotion, "I thought you were lost to us for good!"

After a few ecstatic moments, after she was certain that this was not a dream, that this was indeed her precious flesh-and-blood daughter returned to her, Elizabeth released her tenacious embrace and held Sarah at arm's length to get a better look at her. As she did so, Daniel threw a blanket around his daughter's trembling body.

Elizabeth studied Sarah's face. It was scratched and bruised and dirty, and the left side of it was caked with dried blood. Blood was also in her ear and in her hair. She looked a fright, but there was a strangely peaceful smile on her face.

Elizabeth shook her head in disbelief. "Sarah, Honey, where *were* you?"

"I was lost, Mommy," she replied, her body trembling but her eyes bright, "I was far, far away and I was lost . . . but Kati showed me the way home."

Daniel, who was pouring hot water into the wooden tub for Sarah's bath, looked up at Elizabeth. She was already looking at him. It was the first time Sarah had mentioned Kati in the three years, three months, and ten days they had been in North Carolina.

As soon as it was light enough to see, Elizabeth climbed the ladder into Sarah's loft. She found Sarah lying in her bed awake, staring out the window. She sat down on the edge of the bed.

"How are you feeling this morning?" she asked tentatively. It was evident from the hoarseness of her own voice that she herself was not fully recovered from the terrible agony of the night before.

Sarah turned to her and tried to force a smile, but the best she could manage was a weak and evanescent half-smile. "I'm mixed up, Mommy. I'm all mixed up."

"I know, Honey, I know," replied Elizabeth tenderly. She felt for Sarah's hand under the quilt and found it. "At least you're warmer this morning." Sarah nodded her head. Elizabeth held on to the hand.

Elizabeth could only try to imagine the torment that Sarah was suffering. Sarah had tried to come to terms with the killing of animals for Daniel's sake—because she didn't want her Daddy to be sad. Perhaps in the shallow waters of her mind she *had* accepted it—or thought she had—but she had struggled in vain against an undertow that was both stronger and deeper than any reasoned argument could reach—against an undercurrent that had not accepted it and could not be made to accept it. Elizabeth herself had been horrified at the sight of the dying deer's heroic but futile efforts to escape his slayer. She had had to steel her mind against it, just as later she had had to steel her mind against the sight of it strung up by its hindlegs from a pole out behind the house. It seemed such an inglorious end for such a beautiful and noble creature. But she had known when she came to the mountains that there would be some aspects of this simple do-for-yourself way of living that would offend her finer sensibilities. Before she had been at Nathan and Hester's a week, she had skinned her first rabbit. During that first winter she had seen hogs butchered and had handled their innards. Her natural reaction, had she allowed herself the freedom to feel or express it, would not have been very much different from Sarah's. As a result she had little difficulty now empathizing with Sarah's feelings for the slain deer, or understanding her daughter's terrible dilemma.

"Sarah, tell me about Kati."

Sarah's eyes brightened and a trace of a smile appeared on her lips–the same brightness and the same smile Elizabeth had seen the night before.

"Last night you said that you were lost and Kati showed you the way home."

Sarah nodded but remained reticent.

"Can't you tell me about it, Honey?"

"I really shouldn't, Mommy. I shouldn't have said that last night. I promised I would never talk about Kati again."

"Whom did you promise?"

"I promised myself."

Elizabeth smiled. "When did you make this promise?"

"A long time ago. Before we left Massachusetts."

"But why? Why did you promise yourself not to talk about Kati?"

Because I didn't want to make you and Daddy upset."

Elizabeth remembered the tense night in the kitchen back in Springfield when Sarah first told them about her imaginary friend. Elizabeth had thought at the time that she and Daniel had concealed their anxiety fairly well. "Why did you think that we would be upset?"

"Because when I told you about Kati you talked like you talk when you're upset–not angry-upset, but worried-upset. And Daddy's hands were sweating. Daddy's hands never sweat."

"If I promise not to be upset now, will you tell me about Kati?"

Sarah furrowed her brow and turned again toward the window. Elizabeth guessed from her troubled expression and her hesitation that Sarah was worried about her promise.

"Sarah, since you made the promise to yourself, why don't you ask yourself for permission to break it?"

Sarah turned back to her mother, a surprised look on her face. "Can I *do* that?"

"I don't see why not."

Sarah thought for a moment. "All right then, I give myself permission to break my promise."

"Tell me about last night. Tell me how Kati showed you the way home in the dark."

A painful expression came over Sarah's face as she recalled the frightening events of the previous night. "When Daddy shot the deer," she began haltingly, pausing to choke back the sobs, "I just started running as fast as I could. I ran far, far away. I ran until it got dark, then I crawled under a big rock. . . I cried for a long time . . .Then I started to shiver. It was very cold and I thought I was going to die. But I knew that it would be all right if I died, because then I could go to Heaven and be with Aunt Ruth, and Daddy could go hunting and he wouldn't be sad anymore . . . "

"Oh, Sarah, surely you know that your Daddy would be much sadder if something happened to you. Last night he was nearly out of his mind with worry. We both were."

"I knew that *you* would be sad if I died. It was when I thought about you and how much you would miss me, that I tried to find my way home. But I couldn't see"– she fought back tears–"it was too dark. I kept running into bushes and briars, and I kept falling over rocks. Then I fell and rolled down a steep bank into . . . like a ditch. When I got back out, I didn't know which way to go . . . That's when Kati came."

Elizabeth had been listening in horror to Sarah's story, trying to imagine the mental anguish that had propelled Sarah into flight in the first place–the mental anguish that had been so great that even death had seemed preferable–and the confusion and fear she must have experienced as she tried to find her way home through the forest in the dark. "Could you see Kati in the dark?"

"Oh yes, she's very bright."

"Can you describe her to me? Does she have a face? Does she have eyes, a nose, a mouth? Does she have arms and legs, hands and feet?"

"Of course, Mommy. She's a real person just like you and me."

Elizabeth was intrigued, but confused. "Can you touch her?"

"No, I can't touch her. She's made out of light."

"So you can see her, but you can't touch her?"

Sarah nodded her head. "Just like the light in the lantern, Mommy. We can see it but we can't touch it."

"Was this the first time you've seen Kati since we moved from Massachusetts?"

"Oh no, I've seen her lots of times. She usually comes to see me in the early morning before it gets light."

Elizabeth remembered that it was always in the early pre-dawn hours that Sarah had had her conversations with her imaginary friend. "Do you still talk to Kati?"

"We don't talk out loud, but we talk."

"How do you mean?"

"When I was little, I talked out loud, but that was before I learned we could talk inside my head."

"Inside your head?"

"Yes, you know, like when you read to yourself, you don't hear the words through your ears. You hear them inside your head."

"How long have you been talking to Kati inside your head?"

"Since that winter we lived at Aunt Hester's."

Elizabeth had slept in the same bed with Sarah that winter and had heard nothing. Now she understood why. "What kinds of things do you talk about?"

"All kinds of things. Mostly I talk to her and she listens. But sometimes she tells me about the beautiful place where she lives."

"The White Light World?"

"Yes."

"Sarah, can you show Kati to me?"

"No, you can't see her."

"How do you know?"

"Because that winter at Aunt Hester's she would sometimes stand right next to the bed and you wouldn't see her. And do you remember that time, back in Massachusetts, when you came into my room and I first told you about her?"

"Yes, I thought you were talking to your doll."

"Well, Kati was sitting right *on* my bed. I thought you saw her. That's why I couldn't understand why you made a place at supper for my rag doll instead."

"Kati's not sitting on your bed now, is she?" asked Elizabeth, half-jesting, looking around. She had hoped to coax a smile or even a bit of laughter out of Sarah, but she was unsuccessful.

"No," replied Sarah in the same sad and subdued tone of voice, "but she was here earlier this morning, sitting right where you're sitting now."

Elizabeth felt an eerie chill go up her spine. "The next time you see her," she said, "I want you to be sure to thank her for me and your Daddy for bringing you home last night."

"Oh, I almost forgot!" exclaimed Sarah. "Kati gave me a message for you and Daddy this morning. She wishes you both a very happy Christmas."

Elizabeth descended the ladder and found Daniel waiting for her in the kitchen.

"How is she?" he asked nervously.

"I don't know, Daniel, it's hard to say. She's suffered severe emotional trauma. It could be quite some time before she's fully recovered . . . Also, she's very confused. She finds herself in this awful dilemma. On the one hand, she loves you and wants you to be happy. On the other hand, she loves the animals too and can't bear to see them get shot. When she was lost in the woods last night, she said that she thought she was going to freeze to death and that somehow the idea of dying gave her peace, because if she died, then you could go hunting and you wouldn't be sad anymore."

Daniel buried his face in his hands. "Oh my God!" he murmured.

"I assured her that it would make you much sadder if something happened to her, and, of course, she understands that now, this morning. But last night she was so terribly hurt and confused that she wasn't thinking clearly."

"Did she say anythang more about . . . ?"

"About Kati? Yes, she did. In fact, the only way I could get a smile out of her was to get her to talk about Kati. Kati seems to be the only bright spot in her life right now." Elizabeth smiled in embarrassment at her unintentional pun.

"But I still don't have a very good idea about who or what Kati is. I *think* Sarah is just imagining her, fantasizing her, to fill some need for companionship or understanding or something. Do you know how we thought Sarah had stopped talking to Kati?

Well, it turns out that she never stopped talking to her at all. She's been talking to her all along–inside her head. That suggests to me that that is the only place Kati exists: inside Sarah's head. But if that's the case, then how did she find her way home last night? She says that Kati *showed* her the way."

"Mebbe one of the Little People showed her the way."

"One of the Little People?"

"I reckon you never heard of the Little People. The Cherokee Indians used t' tell of a tribe of Little People who live in the deep woods near the tops of high mountains. They're small, no bigger'n children, an' they're purty like children. They got real long ha'r that comes all the way down to here"–he stooped his shoulders and touched his legs just below his knees–"an' when they dance under the trees, their long ha'r goes a-flyin' in the wind. They're the keepers of the Cherokee legends. . . "

"They sound like elves."

"Whatever they are, they're real happy an' gentle an' peaceful folk. An' they do good deeds–like leadin' lost children home to their parents. . . Well, when I was out in them dark woods a-lookin' for Sarah last night, I remembered about the Little People. I don't expect they really exist, but I didn't think it would hurt t' ask God t' send one of them t' find Sarah just in case. I was a-prayin' ever' prayer I could think up last night."

Elizabeth lost herself in thought for a moment. White light people. Little people. What next? Reality seemed to be slipping away. Suddenly she remembered the message. "Oh, by the way, Kati wishes us both a merry Christmas."

Daniel allowed himself a fleeting smile. "I had completely forgot that it was Christmas."

"I know what you mean. It doesn't seem much like Christmas, does it?. . . But when I think how close we came to losing Sarah. . ."

"Yeah, I reckon we got the best Christmas gift anybody could ask for." Daniel thought seriously for a moment. "Do you reckon I should go up an' see her?"

"I think you should at least go up and say hello to her and tell her that you love her–just to remind her."

289

"You know, she didn't even look at me when she came in last night. Ran right past me. Wouldn't look at me at all."

"And she may not look at you this morning," cautioned Elizabeth. "She may pull the covers over her head. But I still think you should go up and see her, just to let her know that you're hurting too. But be patient with her. Don't expect too much too soon. We're going to have to give her a little time."

Sarah did not come out of her loft at all on Christmas Day, nor the day after. Nor did she eat anything. On the third day she got up early, filled the pockets of her coat with biscuits and went outside. Elizabeth watched from the window as she fed all but one of the biscuits to the birds.

For the next two weeks she remained a solitary creature, spending her days confined to her loft or out in the woods walking alone. She had little contact with either Daniel or Elizabeth, declining even to join them for meals. What little food she ate, she took outside with her or up to her room.

Daniel hoped that Sarah would in time forgive him. He knew she was watching his movements during those days immediately following Christmas Day and carefully avoiding him. Whenever they did chance to meet, her greeting was offered more out of habit or sense of duty than any genuine feeling. No longer did she rush spontaneously into his arms or jump up on his lap when he sat in his rocker in the evening. He missed her exuberance. He had not fully realized how infectious his daughter's enthusiasm for life had been. Now that it had been taken from him, he felt as though something inside his own soul was beginning to die. Worst of all, Sarah was reluctant to be left alone with him. Daniel's heart was breaking.

One morning toward the end of the first week of January, Daniel decided he had to try to set things right. He was standing at the foot of the ladder as Sarah came down out of her loft. Halfway down the ladder she turned and saw him and stopped.

"Good morning, Daddy," she said in a tone so cold and remote that Daniel felt as though he had just been stabbed in the throat with an ice pick. Not until he took a step back would she complete her descent of the ladder.

"Put on your coat an' shoes, Sweetheart, let's go outside. I want t' talk to you."

When she was fully dressed. Daniel held out his hand to her. Cautiously she extended her own. Elizabeth watched from the kitchen window as Daniel led her out into the clearing in front of the house. He sought out a patch of sunlight, then took Sarah's hands in his and crouched down on his haunches, as he did whenever he had something important to say to her. He did not look directly into her eyes, but cast his gaze downward until it fixed on the bottom button of her coat. Even had he not been looking down, their eyes would not have met. Sarah was too tall for that now. Moreover, she was not even looking at him but had turned her head to the side, away from the house, and was staring off into the woods. A chilly morning breeze reddened their cheeks and played with wisps of Sarah's long hair. From her window Elizabeth could see their warm breath penetrating the cold January air. Daniel began to speak very slowly and deliberately. He had not planned a speech in his head. His words would have to come from his heart.

"Sarah, I want you t' know somethin' . . . I want you t' know that I love you very, very much . . . An' I would never do anythang–*anythang*–to deliberately hurt you . . . But sometimes I make mistakes. Sometimes I hurt you without meanin' to . . . I know I hurt you real bad the other day. I wish t' God it hadn't happened. I wish t' God that I had been smart enough to a-knowed that killin' that deer would hurt you so bad . . . I wish I could tell you that I'll never do anythang t' hurt you ag'in. But I cain't promise you that. All I can promise you is, I'll *try*–I'll *try*. . . I've decided I'm a-gwine t' give up huntin' for good. I'm a-gwine t' give it up . . ."

"No, Daddy, no . . ."

"Now, let me finish, Sweetheart . . . You see, the problem is, I'm just a very ordinary man . . . an' you . . . you're a very *extra-*

ordinary little girl. I never knowed anyone quite like you before . . . An' what that means is, even though I'm your father, even though I'm much older than you. . .what that means is, sometimes *you* will haf t' teach *me*. . . But you've got t' believe this, Sarah, I wouldn't trade you for any other little girl in the whole world . . . Ever' day of my life. . . ever' day of my life . . . I thank God for sendin' you to us . . . Ever' day of my life, I pray to God to protect you an' keep you from harm . . . If anythang should ever happen to you . . ."

Daniel could not continue. He was choking on the words. Tears were streaming down his face. "Please forgive me, Sweetheart, please forgive me."

Sarah, also crying, fell into his arms. "No, Daddy, don't cry. Please don't cry."

Elizabeth felt a sudden surge of warmth rush into her breast as she watched the tearful reconciliation. This was the outcome she had hoped for. She wondered what Daniel had said. Then she saw something that she had not expected. She saw Sarah pull herself gently away from Daniel and crouch down in front of *him*. Then taking *his* hands in *hers*, she began to speak. Elizabeth would have given anything to have been close enough to hear, but she knew that this was something that had to be worked out between Sarah and Daniel.

"Daddy, I've been thinking too," began Sarah, also struggling to contain her emotions. "I know you were upset with me because I cried and ran away when you shot the deer. I know it was silly of me to cry. I won't cry again, I promise. And I won't run away again. Only please don't give up hunting because of me. I'm going to do better, really I am. I'm going to be a big girl, you wait and see.

"I know you were right about some things. Not about everything though. I can't believe God put the animals on the earth for us to kill and eat. I can't believe that God would do that. But I know you're right about animals getting killed all the time in the woods, and it's silly of me to cry every time one of them dies. I've made a promise to myself that I won't cry again when you shoot an animal. But I've also made a promise to the animals. I've promised them that I will never, ever eat them again. I'm not going to wait for God's kingdom to come, Daddy; I'm going to start now. As long as I live I will never eat animals again."

"No, Sarah, don't promise that. You haf t' eat meat t' live."

"I can't break this promise, Daddy. I didn't make it to myself. I made it to the animals."

Sarah's decision to never again eat animals came as no great surprise to Elizabeth. She knew that Sarah had always taken great delight in watching the many and diverse creatures with which the Earth seemed to abound. It had started when she was very young with the birds, butterflies, rabbits, toads, and assorted other animals and insects that lived in or visited their backyard garden in Springfield, and with the many wonderful wild creatures that inhabited the lakes, streams, and woodlands of Forest Park. Since coming to the mountains her love of all animals, both wild and domestic, had not diminished in the least. Quite the contrary. Elizabeth had to admit that, given Sarah's feelings toward all living creatures, her refusal now to eat them was a perfectly natural extension of those feelings. Her stand was both logical and consistent. Consequently, Elizabeth respected Sarah's wishes and thereafter saw that no meat of any kind found its way onto her daughter's plate.

There were times when Elizabeth wondered whether Sarah needed to eat anything at all. Her energy had always seemed so boundless, as though she had somehow managed to tap into the power source of the universe itself. Elizabeth half suspected that Sarah could live on mountain air and sunshine alone if she really had to.

Elizabeth herself had never eaten much, but then she had never had Sarah's energy either. Daniel, for his part, was convinced that Sarah would grow weak and die before spring if she persisted in keeping to her promise. He himself continued to eat meat at almost every meal. Elizabeth, caught once again between two competing sympathies–one for her husband, the other for her daughter–found herself eating meat less and less frequently. But she was always careful not to put any pressure on Daniel to change his diet. She assured him that he needed the meat in his diet to keep up his strength since he worked much harder than either she or Sarah did. Besides, she joked, somebody had to to eat all the venison he had smoked.

After the talk with Daniel, Sarah seemed to recover quickly from the traumatic events of Christmas Eve. By the middle of January she had resumed her school lessons, and with the exception of her change in diet and perhaps a tendency to be more serious, her behavior had returned to normal. If she had been left with any emotional scars, she did not show it.

The same could not be said for Daniel and Elizabeth. Daniel continued to feel terrible about killing the deer and was reluctant to take up hunting again, even though Sarah had practically pleaded with him not to give it up. Elizabeth continued to be troubled by something else, by something she considered to be far more serious. It was not something new. It was an old problem come back to haunt them: the problem of Sarah's friend "Kati." Was Kati a creation of Sarah's mind, as Elizabeth suspected, or was she, as Sarah insisted, a real person? If she was real, in what sense was she real? If she enjoyed an existence outside of Sarah's mind, why was it that only Sarah could see her? Elizabeth found the problem as intriguing as it was worrying, and she sometimes found herself pondering on it at great length.

Elizabeth may have concluded that Kati was nothing more–or less–than a fantasy of Sarah's mind–albeit a very real-seeming fantasy to Sarah–and let it go at that, if it had not been for other curious behavior on Sarah's part that she had witnessed over the years. One of the reasons that Elizabeth spent less and less time outside in the woods with Sarah as the years went by, besides her inability to find the time, was that Sarah was a very difficult person to be with out of doors. When Sarah was in the woods she had a pace and rhythm all her own. It was not uncommon, during their now infrequent walks together, for Sarah to run on ahead, as if chasing some elusive bird or butterfly through the lights and shadows of the forest, then to stop abruptly and not move at all for twenty or thirty minutes or more. It was during these still moments that Elizabeth found Sarah the most fascinating to watch. The expression on her face would not be fixed, like that of someone in a daydream or reverie, but rather would be very animated and constantly changing, like that of someone watching a lively performance at the theater. Try as she might, Elizabeth was never able to determine what it was that Sarah seemed to be chasing on her wild gambols through the forest, or what it was that so fascinated and amused her when she stopped to watch. It was almost as if Sarah were seeing and hearing things in the forest which Elizabeth herself was unable to see or hear. Had she witnessed but a single instance of this unusual behavior, Elizabeth might have thought no more of it, but over the years there had been a number of such indications that the world that Sarah perceived was somehow different from the world that she perceived.

Was it possible, Elizabeth wondered, that Sarah was seeing things that other people couldn't see? As difficult as this was for Elizabeth to believe at first, eventually she came to the conclusion that there was no good reason *not* to believe it. After all, there was no reason to assume that everyone perceives the world in exactly the same way. In fact, there was no good reason to assume that *any two people* perceive the world in exactly the same way. She did not wish to go so far as the good Bishop Berkeley and suggest that there might not be a world "out there" at all, but she was prepared to admit that the Bishop was right–irrefutably right–when he said that the only thing we can know directly are our own private perceptions; and they exist only in our minds. The images we "see" are not in the world "out there:" they are on the retinas of our own eyes. Destroy the retina and the visible world disappears. Similarly, the sounds we hear do not come from the world "out there," but from our own eardrums. Destroy the eardrum and the audible world disappears. The same is true of our senses of touch, taste and smell. We are perceiving sensations in our own nervous system, nothing more. We only *infer* that our perceptions are *of* something "out there," that the sensations we experience are caused by something outside ourselves.

Since we cannot know with any certainty that there even *is* a world "out there"–that is, outside our minds–it would be absurd to insist that everyone perceives that world in exactly the same way. But even assuming that there *is* an objective reality "out there," and even assuming that most people do perceive that reality in more or less the same way, why should we assume that our five physical senses are capable of perceiving the totality of it? Perhaps we are capable of perceiving only a small band in the total spectrum of reality. We know that we are capable of *seeing* only a small band in the total spectrum of light waves, and *hearing* only a small band in the total spectrum of sound waves. Is it possible that some people are capable of seeing a broader band in the spectrum of light waves, of hearing a broader band in the spectrum of sound waves–of perceiving a broader band in the total spectrum of reality–than others? Do religious mystics perceive the world in the same way as bankers and shop-keepers? Is the world that the great artists and poets perceive the same world that ordinary people must deal with? Did Rembrandt really see a world that full of light? Did Van Gogh actually see a world that rich in color? Did the saints really see visions of Christ and Mary? Did Joan of Arc really hear the voice of God?

Elizabeth remembered how years ago she had tried to see the world through Sarah's eyes. It was simply a mental exercise at the time, the purpose of which was to force *herself* to try to see the world as a new and fresh creation, to see the world as though it had been created that very morning and she was seeing it for the very first time. But she never imagined at the time that Sarah might actually *be* seeing the world–the world "out there"–any differently from the way *she* saw it. Now she could not help but wonder what the world looked like to Sarah. Now, more than ever before, she wished she really could see the world through Sarah's eyes.

One morning later that winter—it was toward the end of February—Elizabeth decided to make an attempt to get a glimpse into the world that Sarah saw. As Sarah sat down at the kitchen table after breakfast to begin her morning lessons, Elizabeth handed her a sheet of paper.

"Sarah, this morning I'd like you to draw a picture."

Sarah grimaced. She did not share her mother's enthusiasm for drawing. She couldn't see any sense in it. A drawing of something, in her opinion, was never as interesting as the thing itself. "What shall I draw a picture of?"

"Of me."

"Of you?"

"Yes." Elizabeth took the seat across the table from her young pupil.

"That's too hard."

"Just do the best you can."

Without further protest, Sarah began to draw. Elizabeth, from her self-imposed state of immobility, waited with some anticipation. The weak winter sun occasionally broke through the bare branches of the trees outside to strike the window at which they were sitting. Elizabeth watched the elusive sunlight alternately wax and wane on Sarah's face. Elizabeth had never forgotten the pictures that Sarah had drawn for Miss Kinney over three years before. Over the course of those three years she had often wondered about those curious circles that Sarah had drawn around the heads of the three human figures in her "happy" picture. Elizabeth had thought it only a curious oddity at the time that Miss Kinney had shown her the drawings, but as the years passed and Elizabeth had come to suspect that Sarah's perception of the world was somehow different from her own, she had begun to think more and more about those curious circles.

"I'm afraid it's not very good," sighed Sarah when she had finished. "It looks more like Aunt Martha than you." She slid the picture across the table to her mother.

Elizabeth turned it around and looked at it. There was no circle. "Haven't you forgotten something?" she asked.

"I didn't draw your legs and feet because I couldn't see them," apologized Sarah. "They were under the table."

"No, I mean this," said Elizabeth, drawing a circle around Sarah's less-than-flattering caricature of her head. She slid the picture back across the table.

Sarah looked at the altered drawing and her eyes immediately lit up. "You mean *you* can see it too?" she asked, startled and excited. "I didn't think *anyone* else could see it! Otis said *he* couldn't see it. He said *nobody* else could see it! I should have known that he was just telling another one of his stories. He said there was no light. He said if I saw a light, I must be crazy. But I knew there was a light, and I knew other people saw it, and I told him so. I told him to look at the pictures on the wall in the church—you know, where we went to school. The people in those pictures all have light around their heads. Whoever drew those pictures must have seen it."

"Do you see light around my head right now?" asked Elizabeth, fascinated by this startling revelation.

"Oh yes, a lot of it. You have a lot of light. Some people have a lot. Uncle Jacob has a lot. So does Aunt Emily. But other people have only a little. Do you know what I've discovered, Mommy? I've discovered that we can make the light around us brighter just by thinking good thoughts. Watch this!" She closed her eyes and assumed an expression of perfect bliss. "Can you see it?" she asked excitedly, her eyes still closed, "can you see it getting brighter?"

In her excitement Sarah had been talking so fast and what she was saying was so incredible that Elizabeth had almost forgotten that she had, in a way, tricked Sarah into making this remarkable disclosure. Now the moment of truth had arrived. "Sarah," she confessed, "I can't see the light around your head."

Sarah opened her eyes. A look of mortification came over her face. "You can't see *any*?" she asked, the words almost sticking in her throat. Her excitement had suddenly turned to shock and disappointment. "But everybody has *some*."

"No, no, it's not that, Honey. I'm sure you have a lot of light. It's just that I can't see the light around people's heads the way you can. But I believe *you* can see it. I truly believe that. And *I* don't think you're crazy. I think you're just very special. You have a very special gift."

The look of disappointment on Sarah's face could not have been more acute, or more painful for Elizabeth to behold. Nor did the disappointment seem to be mitigated in the least by Elizabeth's words of encouragement. But Elizabeth could not allow Sarah to stop now, could not allow her to draw back and retreat into herself, not at this juncture. This revelation was just too astonishing. She had to try to get Sarah to expound further. "Honey, can you tell me more about this light you see?"

Sarah turned and stared out the window. For a long minute she remained lost in thought and Elizabeth wondered if she was going to respond to her question.

"It's not just around the head," said Sarah at last, speaking slowly, very matter-of-factly, her voice devoid of its earlier enthusiasm, "it's around the whole body." Again she fell silent.

"Around the whole body?" prompted Elizabeth.

"Yes, around the whole body."

Desperate to keep her reluctant daughter talking, Elizabeth thrust out her arm. "Can you see light around my arm right now?"

Sarah turned to face her mother. "Yes," she nodded, "it's yellow."

"The light around my arm is yellow?"

"The light around your whole body is yellow right now. Sometimes it's more orange, and sometimes it's almost red, but right now it's mostly yellow."

"The light can change colors then?"

Sarah nodded.

"And you said it can also vary in intensity?"

Elizabeth waited for a response but none came. Perhaps Sarah had not understood the question. How to rephrase it? "Sometimes the light is very bright, other times not as bright?"

"Yes, sometimes the light is very bright, but other times I can hardly see it . . . Do you remember the squirrel that Daddy shot with his gun?"

"Yes."

"When he laid it on the porch, the light was still in it, but it was going out, so I took it and I petted it, to try to make the light brighter, but..."

"Do animals have this light too?" asked Elizabeth, astonished.

Elizabeth could tell from the stunned expression on her daughter's face that she had just asked the dumbest possible question.

"Yes, of course," replied Sarah. She was trying to be patient, but Elizabeth could not mistake the trace of exasperation in her voice. "All birds and animals have light. So do the flowers and plants and trees... At least they used to."

"They *used* to?"

"Yes," she said sadly, "I can't see the light in flowers and trees anymore, but when I was little I could. I don't think the light in people and animals is as bright as it used to be either. When I was little, it was *real* bright–at least I think it was. It's hard to remember now." Again she turned toward the window.

It was apparent to Elizabeth that Sarah really didn't want to be talking about this anymore. She had lost her enthusiasm for the subject the moment she had learned that her mother had deceived her. Elizabeth decided not to push her daughter any further. Besides, Sarah had already given her enough to think about for the rest of the winter. But there was something else that Elizabeth wondered about, something else that had to do with those drawings Sarah had done for Miss Kinney, and this was something she had tried *not* to think about, something she had tried to put *out* of her mind, something she had closed the doors of her mind *against*, but which had a habit of breaking back in from time to time, and every time it did so, it caused a disturbance. She knew that Sarah would welcome a change of subject, but she doubted very much that this particular subject would be any more agreeable to her.

"Sarah, do you remember the drawings you did for Miss Kinney back when you first started school?"

"Yes, I think so," she answered unenthusiastically, still looking out the window.

"Do you remember what you drew when Miss Kinney asked you to draw an 'unhappy' picture?"

A troubled expression came over Sarah's face. "Do you mean the girl in the fire?" she asked tentatively.

Elizabeth was surprised that Sarah had answered at all. "Yes. Who was the girl in the fire, Sarah?"

Elizabeth watched as Sarah's face became contorted in pain. Her whole body was becoming rigid.

"It was meant to be *me*," she said at last, her voice suddenly quivering with emotion, "only it *wasn't* me. It was someone else. They tied her up and cut off her head and set her on fire."

"They cut off her head?" asked Elizabeth in horror.

"Yes!" screamed Sarah.

"Who did?"

Suddenly, as if no longer able to sustain the tension, Sarah relaxed and turned to face her mother. "It wasn't a very good drawing. I'll never be able to draw as well as you, Mommy."

"Sarah, who did this? Who cut off the girl's head and set her on fire?"

"I don't know. I don't remember. Sometimes it's hard to remember dreams."

"It was a dream then?"

"Yes, it was an awful dream." Sarah shuddered.

Elizabeth shuddered too, in a sudden release of tension. She remembered the nightmares Sarah had had that winter they had spent at Nathan and Hester's. "When did you have this dream, Honey?"

"I've had it more than once. I can't remember all the times."

"The same dream?"

"Yes . . . Where do dreams come from, Mommy?"

"That's a good question. Psychologists say they come from a place deep inside our minds called the 'unconscious.' "

"But how do they get in there?"

"I wish I knew that, Sarah. I truly wish I knew."

"But what do they mean?"

"That's another good question. When you're older, you can read what Sigmund Freud had to say about dreams."

"Do you have any books by . . . Sig Manfroy?" asked Sarah, trying as best she could to reproduce the name that had rolled so glibly off her mother's tongue.

Elizabeth laughed, albeit nervously. "Sigmund Freud," she repeated, enunciating the name more clearly this time. "No, I don't. You may think I have every book that was ever written, but I don't. I think Miss Kinney had some books by Freud though. I know she was interested in psychology. It's too bad she had to leave Rushing Creek. I would have liked to have talked to her again."

She got to her feet. "In fact, I'd like to talk to her right now," she added, speaking more to herself than to Sarah.

There was someone else she wished she could talk to at that moment. For one of the few times in her life she wished she could talk to her mother. If Miss Kinney had been right, if the girl in Sarah's drawing–the girl bound to the post, the girl consumed in flames, the girl who had "lost her head"–really was Elizabeth's Aunt Katherine, then Sarah's disclosure that the girl's head had been *cut off*–that the severed head in the drawing was not meant to suggest mental insanity, was not meant to be symbolic, but was meant to be exactly what it appeared to be: a severed head–cast a wholly new and extremely ominous light on the circumstances surrounding Katherine's death. But Elizabeth was still not sure that Miss Kinney *had* been right. After all, how would Sarah have known of Katherine's death? How would Sarah have known anything about Katherine? Why should she have dreamed of her, had nightmares of her tragic death in the fire? There were so many unanswered questions–not the least of which was, what had Sarah meant when she said that the girl in the fire was "meant to be me?"

Elizabeth was almost glad that she didn't have any of Freud's writings in her small library of books. She knew that Sarah didn't especially like being told that she must wait until she was older–to do *anything* –and if there had been a book by Freud in the house, she would have insisted that her mother read it to her at once. She was impatient in that way. It was as if she only had so much time and had to learn everything as soon as possible. But Elizabeth did not feel that Sarah, precocious as she was, was ready for Freud. She was only nine years old, after all. It was true, her mental development was far ahead of that of most other children her age. No one who had seen Sarah and Otis together that first winter at Nathan and Hester's would have guessed that Otis was the elder by two years. As far as Elizabeth could tell, Otis was not an unusually stupid child: he was simply a boy possessed of normal intelligence. It was just that Sarah was so advanced for her years that she made Otis seem slow by comparison. And Otis had not been able to make any progress in bridging the gap during the three years that had transpired since then. He was progressing at his own deliberate pace, but Sarah was moving ahead like an express train on a fast track. Still, Sarah's body was only nine years old and it would be at least another two or three years before it would begin to undergo the inevitable series of changes that would eventually transform her into a sexually mature woman. Quick as her mind was, she had not yet experienced sexual desire. How could she possibly understand Freud's analysis of dreams?

When spring burst forth upon the mountain, Sarah was still very much alive, contrary to Daniel's dire prediction. In fact, to Daniel's surprise, Sarah had not seemed to suffer in the least from the lack of meat in her diet. She had not grown thin and weak as he had expected, but seemed to be growing taller and stronger with each passing day. Gradually he had come to the realization that his fears had been unfounded. And all this had started him thinking that maybe people didn't have to eat meat to live. He had never thought much about it, but he knew that horses and mules thrived on diets of grain and grass, and they were much stronger than even the strongest man. Why, Jesse could pull *him and the plow* with seemingly no effort at all. And if it hadn't been for Jesse, he would never have been able to clear the land in the first place, or to haul the stove, the sewing machine, Elizabeth's books, and all those other heavy essentials up the mountain.

But Daniel himself continued to eat meat. He liked meat. He had eaten it all his life, and it would have been a very difficult habit for him to break. Hunting too had proved a difficult habit to break. Late in the winter, when the last of the deer meat had been consumed, he had taken his gun and gone out into the woods and shot a grouse. He had felt uneasy bringing the dead bird home, even though he had concealed it in a deer-skin pouch. Sarah had kept her promise to the animals, not to eat them, but Daniel had wondered if she would also be able to keep her promise to herself and to him, not to cry when he shot them. Sarah, true to her word, had only smiled at him upon his return and had pretended to take no notice of the conspicuous bulge in the pouch slung over his shoulder.

But Daniel had vowed that he would never again kill an animal in front of Sarah. He continued to feel terrible about having shot the deer right in front of the house. For all he knew it might even have been one of the young fawns that had come up to Sarah on almost that very spot that first spring. How could he have been so stupid? What had he been thinking? He knew how much Sarah liked deer. Besides, it was a shame to have shot such a young buck. In another couple of years he would have doubled in size and weight. As scarce as deer were becoming in the mountains, it made no sense to shoot them before they were even half-grown.

He also felt ashamed of himself for the manner in which he had gotten Sarah to give her consent to let him go hunting in the first place. "Let me go hunting," he had told her in effect, "or I won't be happy." He had been so anxious to win her approval that he had resorted to emotional blackmail. He could not fault himself, however, for *wanting* to go hunting. That, he felt, was a natural instinctive desire of all red-blooded men—certainly of all men who lived close to the state of nature. Nor could he fault himself for wanting to teach Sarah to become a hunter. He wanted her to be a complete, whole, self-sufficient person, able to provide for herself all the basic necessities of life. He felt that that was what *he* could teach her. This, after loving her and protecting her, was his first duty as a father. The fact that she was his daughter and not his son made absolutely no difference to him. Too many women were made early widows in these mountains and were forced to survive by their own wits, sometimes for twenty or thirty years after they lost their husbands. No, he could not believe his *intentions* had been wrong. If he had made a mistake—and there was no doubt in his mind that he *had* made a mistake—it was in assuming, as everyone in these mountains assumed, that it was necessary to kill to survive. One simply had to eat if one expected to live. And to eat, one had to kill animals. At least that's what everyone assumed. If Sarah could survive without eating meat—and so far she seemed to be doing so remarkably well—then there would be no reason for her to learn to kill. He would teach her instead to grow grains and vegetables, to plant and graft fruit trees, and to find wild foods in the woods.

The Christmas of 1935 had been a turning point. It had produced one of those unexpected events in the course of life, after which things are never quite the same again. Daniel had resumed hunting as he had longed to do, but he would never again enjoy it as he once had. Elizabeth had received the fright of her life, and even though she now had her daughter back, in another sense she had lost her. Elizabeth could no longer look upon Sarah as an extension of herself. Sarah was becoming a person in her own right, with a mind entirely her own. In truth, Elizabeth now realized, Sarah had long been a person in her own right, whose mind had always been her own. But Elizabeth had never realized until now how different from her own that mind was.

As for Sarah, the traumatic events of that Christmas had forced her to make decisions that she might not otherwise have made—or at least had forced her to make them sooner. She had promised never again to eat the meat of animals, a resolution that would allow her the peace of knowing that her actions were no longer in conflict with her thoughts and feelings. But she had also learned to suspend her mind, to deliberately not allow herself to think about some things, to pretend that some things didn't happen. This was not an easy thing for her to do. It was dishonest and untruthful; it was like lying to herself. But at least it allowed her and her father to co-exist peacefully on the same mountain, and, whatever the price, she had promised herself that she would pay it.

She had been forced to accept the fact that no one else felt as passionately about the killing of animals as she did, that, for some reason, she was strange, different. Telling her mother about Kati and the light that shines out of people had served only to reinforce that feeling of strangeness and isolation.

For the next two years life in the mountains remained comparatively tranquil, as the disruptive changes brought about by the events, decisions, and revelations of the winter of 1935-36 became gradually assimilated into the broader stream of their lives. Then, two years later, in the spring of 1938, something happened which would again alter the course of their lives forever—something which, in some respects at least, was so eerily similar to the earlier incident, that Daniel and Elizabeth would think that they were reliving the Christmas Eve nightmare of 1935 all over again. But again it was upon Sarah that the experience would have the most dramatic impact and leave the most lasting impression. For Sarah the experience would be something out of this world.

10

THE WHITE LIGHT WORLD

    The ten-to-twelve-mile trek down the mountain to the town of Rushing Creek was easy enough–it was mostly downhill–but the return trip back up the mountain was arduous in the extreme. Because the trip was so difficult, Daniel usually went alone, but about two or three times a year Elizabeth and Sarah accompanied him. Although Elizabeth was normally quite content in their quiet mountain home, every so often the isolation of the place would get the better of her and she would feel the need to go down to the town, just to be reassured that there were still other people living in the world. An over-night stay with Nathan and Hester and a visit to Walter Lehman's General Store every three or four months or so was sufficient. Further contact with the outside world she did not seem to need.

    By the middle of the spring of 1938 Elizabeth was ready to make contact again. She had not been off the mountain since the previous November, when she and Daniel and Sarah had gone down to the annual Thanksgiving gathering at Isaac and Martha's. She liked to make a trip down to the town in the early spring, in March or April. That was the time of year she most needed to get away, after the long winter of confinement inside the cabin. It was also the best time of year to make the trip. Spring came late to the mountains, two to three weeks later than it came to lower elevations, so that a descent of the mountain in March or April was a descent into ever more advanced spring. In the course of a single day, a downhill traveler could observe a broad spectrum of the season, from the first violets and spring beauties near the tops of the mountains, to the flowering dogwood, redbud, and serviceberry trees at the middle elevations, to full-blown lilac and apple blossoms down in the valleys.

    But spring had come early this year, taking Daniel by surprise. Once they got busy, there was no getting away until the work was caught up. But finally, by mid-May, Daniel felt he had the farm well enough in hand to be able to be away for a couple of days. When he announced one evening at supper that he would be going down to the town the next morning, Elizabeth was more than ready to go with him.

Elizabeth assumed that since she would be going, Sarah just naturally would be going as well. Sarah never had any problem making the trip up and down the mountain. She expended an equivalent amount of energy every day of her life. But to Elizabeth's surprise, Sarah asked if she might be allowed to stay home.

"If I stay home," she pleaded, "I can look after Molly and the chickens."

The chickens had been added to their growing menagerie of animals just two years before, soon after Sarah had stopped eating meat. Daniel had hauled them up the mountain in cages strapped to Jesse's back. Although they had clucked and squawked continuously during the long laborious ascent of the mountain, nearly driving both Daniel and the mule out of their minds, Daniel had considered the effort worthwhile, as the eggs would be an important supplement to Sarah's meager diet. He had discovered later, to his dismay, that Sarah did not especially like eggs, and the only way she could be persuaded to eat them was if they were beaten beyond recognition and baked into bread, biscuits, or pancakes. But whatever her feelings about eggs, she *did* like the chickens, and feeding them and gathering the eggs soon became part of her daily routine.

Daniel assured Sarah that if he put Molly in the pasture and gave the chickens some extra feed before they left, the animals would be just fine until they got back. After all, it would not be the first time they had been left alone, and they had always been all right before. Nevertheless, Sarah still asked if she might be allowed to stay home.

Elizabeth did not think that it was a good idea to leave the child alone by herself for two days–after all, she was only eleven–though she could not imagine what kind of harm could befall her. Few strangers ever came by–the place was too isolated for that–and Sarah had already befriended every beast in the forest, or so it seemed, so Elizabeth had no fear from that quarter. After thinking it over, therefore, she decided she had no good reason for refusing the child's request. Daniel had come to the same conclusion. After all, he was trying to teach Sarah self-sufficiency, wasn't he? So it was decided. The next morning Daniel helped Elizabeth up onto Jesse, and the two of them set off on their long journey down the mountain, looking for all the world like Joseph and Mary on their way to Bethlehem. Sarah shouted and waved after them until they were out of sight.

Sarah had her own reason for wanting to stay behind, and it had nothing to do with Molly and the chickens. It had to do with Kati. Sarah had continued to have her secret conversations with her white-light friend in the early mornings before dawn as she lay in her bed in the loft. Years ago, Kati had promised Sarah that one day she would take Sarah to *her* world–to her White Light World–and now it seems, the time had come. Every morning for the past two or three weeks, Kati had been telling Sarah how beautiful the White Light World was, and that if she wanted to see it, she really must come soon. But Kati couldn't show her here at the house. Sarah would have to come to the top of the higher mountain to the south–to Sarah's "holy mountain"–and she would have to come before dawn!

Sarah had already figured out that the only way to be up on the high mountain before dawn would be to go up the afternoon before and spend the night. Not even she could have found her way up in the dark–unless Kati was prepared to lead her again. But it was foolish to even think about it, because her mother and father would never have allowed it in any case. But now her mother and father were away and would not be coming back that night. She had never done anything like this before and she felt guilty–her parents trusted her so completely–but she had resolved to do it. She simply could not let a chance like this go by, a chance to finally see Kati's world.

Toward mid-afternoon she filled a bag with some garden greens and some corn bread and rolled it up into a blanket she had taken off her bed. She tied the bundle with a length of rope, slung it over her shoulder, and set off down the mountain. She carried no water with her as she knew exactly where to find water along the way, having made the trip countless times before. She walked slowly. The day was warm and there was no need to hurry. She could easily make it to her destination with time to spare before the sun went down.

Her mind, however, was not as much at ease as she would have liked. The further she got from home—and she was now ascending the greater mountain to the south—the more she began to think about the hurt she would cause her parents if they knew what she was doing at that very moment. Or what if—and this was the scariest thought of all—what if something had gone wrong? What if Jesse had gone lame or something on the way down the mountain, and her parents had come back home? What if they were home *right now* and wondering where she was? If she didn't come home at all that night—and that was her plan—they would be worried to death. She thought of turning back. She stopped and looked back down the mountain toward home. If she hurried she could still get back before dark. But no, she could not go back. Some irresistible unseen force—there it was again—was pulling her on. She simply *had* to see Kati's world!

She reached the top an hour before dark, spread out her blanket under the pine trees at the base of the high rocks, and ate the supply of food she had brought with her. Just as the sun was beginning to slide behind the mountains to the west, she bounded up onto the rocks and climbed until she reached the summit. Again the absolute grandeur and magnificence of the vista took her breath away. It had been worth the climb, even if she could only stay for a few minutes. Far off in the valley she could see lights beginning to come on. To the west the sun was just disappearing behind the last ridge of mountains on the far horizon. She waited until the last lingering whisks of color had faded from the western sky, then turned and carefully climbed back down. It was almost dark when she reached the pine trees. She lay down on her back on the blanket and watched the sky as the last light of day dissolved into blackness and stars began to appear. It was the middle of May, the earth was aburst with new life, the night air warm and fresh and fragrant with bloom. How could Kati's world be any more beautiful than this? Sarah could not imagine. She was glad she had come, and she resolved to allow no more troubling thoughts to enter her mind. She closed her eyes, and with a smile on her lips, fell asleep.

About an hour before the first light of dawn, she awoke. It was still quite dark. She studied the sky. The stars had moved during the time she had been asleep. Her heart began to pound with excitement. Quite certain that no one was nearby, or even within miles of her, she allowed herself to do something she had not done in years: she whispered Kati's name aloud.

"Kati, are you there?"

She watched and listened intently. From a nearby tree she heard an owl hoot. From someplace far off in the distance, from down in one of the hollows, she heard a dog howl. Another minute passed. Then suddenly she sat up.

"*There* you are, Kati!"

Slowly she got to her feet.

"Yes, I'm ready. I will follow you."

She moved very slowly in the darkness, with her arms extended in front of her, carefully placing one foot in front of the other. Was she imagining it or was Kati leading her to the high rocks? In the dark Sarah climbed up onto the rocks. Higher and higher she climbed, feeling with her hands, until she reached the very summit. She paused for a moment, on hands and knees, to catch her breath. Still, Kati beckoned her on. Sarah stood up and slowly began to inch her way out toward the edge, groping with her hands at the dark emptiness that surrounded her. As she neared the edge, she began to sway dizzily from side to side. She jerked her arms about wildly as she desperately tried to regain her balance. Then suddenly she felt herself plunging through the blackness.

When Daniel and Elizabeth returned home that evening, it was nearly dark. Elizabeth was exhausted. They had gotten a late start on their return journey as Elizabeth had spent more time at Lehman's store than she had really planned, and so all afternoon they had been pressing hard up the mountain trail with nary a break in order to get home before dark. As if the journey had not been difficult enough, they had been caught in a heavy downpour of rain, adding greatly not only to their own physical discomfort, but also to the treacherousness of the trail. When the cabin finally came into view, Elizabeth's relief was intense. She knew that if she had to walk another mile, she would have been crippled for life.

Normally it would have been Elizabeth who would have sensed that something was wrong, but this time it was Daniel. Sarah had not come to greet them, which he thought unusual. That she would have come running had she heard them coming up the trail, he had no doubt. And as she was usually aware whenever a twig snapped anywhere in the forest, he could not imagine that she had not heard them. Also, he noticed that there was no light coming from inside the cabin, though it was almost dark outside and must be completely dark inside by this time. He called out her name. There was no answer. It was not until she heard Daniel call Sarah's name aloud, that Elizabeth realized that something was amiss. She had been so preoccupied with her own discomfort, with no other thought in her head but to soak her feet in a tub of hot water and go to bed, that she had not even noticed the irregularities that had caused Daniel to be concerned.

Now she too called out Sarah's name, and hobbled to the cabin as quickly as her aching legs and feet would allow. Daniel set to the task of unpacking the mule before complete darkness set in, calling out Sarah's name several more times as he did so. Once inside, Elizabeth called again, then lit the kerosene lantern. She held it over her head. One quick glance around told her that Sarah was not in the cabin. Still holding the lantern, she stepped out onto the porch.

"Daniel, she's not here!"

The agitation in her voice was extreme. She was near to complete physical exhaustion and now this. Sarah was missing! Daniel continued to call, ever more loudly. He carried the bundle of supplies into the house and dumped it unceremoniously onto the floor, then took the lantern from Elizabeth and walked to the edge of the clearing where the woods began. Holding the lantern above his head, he called again. And again. He felt his stomach tighten into a knot.

"Please, God, not ag'in! Don't let this be happ'nin' ag'in!"

How he wished he could just re-live the past hour of his life—could just go back down the mountain a piece and come back up—only this time he would have Sarah run and greet them as they came up the trail to the cabin. He wanted to feel her arms around him right now. More than anything else in the world, he wanted to feel Sarah's arms around him right now.

"Sarah!" he called again in desperation as he moved along the edge of the woods. But there was no one there, only the grotesque shadows made by the unnatural light of the lantern probing into the blackness of the forest. Realizing that what he was doing made absolutely no sense, and unable to think what to do next, he turned and walked back to the cabin. Elizabeth was still standing on the porch in the dark where he had left her. Only one other time had he seen such a frightened look in her eyes. He took her hand and led her inside. Setting the lantern on the kitchen table, he drew her to him. Her hands were cold and her body was stiff. She was all but paralyzed with fear. When he put his arms around her, she collapsed onto him and cried uncontrollably.

How long they stood there in the kitchen clinging to each other, neither of them had any idea. They had lost all sense of time. It was completely dark outside now, but whether it had been dark for one hour, for two hours, or for four hours, neither had any idea. All they knew was that sometime in the near or distant past it had become completely dark, and sometime in the near or distant future it would be light again, and that all the dark hours in between would be indistinguishable one from another. All they could do now was wait. In the morning they could do *some*thing: they could begin to look for their lost child. In the meantime all they could do was wait–and pray.

Daniel remembered only too well the last time he had tried looking for Sarah in the dark. He searched his mind for a reason to be optimistic. Did he dare hope that Sarah's white-light friend would lead her home as she had done that other time? At least it wasn't freezing cold outside as it had been that terrible Christmas Eve. It was May, it wasn't December. If Sarah had somehow strayed too far into the woods and had miscalculated the time it would take her to get back home, she could survive easily enough in the forest overnight. It might be a terrifying experience for any other eleven-year-old girl, but not for Sarah. She was completely at home in the forest. But it was not like Sarah to miscalculate. She had always seemed to have such an unerring sense of time and distance. Why wasn't she here? Surely she would be here unless something had happened to her. Nothing had caused her to run away this time. For all its desperate reaching and grasping, Daniel's mind in the end was forced to accept the same crushing but inescapable conclusion that Elizabeth seemed to have reached almost immediately, intuitively: something had happened to Sarah.

As Elizabeth sobbed helplessly into his shoulder, Daniel continued to pray. Suddenly a sound from the loft above them caused them both to freeze into immediate and absolute silence. Neither breathed as they waited and prayed for the sound to come again. Had they really heard something? Or was it only their desperate need to hear something that had caused them to imagine it? No, clearly, there it was again. Daniel picked up the lantern and stepped up to the third rung of the ladder leading into Sarah's loft. Hoping to find that which he dared not hope to find, he held the lantern over his head and peered in. The sudden intrusion of light caused a small, shadowy creature with a bushy tail to go scurrying across the floor of the loft and disappear under the bed. But Daniel did not even have time to emit a sigh of despair when his attention was drawn to another form moving on top of the bed. Suddenly Sarah, looking absolutely radiant, sprang from the bed and rushed toward him. "Daddy! Mother! I have been to the most wonderful place!"

Daniel was so astonished that he nearly fell backwards off the ladder. He was forced to retreat hurriedly in any case as Sarah came scrambling down.

"Sarah! Didn't you hear us callin' you?" he asked, his voice strained with emotion, his mind suddenly flooded with alternating waves of intense relief and intense anger. All of their terrible anguish had been for nought.

Sarah looked up and saw the desperate faces of both parents staring at her. "No, I... How long have you been here?"

"I don't know how long. A long time," replied Daniel, still struggling to bring his confused emotions under control. "Your mother an' I got home just afore dark, an' we been a-standin' here in the kitchen worryin' ourselves sick over you." He turned to Elizabeth. "Didn't you look up in her room?"

"No," stammered Elizabeth, "I called when I first came in, but it never occurred to me that she'd be asleep already."

"I wasn't asleep."

Daniel took his daughter by the shoulders and shook her. "Sarah, if you weren't asleep, why, in Heaven's name, didn't you answer us?"

"Because I didn't hear you, Daddy. I wasn't here. I mean, my body was here, but *I* wasn't here."

"Sarah, you're not talkin' sense. What do yuh mean, your body was here but *you* weren't?"

Sarah turned to her mother. "Mother, it's true! Souls *are* more real than bodies! And they can do everything a body can do! They can see, they can hear, they can think and feel and remember! I was outside of my body, and I could still do all these things! And I could move much faster! I could go from one place to another just by thinking about it! I could go right through walls and trees and..."

"Sarah, Sarah, slow down." Elizabeth's mind was reeling. She had not yet begun to recover from the agony of thinking Sarah was missing. Now suddenly here was Sarah standing in front of her chattering incoherently about being outside of her body. It was all too much for her weary, battered mind to comprehend. "Tell you what. Why don't we make a nice pot of peppermint tea and sit down at the table. Then you can tell us everything from the beginning."

Daniel built a fire and Elizabeth put a kettle of water on the stove. As they waited for the water to boil, Elizabeth could see that Sarah was making a supreme effort to contain her excitement. By the time the tea was ready, Elizabeth had managed to regain some of her composure. "Now, what's this all about?" she asked, as the three of them took their places at the table. "You say you were *outside* of your body?"

"Yes!"

"How exactly did you get outside of your body?"

"Well, the first time I just sort of fell out."

"You *fell* out of your body?"

"Yes. And the second time I just sort of popped out."

Elizabeth shook her head in total incomprehension.

"The first time was early this morning before the sun came up. The second time was later in the day, just as the sun was going down."

"And you say the first time you just sort of . . . fell out?"

"Yes. It felt like I was falling down a long dark tunnel. It was very dark, and I was falling very fast, but I wasn't scared. I kept falling and falling. And there was a rushing sound, like the sound the wind makes when it blows through the trees just before a big storm. Then I saw a light at the end of the tunnel. When I reached it, there was my friend Kati.

"At first I didn't know where I was. It had been dark, but suddenly it was light, and I didn't know how that had happened. But I wasn't afraid, because Kati was there. I always feel safe when I'm with her. She told me she was glad I had finally come. She didn't actually talk, but I could hear her thoughts inside my head, like always. She asked me if I knew where I was. I looked around. Everything seemed so strange. We seemed to be in a long hallway. I asked her if we were in Heaven. She said, 'Not yet.' Then she took my hand and we started moving. It was like floating, but we could go very fast. At first I thought we were in the Underworld because all along the hallway there were people who looked very sad and confused. Some of them even looked angry. They just seemed to be wandering about as if they were lost. Kati told me they were people who had just died and who didn't know where they were yet. Some of them didn't even know they had died.

"Then suddenly everything changed. We were no longer in the hallway, but outside on a street. We were still moving very fast, still floating. Along the street I saw more people, but these people looked much happier than the people in the hallway. I saw houses along the street too, and flower gardens, and trees. I even saw a house with a white picket fence around it, like our house back in Springfield. Then we crossed a river. The river had a bridge over it, but we didn't use the bridge: we floated right across the water. On the other side of the river was a town . . . " She paused to catch her breath.

"You were in a *town?*" asked Elizabeth, who, up to this point, had been able to make no sense at all out of Sarah's story.

"Yes!"

"Do you have any idea where this town was?"

Sarah shook her head. "It wasn't an Earth town, Mother. At first I thought it was—I thought Kati had brought me back to Earth—but then she told me it wasn't the Earth: it was the first heaven, the first heaven that people go to after they die."

Elizabeth stared at her incredulously. "There are *houses* in Heaven? And *bridges?* And *towns?*"

"Yes, it looked just like the Earth. Kati told me that the first heaven is sometimes called the Dream World or the Thought World because it can be made to look any way the people who live there dream it or imagine it to look. It's also sometimes called the Earth Heaven, because most all of the people who live there imagine it to look exactly like the Earth. If anybody wants to change anything—like the house they live in, or the clothes they wear, or the kind of work they do—they can do it by simply imagining it some other way."

Again Elizabeth shook her head in total incomprehension.

"Then suddenly," continued Sarah, still bursting with excitement, "we were in another place, in a beautiful place like the Elysian Fields where Aeneas went. There were green hills and fruit trees and flowers . . . so many flowers! . . ."

"Sounds like here," interrupted Daniel, who was by this time completely engrossed in Sarah's story.

"It *was* like here, Daddy, it *was*! It had deep forests and rushing streams too! Only it was different. It was like everything was made out of light. Light seemed to shine from inside of everything. It's hard to describe. And I couldn't begin to describe all the different kinds of flowers and fruit trees—more kinds than we have here even. And the colors! I've never seen so many colors! There were colors that I never even imagined were possible.

"We were moving past everything so fast. I thought, wouldn't it be wonderful if we could just stop for a little while and run through the fields of flowers. Just as soon as I thought the thought in my head, we were in a meadow running hand-in-hand through the flowers. We ran up a hill covered with high, soft, green grass—the greenest green I've ever seen—and more flowers, thousands of flowers, every color you can imagine—and lots of colors you *can't* imagine. At least *I* couldn't imagine them. When we got to the top, I stopped to look around. It was then that I noticed that Kati was no longer made out of white light. She was a normal girl just like me, only bigger than me. She had brown hair too, but not quite as dark as mine, and her eyes were blue, not brown. She was so beautiful! Her cheeks were so pink!

"Then for the first time I looked at my own body. It *looked* like my body, but it didn't feel heavy like my body. It was so light it could float . . . and the light seemed to shine right through it. I touched it just to make sure it was real, and it was. I could touch Kati too, and that was something I had never been able to do with my Earth body. We both had on white dresses. Kati just kept smiling at me. She knew that I wouldn't be able to understand everything I was seeing.

"Then we ran together down the other side of the hill until we came to a stream. The water sparkled like . . . You know how the branches of the trees sometimes get in the winter when the rain freezes on them and then the sun shines through? Well, the water sparkled something like that. And it made a happy, tinkling sound, like chimes. We followed the stream into a deep forest of very old trees with thick trunks and lots of branches hanging close to the ground. They would have been great trees for building a tree-house in, Daddy.

"As we walked under the trees, butterflies and birds came down and flew all around us–kinds I had never seen before. They were all beautiful colors and the light seemed to shine right through them. We went a little further and came to a clearing in the woods. There we saw some people gathered around a waterfall and a pool of water. There were children there too. They were all dressed in different colors, and they all looked so peaceful and happy. They were playing music and singing. It was the most beautiful sound I had ever heard–even more beautiful than the songs of the wood thrush and the veery.

"I thought how happy I would be if I could just stay there with Kati and explore that wonderful world of flowers and waterfalls and beautiful colors forever, but Kati reminded me that I had only come for a visit and there was still much more to see. The next thing I knew, she had become white light and we were moving again.

"She showed me some of the buildings where people in the Heaven of Colors live and study and work. They were like palaces, or like those white buildings with the columns that the Greek people built a long time ago."

"You mean temples, like the Parthenon?" suggested Elizabeth.

"Yes, some of them were like that. But there were other kinds too. They were all gleaming white. But they weren't all crowded together like buildings in Earth cities. Each one was surrounded by a garden of flowers and trees. Some of them were on tops of hills. I saw some others on the shore of a lake. I told Kati, this must be a wonderful place to live. She said it *was* a wonderful place to live, but more importantly, it was a wonderful place to *learn*. She said learning was very important in *all* the worlds, including the Earth world. We are *here* to learn, she said. I asked her if it was important to learn arithmetic. She just smiled. She said school lessons were important because they teach us *how* to learn; they prepare us for all the learning we must do when we grow up. She said that one mistake that people on Earth often make is that they think that once they get out of school they can stop learning. She said learning should never stop. We should continue to study and learn as long as we live: there is just so much we need to know. Another mistake we mustn't make, she said, was to think that we've become so smart that we know everything there is to know. She said that even people in Heaven do not know everything there is to know. In fact, people in the first heaven don't know much more than people do here on Earth. They too have a long way to go. They still have a lot to learn. She said the same is true in the Heaven of Colors. As beautiful as that world is, it's not the highest heaven, and the people who live there don't know everything there is to know. But it's a wonderful place to learn. Then she said it was time to see *her* world, the place where *she* lives.

"Suddenly everything was white—bright, bright white. It was the brightest light I could ever imagine, but for some reason it didn't hurt my eyes. Kati was still standing right by my side, but now there were other white-light people standing all around us, some of them even brighter than Kati. At first I was just surprised to see so much light, but then I began to feel something. Whenever Kati is with me, I feel very happy, very peaceful. I know she loves me very much. It's like all that light that shines out of her is . . . is love. It always makes me feel real good inside. It's always been that way, ever since I was a little girl.

"But when I was standing there with Kati in the middle of all that light, it was like standing in the middle of the sun. Only it wasn't hot; it didn't burn. It was the happiest feeling I have ever known. It filled me with a feeling of wonderful, wonderful peace—a feeling of being totally and completely loved. It only lasted for a few seconds. I think I might have died if it had lasted any longer." She laughed. "What a funny thing to say. Because I *was* dead. I mean, I was out of my Earth body, which is what people on Earth call 'dead.' I knew when I was out of my body that *I*—the real me—was never going to die.

"The last thing Kati said to me when I was standing in the light was, 'Remember this love. When you go back to the Earth

World, remember this love, and know that you have been to the fount of all creation. Know that you have touched the heart of God.' . . . The next thing I knew, I was back in my body. That's when I woke up."

Daniel and Elizabeth were speechless. For several minutes after Sarah had finished her incredible narrative, they continued to stare at her in disbelief. Neither of them had ever seen such a peaceful and radiant look on her face. Then Daniel looked down at the cup of untouched tea in front of him. He glanced around the table and noticed that no one had taken so much as a sip of tea.

"I'd better re-heat this tea," he said, getting up and going to the stove.

Elizabeth continued to sit, unable to move. "Sarah, was this a dream?"

"No, Mother, it was not a dream. It was as real as anything could be. If anything, it was more real than *this* even." She made a gesture with her hands to indicate the reality of the present moment. "I remember thinking when I was standing with Kati on top of the hill in the Heaven of Colors that maybe the Earth was the Underworld, because everything seemed so much more real there than here." She looked around the kitchen. "Of course, this seems pretty real to me now."

"Sarah, where do you think these other worlds are?"

Sarah shook her head. "I don't know, Mother. I can't figure that out exactly. I don't think they're any *place*."

"Do you think they might be in your mind?"

"I'm not sure I know where my mind *is* anymore."

Elizabeth looked at her curiously. "What do you mean?"

"I mean, I used to think my mind was inside my head—I mean *this* head"—she touched both hands to her head—"but now I know it doesn't have to be . . . Let me tell you about the second time I was out of my body today. . .

"I had expected you to come home for supper. When you didn't, I ate something myself, then went up to my room. The sun was going down behind the mountain but it wasn't dark yet. I lay down in my bed. I wasn't sleepy—I was much too excited to be sleepy—but I wanted to see if I could get out of my body again. It took me a while but I finally did it. I sort of popped out this time, right out through the top of my head. One minute I was inside my head looking up at the ceiling, and the next thing I knew, I was up on the ceiling looking down. I could see myself lying in the bed. I looked at myself for a long time—it was such a strange thing to be doing. I mean, I have never looked at my face before, except in a mirror . . . Then I just sort of floated right up through the roof, and the next thing I knew, I was outside. I was in my light body again. I kept going higher and higher until I was above the trees. Suddenly I could see the sun again, and I decided I would go toward it, toward the sun. I started moving very slowly at first, staying just above the tops of the trees. But then I started going faster and faster, and suddenly I was whooshing over the tops of mountains and dipping down into the valleys. It was so much fun! I felt as free as a bird! Freer!—because I didn't even have to flap my wings."

"Did you *have* wings?" asked Daniel as he re-poured the three cups of tea.

"No, Daddy, I didn't have wings."

"When you were up in Heaven, did you see anyone with wings?"

"No. People in Heaven don't need wings. They can go anywhere they want just by thinking."

"Hmm," said Daniel, sitting back down, "I reckon that makes sense . . . But what about this friend of yours, this Kati, is she what you'd call an angel?"

"I don't know, Daddy. I don't think I understand what an angel is exactly."

"I don't reckon I do either. But I'd be purty sure your friend Kati is what most folks would call an angel." Daniel sipped his tea, satisfied that he was finally beginning to make some sense out of Sarah's story.

Elizabeth had been fascinated by Sarah's recounting of her second adventure outside of her body and was anxious for her to continue. "You said you were flying over the mountains."

"Oh yes! It was so exciting! I never imagined there were so many mountains out there, and it seemed like they just kept getting higher and higher the further I went. It was so beautiful because it had rained earlier and the mist was still rising out of the valleys. I wanted to keep going and going, but it started to get dark. I couldn't see the sun anywhere anymore. That's when I decided it was time to come home. It's funny, I don't remember actually coming back. All I remember was thinking that it was time to come back, and the next thing I knew, I was back in my room inside my body . . . I lay in my bed for a long time just thinking about all the things I had seen and heard today. I didn't want to forget anything . . . Then suddenly I saw the light shining into my loft. That's when I got up."

Slowly Elizabeth drank her cup of tea. She was exhausted, both physically and mentally. She knew that her mind was in no condition at the moment to make any final judgement on the credibility of the fantastic story her daughter had just related. But she knew that Sarah had experienced *some*thing; she hadn't made it up. She would get some sleep and look at it all again in the morning when her mind was clearer. But for now she felt herself inclined to believe that Sarah had experienced precisely what she said she had experienced. She didn't know how it was possible, but apparently somehow Sarah's mind had slipped through the normal bounds of consciousness and had entered another dimension of reality. She finished her tea, gave her radiant daughter a long and loving embrace, and went to bed.

Sarah had not told her parents everything. She had deliberately failed to mention *where* she had been–where *her body* had been–the first time she had been outside of it. She had not wanted to cause them needless worry, and had they known that she had been climbing around on the top of high rocks in the dark, only inches away from a sheer drop of a hundred feet or more, it would have been just like them to worry. Besides, the holy mountain was her secret place. She couldn't tell anyone about it, not even them.

But she did not understand, even now, why Kati had led her to the top of the high rocks in the first place, unless it had been necessary to make her think she was falling. If so, it had certainly worked: she certainly had thought that she was falling. And when she went out of her body the second time—when she had simply popped out—she had not gone through the tunnel and she had not ended up in the same place. Whatever the reason, it had certainly been an exciting place to wake up upon returning to her body: on top of the high rocks with the sun just beginning to rise on the eastern horizon. It was the first time she had ever seen the sun rise from the top of her holy mountain. She promised herself it would not be the last.

Early the next morning, after she had milked the cow and gathered the eggs, Sarah returned to the house for breakfast, and found both her mother and her father waiting for her in the kitchen.

"Good mornin'," said Daniel cheerily, studying her with keen interest. He had just sat down to breakfast.

"Good morning," said Sarah. She did not seem quite so radiant as the night before.

"Did you sleep well?"

"Not very. I was too excited to sleep."

"I reckon I can understand that. Hit was quite an adventure you had yesterday."

Sarah smiled and sat down at the table.

"I was wond'rin'," continued Daniel, propping his elbows on either side of his plate, "when you were up in Heaven yesterday, did you see Jesus?"

"I may have, Daddy, I don't know. I didn't get to meet anyone by name."

"Do you reckon mebbe Jesus was one of them white-light people you saw?"

"I don't know, Daddy. He may have been. Jesus *may* live in the White Light Heaven. Or he may live in one of the other heavens. Or he may be between heavens—or beyond them."

"Between? Beyond?"

"Yes. Kati told me that after people leave the Heaven of Colors, they travel all over the universe like shooting stars, with bodies made of fire. Then after they've visited lots of other stars and planets and learned what life is like there, they enter into the White Light Heaven. Kati said that she's been all over the universe and to all three heavens, but she's never been beyond the White Light Heaven, where she is now. She said when you move beyond the White Light Heaven, it's like becoming part of God. Maybe that's where Jesus is. Maybe he's part of God."

Daniel shook his head. "I never knowed thar were so many differ'nt places t' go to after we die."

" 'In my Father's house are many mansions,' " interjected Elizabeth.

Daniel and Sarah looked up at her. Both appeared to be stupefied.

"That's from the Bible," explained Elizabeth, "from the Gospel of John. I wouldn't have known it either if Hester hadn't asked me to read the Gospel of John to her that winter that Sarah and I spent at her house."

"Explain this to me," said Daniel, turning back to Sarah. "When a body dies, who decides which heaven he goes to?"

"I think it's like a school, Daddy. You have to start in the first grade and work your way up. The Earth is like the first grade. You can't go from the Earth directly into the White Light World. You have to go through all the other grades first."

"So your friend Kati is real high up in Heaven?"

"Yes."

"An' Jesus might be higher yet?"

"He might be. I don't know."

Daniel chuckled to himself. "Hain't this the dangdest thang? 'Magine me askin' my 'leven-year-old daughter t' tell me about Heaven . . . Tell me this: what do folks *do* in Heaven?"

"I guess they must study a lot, because Kati said learning is very important. But they work too. Kati said everyone keeps busy. Everyone finds something useful to do."

"Do you reckon," asked Daniel with a twinkle in his eyes, "if I went to Heaven, I could find me a patch of corn t' hoe?"

"I don't see why not. Kati said in Heaven thoughts are the most real things there are, and when people come into the first heaven, they often try to make everything exactly the way it was on Earth. And they can do it too, just by thinking it. All you'd have to do is imagine yourself in a cornfield and you'd be there."

"This place sounds too good t' be true," sighed Daniel. He continued to ponder on these things as he sat quietly eating his breakfast.

Elizabeth's mind had been running along a slightly different track. "Sarah?"

Sarah looked up at her mother.

"Do you have any idea why *you* can see Kati but no one else can?"

"Because she's my friend."

"All right, let's suppose for a moment that Kati *is* an angel or a white-light person..."

"She *is* a white-light person. We don't have to suppose."

"All right. But *you're* just an Earth girl. Why did she take *you* to Heaven?"

"Because I'm her friend."

"But how did you get to be her friend?"

"I don't know. I've *always* been her friend."

Elizabeth relented. She could see that she was getting nowhere with this line of questioning, and she was beginning to sound like the Inquisition. She paused for a moment, then addressed her daughter again, this time in a more conversational tone of voice. "Did you talk to Kati this morning?"

"Yes. She told me some sad news."

"Oh? What sad news?"

"She told me that she wouldn't be coming to visit me anymore."

"Why is that?"

"She said that she had shown me the White Light World, and that's what she had always wanted to do. But now I must live my life here. She said I still have a lot to learn here on Earth. She also said I mustn't try to get out of my body anymore."

How ironic, Elizabeth thought to herself. Years before, her most fervent hope had been that Sarah would forget about Kati, that Kati would go away and not come back. Now she too felt sad at this news. It was almost as if she too had come to accept the reality of Sarah's friend from the "White Light World." And perhaps she had.

Daniel smiled and shook his head as he got up from the table. He had not thought much about Heaven before. He believed in Heaven. Everyone believed in Heaven, didn't they? But he had never thought much about it or what it might be like. But Sarah's description of Heaven had fascinated him. Even the previous night, when it was so late and he had been so travel-worn and emotionally exhausted, he had listened to her every word and had not nodded off to sleep once. In Heaven, Sarah said, folks could make their world any way they wanted just by thinking the right thoughts. When he got there, he would make himself a farm in the mountains, just like this one.

"Well, I'd like t' set around in here an' talk about Heaven all day," he said as he headed for the door, "but I got me some corn t' hoe."

"Save some for me, Daddy," Sarah called after him. "I'll be out just as soon as I help mother clean up."

"Sarah," said Elizabeth when the two of them were alone in the kitchen, "do you remember the dream you used to have about the girl being burned in a fire?"

"Yes."

"Do you still have it?"

"I haven't had it for a long time now."

"The girl in that dream . . . Do you think it might have been Kati?"

Sarah looked at her mother intently for a moment, then nodded her head. "It *was* Kati, Mother. It *was.*"

Elizabeth had not expected so direct and so definitive an answer. "But you said it was just a dream?"

"Yes, it was a dream. But I think it really happened. It happened a long time ago, when Kati lived on the Earth."

Just as soon as the breakfast dishes were washed and the kitchen floor swept, Sarah went out to join her father in the cornfield, leaving Elizabeth alone with her thoughts. Over the course of the past twelve hours, so much new and extraordinary raw material had entered the factories of Elizabeth's mind that she hardly knew how to begin to sort it out, much less process it and make sense of it. She decided to begin with the single piece of information that was freshest in her mind: Sarah's positive identification of the young girl who had died in the fire as Kati. For Elizabeth this was a very significant piece of information because it forced her to accept at last an identification that she had long suspected but had hitherto sought to resist. Up to this point, Elizabeth, consciously or unconsciously, had always treated the mystery of Sarah's friend "Kati" and the mystery of Sarah's dream—the dream that had found expression in her "unhappy" drawing—as two separate mysteries, as two separate puzzles. But Sarah's identification of the girl who had died in the fire as Kati now seemed to link quite conclusively the two puzzles into one. To Elizabeth's great distress she was now forced to admit that, however incredible, Sarah's friend Kati was her own Aunt Katherine!

But how was it possible?—it *wasn't* possible!—and what did it all mean? If she assumed for a moment that a mind or soul could exist outside of a physical body—as Sarah was now insisting—and if she further assumed that Sarah's friend "Kati" was the ghost or soul of her own Aunt Katherine, that still did not explain why Katherine's ghost had chosen to reveal itself to a child like Sarah and to no one else. Unless, of course, it had not been a case of choosing. Unless, of course, Sarah, with her unusual powers of perception, was the only one with whom a disembodied spirit was *capable* of communicating. But still, to what purpose had Katherine's spirit made contact with Sarah? Was it to reveal some hidden truth about the circumstances surrounding her death? To shed new light on a dark family secret? To bear witness to the fact that she had not died by accident but had been murdered–had been murdered in a most gruesome and diabolical manner?

Elizabeth shuddered. She felt herself growing faint. It wasn't just the thought that her unfortunate Aunt Katherine might have been murdered–and that her own grandmother and possibly even her own mother might have been involved–that made her uncomfortable. The whole business of ghosts, of disembodied spirits, made her uncomfortable. It was still much easier for her to believe that "Kati" was simply a creation of Sarah's unconscious mind, though she now realized that that particular hypothesis failed to answer too many questions to be any longer taken seriously. In fact, for every question it *did* answer, it seemed to generate two new ones.

But the question of Katherine aside, what of Sarah's extraordinary claim that she herself had been outside of her body? Had not only been outside of her body, but had been to other worlds, to *Heaven*? Like Daniel, Elizabeth had never thought much about Heaven. But it was not because she did not think about ultimate things. On the contrary. She had always been curious about the ultimate questions of life–the eternal mysteries–and never ceased to be amazed that more people weren't. Those questions which to her seemed to be of the utmost importance–Who are we? *What* are we? Why are we here? What is the meaning of all this? What happens to us when we die?–so many people seemed not to be seriously interested in at all. She had thought a lot about these questions when she was in college and had continued to ponder them from time to time over the years since then. She knew that a lot of people *had* answers–or *thought* they did. Most of the people she knew back in Massachusetts and virtually everyone she had met here in North Carolina called themselves Christians, and, as such, accepted the teachings of the Bible and the Church in matters relating to the nature and destiny of the human soul. If she herself had never thought much about Heaven, it was not for lack of thinking. It was because she had never been able to take belief in Heaven, or many other tenets of the Christian Church, seriously. From the point of view of an outsider looking in—which was the only point of view she had ever known—many of the doctrines of the Christian Church were intellectually indefensible.

The Church taught that a man named Jesus, a part-time-carpenter-turned-rabbi from the town of Nazareth near the Sea of Galilee in the land of Palestine, who had lived approximately from the year 1 A.D. to the year 33 A.D. on the Christian calendar, was God, or, at the very least, the son of God, which was, in the view of many of his followers, somehow the same thing. The Church taught that the salvation of every human soul was in the hands of this God or son-of-God Jesus. To be "saved," to win a place in Heaven, a person had to accept Jesus as Lord and Savior. Different factions of the Christian Church had different ideas about what else, if anything, might be required, reflecting the differences of opinion that various Church Fathers, scholastics, and reformers had enunciated over the centuries. Some were of the opinion that "good works" might be of benefit in helping one get into Heaven, so long as one did not make the mistake of thinking that "good works" alone would be sufficient. Presumably even the most saintly men and women would be shut out of Heaven if they did not accept Jesus as Lord and Savior.

It had been suggested by some that exceptions should be made for people of good conduct who had lived before the time of Jesus, or for those who had had the misfortune of being born into a part of the world where news of Jesus had not yet reached, but this was a very sore point, as the Church did not want people in general to get the idea that it was possible to get into Heaven without first accepting Jesus as Savior. As for those who *had* heard of Jesus, but had *not* accepted him, for whatever reason—be it outright rejection or simple procrastination—it would not go well for them come Judgement Day. Again, there was a difference of opinion concerning the fate of those who died without benefit of being "saved," but none of the options was very savory. One could be simply snuffed out, which was what most non-believers expected to happen anyway—to "saved" and "unsaved" alike. Or one might go to Purgatory for a second chance. Or one could burn forever in Hell. This last option seemed to be the most popular one—at least the one most widely believed in throughout the ages, if not the one most favored by those not destined for Heaven. And here in the rural South this doctrine of everlasting hellfire seemed to have lost none of its peculiar appeal. It seemed to be embraced, not with resignation, but with positive enthusiasm. In Elizabeth's opinion, nothing in the teaching of the Church had turned more people against Christianity in particular, and religion in general, than the doctrine of eternal damnation. Anyone who had evolved far enough out of the primordial ooze to have attained a degree of compassion could see that any "God" who says "Believe in me or burn forever in Hell" was not deserving of our respect or even our attention, much less our praise and worship. If anyone other than God behaved in such a ridiculous and petulant manner, he would not be tolerated for an instant. He would be thrown out on his ear. But Elizabeth did not believe for a moment that the deficiency lay in God, but rather in those small, petty, spiteful, malignant minds that had created God in their own image and had foisted their pernicious doctrine upon the world.

Elizabeth had never received religious instruction as a child. Her parents had never read the Bible or gone to church, and, in a way, she was glad for that. She was often critical of her parents, but she never blamed them for not making her go to Sunday School or church. This "negligence" on their part had allowed her to reach the age when she was able to think critically with fewer preconceived ideas than might otherwise have been the case. But she had not gone so far as to reject all religion outright as some of her fellow-students in college had. She had known some who had gone so far as to declare themselves atheists and to refuse to believe anything they couldn't see with their own eyes. Elizabeth had always felt that these self-proclaimed atheists were not so much interested in finding answers to ultimate questions as they were in attacking and ridiculing the teachings of the Church and castigating the sometimes overzealous disseminators of that teaching. While she had to agree with the atheists that much of the theology taught in the Church was unsatisfactory—or, to use their words, "meaningless and absurd"—she could not for a moment accept their materialistic doctrine—which to her mind was equally absurd—that there is no reality other than the one we perceive with our five senses. Even if it were true, how could they possibly know that? It was an act of supreme arrogance, as well as a giant leap of faith, in Elizabeth's opinion, to insist that nothing exists beyond the limits of our own sense experience. It was as arrogant and as anthropocentric as the old pre-Copernican belief that the Earth was the center of the solar system. Just as the medieval Christian said, the Earth must be the center of all creation because *I* live here, so the modern materialist says, Physical reality must be the only reality because it is the only reality that *I* can perceive. As far as Elizabeth knew, the greater part of reality might lie beyond normal human perception, beyond normal sense experience. How could the materialist possibly maintain, with any degree of certainty or even probability, that no non-physical reality exists? In fact—and this for her would have been reason enough for rejecting the doctrine of atheistic materialism as untenable—*consciousness itself* lay outside the purview of normal sense experience—and what could be more real than consciousness? Surely a doctrine that could not even adequately explain a phenomenon as pervasive as consciousness could not be taken seriously. She considered as laughable the claim of some materialists that consciousness was a "secretion" of the brain, much like bile was a secretion of the liver. It was difficult enough to accept the first article of the materialists' faith—that life had evolved from lifeless matter, had "just happened" as a result of a chance collision of atoms—but when they asked her to believe that consciousness had just "appeared" in the world, had somehow been spontaneously generated out of this same fertile seedbed of once-lifeless, once-mindless matter, they were asking too much.

    This terminal inability on her part to come to a rational understanding of the phenomenon of consciousness was the crack in the door for her, the opening through which her mind could be drawn to accept the possibility of the existence of "God." Her inability to believe that mind had evolved from the world of matter—even living matter—forced her, albeit reluctantly, to the conclusion that mind in some form must have always existed. How else to explain its existence now? She could not conceive that it had originated from any combination of atoms and molecules, no matter how complex and no matter how many billions of years Nature had to work on it. It must have been part and parcel of the make-up of the universe from the very beginning—perhaps had even preceded matter—and might very possibly have had a hand in the creation of the physical universe and in the direction of its evolution, either from within or from without. Perhaps the physical universe was even a manifestation, a "secretion," of mind, of consciousness, instead of the other way around as the materialists believed. If some people chose to identify this mind, this consciousness, as "God," she was perfectly willing to allow that—provided they did not confuse *this* God—this Mind that creates, sustains, and perhaps in some sense *is* the physical universe—with any of those lesser gods, either with that jealous and vengeful tribal god of the Old Testament, who thinks nothing of murdering thousands of innocent infants and children; or with that loving and forgiving god of the Christians, who condemns good people to eternal punishment for simple failure to acknowledge a certain Palestinian carpenter-turned-rabbi of the first century A.D. as Lord and Savior.

Yet, if Elizabeth had been asked, "Do you believe in God?" the answer would not have been readily forthcoming. In the first place, any mind capable of framing the question in so simple and childlike a manner, would not likely have been able to understand any answer she would have been able to give. Like many of the questions that Sarah had asked when she was younger, the question, "Do you believe in God?" required more than a simple "yes" or "no" answer. It required at the very least some attempt at a definition of "God," and since defining "God" was tantamount to defining the Undefinable, this was a serious obstacle to any further exploration of the question. But even if this obstacle were overcome, even if some working definition of "God" were arrived at—unless, of course, the definition arrived at was so vague and all-encompassing as to beg the question, such as "God is Energy" or "God is Love" or "God is the name for everything that is"–she still would have had difficulty answering the question of God's existence in the affirmative with any degree of confidence. Even if "God" were defined as "First Mind"–which would have been her preference, insofar as she had a preference–she would have been able to acknowledge, at best, only the *possibility* of "His"–its– existence. Even if mind *had* existed from the very beginning–or from all time, in the event that there was no beginning–how was it to be conceived? Was it to be conceived as a single, universal mind, from which all individual minds had been derived, had been created? Or as the *sum total* of all individual minds? If minds could exist outside of physical bodies, independently of matter, then perhaps *all* minds had existed from the very beginning. Perhaps *she herself* had existed from the very beginning! What an extraordinary thought!

Extraordinary, but purely speculative–and more than a little presumptuous. But virtually any statement she would have been able to make concerning the existence of God or any of the other great metaphysical questions confronting her would have been purely speculative, because the truth of the matter was, she just didn't know. She hadn't yet found the answers. Furthermore, she wasn't convinced that anyone else had either. It had always seemed a little ironic to her that the people who had the most ready and most unequivocal answers were often precisely the same people who had given the questions the least amount of thought. The more one explored the questions, it seemed, the more one came to appreciate the true depth and complexity of the mystery. At times Elizabeth wondered whether people who had received religious education as children had not been short-changed. By having been given all the answers before their young minds had even had a chance to form the questions, might they not have been deprived of some of that sense of wonder which, in her opinion, was every child's–nay, every human's–birthright? Might they not have heard the name of God invoked so often that they had actually come to think that the name "God" referred to something comprehensible?

But even more deserving of pity were those who did not even seem to be aware that a mystery existed, those who had never bothered to seek answers because they had never bothered to ask the questions. Her father had been one of these. His only interest in life had been to make money and to be recognized as a "success" in the community. If life had any meaning or purpose above and beyond that, he seemed not have had any conception of it. He had always considered Elizabeth's preoccupation with questions about the meaning of life as so much foolishness and a waste of time. It was just a temporary brain disorder, he used to say; it came from reading too much poetry. Now in her mid-thirties she apparently still suffered from her "temporary brain disorder." But she was not unhappy. Despite her father's prediction that "she will *always* be unhappy; she *likes* to be unhappy," she could say, without fear of contradiction, that she was *very* happy. In truth, she could not have been happier. Nevertheless, she still found herself wondering at times who she was and why she had been born into the world in the first place, and whether life had any significance beyond the immediate reality of the day. Life on the surface of the pond was pleasant enough, but she could not help but wonder what, if anything, lay hidden in the depths.

Being born into the world, she mused, was like walking into a theater in the middle of a play. If she were to walk into a theater in the middle of a play, the first thing she would have to do would be to get herself oriented. She would have to know, what is this play all about? what's going on here? what did the playwright have in mind? In the theater she could, between acts, ask the person sitting next to her who had seen the play from the beginning. Or, if she wanted more than a summary, if she wanted to know every scene and every line of dialogue in detail, she could later read the play or see it again from the opening curtain. But it was important for her to *know*. Her mind would not be at ease until she got her bearings. The same was true whenever she found herself in a strange house or in a strange town or in an unfamiliar outdoor setting. Before she could feel comfortable, she had to have at least a general idea as to the layout.

But the world at large afforded no such opportunity. Being born into the world was like walking into a theater in the middle of a play in which *no one* had seen it from the beginning, and in which *no one*, not even the actors on the stage, seemed to have any idea what was going on. If there was a script, no one seemed to have a copy, or ever remember seeing one. As to the playwright, no one seemed to know of his whereabouts, or if, in fact, a playwright even existed.

In any such theater there is likely to be at least one philosopher whose humors require him to make sense of the play, to impose order on the chaos, to find meaning in that which, on the face of it, appears to be devoid of meaning. But the great majority of people, it seemed to Elizabeth, are perfectly content to walk into the theater in the middle of the play, watch it for an act or two, then get up and walk out without having the slightest curiosity about what they have just seen and heard. Any slight curiosity they might have is generally satisfied by the speculation of the first philosopher to reach their ears. Here in the mountains of North Carolina the first speculation concerning the meaning of life to reach the ears of most people was that of the Judeo-Christian religion, and it was generally accepted by one and all readily and without question. Elizabeth thought it ironic that these isolated mountain people, who were normally suspicious of anyone and anything that came from the outside world, should so readily accept a system of beliefs that had its origin not in the green hills of the Appalachian Mountains, but far across the ocean in the deserts east of the Mediterranean, amongst a small, relatively obscure tribe of Semitic people whose culture, language, and even alphabet were totally different from their own. And she was almost certain that had any of these same people walked into a theater in another part of the world–in Arabia or China or India, say–had they been born there rather than here, they would just as readily have accepted some other system of beliefs.

What Elizabeth couldn't understand was, why were so many people so indifferent to this intolerable state of affairs? Why weren't people screaming to know the truth? Why weren't more people standing up in the middle of the play and *demanding* to know what was going on? What in all of life could be more important than knowing the answer to that one simple question: *what is this all about?* How could anyone who had passed beyond the threshold of consciousness *not* think about this? How could anyone *not* be curious? How could anyone *not* wonder? Was it because most people had not yet attained the level of consciousness that allowed them to question the meaning of life? According to the philosophers, man was the only animal who had attained self-awareness. This is what separated him from the rest of creation. The "lower" animals were aware of their surroundings, conscious of their environment, but man's consciousness had evolved further. He was not only conscious of his environment, but also of himself. He was conscious of being conscious. At least that's what the philosophers said. But, Elizabeth wondered, just how widespread was this self-awareness? Was it something that every member of the human species possessed, or was it something that only the rare few–the geniuses, the poets, the mystics–attained? From her own limited experience in the world, she would have had to conclude that most people do not exhibit a level of awareness appreciably higher than that of the so-called "lower" animals. They are born into the world, they eat, they sleep, they struggle to stay alive, they reproduce themselves, and they die. How was that any different from any of the myriad "lower" forms of life that inhabited these woods around her? Did not every insect, bird, reptile, and mammal do the same? No, in her experience it was the rare person who reflected on the meaning of life and on his or her place in the grand scheme of things.

When she allowed her thoughts to drift in this direction, she always became angry with herself, because she was saying in effect that she herself was one of those rare people. Yet she did not feel superior to other people. Even if her line of reasoning were correct and she did possess a greater degree of consciousness, a higher level of awareness, than the majority of people with whom she came in contact, she would have been the first to acknowledge that she had not created her own consciousness any more than her brother-in-law Isaac had created these mountains. To her, consciousness was the supreme miracle of creation. She accepted her portion of it as the greatest possible gift, and in a thousand silent prayers every day she gave thanks to Whomever or Whatever had bestowed that gift upon her. But she was under no illusion that greater awareness necessarily brought greater understanding. Having the power of mind to ask the questions was no guarantee that one would ever find the answers. Wondering did not automatically bring wisdom–but, in Elizabeth's view, it was a necessary first step. She may not have found all the answers to Life's big questions, but at least, she thought, she had the power of mind to discern between that which was reasonable to believe and that which was patently absurd. And she would not have traded that power of mind for all the Absolute Truth in the world.

She half-expected to be struck by lightning or have her consciousness snuffed out every time she had thoughts of this kind as divine punishment for her intellectual arrogance. As an antidote to her conceit, she always thought of Daniel. Daniel never asked these metaphysical questions about life. He simply *lived* life. He ate, he slept, he hoed his corn, and, not least, with her help he had reproduced himself in the form of an extraordinary little girl. And one day he would die. But he was a happy man. And if she had suggested to him that his approach to life was little different from that of the beasts of the fields or the wild creatures of the forest, he would not have been insulted. On the contrary, he probably would have taken it as a compliment. The wild creatures knew their place in the scheme of things, and so it seemed did Daniel. It was a though he knew at some deep unconscious level exactly why he was in the world and how to live his life. It was as though, deep inside his being, all those questions which perplexed Elizabeth were answered. He could not have begun to express any of it verbally, but somehow he *knew*, just as the wild creatures of the woods *knew*. Perhaps, Elizabeth thought, the deficiency lay not in other people but in *her*. She always took a strange sort of comfort in this thought. She always felt ashamed when her impatience with other people's lack of curiosity led her to conclude that she had been blessed with greater mental power, and she always felt a sense of relief when she considered this more humbling alternative. Perhaps she too knew at some deep unconscious level the answers to all her questions. She had always thought it unlikely that she would ever know *everything* she wanted to know, and she never would have been so foolish as to stake her own personal happiness on finding the answers. But still, if there was any way of knowing, at a conscious level, in a clear waking state, why she was in the world and what life was all about, she would not have passed up the opportunity to explore that path. And now, just possibly, she had such an opportunity—an opportunity to learn from someone who had been endowed with a gift of consciousness at least as generous as her own, someone whose power of insight into the nature of reality and the reason for being was just possibly greater than that of anyone she had ever known. And that someone was eleven-year-old Sarah.

Had Sarah really been outside of her body as she had claimed?—or, as she believed, as she would not have claimed it if she didn't believe it. According to Sarah, she had been outside her body and actually looking at her own face!—with all her senses and mental faculties in tact. Elizabeth almost envied her the experience. If she herself had had such an experience, the ages-old philosophical question concerning the existence of the soul would have been settled for all time—at least to her satisfaction.

And what about Sarah's extraordinary claim that she had been to "Heaven," that she had been to worlds beyond this earth? Were these other worlds to be understood as real places, as places "out there," or were they to be understood as psychic states, as other states of consciousness? And if they were "only" other states of consciousness, were they somehow less real? She considered again Bishop Berkeley's argument that there may not even be a physical world "out there," that the only reason we even think there is a physical world "out there" is because of our sense impressions—we see it, we hear, we touch it—but these sense impressions are *mental* events, psychic events. They are things happening inside our brains—or wherever mental events take place—not "out there." From this point of view, mental events become not only more real than the physical world—insofar as they alone have any power to affect us—but they become quite possibly the *only* reality. Even if we were to concede the independent existence of the physical world—that is, to concede that the physical world would continue to exist even if no mind were here to perceive it—as Elizabeth was perfectly willing to do—there was still the possibility that the entire physical universe, which seems to real to us, might be nothing more than a mental event after all—a mental event in a much vaster mind: a thought or dream in the infinite mind of "God." Again, pure speculation. But Sarah's statement that "in Heaven thoughts are the most real things there are," suggested that, in this world too, mind, not matter, might be the ultimate reality.

At the first available opportunity Elizabeth fully intended to ask Sarah to repeat her accounts of her journeys outside her body, and to ask numerous questions, in an attempt to come to a better understanding of what Sarah had experienced. In the past Sarah had always shown a reluctance to talk about any private experience which she thought might be out of the ordinary in any way, partly out of a desire not to upset her parents, partly out of fear that people might call her crazy, as her cousin Otis had done when she had first told him that she could see light coming out of people. The world of her mind was her own private world—her secret world—and in the past she had always kept it well-guarded. But the visit to "Heaven" seemed to have changed all that. Apparently the experience had been so exciting, so overwhelming, so positively joyous, that she had felt the need to share it with others. Perhaps she would be more willing now to talk about other subjects as well, subjects which, in the past, she could be persuaded to talk about only after much coaxing, if at all. Elizabeth was determined to make Sarah understand that her purpose in interrogating her was not to ridicule her or to pass judgement on the soundness of her mind, but only to learn, to understand. She hoped to persuade Sarah to open up, to allow her to peer into the secret world of her mind. She would encourage Sarah to talk about her thoughts, her dreams, her perceptions—and her friend Kati. She would especially encourage

Sarah to try to remember things that Kati had told her over the years, because if, as Sarah insisted, Kati really was a being from one of the higher heavens, regardless of what she might have been during her Earth life, then she would certainly be in possession of a great amount of knowledge that would be of interest to a mere earth-bound creature like herself who was seeking answers to Life's great questions. It promised to be a fascinating adventure, an exciting exploration–one to which she was looking forward.

Sarah, for her part, was about to embark upon an exploration of her own. As she helped her father hoe the cornfield on the hillside behind the house, she found herself once again engaged in a conversation about Heaven. Just as at breakfast, the conversation consisted mostly of questions and answers, with Daniel asking the questions and Sarah doing her best to answer them. There was one question, however, which Sarah had been wanting to ask *him*.

"Daddy, at breakfast, why did you ask me if I had seen Jesus when I was in Heaven?"

"Why? Well, I reckon I always figgered that Jesus was sort of in charge up in Heaven . . . What was that that your mother said about Heaven bein' like a mansion?"

" 'In my father's house are many mansions.' "

"Right. Well, I reckon I always figgered that Jesus sort of owned that big house with all them mansions, an' that ever'one who went to Heaven sort of went thar as his guest."

"I don't know, Daddy. I think if anyone *owns* Heaven, it would be God."

"Well, sure, Sarah, but Jesus *is* God."

"Jesus is *God*?"

"'Course he is, Sweetheart. You knew that."

"No, Daddy, I didn't. Mother told me that some people believe that Jesus was the *son* of God, but she never told me that Jesus *was* God . . . Don't you believe that Jesus was the son of God?"

"Yup, Sweetheart, sure do."

"I don't understand, Daddy. How could Jesus be both God *and* the son of God?"

"Well, I reckon I ain't too clear on that myself, but that's what it says in the Bible."

"Do you know where in the Bible it says that?"

"No, don't reckon I do, but hit's in thar somewhar. Your Aunt Hester could tell yuh. Somewhar in thar hit says that God had t' become a man in order t' save us from our sins. He had t' sacrifice hisself . . ."

"What does 'sacrifice' mean?"

"Hit means he gave up his life t' save us. By dyin' on the cross, Jesus took away all our sins. He saved the whole world."

Sarah fell into deep thought. As she worked her hoe in and out amongst the tender young corn plants she pondered her father's words. She decided she had to know more about this man who her father believed to be both God and the son of God, both the owner of Heaven and the saver of the world. After supper she would ask to borrow her mother's Bible. She expected she would also have to ask for her mother's assistance. She had no doubt that the assistance would be readily forthcoming. Whenever she undertook an exploration of this kind, she knew that she could always count on her mother to join her.

11

DEATH IN THE FAMILY

> Am I not more a child today
> Than when I was a child before?
> Did ever first snow thrill me so,
> First flower of spring delight me more?

Elizabeth looked out the window. It was still quite dark, but in the faintest light of new morning, she could see that it was snowing again. She had gotten up earlier than usual. A poem had come stealing silently into her thoughts as she lay in bed in the dark, and she had wanted to write it down before it drifted off into the effluvial dream-mist of the night and was lost forever. In the shadowy twilight darkness that filled the cabin, she had stoked the fire in the stove and added two more chunks of wood, quietly, very quietly, so as not to waken Daniel or Sarah. Then she had wrapped herself in her woolen shawl and sat down at the table in the kitchen next to the front window and started to write down the words that had so gently but insistently roused her from her sleep. She wrote a second verse.

> Did ever clear fresh draught of Life
> Taste so sweet?–like April rain!–
> Or fill me so to o'erflowing,
> Or rush so madly through my brain?

It sounds like a spring poem, she thought to herself, not like something someone would write in the dead of winter. But she felt vibrantly alive, filled with spring energy. The snow seemed to have the same energizing effect on her that it had on Sarah. But it was not only the snow, it was the whole setting: the gently falling snow, yes, but also the solitude of their high mountain abode, the deep forest, the dreamy pre-dawn twilight, the snugness of the cabin, the warmth of he stove. It all combined to have an exhilarating effect on her soul.

> *I want to play! I want to run!*
> *To chase the dancing beams of sun!*
> *To climb the hills and skip the brooks,*
> *To touch the flowers one by one!*
>
> Are flowers not more lovely now
> Than any I had in childhood seen?
> Is not the forest more enchanted,
> First bud of spring more tender green?
>
> Did always birds so joyous sing?
> Was always Earth so filled with song?
> Were younger ears too small to hear,
> Young voice too weak to sing along?
>
> *I want to sing! I want to shout!*
> *Like whirling dervish, spin about!*
> *I cannot screw the cork back in,*
> *The song inside me must come out!*
>
> Did e'er I so delight to know
> Sun's morning kiss upon my face,
> The soft caress of Wind and Rain,
> The peace of Moon's night-long embrace?
>
> Was I once caught in stardust storm,
> Or moonbeam struck while sleeping lay,
> To be seduced each night by Night,
> To fall in love each morn with Day?

Elizabeth wrote the date—January 14, 1941—and laid down her pen. It was not Elizabeth Barrett Browning, she thought to herself, smiling, but at least it had captured some of the childlike joy and delight with which she seemed to be so filled these days.

She and Daniel and Sarah had been in the mountains almost eight years now, and there had been moments during that time when she had thought that if her happiness were any more intense, her heart would surely burst, and the joy it contained would fall like rain upon the Earth for a hundred years to come.

Whenever Elizabeth reflected on her life—and it was in her nature to do so often—she realized that the two people with whom she shared her life most intimately were in no small way responsible for the joy she felt inside. She often wondered what course her life might have taken had she never met Daniel. Would she now be married to some wealthy banker or lawyer or real-estate baron, living in a fine house in Springfield or Boston, hosting dinner parties, frequenting museums, attending the theater? She could see herself in such a role, but she could not see herself finding much satisfaction in it. She wouldn't mind going to the theater. At times she missed the theater, but not so much that she would have been willing to give up her life in the mountains for life in any of the great cultural centers of the Northeast. She was under no illusion that cultural life in itself was sufficient. Quite the contrary. She knew that if she lived in the city, she would spend many hours in the libraries and museums and theaters in an attempt to escape the artificiality of her life, but in the end would become only more desperate and disillusioned. Art had that effect upon her. Again it was her passion for reality that could not be suppressed. She could never be satisfied simply *reading* the great poets: she wanted to live a poetic life, the kind of life that might inspire one to *write* poetry. She could never be satisfied simply *looking* at the great paintings: she wanted to be *in* the paintings. She remembered how, when she was younger, every time she looked at Millet's "The Gleaners," she found herself wishing that she could *be* one of those simple, hard-working French peasant women gleaning grain from the fields: wanting to *feel* the sun on her back and the sweat on her face; wanting to *taste* the dust in her mouth; wanting to *hear* the songs and the shouts of the workers and the creaking of the wagon wheels. Those women seemed to be doing something vital, something real, something useful, while all *she* was doing was looking at a painting. Life–*real* life–was out there for those with the courage to pursue it. It had always seemed a tragic waste of life to her to settle for anything less, to spend one's brief tenure on Earth far removed from the real business of life, to confine one's self to the role of spectator and critic, to experience life only through literature and art, only vicariously. Surely a little perspiration and a few tired muscles was a small price to pay for a real life.

Where would she be had she never married at all? That was a question to which no clear answer was ever forthcoming. It was not likely that at the age of thirty-nine she would still be shutting herself up in a room somewhere with her books. Possibly she would have eventually gone back to college and perhaps become a teacher. Or perhaps she could have supported herself by selling her drawings or doing illustrations for books and magazines. There were any number of things she *might* have done, but would any of them have satisfied her need to live a whole human life?

Fortunately Daniel had saved her from all those other lives she might have lived. She had married him against the most strenuous objections of her parents, but she had never regretted it. She knew that, intellectually, he was not her equal, but she did not respect him any the less on that account. He could not discuss poetry–or even stay awake through a reading of it–but he *could* build a house for poets to live in. He could not follow a philosophical argument beyond the first major premise, but he *could* grow food for philosophers to eat. He could even build a table for eating philosophers to sit at, and chairs for them to sit on. He may not have been able to offer learned critiques on the great works of art, but he knew a fine-looking piece of black-cherry wood when he saw it. No, Daniel did not have the education in literature and the arts that she did, but he had a perfectly good mind and a rich storehouse of practical knowledge. He knew how to survive in the world. Had *he* been the sole inhabitant of a desert island, he would have survived easily–provided he had the raw materials from which food, clothing, and shelter could be derived. He might have had difficulty on an island of solid rock, devoid of vegetation, but if he were given anything at all with which to work, the skill and the ingenuity would not be lacking. For all practical purposes, the remote mountain farm on which they lived might just as well have been an uncharted island somewhere in the far Pacific. They were now producing for themselves almost everything they needed, relying very little on the outside world. In fact, had the outside world not existed, their lives might even have been easier, as then they would not have had to come up with the money each year to pay the tax collector. Not that making money had proved to be difficult. Again, Daniel's skill and ingenuity–and his treasure-house of mountain lore–had served them well. Over the years they had made a little money by gathering and selling nuts and sourwood honey, but most of their income had come from Daniel's whirligig business. Sales had been slow the first couple of years, but gradually, as money became more readily available–especially to city-dwellers–and as more and more of those city-dwellers seemed willing to spend their money on cars and their vacations in the mountains, sales had increased correspondingly. And now that the Smoky Mountains were officially a national park– President Roosevelt himself had come down from Washington just a few months before, on Labor Day, 1940, to dedicate it–Daniel expected to sell his whirligigs almost as fast as he could make them. Already he had acquired a reputation all over the mountains as the "whirligig man." This had inspired him, in a fit of good humor, to make a sign to hang over his workshop door, an oak board with the inscription, "D. Wicker, Whirligig Maker." The sign itself was so beautiful–Daniel having carved out the letters with the same skill and care with which he did everything–that Elizabeth thought it a shame that more people couldn't see it. If Daniel's whirligig business ever failed, she mused to herself, he always had another business waiting in the wings: D. Wicker, Sign Maker. She took comfort in knowing that, one way or another, Daniel would always find a way to survive in the world–even in the civilized world.

Elizabeth was aware that she had always romanticized Daniel and his humble origins. To her he had always been like Rousseau's noble savage: a natural man unspoiled by the excesses of civilization and pompous learning. He was an innocent. There was no sophistry, deceit, or hypocrisy in him. She was also aware that *he* had always romanticized *her*. He had always seen her as a living embodiment of culture and refinement, of elegance and proper learning. He made no secret of the fact that he worshipped her, had always worshipped her, from that very first day that they met in Forest Park. His adoration of her was reflected in his behavior. He was ever solicitous of her physical and emotional well-being, ever anxious that she might be working too hard or finding life in the mountains too austere, too lonely. He was ever kind and considerate, never disrespectful. He never raised his voice in anger at her. He would sooner have had his tongue torn from his mouth than say something that might hurt her feelings. Whenever there was a decision to be made, especially in regard to Sarah's upbringing and education, he would consult with her, and would, more often than not, defer to her greater intelligence. Daniel had always accepted the fact that she had the superior mind. It wasn't just that she had had more schooling. She had, in his words, been "born smarter." More than once she had overheard him tell Sarah, "Go ask your mother. She knows ever'thang." He seemed to have no problem at all accepting this difference in their respective mental capacities. On the contrary, he often tended to exaggerate the difference, depreciating his own and exalting hers. Whether he did this because he was so comfortable in his own sense of self-worth that he had no need to believe himself to be the equal of his wife in intelligence as well, or because he was such a genuinely humble man that the seeds of envy could find in him no soil in which to take root, Elizabeth was never quite sure. Perhaps it was a little of both. Or perhaps it was simply out of his great and generous love for her that he could, without thought for himself, elevate her at his own expense. He had told her over the years— had told her so many times that she could not doubt it—that he loved her more than he loved his own life. But he would not have had to tell her at all. His actions spoke for themselves. Day in and day out, in countless ways, he demonstrated his love for her. It was Daniel's deep and abiding love that was the rock of her life, the foundation of her happiness, the solid ground from which she could launch herself into flights of ecstasy.

It was Daniel too who had brought her to these North Carolina hills. One could not help but feel alive in this wild mountain setting, where the pulse of life throbbed so powerfully, so insistently, that one was almost compelled to fall into resonance with it. It was winter now and the world outside the cabin was a quiet one, but Elizabeth knew that soon enough spring would return and with it would come the great re-awakening of creation. The still, white world of winter, as restful and as alluring as it was, would be transformed in a matter of weeks into a spectacle of color and motion almost too dazzling to behold. Here one did not have to seek out the wonders of creation: here wonders assaulted you constantly from all sides. Beauty beat on you so relentlessly that sometimes you feared that the walls of your mind must surely collapse. Only the old and foolish resisted, Elizabeth mused: the young and the wise surrendered at once. She knew that the physical environment in which she found herself had much to do with her having been able to retain her childlike sense of wonder into middle age. She may have been able to have retained it elsewhere, possibly even within the confines of her white picket fence back in Springfield, but it was so much easier here.

Then there was Sarah. Sarah had been a gift, a bonus. Elizabeth had never thought about having children when she was younger, back when she was in her late teens and early twenties, before she was married. She knew that other young women that age did, and, indeed, for many, their primary objective in life seemed to be to get married and raise a family. Elizabeth had not made a decision *not* to have children. It was just something she had never thought much about one way or the other. As carefully as she had planned other aspects of her life, she had not planned Sarah. She had *chosen* Daniel. In a sense she had even chosen the mountains. From the day of her marriage she had secretly nurtured the hope that Daniel would one day take her back to the home of his boyhood, and when he lost his job during the Depression, it was she who had suggested that they move to

North Carolina. But she had not chosen Sarah. Sarah had been a gift. Being with Sarah, watching her grow up, watching her charge through childhood like an explorer on a great voyage of discovery, had been for Elizabeth an excitement and a joy that had come as a windfall from Heaven.

Now, at the age of fourteen, Sarah was blossoming into a beautiful young woman. She had grown tall, almost as tall as Elizabeth herself. She had changed over the years, from the exuberant little girl who could not keep still, who *had* to be outside, who *had* to be running, to a very composed young woman, graceful as ever in movement, but more serene, less hurried and frenetic. She had lost none of her enthusiasm, none of the brightness in her eyes, but her enthusiasm was quieter now, more controlled, the brightness in her eyes less the brightness of curiosity and excitement, more the brightness of loving tenderness. It was as if all that wild kinetic energy had been transformed into pure radiant energy, pure luminosity. Elizabeth could cite the hour and the day that all this change had started to take place: it was that day in the spring of 1938 when Sarah had been to "Heaven." There was no longer any doubt in Daniel's mind what had happened that day: an angel had come and taken Sarah to Heaven, and now Sarah had become an angel herself. Elizabeth was not quite so certain as Daniel what had happened that day, but she knew that, whatever it was, the experience had left Sarah a changed, almost transfigured, person. She had become, in Daniel's words, an "angel of sweetness and light." Elizabeth may not have used Daniel's exact words, but she had to agree that her little girl—the little girl she had brought into the world and had nurtured so lovingly—had become an extraordinary presence.

Over the years visitors to their remote mountain home had been few and far between. Daniel's brother Jacob had spent the better part of two weeks working with Daniel that first winter, that winter that Daniel had spent mostly by himself, working on the house. But Jacob had not been back up in the eight years since then, though every time he saw Daniel he mentioned how one day he would like to pay another visit to see what Daniel had done with the old Puckett place. Isaac occasionally expressed a similar interest, but Daniel did not think it likely that Isaac would ever go to the trouble of actually making the trip, since it could not be made by motorized conveyance. Nathan, on the other hand, had visited them several times, once in the spring of 1936, when he had helped Daniel plant apple trees, and twice since. As the modern world with its electrical wires, telephones, and gasoline cars pushed ever more intrusively into the hills and hollows of western North Carolina, Nathan seemed to need to retreat from time to time up into the mountains, "back where folks still live the way God intended." He and Hester and Otis had spent two days with Daniel and his family in the summer of 1937, and two years later he and Otis had visited for four days. On each occasion Nathan had had difficulty making his departure—he had come to envy Daniel his isolation—but in the end had decided that it was his duty to go back down the mountain to do battle with encroaching civilization.

Hunters occasionally happened by too, but, in general, visitors were rare, especially so in the winter.

Consequently, it came as quite a surprise when one Saturday evening in February of 1941, as the family had just sat down to supper, a loud knocking was heard on the door. After a brief exchange of looks of wonderment around the table, Sarah got up to go to the door, but before she could reach it, it opened and Isaac stepped in.

"You gwine t' leave me a-standin' out thar in the freezin' cold all night?" he asked in his characteristically brusque but harmless manner. He closed the door behind him.

"Uncle Isaac!" exclaimed Sarah in surprise. She gave him a quick hug and backed away before he had a chance to crush her.

Isaac studied Sarah and shook his head. "Just look at you! Hain't you somethin'! I do believe you get purtier ever' time I see you." He glanced at Daniel and Elizabeth, who had also risen to greet him, but his eyes came back to Sarah. "The last four or five miles I been a-cussin' you all for livin' so gaw-danged far away from the rest of the inhabited world, but lawsy, one look at this young'un of yours an' suddenly I'm a-thinkin' hit was worth ever' sore-footed step of it."

Sarah blushed. Daniel, smiling nervously, reached in front of her and shook Isaac's hand. Daniel knew that Isaac would not have walked all the way up the mountain on a cold winter's day to pay them a social call, and he waited apprehensively to learn the reason for his brother's visit.

"Hit's Emily, Dan'l," said Isaac, turning suddenly gravely serious, "she passed away night before last."

"Oh no!" cried Elizabeth.

"The fun'ral's gwine t' be Monday. I thought you might like t' be thar."

"Yes, of course," said Daniel solemnly.

For the next half-minute the four stood in silence as the shock of the tragic news was absorbed.

"Isaac," said Elizabeth in a subdued voice, "we were just about to sit down to supper. You're welcome to join us. And of course you'll spend the night with us. Daniel can fix you up a place to sleep here in the kitchen. Then tomorrow we'll all go down to your place together."

Isaac agreed. Daniel sadly nodded his consent.

A cold raw wind beat against the fifty to sixty mourners who had gathered in the cemetery on the hill behind the Rushing Creek Baptist Church to pay their last respects to the deceased and to comfort, as best they knew how, the bereaved widower. Standing over the coffin, the Reverend Lewis Eby, Bible in hand, looked around the circle of downcast, tear-lined faces huddled together against the wind as he delivered his eulogy. Over the course of the past forty-two years he had delivered many eulogies among these tombstones, to many of these same faces. He always tried to be generous in his eulogies—as generous as the particular shortcomings of the deceased allowed—but he found himself on occasion wishing that the one being eulogized had, during his tenure on Earth, shown more consideration for the local preacher, for the one who would one day shoulder the burden of finding something good to say about him when he died. Some who presented themselves for burial gave the eulogizer very little with which to work.

Such was not the case with Emily Wicker. She was one of the good ones. What made her eulogy so difficult was that she was *such* a good one. She and her husband Jacob were beloved by all members of the community for their quiet and gentle manner and their Christian charity. The Reverend Eby shared deeply in the sense of loss. He had been good friends of Jacob and Emily Wicker for many years. It was he who had married them, back in 1912, when, as a pair of shy teenagers, they were just beginning their life together. Over the years he had shared their anxieties and disappointments. He had comforted Emily when Jacob went off to war. He had comforted them both when, after years of trying, they learned that they would be unable to have the children they had wanted so badly. He had comforted Jacob when his father died, and again when his mother died. Having never married himself, having never had children of his own, the Reverend Eby had almost come to look upon Jacob and Emily as his own children, as his own son and daughter. Now his beloved daughter had died, and his son was once again sorely in need of comforting.

The preacher closed his eulogy as always with a prayer to the Lord to look after the one he was now entrusting to more capable hands. When he finished he peered tenderly through his spectacles across the coffin at the grief-stricken face of his friend Jacob, and his heart went out to him. He could not help but notice the young teenaged girl who had stood next to Jacob throughout the ceremony, holding his hand. As the coffin was lowered into the ground, the Reverend Eby's eyes once again sought out the face of the young girl. He knew who she was. Even if he had not been told, he could have guessed. On more than one occasion, when he had been to Jacob and Emily's for

Sunday dinner, Jacob had spoken fondly of this young niece of his, his brother Daniel's daughter who lived up in the mountains.

After the service, as well-wishers began to file past Jacob, each in turn to offer his or her parting words of condolence, Sarah left her uncle's side and wandered pensively among the nearby tombstones. Four generations of Wickers lay buried beneath the withered grass on which she trod. She read the inscription on each tombstone in turn and remembered the lines from *Hiawatha*.

> Pause by some neglected graveyard,
> For a while to muse, and ponder
> On a half-effaced inscription,
> Written with little skill of song-craft,
> Homely phrases, but each letter
> Full of hope, and yet of heart-break,
> Full of all the tender pathos
> Of the Here and the Hereafter . . .

Suddenly she came upon a small grave marker that caused her to gasp for breath. She knelt down and read the inscription:

Here Lies Ruth
Beloved Daughter of Benjamin and Hannah Wicker
Died May 2, 1904
Aged 11 Years, 1 Month, 19 Days

Sarah had fought back her grief up to this point, but now she felt the tears coming into her eyes. Suddenly she was aware of someone standing over her. She stood up to find her mother looking at her sympathetically.

"It's sad, Mother," she sobbed, "it's so very sad. Uncle Jacob has lost everyone who was ever dear to him. First, his sister Ruth, then his mother, and now Aunt Emily."

Elizabeth put an arm around her daughter. "He hasn't lost *you*."

Sarah tried to force a smile, then looked down again at the small grave marker. But she was thinking about what her mother had said.

"Do you think it would be all right if I stayed with Uncle Jacob for a few days?"

"Your Daddy and I will miss you," replied Elizabeth after a quiet moment's reflection, "but I think your Uncle Jacob needs you more than we do just now . . . You're right, it's very sad that he should have to suffer like this. He's a good man, Sarah. I'm sure he has many friends, all of whom would be willing to do just about anything for him, but I think you're the one person who might be able to make a difference. He's always had a very special affection for you."

Sarah continued to stare at the small grave marker, lost in thought. Elizabeth looked around for Daniel and found him standing at the grave site a short distance away, between Isaac and Jacob, receiving friends of the family. Since arriving at the cemetery, Elizabeth had noticed a number of women in the crowd casting suspicious glances in her direction from time to time, apparently remembering the winter she had lived at Nathan and Hester's and had not gone to church. She knew that she might never be forgiven by these good Christian ladies for so grievous a sin.

"I wonder what she was like," mused Sarah, as much to herself as to her mother.

"Who?" asked Elizabeth, turning back to her daughter.

"Aunt Ruth."

Elizabeth looked down at the small grave. "Have you ever asked your Uncle Jacob about her?"

"I did when I was little, but Daddy later told me that I shouldn't ask Uncle Jacob about her because it makes him sad."

"Apparently your Aunt Hester doesn't like to be reminded of her either. I once read Wordsworth's poem 'Ruth' to her and Nathan—you know the one—and Hester got so upset she left the room. Ruth's death must have been a terrible loss for all of them. Your father was only four at the time but he heard later that his mother—*their* mother—was never quite the same after Ruth died."

The irony of what they were doing did not escape Elizabeth. They had come to the cemetery to pay their last respects to Jacob's wife Emily, and here they were, she and Sarah, standing at another grave and mourning for a little girl who had died thirty-seven years before—a little girl whom neither of them had ever known.

"She died in May, Mother," lamented Sarah, her voice breaking with pathos. "She died in the spring of the year."

The next morning Daniel and Elizabeth headed back up the mountain but Sarah did not go with them. For the next three days she stayed with Jacob, cooking his meals for him, keeping his house, and providing what companionship she could. Jacob knew that he was not the best of companions during those three days, preferring to be alone and quiet with his grief most of the time, but he was glad that Sarah was there and he made sure she knew it by an occasional teary-eyed smile and a gentle patting of her hand. By the evening of the third day Sarah sensed that her uncle might be willing to talk—or at least to listen—and there was something she had never told him, something which she thought might be of interest, and perhaps even of some comfort, to him now.

"Uncle Jacob, do you remember that first night I ever stayed in your house? You told me about souls. You said, souls are more real than bodies."

Jacob smiled at her and nodded. "As I remember," he said quietly and with effort, "you weren't too sure about souls because I told you you couldn't see them or touch them."

"That's right. But I'm sure now, Uncle Jacob. And you were right. Souls *are* more real than bodies. We *are* souls. We aren't bodies at all. I know, because I have been outside of my body. I have even been to Heaven. I have been to Heaven, Uncle Jacob."

Jacob looked at her curiously.

"When I was a little girl I had a friend named Kati. She wasn't like you and me. She didn't have a body, at least not an Earth body. For some reason, which I've never really understood, I was the only one who could ever see her or hear her. I couldn't see her all the time, only when she would let me. But my mother and father could never see her at all. I haven't seen her myself now in nearly three years, not since she took me to Heaven. But she was so beautiful, Uncle Jacob. She was made of white light, and she came from a world where everything is made of white light. My Daddy says she must have been an angel. I don't know, maybe she was what some people call an angel. All I know is, when I was with her in Heaven standing in the midst of all that white light, I felt totally and completely loved. It was an indescribable feeling.

"I don't know where Heaven is, Uncle Jacob, or if it even makes sense to talk about it as though it exists in some *place*. But I know I was there. I know it's real. And I know that that wonderful white-light love that I felt inside me was real. Kati told me that I had touched the heart of God. It's like, everything that exists–everything that ever comes into being–is part of this flood-stream of loving white light that is being continuously pumped from the heart of God. And this light, Uncle Jacob, this love, is greater and more wonderful than anything we can imagine."

Jacob's eyes glistened. "I have never doubted it," he said, his face suddenly illumined by a beatific smile. "I know that God sometimes works in mysterious ways, an' we cain't always understand some of the thangs He does, but I've never questioned His love." He continued to look at her lovingly, tenderly, curiously.

The next morning Sarah prepared to take her leave. She knew the parting would not be easy for either of them. Jacob asked if he might accompany her as far as the hard road. As they walked together out the long lane, neither of them spoke. The sun was shining brightly but the morning air was still quite cold. When they reached the end of the lane they stopped and turned to face each other. For a long peaceful moment they stood silently in the bright winter sunlight looking into each other's eyes and smiling.

"I'm a-gwine t' miss you," said Jacob wistfully. "That room upstairs will always be yours. You come back any time you like, you hear me?"

"I will, Uncle Jacob. I'll come back soon . . . I love you." She kissed him on the cheek, then turned toward the mountains rising to the west and began her long journey home.

The winter of 1941 did not end on the first day of spring. The warblers did not arrive in March. The serviceberry trees did not bloom the first week in April. As Daniel walked across his still-frozen cornfield, he reconciled himself to a late spring. There was nothing to do but wait until the warring forces of winter and spring had signed their annual truce. Spring would win in the end, but winter sometimes proved a staunch adversary, refusing to surrender until it had occupied much of its enemy's territory.

The war between winter and spring had raged at fever pitch in recent years, with little regard for the vernal equinox–the traditional day of truce-signing–and with no clear victor. The battle had surged back and forth, with spring gaining the upper hand one year, winter the next. Spring had won decisively in 1937, routing winter, nearly driving it off the calendar. It had been so warm in January that year that flowers and trees had bloomed, snakes had revived, and bears, which had only been in hibernation a month, had come out again and had been roaming the woods. If the bears were confused that winter, so were the farmers. Every day for a week during that winter warm spell, Daniel had entertained the notion of getting his crops in early, but in the end had decided that only a fool would plant corn in January.

The following year winter had fared little better. After a short reign, it had been forced to yield once again to a warm, early spring. But two years later winter had come back with a vengeance. January 1940 had been the coldest January in living memory, with the temperature plunging below zero degrees Fahrenheit night after night. Fortunately Daniel and Sarah had been able to lay in a good supply of firewood. Over the years Sarah had become quite proficient at wielding her end of the two-man saw, and even during the coldest days that winter they had gone out into the woods in search of dead trees for cutting. They had so enjoyed the time spent in the woods together, that they had come to look upon the severe cold more as a chance to test their mettle than as a serious threat to their survival. The current winter of 1941 had not been as cold, but what it had lacked in severity it was now making up for in persistence.

But in the waning days of April, as the ever-increasing forces of spring began to advance up the mountainside, winter did at last begin to retreat. The serviceberry, which had waited so patiently, finally bloomed; wildflowers began to poke their faces through the warming leafmold; and the skyways once again began to fill with waves of migrating birds. It was the time of year that Elizabeth felt most restless, when she too felt the urge to migrate rushing in her blood. At the very least she needed to be outside and moving. It was still too early to put in her garden, despite the calendar, as the soil was still too cold and damp for most seeds. This was the time of year, between spring thaw and planting time, that they normally made an excursion down to Rushing Creek. Elizabeth was avid to go. So were Daniel and Sarah.

The trip down the mountain was a romp. They laughed and sang and carried on like three children on a Sunday picnic. Daniel decided that it was as good a time as any to teach Elizabeth and Sarah some of the traditional mountain dances he had learned in his youth, notwithstanding the unevenness and precarious slope of the dance floor. With first Elizabeth and then Sarah, he went stomping and twirling down the trail. Daniel had never fancied himself a *good* dancer, but what he lacked in grace he more than made up for in rambunctiousness. Then Sarah, caught up in the light-hearted spirit of the day, decided to take it upon herself to teach Jesse how to skip.

"You can do it, Jesse, I know you can. Just watch me."

Daniel and Elizabeth doubled over laughing as the mule, incredibly enough, tried to imitate her, albeit not very successfully.

"I think I see what his problem is," laughed Daniel. "He's got two left feet."

Sarah pretended to cover the mule's ears with her hands. "Don't you listen to him, Jesse. I think you did real well."

"Besides," said Elizabeth, poking her husband gently in the ribs, "you're a fine one to talk about having two left feet."

Daniel laughed again.

The further they went down the mountain, the more flowers and trees they found in bloom. Elizabeth was delirious with joy. She recited aloud part of the poem she had written during the winter.

"I want to sing! I want to shout!
Like whirling dervish, spin about!"

She spun around so quickly that she lost her balance and fell. Fortunately Daniel and Sarah were there to catch her. Unfortunately they were not able to keep their own balance. They all fell together in a heap and burst out laughing. From her prostrate position, Elizabeth finished her verse.

"I cannot screw the cork back in,
The song inside me must come out!"

"I think perhaps you've lost the cork altogether, Mother," laughed Sarah.

"I think we better find it quick!" said Daniel, pretending to search the ground with his hands.

Elizabeth laughed. "I think we've *all* gone mad," she said. "I think we've all come down with spring fever and have gone quite mad."

"I think hit's most likely just a tetch of the cabin fever," said Daniel. "Spring is the only known cure . . . 'Course, folks have been known to die from the cure."

They untangled themselves and slowly got to their feet.

" 'Course now," continued Daniel, still laughing, "if we died, we could all go to Heaven. Sarah could introduce us to all her friends up thar. We could build us a cabin in the mountains. I could plant me a cornfield . . ."

They laughed again and continued on their merry way.

They arrived at Nathan and Hester's late in the day, a bit more subdued than they had been in the early morning when they began their long journey. Their plan was to spend the night at Nathan's, go into town the next day, then to spend the second night with Jacob, before heading back up the mountain the third day. As they approached the house they could see Hester bustling about through the kitchen window. They might have felt guilty dropping in on anyone else this close to suppertime, but Daniel knew that Hester would be delighted to see them as always and would not consider herself put upon in the least to have to set three more places at the table. She always seemed to have more than enough food on hand and was only too glad to share it with the right guests—especially if those right guests also happened to be family. Besides, their visit would not come as a complete surprise, as this was the time of year they normally paid Hester a visit. It was something that Hester not only expected, but looked forward to.

"I been expectin' you!" cried Hester, rushing to the door to greet them. "I told Nathan this very mornin', today's the day! Dan'l an' Miss 'Lizbeth an' Sarah will be here for supper. An' sure enough, here you be!"

She embraced them each in turn, talking excitedly as she did so, then took a breath and continued. "I expect you'll want to clean up a bit. Nathan's in the barn; he'll be in soon. Otis, he's s'posed to be doin' his schoolwork, but I expect he's down at the creek fishin'. Mebbe Sarah can help him with his schoolwork after supper. He sure could use it."

"I don't know, Aunt Hester," said Sarah timidly, somewhat overwhelmed by her aunt's effusive greeting, "I've only ever been to the first grade, you know, and I didn't even finish that."

"Aw shucks, child," retorted Hester, dismissing her objection with a wave of the hand, "that makes no differ'nce. You're like your mother. You was born smart." She continued to bustle. "Here comes Nathan now."

After supper the four adults adjourned to the parlor, leaving Otis and Sarah at the kitchen table to work on Otis' homework. In the parlor the conversation soon turned to Jacob.

"How is he, Hester?" asked Daniel.

"I reckon he's mighty lonesome, a-livin' in that big house all by hisself now. But you know Jacob: no matter how bad he's a-hurtin' inside, he don't like to bother nobody else with it. He keeps it to hisself."

"Well now," said Nathan, drawing on his pipe, "he just might not be lonesome for long. Sam Ogle's widow certainly seems to have her eye on him."

"Nathan, that's foolishness an' you know it," snorted Hester. "Jacob will never marry Harriet Ogle. Not after Emily."

"It's true, she's no Emily," replied Nathan in defense, "but he'll never find another Emily. They just don't make them like her anymore."

They don't make them like Jacob anymore either, thought Elizabeth to herself.

"Besides," added Nathan, "Harriet Ogle ain't that bad."

Hester feigned exasperation. "You'll haf t' excuse my husband," she said, turning to Daniel and Elizabeth, "his haid ain't quite thawed out yet from the long winter."

Nathan laughed.

"How old is Jacob?" asked Elizabeth. She could have figured it out easily enough for herself, but she had not participated thus far in the conversation and she wanted the others to know that she too was concerned about her brother-in-law's well-being.

"He'll be fifty next year," answered Hester. "Too old t' go a-courtin' but too young t' spend the rest of his life alone."

"Fifty ain't too old to go courtin'," objected Nathan. "He wouldn't go courtin' no teenager. He'd go courtin' a woman his own age."

"Like Harried Ogle, I suppose?"

"Yes, Hester, like Harriet . . . or someone else."

"I can't imagine Jacob courting anyone," said Elizabeth, anxious to head off another argument over the good widow Ogle. "He seems too shy. How did he court Emily?"

"He never really courted Emily," replied Hester. "They just kind of growed up together. They knowed each other from the time they was young'uns. Jacob, Emily, an' Ruth was all real close. When Ruth died, Emily was the one Jacob turned to. From the time he was about twelve years old, he knowed that one day he was a-gwine t' marry her."

They sat for a while in silence, each absorbed in his or her own private thoughts. Then Nathan turned to Daniel.

"You *are* plannin' t' see Jacob while you're down here, aren't you?"

"Yes," replied Daniel, "we'll be a-gwine down thar tomorruh."

At four o'clock in the afternoon of the following day, the three travelers found themselves walking in the long lane leading to the old Wicker farmstead. Elizabeth was still thinking about things Nathan and Hester had said the night before. She remembered that Daniel had told her years ago that Jacob and Emily had been childhood sweethearts, and she had also known that Jacob and his sister Ruth had been very close. But these had existed as two separate pieces of information in her mind. She had never connected them together. But of course, it only made sense: Jacob, Ruth, and Emily had, all three of them, been close. When Ruth died, Jacob had turned to Emily for comfort. It was only natural. But now Emily had died. Who would he turn to now? Or, Elizabeth wondered, had he already turned to someone? She wasn't thinking of Harriet Ogle.

At his age, Jacob would not court a teenager, Nathan had said. Elizabeth did not think Jacob was courting Sarah. But she knew that the two of them had always had a special affection for each other. There was a bond between them, a beautiful bond of love and friendship–the same kind of bond Jacob had had with Emily. Elizabeth could not help but wonder if the bond between Jacob and Sarah might also develop into something more than friendship.

She found the thought a little disturbing. Sarah was still so very young. Jacob was thirty-five years her elder. He was eight years older than Daniel. Elizabeth had no reason to believe that the relationship between them would ever be anything other than that of loving uncle to loving niece, but here in the Appalachian hill country where girls were often married at the age of thirteen or fourteen, and where there seemed to be no great aversion to marrying blood relatives, Elizabeth decided it would be prudent to be prepared for any and all possibilities. Having so decided, she immediately dismissed the idea from her mind as ludicrous. She was letting her imagination run away with her.

They found Jacob in the barn milking the cows. He appeared to be considerably more composed than when they had last seen him in February. His smile was as tender and sweet as ever, and some of the luster had returned to his eyes.

"I'll make you a deal," Elizabeth said to him after they had all exchanged greetings. "If you invite us to supper, I'll cook it."

Jacob happily agreed to this arrangement, and an hour later the four of them found themselves seated around the table in Jacob's kitchen. Elizabeth could not help but notice the tenderness with which Jacob looked at Sarah, but she decided to make nothing of it, as he looked at *her* with the same tenderness. It was just the way Jacob was.

Before arriving, the three visitors had decided amongst themselves that it would be wise not to talk about Emily to Jacob, or to say anything that might remind him of his recent loss, unless, of course, he himself showed an inclination to talk. Consequently, the conversation that evening revolved around the three visitors themselves and their life in the mountains on the old Puckett place. Jacob sat and listened contentedly as Daniel, Elizabeth, and Sarah took turns giving descriptive accounts and telling of their adventures over the years on their remote mountain farm. Jacob took as much pleasure in the story-tellers themselves as in their stories, in their closeness as a family, in the manifest love they had for one another.

"I reckon I'm just a-gwine t' haf t' get up thar one day for a visit," he said wistfully. It was just what Daniel had expected him to say.

The next morning after breakfast, Daniel went outside to halter the mule and to re-pack the few goods they had purchased the day before. Elizabeth and Sarah stayed in the kitchen to clean up. When they had finished, Sarah approached her mother.

"Mother, I'd like to stay here for a couple more days, if it's all right with you. Uncle Jacob said it would be all right with him."

Elizabeth looked into her eyes and studied her quietly for a moment, then smiled and nodded. "All right, Sarah, but you'd better ask your father. I can't imagine him saying no, but he will be plowing and planting soon and he may need your help."

"Oh, I'd be back in time for planting, but in case Daddy wants to start plowing in the next day or two, I'll talk to Jesse and tell him to behave for him."

Elizabeth knew there was no chance that Daniel would refuse Sarah, and, true to form, he did not. So once again Elizabeth and Daniel and the mule headed back up the mountain alone.

Two days later Sarah was heading out the lane herself. She had thought of staying another day, but the weather was turning warmer and she knew that her father would be anxious to begin plowing and planting. Spring had been late in coming, but now that it was here, farmers would be working all hours to get caught up. The day before, Isaac had sat on his tractor and plowed from early morning until past dark with only brief stops for dinner and supper.

As she neared the end of the lane, she met Isaac's truck turning in. He stopped.

"Leavin' us ag'in, are yuh?" he said, leaning out the window, a wide grin on his face.

"Yes, I've got to get home to help my Daddy plant corn."

"Well, I know that Jacob sure appreciates your visits. We all do. I only wish we had a li'l more time t' visit with yuh. Hit's just that we're a li'l busy right now . . ."

"I understand, Uncle Isaac."

"Well, we'll be a-seein' yuh. You take care of yourself, hear?" He waved, then shifted his truck into first gear and headed down the lane. He had only gone a short distance when he hit his brakes and shifted into reverse. Sarah had to jump off the road as he came roaring back. He stopped again.

"Sorry, I didn't mean t' run over yuh," he grinned.

Sarah watched as his face assumed a more serious expression.

"Listen, Sarah, thar's somethin' I meant t' tell yuh. I was in town just a bit ago, into Lehman's store. Wesley Hicks was in thar buyin' shells for his rifle. Wesley lives over on Whiskey Run Road. You know whar that is, don't yuh? You pass it on your way home."

Sarah nodded.

"Well, I overheard Wesley tellin' Walter about this bear that kilt one of his hogs night before last. Wesley went out huntin' it yesterday, but danged if hit didn't kill one of his dogs. Wesley's got them Plotts hounds. They're as good a bear dog as thar is. Good fighters. Won't quit. An' mean. They'd just as soon tear into another dog or a man as a bear . . . Well, this here bear kilt one of them an' mangled another one purty good. Wesley says he put at least two bullets into this bear. Never even slowed it down. Must be one mean critter, if you ax me. Hit must a-stumbled onto a still in the woods an' drunk a bunch of bad hooch or somethin'. Or mebbe hit took a rifle ball in the haid a li'l while back. Not enough t' kill it, just enough t' make it a li'l crazy . . . Anyway, what I wanted t' tell yuh is, Wesley chased this critter back your way. I know thar's a lot of woods over thar an' thar's prob'bly not much chance of your runnin' into it, but you'd best be careful all the same . . . An' whatever yuh do, if yuh do happen t' see it, don't go tryin' t' get it t' eat out of your hand or anythang foolish like that. Just run for your life."

Sarah smiled. "Thanks, Uncle Isaac. I'll be careful."

Isaac shifted back into first and again headed down the lane. Sarah watched to see if he would stop again. When he did not, she turned and headed for home, singing.

It was a beautiful spring day in the mountains and Elizabeth too was singing as she did the laundry. Daniel had hitched the plow to the mule and had coaxed the animal up the hill to a plot of ground in the upper corner of the field. He had chosen this piece of ground to start his plowing for two reasons. For one, it was newly cleared ground. It was ground which until the previous year had not been plowed–at least, not in recent years, not since the last of the Pucketts had plowed it over thirty years before. Daniel had not yet reclaimed all of the land that the Pucketts had once had cleared, but he was getting close to it. He had deliberately stayed away from the much steeper hillside to the east, not wishing to court the same fate as had befallen old Jeremiah Puckett–if indeed the story was true. This most recently reclaimed plot of ground needed some extra work and Daniel's plan was to make a pass or two over it now, then go over it again when he plowed the whole field.

The other reason he had decided to start on this new ground was that it was the highest point of cleared land on the farm, and, as such, it was the part of the field that dried out first. Also, it afforded the most spectacular view. It was the kind of day that called a man to the high places.

If he had a third reason, it would have been that Sarah would be coming back later in the day, or the next day at the latest, and he knew that she would be disappointed if he had most of the plowing done before she got back. In a sense he was biding his time, but still doing something that would have to be done sooner or later in any case.

He could not help but wonder how many more years Sarah would be with them on the mountain. She was fourteen years old now, almost a grown woman, and though Daniel didn't think there was a man in the world good enough for her, he knew that one day he would lose her. She would one day get married and raise a family of her own. It saddened Daniel to think what life might be like on the mountain without her. He hoped that if she did leave, she wouldn't go too far away. He thought of his sister Hester and how much she had missed *him* during the years he had lived in Massachusetts. He consoled himself with the thought that if Sarah *did* move away, she too might one day come back.

As he followed the plow across the field, he looked down toward the house, at Elizabeth hanging up the wash. He wondered how well she would adjust if Sarah were no longer with them. She and Sarah were as close as any mother and daughter could be. Would Elizabeth be happy living with just him in so isolated a place? Perhaps they *should* have had a second child. Perhaps a third and a fourth. Even if they had *all* been girls. Daniel smiled. Somehow the prospect of having had a houseful of girls did not seem so disagreeable to him now—not if they had all turned out like Sarah.

Suddenly Jesse balked. He stopped dead in his tracks and looked nervously toward the woods, his ears pricked. Daniel looked into the woods but saw nothing.

"C'mon Jesse, hit's just a squirrel."

Still the mule did not move. As Daniel waited, hands on the plow, he again surveyed the breathtaking vista that stretched out before him, allowing his eyes to sink into the soft green spring hills.

"C'mon, Jesse," he repeated, growing a bit impatient, "we got work t' do. Remember what Sarah told you. She told you t' mind me."

Suddenly the mule brayed in alarm and reared up onto its hindlegs. As Daniel had never known Jesse to rear before, he realized at once that this was not one of the mule's normal fits of stubbornness with which he was contending. Jesse had definitely caught the scent of something in the woods—and that "something" was not a squirrel. If the sight of the mule standing, even so briefly, on its hindlegs was a strange one to Daniel, the *sensation* of standing on its hindlegs must have been equally strange to the mule. It was, in fact, so strange that Jesse was unable to recover from the sudden shift in his center of gravity. He would have fallen straight over backwards on top of the plow had he not twisted at the last possible moment, like a cat in the air, and fallen downhill onto his side. The steep incline of the field, which had no doubt contributed to his loss of balance in the first place, had also allowed him to change direction in mid-fall. It all happened so fast that Daniel had no chance whatever to react. His hands were still on the plow when the mule went down, and when the plow overturned, Daniel went with it.

He lay on the ground for a moment, somewhat dazed, as Jesse, still braying in alarm, struggled to his feet and bolted for the barn. Suddenly Daniel found himself being dragged down the hill behind the overturned plow.

"Whoa! Whoa!" he called. But to no avail. As dirt flew into his face, he struggled to free himself from the reins cutting across his neck. Once free, he lay for a moment on the ground, still stunned, and watched as the mule galloped away from him down the hill. Then he looked back toward the woods.

"Elizabeth!" he shouted, "get the gun!"

Daniel's urgent cry caused Elizabeth to look up from her laundry. What she saw caused her to freeze with terror. Before Daniel could get to his feet, the bear was on top of him.

Sarah had deliberated all day whether she should hurry so as to get home as soon as possible to help her father, or to dally and enjoy the spectacle of spring returning to the woods. Unable to come to any clear decision, she had compromised and done a little of both. She had run part of the way, but she had also stopped periodically to watch and listen–and to look in wonder at the dazzling array of blooming trees, shrubs, and flowers that graced both sides of the trail, as if they had been placed there to herald the arrival of some visiting princess or goddess–perhaps Persephone herself. She forgave herself these diversions, and comforted herself with the knowledge that even with these interruptions in her journey, she could still make the ascent of the mountain in less time than anyone else.

She was only about an hour from home when she paused to admire a bed of white-fringed phacelia that covered the forest floor like a carpet of snow. She had seen several such carpets at a distance throughout the course of her journey, but this one was close enough to justify a closer look. Walking into the bed of phacelia, she knelt and examined the delicate white-fringed flowers. Dreamily, she got to her feet and returned to the trail. A short distance further on, at a bend in the trail, she stopped for one last look back at the flower-strewn corridor through which she had just come. When she turned again to resume her homeward journey, she was surprised to find her father standing in front of her.

"Daddy! I didn't hear you."

He had a strange, far-away look on his face, the kind of look he had whenever he stood in his cornfield and looked out across the mountains. Then he turned his head, and Sarah saw that the back of his head behind his left ear was covered with blood.

"Daddy!" she cried. She reached out to support him, but to her utter astonishment her arm went right through him! Suddenly he was gone! She looked around but could find him nowhere. For a brief instant she stood frozen to the spot, trying to comprehend what she had just seen. Then, like a deer fleeing for its life, she ran for home.

When she reached the clearing, she knew that something terrible had happened. Chickens were running loose and she could hear Jesse braying in the woods. The door of the cabin stood ajar, but she did not stop at the cabin. She ran straight for the cornfield. Three-quarters of the way up the hill she found her father lying amidst the rotting corn stubble, his clothing torn, the ground beneath his head soaked with blood. She turned his head to the side and saw the vicious wound. She could see the light leaving his body. Gasping for breath she knelt down beside him.

"Don't leave, Daddy! Please don't leave!"

But she knew that it was too late. Sobbing, choking, struggling for breath, she laid her head down on his chest and cried harder than she had ever cried in her life.

It was nearly dark when she lifted her tear-soaked face from her father's lifeless body. Slowly she got to her feet and walked down the hill. She found Jesse in the woods with the plow overturned and wedged sideways between two trees. She unhitched the mule and led him to the barn. Then she went up into the pasture to get Molly. She fed and watered both animals and locked them in their stables. On the way to the house she inspected the chicken pen and found it in a shambles. The fence had been smashed and chicken feathers were scattered everywhere. The few chickens that had managed to escape had fled into the woods.

Trembling, Sarah pushed open the door to the cabin, afraid of what she might find. Her father's rifle was lying on the kitchen floor but there was no sign of her mother. Carefully she picked up the rifle and returned it to its rack. Then very slowly she pushed open the door to her parents' bedroom. There in the dusky twilight she saw the silhouette of her mother sitting erect on the edge of the bed, facing the wall.

"Mother?" called Sarah, in a trembling voice barely above a whisper.

Elizabeth did not respond. Sarah walked around to the side of the bed and sat down next to her. She leaned her head against her mother's and cried again. After half an hour, Sarah stood up, looked sympathetically into her mother's empty, staring eyes, and kissed her on the forehead. Then she left the room, closing the door behind her.

Climbing into the loft she gathered all the blankets off her bed and carried them downstairs and out the door. As she made her way back up the hillside in the dark, she wondered how a day which had begun so gloriously in sunshine and song could have ended in such devastating tragedy. When she reached her father, she spread a blanket out over him, then, wrapping herself in another blanket, she sat down on the ground next to him. For the rest of the night she sat on the side of the hill keeping watch over her father's body, alone with her thoughts and her memories. She looked up from time to time at the stars overhead, but she did not really see them. Although the night woods were once again alive with the sounds of spring, she heard almost nothing. The only sound that penetrated her consciousness was the plaintive cry of the whippoorwill.

About an hour before dawn she closed her eyes and prayed. "Please, Kati, if you can still hear me . . . please look after him. I can't begin to tell you how much I love him . . . I know he's safe . . . I know he will like it in Heaven when he gets there . . . But I'm going to miss him. I'm going to miss him so terribly much . . ."

For all the next day and all the next night, she continued her wake, leaving her father's side only briefly to tend the animals and to look in on her mother. On the third day it rained, but still she did not move. She continued to sit and pray—and talk to her father's soul. On the morning of the fourth day, when she could see no more light coming from his body, she stood up and gazed far, far out across the mountains.

"When you plant your cornfield, Daddy," she said, her voice quivering with emotion, "plant a big one . . . and wait for me . . . Because one day . . . one day . . . I'm going to come . . . and help you hoe it."

Struggling to force back tears, she lowered her eyes and walked slowly down the hill to the barn. Removing Jesse from his stall, she hitched him to the sledge and began gathering dried brush from the surrounding forest and hauling it to a pile on the hillside just below her father's empty body. To this she added the last of the winter's wood supply from the woodshed. When she was satisfied that the pile of wood and brush was high enough, she rolled her father's body onto it. Then, with tears running down her face, she knelt before the funeral pyre she had constructed, and, with hands trembling, struck a match and lit it.

12

A SOUL RESTORED

Otis hurriedly gathered together the small pile of battered schoolbooks that lay strewn in disarray next to him on the seat, then sprang to his feet and made his way to the front of the bus. With all the desperation of a long-imprisoned convict making a mad dash for freedom, he descended the two steps and lunged through the open doors. The instant his foot made contact with the roadside, a feeling of intense relief rushed through him. Another school day was behind him. In another month school would be out for the summer. Otis was counting the days.

As the creaking school bus groaned into motion again and resumed its slow, lurching movement northward and westward up the hollow, Otis began to amble leisurely down the lane through the woods that led toward home. He had a lot on his mind these days, and always during these walks down the lane in the afternoons, he found himself doing a lot of thinking.

Otis was seriously beginning to doubt his worth as a human being. Primary school had done little to boost his self-esteem, but it was not until he had started going to high school in Haynesville that he had learned the true meaning of humility. Haynesville was only nine miles from Rushing Creek, just on the other side of the mountain, but it might as well have been on the other side of the moon as far as Otis was concerned. The teachers in the high school there seemed to speak another language. Otis hadn't understood one word of algebra all year. He might as well have been sitting in the middle of the Great Arabian Desert as in algebra class, for all the good it did him. He would have been no more lost. History class was little better. His teacher, Mr. Kerr, used big words which he didn't understand, and gave essay questions on his tests, which Otis loathed and dreaded. And English! Otis had thought, when he had first started going to high school in Haynesville, that at the very least he would be able to understand English–his native tongue!–but the teachers there had introduced something called grammar, and had even managed to make English sound like a foreign language!

Otis was sixteen years old, and by the time school resumed again at the end of the summer, he would be seventeen. He was now at an age when he could legally quit school, and hardly had a day gone by since his sixteenth birthday that he had not thought of doing so. He knew that his mother could probably be persuaded to let him quit—she didn't have much use for book-learning anyway—but his father was another matter. His father held doggedly to the view that school served some useful purpose and that Otis and all other boys and girls his age should be grateful that they lived in a country in which education was available to everyone, rich and poor alike. In his father's opinion, universal education was about the only improvement the twentieth century had made over the eighteenth, and, as such, all young people should take advantage of it. Still, if Otis had his way, he'd live way back in the mountains like his cousin Sarah, where he would not be able to take such advantage. On several occasions when he had tried to approach his father about the subject of his quitting school, Otis had argued that a person could learn more by staying home, and he had used Sarah as an example to prove his point. "She's really smart, Pa," he had told his father as recently as last week. "She knows more than any of the kids in school." Nathan was willing enough to concede to Otis one point—that Sarah probably *did* know more than most of the local boys and girls her age who had been educated in the more conventional manner—but he was reluctant to concede the broader argument, that *all* children could learn more by staying home than by going to school.

It seemed to Otis that he had been going to school all of his life. If there had ever been a time when he had not gone to school, he could no longer remember it. He had spent seven years of his life in primary school and, so far, almost four in high school. Normally, four years in high school were all that were required, but as he had failed his freshman year and been forced to repeat it, his sentence had, in effect, been extended to five years. He was now in his junior year, and if he failed it, as he feared he might, his sentence could be extended even further. But even if he passed it, he would not be out of the woods yet. There was still the small matter of his senior year to consider. Every small success he managed to eke out of life seemed to be followed by an even greater opportunity for failure.

If there was any consolation at all in failing, it was that the longer he stayed in school, the longer he could postpone the day when he would have to decide what he would do when he got out of school. Would he stay on the farm with his father and mother? Would he get a farm of his own? Did he even want to be a farmer? A farmer's life was a hard life and a poor one. His father and mother had worked hard all of their lives and had very little to show for it. They didn't even have a car. They never went anywhere. Otis dreamed of one day having a car and going to all the fabulous places beyond the mountains which he had only read or heard about. St. Louis! Atlanta! New Orleans! Richmond! In all his life he had never been further than Asheville. Sometimes on summer evenings he would sit out at the end of the lane and watch cars go by–out-of-state cars from such exotic-sounding places as Virginia, South Carolina, Georgia, Alabama–he had even seen one from Maryland!–cars of tourists who had come to the mountains for a weekend outing and had ventured off the main route to take in the local color. How he wished at times that he could make himself invisible and jump into the back seat of one of those passing out-of-state cars and go home with its occupants, just to see what kind of houses they lived in, what kind of lives they lived. Sometimes he thought that Rushing Creek, North Carolina was the worst place in all the world to have been born. Everyone here was poor and always had been and always would be. Nobody here was going anywhere. How much better to have been born someplace else and to have money–and to have a car!–and to drive through places like Rushing Creek on weekends without ever getting out. His Uncle Daniel and Cousin Benjamin had had the right idea. They had left to go off and look for work elsewhere. Of course, the Depression had forced his Uncle Daniel to return home, but the worst of the Depression was over now. Times were getting better–at least for some people. Times would never get better in Rushing Creek. His Cousin Benjamin was working as an auto mechanic in Raleigh and was making good money. Just last Thanksgiving Benjamin had talked about buying his own auto garage and going into business for himself. When he did, he said that Otis could come and work for him. It was an offer that Otis found well-nigh irresistible. There was only one problem with it. It was the same problem that confounded all of his plans and dreams for a life in the world beyond Rushing Creek: he knew that if he left home, he would break his mother's heart. Would he one day have to choose between his mother's happiness and his own? Just the thought that he might one day have to make such a decision filled Otis with dread.

But perhaps he wouldn't have to decide. Perhaps he might never have a chance to choose. There had been a lot of talk of late about the war in Europe, and what folks were saying was, that if no one else could stop the Germans, then the United States would probably have to get into the war too. In a way Otis almost hoped the United States *would* get into the war—but not too soon. He didn't want it all to be over before he was old enough to enlist. He had never been a very good student, but he figured he could be a pretty good soldier all right. His mother would *have* to let him go into the army. She would understand that. And who knows? He might even return home a war hero. At the very least he would get to see another part of the world. And there would be a further postponement of the day when he would have to decide what to do with his life. Perhaps by the time he got out of the army it would all be clear.

As he emerged from the woods into the orchard, the wondrous spectacle that exploded upon his senses brought him to a full and immediate awareness of the present moment. The apple trees were in magnificent full bloom, and in the warmth of the afternoon sun, bees were busy at work among the fragrant blossoms. But as he walked down the lane between the rows of flowering trees, Otis found himself once again being lulled into reverie, only this time his thoughts drifted, like bees to blossoms, to the sweeter, more pleasant things in his life. His life, much to his relief, did not consist entirely of humiliation and anxiety. Even school had its gratifications. Otis may not have been one of the brightest students in his school, but he was certainly one of the most popular. His polite, shy, and affable manner stood him in good stead with his fellow students, if not with his teachers, and his striking physical appearance–his tall stature, his lithe, muscular body, his conspicuous white-blond hair, and his lucid blue eyes–made him a special favorite of the girls. Why, only that morning Gladys Cole and Tammy Bright had gotten into a fight over him. It was a little embarrassing to have girls vying with one another for his attention–but not so embarrassing that he would have preferred that it hadn't happened. He knew when he invited Gladys to the school picnic that some of the other girls would be disappointed. He had known Gladys practically all of his life, from the time the both of them could walk. Even before they had started to school, they had gone to Sunday School together. She was just a skinny little thing then and Otis had paid her no mind at all, but she had grown considerably in the last ten years, and especially in the last two or three. She had begun filling out in the most interesting places, and it was all Otis could do now to keep his eyes and his mind off her. He realized that any plans he made for the future just might have to include Gladys. Just thinking about her made the apple blossoms smell all the sweeter.

As he approached the house he found a familiar old friend tied to the fence post.

"Hello, Jesse," he said, rubbing the mule's nose, "what're you doin' back so soon?"

He bounded up the porch steps and charged through the kitchen door. The totally unexpected scene of desolation that confronted him caused him to stop dead in his tracks just inside the threshold. His mother was crying hysterically and his father had his arms around her in an attempt to comfort her. His Aunt Elizabeth was sitting in a chair near the table staring fixedly into space, and behind her stood his Cousin Sarah with her hands resting on her mother's shoulders. The grim expressions on all four faces told Otis that something terrible had happened. He turned to his father.

"What is it, Pa?" he asked anxiously, all thoughts of school and girls and war and future suddenly expunged from his mind. "What happened?"

"It's your Uncle Daniel, Son," replied Nathan gravely. "He was killed by a bear."

Otis' mouth dropped open and he looked in dumbfounded disbelief around the room, his face assuming the same grim countenance as those he saw staring back at him. As the tragic news settled into his consciousness Otis found himself awed and transfixed by the horror of it. He felt ashamed for feeling it, but mingled with his genuine feelings of shock and sadness and sympathy, there was a tingling sensation–an excitement, a fascination, a thrill. So seldom did anything so out of the ordinary happen in their lives. He wanted to know more about it.

"How, Pa? How did it happen?"

Not wishing to put the others present through the pain of hearing the details of the tragic news repeated, Nathan demurred. "Not now, Son. I'll tell you later."

An hour later in the barn, as he helped his father clean and bed the stables, Otis found his chance to ask again. "But how did it happen, Pa?"

"Don't really know for sure, Son. Sarah's the only one who'll talk about it an' she didn't see it. She wasn't there when it happened. She stayed on at your Uncle Jacob's for a couple days after they all left here last week. When she got home she found her Pa lyin' dead in that field up behind their house with his scalp tore open. He had lost a lot of blood. He must a-been plowin' when the bear attacked him. Sarah saw tracks but she never saw the bear. The chicken pen was smashed an' some of the chickens were missin'. My guess is, it was the same bear that Wesley Hicks has been after–the one that killed one of his hogs about a week back."

Otis brooded silently for a moment as he tried to imagine the tragic scene in his mind. Also in his mind was something else that had disturbed him, something he had seen in the kitchen. "What's wrong with Aunt 'Lizbeth, Pa?"

"She's had a terrible shock, Son. Apparently she saw the whole thing. She must a-been hangin' up the wash. Sarah says when she got home only half the wash was hung up. The rest was still in the basket. She found her mother in the house sittin' on the bed, just starin' at the wall, same as she is now. Sarah says she ain't said a word since it happened, ain't even cried. It's like her soul ain't even in her body no more. She just sits an' stares, don't eat–ain't et a thing in a week–hardly sleeps neither."

"Is she gwine t' die?"

Nathan heaved a troubled sigh. "It does seem like she's kind of got her mind set on it, don't it? An' Lord knows, when a body makes up their mind t' die, it's no easy thing t' talk them out of it– 'specially when they don't hear a word you're sayin'."

Otis pondered some more. "Are they gwine t' stay here with us?" he asked. For some reason he found himself hoping that his father would say "yes."

"They're certainly welcome t' stay here–for as long as they like or have a need."

For the first time since hearing the news of his Uncle Daniel's death Otis felt a faint ray of light penetrate the terrible gloom that had descended with such devastating suddenness and force upon his soul. He found the prospect of his Cousin Sarah living with them again positively intriguing. He thought of something that his Aunt Emily had been fond of saying in times of crisis: "Every dark cloud has a silver lining." Otis now knew that to be true. Even out of the worst tragedy, fresh possibilities and new opportunities could arise.

Supper was a solemn affair. No one felt much like eating. The only words spoken were those necessary for the conducting of the meal, and they were spoken only in the most subdued tones. Otis had taken a seat across the table from Sarah so as to be able to catch an occasional glimpse of her face. How sad she looked. Her dark eyes, the well-springs of her soul, which had always sparkled with fascination and delight, had become deep pools of sadness which seemed to have no bottoms. Once when their eyes met she tried to force a smile, but could not. Her smile, which had always come so easily, so spontaneously, failed her now. Otis withdrew his eyes from hers so as not to cause her further discomfort. But he had appreciated the effort she had made, and as he stared with total detachment at the plate of food in front of him, he felt his heart breaking with sadness for her. He knew that if he looked at her again he might start to cry himself. He didn't want her to see him cry.

Elizabeth sat next to Sarah but ate nothing. Sarah had forewarned Hester that she would not, but Hester had insisted that she must put *something* on her plate lest it appear that they were *trying* to starve her. After supper Sarah offered to help Hester clean up, but Hester refused.

"You look after your mother, child," she said rather brusquely, her eyes still red from crying, her voice hoarse with emotion. "I'll take care of this. I need t' keep busy just now."

Sarah stopped her aunt in mid-bustle and put her arms around her. "Thank you, Aunt Hester," she sobbed, "thank you for letting us stay."

Hester pushed her away. "You go on now, child, afore you start *me* bawlin' ag'in."

Sarah turned to Nathan. "Thank you, Uncle Nathan."

Nathan was too choked to respond. He just looked at her compassionately. Then Sarah took her mother's hand and led her upstairs to the room they had shared that first winter eight years before. Once inside, Sarah closed the door and surveyed the dusky interior. Even though the world had gone through cataclysmic upheaval and now lay in ruins, the room had changed little. Without lighting the lamp, Sarah undressed her mother and helped her into her nightgown. There was nothing more she could do for her father now, save pray for his soul. Now it was her mother who needed her. For the past week she had dressed and undressed her, bathed her, looked after her every need. She now cared for her mother as she would have cared for a helpless child, just as her mother had once cared for her. But she had been unable to get her to eat anything. She could sometimes get her to swallow water, but in the week that had passed since her father's death, she had not been able to get her to take food of any kind.

Sarah helped her mother into bed and pulled the coverlet over her. Then she walked around the bed to the north window and stared out at the evening shadows. It was not yet quite dark. Beyond the porch roof she could still make out Hester's garden, freshly cultivated, with long faint parallel lines of green running through the dark earth. Beyond the garden lay the orchard, standing out against the darkening woods like a clump of cotton on black velvet. Above the hills to the west the sky glowed red and purple in the wake of the setting sun. She opened the window to let some fresh air into the room. Wafting in on the evening breeze came the sweet fragrances of lilacs and apple blossoms, and from the direction of the run she could hear the sound of the spring peepers. Once again she tried to smile, but could not.

She changed into her nightgown and lay down upon the bed. Then, turning to her mother, who lay with her back toward her, facing the wall, Sarah drew herself up close behind and put an arm around her. Late into the night they lay close together, in perfect stillness, save for the gentle rhythmic motion of Sarah's hand stoking her mother's hair, until finally Sarah–and Sarah alone–fell asleep.

Even before Sarah had arrived, it had seemed to Otis that the days were getting longer. It was spring. The sun *was* rising earlier and setting later each day. But it seemed to Otis that the minutes and hours themselves were expanding in duration. It happened every year about this time, during the last month of school before summer recess. But the longer minutes and hours notwithstanding, Friday afternoon finally came and Otis was once again on the bus going home. Another school week was finished! Now there were only three more weeks left to go. Unfortunately, they would be the longest three weeks of the year.

As he ran down the lane his thoughts were on the weekend ahead. Between his chores and his school homework he had not gotten to see much of his Cousin Sarah during the evenings after school, but now that he would have two whole days at home—save for the two hours Sunday morning that he would be required to be in church—he expected that he would be able to catch more than an occasional glimpse of her at suppertime.

He came downstairs the next morning to find his Aunt Elizabeth sitting in the kitchen on a chair next to the stove. His Aunt Elizabeth made him a little nervous. He was not sure he would ever get used to her gaunt appearance and the strange, hollow look in her eyes. He found her a little spooky.

"Mornin', Aunt 'Lizbeth," he said politely, but nervously. He had learned to expect no response and received none.

"Mornin', Ma," he said to his mother, whom he found at her accustomed place for this time of day: standing over the stove.

"Your Pa's been a-lookin' for you," was his mother's only greeting.

Otis went out the door and walked down the well-worn path to the outdoor privy. The sun was just beginning to illuminate the tops of the mountains. When he returned to the house he found his father sitting at the kitchen table. "Mornin', Pa."

"Mornin', Son. You slept late, didn't you?"

"Yeah, I did a little, I guess."

"We've got a lot of work t' do today, you know. Better have some breakfast."

Otis took his seat. "Whar's Sarah?" he inquired, trying to sound as uninterested as possible.

"Just left," replied Nathan between spoonfuls of grits. "She helped me with the milkin', then took Jesse an' went back up the mountain to get their cow an' some more of their things. She'll be back tomorrow afternoon."

Without saying another word, Otis dug into his grits and tried as best he could to hide his disappointment.

But Nathan was glad that Sarah had gone. In fact he had encouraged her to go. He felt that she had been carrying far too heavy a burden for a girl of her years. Nathan could not help but

382

take pity on her. The death of her father, coming as it had so suddenly and unexpectedly, had dealt her a severe blow—and she was such a gentle young thing to begin with. But not only had she had to learn to carry on her slender shoulders the full weight of her terrible grief, but she had also assumed full responsibility for looking after her mother, who had become, for all practical purposes, an invalid. Nathan knew there was nothing he and Hester could do to mitigate the grief caused by her father's death—only time could do that—but, at the very least, they could relieve her of the responsibility of looking after her mother for a couple of days. Nathan knew that Sarah was becoming increasingly anxious about her mother—and for good reason. If Elizabeth did not soon show some interest in living—if she could not at least be persuaded to take some nourishment—then she too would die. Nathan hoped for everyone's sake that it would not come to that, but especially for Sarah's.

All Sunday afternoon Otis waited impatiently for Sarah to return, but it was not until early evening, just before dusk, that he finally saw her coming in the lane leading the mule and the cow. Otis met her at the barn.

"Uncle Jacob was here," he said as he helped her unpack the mule.

"Oh, I'm sorry I missed him," she replied with effort, dredging the words up from the deep well of grief inside her.

"He came to dinner after church an' sat with your mother most of the afternoon. He just left about an hour ago."

"He sat with my mother?"

"Uh-huh. An' talked to her some."

Sarah's eyes brightened. "Did she . . . ?"

Otis shook his head. "Nope, she didn't say nuthin'. I don't think she even knowed he was thar."

Otis helped her carry some things into the house. Sarah went straight to her mother in the rocking chair and kissed her on the cheek. "Hello, Mother."

Sarah placed her face directly in the path of her mother's fixed gaze, but there was no indication in her mother's dark vacant eyes that her presence was even noticed. Immediately after supper, Sarah led her mother up to their room. Otis hoped that Sarah would come back downstairs, but she did not.

The following morning Otis went back to school, his mind in a turbulent state. He had problems of his own to worry about–he had just been told by his teachers that he was failing algebra and was just barely passing English and history; Tammy Bright was still mad at him for not asking her to the school picnic, and Gladys Cole, whom he *had* asked, was unhappy with him because he had not been paying as much attention to her as she thought she deserved–but he felt his own problems were of little account when compared to his Cousin Sarah's. *He* was only failing a couple of useless school courses: *her* Pa had been killed. All *he* had to worry about was keeping a couple of giddy schoolgirls mollified: *she* had to worry about keeping her mother alive. Once he had put things in their proper perspective, Otis was able to see quite clearly that his own problems were of little significance in the grand scheme of things, and chose therefore to ignore them. He would have had a difficult time bringing his mental energies to bear on his own problems in any case, as he found himself now thinking almost constantly about Sarah.

The days were now interminable, hours without end, minutes without end. From the moment he stepped onto the school bus in the morning, Otis counted the minutes and seconds until the bus brought him home again in the late afternoon. Such patience, such longing, should have been better rewarded, but his hopes of seeing more of Sarah, spending more time with her, were almost invariably frustrated. He had his chores to do after school, and by the time he finished those, it was time for supper. He had learned to look forward to suppertime as that was the one time of day he could count on seeing his cousin, if ever so briefly, before she retired with her mother to their room. But midway through the week even that changed.

Elizabeth had become so weak that Sarah had decided to discontinue the ritual of getting her up and dressed in the mornings, allowing her instead to remain in bed. Sarah herself continued to help out around the farm–working with Hester in the garden, helping Nathan with the milking–as she had done since the day she arrived, but generally she limited her working hours to the forenoon and early afternoon, excusing herself around four o'clock, about the time that Otis came home from school, to tend to her mother. At first it seemed to Otis that she was deliberately avoiding him, and he said so to his father.

"She's not avoidin' you, Son," explained Nathan, "though it may seem that way. She's just helpin' us out when you're not around—fillin' your shoes, so t' speak, til you get home from school."

Once Elizabeth became confined to her bed, Otis saw even less of Sarah, as she sometimes did not even make an appearance at supper. If Otis had hoped to see more of his cousin on the weekend, again he was disappointed, as she spent virtually all of Saturday and Sunday shut up inside her room. Otis understood that his Aunt Elizabeth's condition was becoming quite serious now. He understood why Sarah had to spend so much time with her: any day now might be the last. Otis found himself just wishing it would soon be over, one way or the other. If his Aunt Elizabeth was going to get better, he wished she would get better soon. If she was going to die—he hated himself for thinking it—he hoped she would die soon. It would be better that way for everyone: it was the waiting that was so hard.

Another week slowly passed. As the prospect of his Aunt Elizabeth's recovering grew increasingly dim with each passing day, Otis found that he was not even that anxious to rush home from school, for fear of the news that might be awaiting him. He had learned to tell by reading the expressions on the faces of his mother and father whether there had been any change in his Aunt Elizabeth's condition, and as those expressions became daily more grim, Otis understood without asking that the end would not be long in coming. He also knew from brief murmured exchanges he overheard between his mother and father, that they were becoming increasingly worried about Sarah, who was herself becoming thin and gaunt from lack of food. She seldom bothered to come to meals anymore, despite Hester's pleading, and every minute she wasn't working she spent in her room sitting with her mother. Her death watch had begun.

Finally, by Friday evening of the third week, Nathan decided he had to do something. They had already lost Daniel; they were about to lose Elizabeth; but he was determined that they were not going to lose Sarah as well. Another weekend was coming up, which meant Otis would be home from school for the next two days. If the previous weekend was any indication, Sarah could be expected to spend virtually all of those two days shut up inside her room. Nathan was not about to let that happen.

Early Saturday morning he knocked on Sarah's door. When there was no answer he slowly pushed the door open far enough to poke his head through. He found Sarah fully clothed and lying on top of the bed covers with her arm around her mother. Elizabeth's eyes were closed. It was now Sarah who was staring into space. She looked exhausted.

"Sarah?" Nathan called softly.

Sarah turned slowly toward him, a distant, weary look in her eyes.

Nathan nodded toward Elizabeth's motionless form. "Is she . . . ?"

"She's asleep," replied Sarah numbly.

Nathan breathed a sigh of relief. He paused a moment to re-gather his thoughts. "Sarah, I'm gonna be sendin' Otis down to the mill this mornin' to get some corn ground up. I was wond'rin' if you might like t' go with him."

"Do you *want* me to go, Uncle Nathan?"

Nathan hesitated a moment before replying. "Yes, Sarah, I do."

"Then I will. I'll be down in a minute."

Nathan closed the door and went downstairs, where he found Otis eating his breakfast.

"Son, we're just about out of corn meal. I want you t' shell a couple of bushels of corn this mornin' an' go down to Bryson's to have it ground. Sarah will be goin' with you."

Otis looked up in surprise, temporarily at a loss for words.

"You don't mind, do you, Son?"

"No, Pa, I don't mind," said Otis eagerly, "I don't mind a bit. I'll get to it right after breakfast." He quickly took half a dozen more forkfuls of sausage and johnnycake. "Thar, I'm finished now. I'll get to it right away." He jumped up from his chair and hurried out the door without closing it.

Nathan looked at Hester, shook his head, and smiled. Then, walking to the still-open door, he called out, "Don't leave without Sarah, Son."

"I won't, Pa," came a voice from the distance.

Nathan closed the door and had just turned back to the table when Sarah emerged from the stairwell.

"Where's Otis?" she asked, looking around the kitchen. "Isn't he up yet?"

"He just went out t' shell some corn," replied Nathan.

"I'll go help him," she offered, moving toward the door.

"No," said Nathan, placing his rather sizable frame in her path, "he can manage. You sit down with me an' have some breakfast first."

"But I can shell corn much faster than Otis, Uncle Nathan."

"I'm sure you can, prob'bly even with one hand tied behind your back. But we're in no hurry, are we?"

Sarah studied her uncle's eyes to divine his intention. "You don't need me to go to the mill, do you?"

"No," replied Nathan compassionately, "but *you* need t' go. And I *want* you t' go. But first you have some breakfast."

Sarah acquiesced and sat down at the table. Nathan joined her.

"You're gettin' skinny, girl," remarked Hester as she placed two johnnycakes on the plate in front of her. "You don't eat near enough. I know you won't eat sausage, but at least you can eat a johnnycake or two. An' I've opened up a jar of peaches for you. I know how you like peaches. 'Course, canned's never as good as fresh, but still, hit's better than no peaches at all. In another day or two we'll have fresh strawberries. We'd a-been pickin' them a week already any other year."

Nathan continued to study his niece's face as she obligingly turned her attention to the plate of johnnycakes and the bowl of peaches that Hester had placed before her. Hester was right. She had grown thinner in the two and a half weeks she had been with them. Even her face was thinner, and there were dark circles under her eyes. Her once-lovely face, which had always been so pleasing to behold, with its wide range of animated expressions, was now frozen by grief and anxiety into the single expression of pain. It was a face that was almost too sad to behold. Nathan knew that one day the warm sun would again shine on this young girl's life and begin to slowly melt through the grief that held those other faces frozen within. But he did not know when. He did not think it would be any time soon.

Sarah finished her breakfast and, excusing herself, again made for the door. This time Nathan did not stop her.

"Well, " sighed Hester when she and Nathan were alone in the kitchen, "at least you managed t' breathe some life back into one of them. I ain't seen Otis show that much int'rest in anythang in a week of Sundays . . . But I ain't so sure you did right by Sarah. Did you ever stop t' think, what if Miss 'Lizbeth passes away while Sarah is off at the mill?"

"Yes, Hester, I did think about that, an' I asked myself, would it be any better if Elizabeth died in Sarah's arms? An' if better, better for who? Better for Sarah? I don't see how."

Hester sadly nodded her head in agreement.

Otis waited nervously as Sarah climbed up onto the wagon and sat down next to him on the driver's seat. He wasn't sure why the mere physical presence of this cousin of his had, so all of a sudden, become the one thing he desired most in all the world. He had always liked her, had always looked forward to seeing her at Thanksgiving and at those infrequent other times during the year when she came to visit, or on those even rarer occasions when he had gone up to visit her in the mountains. He had come to feel that they had developed almost a kind of sibling bond between them. Neither one of them had any brothers or sisters, nor even any other cousins near to them in age—at least none living in North Carolina. Otis had been told that he had cousins his own age up north in Ohio, but he had never met them and did not think it at all likely that he ever would. Because he and Sarah were family, related by blood; because they lived close enough to visit; because there was only two years difference in their ages–it was only natural that the two of them would be drawn into each other's company, especially in a family as ticktight as the Wickers. Under the circumstances it could not have been otherwise. Still, that did not altogether explain the feelings that Otis was feeling for his cousin now. He was coming to realize that his feelings toward her had changed–just as his feelings toward Gladys Cole had changed.

As they drove out the lane, Otis' fingers played nervously with the reins. He found himself paying less attention to his driving than to the passenger seated next to him, and as often as he dared–as often as conscience and self-respect would permit–he stole glimpses of her out of the corner of his eye. Sarah was certainly much thinner than Gladys, especially now. But even before she had lost so much weight, she did not have the full figure that Gladys had. Her breasts and hips were not so well developed; she did not appear to be as soft. Of course, Gladys was two years older than Sarah, but even at fourteen Gladys had been the envy of all the other girls and the subject of much talk among all the boys in school. No, Sarah did not now, and probably never would, have Gladys' full figure, but still there was something intriguing about her. She had some strange indefinable quality that neither Gladys nor any of the other girls at school possessed. There had always been something about Sarah that was different, and Otis had always viewed her with a certain amount of awe. He had always been her most severe critic, but he had been her most ardent admirer as well, and it had always been a great source of pride to him that she was his cousin.

"Sure is a purty day," observed Otis dreamily as they drove out the cool, dew-damp, wooded lane.

Spring, so late in coming, was well advanced now. The understory trees–the serviceberry, redbud, and dogwood–which had been in bloom only a month before and had stood out so distinctly, had dropped their petals and faded into green obscurity. The taller trees–the oaks, the tulips, the beeches–were likewise in full leaf now. The tulip trees were in leaf *and* bloom. Sarah looked up at the sunlit greenery overhead but said nothing. Otis had not really expected her to engage in conversation, so he was not disappointed. He was happy just to finally be this close to her. She had been living with him and his family for the past two and a half weeks now, and, in that time, this was the closest he had been to her. And as it would take close to half an hour to get to the mill, at least a quarter of an hour to get the corn milled, and another half hour to return home, he would be assured of her physical proximity for at least the next hour and a quarter, and he figured that if he drove slowly enough, he could easily stretch that into two hours.

When they arrived at the mill, he was glad to see another wagon and a truck already there.

"Looks like we're a-gwine t' haf t' wait our turn," he said, stepping down from the wagon and tying the horse to the hitching rail. "You been here before, ain't you?"

"Yes," answered Sarah, more out of courtesy than any desire to make conversation. "Usually we ground our corn at home on our hand grinder, but whenever my Daddy came down to town, he always brought a sack of corn with him for Mr. Bryson to mill. And whenever my mother and I were along, we'd come to the mill with him . . . We were all here just last month . . . the last time we came to visit . . ."

As she struggled with the words, Otis realized too late that in his attempt to engage her in passing conversation, he had forced her to recall the very memories he had wished her, for a time, to forget. He could have kicked himself in the head. "I'm sorry," he stammered, "I didn't mean . . . I better go in an' see how long it'll be." He turned and hurried toward the millhouse.

When he returned Sarah was no longer in the wagon. He looked around and found her standing on the bank a short distance away, leaning over the wooden flume that carried the water to the mill wheel. He wondered if he should let her be, rather than take a chance on saying something else stupid that might upset her. He found that it was not in his power to let her be, not when she was standing so close to him, and so alone. He walked up the bank toward the flume, vowing with each step that he would not speak unless she spoke to him first. When he reached her side, he found her staring at a small pool of water she was holding in her cupped hands. Otis too stared at her hands, but, true to his resolve, said nothing.

"I was just thinking," she said sadly, after a long moment's silence, "about something my Daddy told me when I was little. He said the life we're given is like the water we can hold in our hands. No matter how tightly we hold onto it, little by little it slips through our fingers. Drink deeply, he said, while you still have it. Don't let it all slip away before you've even tasted it . . .

"My Daddy lived a good life, Otis, the kind of life he wanted to live. He tasted the water and he drank deeply. But I don't think that even he had any idea how fast it would all slip through his fingers. It seems so unfair because really it didn't slip through. It was like the bowl was overturned and it spilled out . . .

"And now I'm looking at the water slipping through my own fingers and I'm thinking of something else my Daddy said. We mustn't grieve, he said. Life is too short for grieving . . . But how do you stop? How do you make it stop? It's been almost a month and it hurts just as much now . . . And my poor mother . . ."

As she broke into sobs, she dropped the water from her hands back into the flume and covered her face. What Otis did next he might not have done had he taken the time to think about it. But he acted instinctively, impulsively. He listened not to his head, but to his heart, which was aching with pity for this poor injured creature by his side. It all happened so fast that he could not be sure whether she had started to fall and he had caught her, or he had simply seized her and pulled her to him, but suddenly she was in his arms, their bodies pressing against each other. Without resisting she buried her face against his shoulder and put her arms around him. How long they stood locked in each other's arms by the side of the flume, Otis could not have begun to guess. Seconds and minutes could not now be long enough. Hours and days could not now be long enough. Over her shoulder he could see the mill wheel turning, once, twice, three times . . .

"Your turn, Otis," came Henry Bryson's cheerful call.

No, it couldn't be, thought Otis, not already. But Sarah had started to release herself at the sound of the miller's voice. She rubbed her eyes with the palms of her hands and headed in the direction of the wagon. Reluctantly Otis followed her. By the time he reached the wagon, Sarah had already heaved one of the sacks of corn onto her shoulder. Otis picked up the other sack and followed her into the millhouse.

Henry Bryson was remarkably well-preserved for a man in his late fifties. He still had a full head of hair, thick and wavy, which for the most part, was seldom seen by anyone other than his wife, except in church, due to his ever-present cap, but some curls of which could still be seen around his ears and on the back of his neck where the hat didn't quite cover. If it weren't for the fact that this fine head of hair was as white as the mountain snow, he might have been taken for a man half his age. The skin of his face and hands was equally well-preserved, as pink and smooth as a prepubescent child's. Whether the youthful appearance of his skin was attributable to genetic factors, or, as some believed, to the beneficial properties of mill dust, would have been difficult to judge. His father had also retained a smooth, rosy-skinned complexion into the later years of his life, but then he also had been a miller. In fact the mill had been in the Bryson family since it was first built by William Bryson back in the late 1820s. Whatever the reason, the skin of Henry Bryson's face and hands was much softer and smoother than the wrinkled, weathered hides of most of the farmers who came to him to have their corn milled. It could not be said that the fairness of his skin was due to his lack of exposure to the elements, because Henry, like all the Brysons before him, was a farmer himself. Operating a grist mill in Rushing Creek was hardly a full-time occupation.

At the sound of footsteps he turned to find Sarah coming through the doorway, a sack of corn on her shoulder. Otis was right behind her.

"Why, hello, Sarah," said the miller with a smile. "What a pleasant surprise! Otis didn't tell me he brung a helper."

"Hello, Mr. Bryson," responded Sarah with difficulty. Again the smile would not come.

"Here, let me help you with that," offered the miller. As he removed the sack from her shoulder, he looked closely at her face. His demeanor changed at once. "Sarah," he said solemnly, "I was terrible sorry to hear about your father. He was a good man . . ."

Sarah lowered her eyes and nodded her head to acknowledge the miller's expression of sympathy.

Henry Bryson emptied the first sack of corn into the hopper. As the huge stone buhrs slowly ground the kernels into a fine meal, the miller and the two teenagers stood quietly and watched, each locked in his or her own world of thought. If Sarah's own mind had not been so preoccupied, if she had been able to read the thoughts of the man and the boy standing next to her in the millhouse, she might have been embarrassed to find that both were thinking of her. Otis, his palms still sweating and his heart still pounding from excitement and confusion, was thinking about what had just happened at the flume and what it might portend for the future. Henry Bryson was thinking about Sarah too, but he was recalling a time seven or eight years in the past, the time he had first laid eyes on this young girl. She could scarcely have been more than a child of about seven then. Her father had just harvested his first crop of corn up at the old Puckett place, and he had brought a sack of it down around Thanksgiving to have it milled, and little Sarah had come along. She had been just about the happiest child he had ever seen–and the most inquisitive. She had been fascinated by the mill and had wanted to know exactly how everything worked, and he had taken great pleasure in explaining it to her. He had not seen her often in the years that had passed since then–each time he saw her she seemed to have grown another hand taller since the last time–but the thing he remembered best about her–the one thing that never changed as she grew older–was her lively and cheerful disposition. He had never met a child who seemed to be so pleased just to be alive. She had a way of smiling that made other people feel good, made other people feel glad to be alive. Henry Bryson remembered one time when Sarah had come to the mill with her father, he had gone into the house to fetch his wife. "Come out here, Mary," he had told her, "thar's someone I want you t' meet." Thinking the visitor was some important dignitary passing through–a judge, perhaps, or a circuit preacher–Mrs Bryson had taken off her apron, tidied herself up, and hurried out, only to find this little mite of a girl looking up at her and smiling. But she had had to admit–and she was no mean judge of children, having raised ten of her own–that little Sarah Wicker was just about the sweetest-natured and best-mannered child she had ever had the pleasure of meeting–and "smart as a whip besides." "That one's a-gwine t' haf t' be careful," she had told her husband after Sarah and her father had left, "or one day she's a-gwine t' sprout wings."

"That should do you for a while," said the miller as he tied up the last sack of meal. "Give my regards to your Ma an' Pa, Otis."

He watched from the doorway as the two youngsters carried the sacks of meal to the wagon. He was still thinking about Sarah. He could not help but wonder what would become of this young girl whose father had been killed so tragically in the prime of his life and whose mother, he had heard, was far from well. He felt sorry for her–and for himself–and for everyone else whose life had once been gladdened by this young girl's presence. As he watched the wagon pull up onto the hard road, he took off his hat and shook the dust out of it, then used it to beat more dust out of his shirt and overalls, before returning it to its proper place on top of his head.

"Mornin', George," he called out cheerfully, greeting his next customer. "What can I do for you today?"

"Otis, stop!" said Sarah as they pulled up onto the bridge.

Obediently Otis reined in the horse. As they sat in the middle of the bridge above the rushing water, Sarah looked up the stream.

"I think I'd like to walk back," she said.

"You cain't walk," objected Otis. "Hit's too far. Hit'll take you too long. Hit's much quicker t' go back in the wagon."

"But we're in no hurry, are we?" replied Sarah, repeating the words her Uncle Nathan had spoken to her earlier. "Besides, I'd like to go back a different way."

"Thar ain't no differ'nt way."

"What about up along the creek?"

"You cain't go up along the creek."

"Why not?"

"You cain't get through."

"Why not?"

"'Cause you cain't."

"Have you ever tried it?"

"Nope."

"Aren't you curious to know what lies between here and your farm?"

"I know what lies between. Right 'round that first bend is the dam. That's whar the swimmin' hole is, whar all the boys go a-jay-birdin' in the summertime. Then a li'l further up is the place whar they hold the baptizin's. An' after that, thar's nuthin' but rocks an' trees."

Sarah started to get down.

"You better not go," urged Otis, half warning, half pleading. "You might get lost."

Sarah turned to him and gave him a questioning look. "How can I get lost if I follow the creek?"

"My Pa will be expectin' you t' come back with me," countered Otis in desperation.

"I think he'll probably be glad to have me out of the house for a while," she replied, her eyes fixing again on the point upstream where the creek made a bend and disappeared from view.

"What about your Ma? Who'll look after her?"

Sarah turned once again toward him. A strange calm came over her face. "There's nothing more I can do for her," she replied, her voice devoid of any feeling, as if drained of all emotion. "I'm going to release her."

"What do yuh mean?" asked Otis, confused by her strange look and cryptic words.

"There's nothing more I can do for her," she repeated, shaking her head.

Otis continued to stare in bewilderment at her as she walked to the end of the bridge, then made her way down over the rock boulders to the edge of the rushing water. He thought briefly of going after her, to try once again to talk her into going back with him in the wagon, but he knew it would be useless. He was forced to move when a car came up behind him on the bridge. Once in motion, he kept going.

Fifty yards upstream, around the bend, Sarah came to the dam. She had known about the dam, but she had never seen it before. Her Uncle Isaac had told her about it on the day that she and her mother and father first arrived in Rushing Creek, and not too long after that, Mr. Bryson had told her that the water that fed into his grist mill came down a mill race from the dam in the creek. It was not a high dam and she had no difficulty getting around it.

For another fifty yards above the dam the water was calm and deep. It did not seem like Rushing Creek at all. Even if Otis hadn't told her, Sarah could have guessed that this was a favorite swimming hole. The evidence was everywhere. Rope swings, suspended from high tree branches, dangled over the water; boards nailed to trunks of trees served as steps to launching platforms higher up; circles of blackened stones and bits of charred wood on the ground bore mute witness to campfires of summers gone by. Sarah looked around at the still, quiet scene with its many signs of past revelry. There was no one swimming here now. She had hoped that there would not be. She didn't know what she would have done had she stumbled upon a group of naked boys. But at this time of morning she had not expected to find anyone. In another few weeks, when school was out, when the smothering heat of summer had settled over the valley like a blanket, then there would be activity here once again. Then the sounds of shouting and laughing and splashing would again be heard as hot, tired farmboys congregated here to seek temporary relief from the heat of corn - and hayfields in the cool waters of Rushing Creek. As Sarah imagined the scene in her mind, she wondered if her father had ever come here as a boy.

Further upstream, at another bend, where the creek was still relatively calm but the water not quite as deep, she came to a clearing. From one corner of the clearing a path led up into the woods. Sarah guessed that this was the place of baptism that Otis had mentioned, and that if she followed the path she would come out at the hard road directly across from the church. Years ago, when she went to school at the church, she had passed by that path nearly every day and had often wondered where it led. She always knew that one day she would have to find out. Now she had.

As she stood on the bank and looked out across the water, she wondered if the Jordan River could possibly be this beautiful. She had never understood baptism exactly, though her father had tried to explain it to her once–it was one of the few times her mother had told her to "go ask your father"–but she reckoned that if a person had to be baptized, this was certainly the place for it–here in this pure, clean water coming down out of the mountains, with the open sky above and the green trees all around. Sarah herself had not been baptized, but she knew that four generations of Wickers before her had been, right here at this very spot. Her father had been baptized here.

With a heaviness in her heart she looked upstream. Did she want to go on? The memories were coming back now, memories of her father, memories of those eight happy years they had lived together in the mountains, just the three of them–she and her mother and her father. It was starting to hurt again. She thought for a moment of sitting down on the bank of the creek and not moving again until the hurting stopped, even if it took a month, even if it took a year, even if it took the rest of her life. The rest of her life! How long could that be? How long could she live with this terrible grief? Surely not for very long.

"Don't grieve," her father had told her. "Life is too short for grieving."

She knew she had to go on. With firm resolve, she pushed the memories from her mind and began moving again.

Rocks and trees, Otis had said. That's what lay upstream from here, nothing but rocks and trees. But he had never been past this point himself. As far as Sarah was concerned, the stretch of creek that lay ahead of her now was unexplored territory.

She could see from the outset that it was not going to be easy. Here along this less traveled section of creek, the rhododendron grew thick on both banks. At first she tried to follow a trail through the thick tangle, but the further she went, the less defined the trail became. Finally it disappeared altogether, forcing her to retreat up the wooded hillside into more open forest. But she continued to follow the course of the creek, never losing sight of it for more than a minute or two at a time.

At the first opportunity she made her way back down the steep hillside to the water's edge. At the sight of the once-again rushing water, she felt a tremor of excitement ripple through her body. She was surprised to feel it, because in the past month she had been too numbed by grief to feel anything. She stepped out onto a half-submerged rock in the creek and looked upstream at the water rushing toward her. It was impossible to take it all in— too much was happening. The water seemed to be moving in all directions at once, as it was being forced to constantly change its course by the myriad of rocks that stood in its path and obstructed its free flow. With reckless abandon she began leaping from rock to rock along the river's edge. The sight and sound of the wild water crashing about her, the feel of the wet spray on her legs and feet and arms and face, seemed for a moment to rekindle something inside her, something she thought she might have lost forever.

As the roaring of the water increased in intensity, Sarah kept her eyes riveted upstream. Suddenly she stopped in breathless amazement. Just ahead of her the creek had metamorphosed itself once again, becoming now a torrent of boiling white foam as it came charging through a narrow gorge. Seeing at once that there was no possible way for her to go through the gorge, she abandoned the creek and once again retreated up the steep wooded hillside.

Skirting the gorge proved to be no mean feat as it required a strenuous climb over rocky, nearly vertical terrain. She had just about succeeded in negotiating the most hazardous part of the climb when her progress was suddenly interrupted by a great pine tree, which had been uprooted and had fallen across the creek, spanning the gorge. She stopped to contemplate the fallen giant and to ponder her next move. When she was a young explorer of about six, she had made up a rule to deal with situations just such as this: when you come to a tree that has fallen across a stream, you must cross over it. The rule had not been completely arbitrary. None of her rules of exploring had been. They had simply required her to do that which she had an irresistible urge to do anyway.

She knew that she was now at an age when she could be forgiven for breaking a rule that she had made for herself at age six, but as she climbed up onto the tree and looked out along the length of it toward the other bank, she was surprised to feel the same youthful urge welling up inside her. She looked up at the sky. It was only about midmorning, maybe nine o'clock. She had plenty of time; she was in no hurry to get back. She estimated that she had come about a mile since the dam and that she probably had another mile to go before reaching her Uncle Nathan's farm. She knew that if she crossed to the other bank, she would eventually have to get back to the side she was on, but that had always been part of the challenge, part of the reason for making up the rule in the first place. There were so many rocks in Rushing Creek that she felt that surely at some point upstream she would be able to cross over by jumping from rock to rock, though that would have been a very risky undertaking along that part of the creek she had traversed thus far, where the water was so deep and the current so strong. If necessary she could continue upstream beyond Nathan's to where the creek was narrower, cross over there, then circle back. Or, as a last resort, she could always come back and cross back to the other side on the fallen tree, even though that meant violating another of her rules:

never retrace your steps. But that rule had never been a hard and fast one. It was one that she had found it necessary to break on more than one occasion in the past.

Halfway across the fallen tree she paused for a moment to watch the water rushing beneath her. With her eyes she followed its course downstream as it plunged relentlessly through its boulder-strewn channel—pounding against the rocks, dashing between them, leaping over them—on its way through the narrow gorge.

Once on the other side she began again to make her way upstream, again following along the bank whenever possible, again jumping from rock to rock along the edge of the stream itself when not. There was buoyancy in her step now. Slowly but surely she could feel the life force beginning to stir within her. She thought of the lines from the Twenty-third Psalm:

> "He leadeth me beside still waters,
> He restoreth my soul . . . "

These could hardly be called still waters—far from it—but she could feel her soul being restored. "Nothing but rocks and trees," Otis had said, but these rocks and trees—and this water rushing with such reckless abandon, with such unrestrained exuberance—were working their healing magic on her soul, and for the first time in nearly a month she remembered what it felt like to be alive, to be truly alive, to be alive and to be glad of it. She knew it would take time. She knew the hurting would not stop all at once. But she knew with certainty that the day would come when the water she held in her hands would once again taste sweet to her. The healing process had begun.

Her attention was diverted from the stream ahead by a smaller stream coming in from the side. Now she had another decision to make: whether to maintain her course up along Rushing Creek without interruption, or to take the time to explore this small tributary. There was no rule to cover this precise situation, but since an explorer's duty in general was to see everything there was to see—and since the smaller stream was especially alluring, leading as it did up the side of the mountain—she decided to allow herself to digress for a moment from her charted course.

She did not know what she would find up along this small stream that came tumbling down the dark side of the mountain, but as she entered the forest, she felt a strange sense of expectation. Suddenly she found herself in a very different world. The sights, the sounds, the smells had all changed. As she followed the stream deeper and deeper into the dark green coolness, the roaring of Rushing Creek faded in the distance behind her. There was nothing to disturb the silence now save the gentle tinkling, splashing sound of this less hurried stream and the twittering of birds in the treetops above her. The earthy smells of wet moss and peat and pine needles permeated the cool damp air she breathed.

As the course of the cascading stream led her further and further up the side of the mountain, she found herself once again climbing over large boulders and traversing hazardous terrain. She thought of turning back—she had never intended to follow the stream all the way to its source—but the sense that there was something still ahead of her, something she *had* to see, persisted. She remembered having had the same sense of expectation that day she had gone off in search of her holy mountain. Suddenly, as she emerged from behind another great boulder, she saw it: a lovely cascade of water, perhaps ten feet in breadth, spilling over the rocks above and making a vertical leap of some sixty feet into the pool of water below. It reminded her immediately of the waterfall she and Kati had seen in the Heaven of Colors.

She made her way out to the edge of the pool of water that had accumulated at the bottom of the falls, stepped onto one of the huge rock boulders that formed the basin, and sat down. As she watched the falling water she could feel the cool spray on her arms and legs. It was an ethereal scene, she thought, a scene of perfect peace—a holy place. She did not know how long she would be staying at her Uncle Nathan's and Aunt Hester's, but as long as she was, she could imagine herself coming back to this place again and again–just as she had returned again and again to her other holy place on the top of the mountain–to think, to pray, to be alone with her soul–to find again, if possible, that peace and love that she had been allowed to feel for that one brief moment in the White Light Heaven.

For the next hour she sat perfectly still, deep in thought, on the rock at the edge of the pool of water. Then slowly she stood up and looked around at the great cathedral of rocks and trees that surrounded her. Finally her eyes came to rest on a point in space above the waterfall.

"Daddy," she began, a slight tremor in her voice, "I don't know if you can still hear me, but if you can, I want you to know that I'm going to be all right... It's been hard... I've missed you... I think I will always miss you..."

Her voice trailed off. She waited for the words to come again, then continued. "I've been worried about Mother. I've been praying for her not to die–I prayed all night last night–but I realize now that I was wrong to do that. I was thinking only of myself and how much I would miss her if she were to die too... She wants to be with you, Daddy... and I'm going to let her go. I'm going to pray for her to die now, so she can be with you... Don't worry about me, Daddy... I'm going to be all right, really I am... I love you."

Quietly she turned, and from her vantage point high on the wooded hillside she looked down through the wilderness of rocks and trees through which she had come. Then, after turning once more to take one last look at the waterfall, she stepped down off the rock and began her descent, this time moving *with* the flow of water as it tumbled and splashed down over the side of the mountain on its journey toward Rushing Creek.

The trip to the mill had been only the beginning of a busy day for Otis. Upon his return he had spent the rest of the morning helping his father spray lime and sulfur on the apple and peach trees. Then in the afternoon he had been conscripted by his mother to help in the garden. He had weeded the strawberries and laid down fresh straw between the rows of nearly ripe berries. No sooner had he finished that than his mother had handed him a hoe and pointed him in the direction of the beans. He had been thinking about Sarah all day, ever since leaving her at the bridge, and now as he worked his hoe down the seemingly endless rows of beans, his thoughts were becoming increasingly anxious. Where was she? Why hadn't she returned? What was taking her so long? Surely she must have gotten lost just as he had warned her she would.

When he finally finished the last row of beans, he slowly straightened himself into an approximately vertical position and looked up at the sun. There was still about an hour left to the day before supper. He looked around for his mother and father. If either one of them saw him standing idle, he could expect to be given another chore to keep him occupied for the last hour. He could see that the sweet corn needed hoeing, but as he had not been told to do it, and as neither his mother nor his father was in sight at the moment, Otis decided that his time would be best spent down at the creek waiting for his cousin Sarah. Shouldering his hoe he set off for the creek.

When he reached the water's edge, he stepped out onto a large flat rock and looked downstream. There was no sign of Sarah. He thought of calling her name but decided against it. She just might hear him, and he didn't want to appear anxious. He squatted down on the rock with the hoe across his knees and waited.

After a few minutes he became restless and changed his position. Seeking a distraction he picked up his hoe and dangled the blade in the water, and for a few more minutes he amused himself by watching the water being diverted this way, then that, around the partially submerged blade.

"Are you fishing?" came a voice from behind him.

Otis jumped to his feet and turned around to find Sarah giving him a very puzzled look.

"Uh, no," he stammered, clutching the hoe, "I was just . . . Hey, wait a minute. How come you're a-comin' from that direction? I always figgered the mill was *that* way." He turned and pointed downstream.

"It *is* that way," replied Sarah, "but I crossed over the creek on a fallen pine tree about a mile down, then I jumped rocks to get back to this side, but then I came to another tree which had fallen across the creek, so I had to cross over again. In order to get back to this side the second time, I had to . . . "

She could tell by the expression on Otis' face that he had not understood a word she had said, but at the moment she had neither the patience nor the energy to repeat herself or to give a lengthy discourse on the rules of childhood exploring. "I'm sorry, Otis. Please forgive me. I'll try to explain another time." She headed up the bank.

"Hey, wait for me," Otis called after her. He caught up with her just as she emerged from the wooded bank into the fields. "Tell me about whar you been. Wha'd yuh see?"

"Rocks and trees," answered Sarah rather perfunctorily, "just like you said."

They met Nathan coming out of the barn.

"I see you made it back in one piece," he said, eyeing her carefully. He could not be sure, but she did not seem to him to look quite so forlorn as she had in the morning.

"Yes," replied Sarah, "I hope you weren't worried about me."

"Well, t' tell the truth, I was . . . a little . . . an' still am."

Sarah looked into her uncle's eyes and could see therein his deep concern and compassion.

"Please, Uncle Nathan, don't worry about me. I'm going to be all right now . . . And thank you for asking me to go to the mill this morning, even though you didn't need me to. You were right. I've been spending too much time in the house."

Nathan smiled, then turned to Otis. "Have you finished hoein' the beans, Son?"

"Yeah, Pa, just finished."

"Then why don't you hoe your mother's sweet corn for a while til suppertime."

Sarah found Hester in the kitchen.

"She's been a-sleepin' peaceful all day," reported Hester, anticipating Sarah's question.

Sarah headed for the stairs.

"You come back down for supper, you hear me, child?"

Sarah ascended the stairs without responding, but half an hour later she came back down and joined the others for supper.

Otis expected Sarah to excuse herself immediately after supper and retire to her room, as had become her habit, and was surprised when she did not. Instead she went back outside, picked up the hoe that he had left on the porch, and began hoeing the sweet corn where he had left off. Nathan and Otis watched her from the porch.

"What's she doin', Pa?"

"Looks to me like she's hoein' corn, Son," replied Nathan wryly, drawing on his pipe.

"I better go help her."

"Son, I know how much you like to hoe corn, but I think you'd best leave her be just now. She needs some time to herself."

"But she's been by herself all day," protested Otis.

Hester, wiping her hands on her apron, joined them on the porch.

"Nathan, why don't you make her come in? Cain't you see, she's so tired, hit's all she can do t' stand up? She ain't had a good night's sleep since she's been here."

"She'll come in when she's ready," Nathan assured her as he opened the door to re-enter the house. "Just leave her be, the both of you."

Hester shook her head in exasperation and followed her husband into the house, but Otis remained on the porch. He was still there an hour later, sitting in the dark, listening to the rhythmic cadence of the hoe striking the earth. Finally it stopped, and by the light coming from inside the house, he was able to make out Sarah's form coming toward the porch. She went directly to the pump and drew a bucket of water. Seeing that she was intending to wash up, and thinking she might like some privacy, Otis got to his feet, reluctantly excused himself, and went into the house.

Shortly thereafter Sarah herself went into the house, said goodnight to Otis, whom she found still lingering in the kitchen, and to Nathan and Hester, whom she found in the parlor. Slowly she climbed the stairs, supporting herself against the railing. She hesitated a moment before opening the door to her room, then opened it and entered. Once inside, she closed the door behind her and hesitated again. Leaning back against the door she stood quietly in the darkness listening for the sound of her mother's breathing. At first she heard nothing, and for one brief heart-stopping instant she thought that her days and nights of dread and uncertainty were finally over. But as she drew closer to the bed she heard the barely perceptible sound of air being inhaled and exhaled. She lit the lamp and changed into her nightgown. She was exhausted and ready for sleep. She lay down on the bed next to her mother's withered body and blew out the lamp. In the darkness she once again reached over her mother's shoulder and stroked her hair.

"Good-by, Mother," she said tenderly.

There was so much more she had wanted to say, so many things she had planned to say, but she was fast losing consciousness. Too many nights without sleep had finally caught up with her. Completely exhausted–completely drained of every last drop of physical and emotional energy–she fell into a deep, sound sleep.

When she opened her eyes again the light of a new day had already begun to fill the room. As she lay on her back staring at the ceiling, she listened again for the sound of breathing. This time she heard nothing.

For a quarter of an hour she lay motionless, scarcely breathing herself, listening for the sound that did not come. Finally she worked up the courage to turn toward her mother. To her utter astonishment she found herself alone in the bed. Her mother was gone! She sat bolt upright and looked around. Her mother was not in the room!

She sprang to her feet, and, still in her nightgown, opened the door and ran down the stairs. There was no one in the kitchen. Where was everyone? Just then Nathan came hurrying through the kitchen door, grinning from ear to ear.

"She's in the strawberry patch," he beamed. "I was just comin' t' get you."

Sarah ran through the kitchen door and out into the garden. There she found her mother, also still in her nightgown, with Hester supporting her, bending over a row of strawberries.

"Look, Sarah!" exclaimed Elizabeth upon seeing her daughter, "ripe strawberries! I could smell them all the way from upstairs!"

Overwhelmed by emotion Sarah rushed to her mother and threw her arms around her.

"Careful now," cautioned Hester, "or you'll knock her over. She ain't got the legs of a newborn colt."

Sarah, crying copious tears of relief and joy, continued to hug and kiss her mother with unrestrained emotion.

"Well," said Hester, her own emotions only slightly more restrained than Sarah's, "I'll leave her to you now. I've got t' get breakfast started, or we'll never get to church on time." She hurried off in the direction of the kitchen.

Elizabeth, startled and confused by Sarah's emotional behavior, tried now to comfort her daughter. "Don't cry, Sarah," she said, holding her close to her breast and patting her back. "Everything's going to be all right . . . Your Daddy came to see us last night. . ."

Sarah backed away and gave her mother a puzzled look.

"You were sleeping so soundly," continued Elizabeth, "I didn't want to wake you. He said he's found us a place in the mountains–a beautiful place, he said. He's got some work to do on it, but as soon as it's ready, he's going to come for us and take us there."

She put her arms around Sarah once again and drew her near. "In the meantime, he said I was to take good care of our little girl."

13

A QUESTION OF BAPTISM

There was a fluid, almost gliding quality to Sarah's step as she slipped down along the edge of the woods toward the creek. From the shade of overhanging oak, hickory, and wild cherry trees, she looked dreamily out across the glittering sunlit field of hay which her Uncle Nathan had just cut the day before. The field appeared to sparkle as she moved, as beads of dew caught the morning sunlight and were transformed into multi-colored jewels. The smell of the new-mown hay, spiced with the other fragrances in the air–those of wild rose, honeysuckle, and wild strawberry–gave the morning breeze a delicious, almost tangible quality. It looked and smelled like June–and indeed it *was* June– that month in which, almost without notice, spring gave way to summer, when the late blossoms of the one co-existed side by side with the early fruits of the other. This was the season when the earth was voluptuously full and sweet-smelling and most tantalizing to the senses.

Sarah smiled. She had reason to smile. In the two weeks that had passed since her mother had been suddenly and miraculously restored to her, Elizabeth's condition had improved steadily. Her appetite had been hearty–as might be expected after nearly a month without food–and she was daily increasing in weight and strength. Yet Sarah was not entirely free of anxiety concerning her mother. While the steady improvement in the state of Elizabeth's physical health was encouraging, the same could not be said for the state of her mind. Elizabeth seemed to have no recollection whatsoever of the tragic event which she, and she alone, had witnessed, and which had brought so much grief to Sarah and to so many others. She had not accepted the fact that Daniel was dead. In her mind he had merely gone up into the mountains to make a home for her and Sarah, just as he had done in reality eight years before. That was the reason he wasn't with them now; that was the reason she and Sarah were staying at

Nathan and Hester's. She seemed to have no memory at all of the past eight years. Sarah knew how happy her mother had been during those eight years the three of them had lived in the mountains, and now those eight wonderful years had been erased from her memory as if they had never existed at all.

There was something else about which Sarah continued to wonder. It was the curious thing her mother had said that morning in the strawberry patch: "Your Daddy came to see us last night." In those days of terrible grief immediately following her father's death, Sarah had hoped and prayed that he might communicate with her in some way, give her a sign, that he was all right, that he was being taken care of, but to no avail. Then, nearly a month after his death, had come her mother's startling assertion that he had come to *her* during the night. Had she really seen him? Had he in fact come to *her*, come to her in his soul body to persuade her that it was not time for her to die, that she must continue to live in order to "take good care of our little girl?" Or had she only dreamed it? The only thing Sarah knew for certain was that her mother was completely unaware of the fate that had befallen Daniel. Elizabeth believed her husband to be still alive, and Sarah had decided, for the time being at least, not to deprive her of the comfort of that belief. Nathan and Hester had agreed that Sarah's decision was the only one possible under the circumstances. Later, when Elizabeth was stronger, both physically and emotionally, she could be told the truth, but until then, they would allow her to believe that Daniel was still alive, up in the mountains somewhere, preparing a home for his wife and daughter.

Nathan and Hester had found a modicum of comfort of their own in carrying out this deception, as they found Elizabeth's view of reality much more congenial than the terrible unrelenting truth. For Sarah the decision not to tell her mother that terrible truth, in its full severity and at once, had not been an easy one. It had run contrary to her every instinct. But, for her mother's sake, she had been willing, this one time, to suppress her need to be absolutely forthright and truthful. Fortunately, she had found, whenever she and her mother talked about Daniel, that she was able to be less than completely truthful without actually being *un*truthful. In fact, her own view of the reality was not so very different from that of her mother. She knew that her father *was* still alive. He was *not* dead. And she believed that quite probably he *was* up in the mountains somewhere preparing a home for them. But she also knew that the mountain on which her father now lived was not to be found on any map, that the home he was preparing for them was not a home in this world.

Just as she reached the creek she heard the sound of church bells ringing in the distance. She knew that Nathan and Hester and Otis would be arriving at the church soon, if they weren't there already. She thought the practice of going indoors to worship a curious one. When she was but a small child back in Springfield, her mother had not taken her to church, but to Forest Park on Sunday morning. They had gone to Forest Park at other times as well, but always on Sunday morning, and in every season of the year, including the winter. Usually her father had accompanied them as well, but sometimes he had gone to church instead. After moving to North Carolina the practice of spending Sunday mornings out of doors in quiet, reverent contemplation had continued, but as Sarah grew older, she had tended more and more to spend the time alone and to wander further and further from home. As a consequence, her Sunday "morning" walks sometimes lasted all day, and over the years she had missed many a Sunday dinner on that account. Once she had found her holy mountain, she had even had a special place to go on Sundays. Now she had another special place to go. She had not been back to the waterfall since first finding it that day she had walked home from the mill two weeks before, but now that some semblance of normality had returned to her life—now that she had settled into the day-to-day rhythm of living and working with her Uncle Nathan and Aunt Hester; now that her mother, though not completely well, was at least out of danger and making progress toward complete recovery, at least of her physical health—she fully expected to resume her weekly Sunday morning walks. Perhaps in a few more weeks her mother would be strong enough to accompany her again, but this morning she was going alone. In all likelihood she would not be back in time for Sunday dinner and her Aunt Hester would be upset with her, but that was something that Sarah was getting used to. Aunt Hester always got upset with her when she missed meals. To Sarah's mind, Aunt Hester attached undue importance to eating. Sarah was glad for the great variety and abundance of food available to her at her Uncle Nathan's farm–a much greater variety and abundance than her family had ever had up on the mountain–but one could only eat so much and so often. Her mother had just gone a whole month without any food at all. Surely it wouldn't hurt to miss one meal now and again.

In the distance she heard the church bells ring again. She thought of Otis and how nice he had looked in his dark blue suit and his red-and-gray-striped tie. She had developed a fondness for Otis. Since her father's death he had been very sympathetic and had tried, on more than one occasion, to comfort her in his own awkward way. He had become very protective of her, reluctant to even let her out of his sight lest some harm should befall her. Earlier in the morning he had asked her if she might like to go to church with him and his parents. He had even tried to lure her with the promise of a ride in the back of the wagon–as if she were still a child!–and for a moment she had thought of accepting his invitation, so as not to disappoint him, but in the end she had politely declined. Perhaps another time, she had told him. This morning she had another place she wanted to go. She would see Otis the next day, and again the day after. Now that school was out for the summer, she would be seeing him every day. She saw no need to go with him to church on Sunday morning as well. But she had to admit, as she jumped out onto a rock in the creek, that the sound of the church bells pealing so joyously in the distance was a pleasant one, and she felt herself in a way drawn to it. Perhaps one day she *would* go to church with her Uncle Nathan, Aunt Hester, and Cousin Otis. But at the moment there was another sound calling to her even more urgently and more joyously: the sound of the water rushing at her feet.

As she stood for a moment on the rock, delighting once again in the sound and the sensation of the water rushing all around her, her attention was drawn to a large butterfly hovering just above the water's surface only a few feet away from her. She held out her hand and the delicate creature immediately fluttered toward her and lit on her fingers. She drew her hand nearer to her face to study it more closely. She marveled that a creature such as this could exist in a state of nature. It appeared not to be something natural at all, but something that had been made by some master craftsman. Its wings appeared to have been cut from a piece of velvet cloth, deep brownish-maroon in color. A handful of luminous blue gems had then been patiently embedded, one at a time, into the dark velvet to form a row all along the outer edge. As a final embellishing touch, a border of shining gold had been added. Sarah recognized the butterfly as the mourning cloak, so named because of the appearance of the *under*sides of its wings, which, in contrast to the brightly colored uppersides, were a dull gray-brown color, approximately the color of tree bark. When the creature folded its wings, the less colorful undersides became its "mourning cloak."

She pursed her lips and gently blew the delicate creature from her hand. She watched as it flew downstream, following the course of the water. Then, jumping to another rock, and another, she set off in pursuit.

The haywagon lumbered slowly across the field under the mid-afternoon sun. Nathan, on foot, kept pace alongside, his pitchfork resting lightly on his shoulder. Beads of perspiration glistened on his thick, dusty forearms. Without waiting for the rig to come to a complete stop, he thrust his fork into the next stack of hay and began forking it onto the wagon. Otis, working on the opposite side of the wagon, began forking from the pile on his side. From her perch on the driver's seat, Sarah passed the time by watching the two horses swish flies with their tails. She interrupted her vigil only long enough to re-adjust the floppy straw hat which had fallen down over her eyes and to bite the end off the piece of hay on which she had been sucking. Spitting out the spent end, she re-inserted the reed between her teeth.

At a command from Nathan she turned the team and headed for the barn. For Sarah, unloading the wagon was the best part. It meant that she too got to work with a pitchfork. Just outside the barn she brought the team to a halt. Quickly she jumped down from the driver's seat, ran into the barn and up the ladder into the loft. She was followed directly by Otis. Then, as Nathan stood on the wagon and heaved great forkfuls of hay into the loft through the open doors in the gable end of the barn, the two cousins picked it up with their forks and carried it to the back of the loft, adding to the already sizable mound which had accumulated. As they did so, they talked and laughed, reminiscing about the time years before when they had played in this very hayloft as children. This had been their refuge on rainy afternoons, and they had spent many breathless hours scaling the slopes of the high mountain of hay, then jumping off the top and sliding down. Now they were helping to erect a new mountain, but neither of them could imagine that it would ever seem as high as the one they had played on as small children.

Otis was all but jumping with joy. It was all he could do to keep from running to the top of the hay mound at this very moment and throwing himself off. School was out at last, and it would be three months before he would have to go back again. He had passed the year, although he had failed one course, algebra, which he would have to repeat in the fall. But fall was a long way off, and he wasn't about to allow his mind to dwell on anything so unpleasant as algebra during his three months of freedom. As the Good Book said, "Sufficient unto the day is the evil thereof." He would worry about school when school started again in the fall. In the meantime he was determined to enjoy his hard-earned freedom.

If Otis had been asked to name his favorite season of the year, he probably would have said summer. It wasn't that he liked summer all that much: it was just that he liked the rest of the year less. And the reason for that was simple enough: he had to go to school all the rest of the year. He had not always disliked school so intensely. In fact, when he had first started going, he had been glad to go, because it had meant deliverance from all the farmwork his mother and father had made him do. Like most farm kids between the ages of six and twelve, he had preferred being in school to being home doing chores. School, even at its worst, had been better than working. In fact, he remembered thinking back when he was about eight or nine, that it was a great injustice that they didn't let kids go to school in the summertime as well, when they most needed the relief. It was during the summers that the workload on the farm became unbearable.

Even a few odd chores can seem too heavy a burden to an eight-or-nine-year-old boy who would rather be down at the creek fishing, but for Otis the burden had scarcely become any lighter in more recent years. As he had increased in stature and strength, his share of the workload had increased proportionately. The hoe may not have seemed as heavy to him at age fifteen as it had when he was eight or ten or even twelve—or the distance from one end of a row of corn to the other as great—but the sun was still as hot and the sweat bees still stung just as mercilessly. Just last summer he had found himself thinking, while out hoeing corn one warm and humid morning, how much easier it would be to just lie down between the rows and die and let the vultures pick his bones.

Otis would have been hard put to name his least favorite summer job, but hoeing corn would have been a leading contender. He *hated* hoeing corn. Not only was the job miserable in itself, but the misery was compounded by the number of hours he was required to spend at it. By his own estimation, he spent half of every summer hoeing corn. But there were other jobs which were equally disagreeable. Picking beans, for one. Picking anything, for that matter. During the summer there was always something or other in the garden or orchard that needed picking. There was just no end to it. If it wasn't strawberries, it was peas. If it wasn't peas, it was tomatoes or beans. The only thing he hated picking worse than beans were those itchy, fuzzy peaches. Then there was the haying–the hottest, sweatiest, dirtiest, most exhausting job of all. No, summers on the farm had never been easy, and up until the time he was about twelve, he couldn't wait for summers to end and for school to begin again in the fall.

Then when he was about thirteen or fourteen, everything began to change. It was about the time he started going to high school in Haynesville. As school became more and more difficult for him, even summers began to look good by comparison. By the time he had finished his freshman year–his *first* freshman year– he had found himself positively looking forward to summer.

And he had found himself looking forward to summer every year since then. The best thing about summer, of course, was the fact that he didn't have to go to school, but there were other good things too. Summer had never been entirely without its amenities, which, while they may not have been sufficient to redeem it completely, at least helped to ease the suffering at times. There were always lots of good things to eat in the summer: strawberry shortcake, peach cobbler, corn on the cob, watermelon. There were fun things to do too, like swimming in the creek and going to church picnics. These, in some small measure, helped to compensate for the long hours of hard work. Otis would never have been able to give summer his unqualified endorsement, but when all things were weighed in the balance, he would probably have had to say that summer was his favorite time of year.

But this summer was no ordinary summer. This summer promised to be the best one ever. Even the work did not seem as hard as in previous summers. The rows of corn did not seem nearly as long when Sarah was hoeing in the row next to him. The most incredible thing of all was that Sarah *liked* to hoe corn. She had always liked to hoe corn, even as a kid. Otis still remembered the day when he had first learned this startling fact. It was four years ago, in the summer of 1937, when he and his father and mother had gone up into the mountains to visit with Uncle Daniel and his family. It was one of only two times he had ever gone up there. He was twelve at the time, Sarah was ten. On that occasion *he* had helped *her* with *her* chores, just as *she* always helped *him* when *she* came to visit. It was while they were hoeing corn up on the hillside behind the house that he had told her how much he hated hoeing corn, and how, in his opinion, it was an act of cruelty on the part of parents to make their kids do it. It was then that Sarah had informed him, flat-out and without shame or remorse, that hoeing corn was *fun*! He had responded as he always responded whenever she said something that was outrageous and indefensible: he had laughed in her face and told her she was crazy. To Otis' way of thinking, any kid who liked to hoe corn just wasn't normal.

But he was glad now that she liked to hoe corn, and he was also glad that she was so fast at it. She also liked to pick strawberries and she was fast at that too. And strangely enough, Otis too, for the first time in his life, found himself almost enjoying these chores which in the past had always left him bent and sore and miserable. Now here they were in the hayloft talking and laughing. Otis could not remember ever laughing before while putting up hay.

He had never imagined that the presence of one person could make such a difference. But it wasn't simply the fact that Sarah was present. It was the way in which she was present. She was no longer sad-eyed and solemn and grieving. She was happy again. She was fun to be with again. Otis knew that he had his Aunt Elizabeth's miraculous recovery to thank for that. Had his Aunt Elizabeth died, his whole summer would have been ruined. But she hadn't. She had sprung back to life, just in the nick of time too, just before school was let out for the summer, and Sarah had catapulted back to life with her. Yes, it was going to be a good summer, he thought to himself, and the summer was only just beginning.

Otis joined his father on the back of the wagon and Sarah reassumed her position on the seat in front. With a shake of the reins the horses turned and headed back toward the field for another load of hay. As Sarah maneuvered the team between two rows of haystacks, Nathan and Otis jumped off and began forking. As they moved slowly along the hillside between the rows, Otis from time to time glanced up at his cousin in the driver's seat and grinned. He found the sight of her in her over-sized straw hat quite amusing. There was a story behind that hat. Otis himself had given it to her the day before, when they had first started working in the hayfield together.

"You're a-gwine t' bake your noodle," he had told her as they gathered the loose, dried hay into stacks. "Bake my noodle?" she had queried, uncomprehending. "Yeah, you know," he had replied, "fry your bean, cook your noggin." She had shot him a brief questioning glance, but whether to ask, "What are you talking about?" or "Why are you being so silly?" he had not been sure. Rather than explain his meaning, or defend his silliness, he had simply said, "Wait here. I know just the thang you need." He had then hurried off to the barn to get an old straw hat that he had found along the road the previous summer. The hat was too big for him—it was even a little too big for his father—so it had been allowed to hang in the barn gathering dust for the past year. If it hadn't been for the fact that one of the horses had chewed up part of the brim, it would still have been a perfectly good hat—for someone with a head big enough to wear it.

"Thar, that'll do just fine," he had declared as he placed the hat on her head and pulled it down over her ears and eyes. She had made no effort to remove it but had simply smiled. He had then picked up a piece of hay and touched it to her lips. "Here, put this betwixt your teeth." Trustingly she had done so. "Now you look like a *real* farmer," he had told her as he stepped back to make an appraisal of his cousin's new look.

His intention had been to make her look comical, but for some reason he had found himself unable to laugh. Instead he had just stood there and stared at her in a kind of stupor. He had found all kinds of unexpected things happening to him. He had suddenly felt a queeziness in his stomach. He had found himself thinking, "How purty she is. How purty her nose is. How purty her mouth is." The picture of her standing there in the hayfield among the stacks of hay with the old straw hat pulled down over her eyes, and the piece of hay between her teeth, and the loose curls of her dark brown hair resting softly on the shoulders of her faded blue calico dress, was a picture that had stayed in his mind.

And all the rest of the day, and all day today, there had been other pictures, and he had been storing them all in his mind. And all the rest of the day, and all day today, she had worn that old straw hat—the hat that he had given her—being careful to balance it just a certain way on the top of her head to keep it from falling down over her eyes. And all the rest of the day, and all the day today, she had kept a piece of hay between her teeth.

"Uncle Nathan?"

Nathan looked up from the empty wagon at his niece standing in the open doorway of the barnloft. He had just pitched the last forkful of the last wagonload of hay into the loft. The first cutting was now dried and out of the weather.

"Uncle Nathan, may I sleep up here?"

"Fine by me. We'll wake you for supper."

"I don't mean *now*, Uncle Nathan. I mean tonight. I mean every night. Would it be all right with you if I made a sort of room for myself up here?"

"You don't like your room in the house?"

"Oh, I do. It's just that it's a little small and there's just the one bed. I thought if I moved out here, I could give my mother more room."

Otis came up behind her and for the third time since dinner pulled the hat down over her eyes. "You cain't sleep up here," he argued, "hit's too hot."

"It wouldn't be too hot at night," she replied, re-adjusting her hat, "not with these doors open."

Nathan smiled. "Just promise me one thing," he said, a very familiar twinkle in his eye. "This winter when it gets bitter cold and that raw wind starts blowin' through them leaky walls, promise me that you won't go settin' the hay afire t' keep warm."

Sarah laughed. "I promise, Uncle Nathan."

"Well now," said Nathan, putting his hands on his hips, "I reckon it's about time we all be thinkin' about gettin' cleaned up for supper. Sarah, you want t' be first one t' jump in the creek? Otis an' I will look after the horses, then we'll come down just as soon as you're finished."

"I'll be quick, Uncle Nathan." Bounding down the ladder, she hit the ground floor running. With half a dozen quick strides, she was out of the barn and running for the creek.

Just before dark Sarah carried her blankets up into the barnloft and made herself a bed in the hay near the open doors. She lay down on her stomach, and, leaning her weight forward onto her elbows, raised her head and shoulders in order to study the view. It was a much grander view, both wider and higher, than her view from either of the two windows in her room in the house. Moreover, this view was to the south, whereas the windows in her room in the house faced north and west. The southern view allowed her to look down across the fields of hay and corn and sorghum to the creek. She could not actually see the creek, but she could see the tops of the trees that lined its banks, and she took some satisfaction in knowing that it was there. On the other side of the creek, dark mountains rose up to meet the darkening sky. The view was sufficiently wide that she knew that if she slept with her head close to the sill, she would be able to see the first morning light appear behind the mountains to the southeast. When she lived up at the old Puckett place, she had been able to see the first morning light from the window above her bed in the loft.

She wondered if she would ever again return to her home in the mountains. She thought she would like to go back someday, if for no other reason than to make sure that it was still there, to assure herself that those eight wonderful years, which her mother did not remember at all, were not something that she herself had dreamed. But would it ever seem like home again? It was almost impossible to comprehend, even now, that her father would not be there if and when she went back up. Her home had always been with her father and her mother. Now her father was in Heaven and her mother seemed to be living in a world that existed only in her own mind. Where was home now? Sarah wondered. Where did she belong now?

Nathan and Hester had very graciously opened their home to her and her mother. But Sarah had never expected to stay at Nathan and Hester's forever—only until her mother was better. But she had not thought about where she might go after that. She had assumed that she would be going back "home," without stopping to think that home as she knew it no longer existed. When she had asked her Uncle Nathan for permission to sleep in the barnloft, and he had first made her promise, in his playful manner, that she would not set it on fire when the weather turned cold, she realized that she had given no thought to the coming winter. For a month after her father's death she had lived one day at a time. Just surviving the day at hand had required an all-consuming effort. There had been no thought of tomorrow or the day after.

But now she realized that she would have to start thinking ahead, planning for the future. If she stayed at Nathan and Hester's through the winter, she would have to go to school. There would be no getting around it: she was only fourteen. Was she prepared to go to school? The prospect did not seem as oppressive now as it did when she was younger, and she supposed that if she really had to go, she would. Still, it was something she preferred not to think about until she absolutely had to, and, like her Cousin Otis, she resolved not to allow thoughts of school to cast a dark shadow over the bright days of summer.

As far as spending the winter in the barnloft was concerned, she expected that if she *were* still living at Nathan and Hester's when the weather turned cold, she would, in all likelihood, move back into the house. She knew that her mother would welcome the additional warmth of her body in the bed, as the upstairs of the house was unheated. And her Uncle Nathan would be relieved of any anxiety he might have about her burning his barn down.

She watched the moon come up from behind the mountains and rise to assume its place among the stars in the night sky. Then as gentle waves of moonlight and starlight washed over her face, she closed her eyes and drifted off to sleep.

"Preacher's comin' to dinner tomorruh," announced Hester about half-way through supper one Saturday evening toward the middle of July, "an I want you all t' be here."

"Hear that, Sarah?" crowed Otis, leaning across the table toward his cousin, "she wants us *all* t' be here."

Sarah *had* heard, and she knew for whose benefit the last part of her Aunt Hester's announcement had been made. Her Aunt Hester had been looking directly at her when she said it.

"I'll be here, Aunt Hester."

"I'm pleased t' hear that," said Hester, "'cause I already told Reverend Eby you *would* be. An' I know you wouldn't want t' make a liar out of me. Lyin' to the preacher is not a habit I want t' get into."

After supper Sarah and Otis walked down to the creek. "Ain't you skeered?" asked Otis.

"Why should I be scared?"

"Well, if I heared the preacher was a-comin' t' see me, I know *I'd* be skeered."

"Reverend Eby isn't coming to see *me*," replied Sarah, "he's coming to dinner. I heard your father say that your mother always invites Reverend Eby to dinner when the peaches are ripe because she knows how much he likes her peach cobbler."

"That may be so, but I also heared Ma say that he 'specially wants t' see *you*. He told her to make sure that you *be* here."

"Why would he want to see *me*?"

"I don't know, but if I was you, I'd be skeered."

The next morning, instead of going off on a walk by herself, as had again become her Sunday morning custom, Sarah decided to spend the time with her mother. Elizabeth was much stronger now, and for the past couple of weeks had been helping Hester in the garden. But whenever Sarah had tried to get her to go walking with her, she had shown an extreme reluctance to venture out of sight of the house, and she would not, under any circumstances, go near the woods. The one time Sarah had tried to coax her into the woods, she had become very nervous and had insisted that they return to the house at once. It was the first evidence Sarah had had that her mother's memory had not been erased completely, that somewhere deep within her mother's mind, buried beneath layer upon layer of disbelief and denial, the painful memory of that tragic event still survived.

Sarah passed the morning sitting quietly with her mother on the porch swing, with hardly a word exchanged between them. Just after half past twelve, Nathan, Hester, and Otis returned home from church. Hester jumped off the seat of the wagon and immediately charged upstairs to change out of her Sunday dress. Before five minutes had ticked off the grandfather clock in the parlor, she was down in the kitchen again, working on dinner. Much of the preparation had been done beforehand—she had baked the peach cobbler the night before—but still the chicken would have to be fried and all the vegetables would have to be cooked. Sarah set the table and tried to be as helpful in other ways as possible, but she soon found that she was best able to do that by staying out of Hester's way. When everything was ready, Hester went upstairs and changed back into her Sunday dress.

At exactly one minute before two o'clock, the sound of a car was heard coming in the lane. The car sputtered to a stop in front of the house and the Reverend Eby stepped out. Nathan, who had been sitting on the edge of the porch, rose to greet him as he came up the walk.

"Hope I'm not too late," said the preacher. He knew perfectly well that he was not. He prided himself on being punctual to the minute.

"Right on time, as always, Lewis," replied Nathan.

At the sound of the screendoor opening behind him, Nathan turned to find Sarah standing beside him.

"Lewis, I don't believe you've ever met my niece Sarah."

"No, I can't say I've actually ever met her. I saw her at Emily's funeral–Lord rest her soul–but I didn't get to talk to her. I've heard a lot about her though. Jacob talks about her all the time."

"I'm pleased to meet you, Reverend Eby," said Sarah politely, offering her hand.

"And I'm pleased t' meet you, young Sarah Wicker," said the preacher, taking her hand and clasping it firmly between both of his own large hands. "I'm very pleased indeed."

The conversation at dinner was dominated by Nathan, who spoke with some passion and at length on the evils of twentieth century materialism and on the difficulty of living a Christian life in a world in which people were becoming increasingly dependent on gasoline motor cars, telephones, and electricity. What, he wondered aloud, should be the Christian's attitude toward all these new worldly conveniences, which were designed, after all, not to improve man's relationship with God, but only to increase his material comfort? He tried on several occasions to get the Reverend Eby to express his views on the matter but without much success. It was apparent that the good preacher had not come to preach or to argue, but to eat.

After dinner everyone adjourned to the parlor, with the exception of Elizabeth, who stayed in the kitchen to clean up.

"That was a fine dinner, Hester," said the preacher, sounding very satisfied. "You make the best peach cobbler in the county."

"Thank you, Reverend Eby, but I cain't take all the credit. Hit's my husband that grows the peaches."

"An' don't forget," interjected Otis, "hit was me who picked 'em. I'm still itchin' all over." He twitched and squirmed inside his dark blue suit to illustrate his point.

Nathan lit his pipe and leaned back in his chair. The Reverend Eby, from his seat on the sofa, peered over his spectacles at Sarah.

"You've been quiet, young lady," observed the preacher. "You hardly said a word at dinner."

"Used t' be you couldn't get her t' shut up," volunteered Otis. "When she first moved down here from Yankee Land, she could talk for days at a time without stoppin'. I know, 'cause I was the one who always had to listen to her. When she moved up into the mountains, hit got so quiet around here, I thought I had gone deef."

Sarah looked at her cousin in utter disbelief. She had never understood why Otis insisted on saying things which weren't true. She may have talked a lot when she was little, but she had never talked for "days at a time without stopping." She could not understand what had possessed Otis to tell such an untruth—and to the preacher at that. Nor did she understand why Otis had said it so loudly. In fact, he had spoken loudly all through dinner as well. Perhaps he really was hard of hearing. Or perhaps he really was afraid of the preacher. She had noticed that he had twitched nervously all through dinner. He had dropped his fork on at least three occasions and had knocked over his glass of milk while reaching for a biscuit. She did not think that his strange behavior could be attributed entirely to peach fuzz. In fact, he hadn't even picked that many peaches. *She* had picked most of them.

"How old are you, Sarah?"

She looked back at the preacher. He had not taken his eyes off her. "I'm fourteen, Reverend Eby. I'll be fifteen in November."

"Have you been baptized?"

"No, sir, I haven't."

"Not even as an infant?"

"No, sir. My mother did not—*does* not—believe in infant baptism."

"Then your mother and we Baptists are in agreement."

"That's about the *only* thang Miss 'Lizbeth and us Baptists agree on," put in Hester.

"Oh?" queried the good preacher, raising his eyebrows and directing his gaze toward Hester without turning his head.

"She wouldn't even 'low the child t' go to Sunday School," explained Hester. "I argued with her over it, but Miss 'Lizbeth could be mighty set in her ways at times."

Sarah felt compelled to come to her mother's defense. "She didn't think—she *doesn't* think—that young children should be taught what to believe before they're old enough to understand it. She always felt that I should be allowed to decide for myself what to believe when I was older."

"Well, now," said the preacher, clasping his hands beneath his chin, "that's not so very different from what we Baptists believe. We believe that the decision to accept Christ has to be a personal decision. It can't be decided for you by your parents or anyone else. Otis here–even though he comes from a good Christian home–wasn't baptized til he was . . . How old *were* you, Otis?"

"Thirteen," replied Otis, grinning. Again he had answered in a voice that was louder than was necessary–and he had twitched again.

"Thirteen. Two years ago already. Seems like it was just the Sunday before last."

"Hit was *three* years ago, Reverend Eby."

"Three? You don't say! Has it been that long? It was in March or April if memory serves me correctly."

"February!"

"Oh yes, February . . . Sarah, let me tell you about your Cousin Otis here. He set an example which should serve as an inspiration to all of us. Most folks who get baptized wait for the big revival meetin' at the end of the summer. But not Otis. No, he couldn't wait that long. He came to me after church one Sunday in February–has it really been three years ago already?– and he said to me, 'Reverend Eby, I'm ready to accept Jesus. I want t' be baptized.' I tried to talk him into waitin' a few months til the water warmed up some, but do you know what that young man said to me? He said, 'Hit ain't for us t' decide, Reverend Eby. When Jesus calls, he don't like t' be kept waitin'.' So we went down to the creek and baptized him right then and there."

"An' I nearly froze to death!"

Everyone laughed. "Rushin' Creek is chilly an' cold," sang Nathan, borrowing rather freely from a popular spiritual, "Chills the body but not the soul . . . Right, Son?"

"I don't know, Pa," replied Otis, "I think Rushin' Creek in the wintertime could chill a person's soul right *out* of their body."

Everyone laughed again.

"How about you, Sarah?" asked the preacher. "Do you think you're old enough now to be baptized in the Lord?"

Sarah hesitated.

"If I was you," advised Otis, "I'd get it over with this summer. I wouldn't be takin' no chance on Jesus callin' next winter when the creek is froze over."

"I don't think I'm ready, Reverend Eby," replied Sarah.

"Oh?"

"I mean, in order to be baptized, I would have to accept Jesus as my savior, wouldn't I?"

"That's right."

"But I don't understand what that means. How did Jesus save me?"

"He died for your sins."

"But that's the part I don't understand, Reverend Eby. Jesus lived so long ago, almost two thousand years before I was even born. How could he have died for *my* sins? That has never made any sense to me. Besides, if I do something wrong, it seems to me that *I* should be the one to make things right again. It's not fair to ask someone else to do it. And I hope I never do anything so terribly wrong that someone else feels they have to *die* for me. That would be awful!"

"But don't you see, child, Jesus died for the sins of *all* mankind. He died that we might have eternal life. 'For God so loved the world that he gave his only begotten son, that whosoever believeth in Him should not perish, but have everlasting life!'"

"In other words, if we believe in Jesus, we will go to Heaven when we die?"

"That's right. We will spend all eternity with Him in Heaven."

"But what about people who don't believe in Jesus? What about people who don't accept Jesus as savior? Surely you're not saying that accepting Jesus and being baptized is the only way of getting into Heaven."

"I'm afraid so, Sarah, the only way. As our Lord Himself said, 'I am the way, the truth, and the life: no man cometh unto the Father, but by me.'"

"But I have already been to Heaven, Reverend Eby. I have been as far as the White Light Heaven. And no one in any of the heavens asked me if I had accepted Jesus as savior, or if I had been baptized. At the time I hadn't even read that much of the Bible. I think it is simply not true that a person must believe in Jesus to get into Heaven."

"Whatever are you talkin' about, child?" gasped Hester. "Pay her no mind, Reverend Eby. She's delirious."

Sarah's startling revelation had taken everyone by surprise. Hester's reaction had been the most immediate and the most vocal, but Nathan too had found himself taken completely off guard by his niece's remarkable statement, and he hoped that his wife's angry outburst would not discourage Sarah from expounding further on her visit to "Heaven." The Reverend Eby also fell into thoughtful silence. He too had been taken by surprise, not so much because of *what* Sarah had said, as by the totally matter-of-fact manner in which she had said it. She had talked of going to Heaven as casually as most people talked of going to a Wednesday night prayer meeting. *What* she had said, however, while quite remarkable, had not come as a complete surprise. Several months before, his friend Jacob had told him this very same story, that his niece Sarah had been to Heaven. That was one of the reasons he had wanted to meet this strange young girl from the mountains. Jacob himself believed the story to be true, but then Jacob was so enamored of this young niece of his, that he would have believed anything she told him. Now the Reverend Eby had heard the same story from Sarah herself. Could he believe that she had actually been to Heaven? He didn't think she was capable of lying. Either she had been to Heaven like she said, or she was–to use Hester's word–delirious. In either case it would be difficult to dispute her claim.

"Have you *really* been to Heaven?" asked Otis, his eyes wide in wonderment.

"Yes," replied Sarah, again quite matter-of-factly, turning to her cousin.

"Wow! How did you get thar? What was it like?"

"Don't ax silly questions, Otis," interrupted Hester, becoming increasingly irritated. "She's talkin' foolishness."

"I've never quite understood how I got there," answered Sarah, a little surprised by her aunt's strenuous objections, "nor do I understand to this day where Heaven is exactly. It's not a place we can go to in our physical bodies. I could not have gone there at all if I had not had help from my friend Kati who lives in the White Light Heaven. She helped me to get out of my body. Kati may be what some people call an angel. My Daddy always thought so.

"What is Heaven like? Well, there's more than one heaven. The first heaven we go to when we die is very much like the Earth. I think that's probably where my Daddy is now. Another heaven I visited is something like the Earth too, only more beautiful than you could possibly imagine. All the meadows and hills and trees and flowers there appear to be made out of crushed glass with light shining through it. And the colors! I couldn't possibly describe all the colors to you! We just don't have the words to describe them.

"Then there's the White Light Heaven, which is filled with brilliant white light. That's where my friend Kati lives. When I was standing with Kati and all her white-light friends in the middle of all that light, I felt completely loved. It was the most wonderful, peaceful feeling I have ever known. I think in a way it was like being baptized. I felt like I was completely filled with God's love."

If anyone had entered the parlor at that moment, they would have thought they had stepped into a burial crypt at midnight, such was the depth and totality of the silence. Even Hester had stopped her fussing and become preternaturally calm. The Reverend Eby removed his spectacles to wipe them, then put them on again to study further the radiant face of the young girl who had just spoken.

"Did you see Jesus?" asked Otis, now completely overcome with awe and admiration.

"You know, my Daddy asked me the same thing, and I didn't know what to say exactly. Jesus may have been there. He may have been one of the white-light people. But no one said anything about Jesus. No one pointed him out to me. If he was there, I didn't get to meet him.

"But my Daddy's asking me about Jesus started me wondering about who Jesus might be and whether he might have come from the White Light Heaven or maybe even from beyond the White Light Heaven. And since then I've read the New Testament. I've read the four gospels many times over, but I still don't have a very clear idea about who Jesus was. I find it all very confusing. Part of the problem is, he lived such a long time ago, and all we really know about him is what's written in the Bible, and it's hard to know what's true and what's made up."

Hester rolled her eyes to the ceiling and gasped again.

"I know that some people believe that the Bible is the Word of God," continued Sarah, "and that every word in it is true. I've heard Aunt Hester say that. I don't suppose that anyone actually believes that God wrote the Bible himself. I guess what they believe is that God talked inside the heads of men who *did* write the Bible and told them what to write and made sure they didn't make any mistakes. I know that people from the White Light World can talk inside your head, because Kati used to talk inside mine—she could put her thoughts right inside my head—so I suppose God could do the same. But whether he actually did or not, I have no way of knowing. I think he probably did not—at least not all the time. It seems to me, if God had written the Bible, or spoken to the men who did, then the Bible wouldn't be nearly so confusing. I should think that if Plato could make difficult ideas easy to understand, then God could do the same... Do you suppose God spoke inside Plato's head, Reverend Eby?"

"What is it in the Bible that you don't understand?" asked the preacher, deliberately side-stepping Sarah's last question.

"Well, lots of things, but it's when I try to figure out who Jesus was that I get most confused. Most of the time Jesus called himself the son of man, but some of his followers called him the son of God. I can see how he could have been both a son of man *and* a son of God, because, in a sense, we're all children of God, and, of course, we were all born of Earth parents as well. But the Gospel of John says that Jesus was the *only* son of God. Do you believe that, Reverend Eby? Do you believe that Jesus was the *only* son of God? Aren't we *all* children of God? When Jesus taught us to pray, didn't he teach us to say, '*Our* Father who art in heaven?' "

"Only those who accept Christ are children of God," retorted Hester, before the Reverend Eby had a chance to respond. "In the case of Jesus, the Father an' the Son are one an' the same. 'In the beginnin' was the Word, an' the Word was with God, an' the Word *was* God.' Jesus was the Word made flesh. If you had read the Gospel of John more carefully, you would not have failed to heed that very important point."

"I admit I haven't read the Gospel of John as many times as I've read Matthew, Mark, and Luke, but I *have* read it. And I remember reading that passage. I remember thinking that it was a very strange use of the word 'word.' "

Nathan smiled as he remembered thinking the same thing the first time he had read the Gospel of John, and he was glad to have finally heard someone else say so.

"Even more strange," continued Sarah, "is the fact that this claim that Jesus was God appears nowhere in the other three gospels. If Jesus *was* God–if he *was* the 'Word made flesh'–why did Matthew, Mark, and Luke make no mention of it? If God spoke any such thing to them, then surely *they* would not have failed to heed such a very important point. And why didn't Jesus call *himself* God? Instead, he called himself the son of man. He always spoke of God as his father."

Hester, having realized that in her zeal she had interrupted the preacher in responding to Sarah's previous question, had vowed not to do so again.

"It's true, he did speak of God as his father," replied the Reverend Eby, "but he also said, 'I and my Father are one.'"

"Oh yes!" exclaimed Sarah, closing her eyes and smiling, her face again assuming a radiant expression, "I know that feeling too! When I was standing in the White Light Heaven surrounded by all that wonderful light and warmth and love, I felt that if I had stayed there a moment longer, my soul would have melted completely and I would have become one with God...

"I'm sure Jesus must have felt that too. Sometimes when I'm reading the Bible, I think to myself, Oh yes, surely Jesus must have come straight from Heaven. He had so much of Heaven's love in him. And he worked so many miracles of healing. He brought dead people back to life. He made sick people well. He made the blind to see again... I tried to imagine what it would be like to be blind, to live in darkness all of my life, and suddenly be able to see. Can you imagine it? I mean, when I think how important sight is to me... If I had been born blind, I would never have known what a beautiful place the Earth is. I would never have been able to see the woods in the spring, or Uncle Nathan's apple trees in bloom, or watch the sun set over those misty blue mountains...

"And he healed lepers and made the deaf to hear and the lame to walk. Oh, I can't even imagine what it would be like not to be able to walk. Or to run!

"And he spoke such beautiful words! I have read the Sermon on the Mountain so many times I almost know it by heart. I think only someone who came from the very highest heaven could have delivered a sermon like that... Resist not evil... Turn the other cheek... Love your enemies... Pray for those who persecute you ... Take no thought for your life... I would imagine that people who think that this Earth life is the only life there is, must have a very difficult time understanding words like that. Only someone who had come from Heaven and stood in the light of God's love could have thought to say such things.

"But Jesus said some other things which I don't understand at all. In the Gospel of Luke he said that anyone who would be his disciple must first *hate* his mother and father. I know I could never have become a disciple because nothing could have made me hate my mother and father. Do you suppose that Jesus really said that, Reverend Eby? Do you think Jesus wants us to *love* our enemies but *hate* our mothers and fathers?"

The preacher did not respond immediately, so Sarah continued. "Personally, I don't think he really said it. He couldn't have said it. I think probably Luke didn't hear it quite right. It would have been a curious thing to say, especially since Jesus also said to keep the commandments, and one of the commandments is to 'honor thy father and thy mother.' But in Matthew too he said he came to bring not peace but a sword, to set son against father and daughter against mother...

"Even more difficult for me to understand are some of the things that Jesus did. Like when he was in the country of the Gerasenes and he cured that man who was possessed of demons. I think it was a good thing to cast out the unclean spirits, but did he have to send them into a herd of swine and cause the whole herd to rush over a cliff and be drowned in the sea? There were two thousand pigs in that herd according to Mark. I know that pigs aren't as pleasing to look at as some of God's other creatures, but they're God's creatures all the same. It's hard for me to believe that a man who was filled with God's love could cause such suffering to innocent creatures. And do you suppose that killing all those pigs really got rid of the demons? I would imagine that when the pigs drowned, the demons simply left and went someplace else, maybe into some other poor man.

"I've tried to explain to myself why Jesus would allow a herd of pigs to perish like that. I want to believe he had a good reason. I've told myself, maybe that's the only way he could get the demons to come out of that poor possessed man, and there were *so many* demons that he had to use up a whole herd. But I've never been very satisfied with that.

"I prefer to believe that it never really happened at all–that it's just a made-up story–though why anyone would make up such a story I can't imagine. And since Matthew, Mark, and Luke all tell pretty much the same story, I suspect something of the sort must have happened. It's not likely that they all heard it wrong– we're supposing now that God actually *did* talk inside their heads—though I've noticed that in Matthew's story there are *two* men possessed of demons, and in Mark and Luke only one...

"There was something else that Jesus did that I never quite understood. For no good reason he cursed a fig tree and caused it to wither and die. I'm sure you know the story I mean, Reverend Eby. He was hungry, so he went to a fig tree, but it had no fruit on it because it wasn't the right season, so he got angry and cursed it and made it die. If that story is true, I can't believe that Jesus was God or even a very good son of God. I should think that if he had the power to cause the tree to die, he would also have had the power to cause it to bear fruit, even if it was out of season. Anyone who could turn water into wine and feed five thousand people with five loaves of bread and two small fish, should never have needed to go hungry.

"Do you see what I mean, Reverend Eby? Do you understand why I can't make up my mind about Jesus? My mother and I explored the question of Jesus at great length, but we were never able to come to any satisfactory conclusion. I'd like to believe that he was a great teacher who came to Earth from one of the higher heavens to show the world what God's love was like. And I'd like to believe that some of those other stories aren't true. I'd like to believe in Jesus because my Daddy believed in Jesus. But my mother always told me that I must be careful not to believe something just because I *want* to believe it. She was right, of course. That's the surest way for a seeker after truth to fall into error."

Even Hester had been rendered speechless by this latest discourse of Sarah's. She could not fault the child for not knowing the Scriptures, but then neither could the Devil be faulted on that count. What had so aggrieved Hester was her niece's arrogance in daring to call into question the truth of God's Word. She had even questioned the divinity of Christ. Hester preferred to believe that Sarah's unforgivable behavior was due to her lack of proper religious guidance as a child, though it had crossed her mind that her slippery-tongued young niece just might be possessed of a demon herself. Hester had been shocked almost to the point of senselessness by Sarah's repeated blasphemies and had half

expected the good Reverend Eby to call down the wrath of God upon her head. But the Reverend Eby had not done so. Hester had cast a number of fearful glances in the preacher's direction during the course of Sarah's long discourse, and on each occasion he seemed to be listening intently, absorbing her words like parched earth absorbs rain. He had given no indication of being even shocked, must less driven to righteous anger. After Sarah had finished speaking, he remained deep in thought for several minutes, his eyes still fixed upon her. Then he smiled and spoke.
"Sarah?"
"Yes, Reverend Eby?"
"You said that you and your mother explored the question of Jesus at some length?"
"Yes."
"How would you like to explore the question of Jesus with me?"
She hesitated before replying. "I think I'd like that, Reverend Eby."
"Then why don't you come to church next Sunday?"
Again she hesitated. "All right, Reverend Eby, I will."
"Praise the Lord!" shouted Hester.
"Reverend Eby?"
"Yes, Sarah?"
"Could you talk about the kingdom of God next Sunday?"
The preacher smiled. "With pleasure! Jesus had quite a lot to say about the kingdom of God, as I am sure you are well aware."
"Yes. I think the most important thing Jesus said in all the gospels was 'Seek first the kingdom of God.' I'd like to find the kingdom of God, Reverend Eby, because I think that if I found it, I would find again that peace and love that I felt when I was in the White Light Heaven. Only, I'm not sure I know exactly how to go about looking for it.

"The winter before last I read through all the gospels and wrote down everything Jesus said about the kingdom of God. It's true, what you said: he did have a lot so say about it. The only problem is, he didn't always seem to be saying the same thing. In one place he said the kingdom of God does not come with signs to be observed. We can't see it when it comes. We can't say it is here, or it is there. He said the kingdom of God is 'within you.'

"But then, in another place, he said something very different. He said when the kingdom of God comes, there would be 'terrors and great signs from heaven.' He said nation would rise up against nation, and there would be disease and famine and great destruction upon the earth. When you see these things taking place, he said, you will know that the kingdom of God is near."

"And then," exclaimed Hester, smiling up at the ceiling and clapping her hands, "we will see the Son of man come in a cloud with power and great glory! What a glorious day that will be! Hallelujah!"

Sarah, taken a little by surprise by Hester's sudden outburst of rapture, interrupted her train of thought and looked curiously at her aunt. Sarah knew that her Aunt Hester was looking forward to the return of Jesus—indeed, she seemed to be expecting it almost any day—but Sarah did not understand her aunt's apparent lack of sympathy for the many thousands who would presumably die in the terrible time of death and destruction that, according to the Bible, would immediately precede the coming of God's kingdom.

The Reverend Eby, who had not taken his eyes off Sarah for more than a few seconds since they had adjourned to the parlor, continued to study her now. He had been listening to her with interest before Hester's interruption and he thought he had discerned the direction in which her train of thought was taking her.

"And so you want to know," he said, anticipating her next question, "how the kingdom of God can be both seen and not seen, can come with signs and not come with signs, and can be outside you and inside you at the same time?"

"Yes," she replied. "Is the kingdom of God something we must wait for to happen, or is it something we can find now if we look for it? If it's something we must wait for, then why did Jesus tell us to seek it?"

The preacher smiled at her approvingly. "In the Bible, God has revealed his holy truth for all the world, and he has promised us that if we seek, we shall find. You are seeking and that is good. If you continue to search the Scriptures, I am sure that one day you will come to understand what Jesus meant by 'the kingdom of God.' And I have no doubt that one day you will find the kingdom itself . . . But we can explore this subject further next Sunday, in church."

Jacob ambled slowly through the garden, pausing frequently to linger among the flowers. At the edge of the garden he stopped again, this time to admire the profusion of white, pink, and purple blossoms of the climbing sweet pea, which had completely taken over one section of the garden fence, running riotously up it, along it, and over the top. He turned and walked along the fence in the direction of the house, but after only a few steps he stopped again, for here were the hollyhocks, standing stately, tall, proudly erect—in sharp contrast to the undisciplined, sprawling, clambering vines of the neighboring sweet pea—standing alert and vigilant, like a column of red-, pink-, and white-eyed sentinels guarding their allotted portion of fence.

As he stood before the hollyhocks, he thought again of Emily. How Emily had loved flowers! She had planted them everywhere —around the house, along the garden fence, in the garden itself—any place she could find a few square inches of earth that didn't already have something else growing in it. It hardly seemed possible that Emily was gone. All of her flowers were still here. Ever since the first snowdrops had pushed through the earth in late winter, there had been a steady procession of flowers, whose seeds or bulbs had been gently placed in the soil by her loving hands. As the crocuses, daffodils, tulips, and irises had each bloomed in turn, each had served as a reminder of Emily. And now the hollyhocks, her favorites! As if Jacob needed to be reminded. As if he would have forgotten even if the spring had never come and all the flowers had remained frozen in the earth.

As he stood and watched the hollyhocks lean and sway in the late afternoon breeze, he heard the sound of a motor car sputtering up the lane. Assuming it was Isaac and Martha returning home from their Sunday drive, he paid it no mind. Not until he heard the car stop in front of his own house did he realize that it was not Isaac but someone come to call on *him*. He walked around to the front of the house to find his good friend the Reverend Lewis Eby getting out of his car.

"Good day, Jacob," said the preacher, "I was hopin' I'd find you home."

"Howdy, Lewis."

"I've brought you somethin'."

"Oh?"

The preacher walked around to the passenger side of the car and reached in through the open window. Jacob watched as he carefully lifted out a flat, rectangular object covered with a dish towel.

"When I told your sister Hester that I was comin' out to see you, she insisted I bring this along."

Jacob lifted a corner of the towel and smiled. "Peach cobbler." He took the pan of cobbler from the preacher. "I must remember t' thank her next time I see her."

The two men began walking toward the house.

"Can I get you somethin' to eat or drink, Lewis?"

"Nothin' to eat, thank you, Jacob. I've just had dinner at Hester's and I don't have to tell you what that is like." He patted his stomach. "But if you offered me a cool glass of water, I wouldn't turn it down."

The Reverend Eby followed Jacob into the kitchen. Jacob placed the pan of cobbler in the bread box and drew two glasses of water from the kitchen faucet.

"I don't think I'll ever get used to the idea of drawin' water straight out of the wall," said Jacob, handing the preacher one of the glasses.

"Nathan still pumps his by hand," observed the preacher, taking a seat at the table. "He told me at dinner that he won't have electricity—won't have it on the place."

"Nathan an' Hester are like a pair of matched mules," mused Jacob. "They're both stubborn, an' they're both agreed that all these new labor-savin' inventions are gwine t' lead to no good. They like keepin' thangs simple. Dan'l was that way too."

"Speakin' of Daniel," said the preacher, "I finally got to meet his daughter Sarah today."

Jacob smiled and studied the preacher's face closely in the hope that he might be able to read thereon a clue to his friend's impressions of his niece.

"She's a very unusual girl," continued the preacher. "I must say, she's not exactly what I expected. To look at her, you'd never guess what's goin' on inside her head. She really is a right good-lookin' girl. She's got a real sweet face, an' the smile of an angel."

"Yes," agreed Jacob, "Sarah's a fine-lookin' girl. She takes after her mother."

"She seems to have been well-brought-up, too. She minds her manners, says 'please' an' 'thank you,' 'yes, sir,' an' 'no, sir.' Durin' dinner she was real quiet, only spoke when she was spoke to . . ."

The preacher paused, then smiled, as he recalled an incident that had happened at dinner. "I noticed that she wasn't eatin' any of Hester's fried chicken, so I asked her if she wouldn't care for a piece. She said, 'No, thank you, Reverend Eby, I don't eat chicken.' Then Otis started teasin' her, tried to get her to take a bite off the chicken leg he was eatin'. He pushed it right up to her nose. Anyone else in her place might have got angry, but she just smiled and said, 'No, thank you, Otis' . . . She said it just as polite as you please: 'No, thank you, Otis' . . . Otis behaved strangely today."

"How's that?"

"He acted skittish as a cat in a fryin' pan. If you ask me, he's been smitten by that young cousin of his . . . Can't say that I blame him. I know if I was sixteen again—Heaven forbid!—she'd turn my head."

438

The Reverend Eby fell silent and seemed to drift into a pleasant reverie. Jacob waited patiently for his friend to return.

"Oh yes, " said the preacher suddenly. "I was sayin' how quiet your niece was at dinner. Sometimes when folks are quiet it's because they haven't got anything to say. That doesn't appear to be the case with young Sarah, however–as I soon found out. She's got a *lot* to say, an' she's not afraid to speak her mind. After dinner I asked her if she had given any thought to bein' baptized, an' she allowed how she didn't think she could be baptized because she didn't understand how Jesus had saved her. Then she said she didn't think a person had to be baptized to get into Heaven anyway. She went on to talk at some length on how she couldn't make up her mind about who Jesus was. I have to admit, your young niece raised some very disturbin' points. I know preachers of the Gospel aren't supposed to have any doubts or qualms about God's Holy Word, but I can tell you as a close personal friend, that there are passages in the Bible that disturb *me*.

"As I sat there listenin' to her, I kept thinkin', this is what the elders in the temple must have felt like when the twelve-year-old Jesus instructed them in the law. She knows her Bible backwards an' forwards–probably better than most folks who go to church every Sunday–and she seems to have done a lot of thinkin' on it–too much for her own good, some might say."

"Hit's the way she was brung up," explained Jacob. "Her mother was always after her to figger thangs out for herself. Elizabeth is quite a smart lady, you know. She's been to college an' she's read a lot of books. She brung a whole trunkload of books with her when they moved down here. When you an' I was a-growin' up, thar was only one book in the house, an' that was the Bible. We was taught that the Bible was God's Holy Word, an' it just never crossed any of our minds t' question it.

"Sarah wasn't brung up that way. She growed up around a lot of books–her mother read to her all the time when she was little–an' Sarah was taught to ax questions about ever'thang. Even when she was a wee young'un, her little haid was always busy tryin' t' figger thangs out."

"Well," said the preacher, "it would appear as though she's still tryin' to figure things out. She hasn't got Jesus quite figured out yet. She can't understand why Jesus told his followers that they must first hate their mothers an' fathers, or why he sent the Gerasene demons into the herd of swine an' caused it to perish, or why he cursed a fig tree an' caused it to die. In all my years of preachin' the Gospel, I've never been called upon to defend the moral character of Jesus against the charge that it wasn't good enough."

Jacob smiled. "Did she say anythang about gwine up to Heaven?"

"Yes, she did. And it's like you said. When she talks about Heaven, you can't help but believe that she's actually been there. Her whole face lights up... Hester doesn't believe it though. She doesn't believe a word of it. She nearly had a conniption on the spot. She thinks Sarah is not altogether sound in the head. Apparently Nathan an' Hester had never heard about this before today. They both seemed surprised to hear it."

"Yes, I think Dan'l an' Elizabeth decided it would be best not to mention it. They were afeared that some folks might get the wrong idea—like Hester. What did you think of her story, Lewis?"

"To tell you the truth, I don't know what to make of it. The way she described Heaven is not exactly the way most of us imagine it. She talked about there bein' more than one heaven. I think most Christians would find the notion of more than one heaven a little strange—though there is that curious passage in Second Corinthians where Paul talks about a man bein' taken up to the *third* heaven. Stranger still, she said she didn't see Jesus."

"Do you think she made the whole thang up?"

"No. I admit it's hard to believe that she's actually been to Heaven, but it's even harder to believe that she made the story up. I don't think she could speak falsely to save her soul."

"Do you think she's...?"

"Crazy? Delirious? No, I can't agree with Hester. Your niece's mind seems perfectly sound to me."

Jacob smiled, glad for his friend's reassuring words, which confirmed his own judgement. Both men remained silent for a moment, as each recalled Sarah's astonishing tale, then Jacob spoke again.

"Did Sarah say how she got to Heaven?"

"I believe she said an angel came an' took her."

"Yes, an angel—what we'd call an angel—though Sarah likes to call her somethin' else. She once told me that when she was younger this angel would come visit her ever' mornin' in her bed . . . Do you remember who else used to see angels in the mornin'?"

The Reverend Eby gave Jacob a curious look, then nodded his head.

"Lewis, let me ax you this—an' I want you to answer me as a friend, not as a preacher of the Gospels . . . Do you think hit's possible for a soul to be re-born?"

The Reverend Eby hesitated before replying. "You think Sarah is Ruth re-born?"

"I don't know what t' think. All I know is, Sarah is so much like Ruth, that I cain't think of the one without thinkin' of the other. I'm always confusin' the two of them in my haid. Dan'l once told me that Sarah spent a good part of her growin'-up years off in the woods by herself—just like Ruth did. Sarah has an unusual way with animals. She can even talk to the wild critters an' handle their young. The only other person I ever knowed who could do that was Ruth. Sarah cain't bear t' see animals kilt. She won't eat meat. She ain't et a bite of meat since she was about nine years old. If you remember, Ruth was the same way. She never et meat neither. She wouldn't touch it. Hit made her sick to her stomach. I don't remember Ruth ever talkin' about bein' to Heaven, but she did talk about seein' angels, 'specially towards the end of her life."

The Reverend Eby remained silent for a moment, contemplating the implications of his friend's words. "I don't know, Jacob. I admit there are some strong similarities, but there are some differences too. I never knew Ruth to question the Scriptures the way Sarah does."

"But don't you see, Lewis? That's just because of the way Sarah was brung up. If Sarah had been raised the way *we* was—the way *Ruth* was—she'd never a-thought t' question God's Word either . . . Don't you think hit's possible that a soul can leave this world, then come back in another body?"

The Reverend Eby breathed a heavy sigh. "Jacob, I know how much Ruth meant to you, and I know it would be a great comfort to you to think she's come back. But souls don't come back to the Earth once they leave it. They wouldn't want to even if they could. Once they have seen Heaven in all its glory, nothin' could persuade them to return to this vale of tears. 'It is appointed unto men once to die.' That's what the Bible teaches."

"Yes, I know, the Letter to the Hebrews. But didn't Jesus himself say that John the Baptist was the prophet Elijah reborn?"

The preacher stared hard at his friend. "Yes," he admitted, "he did, in the seventeenth chapter of Matthew. But in the Gospel of John we are told that when the Jews sent priests and Levites from Jerusalem into the desert to ask John the Baptist himself if he was Elijah, he answered, 'I am not.' "

"But if John the Baptist was not Elijah reborn, why did Jesus say that he was?"

"I have to admit, Jacob, that's one of those passages in Scripture that disturbs me."

"I wonder," mused Jacob after a moment's reflection, "if a soul *was* t' be reborn into this world, if they'd remember bein' who they was before."

"You think John the Baptist might have been Elijah reborn but not remembered bein' Elijah?"

"I wasn't thinkin' of John an' Elijah just then, but yes. Wouldn't that explain why Jesus said John was Elijah, but John himself said he wasn't? Mebbe John just plain didn't remember."

"Jacob," sighed the preacher, "I'm afraid I can't tell you what to believe about souls bein' reborn. That's what makes us Baptists diff'rent from the Catholics. We have no priests or bishops or popes tellin' us what to believe. We have no creeds. The Bible is our sole authority. The answers to all our questions are in the Bible. But it's up to each one of us to find them. It's like I told Sarah this afternoon: search the Scriptures. If you continue to search the Scriptures–and pray–I am sure you will find what you are lookin' for. But we must be careful, my friend, that we don't read into Scripture somethin' that isn't there."

Now it was Jacob who seemed to lose himself in contemplation. It was not unusual for the two old friends to lapse occasionally into prolonged periods of thoughtful silence in the course of a conversation.

"I was just thinkin'," said Jacob at last, "about a time a few years back–the first time Sarah ever spent the night in this house. She was only about seven or eight at the time. We got to talkin' about Ruth. She axed me whar Ruth was. I told her Ruth was in Heaven. Then she wanted t' know how people get to Heaven. I explained to her that it was only our souls that go to Heaven. Then she axed me if I thought *her* soul would go to Heaven when she died. I said, yes, I was sure of it. She was glad t' hear that, 'cause she was very excited about one day gwine t' to be with her Aunt Ruth."

The peaceful smile that had lingered on Jacob's lips as he reminisced about that very special Thanksgiving night in 1934 now gave way to a more troubled expression. "I think in time Sarah will come around to acceptin' Jesus . . . But what if she doesn't, Lewis? Do you think God would condemn someone like Sarah to eternal hellfire for not bein' baptized?"

"I should hate to think it. We must pray for her, Jacob. You will be glad to know that she has agreed to come to church next Sunday. She even asked me if I would speak on the kingdom of God. She's very interested in the kingdom of God, you know. She may not yet be able to accept Jesus as her personal Lord and Savior, and she may have difficulty understandin' some of the things Jesus said and did when He walked the earth, but she seems to take quite seriously his teaching to 'seek first the kingdom of God.' She's seeking, Jacob, she's earnestly seeking. I can't believe God would shut out of Heaven someone who is so earnestly seeking His kingdom.

"Besides, I'm not so sure but that she hasn't been baptized already. Not by me. Not in the waters of Rushing Creek. But by the Holy Spirit Himself."

14

THINGS HEARD AND SEEN

From his elevated position behind the podium in the middle of the raised platform, the Reverend Lewis Eby looked down upon the three folds of his assembled flock and smiled. Directly in front of him, occupying the middle section of benches, sat the younger members of the congregation, mostly teenagers–girls in the front rows, boys in the rear–all scrubbed clean and sporting their finest Sunday attire. The boys, with their hair slicked down and their wrists and ankles protruding from coat sleeves and trouser legs that could not be altered often enough to keep pace with their burgeoning growth, looked especially uncomfortable. But they had learned to live with discomfort. For them, that's what going to church was all about.

The Reverend Eby allowed his gaze to drift to the left of the young members, to the section of benches reserved for the menfolk of the community; then slowly to the right, to that reserved for the women. This division of the faithful into three folds dated back to the founding of the church in 1827, and although there had been some talk in recent years about abandoning the arrangement in favor of more modern ways, the elders of the church had resisted, seeing no need to tinker with something that worked just fine the way it was.

Just off the platform to the preacher's left stood three rows of benches, turned at right angles to the congregation and facing the podium. On these benches sat the choir. Behind the choir, in the corner, stood the old pump organ. On the other side of the platform, to the preacher's right, stood three more rows of benches, also facing the podium. This was the "amen corner." It was the function of the dozen or so men and women who occupied the back two rows of benches in the "amen corner" to punctuate the preacher's sermon with suitably-placed shouts of "amen" or other equally rousing words of approbation. The front-row bench in the "amen corner" was reserved for the "mourners," for those of the faithful who had strayed from the path of righteousness in recent weeks and who had been moved by the Holy Spirit to repent of their waywardness and to ask God for forgiveness. There were few in this mountain community of God-fearing men and women who would not have preferred to shame themselves before their peers for two hours on Sunday morning to the alternative, which was to face God on Judgement Day with sins unconfessed. There were five such "mourners"–three men and two women–kneeling before the front bench this morning.

The Reverend Eby opened his Bible to the sixth chapter of Matthew and began to read in a strong baritone voice:

" 'Therefore I say unto you, Take no thought for your life, what ye shall eat, or what ye shall drink; nor yet for your body, what ye shall put on. Is not the life more than meat, and the body than raiment? Behold the fowls of the air: for they sow not, neither do they reap, nor gather into barns; yet your heavenly Father feedeth them. Are ye not much better than they? Which of you by taking thought can add one cubit unto his stature? And why take ye thought for raiment? Consider the lilies of the field, how they grow; they toil not, neither do they spin: and yet I say unto you, That even Solomon in all his glory was not arrayed like one of these. Wherefore, if God so clothe the grass of the field, which today is, and tomorrow is cast into the oven, shall he not much more clothe you, O ye of little faith? Therefore, take no thought, saying, What shall we eat? or, What shall we drink? or, Wherewithal shall we be clothed? For after all these things do the Gentiles seek: for your heavenly Father knoweth that ye have need of all these things. But seek ye first the kingdom of God, and his righteousness; and all these things shall be added unto you.' "

He paused to allow the words to settle into the hearts and minds of the seventy or so worshippers gathered together within the walls of the small country church. He sought out the new face in the crowd. It was not hard to find. Sarah had taken a seat in the very first row, next to Gladys Cole, directly below the podium. He smiled down at her.

" 'But seek ye first the kingdom of God, and his righteousness,' " he repeated, raising his eyes once again to meet the watchful, expectant gazes of older, more familiar faces, " 'and all these things shall be added unto you.' . . . What wonderful words these are! What a glorious promise! What a magnificent test of our faith!

"This morning we have a young visitor to our church whom I had the great pleasure of meeting last Sunday afternoon. In the course of our conversation I found her to be an earnest young seeker after truth. She told me, among other things, that she thought the most important words spoken by Jesus in all the gospels were, 'Seek first the kingdom of God.' " He smiled. "A very bold statement for one so young, I thought to myself. If someone had asked me what I thought were the most important words spoken by Jesus when I was fourteen, I would have been at a loss for words. Even today I would have to stop and think. There are so many! Trying to find one saying or one passage that stands out above the rest is like trying to find a perfect diamond— in a field of perfect diamonds! One saying that comes to mind however is the one that Jesus himself called the first and greatest commandment: 'Thou shalt love the Lord thy God with all thy heart, and with all thy soul, and with all thy mind, and with all thy strength.' . . . And then comes immediately to mind his second commandment: 'Thou shalt love thy neighbor as thyself.' . . . Then there is his counsel to 'be perfect even as your Father in Heaven is perfect.' . . . And what about his glorious pronouncement, 'I am the way, the truth, and the life: no man cometh unto the Father, but by me.' . . . I could go on and on. So many perfect diamonds!

" 'Seek first the kingdom of God.' The most important words spoken by Jesus in all the gospels? Certainly among the most important. Seek first the kingdom. More important than food. More important than clothing. More important than life itself! 'Be not anxious for your life.' . . .'Take no thought for your life.' . . .

'But rather seek ye the kingdom of God and his righteousness, and *all* these things'–everything you need–'shall be added unto you.' . . . Very important words indeed!

"Now I know that I have talked to you about seeking the kingdom of God before. In fact, some of you may think that this sermon I'm about to preach sounds a whole lot like a sermon I preached just a few weeks back. Some of you right now may be thinking, the Reverend Eby must have slept late this morning: he didn't have time to think up a new sermon . . ."

A badly-timed "amen" from one of the brethren in the "amen corner" caused muffled laughter to ripple through the congregation. No one was more amused than the Reverend Eby himself, who turned to the offending brother and grinned broadly. Then, turning back to the congregation, he continued.

"But I'm hoping that most of you are like the good widow Lawson–Lord rest her soul–who came to me after a Sunday service a few years back and said, 'Reverend Eby, I wouldn't mind if you preached the same sermon every week. I just like to hear the way you say the words.' "

The congregation laughed again, cautiously, nervously. The Reverend Eby always began his sermons with a few light-hearted remarks, but those who attended regularly knew that this was only the calm before the storm.

"Besides, I've always believed that all my sermons are worth hearing more than once anyway. If something is good, it should be heard more than once. Why, I've been reading this same old *book* here over and over again for nigh onto sixty years"–he held up his Bible–"and I haven't got tired of *it* yet. In fact, every time I read through it, I seem to find some new insight, some new meaning, which I had never found before . . . So maybe some of you can find something new in this old sermon.

"Seek first the kingdom of God! Now, some of you may ask, if seeking the kingdom of God is so important–more important even than procuring the necessities of life–how do we go about it? Where do we look? What is it that we're looking for?

"Let us consider this question for a moment. First of all, what is a kingdom? A kingdom is a land or a country ruled by a king.

When David was king of Israel, Israel was his kingdom. The people living in the kingdom are subjects of the king. The kingdom of God is a kingdom ruled by God. Only, the kingdom of God is not a physical kingdom. It is not a physical land or country. It does not consist of physical mountains and valleys and trees. It has no physical boundaries. It is not a kingdom of this earth. It is a spiritual kingdom, a heavenly kingdom. The day will soon come when Jesus will return and establish God's kingdom here on this earth–and it will be a day of great rejoicing when that day comes–but at the moment God's kingdom is not a kingdom of this earth. But that does not mean that we have to wait for Jesus to return in order to enter into God's kingdom. Because God's kingdom is really two kingdoms: it is a kingdom that *will* come on this earth; but it is a kingdom in Heaven *now*. We must wait for God's kingdom to come on earth, but we do not have to wait for God's heavenly kingdom. We can enter God's heavenly kingdom *now*. The moment we accept Jesus as our king–as the absolute ruler of our lives–we enter into the heavenly kingdom of God, we become subjects in God's spiritual kingdom. The spiritual kingdom of God is a kingdom of the mind, of the soul, and of the heart. This is why Jesus said that the first and greatest commandment was to love the Lord thy God with all thy heart and with all thy soul and with all thy mind. Because once we do this, we become subjects of God. By opening our hearts to God's almighty love, by placing our souls in God's hands, by keeping our minds always fixed on God's commandments–by giving ourselves to God in total obedience–thereby do we enter into the kingdom of God."

He turned to the seventeenth chapter of Luke:

" 'And when he was demanded of the Pharisees when the kingdom of God should come, he answered them and said, The Kingdom of God cometh not with observation: neither shall they say, Lo here! or, lo there! for, behold, the kingdom of God is within you.' "

For the next half hour Sarah listened as the Reverend Eby continued to expound upon the nature of the spiritual kingdom of God. As he spoke, he was in almost constant motion, pacing back and forth on the platform, returning to the podium only long enough to catch his breath or read an appropriate passage from Scripture, before setting himself in motion again. Now he was talking about the *power* of God's kingdom.

"The kingdom of God is a mighty kingdom, a kingdom of great power. It is mightier than any of the kingdoms of the earth, and will outlast them all. All the kingdoms of the earth will crumble into dust, but God's kingdom will not pass away. It is a kingdom that is increasing in power every day, increasing in strength and numbers every day, growing mightier every day, as new souls enter in. Jesus compared the kingdom of God to a tiny mustard seed. Now, a tiny mustard seed does not look very powerful, does not look very mighty. But sow it in fertile ground, and water it, and look after it–see to it that the weeds don't choke it out or the rabbits eat it off–and soon it grows into a mighty shrub–so great that the birds of the air come and build nests in its branches. So too does the kingdom of God grow in power as new souls enter in.

"Again, Jesus compared the kingdom of God to a measure of leaven. If he were livin' here today, he might have said 'a teaspoon of bakin' soda.' It doesn't look like much, a teaspoon of bakin' soda, but you add it to a cup of flour with a pinch of salt and a little water, and just watch that flour rise. Hot biscuits for dinner! So too does the kingdom of God grow and swell as new souls enter in. In each case–in the case of the mustard seed and in the case of the leaven–a little water is added. That's the water of baptism. The water is important. The mustard seed would not sprout without it; without it the flour would not rise. Each time a new soul is baptized by water in the Lord's name, the kingdom of God increases. I am pleased to say that even as I speak, the kingdom of God is increasing in strength and numbers all over the world. Our Baptist missionaries are spreading God's word all over the world, to places as far away as China. Already they have won thousands of souls to God's kingdom."

From the moment the Reverend Eby had stepped to the podium to begin his sermon, Sarah had kept her eyes fixed upon him. How different he seemed now from the soft-spoken, retiring gentleman who had come to her Aunt Hester's for dinner the previous Sunday and had talked with her in the parlor. Now he was speaking with great force and passion and she had found herself almost mesmerized by the power of his performance. As he strode back and forth across the raised platform only a few feet in front of her, with his long arms waving about, she was reminded of a great bird about to launch itself into flight. She had not been so completely mesmerized, however, that she had failed to notice what she considered to be an inconsistency and a confusion in the preacher's text. On several occasions he had used the words 'God' and 'Jesus' interchangeably, as though they were one and the same. No doubt he had done so deliberately, but, to Sarah's mind, this peculiar idea that Jesus was God was not one that could be supported by either reason *or* revelation. Jesus had not said, "Seek *my* kingdom and *my* righteousness;" he had said, "Seek God's kingdom and *his* righteousness." Furthermore, even though he had instructed his followers to "be perfect even as your Father in heaven is perfect," he himself had made no such claim to perfection. He had even objected to being called "good." "Why do you call me good?" he had asked. "No one is good but God alone." How could he have said any more clearly that he was not God? If the main foundation for the argument that Jesus was God was that curious passage at the beginning of the Gospel of John about the Word becoming flesh, then, Sarah thought, adherents to that doctrine were on very shaky ground indeed. She could understand why people would *want* to believe that Jesus was God. "God" was a very difficult concept to grasp– perhaps impossible to grasp for earthbound minds. Kati had said that even in the lower heavens people do not have a clear idea about what God is. Not until they reach the White Light Heaven do they begin to understand. Sarah remembered one of the discussions she and her mother had had about God. Her mother had made the observation that mankind, throughout its history, in its desire to know and understand God–in its seeming need to know God *personally*–had persistently sought to reduce God to something more familiar, more comprehensible. If God can be reduced to man, then God can be grasped and held and understood. The only question is, is that which has been grasped really God? Sarah could not forget something her mother had stressed repeatedly whenever the two of them had explored difficult ideas together: it is far better to expand your mind to fit an idea, than to reduce the idea to fit your mind. And in the case of "God," her mother felt, the idea may be forever beyond the grasp of finite minds.

Now suddenly the Reverend Eby stopped again. Sarah watched as the towering figure hovered over the edge of the platform for a moment, then stepped again behind the podium. She waited in hushed silence, scarcely breathing, for the preacher's next words. So quiet and still were those seated behind her and to both sides that if she were to have closed her eyes, she could easily have imagined that she was alone in the church. But she was not about to close her eyes. Suddenly, in a loud, impassioned voice, the Reverend Eby was reading from the twenty-first chapter of Luke:

" 'And as some spake of the temple, how it was adorned with goodly stones and gifts, he said, As for these things which ye behold, the days will come, in the which there shall not be left one stone upon another, that shall not be thrown down. And they asked him, saying, Master, but when shall these things be? and what sign will there be when these things shall come to pass? And he said, Take heed that ye be not deceived: for many shall come in my name, saying, I am Christ; and the time draweth near: go ye not therefore after them. But when ye shall hear of wars and commotions, be not terrified: for these things must first come to pass; but the end is not by and by.

" 'Then said he unto them, Nation shall rise against nation, and kingdom against kingdom: and great earthquakes shall be in divers places, and famines, and pestilences; and fearful sights and great signs shall there be from heaven. But before all these, they shall lay their hands on you, and persecute you, delivering you up to the synagogues, and into prisons, being brought before kings and rulers for my name's sake . . . And ye shall be betrayed both by parents and brethren, and kinsfolk, and friends; and some of you shall they cause to be put to death. And ye shall be hated of all men for my name's sake . . .

" 'And when ye shall see Jerusalem compassed with armies, then know that the desolation thereof is nigh. Then let them which are in Judea flee to the mountains; and let them which are in the midst of it depart out; and let not them that are in the countries enter thereinto. For these be the days of vengeance, that all things which are written may be fulfilled. But woe unto them that are with child, and to them that give suck, in those days: for there shall be great distress in the land, and wrath upon this people. And they shall fall by the edge of the sword, and shall be led away captive into all nations: and Jerusalem shall be trodden down of the Gentiles, until the times of the Gentiles be fulfilled.

" 'And there shall be signs in the sun, and in the moon, and in the stars; and upon the earth distress of nations, with perplexity; the sea and the waves roaring; men's hearts failing them for fear, and for looking after those things which are coming on the earth: for the powers of heaven shall be shaken.' "

The preacher shook the podium violently as he read these last words, causing Sarah to start. In fact she had felt her body trembling throughout the impassioned reading. These words of Jesus, which she had read to herself many times, had never before sounded so angry and fearsome. She was just glad that the Reverend Eby had not been reading from Jeremiah or any of the other Old Testament prophets! As she struggled to calm herself, she felt the whole bench begin to shake. Embarrassed lest others seated on the bench feel the tremor, she placed both hands on it in an effort to still it, but the harder she tried, the more the tremor increased. She glanced to her left to see if the girl seated next to her had noticed. She was a pretty girl, blonde and buxom, but she was perspiring freely–and *also* trembling! Sarah turned to her right to find that the smaller red-haired girl seated there was trembling too! Relieved to know that she was not the only one unsettled by the Reverend Eby's fearsome rendering of Luke: 21, Sarah decided that there was nothing to do but ride out the storm.

But the full fury of the storm was yet to come. Now the preacher was striding once again back and forth across the platform describing the terrors of the end-time in his own words, in details more colorful and graphic than were to be found anywhere in the New Testament. He spoke at length about the wars currently raging in Europe and Asia, and about the possibility of the United States going to war too. Were these the wars and rumors of war that Jesus had foretold would designate the time of the end?

Then just as suddenly as the storm had erupted, it ended. The preacher, his face perspiring freely, once again took his place behind the podium and smiled benignly out across his unsettled flock. He began reading again, this time in a more soothing, more reassuring voice:

> " 'And then shall they see the son of Man coming in a cloud with power and great glory. And when these things begin to come to pass, then look up, and lift up your heads; for your redemption draweth nigh.
>
> " 'And he spake to them a parable; Behold the fig tree, and all the trees; when they now shoot forth, ye see and know of your own selves that summer is now nigh at hand. So likewise ye, when ye see these things come to pass, know ye that the kingdom of God is nigh at hand. Verily I say unto you, This generation shall not pass away, till all be fulfilled. Heaven and earth shall pass away; but my words shall not pass away.' "

The Reverend Eby closed his Bible and for the next twenty minutes spoke with great feeling and anticipation of the day when Jesus would return to establish the kingdom of God on earth.

"In that day God's spiritual kingdom will be made manifest in the world. The spiritual will become physical. The prayer of our hearts–'Thy kingdom come, thy will be done on earth as it is in heaven'–will be answered at last. And all those who accepted Jesus as their king, as their lord and savior, when his kingdom was 'only' spiritual, 'only' a kingdom of heaven, will be allowed to enter in. The children of God shall inherit the earth. Hallelujah!"

Sarah recalled that her mother had had serious doubts about the second coming of Jesus. Jesus himself seemed to have believed that the time of the end would come soon after his own death. In the very passage that the Reverend Eby had just cited, Jesus had said, "This generation shall not pass away, till all things be accomplished."

Also, in an earlier chapter in Luke, he had said to a group of people gathered about him, "There will be some of them that stand here, which shall in no wise taste of death, till they see the kingdom of God." And indeed, some of the events prophesied by Jesus *did* take place soon after his death. His disciples *were* persecuted; some of them *were* put to death. And the temple in Jerusalem *was* destroyed–by the Roman Army in 70 A.D.–and the Jewish people *were* scattered to all lands. Sarah could not understand why, in the year 1941 A.D., the Reverend Eby, her Aunt Hester, and apparently everyone else living in this mountain community were still expecting the return of Jesus. Still, as she had sat listening to the Reverend Eby's splendorous account of life in the earthly kingdom of God under the supreme rulership of Jesus, she could not help but get caught up in it. And she had to admit, that if it did come, and if Jesus would agree to let her in, she would probably find it to her liking. Ever since she was a small child, she had longed to live in a kingdom in which the wolf dwelt peacefully with the lamb, and the lion ate straw like the ox–in which no creature was ever hurt or destroyed in all of God's holy mountain.

The Reverend Eby closed his sermon with the most eloquent recitation of the Lord's prayer Sarah had ever heard. "Thy kingdom come! Thy will be done on earth as it is in heaven!" The words seemed to ring off the very walls!

The members of the congregation stood for the singing of one final hymn–Sarah once again sharing the hymn book with the pretty blonde girl to her left–then returned the hymn books to the benches, and, as the organ continued to play, exchanged greetings amongst themselves. Those who had managed to stay both awake and alert throughout the entire service had been lifted to a state of near rapture by the Reverend Eby's closing remarks about the glories of the kingdom of God to come. The Reverend Eby himself had made his way to the rear of the church and was standing just outside the door as the congregation slowly made its way out. The preacher greeted each of his flock in turn as they descended the steps into the bright sunshine. His long arms again served him well as he reached from hand to hand and shoulder to shoulder.

Once outside, Nathan chatted briefly with those of his fellows whom he had not had a chance to speak with inside the church. For the most part the conversations consisted of a few brief sentence fragments only and centered on one of two subject: the crops and the weather. They were little more than verbal equivalents of handshakes, but, like handshakes, they served their purpose of helping to maintain community bonds.

He was engaged in a friendly dispute with his brother-in-law Isaac when his attention was drawn by a loud commotion to the group of women who had gathered for a little socializing in another part of the churchyard a short distance away. Nathan never ceased to marvel at the ability of women to communicate among their own kind. They all seemed to be talking at once, yet he knew that at the same time, each one was hearing what all the others were saying. He knew that Hester was in the group–he had heard her voice–and he also knew that if there was any gossip worth hearing, she would catch him up on it on the drive home. The preacher would not be coming to dinner today, so Hester would be in no hurry to get home. They would not be able to leave for a while anyway as Otis had not yet come out of the church. The teenaged boys were always the last to emerge, as good manners required them to allow their elders and their female counterparts to precede them. The girls were coming out now. Nathan watched as Sarah came through the door, as she smiled, shook hands, and exchanged a few words with the preacher. Nathan knew there was no blood between himself and this precocious young niece of his, but he took pride in her all the same. The Reverend Eby scared most teenagers to death. The fact that he looked like a great bird of prey did not help. Even now as he stood greeting the girls on the steps he seemed to be hovering over them, ready to sink his talons into their soft flesh. But Sarah seemed to have no fear of him. She was certainly not afraid to talk to him! Nathan had never met a fourteen-year-old with so much poise, and he had never met anyone, young or old, who had the courage and imagination to question the Scriptures the way she had—at least not since coming to North Carolina. At times he wondered which was the more solid and unshakeable, the mountains which had drawn him to this part of the country, or the absolute faith in the Bible that the inhabitants of this part of the country seemed to possess. It would have been easier to move one of the mountains, he had decided, than to get anyone in this mountain valley to question his faith. That the Bible was the word of God was as clear to these mountain people as the air they breathed, and no conceivable circumstance could have caused them to change their opinion. Nor were they inclined to be very tolerant of anyone who did not share that opinion. Having been raised on the Bible himself, Nathan had no difficulty worshipping side by side with his mountain-born brethren, but having also been taught that tolerance was a virtue, he could not approve of their lack of tolerance for anyone who did not conform to their way of thinking. God, in Nathan's opinion, probably liked a little diversity; otherwise why would He have created so much of it? But God's thoughts on the subject aside, *Nathan* liked diversity. He found that whenever everybody thought alike, the air got a little too thick for breathing. The previous Sunday, when Sarah had done all her "blaspheming" in the parlor, it had seemed to him as if a breath of fresh air had suddenly been let loose through this stuffy mountain valley, and he, for one, was glad for it.

The boys were finally coming out. The boys were the worst of all. The best that most of them could manage when the preacher spoke to them as they exited the church were a few hurried, incoherent words uttered under their breath as they stumbled, in headlong flight, down the steps. Finally Otis appeared. Nathan turned his head so as not to be embarrassed.

He could now begin to think about gathering up his family for the ride home. Hester was still busily engaged with her talkative women friends, but Nathan knew that that loquacious group would soon be disbanding now that all of the children were out of the church. Sarah was standing near Isaac's truck talking to her Uncle Jacob. She had already taken off her shoes and was holding them in her hands. Nathan began walking toward the wagon. Each year there seemed to be more and more cars and trucks, fewer and fewer horses and wagons. He didn't mind in the least, as it meant that each year there was all the more room at the hitching rail for him.

Otis, though the last one out of the church, was the first to join him at the wagon. A few moments later Hester came bustling up, an expression of supreme satisfaction on her face. Nathan guessed that either she had become privy to some extraordinary gossip or she was still rejoicing over the fact that Sarah had finally agreed to come to church. Nathan knew how uncomfortable it had made Hester to have to explain to her friends week after week how it was that her fourteen-year-old niece who had been living with them since the first week in May had not come to church. She had gone through the same ordeal with Elizabeth eight years before. Hester could hardly be held accountable for the actions of her sister-in-law–a full-grown woman and an outlander at that–but she *did* feel responsible for her fourteen-year-old niece, her brother Daniel's daughter.

Sarah walked over to the wagon and placed her shoes under the seat. "I'm going to walk home, Uncle Nathan," she said. Then, turning to her aunt, she added, "I won't be home for dinner, Aunt Hester."

"As usual," sighed Hester, adding what she thought should have been the final two words of her niece's sentence.

"As usual," repeated Sarah, smiling. She kissed her aunt on the cheek and started out the lane in the direction of the main road.

"Wait up!" shouted Otis, running after her, "I'll go with yuh."

"Otis, come back here!" yelled Hester, "you'll ruin your suit!"

Otis stopped. He felt the blood rush to his head and a lump come to his throat as he watched Sarah moving further and further away from him.

"Who is that, Otis?"

Otis turned to find Gladys Cole standing behind him. "Uh, hit's my Cousin Sarah," he stammered. "You know, the one I told you about."

"She's your cousin? Really? She sat right next to me in church. She said her name was Sarah, but I didn't know she was your *Cousin* Sarah."

Otis nodded.

"Wasn't she the one who was just startin' school the year we were in third grade?"

"Yeah, that's her."

"She never came back to school after the first grade, did she?"

"Nope, she ain't never been back to school since."

"That explains why she can't read."

"She can too read!" retorted Otis. "She can read good. She can read better'n anybody!"

"Then why didn't she sing any of the hymns. We used the same hymn book, but I was the only one singin'. She never opened her mouth ... Maybe she can't sing."

"Sure she can sing. I've heared her sing. She sings all the time when we're hoein' corn."

"Well, all I know is, she didn't sing the hymns this morning. Maybe she was just nervous on account of it bein' her first day in church and all."

"Yeah," agreed Otis, "I reckon that was it." He looked around for Sarah, but she was out of sight now.

"Otis, I was thinkin'," said Gladys, in a more solicitous tone of voice, "that if you weren't doin' anything this afternoon, maybe you could ask to borrow your Pa's wagon an we could go for a ride."

Otis scratched his white-blond head. "I'd like to, Gladys, but the horses really should rest on Sunday. They work too, you know."

"Well, when *can* I see you, Otis? I've hardly seen you at all since the school picnic."

"I been busy. You know what summers are like on a farm. Your Pa's got a tractor, so hit's easier for you now. Besides, you got all them brothers an' sisters to help out. My Pa still makes do with horses. An' I don't got no brothers or sisters. That means I got to work all the harder."

"What about your Cousin Sarah? Doesn't she help out?"

"She don't help much."

"Well, I should think that you could at least find time to come over and see me once in a while."

Otis was searching his brain for an excuse–*any* excuse–not to go visit her, when they heard her father's voice calling her. They turned and headed back toward the parking lot.

"I'll see you next Sunday–in church," said Otis hurriedly as they parted company. He realized as he climbed into the wagon that his parting words had been of little comfort to Gladys. Three months before, she had been all he could think of. Now he was inventing excuses not to see her. What had changed? Otis knew only too well.

After crossing the road, Sarah headed down the path that led to the creek, to the place where the baptisms were held. But instead of following the path all the way to the end, she cut into the woods to her right and headed for the creek at an angle, so as to meet it at a point further upstream where she knew the water would be flowing more freely. She had a lot to think about, and she was always able to think best in the woods. She would go to the waterfall and spend the afternoon there, reflecting on all the many things she had heard and seen and felt during the course of the Sunday morning church service. She had never experienced anything quite like it. She had listened to the Reverend Eby's sermon with great interest. By making a distinction between the spiritual and the physical aspects of the kingdom of God, he seemed to have resolved the apparent contradictions which she had found in Jesus' various statements on the subject—but she would have to give it further thought. She wished she had been able to ask questions—her mother had always allowed her, even encouraged her, to ask questions during *their* explorations—but had decided that it would be best not to interrupt the Reverend Eby during his sermon, especially as no one else seemed to be doing so. To be sure, there had been some members of the congregation who had spoken aloud during the service, especially those members seated on the benches up front, next to the preacher's platform. They had said "amen" almost every time the preacher inhaled some air. If they had said it once, they must have said it a hundred times. She had also heard people behind her, mostly from the women's side of the aisle, shout "Hallelujah!" and "Praise the Lord!" whenever the spirit had moved them to do so. She had even heard her Aunt Hester's voice on several occasions. But no one had asked questions.

The Reverend Eby had promised her, however, that if she ever wanted to ask questions, or to discuss anything with him, he would be glad to stay after church, or to meet with her anytime that was convenient for the both of them. She appreciated the offer and she fully expected there would be occasions when she would want to do so. Yet at the same time she felt that the number of ideas that she could discuss with him would be limited. The Reverend Eby, like her Aunt Hester, simply had too many beliefs which he seemed unwilling or unable to question. Her mother had always told her that a seeker after truth must be prepared to believe *any*thing, but, at the same time, to be able to doubt *every*thing. Insofar as the Reverend Eby was incapable of doubting the Bible, the extent of the territory that the two of them would be able to explore together would be severely restricted. Perhaps he could help her to understand "the Word of God" as he understood it, but it would be her responsibility to decide whether "the Word of God" had any relevance to her own personal search for God and God's kingdom. Indeed, she wondered now whether it was even the "kingdom" of God she was looking for, or something else, something more. It would be all right, she supposed, to live in a kingdom ruled by God, but she wanted more than that: she wanted to be consumed by God, to be one with God, to be filled with God completely, as she had been for that one brief indescribable moment in the White Light Heaven. That's what finding the kingdom of God had meant to her. That's what she thought Jesus had meant too when he said, "The kingdom of God is within you." She felt there was something inside her, deep within her soul, that belonged to God, that was part of God, that *was* God. She had come to believe that planted deep within her soul was a tiny seed–a tiny seed of God–which, if properly nurtured, could grow into a great shrub or mighty tree. Like a measure of leaven, that small teaspoonful of God could rise and swell and fill her soul completely. That's how *she* had understood Jesus' parables of the mustard seed and the leaven: the kingdom of God was something inside *her*, which could grow and swell and completely fill her with the presence of God. It had nothing to do with missionaries in China. Presumably there were many in Rushing Creek who had found the kingdom of God as the Reverend Eby had defined it. Her Aunt Hester, for example. She accepted Jesus as Lord and Savior, and she obeyed God's commandments. Yet Sarah did not believe that her Aunt Hester had ever experienced anything like what she herself had experienced in the White Light Heaven. She wondered how many, if any, of those others who had gathered for worship that morning in the Rushing Creek Baptist Church, had ever experienced the sensation of being completely consumed by God, completely filled with God's love. How many of them had found *that* kingdom?

    She planned to continue going to church. It made her Aunt Hester happy, and she would still be able to take her walks in the woods in the afternoons. Besides, she liked the Reverend Eby. She had been absolutely enthralled by the power of his preaching, by the resonance of his voice, and by the majestic manner in which he had strode back and forth across the platform. And when he had paused behind the podium for breath, he had a smile almost as sweet as her Uncle Jacob's. She may not have been able to accept everything he said, but she liked the way he moved, the way he smiled, and, like the good widow Lawson—Lord rest her soul—she liked the way he said the words.

But she didn't think she would ever be able to bring herself to sing the hymns. She had liked the music well enough. She had loved the sound of the organ, and she had found listening to all the voices coming together in harmony a very pleasant experience. But the words! The words had seemed very strange to her. Sarah did not think there would ever come a time in her life when she would have a desire to be "washed in the blood of the Lamb!" Or to sing about it.

"Bring the wagon 'round, will you, Son?" said Nathan as he and Otis stepped out onto the porch, "so's your mother don't haf to walk through the dust in her Sunday dress."

"I'll get it, Pa," said Otis as he hurried down the porch steps and headed toward the barn.

Nathan looked up at the threatening sky. "An' better make sure we've got the tarp," he called after him. "It looks like we could be drivin' home in the rain."

"I'll see to it, Pa."

Otis turned the corner of the barn and found the team of horses waiting patiently. His father had hitched them to the wagon earlier in the morning, before breakfast, and for the past hour they had stood just inside the barn awaiting further instructions. Otis rubbed their noses as he walked past. He pulled the storage box out from under the driver's seat and opened the lid. The canvas tarpaulin, which would be their only protection in the event of rain, lay folded inside the box. Closing the lid and shoving the box back under the seat, he walked over to the ladder leading up to the hayloft.

"You 'bout ready, Sarah?" he called up through the opening in the loft floor.

"Yes," came the voice from above, "I was just closing the doors. It looks like rain."

Ten seconds later she appeared at the opening and descended the ladder. Together the two cousins walked to the wagon. Sarah climbed into the back as Otis took the driver's seat. Reluctantly the horses moved from the cool interior of the barn out into the heavy, warm morning air. When they reached the house Otis reined them in, then stepped over the seat and joined his cousin in the back of the wagon. Nathan helped Hester up onto the vacated driver's seat, then walked around to the other side and climbed aboard himself.

He shook the reins and the horses began to move lazily down the dusty lane through the orchard. Sarah kept her eyes fixed on the black thunderclouds gathering in the sky to the west. It certainly *looked* like rain. But on any number of occasions over the course of the past three weeks, it had looked like rain, but each time the storm had spent itself on the mountains to the west or had chosen another valley by which to make its eastward journey to the Atlantic. They had not had more than a few drops of rain through the first two and a half weeks of August.

"If it ain't a flood, it's a drought," muttered Nathan, as he surveyed with dismay his thus-far-disappointing apple crop. "Last summer we couldn't get it t' *stop* rainin'; this summer we can't seem t' get it t' *start*."

Sarah remembered the heavy, almost continuous rains of the previous August to which her Uncle Nathan had alluded. It had rained so much up on the mountain that their cornfield had practically been washed into their garden, and for several weeks the normally small gurgle of water that emanated from their spring house had become a gushing torrent. In fact, gushing torrents of water seemed to have sprung up all over the mountain as underground streams and reservoirs had become gorged and overflowed. She had seen so much water go spilling down over the side of the mountain that it had come as no surprise to her when she later learned of all the terrible flooding that had occurred down in the valleys.

But that was a year ago. Conditions were far different this year. No farmer in Rushing Creek or in the neighboring communities would have wished for a repeat of the previous August, but not one of them would have refused a good soaking rain if it had been offered him. Even before the drought had set in, Sarah had begun to long for the cool of the mountains. August had never been her favorite month, but at least up in the mountains there had been breezes to give relief from the oppressive heat and humidity. As for rain, in the eight years that she and her father and her mother had lived up at the old Puckett place, she could not remember a summer when they had gone more than a week without rain. Rainclouds seemed always to be bumping into the side of the mountain on which they had lived. She suspected that even during the past month, when hardly any rain had fallen in the valley, there had been plenty of rain at the higher elevations. Rushing Creek still had a lot of water in it: all that water had to be coming from somewhere.

It was a strange morning. It hardly seemed like morning at all. The air was eerily still. As they drove through the woods there was no sound, no movement in the trees, no sign of life of any kind. There was something ominous in the air. Ominous yet exciting! It was as if the thunderstorm which had begun building the afternoon before, had continued to build all through the night. If and when it broke, it was going to be an awesome spectacle to behold. Sarah hoped that the storm would hold off until after church was out. It had waited three weeks: it could wait another two hours.

As the horses clopped along the sun-baked clay road, the thick, heavy air suddenly began to reverberate with the sound of the church bells. The sound seemed so close!–so close that Sarah imagined that if she reached out her hand, she could pull it right out of the air. As they drove up the lane to the church, she did in fact reach out her hand, but not to catch the sound of the bells, rather to wave, as Isaac's truck pulled up behind them, with Isaac, Martha, and Jacob in the front seat.

Once they had arrived at the church, Sarah decided to wait until the last possible moment before going inside. She stood on the top step just outside the door as others filed past her into the small church. Her eyes were still fixed on the sky to the west, which was much darker now. The air had also begun to move. She doubted very much if all the prayers on earth could hold back the storm at this point. She was becoming anxious that if she went into the church now, the storm might be completely over by the time she got out. It made absolutely no sense to her to be shut up inside when such primal, elemental drama was transpiring without. For a brief moment she considered running up the hill to the cemetery behind the church to get a better view.

Suddenly one of the deacons clasped her hand, pulled her inside, and closed the doors. The decision seemed to have been made for her. Resigned but uneasy, she made her way to the front of the church and took her accustomed seat on the bench just below the podium. The Reverend Eby smiled down at her from his chair on the platform, and for a moment her anxiety was quieted. But she realized that it was going to be very difficult to maintain her concentration. Her mind was beginning to drift already. She found herself wishing she was standing on the top of her holy mountain—on the very highest rock—watching the storm approach. She had done just that on numerous occasions during those years she had lived up in the mountains. It was the best place she had ever found from which to watch storms gather and break. In fact, there had been many a summer's day just like this one, when it felt and looked like a storm was imminent, that she had run all the way from her house to the top of the high rocks, just in order to be there when the storm arrived.

As the Reverend Eby led the congregation in prayer, Sarah found herself listening more to the wind rattling the window panes of the church. She wished she could be outside right now. She rose with the congregation for the singing of the first hymn of the morning. Again she shared the hymnal with the blonde girl, Gladys, to her left, as she had done each Sunday for the past four weeks. She still found herself unable to sing or utter aloud the words to most of the hymns, as they simply did not express the thoughts and feelings in her own mind and heart, or did not express them in a language with which she was comfortable. Consequently, during the singing of the hymns, she usually found herself simply standing mute while she thought her own thoughts and listened to the music. Every so often, however, she did find a hymn, or at least an odd verse here and there, which she was able to sing in good conscience. She knew that Gladys must be wondering why it was that she sometimes sang and sometimes didn't, but Gladys hadn't asked so Sarah hadn't bothered to explain.

Gladys opened the hymnal to the number the Reverend Eby had indicated, and as the organ played the prelude, Sarah quickly read over the words of the first verse. Deciding that the verse was acceptable, she joined her voice with the others:

> "God of the world! Thy glories shine
> Through earth and heaven with rays divine;
> Thy smile gives beauty to the flower,
> Thine anger to the tempest power."

Before she had a chance to peruse the second verse, a tremendous clap of thunder caused everyone—organist, choir, and congregation—to come to a complete stop and gasp for breath. Satisfied, after several seconds of anxious waiting, that the building was not about to fall on her head, the organist, Harriet Ogle, continued, and the choir and congregation followed suit. Sarah tried to focus her eyes on the words on the page, but for some strange reason, she found herself unable to do so. The words seemed to be getting further and further away. Suddenly she realized that she was no longer in her body but floating toward the ceiling! She looked down at the congregation, at the choir, at the Reverend Eby on the raised platform. They were all receding away from her. Seized with panic, she tried desperately to get back into her body, but to no avail. Suddenly she was through the roof and outside. The sky was almost totally black now. She could not feel the wind, but she could see that it was blowing with gale force. Great trees were being whipped about and bent over under its assault. Torn branches were hurtling through the air. She soared higher still, past the church steeple, above the trees. It was thrilling beyond words to describe! To the west, in the far distance, she could see the rain approaching. Suddenly, a white bolt of lightning ripped through the darkened sky, followed by another crash of thunder.

Gladys Cole cried out in alarm as Sarah collapsed against her and fell to the floor. The Reverend Eby, seeing Sarah fall, motioned with a wave of his hand for the organist and choir to desist, but this was hardly necessary as they had all but stopped already after the second clap of thunder, which was even louder than the first. The Reverend Eby poured a glass of water from the pitcher he kept under the podium, then stepped down off the platform to the spot where Sarah had fallen.

"Is she dead?" asked Gladys Cole anxiously, as the preacher knelt over the prostrate form.

"No," replied the preacher, "she's just fainted. She'll be all right in a few minutes." He sprinkled some of the water onto Sarah's face.

Nathan, sitting half a dozen rows back on the men's side of the aisle, had not seen Sarah fall, but he had heard Gladys Cole scream and he had seen the preacher step down off the platform. Guessing that something had happened to one of the teenaged girls in the front row, and thinking it *might* be Sarah, he worked his way to the aisle and hurried to the scene of the disturbance. He was followed almost immediately by Jacob and Isaac.

By this time everyone in the church had become aware that something had happened to one of the young girls in the front row. The Reverend Eby's assurance that "she's just fainted" had been passed along by word of mouth from the front rows to the very back, but as yet no one seemed to know the identity of the young girl who had done the fainting.

When Nathan saw that it was Sarah, he rushed to her side and knelt down. She was still unconscious. As the preacher, Isaac, and Jacob all hovered anxiously over her, Nathan lifted her into a sitting position with his left arm, then with the thumb and fingers of his right hand began rubbing and patting her cheeks.

"Sarah, can you hear me?" he importuned. Still there was no response. The Reverend Eby sprinkled more water on her face.

As Nathan, with the preacher's assistance, continued to work to revive his niece, yet another clap of thunder was heard, and another. As the shock waves shook walls and rattled windows, the congregation grew more and more anxious.

Finally, after what seemed to Nathan like twenty or thirty minutes, but which in reality was only two or three, Sarah's eyes began to flutter.

"Uncle Nathan?" She seemed startled. "Where . . .?" Confused, she looked around at the faces hovering above her. Then, as she gathered her wits about her, her eyes grew wide with alarm. "The mill!" she exclaimed in an excited voice. "Mr. Bryson's mill is on fire!"

"Here now, hush, child; drink this," said the preacher, holding the glass of water to her lips.

"No, you don't understand," she protested, pushing the glass aside. "The mill is on fire!" She tried to get to her feet.

Nathan, Isaac, and Jacob exchanged curious looks amongst themselves.

"What's she talkin' about?" asked Isaac. "Why is she sayin' the mill is on fire?"

In the meantime, the congregation had been growing more restless with each passing moment. By this time everyone had learned that it was Daniel Wicker's girl who had fainted, but now the rumor being circulated was that Bryson's mill was on fire.

Suddenly Nathan jumped up onto the platform and turned to face the congregation. "Listen, everybody," he shouted, "Bryson's mill is on fire! We've got to get over there an' put it out!"

Sarah was already running for the door.

"I want every able-bodied man," shouted Nathan as he followed her down the aisle.

"Nathan, what's this all about?" asked a gentleman with snow-white hair. It was Henry Bryson.

"You'd better come along, Henry. I have reason to believe your mill is on fire."

Sarah was waiting for Nathan outside the door.

"I'm trustin' you, girl," he whispered to her.

She looked back at him in alarm. "We've got to hurry, Uncle Nathan!" Together they rushed down the steps into the stiff wind. It was not yet raining.

"We'll take my truck," shouted Isaac, who was right behind them, "hit'll be faster."

"But will we survive the ride?–that's the question," joked Nathan as he and Sarah jumped into the back of the truck. They were joined by several others, including Otis. Jacob climbed into the cab of the truck as Isaac cranked the engine.

"I sure hope we ain't makin' fools of ourselves," said Isaac to his brother as he swung himself in behind the steering wheel.

Before he could pull out, a large red nose appeared at the cab window. A pair of wire-rimmed spectacles was perched on top of it; a bushy white mustache hung from the nostrils. It was Walter Lehman.

"Stop by the store, Isaac. We'll get some buckets."

Just as suddenly as Walter had appeared, he was gone. Poking his head out the window and casting a quick glance back, Isaac saw the store-keeper jumping into his own truck.

"Well," said Isaac, turning back to his brother, "that makes me feel better, knowin' that Walter thinks thar's a fire too."

"Looks like Walter's hay fever's been a-actin' up," observed Jacob as they roared out the lane in the direction of the town.

"Lawsy, she was right!" exclaimed Isaac as they entered the town. He could see the smoke in the distance. "How in tarnation did she know that?"

They stopped at the general store. Walter Lehman pulled up right behind them, jumped out of his truck, ran up the steps and unlocked the door. Nathan and Otis followed him in, and in a matter of seconds all three emerged, each carrying a stack of metal pails.

"Go!" shouted Nathan, when he and Otis had secured themselves once again in the back of the truck. Isaac started with such a lurch that Otis was nearly thrown out despite his precautions. Fortunately Nathan managed to grab him in time.

469

"Six fire-fighters killed by maniac driver on way to fire," muttered Nathan under his breath, as he tried to imagine the headline of the Monday edition of the *Haynesville Observer*.

As they approached the millhouse they could see that the east end of the two-story wooden structure was engulfed in flames. Even before the truck had come to a complete stop, Sarah had taken a stack of buckets and jumped out. By the time Nathan and the others got to the run-off pond below the mill, Sarah had already jumped into the water and had begun filling buckets.

"Otis," shouted Nathan, "you take the buckets from Sarah. We'll make a brigade. Men'll carry the full buckets, women'll return the empties. We should have plenty of people. It looks like everyone from the church is comin', includin' the women. . . I'm goin' to the other end."

As Sarah quickly filled the buckets and handed them to Otis, she watched with fascination the incredible drama that was unfolding before her eyes. The scene was unlike anything she had ever before witnessed. The sky above and all around was black with clouds and smoke, while the water in which she stood was brilliantly aglow with the reflection of the burning millhouse. It was as if the sun had fallen out of the sky and into the pond, leaving a black void above.

She looked up at the fire. The flames, driven by the wind, were leaping furiously into the blackened sky. She could feel the heat on her face. The storm alone would have been sufficient to fill all her senses. The storm and fire together were overwhelming. Yet there was still more. The fire brigade which Nathan had organized was itself a spectacle to behold. Thirty men and boys in their Sunday suits had formed themselves into a human chain and were passing buckets from hand to hand from the pond where Sarah was filling them, up along the embankment, to the burning building where Nathan, Isaac, Henry Bryson, and two other men were taking turns throwing the water onto the fire. A second chain, running parallel to the first and consisting entirely of women and girls, was relaying the empty buckets back to the pond to be re-filled. Both men and women were finding it necessary to brace themselves against the wind, which, in addition to its apparent determination to level everything in its path, was also causing some other, equally aggravating problems for each of the two lines of the brigade, as the men were constantly finding it necessary to remove their ties from out of their mouths and the women were in an almost constant struggle to keep their hair out of their eyes and their dresses below their knees. Yet they continued to work on, never slowing, never faltering, passing bucket after bucket after bucket up and down the line. How many buckets would it take? Sarah wondered. She must have filled close to a hundred already, and still the fire seemed to be burning just as furiously as when they had first arrived.

Suddenly the rain was upon them! Torrential rain!

"Keep the buckets comin'!" shouted Nathan over the combined roar of the fire and the wind and the rain.

For the next twenty minutes Sarah and the others stood in the pouring rain and kept the buckets coming. One hundred fifty. Two hundred. Two hundred fifty. Three hundred.

"We got it!" cried Nathan at last. "We got it! She's out!"

A jubilant cheer went up from the brigade. Tired but exhilarated by the effort, and soaked clear through to the skin, Sarah continued to stand knee-deep in the water and stare at the still-smoldering building. The rain was beginning to let up.

"Well," said Otis, who was left holding the last bucket Sarah had filled, "I reckon we won't be a-needin' this one." So saying, he poured it over Sarah's head.

She turned to him with a surprised look on her face, then smiled. It was exactly what he had expected her to do. He knew she wouldn't get mad. She never got mad at anything anymore.

Nathan, Isaac, Henry Bryson, and some of the other men entered the millhouse to survey the damage. All the clapboard siding had burned off the east wall, and the heavy oak beams and posts on that end of the building had been badly charred. About a third of the roof had burned as well.

"Could a-been worse," assayed Nathan.

"Could a-been a heck of a lot worse," agreed the miller. "If we hadn't got here when we did, we'd a-lost the whole danged thang.

As it is, we saved the wheel an' all the machinery. That's what's important."

"I think we can probably round up some volunteers t' help you repair the roof an' that wall," said Nathan.

"Count me in," offered Isaac. "I can be here at six o'clock tomorruh mornin'."

"I'll be with him," added Jacob.

The half dozen other men who had come in to look at the damage indicated their willingness to help as well. George Ownby, who operated the sawmill, offered to cut and haul the lumber. Henry Bryson thanked them all for their generosity.

"But thar's somethin' I don't understand," said the miller, turning back to Nathan. "You were in church with the rest of us. How'd you know thar was a fire?"

"That's a question you'll haf t' ask my niece, Henry," replied Nathan. "It's a question I'd like to ask her myself. *She's* the one who knew there was a fire."

"You mean Sarah? Is she all right? I heard that she was the girl that fainted."

"Is she all right? Well, I'd say she's probably a little tired by now, and maybe a little cold. She was the one who was standin' down there in that pond the whole time, right through the pourin' rain, fillin' all them buckets, while you an' I were standin' up here by this toasty fire keepin' warm."

"I'll be danged. Well then, I reckon I'd better find this niece of yours an' thank her proper-like."

He exited the building and began making his way through the crowd of onlookers–mostly men and teenaged boys–who had gathered around the millhouse in the hope of getting a closer look at the damage. He was followed closely by Nathan. Once beyond the perimeter of the crowd, both men were surprised to see that an even larger crowd had gathered down by the pond. The group seemed to consist mostly of women and teenaged girls, but there were men and boys there as well, including the Reverend Eby, who was never hard to find in a crowd, as he stood half a head taller than most men and a full head taller than most women. He was standing approximately in the center of the group. As the two men approached they heard angry, discordant voices—women's voices—emanating from within. The women involved seemed to be arguing about something, rather heatedly judging by the sharpness of their voices. The Reverend Eby seemed to be trying to calm them down.

Nathan saw Otis emerging from the crowd.

"Pa, I was just comin' t' fetch yuh!" he said excitedly.

"What's goin' on, Son?"

"You should a-been here, Pa. Mrs. Hicks called Sarah a witch!"

"What?"

"Mrs. Hicks, she called Sarah a witch!"

"Where's Sarah now?"

"She's with Reverend Eby."

Nathan began pushing his way toward the center of the crowd. Given his considerable size, he did not meet with much resistance. He found Sarah standing in the very middle of the group with all eyes fixed upon her. The Reverend Eby was hovering over her like a mother hawk protecting its young. Sarah was staring straight ahead, in disbelief, at a woman about ten feet away. It was Lydia Hicks. She was pointing at Sarah and screaming.

"She's a witch, Reverend Eby. I swear to you, she's a witch!"

"What's goin' on here?" asked Nathan.

"I'll tell you what's gwine on here, Nathan Andersson," replied Mrs. Hicks, her voice rife with fear and anger, "this niece of yourn is a witch. Anyone who can leave their body an' fly about in the air like she said she done, is a witch!"

"Come on, Sarah," said Nathan "we're goin' home."

Sarah did not move. She continued to stare at Lydia Hicks.

"Now she's puttin' her evil eye on me," cried Mrs. Hicks. "Mark my words, I'll be daid in my grave afore the fortnight!"

"Come on, Sarah," Nathan repeated. This time he took her by the arm and led her out through the crowd. Behind him he could still hear Lydia Hicks' shrill voice hurling invectives in his and Sarah's direction. But there were other voices too, some of them speaking out in Sarah's defense.

"Leave the child be, Lydia," he heard one voice saying. "She ain't done no harm to you."

"I for one don't care how she knew the place was on fire," he heard another voice saying, this one belonging to Henry Bryson's wife, Mary. "I'm just grateful she knew. If it hadn't a-been for her, the whole thang would a-burned to the ground."

At the edge of the crowd, Nathan met up once again with Mary's husband, Henry.

"Sarah," said the miller, smiling, "your Uncle Nathan tells me that I have you t' thank for savin' my mill."

When she looked up at him, he could see the pain and confusion in her eyes. "Listen, Sarah," he said in a more sympathetic tone of voice, "don't pay no mind to old Lydia Hicks. She don't know what she's a-talkin' about." Then, turning to Nathan, he said, "You'd better get her home, Nathan, so's she can get into some dry clothes. She's startin' t' shiver."

Nathan removed his coat and wrapped it around his niece. "It's wet," he said, "but at least it'll keep some of the heat in."

As they walked up along the embankment together he began looking around for Isaac. He found him standing with Jacob and several other men just outside the mill, planning the repair job that lay ahead.

"Isaac," he said, "could you drive Sarah home? She needs to get into some dry clothes."

"Sure can," he replied with a wide grin, "I reckon we could all do with some dry clothes." He wrung the water out of his tie. "By the way," he asked, nodding in the direction of the crowd gathered by the pond, "what's gwine on down thar? Sounds like a chicken fight."

"Danged if I know," answered Nathan, not entirely truthfully. "Lydia Hicks seems to a-got her dander up about somethin' or other."

Just then they heard the Reverend Eby's booming voice ring out in song:

"Oh Lord, my God, when I in awesome wonder
Consider all the worlds thy hands have made . . ."

Immediately he was joined by the others gathered around him.

"Sounds to me like they're havin' a hymn-sing now," observed Isaac. "I better get Sarah home afore she faints ag'in. If you see Martha, tell her I'll be back for her."

As Nathan walked back down the embankment toward the crowd gathered around the preacher, he was followed by the others who had been hovering around the millhouse. Then, as he and the others in the congregation stood, in their wet Sunday best, singing "How Great Thou Art," the sun broke forth.

At the conclusion of the hymn, the Reverend Eby led the congregation in the Lord's Prayer, after which he made a few humorous remarks about church being held next Sunday in the usual place–"weather permitting."

On the way home Nathan was anxious to hear how the disturbance at the pond had gotten started, and he had fully expected that Hester would give him a full and detailed account without his even asking. But they were halfway home and Hester had not spoken a word. Finally Nathan decided that he had no choice but to ask.

"Hester, you were down by the pond durin' that row between Sarah an' Lydia Hicks. What was that all about? How'd that get started?"

"*I* started it, Pa," volunteered Otis from the back of the wagon. "After the fire was out, I mentioned to Sarah how I couldn't understand how you knowed thar was a fire in the first place. She said *you* knowed 'cause *she* told you. So I axed her how *she* knowed, an' she said she *saw* it. I told her she was crazy. I told her she couldn't a-saw it, 'cause she was in church like the rest of us. Then she said she weren't in church. She said she was outside. I axed her how she got outside without me seein' her, 'cause I was a-settin' in the back right next to the door. That's when she said she didn't go out through the door, she went out through the roof. Ever'body laughed when she said that–by this time ever'one was gathered 'round–but she didn't get mad. You know how she is, Pa. She just said it ag'in. She said she left her

475

body an' went out through the roof an' just kept on a-gwine til she was up above the trees. She said she saw the lightnin' hit the millhouse. An' the next thang she knowed she was a-lyin' on the floor an' you was a-slappin' her in the face an' Reverend Eby was a-throwin' water on her."

"No wonder she looked so scared when she came to," laughed Nathan, "The poor kid probably thought she was bein' baptized."

Hester gave him a scathing look.

"But is it true, Pa, what she said? Did she really see the lightnin' hit the mill?"

"Son, have you ever known your cousin t' tell a lie?"

"Nope."

"Well, neither have I. That's why, when she said the mill was on fire, I figured there was a purty good chance she was right."

"But I don't understand, Pa. How'd she do it. How'd she get outside her body?"

"Well, Son," replied Nathan with a mischievous smile, "maybe it's like Mrs. Hicks says. Maybe your cousin's a witch."

"Wow!" exclaimed Otis. "A real witch?"

"Why don't you ask your mother what she thinks."

"Is she, Ma? Is Sarah a witch?"

Hester directed her response not to her son, but to her husband. "You can laugh an' make fun all you want, Nathan Andersson, but I can tell you this: thar's somethin' mighty peculiar about that girl. Thar always has been. She's been a-puttin' spells on animals ever since she was a young'un . . . An' how can you say you never knowed her t' tell a lie? What about when she told us she's been to Heaven? Surely you ain't a-sayin' you believe *that*. A body would haf t' be a fool or a lunatic t' believe such a story."

"I think your brother Jacob believes it," said Nathan calmly.

"Which is he?"

"Jacob's judgement ain't t' be trusted when it comes to that girl. She done put a spell on him a long time ago."

"I think maybe Reverend Eby believes it too."

"Sometimes I think she done put a spell on him too, the way he's always a-smilin' at her."

Almost too angry to speak, Hester fumed to herself for a moment before continuing. "She had no natural way of knowin' that Bryson's mill was on fire."

"Well," said Nathan patiently, in an attempt to pacify his wife, "both Henry an' Mary are mighty grateful to her. We all should be. We all use that mill."

"I would rather a-seen the whole mill burn to the ground than have this happen . . . An' did you see the way she looked at Lydia Hicks? If that woman gets sick an' dies . . ."

"Don't worry, Hester," Nathan assured her, "nothin's gonna happen to Lydia Hicks."

Whenever Hester got into one of her moods, Nathan always found that the wisest course was to stay clear of her for a few hours, or for a few days, whatever it took. He was glad when they finally reached the house. His first order of business was to get out of his wet Sunday suit, or that part of it which he was still wearing, as he had sent his coat home with Sarah. As he made his way up the porch steps he found Elizabeth sitting on the swing and his coat draped over the back of it, next to her.

"I see that Sarah made it home safely," he said. "With Isaac you never can be sure."

Elizabeth smiled. "Yes, he dropped her off about half an hour ago."

Nathan started to go into the house.

"Nathan?"

He turned back to Elizabeth. She now had a more troubled expression on her face.

"Did something happen in church today? Sarah didn't say anything but she seemed upset about something."

"She didn't tell you about the fire?"

"Fire?" she asked in alarm. "Why, no."

"Well, I reckon she was just bein' modest. You'd a-been proud of your daughter today, Elizabeth. She was a real heroine. She saved Henry Bryson's grist mill from burnin' down. Not only was she the first one t' see the fire, but she also helped t' put it out. She was fillin' water buckets as fast as five grown men could empty 'em."

Elizabeth's eyes gleamed with pride. "Well, I guess I shouldn't be surprised. Daniel and I are always saying what a remarkable child she is."

"She certainly is that," agreed Nathan. "Do you know where she is now?"

"She went out to the barnloft to change clothes, but I don't know if she's still there."

"Well, I'm gonna change clothes myself, then I'll go out an' see. I'd kind of like t' talk to her."

After changing clothes Nathan unhitched the horses from the wagon and put them out to pasture. Then, from outside the barn, he called up through the open loft doors. "Sarah, you up there?" Sarah's face appeared at the opening. "Do you mind if I come up? I'd like t' talk to you."

She nodded her approval but made no verbal response. Nathan entered the barn and climbed the ladder leading up to the loft. He found his niece sitting cross-legged in the hay near the doors, looking out.

"Cozy spot you have up here," he said, looking around. "Nice view. . . A little warm though."

"It's cool at night," she said quietly.

"Yeah, I reckon it would be, sleepin' next to them open doors. I'll bet you wake up with dew on your nose."

She forced a weak smile.

"I'm surprised to find you up here," continued Nathan, half-teasing, hoping to coax more of a smile out of her. "Usually you're out walkin' Sunday afternoons."

"I was thinking I might go out later. I needed to warm up a little first."

"Are you comin' down with somethin'?" He placed his hand on her forehead.

"Uncle Nathan?. . .Is there something wrong with me?"

"Well, you may have a bit of a temperature, but it's kind of hard t' tell. It must be a hundred an' twenty degrees up here."

"No, I mean, is there something *wrong* with me?"

"Sarah, if you're worryin' about what Lydia Hicks said this mornin' . . ."

"It's not *just* that, Uncle Nathan. I'm different from other people, aren't I? Even when I was little girl, I was different. I didn't know it then, but looking back, I can see now that I was."

"Bein' diff'rent ain't necessarily a bad thing, you know."

"No, I know, but . . ." She hesitated.

"But what?"

"But sometimes people don't believe me when I tell them things, and sometimes they even get angry at me. When I was a little girl, my mother and father didn't believe me when I first told them about my friend Kati. Then when Kati took me to Heaven, I'm not sure they believed me then either. I think my father did, but I was never sure about my mother. And you heard how angry Aunt Hester got last month when I told Reverend Eby about it. I don't understand why people get angry. I don't understand what made Mrs. Hicks so angry at me this morning."

Nathan recalled the angry words Hester had just spoken on the way home from church. He was glad that Sarah had not heard them.

"Sometimes folks get angry when they're afraid of somethin'," said Nathan, consolingly, "an' they're usually afraid of somethin' when they don't understand it. Now, maybe you *are* a little diff'rent. An' maybe some folks *are* gonna have trouble understandin' you. Maybe some of them are even gonna get angry. . . But that doesn't mean there's somethin' wrong with *you*. Maybe there's somethin' wrong with *them*. . . Besides," he added in a lighter vein, "you may not be so diff'rent as you think."

She waited for him to continue. When he didn't she looked up. "What do you mean, Uncle Nathan?"

He had been standing over her, but now he squatted down on his haunches directly in front of her, just as her father had done whenever he had had something important to say.

"Do you remember," he said, a comforting smile on his face, "the first time you an' I picked apples together many years ago? I think you were about six at the time."

She nodded. "You wouldn't let me climb up the high ladder."

He laughed. "I might a-known you'd remember *that* . . . Do you remember the story I told you that day?"

"You mean the story about Johnny Appleseed?"

"Yes, that's the one."

She nodded and smiled as she again called to mind the picture of Johnny Appleseed putting on his hat with his supper still in it.

"An' do you remember me tellin' you about the Bible my grandmother showed me when I was a boy?" She knit her brow as she tried to recall. "Well, anyway, this Bible had once belonged to my great-great-grandmother, an' in the back of it..."

"Oh yes," she recalled excitedly, "in the back of the Bible was an old letter or something that Johnny Appleseed had given to your great-great-grandmother."

Nathan was glad to see her becoming more animated. "That's right!" he said. "Only, it wasn't a letter. It was a page from a book. She wouldn't let me touch it 'cause it was so old an' brittle, but she let me read it. It was a page from a book called *Heaven And Hell* by Emanuel Swedenborg. Seems like, wherever Johnny Appleseed went, he carried two books with him. Everybody knows he carried the Bible, but not everybody knows that he also carried Swedenborg's *Heaven And Hell*. He left pages of *Heaven And Hell* with settlers all over the Ohio Valley.

"I remember askin' my grandmother about Swedenborg. She didn't know too much about him—only that he was Swedish an' that he was probably dead. Later, when I was about nineteen or twenty, I read up on him. I read *Heaven And Hell* too.

"This Swedenborg lived back in the 1700s. He was a real educated fella—a scientist, a mathematician—one of the smartest men that's ever lived, they say. He knew just about everything there was to know at the time... You ever heard of Aristotle?"

"Yes, he was a student of Plato's and a great philosopher himself."

"Right. Well, Swedenborg's been called the Swedish Aristotle, on account of he knew so much about so many things. But he was diff'rent from Aristotle in one important respect. In fact, he was diff'rent from purt-near everybody who's ever lived—there's that word 'diff'rent' ag'in. After he had learned just about everything there was t' learn about *this* world, he decided to see what he could find out about Heaven... How many times did you say you been to Heaven?"

"Just once, Uncle Nathan."

"Well, Swedenborg had you beat there, I'm afraid. He made visits up to Heaven purt-near every day for the last twenty-seven years of his life! He had all kinds of spirit-friends an' angel-friends who showed him around all them other worlds an' explained things to him. He wrote a number of books about his travels in Heaven an' the spirit world. *Heaven And Hell* is just one of them, but it's probably the best-known... Maybe you'd like to read it."

"Do you have it, Uncle Nathan?"

"Well now, it just so happens that I do. It's a bit tattered around the edges an' some of the pages are fallin' out, but it's all there. In fact, I've leafed through it a couple times myself these past few weeks, just to refresh my memory. Last month when Reverend Eby came to dinner an' you first told us about your visit to Heaven, the whole while you were talkin', I kept thinkin' to myself, all this sounds very familiar. Purt-near everyone around here believes in Heaven. Most are dead certain they're goin' there when they die, an' the rest are hopin' real hard. But nobody seems to have a very clear idea about what Heaven is like. Most folks seem to have this notion that all they do in Heaven is stand around the throne of God an' sing hymns all day. I never heard anybody from around here describe Heaven the way Swedenborg described it. Til you, that is. Some of the things you said about Heaven–like there bein' more than one heaven, an' not needin' t' be baptized to get in–reminded me of Swedenborg. I wondered at the time whether you might a-read *Heaven And Hell*, but I didn't remember seein' it amongst your mother's books, so I figured you probably hadn't. I'd be glad to loan it to you if you're int'rested."

"Thank you, Uncle Nathan. Thank you very much. I'd love to read it."

"Good. I'll get it for you right after dinner."

Sarah looked into her uncle's eyes and returned the smile she saw therein, acknowledging that she understood that which had not been stated, but which had been clearly implied by his words:

that he expected her to come into the house for Sunday dinner and not to miss it as she usually did. She had just been bribed.

"There's one more thing I wanted to tell you about Swedenborg," continued Nathan, shifting his weight from one leg to the other, then back again, in an unsuccessful attempt to get more comfortable. "How far would you say the mill is from the church?"

"About two miles, I guess." She could not help wondering what this had to do with Swedenborg.

"Yes, I'd say that's about right . . . So, this mornin' when you were passed out on the floor of the church, you saw a fire two miles away?"

"Not exactly. *My body* was passed out on the floor of the church, but I wasn't in it."

"Okay, then, when your body was passed out on the floor of the church an' *you* were up there above the church steeple, you saw a fire two miles away?"

"Yes."

"Well, once when Swedenborg was in the city of Gothenburg on the west coast of Sweden, he saw a fire in Stockholm on the east coast, *three hundred* miles away! There ain't much doubt about this either, 'cause there were plenty of witnesses. Swedenborg himself lived in Stockholm—his own house was there—so he was quite alarmed when he saw the fire break out, as you can probably imagine. He couldn't just jump in the back of a truck an' go put it out like we just done, 'cause it was three hundred miles away!"

"Besides," interjected Sarah, "I don't think they had trucks in the eighteenth century."

"Right. Not a bad century, the eighteenth . . . Anyway, he watched this fire burn for two hours, gettin' closer an' closer to his own house. He saw houses belongin' to his friends an' neighbors goin' up in flames. When the fire was finally put out, he breathed a great sigh of relief: it had stopped just three houses from his own! . . . An' he saw it all happen from three hundred miles away! . . . So, you see, compared to Swedenborg, you're not so very diff'rent after all."

She smiled. "That's a remarkable story, Uncle Nathan."

"Well, I reckon what I'm tryin' t' say, Sarah, is, even if you are a little diff'rent from most folks around here, it doesn't mean that there's somethin' *wrong* with you. In fact, I kind of like you 'cause you *are* a little diff'rent. An' sure, you're gonna shake things up a little around here, but sometimes things need t' be shook up. Remember, it's the folks who *are* diff'rent who *make* a diff'rence in this world. Look at Jesus. He shook things up. An' look at how mad some folks got at him. . . So, don't you be worryin' your head about what old fools like Lydia Hicks think."

He had almost said "old fools like Lydia Hicks and Hester," but he had caught himself in time. Sarah remained silent for a moment as she contemplated Nathan's words.

"She's going to die, Uncle Nathan," she said at last, sadly.

"Who is?"

"Mrs. Hicks."

Nathan felt his heart stop. "How do you know?" he asked nervously.

"She has no light around her."

"No light?"

"I have always been able to see light around people. It shines from inside them. I can't see it nearly as clearly now as I could when I was younger, but I can still see it if I really try. I looked hard, but I couldn't see any at all around Mrs. Hicks. . . She's going to die, Uncle Nathan. She's going to die very soon."

Sarah joined the others for dinner but ate very little. At the conclusion of the meal, she helped her mother and Hester clear the table, then retired to the porch with the book Nathan had given her. Sitting down on the swing, she opened the well-worn volume and read the full title inside: *Heaven and its Wonders, and Hell: from Things Heard and Seen.* With great anticipation and not a little curiosity she turned to the first chapter. She was puzzled by the title: "The Lord is Heaven's God." By the end of the first paragraph it was clear to her whom Swedenborg meant by "the Lord:" he meant Jesus.

Sarah had intended to give the book only a quick preliminary inspection before depositing it in her loft and setting off for the creek, but she was still sitting on the porch swing, perfectly motionless, forty-five minutes later when her mother came out of the kitchen and sat down beside her.

"What are you reading, Honey?"

"An extraordinary book, Mother," replied Sarah abstractedly, without looking up. "It's all about Heaven."

Elizabeth set the swing in motion and leaned back. She allowed her gaze to drift peacefully out across the pasture and orchard to the mountains beyond. "Your Daddy's going to be so proud of you," she said, smiling. "Imagine! Reading already! He's not going to believe how much you've grown."

Sarah smiled, but did not respond. She was now completely absorbed in the book. The chapters were short. She had read four already. She turned the page to Chapter Five: "There are Three Heavens."

"Your Daddy says the place we're going to is a beautiful place," sighed Elizabeth, "more beautiful than we can possibly imagine." Then, in a sadder voice, she added, "I hope he comes for us soon."

Sarah smiled again, again without looking up from the book. But the words were becoming too blurry to make out. Finally she closed the book and laid her head in her mother's lap.

15

WITCH HUNT

Little did Otis suspect when he sat down to breakfast the following morning that he was about to receive a promotion.

"Son," said Nathan, addressing himself to the still sleepy-eyed, slouching figure across the table from him, "I'll be goin' off to the mill this mornin', an' I'll be leavin' you in charge of the farm. In fact, I may haf t' be away for the next three or four days. It shouldn't take any longer than that to rebuild the mill, but it'll depend on how many people show up an' on how fast we can get the lumber. But when I'm away, you're in charge. It's a big job, but I know you can handle it. I want you t' look after the animals—you know what t' do. I'm sure you can get Sarah t' help you with that. An' you'll haf t' hoe your mother's garden again. Now that we've finally had some rain, the weeds'll be growin' faster'n you can hoe them out. It wouldn't hurt t' go over the cornfield again either.

"Also, I need you t' pick the Elberta peaches this week, an' the Rambo apples. In fact, I'd like you t' pick some Rambos today. I've got customers waitin'. Maybe you can get Sarah t' help you with that too."

"Okay, Pa. She can pick the bottoms while I pick the tops."

"Now, Son, you let her pick the tops too. She's been itchin' t' use a long ladder ever since she was six years old." He glanced over at Sarah and they exchanged smiles.

He started to get up from the table. "An' if you get a chance," he added, looking again at Otis, "help your mother out in the garden. She'll be doin' a lot of cannin' this week, an' I'm sure she'll be glad for all the help she can get."

"Okay, Pa," said Otis, straightening himself in his chair, "I'll take care of ever'thang. You can count on me."

"I know I can, Son. I'll see you tonight."

Nathan removed his straw hat from a peg on the wall and was about to go out the door when Hester intercepted him. "Don't forget your lunch," she said, handing him a brown paper poke. "Mary Bryson'll prob'bly fix you all a big dinner, but you best have somethin' along just in case she don't."

He took the poke, gave his wife a peck on the cheek, and went out the door. A few minutes later Otis and Sarah got up from the table and went out as well.

"You gather the eggs an' feed the chickens," said Otis to his cousin as they descended the porch steps, "I'll slop the pigs."

"Yes, sir," said Sarah, saluting him smartly, but at the same time giving him a bemused look. She was impressed by the forceful and decisive manner in which her cousin had issued his first orders of the day, but the orders themselves had hardly been necessary as she *always* gathered the eggs and fed the chickens.

After they had tended the animals, they carried two long ladders and a stack of baskets out to the orchard.

"We'll pick this tree," instructed Otis, as he raised his ladder to a vertical position and leaned it against the first of the six large Rambo trees. "I'll go this way an' you go that."

"Yes, sir." She did not salute this time, as she was too busy at the moment struggling with her ladder. When she finally succeeded in lifting it to an upright position, she leaned it into the tree, next to Otis'.

They unstacked the baskets and set them in the shade of the tree, then strapped themselves into their canvas picking bags. Immediately Sarah climbed to the top of her ladder and began picking the highest apples on the tree.

"No! no!" cried Otis, "you're doin' it all wrong. You got t' pick the bottom ones first."

Sarah stopped and looked down at him, peering out from beneath her straw hat which had fallen down over her eyes. "Why?"

"So's you don't bruise the apples."

She gave him an uncomprehending look. "How will picking the top ones first bruise the apples?" she asked, adjusting her hat.

"You'll drop 'em, an' they'll fall down an' hit the bottom ones," explained Otis. "If you pick the bottom ones first, then when you drop the top ones, thar won't be nuthin' for 'em t' hit."

"I'm not going to drop the top ones, Otis. I'm not going to drop *any* of them."

Otis deliberated for a moment, trying to decide how to deal with this first challenge to his authority. "Okay," he relented, "you can pick the top ones first. But you better not drop any. Pa don't like bruised apples."

He watched her for a while, waiting for her to drop an apple, but when she had filled nearly half a sack without dropping one, he turned his attention to the job at hand, and, per habit, began picking from the bottom of the tree. But he found he could not keep his mind on his work. He was still much too agitated. How dare she disobey his order? His Pa had put *him* in charge, not *her*. He should not have given in to her. The whole chain of command had been upset. Suddenly an apple came thudding down.

"See!" he cried, as if vindicated, "you dropped one already!"

"I didn't drop it," she replied calmly, "I threw it down. It's no good. There's a big hole in it. Birds, I suspect."

Otis picked up the apple and examined it. It was, as she had said, badly bird-damaged. Having been deprived of yet another chance to vent his irritation, he decided the easier course was to allow Sarah to pick the apples the way she wanted and to fret no more about it. After all, he really was glad for this opportunity to be working alone with her, and to conceal this fact from her, he had probably been more critical of her than he should have been. He didn't dare to reveal to her his *true* feelings, but, on the other hand, neither did he want her to get the idea that he despised her by being too severe with her. He resolved to be nicer to her when he saw her again. She was out of sight now, working on the opposite side of the tree, and he would not see her again until they met again on the back side. Otis began to pick faster.

As he moved his ladder to a new position, he thought again about silver linings. Aunt Emily had been right. Every dark cloud *did* have a silver lining. If his Uncle Daniel had not been killed in the spring, his cousin Sarah would never have come to live with them. And now, once again, something good had come about as a result of a catastrophe. If it hadn't been for the fire at the mill, Sarah would not now be picking the Rambos with him. He and his father would be picking the Rambos, and Sarah would be helping his mother and Aunt Elizabeth in the kitchen with the canning.

Otis was only about a third of the way around the tree when he met Sarah coming toward him. Halfway up his ladder he turned and leaned back on the rungs to observe his cousin as she pulled her ladder out of the tree, lifted it off the ground, and carried it in a perfectly vertical position, then set it down and leaned it into the tree only a few feet away from. He was not at all surprised that, once she got used to the feel and the weight of the heavy wooden ladder, she was able to handle it so easily. He had learned early in the summer that she was much stronger than she appeared. She was not as strong as he was, to be sure, but whatever she lacked in physical strength, she more than made up for in determination. In fact, so fierce was her determination that, to Otis' mind, it often bordered on contrariness. She always insisted on doing everything herself. It was pointless to offer to help her do anything, because she always refused. She was never rude about it—she always refused politely—but she always refused just the same.

Otis watched as she again climbed nimbly as a squirrel to the top of her ladder and began picking the apples from the higher branches of the tree. How quickly her hands moved! How fearlessly she moved about on the ladder, leaning this way, then that, seemingly oblivious to the fact that she was fifteen feet above the ground. She seemed to be enjoying herself immensely.

"You like doin' this, don't you?" he asked, looking up at her.

"I told you I was going to be an apple-picker when I grew up," she said, without interrupting the fluidity of her motion.

"*And* a great explorer," Otis reminded her.

She smiled. "*Definitely* a great explorer."

Otis picked a few more apples and put them in his sack, then stopped again to study his cousin. He was recalling the events of the day before and the exchange of words between his father and mother on the way home from the mill after the fire.

"Are you a witch?"

This time Sarah stopped and looked at him. She was not smiling now. "What do you think, Otis?"

"I dunno. On the way home from the mill yesterday, I axed Pa if you was a witch, an' he said mebbe you was."

"Uncle Nathan said that?"

"Cross my heart an' hope t' die. I think he was just teasin' though. You know how he's all the time teasin'. Then he told me to ax Ma what she thought. When I axed her, she got real mad an' said thar was no natural way that you could a-knowed the mill was on fire. She said thar was somethin' peculiar about you. She said thar's *always* been somethin' peculiar about you, even when you was little, puttin' spells on animals an' such. She don't believe you been to Heaven neither."

"Yes," replied Sarah distractedly, "I know Aunt Hester doesn't believe that I've been to Heaven." But she had *not* known that her Aunt Hester considered her peculiar or had been so upset by what had happened at the mill. Now she understood why her Aunt Hester had been so cool toward her at Sunday dinner and again at breakfast that morning.

Otis had watched as the expression on his cousin's face had become increasingly grave, and now he felt obliged to cheer her up.

"But if you ax me, I don't think you're a witch. You don't *look* like a witch."

"Oh?" she queried, scarcely paying attention, "what do witches look like?" She was thinking about what her Uncle Nathan had said to her in the loft the day before: there's nothing wrong with being different. "Peculiar" was just another word for "different."

"They're old an' ugly," replied Otis. "You're ugly enough but you ain't old enough."

As soon as Otis heard with his ears the words he had just spoken with his mouth, he winced in anguish. Whatever had possessed him to say such a thing? She was certainly not ugly. Moreover, only minutes before, he had vowed to be nice to her. He had no one to blame but–his father. His father had teased him ever since he was a small boy, and over the years he had learned to tease back in self-defense. All summer long he and his father had exchanged playful insults. Sarah had often overheard their silly banter, and, at times, even seemed to be amused by it, but she had never participated in it herself. Now she had become the victim of a misdirected shot.

She did not respond. Otis hoped that she hadn't taken him seriously, but knew that she probably had. She took *everything* seriously. He felt awful. He had already upset her once by blurting out without thinking what his mother had said; then, in his stupid attempt to correct *that* mistake, he had upset her again by calling her ugly. He wondered if he should try to think of something else to say, or leave well enough alone. The one thing he *couldn't* do would be retract his statement. If he told her she *wasn't* ugly, that would be tantamount to admitting to her that he thought she was pretty, and he couldn't do that. The best thing to do, he decided, would be to change the subject altogether. But before he could do that, he had to ask her one more question. It had been for the express purpose of asking this one question that he had brought the subject of witches up in the first place.

"But thar's still somethin' I don't understand," he said.

"What's that?" she asked. She had resumed picking.

"I don't understand how you knowed the mill was on fire."

"It's like I told you yesterday. I saw the lightning hit the mill. I saw the fire start."

"When your soul was a-flyin' around outside your body?"

"I wouldn't call it flying exactly. You make me sound like a bird."

"But how'd you do it? How'd you get outside your body?"

"I'm not sure. I didn't try to do it. It just happened. I was standing with everyone else, singing the hymn, when suddenly I felt myself floating toward the ceiling. The next thing I knew, I went through the roof and was outside in the storm."

"Wow!" exclaimed Otis. "I wish I could do that. I wish I could just jump out of my body an' go a-flyin' around in the air."

Half day-dreaming he reached for an apple that was hanging just out of reach, midway between the two ladders. Suddenly his ladder flipped over, and before he could grab onto anything–

branch, rung, or rail–he went crashing through the tree to the ground.

"Otis, are you all right?" asked Sarah anxiously, as she hurried down her ladder. She removed the nearly-full sack from around her neck and ran under the tree to the spot where Otis had fallen. She found him lying on his back with the strap of the picking bag still around his neck and the bag itself pinned beneath him. As he slowly picked himself up, he removed the strap from around his neck.

"Good thang this sack weren't full," he groaned, rubbing his neck, "or hit would a-took my whole haid clean off."

Sarah picked up his picking bag and turned it upside down. Out tumbled about a dozen apples–no more–badly crushed and oozing juice. "Are you sure you're all right?" she asked.

"Yeah, I'm all right," replied Otis, now rubbing his backside. "I reckon we better eat them apples before Pa sees 'em."

She handed him an especially badly bruised specimen. He took a huge bite out of it. She selected another for herself.

"Better gimme another one," he said.

She handed him another and he took a huge bite out of it as well. As she watched him devour the two apples almost simultaneously, she began to laugh.

"What's so funny?" he asked, wiping the juice off his chin with the sleeve of his shirt.

"I forgot to tell you," she said, a very uncharacteristic, but unmistakably impish gleam in her eyes, "When you jump out of your body, you've got to make sure that your body doesn't try to follow you."

"Very funny," groaned Otis. "Very, very funny."

It took exactly four days to rebuild the mill, which was just about the length of time Nathan had estimated. A work force of ten men had turned out on Monday and by the end of the day all the damaged siding and shingles had been removed. The first truckload of new lumber had arrived on Tuesday morning, allowing Nathan and the others to begin the job of replacing the burned-out posts and beams and reinforcing those that could be saved. But then there had been a delay. A belt had broken at the sawmill and George Ownby had had to shut down for the better part of an afternoon to repair it. But once the lumber had started arriving again, the work had progressed steadily and without further interruption. Fourteen men showed up on Thursday morning for the final day. With hammers rat-tat-tatting they swarmed all over the building, with about a third of their number working on the siding and the other two-thirds up on the roof nailing on the shingles. Each day throughout the week Mary Bryson had prepared the men a hearty noonday meal. On Monday they had sat on the lawn in front of the Brysons' house to eat their dinner, in the shade of a huge sycamore tree, but by Tuesday noon they had built themselves a makeshift picnic table, using some of the discarded lumber from the millhouse. On Thursday Hester had sent along half a dozen apple pies with Nathan, and Nathan himself had loaded up the wagon with baskets of apples that Otis and Sarah had picked, and had used the gathering as a marketplace for his produce. By three o'clock Thursday afternoon the work on the mill was completed and Nathan's wagon was empty.

All through the week Nathan had continued to think about Lydia Hicks. Lydia's husband, Wesley, had not been among those who had come to help out at the mill, but Nathan had not really expected him. Nor would Nathan have found his presence entirely desirable. Wesley Hicks had a reputation for being a very difficult man to get along with. When he was younger, he had been a wild man. He had drunk heavily, picked fights, and had been habitually in trouble with the law. After he married Lydia Jennings, he had settled down somewhat, but his dissolute early years had done nothing to prepare him for the responsibilities of family life. He had fathered eight children in eight years—seven sons and a daughter—and would surely have fathered more if Lydia hadn't "dried up" on him. The seven sons had all survived; the only daughter had lived only a few weeks.

It was generally agreed by all the upstanding citizens of the community that Lydia's inability to have more children had been a blessing for all concerned: for Wesley himself, who had never been able to provide for the seven he already had; for Lydia, on whom childbearing had taken a terrible toll (she had been an attractive woman at one time, but the years had not been kind to her); and for none more so than for all those children who had remained unborn, as Wesley's brutal mistreatment of his children was legendary. The community too had been a beneficiary of Lydia's early barrenness, as the seven children she had already unleashed onto an unsuspecting world had wreaked havoc in three counties. They had stolen from their neighbors, had vandalized property (the third son, Rodney, had burned the schoolhouse down when he was only twelve), had killed livestock for sport, and the oldest son, Wesley Jr., at the age of seventeen, had killed another teenaged boy in a quarrel over a girl. A pack of wild dogs could not have caused so much destruction to property and life. Had the Hicks boys *been* a pack of wild dogs, the law-abiding citizens of the community would surely have risen up in self-defense, hunted them down and shot them. As it was, three of them were currently in prison: Wesley Jr. for manslaughter, and two others, Bart and Stanley, for armed robbery. Rodney, the one who had burned the schoolhouse down, and another brother, Charles, were, as of last report, running loose somewhere in Tennessee, wreaking their havoc there.

So, with five of the seven either behind bars or terrorizing other communities, the farmers and shop-keepers of Rushing Creek had been able to relax their vigilance in recent years. The two youngest boys, Frank and James, were still living at home, but thus far they had not shown the same tendency toward criminal behavior that their older brothers had. Perhaps the wild seed that Wesley had sown so liberally in Lydia's womb had lost some of its potency over the years, allowing these last two sons of his to have a chance at a normal life. There was a possibility, of course, that the two younger boys might yet follow in their older brothers' footsteps, but Frank was already fifteen. By the time Wesley Jr. was fifteen, he had already left a long trail of destruction in his wake. Frank was no angel, but compared to his brother Wesley, he was the next thing to it. James, the youngest, who was now thirteen, showed even less tendency toward aggression. He was a shy, brooding boy, who, in his physical appearance at least, seemed to take more after his mother than his father. He was the only one of the seven who had his mother's dark curly hair and blue eyes. The other children had all inherited their father's straight reddish-brown hair and green eyes. Lydia had never made a secret of the fact that she was much fonder of her youngest son than she had ever been of the other six—James was hers; the others were Wesley's—and she was determined not to allow Wesley to ruin her little Jemmy the way he had ruined all the others.

The marriage between Wesley Hicks and Lydia Jennings had been an unhappy one from the start. In the early years of their union, Lydia had been completely submissive. Not all of her husband's violent outbursts of temper had been vented on the children: she had received her share of beatings as well. He had always been a hard drinker, and it was when he was drunk that he was the most dangerous. There had been times when she had feared for her life and for the lives of her children. She had watched in horror one day as Wesley picked up an ax and chopped off the ends of three of Bart's fingers because he had touched a bottle of whiskey that Wesley had left sitting on the table. Bart was five years old at the time.

Lydia never knew where Wesley had gotten all the liquor in those early years. She suspected he had stolen it, as he had never seemed to have any money. Then, in about the sixth year of their marriage, during the Prohibition, he had built himself his own still. Lydia had feared that, fueled by a steady supply of whiskey, her husband's violent outbursts of temper would become even more frequent, and for a time her fears were realized. But as the years passed, Wesley began to pay the price for his lifetime of intemperance. As his health deteriorated, he began to spend days at a time in bed in a state of semi-consciousness. As Wesley became less and less capable of running his own life, much less anyone else's, Lydia began to assert herself. She took a long, hard look at her life—at the low state to which Wesley had brought her—and made a determination to try to salvage what she could. She made Wesley to understand that under no circumstances was he ever to hit her or the children again. She also broke up his still and advised him that she and the children were going to start going to church, and that Wesley was going to accompany them, drunk or sober, even if she had to tie him up and carry him there in the back of the wagon. For the past two and a half years, Wesley, Lydia, and the two youngest boys had attended church regularly.

Nathan could not help wondering if Lydia would be in church come Sunday morning. During the work on the mill there had been some discussion among the men about the incident that had taken place down at the pond. Most of them had not witnessed it firsthand, as they had been looking over the damage to the millhouse at the time, but they had all heard about it from their wives or daughters or one of the neighbors. Most of them, like Nathan, considered Lydia Hicks to be a superstitious old fool. The belief in witches, while it may have been quite prevalent a hundred years ago among the inhabitants of these mountains and hollows, was not one that was generally subscribed to at the present time. If any of the men who came to work on the mill that week shared Lydia Hicks' opinion, they had not said so in front of Nathan. Yet many of them could not help wondering aloud how Nathan's niece had known the mill was on fire. The general consensus seemed to be that "she had no natural way of knowin' "—the same conclusion Hester had reached. Most were unwilling to speculate further until all the evidence was in. If Lydia Hicks died within the fortnight, as she had predicted she would, then her charge of witchcraft might have to be taken more seriously. Nathan would have found the whole thing amusing if it hadn't been for the ominous prediction that Sarah herself had made: "She's going to die, Uncle Nathan. She's going to die very soon."

Nathan paced nervously under the great oak tree in front of the church, waiting for the last parishioners to arrive. When he could see no more cars or wagons coming up the lane, he went inside and took his seat alongside his brethren. The Hickses had not come–neither Wesley, nor Lydia, nor the two boys. The murmuring among the congregation, especially the women, told Nathan that he was not the only one who had taken notice of the Hickses' absence.

Outside in the churchyard after the service the murmuring continued. No one, it seemed, had seen any of the Hickses in the week gone by, but this was not considered unusual, as they lived out of the way and were in the habit of keeping to themselves. It *was* considered unusual, however, that they had not come to church, as they had not missed a Sunday service in two and a half years. Yet no one–no one within Nathan's hearing at least–suggested that this had anything to do with the incident at the mill pond the week before, though Nathan suspected that a good many were thinking it. He also suspected that some who might otherwise have said something were being restrained by the Ninth Commandment–"thou shalt not bear false witness against thy neighbor"–which was fresh in their minds, as the Reverend Eby had emphasized it repeatedly in his sermon on "Loving Thy Neighbor." It seemed to Nathan almost as if the Reverend Eby had prepared the sermon with Lydia Hicks in mind, to chasten her for the way in which she had attacked Sarah the week before, but it had served just as well in Lydia's absence, as a reminder to any others in the congregation who might be tempted to engage in mischievous gossip or to point accusatory fingers in the event that something actually did happen, or had already happened, to Lydia Hicks.

Sarah herself seemed oblivious to the fact that all eyes were upon her as she took off her shoes, placed them under the seat of the wagon, and set off once again in the direction of the creek. Hester spoke not a word on the way home, but by the grave expression on her face, Nathan knew what she was thinking. When they arrived at the house, she continued to sit on the wagon seat for several minutes after the wagon had stopped, staring straight ahead, as though struck dumb.

"I'm gonna be takin' a load of apples up to Hobblebush tomorrow," ventured Nathan cautiously, as if approaching a hornet's nest. "If it'll make you feel any better, I'll stop in an' see the Hickses on the way home."

Without looking at him or saying a word, Hester helped herself down off the wagon and went into the house.

Early the next morning, after the milking and feeding, Nathan hitched the two horses to the wagon and drove the rig around to the apple cellar. There, with Otis' and Sarah's help, he hauled a dozen baskets of Rambo apples out of the cool, damp earthen chamber and loaded them into the wagon. Nathan smiled to himself as he remembered the first time Sarah had seen the inside of the apple cellar. It was back in the fall of 1932, soon after Sarah and her family had moved down from Massachusetts. She had not been able to understand why it was called a "cellar" when it was not located underneath a house but in the side of a hill, and for the rest of the winter she had insisted on calling it the "apple cave." She was such a bright-eyed, innocent child then, Nathan remembered, with such tender feelings. He would never forget as long as he lived how she had cried that time she had seen him shoot the rabbit in the garden. She was eight, almost nine, years older now, but in many ways she was still the same innocent and tender child. Nathan wondered if Sarah had any idea of the repercussions that might result if Lydia Hicks were to die—or had already died.

Nathan closed the door to the cellar and looked to the east. The sun had not yet emerged from behind the mountains, but it had been light for the past hour and the air was already starting to get warm.

"Looks like it's gonna be another scorcher," he predicted, quite safely, as it was, after all, August. "I'd better get started or these apples'll be baked before I get there. I want you two t' help out in the garden this mornin'. The tomatoes, beans, an' sweet corn are all gonna need pickin'. It's gonna be a real busy week, an' before it's over, you'll probably be wishin' that you never see another tomato or ear of corn as long as you live . . . Just keep remindin' yourselves how good everything is gonna taste this winter when the snow is on the ground . . . An' Sarah, maybe you could help out in the kitchen today as well. Otis, after you finish in the garden, maybe you should hoe some more corn."

Otis groaned. Nathan put a comforting hand on his shoulder. "Enjoy it while you can, Son. School starts next week."

"Don't remind me, Pa."

Nathan climbed up onto the driver's seat, took the reins, and coaxed the horses into motion. Otis and Sarah watched as the wagonload of apples lumbered slowly out the lane.

In the garden they found Hester and Elizabeth already seriously engaged in the business of bean-picking. Sarah picked up an empty basket and began picking in the row next to her mother. Otis grabbed another basket and fell in beside his cousin.

By half-past nine, after nearly four hours of steady labor, everything in the garden that had been in urgent need of picking, had been picked. Hester looked around at all the full baskets sitting in the garden and shook her head.

"Hit's too much for us t' put up in one day," she decided. "We'll do the beans an' corn today an' the 'maters tomorruh. Otis, you carry the 'maters down to the spring house, then take the beans into the kitchen. The rest of us will start huskin' corn."

Otis did as he was told and when he had finished he joined the corn-husking party at the foot of the porch steps. But when it came to removing the husk from the corn, he found that he was no match for the three women. His Aunt Elizabeth was the slowest of the three, but even she was faster than he. He tried to make his hands go faster, but he found he was unable to do so and hold onto the ear at the same time. After dropping half a dozen ears on the ground, he decided to ignore the others and work at his own pace. But Sarah was hard to ignore. Otis had never seen anyone whose hands could move as fast as his mother's, but

Sarah was matching her ear for ear. When the husk had been removed from the last ear of corn, Otis trudged off to the cornfield and Sarah reported for duty in the kitchen.

"Are we going to can the beans or dry them, Aunt Hester?" asked Sarah.

"Dry 'em," replied Hester curtly.

"Could I do that? I used to make leather britches all the time at home."

Hester nodded. "I'll get you the needle an' twine."

She went to her sewing chest in the parlor and returned with a heavy sewing needle and spool of twine. Sarah carried the baskets of beans to a far corner of the kitchen, so as to be out of the way, then sat down cross-legged on the floor and began stringing together the six-inch-long green pods. Meanwhile her mother and Aunt Hester took their places at the kitchen table and began the task of cutting the corn from the cobs.

As Sarah quickly ran the needle through the stem-end of one bean pod after another, she glanced up from time to time at the two women working at the table. Whenever she had the choice, Sarah preferred to work outside, but she was always willing to help out in the kitchen when she was needed, even though it almost always filled her with sadness to do so. Whenever she worked with her mother and her Aunt Hester—whenever it was just the three of them—she almost always found herself, sooner or later, thinking about her father. When she worked outside with Nathan and Otis, she sometimes thought about him too, but not nearly as often and never so intensely. For one thing, there were so many more distractions outside: the sky and the wind; the birds, the animals, the insects; the creek, the trees, the mountains all around them; not to mention the almost constant bantering between Nathan and Otis themselves. But there was something else too, something that she would have had difficulty articulating. Ever since her father's death, it had seemed to Sarah as if there were a part of her missing. She was often acutely aware of a feeling of an emptiness inside her, of a great empty void that cried out to be filled. When she worked with Nathan and Otis—with Nathan especially—she felt more like a complete person. The emptiness inside her did not seem so vast and so deep. Nathan, in some way, managed to fill some of that awful void.

It was very different when she found herself in the company of her mother and Hester. The mood was always more somber. The three of them never joked or laughed; they seldom even spoke to each other. They almost always worked in silence, as they were doing now, each busy with her own particular task, each alone in a world of her own thought. Yet Sarah knew that if the silent cries of the heart could be heard, the sound in the kitchen at that very moment would be deafening. In all the world, these were the three people who had loved Daniel the most; these were the three people who had been most devastated by his death. Even though Elizabeth had not yet consciously acknowledged the fact of Daniel's death, she perhaps had been the most devastated of all. Daniel had brought them together; memory of him bound them together now. Daniel had been something different to each of them–to Hester, the kid brother, whom she had practically raised as her own child; to Elizabeth, the devoted husband, the compass, the rudder, the anchor of her life; to Sarah, the doting father, her corn-hoeing partner, half of her world–and each remembered him in her own way. For two of them–for Hester and Sarah–those memories were steeped in grief. It was this shared grief which had bound Hester and Sarah so closely together during those long empty days and weeks immediately following Daniel's death–that, and their common concern for Elizabeth.

But now Sarah felt as though the bond between herself and her Aunt Hester were slipping. She felt as if a rift had opened between them, a rift which was widening with each passing day. Sarah felt that she herself had not changed; it was Hester who had changed. However carefully Hester may have guarded her affections in public places, she had always been open and friendly in the sanctuary of her own home. Whenever members of the family came to visit, she always had a warm welcome for them. Sarah did not feel that warmth now. She did not expect her Aunt Hester to lavish affection upon her–to spontaneously pull her to her bosom and embrace her, as her mother had done–but she would have appreciated a smile and a kind word now and then. In the past week or so, Hester had hardly even looked at her or spoken a word to her, except when it was absolutely necessary. Sarah knew that her Aunt Hester was upset with her, that her Aunt Hester considered her peculiar. It had hurt a little, when Otis had told her that, but she had tried not to let it affect her. She had promised herself that no matter what her Aunt Hester said or did, she would continue to love her just as much. She would continue to act as though nothing had changed. She would continue to be polite and respectful, and to work just as hard—even harder if possible—in the hope that one day her Aunt Hester would once again look upon her more kindly. If she had thought it would make a difference, she would even have promised her Aunt Hester that she wouldn't miss any more Sunday dinners.

When she had finished the first basket, Sarah placed the long strings of beans into a wash tub, folding them back and forth, being careful not to tangle them. Then she picked the tub up and carried it upstairs. Pushing open the door to the attic, she was met by a wall of hot air. Undaunted, she climbed the narrow steps into the attic and began hanging the strings of beans from the hooks which had been screwed into the log rafters expressly for that purpose.

It was while Sarah was in the attic that Hester's and Elizabeth's work was interrupted by the sound of angry shouting outside, followed by a loud banging on the screendoor. Hester wiped her hands on her apron and went to the door to investigate the commotion. She found herself staring through the screendoor at the grizzled face of Wesley Hicks. He was holding a shotgun.

"We come for the witch!" shouted the grizzled face. "We ain't got no quarrel wit you, Hester. All we ax is that you hand over the witch an' thar won't be no trouble."

Hester could smell the whiskey through the screendoor. For a moment she stared into Wesley's glassy, bloodshot eyes, then looked past him to see if she could determine who it was that he had meant by "we." Just off the porch she saw one of Wesley's sons, Frank, holding two bloodhounds on a leash. Another son, the dark-haired one, the youngest, was sitting in the back of

Wesley's wagon with his eyes directed at the ground. There was no sign of Lydia.

"What's this all about, Wesley?" asked Hester in a cold, steely voice. She was almost certain that she knew the answer to that question, but she wanted confirmation.

"Hit's my Lydia," he cried, his voice quavering with anger and grief. "She died this mornin'. She took sick the very day that niece of yourn put her curse on her, an' she died this mornin', just afore sun-up." He paused for a moment to recover himself. "Like I say, Hester, we ain't got no quarrel wit you. Hit's your niece we be a-lookin' for. You just hand her over, an' we'll leave you be."

Hester continued to stare coldly at the frightening visage on the other side of the screendoor. She knew that in his present condition Wesley Hicks was drunk enough and distraught enough to do just about anything. She herself was scarcely more calm, despite her icy exterior. She felt a torrent of emotions surging within her. Every day for the past week she had waited anxiously and fearfully for news of Lydia Hicks. Now the waiting was over, and that which she had dreaded most had come to pass.

"Wait right here," she said at last, dispassionately, "I'll go fetch her for you."

Hester turned and stepped back into the kitchen, where she found Elizabeth standing at the table, an anxious and confused look on her face.

"Hester, what's going on?" she asked.

Hester gave her a passing glance, but made no response. Instead, she turned and made straight for the staircase. There she found Sarah standing in the doorway, frozen to the spot.

"You heared?"

Sarah nodded.

"Lydia Hicks died this mornin'."

"Yes, I know," replied Sarah sympathetically, in a voice barely above a whisper.

Hester stared coldly for a moment into her niece's soft, brown, trusting eyes.

"Now you do as I say, you hear?"

Sarah nodded.

"You get back up in the attic, an' don't you come down til I say so."

Sarah hesitated.

"Now you mind me, hear?" snapped Hester.

Sarah retreated up the stairwell. Hester turned and took Nathan's shotgun down off the wall, loaded it, and dropped a handful of extra shells into the pocket of her apron. She then strode across the room and pushed the screendoor open with so much force that she nearly knocked her visitor off the porch. Before he had time to regain his balance, she had the muzzle of her shotgun pressed into his nostrils.

"Now you listen an' you listen good, Wesley Hicks. I want you an' your young'uns off my property this minute."

Hester's sudden movement had taken Wesley so much by surprise that he had stumbled backwards down the porch steps and had nearly stepped on one of his own dogs.

"Now put that gun down, Hester," he grumbled, "afore someone gets hurt. My quarrel ain't wit you, hit's wit your niece."

"If you got a quarrel with any of mine," retorted Hester, "you got a quarrel with me. I want you t' stay away from Sarah, you hear me? If any harm comes to that girl, so help me God, I'll hunt you down an' shoot you myself. I'll shoot you so full of holes, you'll bleed whiskey for a week. I'll shoot you so full of holes, thar won't be enough of you left for the worms t' bother with."

Hester lowered the barrel of her gun from Wesley's face to his chest and waited for him to consider his options. He had stopped retreating and was now standing his ground and glaring at her. She watched as his hands tightened around his shotgun and as he swung the barrel around to point directly at her midsection. For a tense moment Hester waited, and prayed that Wesley still had enough sense left in his head not to pull the trigger. Suddenly, to Hester's surprise, his face turned white and he began to tremble from head to foot.

"Lydia!" he gasped.

Uncomprehending, Hester gave him a curious look. What had come over him? He looked like, and was acting like, he had just seen a ghost. As Hester continued to stare at him, she noticed that he was no longer looking at *her*, but at something *past* her, over her shoulder. Cautiously she turned her head and saw Elizabeth standing inside the screendoor.

"No, Pa," said Frank, struggling to restrain the dogs, "that ain't her. That ain't Ma."

"Hit's her *soul*, boy," cried Wesley, stumbling sideways. "Don't yuh see, they got her soul. These devils done got her soul." He continued to stare through wide glassy eyes at the ghostly image on the screendoor.

"Come on, Pa, let's go home," pleaded the younger boy on the wagon.

Suddenly Wesley dropped his shotgun and slumped forward onto the ground, unconscious.

"Pa!" yelled Frank, rushing to his father's side. Excitedly the two dogs began crawling over Wesley's prostrate form and licking his face. Frank tried to pull them off. When they refused to be deterred, he gave one of them a hard kick in the stomach and sent it sprawling. Immediately the hound came back at him, snarling. Startled, Frank dropped the leashes, and both dogs went tearing out across the barnyard. Frank turned to his younger brother. "C'mon, Jemmy, help me get him into the wagon."

Nervously the younger boy climbed down out of the wagon and joined his brother at his father's side, but his eyes were still fixed on the screendoor. "It *is* Ma, Frank."

Frank squinted his eyes and looked again. He seemed unable to make up his mind. "Let's get outa here."

Hester watched as the two teenaged boys wrestled their father into the back of the wagon. Both of them continued to cast nervous glances back at the screendoor as they did so. As soon as they had Wesley secured in the back of the wagon, they practically climbed over each other to get into the driver's seat. Frank took the reins and shook them vigorously. "Hah! Git up! Git up!"

The horses bolted into motion, throwing the two boys backwards. Hester watched as the wagon rumbled out the lane, throwing up a cloud of dust in its trail. The dogs, fearing they might be left behind, tore out after the wagon and jumped into the back with Wesley.

Elizabeth stepped aside as Hester came back into the house. "Time's a-wastin'," said Hester curtly. "We got work t' do." She returned the shotgun to its place on the wall and put the shells back in the drawer. Then, returning to the table, she picked up her knife and began working on the next ear of corn.

Nathan knocked again. Still there was no answer. He stepped back off the porch and looked around. The house, like all the buildings on the place, was in a state of disrepair. The roof sagged badly in the middle; some of the windows were broken out; a corner of the porch looked as though it were about to collapse. The yard and surrounding woods were littered with junk.

There seemed to be nobody home. Perhaps the Hickses had gone away. Perhaps that was the reason they had not been in church on Sunday: they had gone away for several days, perhaps to visit one of the older sons in prison. Nathan stepped back up onto the dilapidated porch and peered in the window. The interior of the house was in the same state of disorder as the outside. Dirty dishes were piled up on the table. An old sofa in the corner of the kitchen was faded and soiled and had about as many holes in it as the roof. The floor was littered with yet more junk. Nathan could not help thinking that his hogs lived better than this. He cast a glance at Wesley's hog pen. Even *Wesley's* hogs lived better than this.

He walked around to the back of the house, wending his way through piles of rotting lumber, rusting farm implements, tin cans, and assorted other debris. He went to another window. Cupping his hands around his eyes, he pressed his face against the glass. Instantly he drew back and ducked to the side, away from the window. For a long moment he remained pressed against the wall, too embarrassed to move. How awkward! He had just peeked into Lydia Hicks' bedroom and had seen Lydia lying in her bed and staring back at him! By the expression on her face, he had scared her half to death.

He tried to think, what to do next. He couldn't look in the window again. It had been embarrassing enough the first time. Nor could he just leave. He knew that she had seen him. He decided that the least embarrassing course of action was to go back around front, knock on the door again, and apologize for his ill manners.

Again he picked his way through the litter in the yard. Stepping cautiously onto the shaky porch, he knocked again. Again there was no answer. "Lydia," he called, "are you there?"

He pushed open the door and called again. Still there was no answer, no sound of any kind. He stepped into the house and called again. Cautiously he made his way to the back room and pushed open the door. "Lydia," he whispered.

She was lying in the bed with her face toward the window. Nathan did not touch her. He did not have to. He knew she was dead. The smell of death was in the room.

He closed the door and walked back out into the kitchen, his mind suddenly flooded with anxious thoughts. Desperately he tried to sort them out. Where were Wesley and the boys? He looked around the kitchen, at the squalor, at the clutter of dishes, bottles, and jars on the table, at the multitude of flies crawling over everything. He picked up one of the Mason jars, chased out the flies, and lifted it to his nose. It smelled of alcohol. Nathan decided that the prudent thing to do was to get home as soon as possible.

As he drove the horses down the clay road, all sorts of dire thoughts were going through his mind. As he approached his own lane, he saw Wesley's horse and wagon coming out. Immediately a feeling of dread came over him. As the wagon came nearer, he noticed that Wesley was not driving. The two boys were in the driver's seat. Where was Wesley? Nathan signalled for the boys to stop, but they sped by him without even slowing down. As the wagon went past, Nathan saw Wesley's crumpled form lying in the back with two hound dogs crawling over him hungrily licking their master's hands and face. What had happened to Wesley? My God, had Hester shot him?

As Nathan reined in the team in front of the barn, he saw Otis with his hoe on his shoulder, coming up out of the cornfield.

"What's happened, Son?"

"Whatta yuh mean, Pa?"

"Where's your mother? Where's Sarah?"

"I dunno. In the house, I reckon."

Nathan ran to the house with Otis close at his heels. "What's gwine on, Pa?"

Nathan burst into the kitchen. There he found Hester and Elizabeth standing at the table, bent over a tub of cut corn.

"Hester, what happened to Wesley Hicks? You didn't shoot him, did you?"

"Not yet," replied Hester perfunctorily, without looking up from her work.

"Then what happened to him? I just saw him go out of here in the back of his wagon."

"Passed out. He was drunk."

Nathan was beginning to realize that Hester wasn't about to volunteer any information: he was going to have to extract it one piece at a time. "What did he want?"

"Lydia died this mornin'."

"Yes," sighed Nathan, "I know. I just came from there."

"You told me she weren't a-gwine t' die, Nathan. You told me nuthin' was a-gwine t' happen to her."

"I know, I know," replied Nathan contritely. The last thing that he wanted to tell Hester was that he had changed his mind, that he had been half-expecting Lydia Hicks to die ever since Sarah had told him that she was going to. Sarah had no natural way of knowing that either. "What exactly did Wesley say?"

"He said, 'we come for the witch.'"

"He wanted to *take* Sarah?"

"That's what he said."

"But you say he passed out?"

"Fell right over on the ground. His boys had t' load him into the wagon."

"The boys didn't waste any time gettin' out of here. You must a-done somethin' to put the fear of the Lord into them."

"Weren't me. Hit was Miss 'Lizbeth. An' hit weren't the fear of the Lord she put into them. Hit was the fear of the Devil."

Otis, who had been completely bewildered by everything he had heard since coming out of the cornfield, turned to his father. "Pa, can you explain to me what's gwine on? I don't understand any of this."

"I'd be glad to, Son," said Nathan, putting a hand on Otis' shoulder, "just as soon as I understand it myself."

"But whar's Sarah?" asked Otis anxiously. "Did Mr. Hicks *take* her?"

"Oh my word!" exclaimed Hester, suddenly looking up. "I plum' forgot about Sarah. I sent her up to that hot attic an' told her not to come down til I said so. That poor child must be dried to leather herself by now."

"I'll go get her," offered Nathan.

He went upstairs and opened the door to the attic. Thrusting his head through the narrow doorway, he saw Sarah sitting at the top of the staircase with her eyes closed.

"Are you *in* your body or *out*?" he asked.

She opened her eyes and smiled. "I'm *in*, Uncle Nathan."

Braving the heat, he started up the steps. Sarah stood up and stepped back to make way for him. When he reached the floor of the attic, he looked around at the ropes of green beans, strung like clotheslines from one end of the attic to the other.

"Well, what have we got here?" he asked, a diabolical twinkle in his eye. "Looks to me like lots of little leather britches–an' one little leather witch."

Sarah laughed. It was just like her Uncle Nathan to say something like that. No matter how serious the crisis, he never lost his sense of humor. At once she felt the tension go out of her body. It was as if a wire which had been pulled taut inside her had suddenly been released. "Did Aunt Hester say I could come down now?"

Nathan nodded. "Yeah, she doesn't want you t' miss dinner."

Sarah waited for him to move, as he was standing between her and the steps, but he did not do so. She looked up into his eyes to determine the reason for his hesitation, and found him studying her with a look of concern and compassion. There was no mischief in his eyes now. Suddenly he did something he had never done before. He reached his arms around her shoulders and pulled her against his large chest.

"I'm glad you're all right," he said tenderly, breathing a heavy sigh of relief. "I don't know what I would a-done if somethin' had happened to you . . . If you were my own daughter, I couldn't love you any more than I do already . . . I just wanted you to know that."

He placed his hands on her shoulders and held her at arm's length. He was surprised to see tears in her eyes. He was even more surprised when, quite spontaneously, she threw her arms around him and once again buried herself in his chest.

"Thank you, Uncle Nathan. Thank you very much."

Moved almost to tears himself, Nathan continued to hold her close to him.

"Well," he said, when she had finally made a move to release herself, "I reckon we better go downstairs before we both expire."

He pulled a handkerchief from his hip pocket to wipe his face and brow, then stepped aside and allowed Sarah to pass.

Feeling very full inside, more full than she had felt at any time since her father's death, Sarah wiped her eyes and headed down the stairs.

All the next day and the day after, Nathan kept one eye on the lane, just in case Wesley Hicks decided to pay a return visit. But the only visitors to call during those two days were an elderly couple who had seen the "Apples For Sale" sign at the end of the lane, and the Reverend Eby, who had taken upon himself the duty of informing the community of the passing of Lydia Hicks and of notifying friends of the deceased that the funeral would be at eight o'clock Thursday morning.

On Thursday morning, at the designated hour, Nathan and Hester found themselves standing, heads bowed, in the crowd of mourners and onlookers gathered together in the small cemetery on the hillside behind the church. There had never been any question in either Nathan's or Hester's mind that they would attend the funeral. Whenever anyone in the community died, from the most beloved to the most reviled, everyone within a two- or three-mile radius of Rushing Creek attended the funeral, to pay their last respects, and to wish the departed brother or sister a safe journey to the next world. Common courtesy demanded it.

But Nathan had reasons other than common courtesy for wanting to be present at Lydia's funeral. He knew that the news of Lydia's death would stir up a hornet's nest of gossip, and he felt that his presence at the funeral might help to keep the gossip from getting out of hand. For the same reason he had driven over to Isaac and Jacob's the evening before to make certain that his in-laws were planning to attend the funeral as well. The Wickers were one of the oldest and most respected families in Rushing Creek, and Nathan felt that the presence of Isaac and Jacob might help to remind anyone who might need reminding that Sarah was a Wicker too, that she was one of their own, even if she hadn't been born in Rushing Creek, and even if she didn't exactly look like one of them.

Nathan looked around at the crowd of people standing around the coffin. Nearly everyone in attendance had also been at the mill the day of the fire. Many of them had witnessed firsthand the confrontation between Lydia and Sarah. They had heard Lydia call Sarah a witch. They had seen Sarah stare back at Lydia. They had heard Lydia's dire prediction that she would die within the fortnight. The news that Lydia had taken sick the very same day and had died eight days later—well within the fortnight—had come as a shock to many, even to those who had chastised Lydia for her hysterical behavior and ridiculed her for her superstitious beliefs.

Nathan knew that Sarah had had nothing to do with Lydia's death, at least not directly, not intentionally. He knew that Lydia Hicks had been very sick and would have died soon anyway. It was conceivable that she might have lived a few weeks longer if she hadn't worked herself into such a frenzy that day at the mill, but she would have died soon anyway. Nathan knew this, but would he be able to convince anyone else of it? He hadn't even been able to convince his own wife.

And suppose someone were to ask him how he knew that Lydia had been sick, when no one else seemed to have been aware of it. He couldn't very well tell them what Sarah had told him, that Lydia had no light coming out of her. That would only make matters worse. He was trying to exonerate Sarah from the charge of witchcraft, not convict her.

He *could* say that he had been out to the Hickses' house and had seen all the clutter and filth in the kitchen, which Lydia would never have permitted to accumulate had she been well. There was at least that much tangible evidence that she had been sick for quite some time before her encounter with Sarah at the mill. Perhaps she had even had a fever in the brain. Perhaps that was the reason she had attacked Sarah so vehemently in the first place.

Nathan decided that that was how he would make his case for Sarah's defense: he would argue that Lydia had been sick for a long time and would have died anyway. As evidence he would cite the unkept house and her hysterical behavior the day of the fire. But Nathan knew that even if he were successful in getting a verdict of "not guilty," there would still be one unanswered question lingering in the back of every juror's mind: how had Sarah known there was a fire at the mill in the first place?

Nathan found Isaac's face in the crowd, then Jacob's. He was glad they had come. There were others in the crowd too, whom he knew could be depended upon to stand up in Sarah's defense, not the least of whom was the Reverend Eby himself. With the Reverend Eby on her side, Sarah was hardly in need of any other allies, but if she needed them, there were others too who were prepared to stand by her, including some of the most prominent people in the town, like Walter Lehman and Henry and Mary Bryson. These were people who had known Sarah before the incident at the mill. It was not possible, in Nathan's view, for anyone to know Sarah and not like her. But the majority of the people who now stood around Lydia Hicks' coffin had never met Sarah. Up until the day of the fire, they had only seen her a few times in church and knew her only as "Hester's niece" or as "Dan'l Wicker's girl–Lord rest his soul." Of course, after the fire, *everyone* knew Sarah by name, and for many she had been the main topic of conversation ever since, even though most of them still had never made her acquaintance or spoken to her. Sarah had not come to the funeral. Nathan had thought it best that she not come. He was not sure how Wesley would react to her presence, nor was he that anxious to find out. Consequently, he had left Otis and Sarah at home to look after the farm in his absence.

As the coffin was lowered into the ground, Nathan studied the faces of Wesley and the two boys. Wesley looked deathly ill. His face was haggard and drawn, and had a sickly yellow cast that even a week's growth of white whiskers could not hide. He was bent over, stooped forward, and at times appeared ready to topple into the open grave himself. Every time he tried to straighten himself up, he winced in pain. Nathan had also observed Wesley's body to shudder spasmodically on several occasions during the service, as if shivering from cold, despite the ninety-degree heat. Wesley Hicks was clearly a man in pain, but it was difficult to know how much of that pain was due to grief over his wife's death and how much was due to the poor state of his own health. Nathan could not help wondering if Wesley himself would live another fortnight, but he was not about to make any predictions– at least not within earshot of another human being.

Nathan allowed his gaze to move from Wesley to the two boys. Frank, the older of the two, appeared to be very uncomfortable. He had had difficulty remaining still during the Reverend Eby's eulogy, even though the eulogy was not nearly as long as some others which Nathan had known the good preacher to deliver over the years. Frank had shuffled his feet, had repeatedly shoved his hands into his pockets and withdrawn them again, and had cast furtive glances from side to side, as if anxious to know if anyone was watching him. The look on Frank's face at the moment was properly mournful, but it was a face that he had had difficulty maintaining. It was almost as if the act of grieving was one for which he did not have sufficient concentration.

The younger boy, James, on the other hand, had struggled throughout the service to hold back tears, most of the time unsuccessfully. Of the three, it was young James who seemed to be taking Lydia's death the hardest. While looking at his face, Nathan was reminded of Sarah's face, the way Sarah had looked back in the spring, for a month after her father's death. Nathan found that he could not help but be moved to pity by this young boy, who was even younger than Sarah, and who had also lost a beloved parent.

At the conclusion of the service, Nathan was among the first of those assembled to shake hands with Wesley and his two sons and to offer his heartfelt sympathy and condolences. He then spent the next three-quarters of an hour mingling with the other mourners and describing the state in which Lydia Hicks had left her house—"due no doubt to her long illness." It was not until most of the crowd had dispersed that he gathered up Hester and headed for the wagon.

"He's a beaten man," sighed Nathan on the way home, "hardly anything like the Wesley Hicks of old."

"He's a creature t' be pitied, that's for sure," agreed Hester. "Almost makes me feel sorry for the way I took after him with the shotgun the other day . . . That's not t' say I wouldn't shoot him daid in the dirt if'n he ever dares t' set foot on our place ag'in."

"I don't reckon we'll be seein' any more of Wesley Hicks," said Nathan confidently. There! he thought, that's as close as I'll come to telling the world that Wesley Hicks' days on this earth are numbered.

"He won't be around any more today, that's for sure," agreed Hester, again, "not unless he comes a-crawlin' on his hands an' knees. Hit was all he could do t' keep from fallin' over back thar . . . Did you smell the liquor on his breath? He's been a-drinkin' ag'in. Now that Lydia's gone, he'll prob'bly drink hisself straight into the grave."

There! thought Nathan, Hester had just confirmed his own prognostication.

" 'Course, I could be wrong," continued Hester. "I been wrong about Wesley before. I gave him up for daid three or four times some years back when he was so awful sick, an' each time he fooled me. He just refuses t' die. He's as stubborn as he is mean. Hit wouldn't surprise me if'n he don't outlive us all."

Nathan felt suddenly ill. He stared at the road ahead and gritted his teeth. He did not find the thought of Wesley Hicks outliving them all an especially comforting one.

16

RULING AFFECTIONS

"Today's Labor Day, Pa," said Otis at breakfast the following Monday, the first day of September. "We should do somethin' special today."

"Somethin' special, you say? You mean, to celebrate Labor Day?"

"Yeah, Pa."

"What do you have in mind, Son?"

"We could pack a big picnic lunch an' go up in the mountains."

"Picnic, you say? That sounds like a mighty fine idea, but I don't think it would be exactly fittin'. It's Labor Day, after all, not Picnic Day."

"Well, then, how about you an' me go swimmin' down at the dam?"

"Son, if today was Swimmin' Day, I'd be the first one t' say, let's go down to the dam an' go swimmin'. But the simple truth of the matter is, it ain't Swimmin' Day, it's Labor Day. We should do somethin' that would be appropriate for Labor Day."

A frown came over Otis' face. He did not like the direction in which the current of this conversation was running. "You mean we gotta *work* today, Pa?"

"Good idea, Son," exclaimed Nathan. "I'm glad you thought of it. We can celebrate labor by laborin'."

"But we work *all* the time, Pa," protested Otis.

"No, Son, your mother and I work *all* the time. You work *some* of the time."

"But don't you ever get tired of it, Pa? Don't you ever wanna do somethin' else?"

"I can't think of anything I'd rather do than work. I'm just grateful that I have so much of it t' do."

Otis watched his father's eyes, waiting for the telltale twinkle. "Are you teasin' me ag'in, Pa?"

"Listen, Son," replied Nathan quite seriously, "I think a man has t' do what he likes in this world. That's important. But what's even more important is that he *likes* what he *has t' do* . . . Keep that thought in mind today while we're cuttin' sorghum."

"May I help, Uncle Nathan?" interjected Sarah. "I've never cut sorghum before."

"I reckon you may—if you're not needed in the kitchen, that is." Both Nathan and Sarah cast a glance in Hester's direction.

"You might as well take her," sighed Hester. "She'd rather be outside with you anyway."

"Are we going to make molasses, Uncle Nathan?" asked Sarah.

"That we are. An' tomorrow your Aunt Hester is gonna bake us a fresh molasses cake, 'cause don't be forgettin', somebody sittin' right here at this table is gonna be celebratin' a birthday tomorrow."

All eyes fell upon Otis. "Yeah," he grumbled, "I s'pose I'll haf t' celebrate my *birthday* by bein' *born* ag'in."

"No need t' put yourself to so much trouble, Son," laughed Nathan. "You can celebrate your birthday by goin' back t' school."

Otis groaned.

"You should consider yourself lucky, Otis," ventured Sarah, impishly. "Not everyone gets to celebrate two days in a row." She exchanged glances with Nathan and they both laughed.

"Oh yeah?" countered Otis, addressing himself to his cousin. "You won't be laughin' tomorruh, Miss Smarty Pants. You gotta go to school too, don't forget."

Properly chastised, Sarah fell silent.

"I'm certainly gonna miss the both of you," said Nathan. "You've both been a big help around here this summer."

"But there's still a lot of work to do, Uncle Nathan," said Sarah. "There are still all the apples to pick. Shouldn't I stay home to help you?"

"You cain't stay home," argued Otis. "You're only fourteen. If you don't go to school, the sheriff'll come an' arrest you."

"It's not that I don't appreciate the offer," replied Nathan, "but it's more important that you get yourself an education. The work around here will get done; it always does. Besides, it's not like you're goin' off to boardin' school or anything like that. You'll still be here t' help out after school every day and all day on Saturdays . . . In fact, if you want, we could let you do *all* the work on Saturdays while Otis and I go fishin'."

"Cain't we go fishin' today, Pa?" pleaded Otis.

"Son, are you forgettin' what day today is?"

"No, Pa," groaned Otis, "hit's Labor Day."

"That's right. But I guess we wouldn't haf t' celebrate all day. Maybe this ev'nin' after supper you an' me can sneak down to the creek an' do us a little fishin'. How does that sound?"

"Sounds good to me, Pa."

The next morning Nathan watched anxiously as Otis and Sarah headed out the lane to meet the school bus. He had not told anyone, but for the past two weeks, he had been thinking quite seriously of keeping Sarah out of school, the law notwithstanding, out of concern for her safety. The day that Wesley Hicks had come to the house and demanded that Sarah be handed over, Nathan had decided that, under no circumstances, even if it meant going to jail himself, would he allow Sarah to go to school—only to change his mind after the funeral. Now he hoped that he had not made a mistake in not adhering to his original decision.

He had instructed Otis to keep an eye on Sarah and to report back to him if anyone at school threatened her or showed any kind of hostility toward her. He was especially concerned about the two Hicks boys, who rode the same school bus. At the first sign of trouble, Nathan was prepared to take Sarah out of school and keep her home, where he could look after her himself.

But when the first month of school passed without incident, Nathan began to relax. Sarah herself seemed to be enjoying school. The whole experience of being with so many other young people her own age seemed to be in itself an exciting one for her—

exciting and perhaps a little overwhelming. It was, after all, quite a change from the solitary life she had lived in the mountains.

Despite the fact that every day during that first month Nathan expected Sarah to come home from school upset or crying—or worse, his fears were for nought. Most days she came home laughing. In fact, it was the sound of Sarah's laughter coming from out of the woods in the late afternoons that usually alerted Nathan to the fact that the children were home from school.

"How's she doin', Son?" Nathan had asked Otis on more than one occasion during that first month of school, when the two of them were alone.

"She's doin' fine, Pa," Otis had always replied.

"Is anybody pickin' on her?" Nathan had asked on one of those occasions.

"Some of the boys tease her," Otis had replied on that occasion, "but the boys tease *all* the girls."

"How about the two Hicks boys? Do they tease her?"

"No, Pa, they don't say nuthin'. When they get on the bus, they don't even look at her. They look the other way. Some of the other kids on the bus, they tease her though. They call her the Wicker witch."

"The Wicker witch, eh? Well, if it starts to get too rough, you let me know, okay?"

"I sure will, Pa."

The first hours of the morning had passed quietly. The chill in the air and the heavy dew on the grass and trees had caused the three moving figures to remain tightly huddled within themselves. Through the dripping branches of apple trees Nathan had, from time to time, caught glimpses of his two young assistants working silently in the next row of trees, but had said nothing. It was Saturday, the first Saturday of October, and the annual harvest of the Winesaps had begun on a cold, damp note.

Toward mid-morning, however, as the gradually strengthening sun began to warm the air and dry the trees, Nathan felt the life-blood beginning to circulate a bit more freely. Each of the three laborers had begun the day working in his or her own separate tree, but now as Nathan finished the tree in which he had been working, he moved his ladder into Sarah's tree. It was apparent that he was seeking conversation, because he lost no time at all in getting started.

"So, Sarah," he began, "tell me about school."

"What do you want to know, Uncle Nathan?"

"Well, do you like it any better this time than the first time you tried it?"

She laughed. "I think I'd still prefer to be out exploring in the woods—or picking apples."

"Are you learnin' anything?"

"Oh yes, lots of things, including some things I probably would not have learned if I hadn't gone to school."

"You hear that, Otis?" said Nathan, addressing himself to the picker in the next tree. "It *is* possible to learn something in school."

"Ax her what class she's in, Pa," suggested Otis, deftly changing the subject.

"I'm a sophomore, a junior, and a senior," replied Sarah without waiting for Nathan to re-iterate Otis' question. "I take plane geometry with the sophomore class, chemistry and American history with the junior class, and English with the senior class."

Nathan laughed. "Yes, I can see how you would a-presented a rather unusual problem for the folks who run things over at Haynesville High."

"Yeah, she's in *my* English class," said Otis indignantly. "She's prob'bly the first kid in the history of school t' jump from first grade element'ry school straight into senior year high school."

Sarah came down the ladder and emptied her sack, then moved her ladder to a new position and climbed once again to the top. She worked quietly for the next few minutes as she pondered what Otis had just said.

"Uncle Nathan," she said at last, "can I ask you a question about Swedenborg?"

"I guess that's allowed. No law says we haf t' talk about school . . . Have you finished *Heaven And Hell*?"

"Yes, I've read it all the way through once, and now I'm reading back over the parts I didn't quite understand the first time."

"There were only *parts* you didn't understand the first time? I don't think I understood *any* of it the first time . . . 'Course, I guess if you've been to Heaven yourself, you have a certain advantage . . . What's your question?"

"Do you believe Swedenborg really made all those visits to Heaven like he said, and spoke to all those spirits and angels?"

"Oh, I see, you want t' know the answer to *the* question about Swedenborg. Well, I'm afraid I don't know the answer to that one. In fact, I was kind of hopin' that *you* could tell *me*. But I'm not sure it makes any real diff'rence to me whether he did or he didn't. I read Swedenborg the same way I read the Bible. If a partic'lar passage inspires me—lifts me up closer to Heaven—then I figure that passage was inspired. The way I see it, all inspiration comes from Heaven. We judge a tree by its fruit. Take this fruit, for example." He held up an apple. "If it looks like an apple, smells like an apple, an' tastes like an apple, then I say it's an apple, an' it's a purty safe bet that it came from an apple tree. It's the same with words in books. If they look like Heaven, smell like Heaven an' taste like Heaven, then I say they came from Heaven.

"As for the Bible, I think some of it is inspired. Some of it came from Heaven. Some of it is the Word of God, just like your Aunt Hester says. But not all of it. As for *Heaven And Hell*, I think a lot of it came from Heaven, maybe most of it. I think you'll agree that Swedenborg's interpretation of the Bible is much more inspirin' than your Aunt Hester's."

"Yes, much. And it makes a lot more sense too."

"But whether Swedenborg was actually ever *in* Heaven, I couldn't say. But there's no doubt in my mind that Heaven was *in him*—an' I ain't so sure that don't amount to the same thing . . . Do you understand what I'm sayin'?"

"I think so, Uncle Nathan, at least the part about being in Heaven being the same thing as Heaven being in us."

"That's a lot of 'bein's' there, girl."

"Yes, I couldn't think of any other way to say it. When I was in the White Light Heaven I was completely filled with warmth and light. I think it would have been just as correct to say that Heaven was in me as to say that I was in Heaven. And Swedenborg himself says that we enter into Heaven by recognizing the Heaven within us—by recognizing it and by allowing ourselves to be led by it. In other words, Heaven—or the kingdom of God—is *within us*, just like Jesus said, and exactly to the degree that we recognize it and accept it, we are *in it*. I think that's a very exciting idea!"

"Not an easy idea though."

"No, not at all. In fact, that's one of those parts that I didn't quite understand the first time I read *Heaven And Hell*. And I'm still not sure I understand it completely. Every time I think I understand it, it seems to slip away again. But part of what it means is that we don't have to *go* anywhere to experience Heaven; we don't even have to die. Heaven is not some far-off place in the sky. Heaven is *right here*, just like Jesus said." Despite the fact that she was at the very top of her ladder, she made a gesture with both hands, holding an apple in each, to indicate "right here."

"Right here in this apple tree, you mean?" teased Nathan.

"Yes," she said, taking a deep breath and looking out across the orchard at the mountains of glittering autumn gold and the deep blue sky beyond, "right here in this apple tree!"

"You better grab her quick, Pa," advised Otis. "I think her soul is about t' jump out of her body ag'in."

"If I do decide to jump out of my body," laughed Sarah, "I'll be sure to come down off my ladder first."

"Very funny," sniveled Otis.

Then turning serious again, she continued. "But I'm a little confused about something else you said, Uncle Nathan. You said we judge a tree by its fruit..."

"I think Jesus said it first."

"Yes, I know. And I understand about the apple and the apple tree, but I'm not sure I understand what you meant when you said that if something looks like Heaven, smells like Heaven, and tastes like Heaven, then it must have come from Heaven. Are you saying that you can tell whether a particular passage in the Bible, or in any other book, is true just by looking at the words on the page—or by smelling them?"

Nathan laughed, "It did sort of sound like that, didn't it? No, that's not what I meant."

"But *can* you tell if something in the Bible is true or not just by reading it?"

"Yes, I think so, most of the time."

"How?"

"By the Heaven-inside-us you were just talkin' about. Our ability to recognize Divine Truth comes from Heaven. Because we have Heaven's light inside us, we are able to discern what is true..."

"Yes, and because we have Heaven's warmth inside us, we are able to intend what is good."

"Right. Divine Truth is Heaven's light and Divine Good is Heaven's warmth, and both come from Heaven's sun, which is the Lord."

"And every single thing that exists in Heaven and Earth depends on the light and warmth of Heaven's sun."

"Which is the Lord. That's right! You *have* been readin' Swedenborg, haven't you?"

"Yes, but now we're going in circles."

"*I'm* gwine in circles, that's for sure!" interjected Otis. "What *are* you talkin' about?"

"What do you mean, Sarah?" asked Nathan, ignoring Otis for the moment.

"I mean, we've just assumed something in order to prove the very thing we've just assumed."

"Now you sound like your mother."

"Swedenborg says we are able to discern what is true because we have Heaven's light inside us, right?"

"Right."

"But how do we know that *that* is true? We can't say that we discern it to be true because we have Heaven's light inside us. I mean, I feel that I *do* have a little of Heaven's light inside me still, but I don't always know whether something is true or not. There are lots of things in the Bible that I'm still confused about."

"Maybe it's just that you don't have enough trust in the Heaven inside you."

"What do you mean?"

"That day last summer when the Reverend Eby came to dinner, you said that every time you read the Sermon on the Mount, you can't help thinkin' that Jesus must a-come straight from Heaven t' be able t' say words like that."

"Yes, I remember."

"Well, what is it in *you* that causes you to react that way to those words? I say it's the Heaven in you that recognizes the Heaven in Jesus' Sermon on the Mount. It's Heaven's light in you that allows you t' see the Divine Truth in those words. You just haf t' learn t' trust yourself t' know what's true an' what ain't."

Sarah climbed down her ladder to empty another sack, but instead of returning to the back side of the tree where she had been picking, she stopped at the foot of Nathan's ladder and remained there, absorbed in thought.

"Then what you're saying is, if I read something in the Bible and it sounds *right* to me, then it's probably true and came from Heaven. But if it sounds wrong, then it's probably not true: it just came out of the head of whoever wrote it."

"Something like that."

"But when Aunt Hester reads the Bible, *everything* sounds right to her. What happens when two people disagree? Take the idea that Jesus was God, for example. That sounds wrong to me, but it sounds right to Aunt Hester. Who's right?"

"Whichever of you is better able to discern what is true."

"Who is that?"

"Whichever of you is more open to Heaven's light."

"But who is that?"

"That's not for me t' say, but I should point out that Swedenborg too says that Jesus is Heaven's God."

"Yes, I know, in the very first chapter. But I can't help it, Uncle Nathan, it still sounds wrong to me."

"Well, Swedenborg does say that the Lord appears diff'rently to diff'rent people, accordin' to how he is accepted . . . What do you think of Swedenborg's idea that you don't haf t' be baptized t' get into Heaven?"

"Oh yes, I discern that to be absolutely true."

"And that heathens can get into Heaven just as easily as Christians?"

"I was glad to hear that too, because I guess I'm what you'd call a heathen. At least that's what Aunt Hester used to call me. Swedenborg says Heaven is open to everyone who loves goodness and truth for the sake of goodness and truth, and that sounds right to me."

"But what about Heaven itself? Does the way Swedenborg describe it sound right to you? Is it the way you remember it?"

"Yes and no. The number of heavens sounds right. Swedenborg says there are three, and I was in three. Swedenborg calls the three heavens the natural, the celestial, and the spiritual. The three worlds I visited—the one that looks like the Earth, the one I call the Heaven of Colors, and the White Light World—correspond very closely with the three heavens Swedenborg describes.

"As for the way he describes Heaven, yes, it's very much the way I remember it. He says the angels in Heaven look just like people do on Earth, except more beautiful. That's true. He says there are flowers and trees in Heaven, and houses and other buildings. That's true too. I don't *discern* these things to be true: I know them to be true because I saw them with my own eyes—not with the eyes in my physical body, but with the eyes of my soul body. But I was only there once, and only for a very short time, so I didn't get to see as much as Swedenborg did, or to learn all the details about how things work."

"What about Hell?" asked Nathan. "Did you get t' see Hell?"

"No."

"So I guess you don't believe in Hell?"

"Well, before I read Swedenborg I didn't. According to Aunt Hester, everybody who doesn't accept Jesus goes to Hell. That's most of the people who've ever lived, Uncle Nathan. I can't believe that's true. That sounds absolutely wrong to me. But the way Swedenborg explains Hell sounds . . . well, more right."

"More right?"

"Yes."

"But not absolutely right?"

"No."

"Let's talk about this for a minute, 'cause I believe in Hell, an' I discern what Swedenborg says about it to be true. What is it about Swedenborg's Hell that doesn't sit right with you?"

"Before you asked me about Hell, I was about to tell you something about Swedenborg's Heaven that doesn't sound right to me."

"All right then, forget about Hell for the moment an' tell me about Heaven. What's wrong with Swedenborg's Heaven?"

"I think I can answer both questions at the same time, because what doesn't seem right to me isn't the way Swedenborg describes Heaven and Hell, but the way it all works. It was something Otis said—about my being the first person in the history of school to jump from first grade elementary school straight into senior year high school—that started me thinking about all of this in the first place.

"I was only eleven years old when Kati took me to Heaven, so there were a lot of things I wasn't able to understand. But one thing that seemed quite clear to me at the time—both from things I saw myself and from things Kati told me—was that the Earth and the heavens together are like a school. We start in the first grade—that's the Earth—then after we learn what we can here, we go into the second grade, into the first world beyond this one. We learn everything we can in each grade, then we move on to the next higher grade—to the next higher world, the next higher heaven—until we reach the highest heaven of all, which is like being one with God.

"But according to Swedenborg, it doesn't work that way at all. He says it is our 'ruling affection' that determines where we go when we die. If we have a strong affection for goodness and truth while we live on the Earth—if we strive to do good and gain knowledge—then we can go straight into the highest heaven when we die. That's like going from the first grade of elementary school straight into the senior year of high school. If we have *some* affection for goodness and truth, but not enough to get us into the highest heaven, then we go to one of the lower heavens. And if we have no affection at all for goodness and truth, but love evil and false things instead, then we go to Hell. But no matter which place we go to—whether to one of the heavens or to Hell—Swedenborg says that's where we stay for all eternity."

"And that doesn't sound right to you?"

"It doesn't sound right to me that someone should spend eternity in Hell just because he was not able to discover the Heaven inside himself during the short time he was on this Earth."

"If you had your way, I s'pose everyone would end up in the highest heaven?"

"Yes, eventually."

"But what if someone didn't want t' go to the highest heaven? What if they wanted to stay in the middle heaven, say? What if they *begged* you t' let them stay in the middle heaven? Would you let them stay?"

Sarah remembered running up the flower-covered hill with Kati in the Heaven of Colors. "Yes, I guess so, if they really wanted to."

"Well, what if someone begged you t' let them go to Hell? Would you let them go?"

"Nobody would *want* to go to Hell, Uncle Nathan."

"Don't be too sure, Sarah. If people in this world were given a choice between Heaven an' Hell, I think you'd be surprised, just how many would choose Hell. And if Swedenborg is right, we *are* given a choice. Nobody is *condemned* to Hell. People throw *themselves* into Hell, because they would rather be in Hell with the evil things they love than in Heaven with the good things they despise. It would be as cruel to send wicked people to Heaven as it would be to send good people to Hell–an' their torment would be just as great. You wouldn't make people go to Heaven who didn't want to, would you?"

"No, but I would allow them to change the quality of their affection over time, so that one day they would want to go to Heaven. If Swedenborg is right, we can never rise above the level of affection we attain during our short life on this Earth. We can perfect ourselves at that level, but we can never rise above it. That doesn't sound right to me. If we have all of eternity stretching out before us, why can't we continue to learn, continue to grow in our love for goodness and truth, continue to rise from level to level, from heaven to heaven? We're talking about all eternity here, Uncle Nathan, forever and forever and forever. Why should our place for all eternity be determined by one short life here on this Earth? Why shouldn't everyone have the opportunity to eventually know what it feels like to be completely filled with God's love?"

"Well, when you put it that way, it doesn't sound right to me either."

"Does that mean you think Swedenborg is wrong when he says that 'our ruling affection is not uprooted to all eternity?' "

"Either that or my ability to discern what is true is not as good as I thought it was."

Sarah walked around the tree to her ladder and moved it to a new setting. She and Nathan were now closing in on the last corner of the tree and were once again within view of one another.

"Let me ask you another question," said Nathan. "What do you think of Swedenborg's idea that Heaven itself is in the shape of a giant man? What's he call it? A Great Man? A Divine Man?"

"Yes, 'the Greatest and Divine Man.' . . . I thought it very strange at first. I mean, it's hard to imagine angels living in Heaven's eyes or in Heaven's nose or in Heaven's belly button, not to mention any of Heaven's internal organs. But I've passed some pleasant moments thinking about it. One day when I was working in the kitchen with my mother and Aunt Hester, I tried to imagine which part of Heaven's body each of them would likely end up in. I decided that Aunt Hester would definitely become part of Heaven's hands, because she works so fast with her hands. I decided my mother would probably end up in the brain, because she *thinks* all the time—at least she used to. I couldn't quite decide which part of Heaven I'd end up in . . ."

"You'd end up in the *mouth*!" interjected Otis, who had been picking quietly in the next tree.

"Son!" exclaimed Nathan, "I'd almost forgotten you were there."

"Well, hit's a good thang I am," retorted Otis. "Somebody's got t' pick these apples. The way you two been a-jabberin' away, you ain't gettin' *nuthin*' picked."

"Hey, that's not true. We've almost got a whole tree picked."

"*I* almost got a whole tree picked all by myself. You guys should a-picked two or three by this time."

"Is that so?"

"Yeah, that's so."

"Sarah," called Nathan, "what part of Heaven's body do you think Otis is gonna end up in?"

She thought for a moment. "Probably in the ears, because he's such a good listener. He's had to be, because, as we all know, I used to talk to him for days at a time without stopping."

"I think he'll prob'bly end up in Heaven's backside," opined Nathan.

"Why is that?" asked Sarah. "Is it because he spends so much time sitting down by the creek fishing?"

"No, it's so he can be a pain in Heaven's backside the way he's been a pain in mine these past seventeen years."

"Very funny, Pa," groaned Otis.

"I'm just teasin'. You know that, don't you, Son?"

"Yeah, I know. . . How about you, Pa?"

"How about me what?"

"What part of Heaven are you a-gwine to end up in?"

"I don't know. What do you think?"

"Prob'bly the arms."

"I think the heart," said Sarah, with affection.
"How about your Uncle Jacob?" asked Nathan.
"Definitely the heart," replied Sarah without hesitation.
"And your Uncle Isaac?"
"In the mouth with Sarah," quipped Otis.

At the end of October, with the return of colder weather, Sarah abandoned her "room" in the barnloft and moved back into the house. Ever since the start of school she had spent most of her evenings in the house anyway, sitting at the kitchen table doing her schoolwork or helping Otis with his. She had also gotten into the habit of staying up late, sitting by the stove and reading, after everyone else had gone to bed. She had come to especially enjoy these solitary late-night hours in the hushed shadowy stillness of the kitchen—in the very kitchen which during the day was the center of so much hurry and bustle.

During the summer the barnloft had served as her retreat, and sometimes she had spent the evening hours lying in the hay just inside the open doors, reading, until darkness forced her to close her book and go to sleep. It had been during those quiet twilight hours in the barnloft that she had read *Heaven And Hell*. But the days had been longer then. With the coming of fall, she had found herself drawn, like a moth to flame, to the light of the house. She had not dared to introduce a lantern into the hayloft for fear of setting the hay afire and burning the barn down, which was something she had promised her Uncle Nathan she would not do. Then, with the coming of colder weather, she decided to make the house her permanent abode for the winter.

It had been over two months since Lydia Hicks' funeral and most of the gossip had long since died down. Nathan continued to be concerned about Wesley, however. Wesley had not set foot again on Nathan's property, nor had he made any more threats against Sarah. Yet neither had he died. Two weeks after the funeral Nathan had passed him on the road. Wesley had sat stiff as a corpse on the driver's seat of his wagon, slumped slightly forward, and had stared straight ahead at the road as they passed. He had not returned Nathan's greeting, or even looked in Nathan's direction, but he had been unmistakably alive. He had not been to church since the day of the fire, but that had come as a surprise to no one. Everyone knew that the only reason Wesley had ever come to church in the first place was because of Lydia. What *had* come as a surprise to many, however, was the appearance of Wesley's youngest son, James, in church the Sunday following his mother's funeral. He had come alone and had walked the entire four miles in order to attend the service, after which he had walked the four miles home, refusing all offers of rides. And he had continued to do the same thing every Sunday since then.

The last person that Nathan had talked to who had seen Wesley himself was Walter Lehman. According to Walter, Wesley had come into the store one day around the middle of October and had bought a hundred pounds of sugar.

"Either Wesley's built himself another still," Nathan had told Hester after learning this news, "or he's fixin' on bakin' himself a lot of pies."

On the twelfth of November Sarah turned fifteen, and as the twelfth of November was a Wednesday, she celebrated her birthday the same way Otis had celebrated his: by going to school.

Thanksgiving was celebrated in the usual manner, with all the family gathered at Isaac and Martha's, but the occasion was a solemn one compared to Thanksgivings of years past. The loss of Emily and Daniel in the same year had left more than empty seats at the dinner table. Elizabeth had expressed a hope that Daniel might take some time off from his work in the mountains in order to join the rest of the family for Thanksgiving dinner, but Hester had warned her not to set her heart on it, lest she be too disappointed if he didn't come.

The pall that hung over the gathering was mitigated in part by the presence of the children. It had been quite a few years since Otis and Sarah were the youngest members of the family. Isaac and Martha now had four grandchildren. Their daughter Lucy and her husband Charles Fox had three little Foxes running around underfoot—two boys and a girl—ranging in age from two to five. But the youngest member of the family—and Isaac's pride and joy—was his son Benjamin's first-born, three-month old Jonathan Wicker. But even with the seeds of a new generation sprouting up beneath their feet, it would be quite some time before those seated at the table would forget the ripe ears already harvested and gathered into Heaven's barn. As Nathan looked around the table, he wondered who would be the next to fall before the silent scythe of the Heavenly reaper—and how soon. What seats, if any, would be empty at the next Thanksgiving? So much could happen in a year's time, as the year just past had so painfully attested.

The after-dinner gathering in the parlor, normally a time for quiet conversation, was interrupted by a bout of yelling and screaming. The problem started when Lucy's three children, who had been placed in an opposite corner of the room and instructed to play quietly, discovered the radio, which happened to stand in the same corner of the room to which they had been consigned. Once they made the further discovery that they could operate the radio by turning two easy-to-reach knobs, they lost all interest in any other kind of play. For the next two minutes they were in ecstasy as they turned the radio on and off, raised and lowered the volume, and spun the tuning dial from one end of the band to the other and back again, without once stopping at any of the stations along the way. Nathan had waited patiently for Lucy to discipline her children, as conversation was becoming difficult, but when she failed to do so, he decided to take matters into his own hands.

"Otis," he shouted in a voice loud enough to be heard above the blare of the radio, "shut that thing off an' see to it that it stays off!"

Otis jumped from his chair and did as he was told, but to Nathan's chagrin, the cessation of the one noise was followed immediately by the commencement of another: that of all three children screaming. In order to appease the unhappy youngsters Otis got down on his hands and knees and allowed them to mount him like a horse. When he had all three on board, he rode them out of the parlor and into the kitchen. Sarah also removed herself to the kitchen to help with the baby-sitting chores.

About an hour later, just as Charles and Lucy were getting up to leave and others were thinking of doing the same, Nathan heard the radio playing again. Looking over, he was surprised to find, not the children, but Sarah, kneeling in front of the radio with one hand on the volume knob and the other on the tuning dial. She was listening at the lowest possible volume and slowly turning the tuning dial from station to station. She remained completely absorbed in the radio for the next two or three minutes, until Lucy tapped her on the shoulder to say good-by and to thank her for helping to look after the children. On the way home Sarah sat quietly in the back of the wagon with her mother and Otis, lost in thought.

Later that night, just before going to bed, Nathan made a visit to the outdoor privy. On his way back to the house, just as he was about to step onto the porch, he caught a glimpse of a silhouette in human form standing in the driveway. Startled, he froze in his tracks and peered into the darkness at the shadowy form. It was not moving; it was standing perfectly still.

"Who's there?" he called nervously.

"It's me—Sarah," came a familiar voice from the darkness.

Nathan breathed a sigh of relief. "You purt-near scared me to death, girl."

"I'm sorry, Uncle Nathan."

"What're you doin' out there standin' in the dark?"

"Thinking."

Nathan chuckled to himself. "I reckon that was a silly question, wasn't it?" He thought he had detected a note of sadness in her voice. He walked over to where she was standing. "You're thinkin' about your Pa again, ain't you?"

"Yes, about him—and other things." She was looking up at the stars.

"Sure is a clear night," observed Nathan, looking up himself. "I do believe we can see every star in the sky."

For the next couple of minutes they stood together in perfect silence looking at the starry spectacle above.

"I just can't imagine it," said Sarah at last, "I just can't imagine how it can go on *forever*. How can *anything* go on forever?"

"It does sort of boggle the mind, don't it?" agreed Nathan.

"We've been studying the universe in school. I should say, Otis has been, but I've been helping him. The distances are just so *vast*. Do you know what the speed of light is, Uncle Nathan?"

"I don't remember exactly, but I know it's purty fast."

"It's over 186,000 *miles per second!* That in itself is hard enough to imagine."

"It's a darn sight faster than I'd care t' go, that's for sure."

"I agree. At that speed, in just one second we could go all the way around the world seven and a half times."

"I reckon it would be kind of hard t' make the corners at that speed though, don't you?"

Sarah laughed. "Yes, but suppose we went straight up instead of around. By the time we could count one-thousand-one, one-thousand-two, we'd be 100,000 miles past the moon. But even at that incredible rate of speed it would take over eight full minutes to reach the sun, which is 93,000,000 miles away, and *over four years* to reach the next star after that. Most of the stars we see up there are so far away we couldn't reach them in our lifetime. It would take thousands, maybe millions, of years to get to some of them, even at the speed of light. I wouldn't even want to try to figure out how many *miles* that would be! And those are just the stars we can see!"

Nathan shook his head. "It wears me down just thinkin' about it."

"Yes, I know what you mean. And that's just the physical universe, just the universe we can see! If our poor brains get exhausted when they try to comprehend the physical universe, it's no wonder they have trouble comprehending all those other worlds out there."

"Out there? You think those other worlds are out there? I thought we decided that Heaven was right here—right over there in that apple tree, I think you said."

Sarah smiled. "You know, ever since my friend Kati took me to Heaven, I've been trying to figure out where those other worlds are. I remember telling my mother that I didn't think they were in any *place*. Well, I think I figured it out today, Uncle Nathan, while I was listening to Uncle Isaac's radio. I think I finally understand where all those other worlds are. They *are* right here! But they're out there too! They're everywhere the physical universe is, only we can't see them because we're not tuned to the right station. Our physical brains are like radios that can only get one station. They're tuned to the physical universe and there's no way to change the station. When I was turning the radio dial from station to station, I suddenly remembered that that's what it was like going from one heaven to another. It wasn't like we *moved* from one to another; it was like we'd be in one, then suddenly we'd be in another. One minute we'd be receiving one station, and the next minute, another. All those other worlds, like all those radio signals out there, are out there all the time, and which one we're experiencing, which one we're receiving, at any given moment, depends on which one we're tuned in to. Right now we're experiencing *this* world because that's the only one *these* brains and *these* bodies *can* experience. Only when we leave these bodies can we experience other worlds."

She paused for a moment before continuing. "But what worries me is, if all those other worlds are as vast as this one, how will I ever find my Daddy when I die?"

Nathan put his arm around her. "I don't think you'll haf t' worry about that, Sarah. Remember what Swedenborg says: in Heaven, folks can get t' see anyone they want just by thinkin' about them . . . Besides, I don't think *you* will haf t' find *him*: I think *he* will find *you*."

It was late on a Monday night in December, about a week and a half after Thanksgiving, as Sarah was sitting alone in the kitchen reading, that she was startled by a loud knocking on the door. She remained frozen in her chair for a moment, trying to decide what to do. Her Uncle Nathan had made her promise that she would never, under any circumstances, go to the door when someone knocked. She was always to let someone else go. But everyone else had gone to bed. The easiest thing and the most natural thing would be just to go over to the door and open it. But a promise was a promise. She decided to go upstairs and wake Nathan.

But before she had a chance to move from her chair, the door opened and a voice called, "Anyone home?"

"Uncle Isaac!" exclaimed Sarah.

"Why, if hit ain't my fav-o-rite niece!" said Isaac, stepping into the kitchen. "I was kind of hopin' someone would still be up. I might a-knowed hit'd be you. Whar's Nathan? He asleep?"

"Not any more," grumbled Nathan, emerging from the stairwell in his red flannel underwear. "It's kind of hard t' sleep when you got a lunatic bangin' your door down in the middle of the night . . . What brings you around at this ungodly hour? Not bad news, I hope."

He looked closely into Isaac's face. "It *is* bad news, isn't it?"

"We're at war, Nathan," said Isaac solemnly. "I just heared it on the radio. Yesterday the Japs bombed some 'merican navy base out in the Pacific. Today Roosevelt axed Congress t' declare war an' Congress declared it."

Nathan stood silent for a moment, absorbing the news. "Well, I guess it was bound t' happen," he said quietly. "We've seen it comin' for quite some time . . . I only wish I didn't have a seventeen-year-old son right now."

Isaac nodded, then looked at Sarah. "Be glad you're a gal, purty little Sarah," he said, pinching her cheek and stroking her hair with his rough, cold hand.

He turned back to Nathan. "Well, I got t' be a-gettin' back home. I just thought.you'd want t' know."

"Thanks, Isaac."

Nathan saw Isaac out, then closed the door. He continued to stand in his red flannel underwear and stocking feet, staring at the door, for the next half minute.

"Does this mean Otis will have to go away?" asked Sarah, who had been quietly watching her uncle.

"Not for a while," replied Nathan, turning to face her. "He won't be eighteen til next September."

"Maybe the war will be over by then."

"We can hope, Sarah. We can only hope."

Three days after the United States declared war on Japan, Germany and Italy declared war on the United States. The United States reciprocated in kind. Otis, who, only a few months before, had looked forward to the United States' entering the war, now had mixed feelings. Back in the spring he had seen the war as a means of escaping, for a time, the hopelessness and the poverty of Rushing Creek. War would be exciting, he remembered thinking. It would allow him to see a whole other world, a world beyond the mountains, maybe even foreign countries which he had only read about in his school books. And it still sounded exciting, even now, when he thought about it. Only now he found that he was not as anxious to get away from Rushing Creek as he had been before. His prospects for the future did not now seem as hopeless as they had in the past. Even being poor did not now seem to be so bad. He was beginning to understand something he had never clearly understood before, something his father must have told him a million times: a person doesn't need a lot of *things* to be happy. His mother and father didn't have much, had never had much, not in the way of material things, yet they seemed to be happy enough. They just didn't seem to need all the things Otis thought *he* would need if he were in their place. How many times had he heard his father say, "Why should I spend my hard-earned money on somethin' I don't need anyway?" or "Why should I want t' go to some big city when everything I need is right here?" His parents did seem to have everything they needed, and one of the things they had was each other. Before Sarah had come to live with them, Otis had never fully realized how important another person could be.

Did he need Sarah? That was the question Otis now found himself contemplating during his reflective moments. His life had certainly changed since she had come to live with them. There was no denying that. He had never spent a more enjoyable summer. He would have been content if the summer had never ended, if the hayfields and the cornfields had just stretched on to eternity. Even school had become tolerable. Sarah seemed intent on helping him get through it in spite of himself. She often worked with him on his school lessons long after he would have given up had he been left to himself, even though that often meant that she had to stay up late to do her own schoolwork. As a consequence, he now found himself better prepared in his classes and able to answer questions put to him by his teachers, something he had never been able to do in the past, except on rare occasions, and then only by virtue of dumb luck. He was passing all of his courses, including the algebra course he had failed the previous year, and his graduation in June, which at one time seemed very much in doubt, now seemed all but guaranteed. Even the days seemed to be passing more quickly now—perhaps, Otis thought, a little too quickly.

Did he need Sarah? If he did have to go off to the war, he would certainly miss her. There was no doubt about that. He would think about her every day, just as he now thought about her every day. He wouldn't turn eighteen until September. That meant he would get to spend another full summer at home. After that, if the war was still going on, he would go when the army called him. He would go marching off to war with his head held high, and he would make everyone proud of him. He would make Sarah proud of him. He would fight real hard and win lots of medals and give them to her when he came home. After that, they could settle down for the rest of their lives in Rushing Creek. They could stay on the farm with his mother and father. They could all live and work together just as they were doing now. Or he and Sarah could find a place of their own, maybe even a place way back in the mountains, a place like the old Jeremiah Puckett place.

One day in March Otis came home from school to find his father plowing the fields. All too quickly and almost without notice, winter had passed into spring. The first weekend in April found him helping his father plant the feed corn, and it gave him a funny feeling in his stomach to think that he might not be there in the fall when it came time to harvest it. April dissolved into May, and May into June, and suddenly the day which Otis, at one time, had thought would never come, the day that had always seemed to hover like a will-of-the-wisp in the mist of the far-distant future, was upon him. As he stood with the Class of '42 on the steps in front of Haynesville High School to receive his diploma, he kept thinking how unreal it all seemed. He didn't *feel* any different than he had felt the day before, but things *were* different. His world had changed. He could no longer think of himself as a boy. He was a man now, and nothing in his life would ever be the same again.

The day after graduation he discovered that nothing had changed at all. He found himself once again crawling on his hands and knees through the strawberry patch, trying to keep up with his cousin Sarah. Again he found himself stealing frequent glimpses of her, just as he always did whenever the two of them worked together, perhaps more than usual. He would be stealing glimpses of her all summer and storing them in his head. He would be needing these pictures of her, by which to remember her. There was little doubt now that he would be going away at the end of the summer. From what people were reading in the newspapers and hearing on the radio, it looked now as though the war was going to be a long one. Some of his high school classmates, who were only a few months older than he, had already received their draft notices.

The sense of unreality which Otis had felt the day of his graduation remained with him throughout the summer. Even the most mundane chores, like picking beans and hoeing corn, seemed to take on a dream-like quality. It was all passing too quickly, slipping through his fingers. He wanted to hold on to everything, not let it go. He tried to fix everything in his mind—the house, the barn, the fields, the orchard, his mother's garden—but he worried that he would not remember, that, once he was away from these things he had known all his life, they would all evaporate from his memory like the morning dew from the orchard grass, and leave no trace. He worried especially that he would not remember Sarah's face once he was away from her for a few weeks or months. Even with all the pictures of her which he had stored in his head over the course of two summers, he still had trouble visualizing her clearly in his mind as he lay alone in his bed at night.

Worse still, he wondered if *she* would remember *him*. She didn't even know how he felt about her. He had never told her. He had always done his best to hide his feelings. Perhaps that had been a mistake. Perhaps he should have told her. He would certainly have to tell her before he left. That would not be easy. He would probably be so nervous that he would just stand there and stutter, or, if by some intercession from Heaven, he were given the necessary power to speak, he would probably say something stupid and make a big fool of himself. He thought of writing her a letter, but dismissed the idea as silly. After all, he saw her every day.

The thought that troubled him most was, what if she didn't feel the same way about him? What if he told her he loved her and she laughed in his face? No, she wouldn't do that. That wouldn't be like her. More than likely she'd give a long speech about love being Heaven's light or Heaven's warmth or something like that—which he wouldn't understand anyway. Out of fear of making a fool of himself, or being rejected, Otis decided to wait until the last possible moment to reveal his feelings to Sarah. He would wait until they were at the bus depot in Haynesville, then just before stepping onto the bus, he would embrace her, maybe even kiss her, and declare his undying love for her. Then, if he totally humiliated himself, he would slink off to the war and throw himself on the first enemy bayonet he could find.

Throughout those final weeks of summer he rehearsed over and over again in his mind the parting scene at the bus depot. In his imagination he could see himself embracing her and maybe giving her a quick parting kiss. Except for that one time at the mill in the spring of the previous year, when she was so overcome with grief over her father's death, they had never really touched each other, except incidentally in the course of their working or studying together. Yet he longed to touch her. Every so often, whenever they were alone, he would feel an almost irrepressible urge to pull her close to him and not let her go. But he always fought the urge. He was never quite sure how she would react. He could almost hear her saying, "Otis, what *are* you doing?" as she struggled to free herself. She had not struggled to free herself that day at the mill, but circumstances had been different then. She had needed somebody then, somebody to comfort her, and probably any shoulder would have sufficed. She was not so vulnerable now; she was much stronger now, much more independent.

Yet the desire to touch her persisted. Often when they worked together, in the hayloft or in the cornfield, he felt a desire to just reach over and touch her hair or her shoulder. She was often so close, within easy reach, yet he had never dared to act on his desire. He always felt ashamed of himself for even feeling the urge.

All day long Otis had been watching Sarah through the stalks of corn. It seemed to him that she was going slower than usual. It was a hot day, even for August—over one hundred degrees in the shade, his father had said at dinnertime—and the air was almost too thick to breathe. Sarah had never made a secret of the fact that she didn't care all that much for hot weather, but Otis had never known it to slow her down before. He suspected that she was going slower today so that he could keep up with her. They both understood that this might be the last time for quite some while that the two of them would be hoeing corn together.

Otis straightened himself up and wiped the perspiration from his forehead. Sarah stopped too and looked at the dark clouds gathering in the west.

"What time do yuh think it is?" asked Otis.

Sarah looked at the sun. "About half past three."

"I'll bet you a nickel the rain gets here before four o'clock."

"If we hurry, I think we can finish before it starts," said Sarah, returning to her hoeing with renewed vigor.

"Hey, wait up!" yelled Otis. "You're gwine too fast."

They came to the end of the two rows they had been working in, turned themselves around, and headed down the last two rows. Whenever they hoed this field of corn, they always started at the top of the hill and worked their way down, so that they would end up near the creek, in which they would then dunk themselves to celebrate the completion of their task. At the moment it did not appear as though they would have the opportunity to do so today.

"We ain't a-gwine t' make it," predicted Otis, as the wind began to blow and the sky suddenly darkened.

"Work faster!" cried Sarah.

As quickly as their hoes could be made to move, they worked their way along the bottom two rows, loosening the earth and pulling it up against each stalk of corn. It was a race against the storm and it was exhilarating. Suddenly the rain was upon them.

"First one t' run for the barn is a dirty Yankee!" shouted Otis, loud enough to be heard above the din created by the deluge of rain beating on the leaves of corn all around them.

Sarah finished her row and headed back Otis'. Finally their hoes clinked together as they descended on the last stalk.

"Last one to the barn is a dirty Nazi!" yelled Otis, already in full flight up the mud-slickened hill.

"A what?" asked Sarah, taking off in pursuit. Halfway up the hill her hat blew off and she was forced to retreat partway back down the hill to retrieve it. By the time she reached the barn, Otis was already standing inside waiting for her.

"What took yuh so long?" he teased.
"My hat blew off," she explained. "I had to run back for it."
"You ran back for that beat-up old thang?"
"Yes, I like this hat."
Otis shook his head and smiled, incredulous, but pleased to know that she had become so fond of the hat he had given her the previous summer.

For the next couple minutes they stood, dripping wet, looking out at the pouring rain while they caught their breath.

"I'd better go up to the hayloft," said Sarah, "to make sure the rain isn't coming in." She disappeared up the ladder into the loft.

Otis waited for her to return. When, after what he considered to be more than a sufficient length of time, she had not done so, he ascended the ladder himself. Thrusting his head into the loft, he found her standing quietly by the open doors with her back toward him, looking out at the rain. He stood on the ladder for a moment debating whether he should enter the loft–which was, after all, her "room," her own private sanctuary–or retreat and leave her to her thoughts. He felt himself drawn to her, and he did not find within himself the will to resist: they had so little time left together. He entered the loft and allowed himself to be drawn to her side. She smiled sweetly to acknowledge his presence, but did not look at him. She continued to stare, almost trance-like, into the rain.

"I have always loved rain," she said softly, wistfully. "When I was little, whenever I saw a storm coming, I would run into the woods and try to get as far away from the house as I could before the storm broke. Then when it started to rain, I would try to find shelter. It was like a game. Even during the hardest rains, there are dry places in the woods. Sometimes I would find a cave to crawl into. Other times I would squeeze myself into a hollow tree. But usually I just squatted under a big rock or stood against the trunk of a pine tree. Then I would watch the rain come down and make everything wet while I stayed dry." She laughed. "Of course, sometimes I didn't find shelter in time and I'd get soaking wet, like I am now... But that was all right too."

She lapsed into silence and for the next few minutes the two of them stood together watching the rain make everything wet while they stayed dry—or, at least, while they got no wetter.

"Then when I was older," she continued, "I had a special place I would sometimes go on days like this, when it looked like rain. It was on top of a high mountain with great rock boulders. I would stand on top of the rocks and watch the storm approaching from the west or from the south, then just before the storm broke I would climb down and duck into one of the caves. As soon as the rain stopped, I would climb back up onto the rocks and watch the storm go out across the valleys to the north and east...

"Funny... I've never told anyone about that place before. I never even told my mother and father. It was my secret place. I'm not sure why I'm telling you now. It was there on those rocks that I first went outside my body, the time that my friend Kati took me to Heaven."

Otis was hardly hearing a word she was saying. He had become completely mesmerized by her presence. Her face was radiant. Without willing it or even knowing fully what he was doing, he lifted his left hand to her wet face and touched her cheek just below her left eye with the tips of his fingers. Then slowly, very slowly, he allowed his fingers to run down over her cheek to the corner of her mouth, then back along the line of her jaw to the strings of her wet hair. With his frozen eyes he followed his fingertips as they moved again and ran down along the side of her neck and out along the shoulder of her wet dress. For a moment he stood there, scarcely breathing, all but trembling with emotion, with his hand resting on her shoulder, and watched her face for some reaction. But she continued to stare out at the rain, seemingly lost in thought.

Slowly, very slowly, he moved his hand off her shoulder and retraced with his fingers their earlier course back toward her neck. He stopped at the collar of her dress, but instead of retracing the course back up along her neck, he found his hand gravitating down over the front of her dress until he found it cupped gently over her left breast. Nervously he watched and waited for her to react, to respond in some way, but she continued to stare out at the rain seemingly oblivious to his presence.

"Otis!" It was his father's voice. It had come from below, in the barn.

Quickly he withdrew his hand from Sarah's breast and stepped away from her. "I'm up here, Pa."

"What're you doin' up there, Son?"

"Just makin' sure the rain don't come in," he stammered.

"Is Sarah up there too?"

"Yeah, Pa, she is."

"Why don't you come on down, Son? It's time t' start the milkin'."

"I'll be right down, Pa." He turned to Sarah. "You comin'?"

"I'll be down in a minute," she answered distractedly, without turning to face him. "I want to put on a dry dress first."

As soon as Otis had left, Sarah, still staring out at the rain, unbuttoned her wet dress, slid it down over her hips, and stepped out of it. Then, as she continued to stand for a moment, watching the rain, clad only in her underpants, she lifted her right hand and touched it to the nipple of her left breast, the one that was still tingling. It was not raining nearly as hard now. The storm was passing. Already she could make out the outline of the mountain on the other side of the creek through the thinning shroud of rain and mist. Then, suddenly waking from her reverie, she sprang into motion. She picked up her wet dress, hung it on a nail, and quickly slipped into a dry one. Before she had half the buttons buttoned, she was hurrying down the ladder to join the others.

Otis' eighteenth birthday came sooner than anyone would have liked. Hester had awaited the day with so much apprehension in fact, that she had been unable to keep food in her stomach for as much as a week beforehand. In an attempt to mitigate the anxiety that everyone was feeling, Nathan decided to declare Otis' birthday an official holiday.

"Today's your day, Son," he informed Otis at breakfast. "We'll do anything you want today."

"Really, Pa?"

"Really."

"Can we go fishin'?"

"If that's what you want, Son."

"You mean we don't haf t' work?"

"Nope, not today. We'll have your Ma pack us a big picnic lunch an' you an' me can go down to the creek an' fish all day if you want."

"How come, Pa?"

"In case we get hungry."

"No, I mean, how come we don't haf t' work?"

" 'Cause it's Son Day."

"No, Pa, hit's Wents-dy."

"No, Son, it's Son Day. It's the day when sons get t' do whatever they want."

"I never heared of that before, Pa."

"Are you sayin' you'd rather not celebrate?"

"No, Pa, I ain't a-sayin' that. I sure ain't a-sayin' that. If you say hit's Son Day, I'll take your word for it . . . But what about Ma an' Aunt 'Lizbeth an' Sarah? Do they got t' work?"

" 'Fraid so. They're gonna be real busy gettin' ready for the big birthday party tonight."

Otis looked around at all the smiling faces. "I think I'm a-gwine t' like Son Day," he beamed. "I think I'm a-gwine t' like it just fine."

Immediately after breakfast Nathan and Otis headed for the creek, fishing poles in hand. For the remainder of the morning they sat quietly on the creek bank, about ten feet apart, fishing and reminising. By noon they had only one small brook trout between them to show for their efforts, but Nathan considered the morning well-spent.

"Why are we doin' this, Pa?" asked Otis as they sat in the shade of a sycamore tree eating their lunch.

"Why are we fishin', or why are we eatin'?"

"Both. Why are we doin' what *I* want today?"

"I told you, Son. It's Son Day."

"No, I mean really."

"Well," said Nathan, in a more serious tone of voice, "I guess I wanted t' spend some time alone with you before you haf t' go away... Besides, I figured, once you get away from here, if all you can remember is the work, you might just decide not t' come back."

"That's not true, Pa. I'd always come back, you know that."

"Have you given any thought to what you might want t' do when you come home?"

"A little."

Nathan waited for Otis to expound further. When he didn't, he decided to do a little fishing on his own.

"I was talkin' to Charlie Cole last Sunday after church. His two oldest boys are in trainin' camp now, an' his daughter Gladys has got herself a job in one of them textile mills in the east, makin' soldiers' uniforms. I reckon, one way or another, this war's gonna take all our young people away from us . . . I always thought you an' Gladys would make a good couple. If I'm not mistaken, you were kind of fond of her at one time. Charlie says she still asks about you all the time in her letters."

Otis lowered his head.

"How about it, Son? Have you given any thought to who you might want t' marry?. . . 'Course, there's no hurry, an' even if you do have someone in mind, you don't haf t' tell me if you don't want to. Just so's you invite me an' your Ma to the weddin'."

Otis continued to stare at the ground as he deliberated whether to tell his father of his innermost feelings. "I love Sarah, Pa," he said at last, in a voice that was barely audible.

"Sarah? 'Course you do, Son. She's your cousin. But you can't very well marry her."

Otis looked up. "Why not, Pa?"

" 'Cause she's your blood cousin."

"What differ'nce does that make? Lots of folks marry their blood cousins."

"That's true, but they shouldn't. For the sake of the children they shouldn't. I ain't sayin' you an' Sarah wouldn't have healthy children, but you got a lot better chance if you marry someone outside the family."

"We wouldn't haf t' have children, Pa."

Nathan studied his son's face. He could see that Otis had given this more than passing thought and was completely serious. "Have you talked to Sarah about this, Son?"

"No, Pa. But I know she likes me."

" 'Course she likes you. But likin' someone ain't the same as wantin' t' marry 'em." Nathan could see the dejection in Otis' eyes. "Listen, Son. Sarah will always be your cousin. Nuthin' will ever change that. You can always love her as a cousin. But don't set your heart on marryin' her, okay?"

For a long moment Otis stared hard at the ground. "Okay, Pa," he replied at last, despondently.

"Now, what do you say we get back to fishin'?"

"Pa?"

"Yes, Son?"

"Would it be all right with you if we don't fish any more today?"

"Whatever you say, Son. It's your day. What would you like t' do? You want t' go swimmin'?"

"No, Pa, I think I'd just like t' work the rest of the day."

The day after Labor Day Nathan drove Otis into Haynesville to sign up for the draft. During the long ride Otis continued to think about what his father had said on his birthday the week before. He decided to take his father's advice and put aside any thoughts he might have of marrying Sarah, for the time being at least. It would be at least two years before he would be able to think seriously about getting married anyway–unless, of course, the Allies, with his help, should happen to rout the enemy in less than two years, in which case he might get to come home early. He decided instead to make the most of the precious little time that he and Sarah had left together. He knew that he would not have long, perhaps only a few days before he received his draft notice and another few days before he would have to report–a total of two weeks at most. He realized that he might have gained for himself another extra day or two if he had not registered so soon after his eighteenth birthday, but even that was far from assured. He knew of several classmates who had hoped to defer the inevitable draft notice by waiting until the last possible day to register. But while *they* had been prepared to wait, the draft board had not: after a few days, Selective Service had simply come and got them.

But to Otis' utter anguish, much of the precious time that he and Sarah had left together was stolen from him. The same day that he registered for the draft, school re-opened, and for the first time since the seventh grade he found himself wishing that he too were going back to school. Again he found himself counting the hours, minutes, and seconds of each day until the school bus stopped at the end of the lane in the late afternoon, just as he had done in the spring of '41, when Sarah had first come to live with them. Only this time, *she* was the one going to school, and *he* the one staying home. But just as before, *he* was the one counting and waiting. During the course of each long day, it seemed to him that hours and minutes had never passed so slowly, not even when he was in school himself. But when the time for his departure came, it seemed to him that two weeks had never passed so quickly.

Suddenly the scene which he had lived and relived in his mind all summer long, he was now reliving again, only this time it did not seem nearly as real. It was all there just as he had imagined: the depot, the bus, the crowd of people, his mother crying, his father offering words of encouragement. But it was all happening so fast now. In his mind there had always been time, lots of time. Now there was no time. Suddenly there was Sarah standing in front of him, pretty dark-eyed Sarah. But there was no time. There was something he had wanted to say to her, but he couldn't remember what it was. There was something he had wanted to do, but there was no time, no time to think. The bus was getting ready to pull out. Suddenly Sarah threw her arms around him and kissed him on the cheek.

"Write to me, Otis. Please write."

"I will," stammered Otis, "I will, I'll write."

He boarded the bus and was gone. Sarah watched for him to appear at one of the windows but she did not see him. She waved as the bus pulled out of the station and continued to wave until it disappeared from view. She then turned and buried her face in Nathan's chest.

17

LETTERS FROM AFAR

Hester's heart was heavy as she walked through the gray drizzle out the lane to the mailbox. The leaves had mostly fallen now, and the sodden carpet of gold squished beneath her feet as she walked. Surely there would be a letter from Otis today. It had been almost six weeks since he left, and aside from one half-page letter which had arrived the week following his departure, he had not been heard from. What aggrieved Hester most was that he had not answered the letter which she had written to him. She had put a lot of time and effort into that letter—and all of her soul. She had poured out all of the feelings that she had not been able to express to his face, had said all the things she had wanted to say at the bus depot, but could not. At the very least he could have written a line or two to acknowledge that he had received her letter.

It had been over ten years since she had last written a letter. That one had been to Daniel. For those twelve long years that Daniel had lived in the north, she had written to him two or three times a year, usually in the spring of the year, and again at Christmas, and at any other time of the year when there was some news to tell. In the ten years that had passed since then, she had had no reason to write. Now another loved one had been taken from her, and she would have to learn to write letters all over again. At least Otis would not be gone for twelve long years.

Nathan had also written to Otis, as had Sarah. In fact Sarah had written about two letters a week since Otis' departure. The mail carrier, Hugh Ogle, Harriet's brother-in-law, had joked with Nathan that he had not seen the flag raised on the Andersson mailbox so often in all the years he had been delivering mail, and had commended Nathan for displaying the flag so proudly in this time of national crisis. Hugh Ogle had a sense of humor much like Nathan's, which, in Hester's opinion, was unfortunate, as she had always found her husband's sense of humor inscrutable.

Upon reaching the mailbox she found the flag was again raised, which meant that the day's mail had not yet come. Opening the lid, she found the letter that Sarah had written to Otis the night before, which she had apparently dropped in the box on her way to school. Hester removed the letter and stuffed it into the pocket of her coat.

For the next ten minutes she stood along the side of the road in the drizzle, awaiting the mail carrier. Why was it that he was always late on rainy days? Finally she saw the familiar car coming around the bend in the road.

"Mornin', Hester," said the driver, as the car pulled up alongside her. "Nice day, eh?"

"Mornin', Hugh."

"Sorry, still nuthin' from Otis. But I do have a package for you." He reached behind his seat and picked up a bulky cardboard carton. "Careful, hit's a little heavy."

"For me?" asked Hester, a little surprised, as she took the carton. "I ain't ordered nuthin'."

"Hit's for your niece actually—you know, the letter-writer."

"That reminds me," said Hester, shifting the weight of the box to her left hip, "here's a letter t' go out." She reached into her pocket and pulled out Sarah's letter. "I put it in my pocket t' keep it dry. Our mailbox has a leak in it. I been after Nathan for years t' fix it, but he ain't got around to it yet."

"Hit'll stay good an' dry with me," said the mailman. "Anythang else t' go out?"

"No, that's all for today."

He drove forward about ten feet and stopped at the mailbox. "I hate t' keep doin' this," he joked as he reached through the window and lowered the flag. "Makes me feel unpatriotic." He eased his vehicle back onto the road and continued on his appointed rounds.

As she walked back down the lane, Hester looked at the return address on the package. "S. Baker," she mumbled to herself, "I wonder who that could be?"

Returning to the house, she placed the box on the kitchen table next to her fresh-baked pies. Half an hour later Nathan came in.

"What's this?" he asked, spying the carton on the table, "somethin' from the Sears catalog?"

"Nope. Hit's for Sarah from someone in Chapel Hill."

"What's in it?"

"How should I know, Nathan? I didn't open it."

Nathan looked at the name on the return address. "S. Baker ... Must be bread," he wise-cracked. He picked the package up. "It ain't bread, that's for sure. It's much too heavy for bread."

"You don't haf t' tell me how heavy it is. I was the one who carried it all the way in from the mailbox."

"Well, there's only one way t' find out what's inside."

"Nathan you *cain't* open it."

"Who said anything about openin' it? I meant, we'll just haf t' wait til Sarah comes home from school, an' let *her* open it."

Sarah too appeared to be baffled by the name on the return address. With Nathan, Hester, and Elizabeth all watching over her shoulder, she opened the package.

"Why, hit's books!" glowered Hester, making little effort to conceal her disappointment and disapproval.

"They're from Miss Kinney!" exclaimed Sarah excitedly.

"Who's Miss Kinney?" asked Nathan.

"You know, Uncle Nathan. Miss Kinney, who taught elementary school here a few years ago."

"Oh, you mean, '*mean, old* Miss Kinney?' "

"Why would she be a-sendin' *you* books?" inquired Hester suspiciously.

"Because I asked her to," replied Sarah, as she opened the letter that she found protruding from the pages of the top book. "I wrote her a letter about two weeks ago. I got her address from the principal's office at the high school."

"What does the letter say?" asked Elizabeth.

"'Dear Sarah' (Sarah read aloud),
'Of course I remember you! I must say, I was surprised and delighted to receive your letter! After leaving Rushing Creek I decided to go back to school myself, here at the university in Chapel Hill. I now have a degree in psychology. I had planned to look for a job, working with disturbed children, but while at university I met a wonderful man named David Baker, and we were married six years ago. I have two children of my own now. The oldest, five-year-old Ella, reminds me a lot of you. Of course, I expect you've grown some since I last saw you almost ten years ago! (Has it really been that long?) Perhaps when the children are grown, I will do something with my degree, but right now I think it's more important that I be home with them.

'I am sending you a good introduction-to-psychology book, also several books by Freud, including the one you asked for, *Interpretation of Dreams*. I am also sending you a collection of writings by Dr. Jung. Jung's idea of the Collective Unconscious is an interesting one, though not one that most Freudians can accept. I have tons of books just sitting on my bookshelves gathering dust. I would be glad to loan you anything you like. Just let me know what you're interested in. If I don't have the books you need in my own small library, I can always get them from the university library. My husband has a good job, so I would be happy to pay postage both ways.

'Give my best regards to your mother. I hope she is in good health. I'd like to hear from her as well. I have always considered her the model mother.

'Happy reading!

Sincerely,

Susan (Kinney) Baker

'P.S. I hope the change in name did not throw you off.'"

"It was nice of Miss Kinney to send you books," said the "model mother" as Sarah refolded the letter.

"Yes, wasn't it? I must write and thank her . . . Do you remember Miss Kinney, Mother?"

"Oh yes, very well. She and I had a very interesting conversation one day last fall."

Nathan, who had been patiently waiting for Sarah to remove the books from the carton so he could take a look at them, glanced up at Elizabeth, then over at Sarah. They were looking at each other, and both were smiling, but he could see a difference in their smiles, despite the similarities in their features. Elizabeth's was more a smile of childish delight, Sarah's a smile of pity and compassion. How many times had he seen this same scene re-enacted, in one form or another, over the past year and a half? Elizabeth's conversation with Susan Kinney, which she remembered as having taken place "one day last fall," had in reality taken place in October of 1932, over ten years ago. There was a period of about eight years, from March of 1933 to May of 1941, which had simply been blotted out of Elizabeth's memory, and she did not seem to be at all disturbed by the contradictions that this truncated version of reality sometimes presented. In Miss Kinney's letter, which Sarah had just finished reading, the former school teacher had even mentioned the fact that it had been almost ten years since she had last seen Sarah, but Elizabeth seemed to have chosen to take no notice of that discrepancy. For better or worse, Sarah had decided never to correct her mother when she made misstatements of fact as a result of her inability—or unwillingness—to remember those eight years that she and Daniel and Sarah had lived in the mountains. Sarah would not now say, "No, Mother, that was ten years ago." Neither would he or Hester. They had agreed never to point out the contradictions in Elizabeth's view of reality, but instead to allow her to live peacefully in the world which she had created for herself.

Nathan glanced over at Hester. *She* was *not* smiling. He knew that she would not be. She was probably wishing now that she had left that mysterious package from "S. Baker" sitting at the end of the lane—or had dumped it in the woods. It was plain from the frown on Hester's face that she did not welcome the return of Susan Kinney into their lives, as she had been one of those irate parents who had banded together eight years ago and demanded that the school teacher be dismissed in the first place.

After supper Nathan retired to the parlor, leaving the three women in the kitchen to clean up. He had just made himself comfortable in his favorite chair and lit his pipe when Sarah appeared at the door.

"May I talk with you, Uncle Nathan?"

"Of course you can. You can always talk to me. You know that."

She entered the room and took a seat opposite him. He waited for her to speak but she seemed to be having trouble working up the courage to begin. Nathan could see that something was troubling her.

"It's about school, Uncle Nathan," she said at last, hesitantly.

Suddenly Nathan's protective instincts were aroused. "Did somethin' happen in school today?" he asked anxiously. "Did somebody . . . ?"

"No, no, it's not that." Again she hesitated and waited for the courage to come again. Finally she said meekly, "I want to *quit* school, Uncle Nathan."

Nathan breathed a sigh of relief. "Oh, is that all?"

"I'll be sixteen next Thursday and . . . What did you say?"

"I said, 'Oh, is that all?' "

"Does that mean . . . that you'll let me quit?" she asked tentatively.

" 'Course I'll let you quit."

She seemed to be at a loss for words. "I don't understand. Otis told me that he wanted to quit when he turned sixteen, but you wouldn't let him."

"That's right. He was always tryin' t' tell me that he could learn more by stayin' home than by goin' to school . . . Did you ever hear such nonsense?"

"But I think it's true, Uncle Nathan. I think you *can* learn more by staying home."

"Oh, there's no doubt about it."

Sarah was confused. "I don't understand. Are you saying you *can* or you *can't* learn more by staying home?"

"Who?"

" 'Who?' "

"I mean, who are we talkin' about here? Are we talkin' about you or are we talkin' about Otis? If we're talkin' about Otis, then the answer is no, you can't learn more by stayin' home, 'cause you'd be spendin' all your time down at the creek fishin' . . . If we're talkin' about you, then the answer is yes, you can learn far more by stayin' home. School is only gonna slow you down . . . Besides, with as many books as you have t' read now, I don't see how you'd find time for school anyway."

Nathan could see by the look on her face that his response had taken her completely by surprise. She seemed stunned but elated.

"I don't know what to say . . . Thank you, Uncle Nathan, thank you." She jumped up and kissed him on the cheek. "It's funny. All the way home on the bus today, I kept trying to think up arguments I could use to persuade you to let me quit. And I didn't even get to use one of them."

"I'm sorry I didn't get to hear them," laughed Nathan. "I'm sure they would a-been better than Otis' . . . Have you thought about what you might want t' do after you're out of school?"

"Well, I *had* thought about going away to get a job in a factory making uniforms like Gladys Cole did . . . It's not fair that only boys should have to fight this war . . ."

Nathan felt his heart sink.

"But," she continued, "I decided against it. I decided it wouldn't be right to leave Mother here with you and Aunt Hester. She's my responsibility, not yours. So I've decided to stay here and help you until Otis comes home—if that's all right with you, that is."

" 'Course that's all right with me. In fact, if I'd a-known that you were even *thinkin'* about leavin' here, I'd never a-consented so easy to lettin' you quit school . . . An' there's no need for you t' leave when Otis comes home neither. You an' your mother are both welcome t' stay here for as long as you like."

"I know that *you* wouldn't mind if I stayed, but I'm not so sure about Aunt Hester."

"Don't mind Hester, Sarah. You leave her to me . . . Besides," he smiled, "if she had wanted t' get rid of you, she could a-handed you over to Wesley Hicks when she had the chance. Instead she went after Wesley with the shotgun. She could a-got herself killed lookin' out for you."

"Yes, I know. I heard it all from the attic. She was very brave. I don't know if I could have done that."

Nathan studied her for a moment. "Have you given any thought about what you might do later on–I mean, after Otis comes home? . . . Besides seekin' the kingdom of God, of course . . . Have you given any thought to gettin' married, say?"

"Married?"

"Yes, married. You needn't act so surprised. Girls your age do start t' think about gettin' married, you know."

"No, I've not thought about that at all. My mother was twenty-two before she got married."

"Got any boyfriends?" asked Nathan, more teasing than inquiring.

She shook her head.

"I can't believe that none of the boys in school has shown an int'rest. When I was in school, a girl as purty as you would never a-gone unnoticed."

"Some of the boys in school tease me."

"Well, did you ever stop t' think that that just might be their way of showin' they're int'rested?"

Nathan could tell that she was not entirely comfortable discussing the subject of boys. In fact, she was getting up to leave. But before she left, he wanted to discuss another subject with her, one with which she'd be even less comfortable.

"Sarah, I'm gonna be butcherin' some hogs the first week in December. I was hopin' t' do it while you were at school, but since you're gonna be quittin' school next week, maybe you'd like t' spend the first week in December visitin' with your Uncle Jacob."

"That's a good idea, Uncle Nathan! I've been meaning to visit Uncle Jacob for a long time now anyway . . . Thank you again for letting me quit school."

She gave him another kiss on the cheek and left the room. Nathan settled back in his chair and smiled to himself. He was almost glad that Sarah had decided to quit school He had never been entirely comfortable with the idea of her going in the first place. It had been over a year since Lydia Hicks' untimely demise, and though most people seemed to have forgotten all about the incident at the mill, he feared there might still be a few disturbed souls out there, including Wesley himself, who might be capable of doing mischief. And now that Otis was no longer in school to look out for her, Nathan was just as glad that she'd be staying home.

Once upstairs, Sarah lit the lamp and sat down on the edge of the bed. She removed from her pocket the crumpled piece of paper that she had brought home from school with her, and looked at it again. This was another reason she had decided it might be a good idea to quit school, though certainly not the main one, and not one that she would have used to persuade her Uncle Nathan. Nathan had said that when the boys teased her, it might just be their way of showing they were interested. If the boy—and she only presumed it was a boy—who had left her this piece of paper was interested in her, he certainly had a strange way of showing it. On the piece of paper which she now held in her hands was a drawing of a dark-haired girl with no eyes. On the chest a large heart had been drawn. The piece of paper had been stuck to her desk with a pocketknife through the heart.

When Sarah arrived at Jacob's she found his house badly in need of cleaning. Immediately she set to work, sweeping, scrubbing, and putting things in order, taking only enough time off from her housecleaning activities to help Jacob with the evening milking. When Jacob came in to supper, she had it waiting on the table for him.

"You'd make somebody a good wife," remarked Jacob, smiling his beatific smile, as he sat down at the table.

Sarah blushed and lowered her eyes as she sat down opposite him at the table.

"Thar are some thangs I just cain't seem t' find time for," continued Jacob, "an' cleanin' house is one of them." If he was at all embarrassed by the state in which Sarah had found his house, he did not show it. The only expression on his face was one of pure joy. He was absolutely delighted that Sarah had come to stay with him for a week. It had been much too long since her last visit. "What have you been doin' with yourself since you quit school?"

"I've been helping Uncle Nathan around the farm, looking after the animals, milking, and such. We've been gathering firewood too. And last week we made cider. In the evenings I've been doing a lot of reading."

"Yes, Nathan says you've become quite a night owl. Are you still readin' *silly* books?"

She laughed. "I'm reading psychology books, and I guess, in a way, you could say that they're silly books."

"How's that?"

"Psychology is supposed to be the study of the psyche—at least that's what I thought. 'Psyche' is the Greek word for soul. But Mr. Freud, who some people seem to believe was a very important psychologist, doesn't even talk about the soul, at least not a soul that can exist apart from the body. I don't think he even believed in it."

"You shouldn't be too hard on Mr. Freud, Sarah," laughed Jacob. "If memory serves me right, thar was a time when you didn't believe in the soul yourself."

"But I was only eight years old, Uncle Jacob . . . Of course, I still might not believe in it if I hadn't seen the evidence for myself. I mean, it's kind of hard to believe that we're nothing more than these physical bodies when you find yourself outside your body looking at your own face."

"I reckon if you cain't take it on faith, then seein' is believin'."

Sarah sat quietly for a moment, considering her Uncle Jacob's words. "Reverend Eby and I had a long talk about faith after church one Sunday. In fact, most of our talks end up in a discussion about faith, because no matter what we talk about, he always ends up by saying, 'I know it to be true, because it says so in the Bible.' Then when I ask him how he knows the Bible is true, he says, 'We just have to take it on faith.' Taking something on faith, Uncle Jacob, is believing in something for no reason at all. I can't see the virtue in that. Swedenborg says that we can discern what is true by the Heaven inside us. Well, I discern that taking something on faith is absolutely the wrong way to go about seeking truth . . . Of course, Swedenborg himself believed in the truth of the Bible—when properly interpreted, that is."

"Sounds to me like you an' this Mr. Freud have a lot in common," observed Jacob, "the only differ'nce bein' that you got to go outside your body t' see for yourself, an' he didn't."

"Oh, I think he's seen for himself *now*."

"How's that?"

"He died three years ago. If Swedenborg is right, then Sigmund Freud is probably in the company of angels right now, being instructed in the truth."

The following evening after supper, Jacob was anxious to continue the conversation they had started the night before. There was one idea in particular which had captured his imagination, and he wished to hear his niece's thoughts on it.

"Sarah?"

"Yes?"

"You been a-studyin' on the soul for quite some time now, haven't you?"

She laughed. "I guess you could say that. At least I've been *interested* in it for a long time. My mother was reading me Plato when I was only eight. Plato was a *true* psychologist."

"Well, let me ax you a question. Do you reckon hit's possible for a soul to leave this world then be born again?"

"Well, Jesus says we *must* be born again. I was a little confused about what that meant at first, but Swedenborg explains that he meant that after we leave this world we are born into the spirit world. That's what 'resurrection' means: to be raised up or 'born again' into the spirit world."

"What about the resurrection of the dead on Judgement Day?"

"Swedenborg says there will be no resurrection of the dead on Judgement Day. In fact, he says there will be no Judgement Day. He says the belief that the dead will be raised up out of their graves on Judgement Day is based on a misunderstanding of the Bible. Only the soul is raised up, into the spirit world, and that happens immediately after death. That sounds right to me. Besides, once dead people see how beautiful their soul bodies are, they would never think for a moment of returning to their old, rotting physical bodies. Swedenborg says the only person who was ever able to raise up his physical body was Jesus, and that was because he was divine in both soul *and* body."

As interesting as all this was, this was not the answer for which Jacob had been looking. He decided to try again.

"I remember you once told me that a soul could live outside a body. We don't need these bodies at all, I think you said."

"Yes, that's true."

"Well then, let me ax you this. Do you reckon hit's possible that our souls might a-lived somewhars else *before* they came into these bodies?"

"You mean, before we were born?"

"Yes, before we were born."

"That's a very interesting question, Uncle Jacob. Some philosophers say that if the soul is immortal, then it must have always existed: it couldn't have been created at a particular moment in time. I have never understood that argument, to tell you the truth. It seems to me that a soul could be created at birth and still be immortal–at least from that point on.

"But I think the idea that our souls might have existed before we were born is a fascinating one. Plato believed in the pre-existence of the soul. In fact, he believed that we *learn* by *remembering*. All knowledge is reminiscence, he said. We have all these memories stored up from some previous state of existence, and we learn by drawing them out. That's what the word 'educate' means: to draw out, not to put in.

"I tried to explore the question of pre-existence with my mother on a number of occasions, but she was always reluctant to talk about it. She always tried to change the subject. In fact, the pre-existence of souls was one of the few subjects I can think of that my mother seemed uncomfortable talking about, which I thought was curious because one of her favorite poets, William Wordsworth, seemed to have believed in it. I've even memorized some lines from one of Wordsworth's poems in which he deals with this very subject:

> " 'Our birth is but a sleep and a forgetting:
> The Soul that rises with us, our life's Star,
> Hath had elsewhere its setting,
> And cometh from afar:
> Not in entire forgetfulness,
> And not in utter nakedness,
> But trailing clouds of glory do we come
> From God, who is our home:
> Heaven lies about us in our infancy!'

"That's from a poem called—let's see if I can remember it— *Intimations of Immortality From Recollections of Early Childhood* . . . It's almost easier to memorize the poem than it is to remember the title. Still, it's one of my favorite poems."

"Mr. Wordsworth seems t' think souls come from Heaven," observed Jacob.

"Yes, from God, from Heaven."

Again, this was all very interesting, but *still* it was not the answer for which Jacob had been looking. He decided to try a third time.

"Let me ax you this, Sarah. Do you reckon hit's possible that our souls might not a-lived in Heaven before we were born, but here on Earth?"

"Here on Earth?"

"Yes, in other bodies."

"You mean, as other people?"

"Yes."

A very serious and troubled expression came over her face. "It's funny you should ask that, Uncle Jacob," she said, in almost trance-like cadence. "When I was little, about five or six, I used to have dreams in which I seemed to be someone else, someone bigger and older. They were mostly very frightening dreams."

"Can you remember any of those dreams?"

"There was only ever one dream, Uncle Jacob. When I said 'dreams,' I meant I dreamed it more than once. I've always wondered where dreams come from. My mother and I talked about it once. And I'm reading a book right now called *Interpretation of Dreams*—by the same Mr. Freud we were talking about last night."

"Can you tell me about your dream?"

"I'd rather not, Uncle Jacob. It was just too horrible to talk about. And I haven't had it for a long time now."

Jacob sympathized with her. He understood well that some things were just too difficult to talk about.

"But I think the idea is an exciting one," continued Sarah, becoming more animated, "the transmigration of souls, I mean. That's what it's called: the transmigration of souls, or rebirth. The Greek philosopher Pythagoras believed in it. I think maybe Plato did too, but I'm not too sure about that. I know that Plato believed that all souls born into the Earth existed somewhere else before, but whether he believed that that earlier existence was also here on the Earth, like Pythagoras, or in one of the other worlds, like Wordsworth, I don't know. I'll have to look that up. I'll have to do some more studying on the whole subject really. I don't know too much about it. I was never able to discuss anything of this sort with my mother. Since it made her uneasy even to talk about souls pre-existing, I never dared to ask her about souls transmigrating from body to body."

Finally Jacob had succeeded in getting her to address herself to the question to which he had given so much thought himself over the course of the past year and a half, and on which he had hoped to elicit her views. Unfortunately, it was a question about which she did not seem to have much knowledge and, consequently, no opinion. He was not about to give up however.

"How about when you went up to Heaven? Did anyone up thar say anythang about souls bein' reborn into the Earth?"

"Well, it was my friend Kati who took me to Heaven, and *she* didn't say anything about souls coming back to Earth. Of course, she was more interested in showing me Heaven, especially the White Light Heaven, so the fact that she didn't mention it, doesn't necessarily mean anything. I'm sure there were lots of things she didn't tell me. She didn't say anything about Hell either.

"But Swedenborg, who made many more visits to Heaven than I did, did not believe that souls are reborn into the Earth. According to him, even children who die very young do not come back to Earth. They go to Heaven where they are raised by angels. Incidentally, he says it makes absolutely no difference if they've been baptized or not: they all go to Heaven . . . I should think that if anyone would get another chance at Earth life, it would be children who die at a very early age. I know if I had died as a child, I would have wanted to come back. Even if I died now, I think I would want to come back, because there are still so many things I have to learn here, so many more things I have to explore."

"That Sweden-feller you keep a-talkin' about . . ."

"Swedenborg?"

"Yes. You say he made visits to Heaven too?"

"That's what he says. Many, many visits. *Thousands* of visits, in fact. And, by his own estimate, he spoke to over a hundred thousand spirits and angels."

"Do you think he's right, about children not comin' back, I mean?"

"I don't know, Uncle Jacob. Swedenborg says some very interesting things, but not everything he says sounds right to me."

"So you think he could be mistaken?"

"I guess I haven't come to a clear discernment on the idea of rebirth one way or the other." She smiled. "I guess I don't have enough Heaven inside me yet to sort that one out . . . But I don't know that it makes a whole lot of difference really, whether we live one life on Earth or many. It seems to me that we're still here for just one purpose, and that's to seek the kingdom of God."

Jacob smiled at her. He would have liked to have stopped right there and gone to bed with the fragrance of that thought still lingering in his mind. He studied her for a long time. At the age of sixteen she was just as beautiful, just as radiant, just as delightful to behold, as she was on that Thanksgiving night eight years ago, when she lay in the bed upstairs reading her "silly" books and asking him all those serious questions. Now *he* was asking *her* questions. He would have liked to have gone upstairs to bed at that very moment with the lovely image of her face still lingering in his mind, but there were still other questions he wanted to ask her.

"Last night you said that you might never a-believed in the existence of the soul if you hadn't seen it for yourself."

She nodded.

"What about souls bein' reborn? Would you believe *that* if you saw it for yourself?"

"You mean, if I had some evidence?"

"Yes."

"What kind of evidence would that be, Uncle Jacob?"

"Well, s'posin' you *remembered* bein' someone else–someone in another life, I mean."

"But I *don't* remember."

"What about your dream?"

"I'm not sure where dreams come from. And despite Mr. Freud's big book on the subject, I'm not sure he understands where dreams come from either–at least, not *all* dreams.

"But even if I had waking memories of a previous life as someone else, how could I be sure they were *my* memories and not someone else's? Swedenborg says that every person who lives on the Earth has spirits and angels bonded to him. I think Kati was an angel bonded to me. She could put *her* thoughts right inside my head. Swedenborg says spirits can do the same. It's perfectly normal. It only gets confusing when spirits speak from their own memories and not from ours. Since all spirits and angels once lived as people on Earth, just like us, they have their own memories of the Earth life. They're not *supposed* to speak to us from their own memories, but they do sometimes. When that happens, *their* memories can get confused with *ours*, and we think we remember things that happened to *us*, which really happened to *them*. I suspect that some of our dreams come from spirits too. Of course," she added, smiling, "they can also come from angels."

"I think you lost me," said Jacob, shaking his head.

Sarah laughed. "I know what that feels like. My mother used to lose me all the time. There was a period of about three years, between the ages of eight and eleven, when just about every time I'd ask her a question, I'd end up 'lost in the thicket,' as we used to say. But that never stopped me from asking. I'm still not sure I've found my way out of that thicket though."

"Well, hit's gettin' late," said Jacob, rising from his chair, "I think I better be gettin' me off to bed. Mebbe I can dream me one of them angel dreams you was a-talkin' about . . . Would you turn off the lights before you come up?"

"I will, Uncle Jacob. Good night."

"Good night, Sarah," he said tenderly, taking one last whiff of the fragrance, one last glimpse of the loveliness.

He went upstairs to the master bedroom and closed the door behind him. Then kneeling down beside the bed–the bed that he and Emily had shared for thirty years, except for the year and a half he had been away during the Great War–he prayed. Every night he concluded his prayer with the same words. Tonight was no different.

"Dear Jesus. Please look after all those womenfolk named Wicker you have up thar in Heaven with you: my dear mother Hannah . . . my beloved wife Emily . . . and especially my little sister Ruth . . . I know they are as precious to you as they were to me . . . In your name, I pray. Amen."

He always included Ruth in his prayers, just to be on the safe side, even though he was almost certain that Ruth was no longer in Heaven. As he lay in bed, he wondered if he should have asked Jesus to send an angel with a dream, then decided that it was just as well that he had not. That would have been asking too much of Heaven. Heaven had already sent him an angel.

Jacob awoke early the next morning. If he had dreamed during the night, he did not remember. But his sleep had not been entirely without visitation. Sometime during the early morning hours, an idea—a plan—had come to him. Whether given to him by some spirit or angel, or conceived out of his own mind, he could not be certain. There were some things in the attic which he had wanted Sarah to see for quite some time, but he wanted her to see them without knowing to whom they had belonged, and he wanted her to see them as if by chance. The plan would require a bit of deception on his part, for which reason he had resisted it at first. Normally Jacob Wicker was a man totally without guile, but once he conceived his plan in its entirety, he was determined to carry it through. There was something he just had to know.

He met Sarah downstairs and together they went to the barn to milk the cows and feed the animals. After breakfast Jacob set his plan in motion. "As long as you're here, Sarah, I wonder if you might help me clean up the attic. I been a-meanin' t' do it for quite some time, but I never seem t' get around to it . . . I know it's hardly fair t' ax you t' help clean the attic after you spent a whole day a-cleanin' the house . . ."

"I'd be glad to help, Uncle Jacob."

"Better put on your coat then. Hit'll be cold up thar."

With broom and scrub bucket in hand, Sarah followed her uncle up the stairs. They traversed the hallway between the bedrooms, then climbed a second flight of stairs into the attic. It was the first time Sarah had ever been in the attic. She smiled to herself as she remembered, years ago, asking her Uncle Jacob if Heaven was in his attic. She stood at the head of the staircase for a moment, exploring the dusky interior with her eyes. She could not believe it! Jacob's attic was as crammed full as Walter Lehman's General Store! There were stacks upon stacks of wooden crates, pasteboard cartons, and metal trunks of every size and description. It was a good thing Heaven was not in Jacob's attic, she thought to herself: there would not have been room for it!

"What *is* all this stuff?" she asked incredulously, pushing aside some of the cobwebs with her hand.

"Wicker family history," sighed Jacob, "four generations of it . . . Most of it was in the attic over at the old house. After your Gran'ma Wicker died, Isaac started throwin' it all out. I rescued it an' brung it up here . . . 'Course, Emily an' I have added our share."

"I think the first thing I'll do is wash the window," said Sarah, glancing at the single small, dirty, fly-specked window in the west end of the attic, "so we can see what we're doing."

For the next two hours she worked diligently, sweeping up the dirt, removing the cobwebs—being careful not to crush the spider eggs—and wiping the dust off all the surfaces with a damp cloth, as Jacob re-organized and consolidated the attic's contents. Every fifteen minutes Sarah found it necessary to go down to the kitchen to empty her bucket of blackened water and to draw fresh. About midway through the morning, in an attempt to bring some cheer into the gloom of the dark attic, she burst into song. To the tune of "We Are Climbing Jacob's Ladder," she began singing "We are cleaning Jacob's attic." Jacob himself soon joined in and for the next half hour they entertained themselves with ever-louder song and laughter, after which they relented and allowed the quiet to settle again.

"I wonder what's in this one," mused Jacob as he lifted a small black metal trunk out of a dark corner. "What say we take a look?"

He carried the trunk to a spot near the window and set it down on the floor. Sarah knelt down beside the trunk and wiped it carefully with her damp cloth. Jacob's eyes were on Sarah as he opened the tarnished brass clasps. The rusty hinges creaked as he slowly lifted the lid.

Immediately Sarah's eyes lit up. "It's my rag doll!" she exclaimed.

"You can pick it up," Jacob assured her, his eyes suddenly moist with tears.

Sarah lifted the doll out of the trunk. She continued to smile with surprise and delight at the doll which was almost identical to the one her mother had made for her when she was a little girl back in Springfield. "I had one just like this when I was little! Who's was it, Uncle Jacob?"

Jacob did not answer. "Let's see what else is in here ... Looks like some old dresses ... a pair of shoes ..."

He handed the items to Sarah one at a time as he removed them from the trunk. He watched as Sarah examined each of the items of clothing. She seemed to be especially fascinated by the pair of black leather high-button shoes. "Whoever it was, had small feet," she mused.

"Looks like an old Bible," said Jacob, peering into the bottom of the trunk. He picked up the Bible, held it in his hands for a moment, turned a few pages, then handed it over to Sarah. He watched her eyes closely as she too opened the Bible and turned the pages.

"This is curious," said Jacob. "I wonder what this is."

Sarah looked up from the Bible. He was holding what appeared to be a bundle of old postcards tied together with a string.

"I don't reckon anybody'll mind if we open it up, do you?" Carefully he untied the string.

"They're pictures, Uncle Jacob!" said Sarah, becoming ever more curious. "They're pictures of birds and animals that somebody drew!"

Jacob handed her the bundle of postcard-sized drawings and studied her closely as her eyes filled with wonder. He had hoped that she would remember these.

Sarah stared in astonishment as she looked through the stack of pictures. There must have been three dozen of them at least. Each was a small pencil drawing of an animal. There was a deer, a rabbit, a possum, a fox–every animal she had ever seen, even a raccoon. And there were many, many drawings of birds. She wished her mother could see these. Her mother had always liked to draw pictures. But she wished her mother could see these drawings for another reason: around the head of every bird and every animal there was a circle of light.

"Who drew these, Uncle Jacob?" she asked in utter astonishment. "Do you know?"

Again Jacob did not answer. He only smiled.

"What's this?" she asked as she came to the bottom of the stack of pictures. "It looks like a letter."

"Why don't you open it up an' see," suggested Jacob.

He watched as Sarah unfolded the piece of yellowed paper. Immediately a look of puzzlement came over her face. Uncomprehending, she looked up at him. "It's to you, Uncle Jacob."

"It is?" he asked, feigning surprise. "What does it say? Can you read it to me?"

Jacob swallowed the lump in his throat and fought back tears as Sarah, with the bundle of pictures still in her lap, and the other articles from the trunk scattered about her on the floor, began to read the letter.

" 'Dear Jacob,

'I have seen the angels, my brother. Sometimes in the early morning I can see them gathering in the shadows around me. I know I will be going with them very soon now.

'I am not sad for myself. I know that death is not an ending, but a glorious new beginning. I am only sad for all the dear ones I must leave behind, especially for you, my brother. No one could have loved me more than you. It is the thought that my death will cause you great sorrow that is the hardest for me to bear. Please do not be sad, dear brother. We will be together again, I promise. Our life on Earth is so short compared to the Eternity beyond.

'Good-bye, dear Jacob. I will never forget you. I love you, I love you, I love you forever.

Ruthie' "

As soon as Sarah had read the words "my brother," she knew who had written the letter, and long before she had finished, tears were running down her cheeks. It was all she could do to read the last few lines.

"All these things," she asked, sobbing quietly, "they belonged to Aunt Ruth?"

Unable to speak, Jacob nodded his head.

With new eyes Sarah looked again at all the things on the floor around her, at the last remaining earthly possessions of the little girl who had died almost forty years ago. Now she hesitated to touch them. It seemed wrong, sacrilegious even. But Jacob had touched them, Jacob, who venerated the memory of his younger sister more than anyone else in the family. Surely if Jacob felt it was all right to disturb Ruth's things, then there could be nothing terribly wrong with it.

She looked again at the letter. In the upper left-hand corner there was another drawing–a picture of a bird, a bird with open wing, a bird in flight, going straight up, toward the sky, toward Heaven. Around its head was a circle of light.

She looked up at Jacob. He was smiling sweetly down at her, but his eyes too were filled with tears. She felt terribly sad for him. She wondered how he had been able to bear to look at these things at all. It had even been hard for her–and *she* hadn't even known Ruth.

Sarah returned to Nathan's to find another letter had arrived from Otis. Like the first, it too had been addressed to Nathan and Hester.

Throughout the winter she continued to write to Otis about twice a week. She knew that he appreciated receiving her letters even though he had not written back, as he had said so in his letter to his parents. She also continued reading the books that Miss Kinney had sent, even though she often found her mind wandering as she sat alone in the kitchen at night, to thoughts of Otis, and to thoughts of the things she had seen in her Uncle

Jacob's attic, especially to those pictures of the birds and animals that her Aunt Ruth had drawn as a little girl. So Aunt Ruth had seen the light too!

Throughout the winter she continued going to church, more to please her Aunt Hester now than for any other reason, and taking her Sunday afternoon walks. In fact, she found she had a lot of time for walking now that there was not so much work to do, and she began once again to spend long hours in the woods. She was beginning to understand why her mother had so enjoyed winters.

Another letter from Otis arrived in January, and another in February, both addressed, once again, to Nathan and Hester. Before Sarah knew it, it was March, and spring had come again to Rushing Creek. When she saw Nathan hitching up the plow, she knew that winter was over.

"It's enough to make a grown man cry," muttered Nathan, as he rummaged through the last of several tobacco tins of assorted nuts and bolts which he kept under his work bench in the barn.

"What's wrong, Uncle Nathan?" asked Sarah, entering the barn. She had been helping her mother and Aunt Hester plant peas in the garden when she had happened to notice Nathan trudging up from the cornfield where he had been plowing, carrying pieces of his plow in both hands.

"Hit a rock," he grumbled, as he emptied one of the cans onto the work bench and rooted through its contents a second time, "busted a share, sheared a bolt, bent up a moldboard. There, look, you can see for yourself."

Sarah examined the bent and broken pieces of metal.

"I can prob'bly straighten out the moldboard with a hammer," continued Nathan. "I even got some extra plowshares lyin' around, but, danged, I can't find a bolt t' bolt the share to the moldboard. That means I'm gonna haf t' run all the way back into town just for one danged bolt."

Sarah knew that Nathan had just come back from town about an hour earlier. He had been to the mill and to Walter Lehman's.

"I just got finished unhitchin' Blackie from the wagon an' hitchin' him up to the plow. Now I'm gonna haf t' unhitch him from the plow an' hitch him back up to the wagon. He's gonna think I'm crazy . . . I'm just glad Otis isn't here t' tell me I need a truck an' a tractor, so I wouldn't haf t' be hitchin' an' unhitchin' the horses all the time."

"I could *run* into town, Uncle Nathan."

Nathan gave her a skeptical look. "You mean run, like on foot?"

"Yes. It's only two miles. It wouldn't take long. I could be back in half an hour–unless Mr. Lehman starts talking."

"Hmm. It might only take you half an hour t' run into town an' back, but it would take *weeks* before your Aunt Hester would forgive me for lettin' you do it. She already thinks you act too much like a boy. She's still mad at me for lettin' you wear Otis' clothes."

"I know, but overalls are so much more practical than a dress, even if they are a little baggy." She hooked her thumbs into the bib just above the waist and pulled it away from her body to demonstrate the airiness of her newly acquired wardrobe. "Besides, they go well with my hat, don't you think?"

Nathan gave her a quick glance and smiled, but his mind was preoccupied with the problem of the broken plow.

"Listen, Sarah," he said, "I think I *will* let you run into town, but I'll let you run in with the wagon. You unhitch one of the horses from the plow an' hitch him up to the wagon–take Old Blue this time: that way maybe Blackie won't think I'm crazy–then go into Walter's an' tell him I need a plow bolt. Better make it half a dozen. That way I'll have some extras on hand. In the meantime I'll try t' hammer out this moldboard."

"I'll be back as soon as I can, Uncle Nathan," she exclaimed enthusiastically, as she took off running for the cornfield to get Old Blue.

She was in the wagon heading out the lane when Hester spied her from the garden. "Just whar do you think you're a-gwine, young lady?"

Sarah reined in the horse. "Into Walter Lehman's to get a plow bolt. Uncle Nathan broke his plow."

"Not dressed like that you ain't," retorted Hester. "You take off them britches an' put a dress on first. You're a young lady, not a boy. Why do I haf t' keep remindin' you of that?"

"Yes, ma'am," answered Sarah contritely. She jumped down from the wagon seat and ran for the barn.

"An' stop runnin'!" shouted Hester in exasperation.

"I told you so," laughed Nathan, as Sarah re-entered the barn. She climbed the ladder into the loft and in a matter of seconds reappeared wearing a gray cotton dress. She did a twirl for Nathan as she walked past him at the work bench and they both broke out laughing.

As soon as she re-emerged into the sunlight she changed her demeanor, and, under Hester's watchful eye, walked lady-like back to the wagon.

As she entered the town she was surprised at the amount of traffic. It was a beautiful early spring day and she figured that all the farmers in Rushing Creek, like her Uncle Nathan, would be out plowing their fields. As she passed Lloyd Stanley's weld shop on the left, she noticed a green Chevy truck parked in front. She recognized it as Charlie Cole's. Just beyond the weld shop, her attention was caught by the excited cries of young boys. She looked and saw a number of them running amongst the wreckage of old and rusted farm machinery that littered the lot adjoining the weld shop. She wondered that they were not in school, then remembered that it was Saturday. That also accounted for the heavier-than-usual amount of traffic.

As she drove by she continued to keep her eyes fixed on the boys running through the lot across the street. She counted five of them. Each had a handful of stones and they seemed to be chasing something. Suddenly they all descended on a rusty old disc, formed a circle around it, and, with arms cocked, waited for their quarry to reappear.

Sarah looked down the street. Walter Lehman's was just another hundred feet ahead on the right. She decided she could walk the rest of the way. Pulling Old Blue off to the side and reining him in, she jumped down from the wagon and ran across the street. The five boys were so absorbed in their hunt, their attention so riveted on the "thing" hiding in the tall, dried grass growing up between the rusty blades of the disc, that they did not see or hear her coming until she was almost upon them.

"Look out! Hit's the witch!" cried the tallest of the five, a boy of about eight or nine years of age, wearing a red flannel shirt. Immediately all five boys turned to run.

Suddenly the "thing" under the disc flew up about three feet in the air and fell again to earth a short distance in front of Sarah. She could now clearly see that the "thing" she had thought might be a rabbit was not a rabbit at all, but a mourning dove with a broken wing. It tried to fly again, but again fell, this time at her feet. She picked it up.

Suddenly she felt a sharp, stinging blow strike her head with so much force that it knocked her off balance. Immediately she dropped to her knees, and while clutching the dove against her stomach with her left hand, instinctively reached with her right hand to the point of impact, to the corner of her brow just above her right eye. For an instant everything went black. As she struggled to retain consciousness, she opened her left eye to see the blurry back of a red flannel shirt running away from her. She removed her right hand from the corner of her eye and looked at it. It was covered with blood. She did not feel any pain, only a sensation of numbness, but she could see that she was bleeding profusely. She laid the injured dove on the ground and tore a six-inch strip of cloth from the hem of her dress and folded it over several times.

Pressing the wad of cloth against the corner of her right brow, she picked up the dove with her free hand and got to her feet. She steadied herself for a moment, long enough to be sure that she had her balance, then headed back to the wagon.

"You stay here," she said, comfortingly, addressing herself to the injured bird, as she placed it in the storage bin under the seat. "I'll be back for you."

She walked up along the side of the street to Lehman's store.

"Good morning, Mr. Ephraim," she said, greeting the old gentleman sitting on the bench on the porch just outside the door. She always called him "Mr. Ephraim," though she knew that Ephraim was not his surname. She did not know his surname. Everyone in town just called him "Ephraim," or, more commonly, "Old Ephraim," as he appeared to be at least eighty years of age, perhaps ninety. Sarah knew that he lived somewhere in town, but she was not sure exactly where. In the summertime he was an almost permanent fixture on the bench on Walter Lehman's porch, and on any other days of the year when the weather did not aggravate his arthritis. On most Saturdays during the winter he could be found inside the store huddling near the pot-belly stove and seeking to engage in conversation anyone who passed through the door. He said nothing now to Sarah as she walked past him, but he gave her an inquisitive look.

The bell above the door jingled as Sarah entered the store. She could see that Mr. Lehman was busy with another customer, so she decided to walk around the store a bit, to browse amongst the counters and shelves, which were crammed full of all sorts of interesting things, from foodstuffs and clothing to kitchenware and hardware and to just about anything else anyone could use around the house or farm. Ever since coming to Rushing Creek she and her mother had always enjoyed visiting Walter Lehman's General Store. In the early years the two of them had played a sort of guessing game, as they had tried to figure out what some of the more curious-looking items were and what they were used for. Sometimes they had been able to guess, but more often they had had to ask Daniel or Walter.

She removed the blood-soaked cloth from the corner of her brow, refolded it, and pressed it back into place.

"Is that you, Sarah?" It was Walter Lehman's voice.

"Yes, Mr. Lehman."

"I thought I saw you over there behind the men's clothin' counter. What can I do for you?"

"I need six plow bolts," she replied, stepping out from behind the counter. Walter had not looked up. He was standing behind the cash register, busily writing in his account book.

"Nathan sheared a bolt, did he? Seems like everybody's havin' plow problems today. Charlie Cole was just in here a bit ago. He *overturned* his plow an' twisted the tongue. He's over at Lloyd's now havin' it straightened . . . Good Heavens! What happened to you?"

"It's nothing, Mr. Lehman."

"Here, let me take a look at that."

She removed the bloody wad of cloth from her eye, revealing the bruise and deep cut at the corner of her brow.

"Nuthin'? You call that nuthin'? You look like you just went fifteen rounds with Joe Louis!"

He took a handkerchief from his pocket and mopped up some more of the blood, studying her face as he did so. "You don't even know who Joe Louis is, do you?"

"Is he a boxer?"

Walter nodded. "I'm gonna have Henrietta take a look at that."

He went to the back room and called up the stairwell to the living quarters above the store. A few moments later Sarah found herself being examined by Mrs. Lehman, a short, rather robust woman, with white curly hair.

"What happened to *you*?" she asked in alarm.

"It's nothing really," replied Sarah.

"She had a fight with Joe Louis," explained Walter.

"Well, he should be locked up!" exclaimed Henrietta indignantly. " 'Magine, beatin' up on a girl! . . . Come upstairs, Sarah. I'll put some iodine on that cut and bandage it for you."

"I can't, Mrs. Lehman. I don't have time. I have to get home. My Uncle Nathan is waiting for a plow bolt."

"I think he'd sooner wait another ten minutes than have you bleed to death on the way home," retorted Henrietta, a little impatiently.

"You go with her, Sarah," urged Walter, in a reassuring tone of voice. "I'll have those bolts ready for you when you come back down."

Reluctantly Sarah followed Mrs. Lehman upstairs.

Walter looked up as another customer entered the store. "Mornin', Wesley. What can I do for you today?"

"I need sugar. How much can I have?"

"Five pounds is the limit."

"Damn war! All right, I'll take five pounds . . . I need flour too."

"Twelve-pound bag?"

"Yeah. Also some bakin' soda, some salt, some coffee . . . an' some t'bacca."

"How much coffee?" asked the storekeeper, as he began removing the items from the shelves behind him. He continued to keep one eye on the two boys who had come into the store with Wesley.

"How much can I have?"

"As much as you can pay for."

"I'll take a pound."

Walter placed the groceries on the counter next to the cash register. "Anything else?"

"I need a muskrat trap. One of mine got stoled."

"Prob'bly by a muskrat," mumbled Walter under his breath. He turned and disappeared into the adjoining room. A moment later he returned with the trap. "Anything else?"

"That's all."

"Let's see," said the storekeeper, writing in his book, "that'll be thirty-three cents for the five pounds of sugar, forty-eight cents for the twelve pounds of flour, nickel for the bakin' soda, nickel for the salt, twenty-six cents for the coffee, seventy-five cents for the tobacca, a dollar for the trap . . . and fifteen cents for that pack of cigarettes Frank put in his pocket when I was in the back room."

Frank lowered his head.

"Put 'em back," scowled Wesley, taking the older of the two boys by the collar of his shirt. "If you're gwine t' smoke, you're gwine t' roll your own, same as I do."

Grudgingly Frank returned the pack of cigarettes to the counter.

"That'll be two dollars and ninety-two cents," said the storekeeper, tallying the figures.

Wesley turned to his younger son. "Jemmy, you got the chicken?"

"Yeah, Pa," replied the smaller, dark-haired boy, dragging a gunny sack across the floor.

"Thar, will that do?" asked Wesley, swinging the sack up onto the counter. The sack emitted a loud unhappy squawk as it made contact with the hard surface.

"It'll do for a start," replied the storekeeper casually, once again writing in his book. "I'll add the two dollars and ninety-two cents to your bill and give you credit for one more chicken. I'll decide how much the chicken is worth after I've tasted it."

"Okay, Frank," said Wesley, turning again to his older son, "make yourself useful for once. Carry this stuff out to the wagon."

Frank was about to pick up the supplies on the counter when suddenly Sarah emerged from the back room. He did not recognize her at first with the patch at the corner of her eye and the bandage around her head. When he did, he immediately averted his eyes.

"Dammit!" growled Wesley. "Hit's the witch! Why didn't you tell us she was here, Walter?" Quickly he turned to his younger son. "Don't look at 'er, boy. Look the other way. You wanna end up daid like your Ma?" He quickly removed his hat to cover his eyes as the younger of the two boys ducked behind a counter.

Walter Lehman looked at Sarah to see if she was finding the behavior of Wesley and his two sons as ridiculous as he was, but she appeared to be more frightened than amused.

"Here's the bolts. Tell your Uncle Nathan I said hello. On second thought, no need t' do that. I said hello to him once already today."

"Thank you, Mr. Lehman," she said, taking the six bolts. Then, without looking back, she walked to the door and went out.

"Is she gone?" asked Wesley, still shielding his eyes with his hat.

"She's gone," replied the storekeeper, making no effort to conceal his contempt.

"You think I'm superstitious, don't yuh?"

Walter Lehman stared hard at the grizzled face across the counter. "You wanna know the truth? . . . I think you're a sick man, Wesley Hicks."

"Then you tell me one thang, Walter Lehman. How'd that girl know Bryson's mill was on fire?"

"Wesley, that was almost two years ago. Let bygones be bygones."

"She said herself she was a-flyin' around outside her body. If that don't make her a witch, I don't know what does. My Lydia was the only one wit enough courage t' stand up an' call her a witch to her face . . . An' you know what happened to her. An' don't you be too sure that my Lydia was the first one t' be kilt by that witch."

"Wesley, what are you talkin' about?"

"I'm a-talkin' about Dan'l Wicker, that's what I'm a-talkin' about."

"Dan'l was killed by a bear."

"If you believe that, you're a bigger fool than I had you figgered for, Walter Lehman. Did anyone ever see the body? If you ax me, them witches done kilt him an' et him."

"*Them* witches?"

"The young'un an' her mother both. They're both witches. They done kilt Dan'l Wicker up thar on that lonesome mountain an' et him."

Walter Lehman continued to stare in disgust at Wesley Hicks, unable to believe that even Wesley's deranged mind could conceive such an idea. Suddenly the door burst open and Old Ephraim stumbled in.

"You better come quick, Wesley!" he wheezed. "Your dawgs are loose an' they're a-chasin' atter one er Charlie Cole's boys!"

Before Wesley could reach the door, Walter Lehman was already through it. The storekeeper rushed out into the street. What he saw was terrifying. Just down the street, a small boy, about eight or nine years of age, whom Walter recognized immediately as Timothy Cole, was screaming and struggling desperately to extricate his shirtsleeve and pantleg from the teeth of Wesley's two snarling hounds. As Walter ran down the street, the dogs suddenly pulled the boy to the ground and set upon him with ferocious intensity, tearing through his clothing with their claws and teeth to get at the tender flesh and blood beneath. A number of people, including the boy's father, were also hurrying to the scene, but their efforts to frighten the dogs off or to distract them had thus far proved futile.

"Somebody get a gun!" shouted Charlie Cole in desperation.

Walter turned to run back to the store, but Wesley Hicks grabbed him by the arm. "You cain't shoot my dawgs!" shouted Wesley. "I won't let you shoot my dawgs!"

"Then *you* do somethin'!" shouted Walter back at him. "They're killin' that boy!"

Trembling nervously Wesley approached the savage fray. The boy was unconscious now and the dogs were attacking his limp body even more viciously, dragging him and rolling him about in the street as though he were a dead rabbit. Wesley reached for one of the leashes, and immediately the hound on the other end turned on him and tore a chunk of flesh out of his hand. In a frantic effort to escape, Wesley fell backwards. Fortunately for him, the hound did not pursue him, but returned instead to the boy.

"Somebody get a gun!" shouted the boy's father again.

"No!" screamed Wesley, struggling to his feet. But this time he was too late. Walter Lehman was already running up the street in the direction of the store. Wesley was about to make another attempt to pull his dogs away from the boy when he saw something that filled him with even more fear. "My Gawd," he cried, trembling, "hit's the witch!"

Having rushed to the scene from further down the street, where she had left the horse and wagon, Sarah now emerged from the small circle of anxious bystanders. She watched intently as the hounds dragged the unconscious boy by his sleeves to a sitting position, then seized the moment. Throwing herself down on her knees just behind the boy, she quickly wrapped her arms around his chest. For the next few tense moments it was a game of tug-of-war as Sarah tried to pull the boy in one direction and the dogs in another. Suddenly the hound pulling on the boy's right arm lost its grip as more of the red flannel shirtsleeve and part of the flesh beneath tore away. Fearing that his prey was being taken from him, the dog attacked with even more ferocity, but before he could take hold of the boy's arm again, Sarah thrust her own arm into the hound's frothing mouth. She bit her lower lip in pain as the sharp fangs sank deep into her flesh. She saw Walter Lehman rush forward and shove the muzzle of his rifle into the dog's ribs.

"No, Mr. Lehman," she cried, "don't shoot him!"

"I haf t' shoot it, Sarah! It'll kill you!"

"Please don't! Please, please don't!"

Confused, but moved by her distraught plea, the storekeeper pulled his gun away. Gradually the dog's fury seemed to abate. It released its grip on her arm and backed away.

Now Sarah turned her attention to the other dog, to the one tearing at the boy's left sleeve. Holding the boy now with her bleeding right arm, she tried to force the fingers of her left hand between the dog's teeth. "Look at me!" she cried, "look at me!"

The hound seemed to study her curiously for a moment as it continued to growl, then it too released its grip on the boy's bloody arm and backed away. Together the two dogs ran up the street and jumped into the back of Wesley's wagon.

Suddenly everyone descended on Sarah and the unconscious boy in the middle of the street. Walter Lehman and Charlie Cole were among the first to reach the boy's side.

"You're gonna haf t' get him to a doctor quick, Charlie," said Walter. "I only hope he's still alive."

"He's still alive," Sarah assured them both. "I can feel him breathing." She handed the boy over to his father and got to her feet.

"I think we'd better get *you* to a doctor too," advised Walter, looking at the blood soaking through the sleeve of her dress.

"No, I'll be all right. I've got to get home."

"Never mind about Nathan and his danged plowin'," snapped the storekeeper. "You've got t' see a doctor. That dog could be rabid."

"No, neither of the dogs is rabid," replied Sarah calmly.

Charlie Cole carried the bloody, limp body of his son to his truck and laid him on the front seat. "I'll be glad t' take her if she wants t' go," he shouted back to Walter. "Hit's the least I can do."

"She says she ain't a-goin'," returned Walter, resigning himself to Sarah's wishes.

Charlie looked around for his other children. "All right, you two, get in the back of the truck an' hang on tight. We're gwine t' haf t' get your brother to the doctor an' we ain't got time t' waste." He started up the truck and roared out of town in the direction of Haynesville.

"At least let Henrietta bandage that arm for you," pleaded Walter, turning his attention again to Sarah. "It looks purty bad."

"It's not as bad as it looks, Mr. Lehman," she said, tearing off the already-torn sleeve of her dress and using it to soak up the blood.

"It looks every bit as bad as it looks, if you ask me," replied the storekeeper, "maybe worse. Now I insist, Sarah, you come back to the store and let Henrietta clean that up and bandage it for you."

Sarah submitted and followed Walter up the street. Together they wended their way through the excited bystanders. A hush fell as Sarah passed through the crowd.

"Somebody should shoot them damn dogs!" shouted a voice from the crowd. "Them Plotts hounds is killers!"

"No!" shouted Sarah in alarm, turning in the direction from which the voice had come. "It wasn't the dogs' fault."

"She's right," came another voice—it was Old Ephraim's. "Dat boy had no bus'ness t'rowin' stones at dem dawgs."

Long after the crowd had dispersed, Wesley Hicks continued to stand in the street next to his wagon, trying to comprehend the meaning of the events he had just witnessed.

Nathan ran out of the barn the moment he heard the sound of the wagon coming in the lane. He had become impatient when Sarah had not returned after an hour, but when she still had not returned after two hours, his impatience had given way to anxiety. Now, the sight of her driving in the lane, with a bandage around her head, another bandage around her arm, and her dress torn and bloody, did little to allay that anxiety. She stopped the rig alongside him, as Hester and Elizabeth came running from the garden.

"Here are the bolts, Uncle Nathan," she said, extending her hand. "I'm sorry I took so long."

"What *happened* to you?" asked Nathan, staring at her in disbelief and alarm. "I sent you into town for a bolt. You look like you've just come back from the war."

"It's a long story, Uncle Nathan, and I'd be glad to tell you all about it, but first there's somebody under the seat I've got to take care of."

Nathan, Hester, and Elizabeth watched with curiosity as Sarah pulled the storage box out from under the seat and opened it. A look of disgust came over Hester's face. "Why, hit's nuthin' but a dirty pigeon."

"No, it's a dove," said Elizabeth, smiling, "the bird of peace."

"Yes," replied Sarah. "It has a broken wing, and it needs some time to heal . . . Here, Mother, would you hold it til I get down?"

Elizabeth took the bird and Nathan helped Sarah down off the wagon.

"You mean you're a-gwine t' try an' *nuss* that bird?" inquired Hester skeptically, and not entirely approvingly.

"Yes, Aunt Hester, I've nursed birds before."

"How you a-gwine t' keep it from flappin' around?"

"I'll bandage its wings together . . . Fortunately," she said, unraveling the dressing from her head, "I have lots of bandages now."

Nathan continued to stare at her aghast. "Are you sure you're all right?"

"Yes, Uncle Nathan, I'm fine. Really, I am."

"Well, I'll take your word for it for now, but I want t' hear all about this just as soon as you're done tendin' to that bird."

With bolts in hand, he headed back to his work bench.

"I don't like the looks of this," said Nathan apprehensively, as he stood on the porch one evening in mid-April and watched the sun set behind the mountains to the west. He was talking to himself.

"Nathan, shut that door!" came an angry voice from the kitchen. "Hit's gettin' cold in here! I'd swear you was born in a barn!"

"Hester, come out here a minute."

Hester stomped out onto the porch and slammed the door behind her. "Whatta yuh want, Nathan? I'm busy."

"Tell me what you think. Is it gonna freeze tonight?"

Hester stepped down off the porch, sniffed the air, and looked up at the sky. Almost instantly her anger was transformed into another emotion, that of alarm. "We gotta cover the 'maters an' melons an' beans," she said, casting a fearful eye toward her garden. "Hit's a-gwine t' freeze good!"

"I wish we could cover the apple trees," sighed Nathan, as he looked out across his orchard white with bloom, "but I don't reckon there's enough straw in the whole county t' do that . . . Well, we better get started. We're gonna have a long night. I'll get Sarah an' we'll bring a wagonload of straw over to the garden, then while you and Elizabeth are coverin' up the perishables, Sarah and I will start haulin' wood out to the orchard."

Shortly after midnight Nathan began torching the teepees of brush and wood that he and Sarah had erected all over the orchard. For the rest of the night, all four remained in the orchard, feeding the fires. As roaring sparks and flames leapt into the clear night sky, illuminating the full-blown apple trees, Nathan held his breath. As soon as the sun appeared from behind the mountain to the east, he ordered the others to desist. As he walked back to the house, he could tell by the heavy frost on the garden that the freeze had been a hard one. He looked at the thermometer on the porch and shook his head. "Twenty-two degrees! Twenty-two degrees on the sixteenth of April! Can you believe it?"

585

The killing frost on the sixteenth was not the last bad tidings April would bring. A week later another letter came from Otis, this one bearing the news from which Hester had prayed to be spared: Otis was being sent overseas; he was going to the war. As distressed as Hester had been over the death and destruction visited upon her tender garden by the killing frost, she was even more distressed by the news borne by Otis' letter. She could always plant another garden; she could never have another son.

Sarah thought it a little curious that Otis had not written to her. All of his letters had been addressed to Nathan and Hester. She was glad, however, that it was that way and not the other way around. She would not have wanted him to write to *her* and not to *them*. She knew how much Hester looked forward to his letters. And Nathan and Hester always allowed her to read the letters that he sent to them. She knew that Otis had not forgotten her completely. He sometimes included a few words to her in his letters to his parents, mostly just to say hello and to thank her for all the letters she had sent to him.

His letters were always short, seldom more than a page or a page and a half long, and from reading them she got the impression that he had labored over them for hours. She knew from helping him with his schoolwork that writing did not come easy to Otis. For him a pencil in his hand was as uncomfortable as a splinter in his finger. So, while she thought it a *little* curious that he wrote so seldom to his parents–and to her not at all–she thought she understood the reason for it and forgave him readily.

Then the letters stopped altogether. There was no letter in May, none again in June. Hester was certain that something had happened to him. When July passed with still no word from him, even Nathan could not calm her. Then in the second week of August, as Sarah was hoeing corn at the bottom of the hill near the creek, she heard Hester excitedly calling to her from the top of the hill. She was waving a letter. Sarah started walking up the hill.

"Hurry, girl, hurry!" called Hester. "Run!"

Sarah dropped her hoe and ran the rest of the way. When she reached the top she found Hester out of breath and bursting with excitement. "I run all the way from the mailbox!" she panted. "Here, hit's for you!"

"Is it from Otis?" asked Sarah, taking the letter. She knew that she need not have asked the question. The anxious expectation written all over Hester's face told her that it could be from no one else. She opened the letter. "It's dated July ninth," she said, "over a month ago."

She would have preferred to have read the letter to herself first, but since Hester was dying to hear the news, and probably would have read it over her shoulder anyway, she decided to read it aloud.

" 'Dear Sarah,

'I'm in a place called Tunisia. I know the spelling is right because I coppied it off a map. They tell me it's in Africa, but they could have fooled me. There's no elefants and jirafs here, no jungles neither. There's hardly even no trees. It's all dessert. I never knew how beutiful Rushing Creek was til I came here.

'I been here almost a month now, mostly just waiting around. War is mostly just waiting around, that's what everybody tells me. I ain't seen no real fighting yet. There was a lot of fighting here before I got here though, and our guys beat the Gerries real good. Everybody says we're winning now.

'It looks like my outfit will be seeing action any day now, maybe even tomorrow. We are part of a big army that will be attacking the Football. That's what all the guys call Sicily. That's the little island that looks like it's being kicked by Italy. But I guess I don't have to tell you that. There are a lot of guys from England here too. They tease us Americans a lot. They say we don't even know what a football looks like. I'm looking at Sicily on a map right now. It don't look much like a football to me neither.

'I think about you a lot. I bet you're hoeing corn right this minute. Unless it's night time over there now. Or maybe you're hoeing corn at night now too, without me there to help you. I seen you do it before.

'I save all your letters. I read them over and over again, even though I don't always understand everything. I have a real good buddy named Larry who I met in training camp. He's from Lake Junaluska, which isn't too far from Rushing Creek. He's a real smart guy. I guess you have to be if you come from a place that hard to spell. He even wears glasses. I sometimes let him read your letters, but he don't always understand them either. He once asked me if you were a college perfesser or something. He didn't believe me when I told him that you were just a sixteen-year-old girl.

'I been meaning to write to you for a long time now. It's always hard to know what to say. I must of wrote "Dear Sarah" a thousand times already, but that's as far as I get. When I was in training camp I figgered there was a chance that the war would be over before I got to go anyway, and then I could just come home and tell you everything.

'I don't know how long it's going to be before I can come home. Not long I hope. Would you do me a big favor? Would you have a picture took of yourself and send it to me? Lots of the guys have pictures from home, and I'd kind of like to have one of you. Could you wear that old straw hat I gave you?

'Also, would you promise me one thing? Would you promise me that you won't get married before I come home? I'd kind of like to be at your wedding.

'Please tell Ma and Pa that I said hello and that I will write to them soon.

         Yours truly,

         Otis

'P.S. Larry helped me with the spelling, so if there's any mistakes, it's his fawt.' "

"Four whole pages!" exclaimed Hester enviously, looking over Sarah's shoulder, "four whole pages!"

"Four pages in ten months," Sarah reminded her, "about one for every fifty I've sent him."

"Could I show it to Nathan?" asked Hester, already reaching for the letter. "I know he'll be a-wantin' t' see it."

Sarah handed her the letter and watched as Hester hurried off in the direction of the barn. She wondered that Hester did not trip and fall, as she certainly was not watching where she was going. She was already re-reading the letter.

As Sarah walked back down the hill to resume her hoeing, she thought about the favor Otis had asked of her. She didn't know of anyone in Rushing Creek who owned a camera. Perhaps Nathan would allow her to drive the wagon into Haynesville to have her picture taken. Or perhaps Isaac would take her in the truck.

As for the promise that Otis had asked her to make—not to marry before he came home—she thought it a strange thing for him to ask, as she certainly had no plans of getting married any time soon. Apparently he needed to be reassured that the home he came home to would be the same as the home he had left, that everything would be just the same as he remembered it. He was obviously missing his home and family a great deal. She decided, therefore, that there would be no great harm in granting his request, no matter how unnecessary it seemed to her. In her next letter to him she would enclose a picture and a promise—a picture of herself in the old straw hat, and a promise that she would not get married before he returned.

18

A SUNDAY IN OCTOBER

Sarah lingered for a moment at the top of her ladder to watch the last vestiges of color fade from the western sky, then climbed down and emptied her half-full sack of apples. The last apple had been picked. The long harvest was finally over. It had been a light crop. The killing frost in April had reduced it to half of what it otherwise would have been. Their all-night vigil had not been for nought however. Nathan considered himself fortunate to have had even half a crop. Most orchards in the western counties had not fared nearly as well.

Sarah had virtually picked the entire crop herself. Late in August, at the very outset of the season, Nathan had fallen and injured his back. He had been up on a ladder, with nearly a full sack of apples, when a rung had broken, sending him and the sack of apples both crashing to earth in rather spectacular fashion. Since then his work activity had been restricted to jobs requiring little or no lifting, of which there were precious few on a subsistence farmstead. For the past month and a half Sarah had worked heroically to harvest the apples before they dropped, starting each day as soon as it was light enough to see, and often working until it was so dark that she had to feel for the apples on the trees. She had not worked in hard, pouring rain, but on more than one occasion she had worked in light rain and drizzle. And to Hester's unbridled shock and dismay, she had even worked on a Sunday afternoon. Whenever possible, Hester and Elizabeth had taken time out from their canning and other kitchen activities to help, but as both were afraid of heights, they had confined their picking to the bottoms of the trees.

Sarah had found the experience wearying but exhilarating. From the tops of apple trees she had witnessed miracles as the leaden days of late August and early September had been transformed, as if by divine alchemy, into golden drops of pure October. She was tired now, needed rest now–the number of times she had climbed up and down her ladder she would not have cared to count, nor the hundreds of times she had filled her picking sack and emptied it out again–but she knew that in another year, when another summer had passed into fall, and apples were once again ripe for the picking, she would be ready to take up picking sack and ladder and do it all over again.

As she loaded the last of the baskets of apples onto the wagon and hauled them to the apple cellar in the twilight darkness, she thought how good it would be to finally have a day off. Tomorrow would be Sunday. She could rest all day. She wouldn't even have to get up early to help milk the cows, as Hester had been helping Nathan with the milking since the beginning of apple season. She would sleep late–perhaps as late as seven o'clock–go to church with Nathan and Hester, then spend a relaxing afternoon at the waterfall. As she drove the wagon back to the barn, she kept her eyes fixed on the silver moon, which was already high in the night sky. The moon, which had been so full and so golden only two or three days before, was now on the wane.

"Better not go in thar right now," warned Frank, emerging from the house and wiping the blood from the corner of his mouth with his sleeve. "Pa's been a-drinkin' ag'in, an' he ain't exackly in a good mood."

He sauntered down off the porch, cuffing Jemmy on the head as he went by. Hands in his pockets, he paced angrily about the yard in the dark, cursing to himself. Stumbling over a bucket, he cursed aloud and kicked it. The ensuing racket started the dogs barking.

"Keep them gaw-dam dawgs quiet!" growled a gravelly voice from inside the house.

"Shut up, you gaw-dam hounds!" shouted Frank, picking up a stick and throwing it in the direction of the barking. There was a single yelp, then all was quiet. He paced some more. When he had cooled down, he came back to the porch and looked at Jemmy. "Yo a-gwine t' set thar all night, li'l brother?"

Jemmy did not respond. Frank continued to study him, but the faint light coming from the house window was not sufficient to illuminate his younger brother's brooding features. But even in the dark Frank could see the pathetic look on Jemmy's face. He could not actually *see* it, but he could see it in his mind, as the expression on Jemmy's face never changed. Since their mother's death over two years ago Frank had not seen his younger brother smile once.

"How old are yo, Jemmy?"

"I'll be sixteen in December," replied Jemmy grudgingly.

"Ever had a woman?"

"None of yo damn bus'ness!"

"I was just axin'. Why is yo so jumpy all the time? Whatsa matter wit yo anyhow? Yo been ackin' peculiar ever since Ma died, a-mopin' around here wit yo tongue hangin' out like some tired old houn'dawg, a-gwine off in the woods by yo'self all the time . . . an' now here yo be a-settin' out here in the dark all by yo'self an' a-starin' up at the moon. Hit just ain't natural. If yo ax me, Pa's right: that witch done put her spell on yo too."

Jemmy continued to stare forlornly at the moon. Frank cast a quick glance up through the trees at the pale lop-sided disc in the clear October night sky, but he could find nothing there to hold his attention. His brain was too agitated.

"We's a-gwine t' haf t' do somethin' about her, yuh know."

"About who?"

"About the Wicker witch, that's who."

"Whatta yuh mean?" asked Jemmy, finally retracting his face from the moon and looking quizzically at his brother.

"I mean we's a-gwine t' haf t' *do* somethin' about her . . . Look, she's already done kilt our Ma, an' now she's got Pa so sick he ain't in his right mind half the time . . ."

"Yo know as well as I do, Frank, that Ma was sick a long time a-fore Sarah Wicker ever laid eyes on her. She could a-died anytime. As for Pa, he's sick 'cause he's a-drinkin' all the time."

"Yeah, but don't yuh see? That witch done put a spell on him. That's what's a-makin' him drink . . . An' yo! Look at yo! I never seed a body ack as sorry as yo been a-ackin' these past two years

... Well, I ain't a-gwine t' set around here an' wait for her t' put a spell on me. I'se a-gwine t' do somethin' about it."

A worried look came over Jemmy's face, but Frank could not see it in the dark. "What yo be fixin' t' do, Frank? Yo ain't a-fixin' t' hurt her, are yuh?"

"Mebbe I is an' mebbe I isn't. I ain't exackly made up my mind yet... But I'se a-gwine t' need yo help."

"Count me out, Frank. I don't want nuthin' t' do wit it."

Frank sat down on the porch step next to Jemmy and put his arm around his shoulders. "Now, I didn't say I was a-gwine t' hurt her, did I, li'l brother?"

"Yo said 'mebbe.' "

"Okay, we won't hurt her. We'll just skeer her a li'l bit. Will yuh help me?"

"Promise not t' hurt her?"

"I promise."

"Cross yo heart an' hope t' die?"

"Cross my heart an' hope t' die."

"Okay, I'll help yuh, I reckon. Whatta yuh want me t' do?"

"Yo be a-gwine t' church t'morruh mornin'?"

"Yo know I is. I promised Ma I'd keep a-gwine."

"An' after that, what?"

"Whatta yuh mean?"

"C'mon, Jemmy, don't yo be a-foolin' wit me. I ain't stupid, yuh know. Hit ain't exackly no secret that yo ain't been a-comin' direckly home after church on Sundays. An' I doubt that yo been a-stayin' late t' do some extra prayin'. Yo been a-follerin' that witch an' a-spyin' on her, ain't yuh?"

"None of yo damn bus'ness!"

"I know she used t' go into the woods after church, back towards the baptizin' hole. Is that whar she goes, back to the baptizin' hole t' cast her spells upon the holy water?"

"No, she don't go to the baptizin' hole."

"But yo know whar she *do* go, don't yuh?"

Reluctantly Jemmy confessed his secret. "Yeah, I know. But I ain't a-tellin' *yo*. I'll take yuh thar, but I ain't a-tellin' yuh."

"T'morruh after church?"

"Okay, t'morruh after church. Meet me in the woods next to the path that goes down to the baptizin' hole after church . . . Less'n of course yo wanna come t' church wit me."

"I'll meet yuh in the woods."

Sarah opened her eyes and rolled over onto her stomach. From her warm bed in the hay she looked out through the open doors of the barn loft toward the mountain to the south. In the early morning light she could see the mist rising off Rushing Creek. She could not see the creek itself, as it was hidden behind the trees that lined its banks, but she could trace its course by the telltale trail of white vapor. Through the mist she could see the yellow and orange hues of the mountain beyond, still subdued in the shadows of night. The leaves would be beginning to fall soon, now that cooler weather had come. In another couple of weeks she would be moving back into the house for the winter.

Although she had tried to sleep late, she had been awake since about four o'clock, and for the past two hours had lain in bed staring up into the ghostly gloom of the barn's interior. In the dark she had heard the soft cooing and the fluttering of wings of the pigeons with whom she shared the barn loft. She had been thinking of Otis. In his last letter to Nathan and Hester he had sounded distraught. He had finally seen the war at close hand, and apparently he had not liked what he had seen. He had sounded frightened and homesick. She worried about Otis. She had said a special prayer for him the night before—in fact, had fallen asleep while praying—and again that morning when she had first awakened—just as she had done every day for the past year.

As the sky grew progressively lighter, Sarah put her dark thoughts aside and focused her attention on the eastern slope of the mountain to the south, where she knew the sun would soon be rising. She smiled as the first burst of sunlight appeared. As shafts of sunlight entered the loft, she threw off her covers. A new day was beginning—an October day!—and it was time to get up. She finally had a day off and she wasn't about to waste it lying in bed.

She rolled out of her cozy nest in the hay and raised herself to a kneeling position. It was deliciously cool! She could see her breath! Vigorously she rubbed some warmth into her arms, then hurriedly pulled the nightgown over her head and reached for her dress. As she did so she suddenly became aware that there was someone else in the loft with her. Instinctively she pulled the crumpled dress against her body to cover her nakedness. She had caught a glimpse of a man's shoes and trousered legs standing near the open trapdoor in the floor of the loft. How had he gotten there? She had not heard anyone come up the ladder. She looked up to find Otis dressed in full army uniform standing before her.

"Otis, you're home!"

But her sudden elation was short-lived. As she looked into Otis' face, she noticed that his expression did not change. He looked lost and confused, as though he had no idea where he was. He continued to stare straight ahead, a distant look in his eyes, as though searching for something familiar, something he could recognize. Sarah tried to meet his gaze, but he was not looking at her, but past her. He neither spoke nor moved. Sarah knew what it meant.

"Are you dead, Otis?" she asked, her voice quivering.

As she watched the image dissolve amongst the shafts of sunlight, she felt a lump come to her throat. Still staring at the illuminated particles of dust that now filled the space where Otis had stood, she mechanically pulled her bedcovers around her shoulders and fell slowly, stiffly onto her side, as if pulled down by the weight of her grief. As she lay there, still staring, frozen in grief, warm tears filled the pools of her eyes, over-ran their banks, and streamed slowly down her face. Drop by drop they were absorbed in the mat of hay on which she lay.

"Sarah?"

It was her Uncle Nathan's voice. Sarah bolted to an upright position and reached again for the dress she had started to put on earlier. Quickly pulling it over her head, she crawled the short distance to the trapdoor and looked down.

"Good morning, Uncle Nathan." He was dressed in his Sunday suit.

"Just wanted t' make sure you were all right. When you didn't come down to breakfast, your Aunt Hester started worryin' about you. I told her you were prob'bly just readin' or somethin' an' we should let you be, but you know Hester. Once she gets a notion in her head, it keeps festerin' in there like a thorn, an' there's just no peace til she gets it pulled out. She insisted I make sure you were all right . . . Are you about ready for church?"

"What time *is* it?"

"About nine-fifteen."

"I guess I overslept."

"Well, if anyone has a right to, you sure do, as hard as you've worked these past couple months." He studied her face. "You been cryin'?"

Sarah wiped her still-moist eyes with the knuckles of her fingers and tried to laugh. "Yes, I guess I have."

Nathan looked at her sympathetically. "You're worried about Otis, aren't you?"

She nodded her head.

"We all are, Sarah," he said solemnly. "Let's hope this war will soon be over . . . Well, we better get a move on if we're gonna get to church on time."

"I'll be right down, Uncle Nathan."

Frank was waiting in the woods just off the path when Jemmy arrived. "Hurry up or we'll lose her. She went by here ten minutes ago."

"No, we got t' let her get on a-haid, or she'll hear us. B'sides, I know whar she be a-gwine."

"I don't think she'd hear anythang t'day. She was like in a trance when she come by here. D'yuh s'pose witches put spells on their-selves? She went a-walkin' by right over thar, not more'n a good spit from whar I was a-settin', an' she never even saw me, never even looked in my direction. Lucky thang too. She took me by surprise. I didn't figger she'd be a-comin' through the woods. I figgered she'd be a-gwine down the path."

Jemmy noticed that Frank's right index finger was curled around the handle of a jug. He watched as his older brother lifted the jug to his lips and took a swig of its contents. "If Pa finds out yo been a-drinkin' his whiskey, he's a-gwine t' skin yo alive."

"That's *if'n* he finds out. But he sure ain't in no condition t' find out for hisself, an' I sure as hell ain't a-fixin' t' tell him. The way I got it figgered, the only way he'll find out is if'n someone else tells him." He glared at Jemmy.

"I won't tell him, Frank, honest I won't. Only don't yo go a-drinkin' that whole jug. Hit's bad enough that Pa's drunk all the time. I don't think I could stand it if'n *yo* started a-beatin' up on me too."

Frank put his free arm around Jemmy's shoulders. "Now, don't yo ever worry about that, li'l brother. I swear t' God I'll never lay an unkind hand on yo as long as yo live. That's a promise."

Jemmy watched nervously as Frank took another swig.

"Don't yo think hit's about time for us t' be a-gettin' started?" asked Frank, growing impatient. "She should be far enough a-haid by now."

"Yeah, we can go now."

Frank wiped his mouth with his hand and put the cork back in the jug. "I'll be right wit yuh. First I got t' get me a coupla thangs I left over here behind this tree."

Jemmy watched as Frank hurried to a nearby tree. "What yo got thar?"

"Just an old feedsack an' some rope."

A look of horror came over Jemmy's face. "Yo said yo weren't a-gwine t' hurt her."

"We *ain't* a-gwine t' hurt her."

"I don't know, Frank. I don't think this is such a good idea."

"C'mon, Jemmy. Yo ain't a-gwine t' back out on me now, is yuh? R'member, we's a-doin' this for Ma an' Pa. Yo's the one who's always a-gwine t' church. Don't they teach yuh t' honor yo Ma an' yo Pa?"

"Yeah, but . . ."

"Well, come on then." Frank started off in the direction of the creek. When he realized that Jemmy wasn't following him, he stopped and turned. "C'mon, Jemmy!"

"Yo promise that yo ain't a-gwine t' hurt her?"

" 'Course we ain't a-gwine t' hurt her. We's just a-gwine t' skeer her a li'l bit."

"What's the sack for?"

"For over her haid. So's she cain't put her evil eye on us."

"Yo ain't a-gwine t' hang her?"

"Hell no, we ain't a-gwine t' hang her. We'll just tie her up an' leave her in the woods overnight. That'll teach her a lesson."

Frank knew that the only thing he could do now was wait for Jemmy to make up his mind. He removed a pack of cigarettes from his shirt pocket, selected one, and lit it. A full minute passed, then two. Frank was getting angry, but he knew that he dared not show his anger to Jemmy. His whole scheme depended on his younger brother's cooperation. "C'mon, Jemmy," he implored again, "if'n yo don't wanna do it for Ma, won't yuh do it for me? I just turned eighteen, an' yo know what that means. Hit means that soon they's a-gwine t' come an' get me, put me in the army, an' send me t' some furrin country somewhar, whar I'll prob'bly get my haid blowed off, an' yo'll never see me ag'in."

Still Jemmy did not move. If he felt any sympathy for Frank's plight his face did not register it.

"C'mon, Jemmy. Yo got t' go first. Yo's the one who knows whar she be a-gwine." Frank was almost begging now.

Jemmy was only too painfully aware that he and he alone knew where Sarah was going. He knew that if he refused to go along with Frank's scheme that Frank would never find her. He knew that if anything happened to Sarah Wicker that he and he alone would be responsible. Never in his young life had he faced a more agonizing dilemma.

Was Sarah Wicker a witch? His mother had thought so, and his father still thought so, but Jemmy wasn't so sure. He thought about what Frank had said the night before, about the reason their Pa had been drinking so much was because Sarah had put a spell on him. The truth of the matter was, their father had started drinking again immediately following their mother's death, and he was sick more days than he was well, but Jemmy had to admit that their father had gotten much worse since that day in the early spring when they had encountered Sarah unexpectedly at Walter Lehman's General Store. None of them had recognized her at first with the bandage on her head, and so before they had had a chance to turn away, her eyes had met their eyes. And it was their father whom she had looked at the longest.

If their father had had any doubts before that Sarah Wicker was a witch, the incredible drama that took place outside in the street immediately afterwards had served to dispel them. Jemmy too had seen Sarah throw herself fearlessly into the midst of the two attacking hounds to save Timothy Cole. He and Frank and their Pa had all watched in fascination and disbelief—it was impossible not to watch!—as she deliberately thrust her own arm into the one dog's mouth. Jemmy thought it was the bravest thing he had ever seen. Like everyone else who had witnessed the spectacle, he had fully expected the dog to tear her apart, and like everyone else he had been amazed and stupefied when the hound released her and backed off. Like everyone else he had again been mystified a minute later when the second dog backed away from her. And all she had made that dog do was look into her eyes! Jemmy had never seen anything like it. If ever there was to be proof that his mother was right—that Sarah Wicker had power in her eyes—then surely that was it. But he had not understood why she had allowed the first dog to bite her, or why she had tried to force her fingers into the mouth of the second dog. Even his Pa had at first been at a loss to understand why she had done this. It was not until they were almost home later that morning that his Pa had been able to explain it to him.

"Don't yuh see, boy? She wanted the dawgs t' bite her. She knew that just as soon as the dawgs got a taste of her blood, they'd leave her be. Witches' blood be p'ison. If anybody or anythang gets a taste of it or even touches it, they'll die. An' if any of it gets spilt on the ground, nuthin' will ever grow thar ag'in. That's why witches are always hanged or burned, never butchered . . . Mark my words, both them dawgs'll be daid in a fortnight. The one got a taste of her blood; the other looked into her evil eye. Both them dawgs'll be daid in a fortnight, just like your Ma was."

But the dogs had not died. Their behavior had been strange for the next several days—they had been more docile, less aggressive—but they had not died. His Pa had been wrong. Nor had his Pa explained why a witch would try to save a nine-year-old boy in the first place.

There was something else that Frank had said that Jemmy now wondered about. He had said that Sarah had cast a spell upon *him*, Jemmy. Jemmy knew that Frank had only been shooting off his mouth, as usual, but there had been many occasions over the past two and a half years when Jemmy himself had wondered if Sarah Wicker had not cast a spell upon him. In fact the spell may have been cast as long ago as five years. He would never forget the first time he had ever seen Sarah Wicker. It was on a Saturday morning in November of 1937 in Walter Lehman's store. He was not quite ten at the time; she must have been no more than eleven. He had come into the store with his father; she had come in with her father. For the longest time he had hidden behind a counter and watched her. He had wondered that he had never seen her before. He had never seen her in school. For days afterwards he had not been able to get the thought of her out of his mind. Every time his father went into town after that, he had asked to go along in the hope that he might see her again, but he never did, not, that is, until she had suddenly reappeared one Sunday morning in church almost four years later. Jemmy would never forget the date: July 20, 1941. She was older and she had grown some in the nearly four years since he had first seen her, but it was unmistakably her: the same dark hair and dark eyes, the same smile, the same . . . Jemmy did not know how to explain it, but there was something about her that was different from any other girl he had ever seen. Something bewitching.

Had she bewitched him? *Had* she cast a spell upon him? Was that the reason he thought about her almost constantly, the reason why, for the past two and a half years, he had been able to think of nothing else? Was that the reason he ached inside, in the hollow of his chest, the reason he couldn't eat or sleep? Was that the reason he longed to be close to her, longed to touch her, in spite of his mother's conviction that she was a witch, in spite of his father's warnings not to even look at her? Was that the reason he sometimes followed her after church? Had she *lured* him to her haunt at the waterfall? Maybe his Pa and Frank were right. Maybe she *had* cast a spell upon him. But he would almost have preferred to live under her spell–or even die from her curse– than see any harm befall her.

In the end it was not Frank's importunings that caused him to yield, but rather his need to be near to the creature that had haunted his days and nights for the past two and a half years and had made his heart ache so terribly with longing. Jemmy wasn't sure what Frank planned to do to Sarah exactly, but at the very least it would involve physical contact. Once Jemmy had framed his dilemma in those terms–to go along with Frank's scheme with its promise of satisfying the deepest and most powerful yearnings his young body and mind had ever known; or to turn away and go home to more of the same emptiness, more of the same awful longing–once he had framed his dilemma in those stark terms, Jemmy's will to resist dissolved.

"Okay, Frank," he said, resigning himself to his fate, "I'll go wit yuh."

"Good boy, Jemmy. Your Ma would be proud."

Jemmy led Frank down through the woods toward the creek. At the first sight of reflected water coming up through the trees he stopped and scanned the bank for signs of movement. Seeing nothing, he pressed onward, but rather than proceeding down the embankment to the water's edge, he set off through the woods on a course parallel to the creek, but at a safe distance from it, so as not to be seen. Quietly Frank dogged his brother's steps.

Not until they had reached the gorge did they venture near the water. Crossing over on the fallen tree, they continued upstream along the other bank. At the place where the smaller stream came rushing down out of the mountain, Jemmy stopped and turned to Frank. "No talkin' from here on. She's right up thar."

As stealthily as two hunters stalking their prey they followed the tumbling stream up the side of the mountain. When they reached the spot just below the waterfall from which Jemmy had seen Sarah the first time he had followed her, he motioned for Frank to stop. "I'll see if she's thar," he whispered.

Frank waited as Jemmy climbed up behind the huge boulders and peered over the top. Excitedly Jemmy hurried back to where Frank was waiting. "She's thar all right, an' her back's to us!"

"Lemme see! Here, hold this stuff." Frank thrust the sack and rope into Jemmy's hands and set off to retrace his brother's course. Jemmy looked around for the jug of whiskey but did not see it. Had Frank drunk the whole thing and discarded the empty jug somewhere in the woods? He looked at the sack and rope in his hands and noticed that Frank had fashioned one end of the rope into a noose. Again an uneasy feeling welled up inside him, but he fought it off. There was no turning back: Frank knew where Sarah was now. Jemmy looked up and saw Frank returning.

"Okay, here's the plan," whispered Frank.

The strong smell of whiskey on his breath caused Jemmy to jerk his head back violently, as if he had just been hit in the face by one of his Pa's fists.

"Whatsa matter, li'l brother?" asked Frank. "Cain't yuh stand the smell of a li'l hooch?"

"A li'l? I'se a-gettin' drunk just a-smellin' yuh."

Frank laughed. "Listen up, here's the plan. See that flat rock in the water over yonder?"

"Yeah."

"Well, I'se a-gwine t' sneak up behind her an' t'row the sack over her haid, then I'se a-gwine t' drag her to that rock. When I get her thar, yo be a-waitin' wit the rope, an' yo slip the noose around her neck."

"We ain't a-gwine t' hang her?" asked Jemmy in alarm.

"For the last time, Jemmy, no, we ain't a-gwine t' hang her! Now stop yo worryin', will yuh?"

Sarah had thought of nothing but Otis since she had seen him standing in full uniform in the hayloft early that morning. She knew that he was not dead. Even if he had been killed in the fighting in Italy, even if it had been his soul body that she had seen, she knew that he was not dead–not in any final sense. She took some comfort in this knowledge–and for her it *was* knowledge–not a pious hope, not something she accepted on faith, but knowledge: she knew the dead survived; she knew that *he*– his soul–was still alive. He had merely gone to another world. But she knew that she would never again see Otis in his Earth body, and she knew that she would miss *that* Otis, miss him terribly, just as she had missed her father so terribly for a long time after his death–missed him still, after two and a half years, missed him still–even though she knew that he, like Otis, was not dead in any final sense. She knew that when enough time had passed, when a sufficient number of years had accumulated to buffer her from the pain of her losses, she would take comfort in this knowledge, but now the pain was too close to her, especially the pain of losing Otis, and it hurt. This most recent wound had not yet even begun to heal; it was still opening.

She remembered the first time she had ever seen Otis, a boy of eight lazily fishing from the creek bank. She remembered thinking he had the blondest head of hair and the bluest eyes she had ever seen. She would never forget how they had both jumped into the creek to retrieve his fishing pole, and how upset her Aunt Hester had been with both of them. But neither one of them had received the scolding that Otis had feared.

Her memory drifted wistfully now to those early years, especially to that winter that she and her mother had stayed at Nathan and Hester's. Even as a boy, Otis had always been so good-natured, so easy-going, so patient, always willing to set off with her on any adventure she happened to dream up, always willing to listen when she talked "for days at a time without stopping." She smiled as she remembered all the times Otis had told her she was crazy. She even remembered with fondness all of the outrageous lies he had told *to* her and *about* her, which to his convoluted way of thinking were not lies at all, but merely interesting "stories," which could very easily have been true if only hard facts and cold reality had been somewhat different. She remembered getting angry at him then, but she could not be angry with him now. If she could have him back–if she could have him back for even a day–she would gladly listen to all of his stories all over again, and she would believe every one of them.

Who knows? She might even agree to play soldier with him again. She remembered the first time that she and Otis had played soldier together, how he had repeatedly threatened to shoot her, first for not obeying orders, then upon discovering that she was a Yankee. In the end he had *not* shot her, neither for being traitor nor for being the mortal enemy–indeed, he had even gone so far as to change wars so that they might once again be comrades-in-arms rather than enemies–but, even so, she had not much enjoyed playing soldier. She certainly had not enjoyed it when Otis had pretended to be mortally wounded, and had lain still and unresponsive on the ground until she, fearful that he actually *had* hurt himself, had begun to cry. Nor had she enjoyed it when he had then jumped to his feet and said, "Ha ha, made you cry, made you cry!" It had been a cruel joke, but, in the end, it had been only that: a joke, a game. If only it were a game they were playing now. If only Otis were pretending to be dead now as he had done so well and so convincingly when the two of them had played soldier as children. If only he would appear to her now– suddenly jump to his feet right in front of her–right in front of her now with the tears pouring from her eyes and streaming down her face–and say, "Ha ha, made you cry, made you cry!" It would be the cruelest possible joke, but she would not be angry. No, she could not be angry with him now. Instead, her tears of pain would instantly become tears of joy, and she would laugh. She would laugh without ceasing for days.

As she sat on the rock, her eyes fixed on the waterfall, memories of Otis continued to wash over her mind, memories of play, memories of work, memories from their childhood merging and mingling with memories from their adolescent years. They flowed through her mind like leaves in a stream, in completely random fashion, in no discernible order: memories of the many hours the two of them had spent together hoeing corn (his always complaining about the heat, always complaining about the flies, always complaining that she was going too fast for him); memories of all the happy hours they had spent in the hayloft, playing together as children, working together as teenagers; memories of all the times they had picked apples together, first as children (him on the step-ladder, her on the ground under the tree, both listening to Nathan tell stories), later, with both of them picking from the straight ladders. (And how could she ever forget the time he had fallen out of the Rambo tree and had tried to eat all the apples he had bruised? He had been sick for two days afterwards.) She remembered fondly the time in the hayfield when he had given her that old straw hat and all the times over the course of the next two summers that he had sneaked up behind her and pulled it down over her eyes. He had even written from Africa asking her to have her picture taken wearing that hat. She wondered where that picture was now. Had he had it in the pocket of his shirt when he was killed? And where now were all the letters she had written him?

She had not told her Uncle Nathan and Aunt Hester that Otis was dead. Her Aunt Hester would not have believed her anyway. She would have said that she had "no natural way of knowing" such a thing. Sarah wondered if she *might* be mistaken. She had no doubt about *what* she had seen–she had seen Otis' soul body– but she wondered if she might have drawn the wrong conclusion from it. After all, *she* had been outside her physical body without being dead, and more than once. But as she remembered the distant gaze on his face, the confused look in his eyes, she remembered where she had seen that look before: it was on the faces of those first people she had seen that time that Kati had taken her out of her body and into other worlds. She remembered that she had thought at first that she was in the Underworld because all the people there looked so sad and confused and seemed to be wandering about as though they were lost. Then Kati had explained that they were people who had just died, people who hadn't yet realized they were dead.

She had come to the waterfall in the hope that the rushing water would soothe her soul, just as it had done once before. But the falling water seemed to be having the very opposite effect upon her. As she allowed her soul to merge with the falling water—as she *became* the waterfall—she felt her pain and her tears increase a thousand-fold. She had become one with Nature, and all of Nature—the falling water, the falling leaves—was mourning the death of Otis.

The only warning she had was the sound of water splashing behind her. But it came too late. Suddenly she was in darkness. As she quickly tried to divest herself of the foreign object that had been pulled down over the upper part of her body, she felt an arm encircle her tightly about the shoulders and chest and pull her backwards off the rock on which she had been sitting. Suddenly she was in the water. Whoever had grabbed her had dropped her. Instinctively she struggled to get to her feet, to get free of the bag or whatever it was that had been pulled over her. But she found it difficult to move her arms. The sack, or whatever it was, was too tight-fitting and had been pulled too far down over her body to allow for any freedom of movement. Suddenly she felt her head being pushed down into the water. Before she had a chance to take a breath, her nose and mouth were under water. She choked as the water entered her lungs. She coughed to get the water out, but more came in. What was happening to her? Who could be doing this? For one long terrifying moment she thought she was going to drown without ever knowing who was assaulting her, or why. Just as suddenly her head was out of the water again. As she gulped for air, she felt the sack being pulled even further down over her body, all the way down over her hips. Again she felt an arm encircle her body, this time around the stomach, and suddenly she was horizontal. Someone—a man she supposed, judging by the strength—had picked her up and was carrying her on his hip like a sack of potatoes. In desperation she lurched her body in a twisting motion and again she felt herself falling from her abductor's grasp. This time she landed on rocks. She heard a man's voice cry out in anger. "Gaw-dammit!" Again she tried to free herself from the hideous thing over her head, but before she had a chance to do so, she again felt the arms locking around her, both of them this time. Now she was being dragged backwards over rocks and through shallow water. She dug in her heels to retard her abductor's progress. Again she heard him utter a cry of vexation, and again he released her, only to pick her up out of the water and heave her onto his shoulder. He stumbled over more rocks, splashed through more water. Suddenly she felt herself hurtling through the air. Had he stumbled again and dropped her, or had she been thrown? The terrific impact with which her head and back struck the rock simultaneously knocked both wind and senses out of her. As she lay there on her back gasping for air and waiting for full consciousness to return, she struggled once again to free her arms, but before she could do so, she felt a man's weight on her legs, his thighs straddling her knees, and two vice-like hands grip her wrists and pin them to the rock. At the same time she felt the sack tighten around her neck. Were there two of them now?

As she lay there trying to catch her breath and still coughing water from her lungs, she wondered what they were going to do to her next. Were they going to kill her? Of all the dreadful thoughts that came rushing into her mind during those next few seconds, the most dreadful of all was that they would kill her and no one would ever know what had happened to her. Her mother, her Uncle Nathan, her Aunt Hester, her Uncle Jacob—no one would ever know what had happened to her.

The events of the past few minutes had happened so quickly and had been so terrifying that Sarah had been forced to act on her instincts alone. She had had no time to think. It occurred to her now, as she lay on the rock struggling for breath inside the wet sack, that these were actual human beings who were doing this to her, probably men, at least two of them. She could not see them. She had not heard them speak, except for the brief profanities the first one had uttered when she had lurched away from him. Nevertheless, they were actual human beings, not some impersonal evil forces, not some dark lords of the Underworld. She decided to appeal to them as human beings.

"Please. Please don't do this," she begged through the cloth that covered her face and mouth.

She waited. Suddenly the one on top of her released her wrists and began to pull up on the cloth sack, working it up over her hips. They were going to release her! Putting her weight on her elbows she lifted her hips and lower back off the rock, allowing the sack to slide further up. When her forearms were free up to her elbows, she reached for the edges of the sack herself to help get it off. No sooner had she done so than she immediately felt herself being strangled around the neck. With her freed hands she reached for her neck and felt the noose. Desperately she worked her fingers in between the rope and the sack to allow air to pass through her windpipe. She felt the rope being pulled tighter, pinching her fingers. With all the strength in her fingers she tried pulling the tightening noose away from her windpipe. Suddenly she heard and felt the front of her dress being torn from the hem up to her waist. She tried to cry out, but could make no sound. She twisted her body to get away, but the weight on her legs was too great. She felt a hand grappling for her underpants and, in one sudden, violent motion, tear the crotch out of them.

The man who had been straddling her knees was now changing positions. She felt her legs being forced apart and suddenly his full weight was directly on top of her. Through the cloth sack she could make out the shadowy silhouette of a head descending toward her. As the mouth pressed against her own through the wet cloth, she tried to turn her head, but with every movement she made, the noose around her neck was being jerked tighter. Warm alcohol-saturated breath filled her throat and nostrils. Just when she thought her agony could get no worse, she felt two hands force themselves up under the sack, grope for her breasts, then crush them against her rib cage. For the next thirty seconds the weight on top of her undulated to and fro and was accompanied by coarse, grunting sounds. Then suddenly it stopped.

"Gaw-dammit t' Hell!"

Sarah felt the grip on her breasts loosen. Was she imagining it or was the man who had been writhing on top of her, crushing her to the rock, getting off of her? He was! She heard the sound of shoe leather scuffling across the rock. She listened nervously. The next sound she heard was that of water hitting water. He was urinating into the stream! She pulled vigorously on the rope around her neck. Again the noose was jerked tighter. There were definitely two of them—at least two of them! The one who had been on top of her, the one who had just relieved himself in the stream, was coming back—Sarah could hear his footsteps on the rock—but before he had a chance to resume his position, she saw the shadowy silhouette of another figure move quickly from behind her head and assume the position vacated by the first. Once again she felt her legs being forced apart. Again she felt the weight descend upon her. Again she felt the mouth seeking out her own through the wet cloth, but this one did not reek of alcohol. And the weight of this body was not so heavy as the first one. This one too was groping under the sack for her breasts, but this one was not so rough as the first. He was not crushing her, but gently fondling her. But the noose was getting tighter and tighter! She couldn't breathe! She felt the hand on her left breast withdraw and reach down between her legs. She froze in terror. Something warm and hard was probing for the opening between her legs. Suddenly it was inside her! It hurt! It hurt! She couldn't breathe! Couldn't breathe! Desperately she tried once more to pull the rope away from her windpipe. But the feeling in her fingers was gone. The strength in her arms was gone. She was struggling now just to remain conscious. But all of her resources were exhausted. Suddenly a feeling of infinite peace rushed through her. It was accompanied by a flash of brilliant light. It lasted only an instant. Then there was darkness. Then there was nothing.

"Whatsa matter wit her, Frank? She went limp." Anxiously Jemmy withdrew from Sarah and buttoned up his trousers. He pulled the torn dress back over her body to cover her as best he could.

"She ain't a-breathin', Frank, she ain't a-breathin'! Get that rope off her!" Jemmy looked up only to discover that Frank had passed out and lay sprawled on the rock only a few inches from Sarah's head, his hand still clutching the rope. Frantically Jemmy worked to loosen the noose around Sarah's neck, his fingers trembling with fear. Finally he succeeded in getting enough slack to allow him to slip the noose up and over her head. Next he set about to remove the sack. He rolled her onto her stomach and pulled the wet sack up her back, then rolled her over onto her back again and pulled the front of the sack up to her shoulders. Again he stopped to cover her bare legs with the torn dress. Then quickly moving around to a position behind her, he pulled the sack off her head. He had never even stopped to think that her eyes might be open. Even if she were dead, as he feared, her eyes might still be open. He knew that people sometimes died with their eyes open. His own mother had died with her eyes open.

Apprehensive but curious, he moved slowly around her, casting nervous glances in the direction of her face. Her eyes were closed. Kneeling down beside her, he studied her face. It was the first time he had really looked her full in the face. The first few times he had seen her, he had only looked at her when she wasn't looking at him. The moment she had turned toward him, he had lowered his eyes or turned away. He had never dared to look *any* girl directly in the face. Then once all the trouble began, his father had forbidden him to look at her. The few glimpses he had gotten of her face had been hurried ones, stolen ones. Now here she was, lying perfectly still before him. He could gaze upon her to his heart's content. His heart's content! Oh, the irony of it! For as long as he could remember, he had thought that if he could just look at her, if he could just touch her, his heart would be forever content. Now he *had* touched her—had touched her more intimately than he had ever dreamed possible, even in his wildest fantasies. And now he *was* looking at her, looking her full in the face, but his heart was far from content. He felt shame and guilt and grief. She was so beautiful! Even with her wet hair plastered to her face and head, she was beautiful! This was no witch! His mother had been wrong! His father was wrong! Frank was wrong! They were all wrong! This was no witch! This was a beautiful and gentle girl, and he had killed her! He and Frank had killed her! They had defiled her and killed her!

"Please, please wake up!" he begged. "Don't be daid, please don't be daid!"

Overcome by remorse and nearly out of his senses with fear and grief, Jemmy frantically rubbed her cheeks, then leaned over and kissed her on the mouth again and again and again. But she did not move. He buried his head between her breasts and sobbed helplessly.

"I never meant t' hurt yuh. Yo gotta b'lieve that. I never meant t' hurt yuh."

He lay down next to her and pressed his warm tear-wet face against hers. Again he touched her breasts. Again he reached his hand down between her legs. No, it wasn't right! He had never meant it to be like this. Again he rubbed her cheeks. "Please, please, yo got t' wake up!"

Suddenly he noticed that she had blood on her face. Where had it come from? It had come from his hand! How had he gotten blood on his hand? Quickly he scrambled to a kneeling position and examined her body. Pulling back her torn dress, he discovered the blood between her legs. He had not seen it before. He looked in horror at the blood on her legs, on her face, and on his fingers. He remembered what his father had said about witches' blood. Desperately he wiped the blood from his fingers onto her dress, then immediately felt ashamed for having done so. This was no witch.

Suddenly he heard Frank groan. Jemmy jumped to his feet and began pulling on his intoxicated brother. "Get up, Frank, get up! We gotta get outa here! We kilt her!"

Groggy-eyed, Frank looked down at Sarah, then up at Jemmy. "She's daid?"

"Yeah, she's daid! We kilt her!"

"Yo mean, *yo* kilt her. Yo pulled the rope too tight."

"*Yo* was a-holdin' the rope when she died!"

Frank tried to bring Jemmy into focus. "I was? Yo mean *yo* was on top of her when she croaked? Yo must a-been too rough wit her, Jemmy. I told yuh, yo gotta be real gentle wit women." He belched, then shook his head and laughed. "Oo-ee! I never knowed yo had it in yuh, li'l brother. Jemmy Hicks, mighty lover! Kilt the first woman he ever made love to! What a man!"

"Yo's drunk, Frank!"

"An' mighty lucky for yo that I is, or I'd a-got to her first."

"Yo's sick!"

"Yeah, that too, li'l brother, that too." He leaned over the edge of the rock and threw up into the stream. "Oh, that's better."

Slowly he raised himself to a squatting position. "Oh, my haid!" he groaned, pressing the palms of his hands into his eye sockets. When he felt quite sure that both feet were planted firmly beneath him, he slowly straightened himself up and looked around. "How'd I get up here?"

Jemmy did not answer. He watched as Frank shuffled cautiously to the edge of the rock, paused for a moment, then took another step and fell two feet into the water. Picking himself up, Frank waded to the bank.

"Whar yo gwine?" asked Jemmy.

"I reckon I'se a-gwine home, if'n I can find it. Our work here is done."

"What about her? We cain't just leave her here."

"Why not?"

"Somebody'll find her."

"Nobody'll find her, an' so what if they do?"

612

"She's not a witch, Frank."

"I never thought she was. That was just some crazy notion that Ma an' Pa had."

Jemmy watched as Frank groped his way down along the edge of the tumbling stream and disappeared into the woods. In the distance Jemmy could hear him singing.

"Damn yo, Frank!" he yelled after him, "damn yo!" He jumped into the water and picked up a stone from the bottom of the stream. He hurled it in the direction of the trees where he had last seen Frank. The stone clattered harmlessly on the rocks below. Then Jemmy broke. Overwhelmed by rage and grief and shame, he fell on his knees in the water and wept. "Oh, Gawd, why?" he cried. "Why?"

The words echoed off the side of the mountain and came back to him, as if to mock him. He climbed back onto the rock and knelt down once again beside Sarah's lifeless body. "Please, Sarah, please wake up!" Sobbing uncontrollably he stroked her wet matted hair away from her face and pressed his trembling mouth against her forehead. "I loved yuh," he sobbed. "Yo never knowed it, but I loved yuh."

When the first rush of emotion had spent itself, he stood up again. He looked down the mountain. He couldn't go home, not now, not ever. He had just killed someone. Sooner or later the county sheriff would find out and he would be arrested for murder. If Frank hadn't been so drunk, he'd have realized that he couldn't go home again either. There was nothing to go home to anyway. For the past two and a half years, his thoughts and dreams of Sarah had been the only things that had made his miserable life worth living. And now she was dead–and *he* had killed her. There was nothing to live for now. He turned and looked up the mountain toward the waterfall, toward the place where Sarah had been sitting when they had found her. As he stared at the waterfall, an idea suddenly entered his tormented brain. All at once he knew what he had to do. The only way to make this unbearable raging and grieving stop was to kill himself. The only way to atone for the sin he had committed against this innocent creature was to take his own life. An eye for an eye, a tooth for a tooth.

He grabbed the rope that lay near Sarah's head and rushed madly over the rocks toward the falls. Feverishly, tearing at shrubs and roots, he clawed his way up the steep wall of rocks. When he reached the top of the falls, he leaned out around a hemlock tree growing on the very brink of the chasm and peered over the edge. He watched as the water rushing past his feet plunged over the edge and was pounded into white foam in the great cauldron of rocks below. In the distance he could see Sarah's body stretched out on the large flat boulder, where he and Frank had dragged her and raped her and killed her. The sight of her desecrated body caused another wave of grief and shame to rush through him. Feverishly he threw one end of the rope over the hemlock branch above his head and secured it. He slipped the noose around his neck and pulled it tight. Again he peered over the edge. It would be so easy. It would all be over in a matter of seconds. All he had to do was jump.

"Jemmy, don't!"

Who said that? Someone had said "Jemmy, don't." Even over the din of his own inner raging he had heard it quite distinctly. It had sounded very close, almost like it had come from inside his own head. Nervously he looked around. Someone was watching him, but who was it? He loosened the noose from around his neck and slipped it off over his head. He had seen no one yet. No one was behind him. Where had the voice come from? As he turned to look across the stream to the other bank, he saw something that nearly caused his heart to leap out of his mouth. There, floating in the air out over the falls, directly in front of him, was Sarah! She was more beautiful than he had ever seen her. Her long shining hair flowed out behind her head. It was not wet as it had been just a few minutes before. And her eyes were open now—and she was looking directly at *him*! He could see no evil in her eyes, only kindness and love—love for *him*! She was looking at him and smiling. Her smile—her beautiful radiant smile—was smiling at *him*! Without taking his eyes off her for even an instant, he reached for the trunk of the hemlock tree and wrapped his arms tightly around it. He did not want to take a chance on falling into the water in his dazed condition and being swept over the falls. He continued to stare, his eyes riveted on the vision of loveliness floating in the air before him, until it dissolved slowly into the mist. It was not until it had vanished completely that Jemmy began to breathe again. What had he seen? It *was* Sarah, but it *wasn't* Sarah. It was not the same Sarah he had just left on the rock below. This Sarah was not wearing a torn wet dress. This Sarah had been wearing a bright, shining, shimmering white robe. And her hair was not plastered down. Her hair had flowed luxuriantly out from her head in long streams. But the face was the same. It was Sarah's face, and she had been looking at him with the tenderest possible expression. Jemmy knew in his heart—he *knew*—that she had forgiven him.

For the next half hour he clung to the tree, unable to move, thinking about what he had seen and what it meant. The voice had said "Jemmy, don't," just as he had been about to jump from the ledge. He knew now that the voice had come from Sarah. She didn't want him to kill himself, of that much he was certain. Her words had said it, her eyes had said it, her smile had said it. But what *was* he to do? He had still killed her. There was no changing that. He could not un-do that which he had already done. At least he had killed the Sarah down there on the rock. She was still down there, wasn't she? He leaned out from behind the tree and looked down over the falls to be sure. Yes, her body was still on the rock just as he had left it. What had he seen then? Was it her soul on its way up to Heaven?

At last the blood began to return to his arms and legs. When he felt he had sufficient strength and control over his body, he released his bear hug on the tree and stepped back from the edge of the falls. He had no desire to kill himself now, by design or otherwise. Slowly, nervously, he climbed back down the side of the waterfall. When he reached the bottom, he stepped out onto the rock in the pool of water, the rock on which Sarah had been sitting when they found her, and picked up her coat. Then, returning once again to the rock on which her body lay, he listened again for the sound of breathing, felt again for a heartbeat, then placed the coat over her. With tears running down his face, he again kissed her full on the mouth. Then, standing up, he again turned toward the top of the falls. "Come back!" he screamed. "Please come back!"

Again the words echoed back to him. For the next several minutes he stood and watched the top of the falls, where he had seen the vision. But now he saw nothing.

"I'se sorry," he sobbed, a note of finality in his voice.

Turning quickly, he jumped down off the rock and plunged through the water to the bank. Then, with his mind still in a state of wild confusion, he took off running down the side of the mountain in pursuit of Frank.

"If hit ain't bad enough that she's already missed breakfast an' dinner," grumbled Hester as she placed the food on the table, "now she seems to a-forgot about supper as well. You'd think she'd be grateful that the Good Lord has blessed us with so much bounty . . . Whar could she be, Nathan? Hit's a-gwine t' be dark soon."

Nathan thought for a moment of responding, but decided not to. He knew his wife well enough to know that she was more anxious than angry. He himself was becoming a little anxious. It was, as Hester had said, almost dark, and though there would be better than a three-quarter moon rising, it was not like Sarah to be late for Sunday supper. She had always made it a point to be home from her Sunday walks in plenty of time for supper, as if to compensate in part for having missed Sunday dinner.

Nathan had been a little concerned about Sarah all day. She had seemed unusually sad and subdued on the way to church, so subdued in fact that she had not said a word, had not even responded to a question he had asked her. Then, after church, when he had asked her if there was anything wrong, she had been evasive, had said once again that she was worried about Otis, but nothing more definitive. Now, as he thought about how distracted she had seemed when she left the church to go off on her walk, he could easily believe that she may very well have forgotten about supper.

"If she's not back by the time we finish supper," said Nathan at last, halfway into the meal, "I'll go down to the creek an' look for her."

After supper Nathan walked down through the fields toward the creek. It was nearly dark now and the moon had already risen above the mountains. When he reached the water's edge, he called Sarah's name several times, but aside from the sound of the rushing water splashing on the rocks and lapping at the bank, he received no reply.

Returning to the house, he was met by Elizabeth at the door. He could tell by the anxious expression on her face that she too was becoming alarmed by Sarah's absence. "I'm gonna run down to Isaac an' Jacob's," he said, as much to ease his own mind as to comfort Elizabeth. "Maybe she went down there."

"Why would she go down thar?" asked Hester, the irritation in her voice increasing as she became more anxious. "She wouldn't a-gone down thar without tellin' us."

"It won't hurt t' make sure," replied Nathan, as calmly as possible.

He hitched Blackie to the wagon, procured a lantern with a reflector from the barn, and set off for Isaac and Jacob's. When he reached the Wicker farm, he decided to go to Jacob's house first, as that was where Sarah was likely to be if she was there at all. Receiving no answer at the door, he walked around the barn and across the barnyard to Isaac's house. The light in the window and the sound of voices emanating from within told him that the old house was not as deserted as Jacob's had been. He knocked at the door and Martha opened it.

"Why, Nathan, what brings you around this time of night?"

Nathan removed his hat and stepped inside. "Sarah went walkin' after church an' hasn't come home yet. I was wond'rin' if she might a-come here."

"Nope, she ain't a-been here. I ain't seen her since church."

"Is Isaac here?"

"Isaac an' Jacob are both here. They're in the parlor." Then, drawing herself up close to Nathan's ear, she whispered, "Harriet Ogle's here too."

Nathan entered the parlor and Isaac and Jacob rose to greet him. "Ev'nin', Miss Ogle," said Nathan politely, nodding to the widow seated on the sofa next to Jacob. Then he turned to his brothers-in-law. "Sarah didn't come home for supper. I thought maybe she might a-come here."

"No, ain't seen her," replied Isaac, "ain't seen her since church."

Jacob shook his head to signify that he had not seen her either.

"Well," said Nathan, "I didn't think she'd come here without tellin' us, but I just wanted t' make sure. She'll prob'bly be home by the time I get back." He turned to leave.

"Now hold on just a danged minute," called Isaac after him. "If my fav-o-rite niece is missin', we got t' find her. I'll go with yuh." He went to the kitchen and removed his hat and coat from a hook on the wall.

"I'll go with yuh too," said Jacob. He turned to Harriet Ogle, patted her hand, and said a few words to her that neither Nathan nor Isaac was able to overhear.

"Why don't yuh come with us in the truck?" suggested Isaac to Nathan as they walked across the barnyard in the moonlight. "You can come back for your horse an' wagon in the mornin'. I don't know how yuh found your way here in the dark anyway."

"I think I *will* ago with yuh," replied Nathan. "It ain't 'cause I can't find my way home in the dark though. And even if *I* couldn't, *Blackie* could. More'n I can say for your beat-up old truck here. Just try drivin' this thing five miles from home an' leavin' it set. Just see how long it takes *it* to find its way home."

"You mean t' tell me that that horse of yourn can find its way home in the dark by itself?" asked Isaac skeptically, as he, Jacob, and Nathan climbed into the cab of the truck.

" 'Course he can," replied Nathan in a tone of voice which expressed surprise that Isaac would even think to question his word.

"You're pullin' my leg."

"Go home, Blackie! Go home!" shouted Nathan as they rattled out across the barnyard past the horse and wagon. He looked back as they roared out the lane. "Here he comes!"

"Get outa here."

When they reached Nathan's, they found that Sarah had still not returned and that Hester now had her hands full trying to restrain Elizabeth. At the sight of Nathan, Elizabeth broke free of Hester's grasp and rushed to him. "Where is she, Nathan?" she cried hysterically. "Where is she? We've got to find her!"

"I don't know where she is, Elizabeth, but we're gonna find her. Isaac an' Jacob are here too."

"I'm going to go with you!"

From behind Elizabeth's back, Hester signalled to Nathan by shaking her head in disapproval, but, after a moment's consideration, Nathan nodded his consent. "Isaac, come with me. We'll round up some lanterns."

A few minutes later they returned to the house with four freshly-refueled lanterns. "Hester," said Nathan, turning to his wife, "you'd best stay here in case she comes back. If she *does* come back, fire a shot, so we won't be out there lookin' for her all night for nuthin'."

Hester watched from the top of the hill as the four spots of light jiggled and bounced down through the fields and finally disappeared amongst the trees lining the creek bank. When she could see them no more, she returned to the house.

"This ain't gonna be easy," said Nathan, as the search party of four began fighting its way through the tangle of rhododendron that grew thick as brambles along the creek's bank. Again he called Sarah's name. Again there was no reply.

After nearly an hour of incessant struggle against the relentless rhododendron and the treacherous terrain, Nathan began to see the pointlessness of what they were doing. "I think we might be smart t' wait til mornin'," he said at last, an unusual note of despair in his voice. "For all we know, she might not even be out here. She might be standin' in the middle of some field somewhere, starin' up at the moon an' thinkin'."

"No!" cried Elizabeth. "We've got to find her." Recklessly she pushed past Nathan and forged ahead.

Nathan turned to Isaac and Jacob and sighed. "I reckon we better follow her."

Before Nathan could catch up to her, he heard Elizabeth scream. The scream was followed immediately by the sound of glass smashing on rock, and suddenly, where there had been a light, now there was only more darkness.

"Elizabeth, where are you?" shouted Nathan in alarm. He fought his way through the rhododendron to the spot along the water's edge where he had last seen the light. He was soon joined by Isaac and Jacob. All three men held their lanterns over the dark water, but they saw no sign of Elizabeth. They proceeded down along the bank.

"Thar she is!" called Jacob.

Nathan rushed to the sound of Jacob's voice and looked in the direction in which Jacob was pointing. He saw Elizabeth about fifteen feet out from the bank, clinging to a rock in the midst of the dark rushing water. As Isaac and Jacob held the lanterns, Nathan jumped into the water, and, struggling against the current, made his way out to her. He found her coughing up water and gasping for air. He waited a few moments until she had recovered herself, then picked her up and carried her back to the bank.

"We've got t' get her back to the house," he said, as Jacob helped her onto the bank, "before she catches pneumonia." As he climbed onto the bank himself he grimaced in pain and clutched his back.

"No, Nathan!" she screamed in protest, "we've got to find her!"

"Listen, Elizabeth," said Nathan, trying desperately to think of something reassuring to say, "Isaac an' I will keep lookin', but I want you t' let Jacob take you back to the house. You're wet an' cold..."

"No!" she screamed. She made an attempt to rush past Nathan again, but this time he restrained her. He encircled her with his arms and pulled her tightly against his chest so as to prevent further movement.

"Listen to me!" he pleaded, his mouth pressed against her ear, "I love Sarah—we all do—an' I promise you we're gonna find her. But we love *you* too, an' we don't want t' lose *you* tryin' t' find *her*. I want you t' let Jacob take you back to the house."

Nathan held her as he waited for her consent. Finally she stopped struggling to free herself and began sobbing quietly into his shoulder. "All right, Nathan, I'll go back to the house—and I'll pray. Hester and I will pray. When we lived up in the mountains, whenever Sarah was lost—or whenever Daniel and I *thought* she was lost—Daniel would pray. He'd always pray—and she'd always come back to us."

As Nathan continued to hold Elizabeth in his arms, the three men exchanged surprised looks amongst themselves. It was the first time since Daniel's death that Elizabeth had shown any indication that she remembered anything at all of the eight years that she and Daniel and Sarah had lived in the mountains.

When he was satisfied that she was sufficiently calm and would not do anything reckless, Nathan released her into Jacob's custody. As Jacob led her back up along the creek bank through the wilderness of rhododendron through which they had come, Nathan turned to Isaac. "She remembers, Isaac! She remembers!"

Isaac nodded. "She remembers all right. I ain't so sure hit's such a good thang though."

"Why do you say that?"

"Well, if hit was Dan'l's death that caused her t' lose half her mind the first time, what's she gwine t' do if somethin's happened to Sarah?"

"Don't even think such a thing, Isaac. We'll find her. We've got to. I promised Elizabeth we would."

"We ain't a-gwine t' find her out here tonight, that's for sure."

"No, but we'll look a little longer, 'cause I promised Elizabeth we would. If Sarah still hasn't come back by mornin', we'll organize a search party. We'll get every able-bodied man in Rushin' Creek, an' we'll keep lookin' til we find her."

They searched another hour and shouted Sarah's name until they were both hoarse, then made their way back up along the creek bank to Nathan's farm. As they climbed the hill under the moonlit sky, Isaac noticed that Nathan was laboring. "You gone an' hurt your back ag'in?"

"Yeah. I must a-strained it when I pulled Elizabeth out of the creek."

"Here, let me help you," said Isaac, offering himself for Nathan to lean on as they neared the top of the hill.

"Thanks, old man. Maybe you could do me another favor too?"

"What's that?"

"Unhitch Blackie for me an' put him in the barn."

Isaac looked up and saw the horse and wagon standing in the driveway. "Well, I'll be danged!"

Isaac and Jacob arrived at first light the next morning, hoping to be greeted with the news that Sarah had returned during the night. Nathan, regretfully, was not able to oblige them. Instead he offered them a plan.

"Isaac, I think we should form two search parties. Jacob an' I will start here an' work *down* the creek. You go into town, get Walter, Henry, an' anybody else you can round up, an' start at the dam an' work your way up t' meet us."

"Sounds like a reasonable plan," said Isaac, "but we should have a signal in case one of us finds her?"

"You got your shotgun?"

"Yup."

"Okay, I'll take mine. We'll fire a shot if we find her."

"No good," objected Isaac. "I might haf t' shoot a rattler or somethin'. How about two shots if we find her?"

"Couldn't you just step around the rattler?" protested Nathan. "All right then, two shots if we find her."

"An' three shots if hit's good news," suggested Isaac.

Grimly Nathan nodded his head in consent, but he would have preferred not to consider the possibility that Isaac's last suggestion had implied: that the news might be something other than good.

Nathan watched Isaac's truck disappear out the lane, then he and Jacob made their way down to the creek and resumed the search they had begun the night before. Even in the daylight their progress along the steep, thickly-wooded bank of the creek was slow, but at least they were able to see where they were going, something they had not been able to do the night before, and it was reassuring to know that if Sarah *was* out there along the creek somewhere—if she had slipped and broken a leg or knocked herself out or something—they might at least be able to see her before they actually fell over her.

Nathan found himself in almost constant pain as he labored over the uneven terrain, but the thought of quitting did not enter his mind. After two hours, as he and Jacob neared the gorge, they heard a shot ring out from downstream. They looked at each other and listened nervously for a second shot. Had Isaac shot at a snake or some other hapless creature that had chanced to cross his path, or was this his signal? Would they be able to hear a second or third shot over the roar of the gorge?

Finally they heard a second shot. They listened for a third. It did not come. Nathan felt his heart sink. Two shots meant they had found her, but *only* two shots meant the news was not good. Perhaps the two shots they had heard were not a signal. They had not been fired in rapid succession. Perhaps Isaac, despite his self-proclaimed hunting prowess, had found it necessary to fire two shots to dispatch the snake or frog or muskrat that had threatened his life. Or perhaps there *had* been three shots, but he and Jacob had not heard the *first* over the roar of the water rushing through the gorge.

But try as he may, Nathan was unable to convince himself that there was any reason to be optimistic. With his heart heavy with dread, he hurried downstream. He was followed closely by Jacob.

Even if Nathan's mind had been free of anxiety, even if his back had been free of pain, he would have found the task of getting around the gorge an extremely difficult one. In his present condition, he found it well nigh impossible. Jacob, despite his comparatively sound back, was not able to render much assistance, as he too had difficulty keeping his footing on the steep hillside. However, after several close calls, both men succeeded in getting beyond the gorge and onto safer terrain. Several hundred yards below the gorge they saw Isaac and a number of other men–Walter Lehman, Henry Bryson, and Charlie Cole among them–standing in a circle on the creek bank and studying something in their midst.

"What is it?" shouted Nathan as soon as he and Jacob were within earshot of the larger party.

Isaac shouted something back, but the only word that Nathan was able to make out was the final word: "body."

"Oh my God!" cried Nathan, turning to Jacob, "they found her body!"

Trembling with emotion, he drew nearer. As he did so, the circle parted, and there, lying on the rocks, he saw the body.

"Hit's Frank Hicks," said Isaac. "He's drowned."

Nathan breathed an immense sigh of relief. For the next two minutes he stood staring at the body, as he tried to catch his breath and collect his thoughts. Finally he looked up at Isaac. "I think it might be a good idea if I go have me a talk with Wesley Hicks... Mind if I borrow your truck?"

"Well, I'll be danged," exclaimed Isaac. "I never thought I'd see the day... Hit's down at Henry's. The key's in it." He watched as Nathan hobbled off in the direction of the mill. "Hey!" he shouted after him, "can you drive?"

"We'll soon find out," Nathan shouted back.

Isaac grinned, then assuming a more stern expression, turned to the others. "C'mon, fellas, we got work t' do. My fav-o-rite niece just might be out here somewhar, an' we got t' find her."

Nathan roared up through Wesley Hicks' yard, scattering chickens and litter in all directions. "Whoa!" he shouted. "Whoa, you stupid beast!" He hit the brake and the clutch and brought the truck to a stop only a few inches from Wesley's porch. He swung open the door and jumped out. Immediately the truck lurched forward and smashed into the corner post of the porch, bringing part of the porch roof down upon its hood.

"What the hell . . . ?" cried a startled voice from inside the house. The door to the house swung open and Wesley came stumbling out.

"Sorry, Wesley," said Nathan as he jumped back into the cab of the truck, "I forgot t' take it out of gear." He looked up to find Wesley staring in wide-eyed disbelief at the damage that Isaac's truck had just done to his porch. "I'm afraid I've brought bad news, Wesley."

"I can see that, plain as day. Now I'd be grateful to yuh if yuh'd just leave b'fore yuh knock the rest of muh house down."

"I'm sorry about your porch, Wesley," said Nathan, getting out of the truck once again. "I'll help you fix it when I get the time. But right now I've got a more important matter on my mind. My niece Sarah didn't come home last night, an' I thought that you just might know somethin' about it."

"I don't know nuthin' 'bout your niece, Nathan Andersson. Now go away an' let me be."

"Do you know where your boys are?"

"The young'un's in school. I don't know whar Frank is. He didn't come home last night. Mebbe he run away like all the rest of them. Good riddance, I say."

"Frank's dead, Wesley. Drowned. We just found his body in the creek down below the gorge."

Wesley was silent for a moment as he mulled over this piece of news, but if he was at all shocked or saddened by it, he did not show it. "If Frank wants t' drown hisself in the creek, that's his bus'ness. That ain't got nuthin' t' do wit me."

Nathan was surprised that even Wesley could be so unmoved by the death of a son. "Well, maybe it's got somethin' t' do with you an' maybe it don't. If I find out that somethin's happened to Sarah, an' if I even *have a suspicion* that either of your boys had anything t' do with it, I'm holdin' you responsible. You're the one who's been fillin' their heads with this nonsense about Sarah bein' a witch."

"She *is* a witch an' so's her mother."

Nathan glared at him. "Listen, Wesley. If anything's happened to that girl, it's not her *or* her mother you're gonna haf t' worry about. It's my wife, 'cause she's gonna be comin' after you with a shotgun. An' I'm gonna be right behind her."

Nathan climbed back into the cab of Isaac's truck and released the brake. He tried one gear after another until he finally found reverse, then backed away, sending the part of the porch resting on the hood crashing to the ground.

When he came to the crossroads at Lehman's Store, he stopped and looked in both directions. He was about to make a right turn and go back to Bryson's mill to rejoin the search party, but at the last moment changed his mind. He turned left and headed the other way. Before rejoining the others, he wanted to talk to one more person. He would take a small detour over to the high school in Haynesville and talk to Jemmy Hicks.

It was late in the afternoon before Nathan caught up to the others. In his absence the search party had been up and down both banks of the creek between the dam and his farm and, aside from an empty whiskey jug, had found nothing of any consequence.

"What'd Wesley have t' say?" asked Isaac.

"He says he don't know a thing. Normally I wouldn't trust Wesley Hicks as far as I could spit, an' I ain't so sure I trust him now. But until I have a reason t' doubt him, I guess I'll haf t' take him at his word . . .

"I talked to his youngest boy, Jemmy, too. Drove over to the high school an' had the principal call him out of class. Nearly scared him to death. He's the most skittish boy you'd ever wanna meet. Always has been. I tried talkin' to him once before, after church, about a year ago. He nearly wet his pants. He says he don't know nuthin' either. He says he remembers seein' Sarah in church yesterday mornin', but he ain't seen her since. I don't *think* he'd lie to me.

"I didn't tell him about Frank. I figured his father could do that–if Wesley can be bothered to remember. Could be that Frank was the only one that could a-told us anything about Sarah, an' we ain't even sure that *he* knew anything. We don't even know for sure that anything's even *happened* to Sarah. Until we find *her* . . ."

Isaac nodded. "Well, we'll just haf t' keep a-lookin' til we find her. Tomorruh we'll recruit us some more volunteers an' begin combin' the woods. We'll turn over ever' leaf an' stone if we haf to . . . By the way, how'd you make out with the truck?"

"I suffered no permanent injuries."

"I wasn't axin' about *you*. I was axin' about *my truck*."

"I'm afraid it's got a few more dents in the hood."

"Oh?" queried Isaac, one eyebrow raised.

"It jumped onto Wesley's porch when my back was turned, an' the porch roof sort of fell on it. I told Wesley that you'd be around one day soon t' help him fix it."

Both men attempted to laugh, but neither succeeded. Their unflagging senses of humor, which had seen them through many crises, including the darkest years of the Depression, failed them now. This was one crisis that could not be ameliorated by humor. Both knew that the longer it took to find Sarah, the less chance they'd have of finding her alive.

The next morning the search began again, but though the number in their search party had doubled, when darkness fell at the end of the day, they still had found nothing.

Sarah felt herself to be floating, but she could not be sure whether it was she that was moving, or whether she was fixed at a point in space and everything else was moving past her. It all had a dream-like quality. She seemed to be passing through a vast expanse of murky darkness. Nothing was clear. The forms that passed before her were shadowy, vapory. Suddenly, from out of the darkness, a face appeared before her.

"Daddy!" she cried.

Then another.

"Aunt Emily!"

The two faces hovered before her for a moment, then were gone. As she continued to drift through the twilight gloom, she became aware of a point of light shining in the distance. It flickered for a moment, then it too was gone.

19

A VERY LONG JOURNEY

Time no longer existed. Awareness existed only as a series of disjointed impressions. Indistinct images of the two faces continued to appear and disappear. The patch of light continued to brighten, then fade. She seemed to be drifting, dream-like, through space.

The next impression of which she had any clear awareness was of a large luminous spheroid, like a moon or planet, hovering in the distance, suspended like a jewel in the blackness of space. At the same time, she felt herself moving toward it, slowly at first, then faster. She continued to accelerate. She was moving faster now, much faster, as though suddenly caught in the planet's gravitational pull. The sphere was rapidly coming closer, filling more and more of her field of vision. She was falling, plunging through space, heading directly for the planet! She couldn't stop, couldn't slow down! It was completely filling her field of vision now! She was rapidly approaching the planet's surface! For one dizzying, terrifying, panic-filled moment, she awaited the sudden, terrible impact and the annihilation that was certain to follow. But the impact did not come. Instead, she seemed to enter right *into* the sphere. Deeper and deeper into the sphere she plunged. Like a breath of air being exhaled into the atmosphere, the atoms of her body seemed to be filtering themselves into the spaces between the atoms of the much greater body. She was dissolving into the sphere, becoming one with it. Then the process stopped and everything was still. Her being had been completely absorbed by the greater being. When she realized that she was still alive, still conscious, a feeling of euphoria rushed through her.

She opened her eyes. It was light. As she struggled to bring things into focus, she became aware once again of a face hovering before her. It was a man's face, but it was not her father's.

"Who are you?" she whispered weakly, unable to find her voice.

The face smiled at her, but did not respond. Then it disappeared.

She continued to watch the space where the face had been. As the images became clearer she realized that she was staring at a ceiling. A moment later the face returned, but this time there was another face beside it, the face of a woman.

"So you've decided t' stay with us, have you?"

Sarah looked around. "Where am I?" she asked, confused.

"You're in Annie Whitehead's house."

Sarah turned toward the face from which the voice had come. It was an old, wrinkled face and it was peeking at her through curtains of long white hair. "Who are you?"

"I'm Annie Whitehead. You can call me Annie."

Sarah could now see that the old woman was very small, less than five feet in height, and that the curtains of white hair hung all the way down to her waist. "How did I get here?"

"Edgar brung you here."

Sarah turned toward the other face. It was the face of a young man of about twenty, a long, thin face flanked by two large protruding ears. The broad sheepish grin on the face extended from the lobe of one large ear to the lobe of the other. Suddenly, quite unexpectedly, the young man stuck out his tongue at her, then quickly retracted it and smiled again.

"Don't mind Edgar," said the old woman, apologizing for her companion. "He cain't talk. All his life folks a-been a-axin' him if the cat's got his tongue. Now he just shows them his tongue first thang, so's they don't haf t' ax."

Sarah looked out the window. "It's still light. I've got to get home before dark."

"Hit just got light," said Annie. "Hit's mornin'."

"Oh no!" cried Sarah, trying to force herself up onto her elbows. "You mean I've been here all night? My Uncle Nathan will be worried sick."

"You been here *three* nights. Hit's Wentsd'y mornin' . . . Now, you rest. You're in no condition t' move."

630

"Annie, I've got to get home," protested Sarah with as much vigor as she could muster. "My Uncle Nathan will think I'm dead."

"An' he wouldn't be too far wrong neither. You nearly *was* daid when Edgar found you. You was scarcely breathin', an' for a while thar your heart had stopped altogether . . .

"Edgar an' me was over on the north side of the mountain diggin' gin-shen when Edgar heared some shoutin' from down in the holler. I didn't hear nuthin', but Edgar, he's got real good ears. He got real excited an' kept a-pointin' down the holler. Finally I told him t' go an' see what it was. He was gone for about an hour. When he come back, he was a-haulin' you. I could see that you needed doctorin' bad, so I decided t' bring you back to the house straight away. Edgar thar, he carried you the whole five miles. If it hadn't a-been for him, you'd be a-talkin' to Jesus right this minute, instead of to old Annie Whitehead here."

Sarah directed her eyes to Edgar and tried to speak. She succeeded, but the words were barely audible. "As much as I'd like to talk to Jesus and ask him a few questions, I'm grateful. Thank you, Edgar."

Edgar was still smiling at her with his big childlike grin.

"You'll haf t' forgive Edgar," said Annie, apologizing once again for her companion. "Hit's not ever' day he finds a girl as purty as you just a-lyin' in the woods. He's scarce took his eyes off you since he found you. Once you get better, I expect he's prob'bly a-gwine t' want t' keep you . . . Go away now, Edgar. Leave her be for a while."

Edgar did not move. Annie turned again to Sarah. "This Uncle Nathan you keep a-talkin' about. Would that be Nathan Andersson?"

"Yes. Do you know him?"

"Know *of* him. Know that he came down from Ohio twenny, twenny-five years ago, bought the old John Hyatt place over in Rushin' Creek, married Hester Wicker. Never met him though, wouldn't know him t' see him. Knew Hester though. Knew all the Wicker children. I used t' live over that way. I was the one who birthed them an' looked after them when they took sick."

"Then you must have known my father."
"Which one might he be?"
"Daniel."
"Oh yes, Dan'l, the baby. Moved up north after the war, came back a few years ago, bought the old Jeremiah Puckett place. I heared he was kilt by a bear."

Sarah nodded sadly. She tried once again to get up out of the bed. "I think you're right, Annie. I'm in no condition to move. But I've got to get word to my Uncle Nathan that I'm all right."

"You know how t' write?"
"Yes."
"Can you move your fingers?"

Sarah flexed the fingers of her right hand. "Yes, a little."

"Then why don't you write your Uncle Nathan a note? Edgar can take it to him."

"That's a good idea, Annie. Do you have a piece of paper and a pencil?"

"I don't write myself, but I reckon I can skeer somethin' up." She went behind the curtain into the next room and returned shortly with a scrap of paper, a bottle of dark fluid, and a quill. "I reckon pokeberry juice and a goose feather'll do."

Sarah lifted herself up onto one elbow. "I'll tell Uncle Nathan where I am, that I'm all right, and that I'll be home in a few days."

She wrote the note, folded it, and handed it to Annie.

"Edgar," said Annie, addressing herself to the young man with the big ears and the silly grin, "I want you t' take this to Nathan Andersson over in Rushin' Creek. He lives at the old John Hyatt place right along the creek. Do you know whar I mean?"

Edgar nodded his head enthusiastically. He took the folded note and smiled once again at Sarah, this time with a smile even more egregious than the one he had previously exhibited, if that were possible. He was obviously pleased to be able to perform this small service for her. He bowed to her several times, then turned and hurried through the curtain and out the door.

"He's a good boy," said Annie. "You can trust him to deliver your note to your Uncle Nathan. Now you stop your worryin' an' get some sleep."

"Why can't he talk, Annie?"

Annie could see that her young patient was not about to sleep. She sat down on the edge of the bed. "Don't know. He's never talked. When he was a young'un, his folks figgered he'd start talkin' when he got older. He's got a perfectly good tongue, as you saw for yourself. But he never did. I don't think he ever will talk now. He's got no need. He gets along just fine the way he is . . . Ever'body likes Edgar. He's like an overgrown child . . ."

"How old is he?"

"Nigh onto twenty-two years . . . Besides, I ain't so sure he ain't better off *not* talkin'. Sometimes talkin' gets folks in trouble."

Sarah nodded her head in agreement. "How long has he lived with you?"

"Oh, he don't live with me. He still lives with his folks, on a farm down at the foot of the mountain. He just helps me out from time t' time, mostly on weekends. 'Course, since you been here, he's been a-hangin' around more than usual. But still, he's been a-gwine home ever' night and a-comin' back in the mornin's."

Sarah had so many questions to ask the old woman she didn't know where to begin. "You said you birthed all the Wicker children and took care of them when they were sick. Are you a doctor?"

Annie smiled. "I'm what they call a granny woman. Before thar was doctors, us granny women was all thar was. We birthed all the babes an' looked after folks when they took sick. I still do some birthin' an' some doctorin'—mostly for older folks who ain't never learned t' trust city doctors, an' for folks who live way back in the mountains. You can see some of my med'cines dryin' above the fireplace thar."

Sarah turned her head in the direction of the fireplace and saw there the patch of light that had flickered in and out of her consciousness over the course of the past three nights. Dangling from a rope stretched along the mantel of the fireplace were bunches of drying leaves and roots.

"That reminds me," said Annie, getting up from the edge of the bed, "I brewed you some tea. Now that you're awake, I want you t' drink some."

She went to the fireplace and swung out the blackened kettle that had been suspended above the flames. She dipped a ladle into the kettle and transferred some of its steaming contents into a cup. Returning to the bed, she set the cup on the window sill above the headboard. "We'll let it cool for a bit, while I get you propped up."

She lifted Sarah's head and pushed another pillow under it. When the tea had cooled sufficiently she held the cup to Sarah's lips. Sarah took a sip and immediately grimaced. "What *is* this stuff?"

Annie laughed. "Just a li'l of this and a li'l of that . . . some black snakeroot . . . some comfrey . . . a tetch of purple foxglove . . . I been a-drippin' it down your gullet for three days now an' you never complained before." Again she pressed the cup to Sarah's lips.

Sarah took another sip and again grimaced. "Purple foxglove? Isn't that poisonous?"

"Now, rest easy, child," replied the old woman, "I said, just a tetch. You don't think we hauled you all the way back here just so's we could p'ison you, do you? If we wanted you t' die, we could a-left you whar we found you–saved ourselves a lot of trouble. Now trust old Annie here an' drink your tea."

As Sarah slowly sipped the tea, Annie studied her face. "Mind if I ax *you* a question?"

"No," replied Sarah.

"What's your name?"

"My name is Sarah," she answered, still grimacing, "Sarah Wicker."

634

By afternoon Sarah was ready to get up. She waited for Annie to go outside, then pushed aside her covers and sat up on the edge of the bed. The first thing she noticed was that she was no longer wearing the dress she had worn to church. She was wearing a dress that Annie had apparently made from an old feedsack. At once her mind flashed back to the incident at the waterfall and to the feedsack that had been pulled over her by her attackers, the feedsack inside of which she had been trapped for so many terrifying minutes—the feedsack that had very nearly been her death shroud. She shuddered at the thought.

She stood up and began to move slowly about the room. The dress was comfortable enough, but as it was considerably shorter than the dresses to which she was accustomed, she found herself tugging at the hem, in an attempt to cover more of her legs. She wondered what her Aunt Hester would think of a dress that stopped several inches short of the knees!

After briefly exploring the room she was in, she pushed aside the curtain and peeked into the next room. She was surprised by what she found. The few bunches of leaves and roots drying above the fireplace were as nothing compared to the forest of dried leaves, roots, and flowers she now found suspended from the ceiling in the room behind the curtain. As she walked slowly around the perimeter of this inverted forest of dried and drying vegetation, she noticed that the shelves on the back wall were lined with dozens of jars, bottles, and tins, all filled with strange-looking substances and all unlabeled.

Just then Annie came in from outside carrying an armload of firewood. "I see you found my med'cine cab'net," she said, smiling.

Sarah continued to peruse the contents of Annie's "medicine cabinet" with awe. "There's something I don't understand, Annie. How do you know what's in these bottles and jars? Nothing's labeled."

"I tell by lookin'. If I cain't tell by lookin', then I tell by sniffin' . . . Besides, I know whar ever'thang is. You ain't a-been a-movin' thangs around, I hope."

"No, I haven't touched anything."

Annie carried the armload of firewood to the fireplace, placed one log on the fire, then rejoined Sarah in the adjoining room. "Here, let me show you," she said, taking one of the jars down from the shelf and opening it. She shoved the jar under Sarah's nose. "What's this smell like to you?"

"It smells like sassafras."

"An' so it is. Sassafras root tea is a blood tonic. Hit purifies the blood. Hit cleans out the liver an' kidneys too."

She resealed the jar and returned it to its place on the shelf. She continued down the row of jars and tins, pointing to one after another. "Bloodroot here's good for the blood too . . . So's spikenard . . . so's black snakeroot. You had some black snakeroot in your tea this mornin'. That's prob'bly why you're up an' around already. Black snakeroot also helps t' stimulate the heart. Hit stimulates the heart an' calms the nerves at the same time. Hit's also good for pain in the back of the haid. For rheumatism pain too. Hit's good for lots of thangs . . ."

"Black snakeroot? I'm not familiar with that."

"Mebbe you know it by another name—black cohosh."

"Oh yes, I know black cohosh. It grew up in the mountains where I used to live."

"This here's purple foxglove," continued Annie, "that 'p'ison' that I been a-makin' you drink. Hit stimulates the heart too. When a heart is just about stopped like your's was, foxglove's 'bout the only thang I know that'll start it up ag'in . . . Lily-of-the-valley root is good for the heart too . . .

"Then over here is cocklebur root. Hit's good for stomach troubles . . . Do you ever get p'ison oak or p'ison ivy?"

"No."

"Me neither, but cocklebur's good for that too. You just crush the fresh leaves an' rub the juice onto your skin . . . Pokeroot juice is good for skin rash too. Pokeroot's also good for locked-up bowels. So's may apple. Loosens them right up. If your bowels are *too* loose, then ground ivy is the thang. Ground ivy's good for kidney problems too. Hit's also good for colic in babies . . ."

Sarah listened in fascination as Annie continued to show her through her pharmaceutical laboratory.

"Yarrow for colds an' flu, spikenard an' comfrey for coughs, cocklebur for sore throat, wolf's-bane root for fever... Pennyroyal here makes you sweat. Good for pneumonia... See this here? This here's flaxseed. You take some of this, mash it up, then mix it with sourwood honey. Makes a salve. When you come down with the whooping cough, just rub it on your chest. That, together with some black snakeroot tea, will fix you right up."

She took a bottle of dark-colored liquid down from the top shelf and removed the cork. This also she held up to Sarah's nose. "Do you know what this is?"

Sarah wrinkled her nose, then shook her head.

"Hit's creosote, from pine tar. That's good for coughs too."

Sarah was dubious, but she didn't argue. She was just glad that she had never been sick.

"Then ever'thang over on this shelf is for female complaints: milkweed, squaw vine, black haw, yarrow, smooth sumac, brown cedar..."

"Annie, how do you know all these things?"

"Learned them from Sophie. She was my Ma. She was a granny woman too. An' *she* learned a lot of it from an old Cherokee Indian squaw. The Cherokee believe that ever' plant in nature was made for some purpose, and if we know how t' read nature, we can figger out what that purpose is. Ever' plant has a signature. Take the hepatica, for example. The leaf of the hepatica is shaped like a liver. That's its signature. That's nature's way of tellin' us that the hepatica is good for liver ailments... The leaf of the rattlesnake plantain looks like a snakeskin. That's nature's way of tellin' us that rattlesnake plantain is a good cure for snakebite... The red sap in the root of the bloodroot tells us hit's good for the blood... Plants like milkweed with a lot of milk in them help nursin' mothers keep full of milk."

She led Sarah back into the other room. "Loot at this root here," she said, directing Sarah's attention to the roots hanging from the fireplace mantel. "This is gin-shen. This is what Edgar an' me was a-diggin' over on the other side of the mountain last

Sunday afternoon when we found you ... What's hit look like to you?"

Sarah studied the root for a moment. "I guess if you have enough imagination, it looks like a person. There's the arms, the legs, even the ... It's a man."

"That's right. Accordin' to the doctrine of signatures, that's nature's way of tellin' us that gin-shen is good for *ever'thang*. A cup of gin-shen tea ever' mornin' will cure whatever ails you an' keep you fit an' spry to a ripe old age."

"Do you drink it, Annie?"

"Sure do. Ever' mornin'."

"How old are you?"

"Eighty-four. And I can still climb up an' down these mountains better'n most of the young folks nowadays." She looked down at Sarah's uncovered legs. "I ain't so sure I'd want t' race you though. I never seen so many muscles in the legs of a girl."

"That comes from climbing up and down the ladder. I've been picking apples for the past two months."

"I reckon that would explain it."

Sarah was thinking about something else. "The doctrine of signatures that you were talking about reminds me a little of Swedenborg's Law of Correspondence. Swedenborg said that everything in the natural world, right down to the last detail, corresponds to something in the spiritual world, and by studying the natural world, we can come to a better understanding of the spiritual world ... Have you ever read Swedenborg, Annie?"

"Would that be a person or a book?"

Sarah's attempt to laugh came out sounding more like a cough, and she was glad of it when she realized that Annie had not intended her question to be facetious. "Swedenborg was a person, but I meant, have you ever read any of his books?"

"Never learnt t' read books. Sophie never had much use for them. She always said, if you can read nature an' you can read the soul, that's all the readin' you need t' know. Thar's nuthin' you can learn from readin' books, she said, that you cain't learn from readin' nature an' the soul."

"What did she mean when she said, 'if you can read the soul?' How can you read the soul?"

"I don't know *how* you do it. You just *do* it. Sophie could do it, an' so can I."

"But what does it mean, 'read the soul?' A soul isn't something you can read like a book."

"Neither's nature, but that never stopped the Cherokee Indians and us granny women from readin' it all the same."

Annie could tell by the deeply inquisitive look on Sarah's face that her young house guest was struggling desperately to make sense out of her words. "Can I trust you, Sarah Wicker? No need t' answer that: I know I can. How do I know I can? Because I can read it in your soul. I can read some other thangs in your soul too. For one, you're real smart—you know lots of thangs. For another, you're real curious. That's an easy one 'cause the two go together like dogs an' ticks. Hit's the smart folks that's the most curious, an' hit's the bein' curious that makes them so smart.

"Also, you're real carin' about other folks. When you woke up this mornin' the first thought that come into your haid was, how worried your Uncle Nathan would be. You came within a breath of dyin', but you never gave a thought for yourself . . . So you see, I done a li'l readin' on your soul already.

"Now, if you was anyone else, I'd say that's all thar was to it. But I know I can trust you, so I'm a-gwine t' tell you, thar's more to it than that. Thar's a *heap* more to it than that. And if you're int'rested, I'll show you what I mean. And I know you're int'rested 'cause you're smart an' that makes you curious. I'll haf t' make you promise not t' tell anyone though, and I know I can trust you t' keep any promise you make. Sophie made the mistake of talkin' about soul-readin' to the wrong folks. That's what I meant when I said that talkin' sometimes gets folks into trouble. Some folks around these parts sort of took the notion that Sophie was a witch on account of her soul-readin's. That's why I try t' be careful about who I tell and about who I read for."

"I can sympathize with your mother," said Sarah. "There are some folks around these parts who seem to have taken the notion that I'm a witch too."

Now it was Annie who had the puzzled look on her face. "Why on earth would anyone think a sweet young girl like yourself was a witch?"

"They say it's because I know things that I have no natural way of knowing."

"That's what they said about Sophie too–that an' worse. Some folks said she was possessed by demons. They done had their 'spicions about me too."

"I don't *think* I'm a witch," said Sarah, "though I'm not sure that I know what a witch is exactly, and I don't *think* I'm possessed by demons, though my Aunt Hester sometimes says I am–but ever since I was eleven years old, I've been able to go outside of my body. I've hardly ever done it because a friend of mine told me it wasn't a good thing to do, but one Sunday morning in church, three summers ago, during a tremendous thunderstorm, I was standing with everyone else singing a hymn, when suddenly I felt myself leave my body. I tried to get back in, but I couldn't. I just kept going, right up through the roof. When I was outside above the trees, I saw lightning start a fire two miles away."

"Bryson's mill?"

"Yes."

"Of course! You're Dan'l Wicker's girl. Now I remember! A coupla years back folks all over these mountains was a-talkin' about you."

"But what was I to do, Annie? *Not* tell anyone the mill was on fire? I couldn't have done that."

Annie did not answer. She was now studying Sarah with a great deal of curiosity. "You're a real unusual girl, Sarah Wicker," she said at last. "If I was you, I'd be a-wond'rin' how I got that way. If you'd agree t' let me read your soul, you just might find out some thangs about yourself that would surprise even you."

"I suppose I have no objection, Annie, though I'm still not sure what you mean by a soul-reading exactly."

"You'll see, you'll see," replied the old woman. "We'll do it tonight after dark. Hit's always best after dark. Hit's easier for me t' go to sleep. An' thar's less chance of our bein' disturbed."

Edgar picked his way through the junk and litter in the yard and approached the house. He could see that the house was in a state of disrepair. Part of the porch roof had collapsed and the rest of it appeared ready to follow. Nervously he ducked under that part of the porch roof that was still standing, gave two hurried raps on the door, then quickly retreated. In his haste to get off the porch his foot went through a floorboard and he fell backwards into the dirt. As he picked himself up, he kept one eye on the roof.

"Whatta yuh want?" came a loud gravelly voice. The voice had not come from the house. It had come from behind him. Turning, Edgar saw a man standing next to the hog pen, and, with long strides, Edgar headed toward him. Smiling, he held out the folded note.

"What's this?" growled the gravelly voice. Wesley took the note, opened it, and turned it around several times. He looked again into Edgar's silly grin. "Get outa here, you half-wit!"

Edgar bowed graciously and hurried off. When he was out of sight, Wesley turned the note around several more times, then crumpled it up and threw it into the hog pen.

Annie pulled her rocking chair up to the fireplace and sat down. "Are you ready t' get started?"

"I guess so," replied Sarah. "What do I have to do?"

"All *you* haf t' do is set an' listen. Why don't you set here on the bench by the fire? Blow out that lamp first. The light of the fire is all we'll be a-needin'."

Sarah blew out the lamp and sat down on the bench that Annie had indicated. In the warm glow of the fire Annie started rocking gently to and fro. "Hit's gwine t' take me a li'l while t' get into it, so be patient. Once I start a-talkin' you can stop me anytime you want to ax questions."

"Annie, I don't understand what it is you're going to do."

"You'll see, you'll see. Be patient, be patient."

Sarah made herself as comfortable as possible on the hard oak bench and watched quietly as the old woman sat with hands folded in her lap and rocked rhythmically back and forth, toward the fire, then away from it, toward it, then away from it, forward, back, forward, back. Suddenly the rocking stopped and Annie's head fell forward.

"Annie!" cried Sarah, jumping up from the bench, "are you all right?"

"Please be seated," came a voice from somewhere—Sarah could not be sure from where. "Annie is in no danger."

Sarah returned to her seat as instructed, but she was totally confused by what was happening. The voice that had just spoken to her had apparently come from Annie, but it was *not* Annie's voice!

"Please state the purpose of this inquiry."

The voice had definitely come from Annie this time, but again it was not Annie's voice. It was much deeper, and the manner of speech—the diction and inflection—were altogether different. "I beg your pardon," stammered Sarah.

"What is your name?"

"Sarah Wicker."

There was a long period of silence as Annie, or whoever it was who had just spoken, seemed to be trying to find the name in some vast mental directory. Finally the voice spoke again.

"We have before us a very old soul," it began, in a slow, methodical cadence, "one that has made many sojourns in the Earth. Throughout its long journey, this soul, which is now known by the name Sarah, has been a persistent seeker after truth and a vigilant defender of those truths she has found. This unquenchable thirst for truth and steadfast adherence to it, has made her many enemies in recent experiences and caused her to suffer much persecution."

Sarah was astounded. She could not believe what she was hearing.

"It is a hard road this soul has chosen to travel," the voice continued. "Fortunately it is not one she has had to travel alone. Throughout this long odyssey she has, on many occasions, been closely associated with another old soul–a sister soul, if you will–who has provided both comfort and companionship. This other old soul has now finished her sojourn on Earth and has no need to return. Even so, this sister soul, this companion, has elected to remain in contact with the Earth plane in order to continue to be of assistance to the soul Sarah and to others still here. The soul Sarah has been in communication with this advanced soul even during the present experience."

"Do you mean Kati?" inquired Sarah breathlessly.

"Yes, the one you know as Kati. The soul Sarah and the soul Kati have shared many Earth experiences. You were husband and wife in Sumer, father and son in Egypt at the time of the building of the pyramids, mother and son in Persia, sisters in China, master and slave in Greece . . . Many, many experiences . . . too many to enumerate.

"Of these, an experience in the subcontinent of India proved to be one of the most profound for the soul Sarah–one that would change her destiny. It was also one of the last Earth-plane experiences that she and the soul Kati would share. It was in the land of the five rivers, in that part of India which is now called the Punjab, at the time when the Master walked the Earth. The soul Sarah and the soul Kati were both in male form then and were adherents of the religious faith known as Jainism. As Jain monks they traveled together throughout the Punjab, teaching the gentle doctrine of *ahimsa*–the non-harming of any living creature–and the supremacy of the soul over the body. It was during this time that they met the young Jesus during those years of his life when the Master traveled in the East. The soul Sarah was especially moved by the power of his presence, by the gentleness of his manner, and by the truth of his teachings."

"Are you saying Jesus was in India?" asked Sarah incredulously.

"Yes, this is so. During those years of the Master's life, between the ages of twelve and thirty, of which you in the West have no accounting, the young Jesus traveled extensively in other lands, most notably in India, where he spent over twelve years studying the sacred scriptures of the Jains, Hindus, and

Buddhists. Not until the age of thirty, after he had traveled in many lands and accumulated much wisdom, did he return to his native Palestine to begin his ministry.

"The soul Sarah was so moved by the experience of being in the presence of the Master, that in her next incarnation she chose to be born into the Greek peninsula in the northern Mediterranean, where the Master's teachings were just being introduced. She had hoped to be of some service in helping to spread this teaching. She was in male form during this sojourn also.

"This was not her first experience in Greece. Five hundred years earlier she had been a male slave in the household of a prominent Athenian statesman. This was not so hard a life as it may sound, as the master of the house, being a man of progressive thought, had treated all his slaves with kindness and respect, even allowing the younger and more quick-minded of these to be educated along with his own children. Needless to say, the soul Sarah was among those so favored. It was during her many hours under common tutelage with her more privileged schoolmates that she developed a close bond with the master's youngest son. When the master died, she became the property of this son. Although her relationship to the son during her latter years of service was technically one of slave to master, in actuality the relationship was more like that of two old friends. In fact, you *were* two old friends. The son was the soul that you now know as Kati.

"In the Greek experience referred to now, the one spanning the period 50 A.D. to 125 A.D., she was the son of a wealthy nobleman herself and an ardent student of philosophy. When, still as a young man, she came into contact with the teachings of the Master, she found herself once again strongly attracted to it, just as she had been in India. But as many tenets of the Master's teaching had already found expression in the writings of the Greek philosophers, especially in the writings of those philosophers who, like Jesus himself, had derived much of their wisdom from the secret teachings of the Ancient Mystery schools, she saw no reason to abandon her own course of studies. Later, when she founded her own school of philosophy, she simply incorporated the Master's teaching into her curriculum. While she was not directly engaged in preaching the gospel of Christ during this lifetime, she felt as though she were working in parallel with those who were.

"Toward the end of her life, however, she became concerned that the true teaching of Jesus was not being adhered to by many of those who called themselves his followers, that, either through misunderstanding or purposeful misrepresentation, the wisdom that Jesus had taught was being subordinated, and in its place a strange new religion–a religion *about* Jesus, a Jesus *cult*–was taking root. She felt that the apostle Paul had been much to blame for this . . . for this change of emphasis, shall we say. He, more than any other, seemed to have confused the Messenger with the Message. But the writers of the gospels too, she felt, had contributed to this confusion. In their zeal to promote the new teaching, they had, perhaps understandably enough, made some exaggerated claims on behalf of the teacher. By elevating the Master to almost mythical stature–by introducing into the narrative of his life certain elements of the dying and resurrecting sun-god myth–and, in the case of John, by identifying the Master with the Creator himself–the gospel writers had furthered the process of shifting the emphasis from the Master's teaching to the Master himself. In an age when earthly rulers and religious teachers alike commonly pretended to God-hood, it is perhaps not surprising that such claims on behalf of the Master should have been made, but to the soul Sarah, who had always insisted on speaking plainly and truthfully, such developments were disturbing.

"Of the dozen or so gospels in circulation in the second century, it was the one known as the Gospel of John which the soul Sarah considered to be the most problematical. While she recognized it as a brilliant piece of esoteric writing, which contained many hidden truths for those trained to interpret such writing–indeed, it was a gospel she would come to love in subsequent incarnations–she was, at the same time, concerned that much misunderstanding might result, and even blood be shed, if this gospel were to fall into the hands of the uninformed masses and be accepted as literal truth. Little did she know at the time how prophetic her concerns would prove to be. Even now, eighteen centuries later, it would be impossible to calculate the number of souls who have been led astray—and will continue to be led astray—or the amount of suffering that has been inflicted upon mankind—and will continue to be inflicted—as a result of placing too literal an interpretation on this richly allegorical document. If ever there was a case wherein it can be truly said that 'the letter killeth, but the spirit giveth life,' it was, and continues to be so, in the case of the Gospel of John. For the few remaining years of her life in second-century Greece, the soul Sarah worked tirelessly to correct the errors that the apostles and evangelists had made and to promote the true teaching that Jesus had taught.

"The pattern established during this experience in Greece was repeated time and again in subsequent incarnations, with the soul Sarah choosing to be born again and again into that part of the world where this strange new religion about Jesus was being taught and received, in order to bear a true witness. She often found herself working in conjunction with others to this purpose. In the land of Egypt, in the fourth century, she was among those of a Christian Gnostic sect who were forced to go into hiding to escape persecution at the hands of the Archbishop of Alexandria. This was a period in the early history of Christianity when the Church's teaching had not yet been officially codified, and so many and diverse ideas were in circulation and competing for recognition. Many of these ideas, including some from so-called 'pagan' sources—the worship of the Master's earthly mother, for example—were eventually incorporated into official church doctrine and ritual, but one idea that could not be incorporated, because it threatened the very authority and legitimacy of the Church itself, was the Gnostic idea that each soul can know and experience God directly. If each soul can know and experience God directly—as the Master himself had taught—of what use then are priests and bishops and other earthly intermediaries between man and God? Of no use, said the Gnostics, and by so saying sealed their own fate. Throughout its long history, whenever the Church has been forced to choose between truth and political power, it has never hesitated to opt for the latter.

"The Archbishop of Alexandria determined that Gnostic teaching had to be suppressed and all Gnostic writings destroyed. The persecution was not as thorough as it might have been, however, and many of the Gnostics survived, including the soul Sarah. Some of the writings of the early Gnostics also survived, including some gospels which are not included in the New Testament. The world does not yet know of these, but they will be discovered in a few years.

"In the sixth century, as a church bishop herself, the soul Sarah was one of those who defended the teachings of the great Church Father Origen against the attacks of the Byzantine Emperor Justinian. She was not successful in this endeavor, however, and at the Fifth Ecumenical Council in Constantinople in the year 553, at Justinian's behest, many of the teachings of Origen were declared anathema. Among the doctrines condemned as evil and accursed was that of the pre-existence of the soul, a doctrine taught by Jesus himself. It was not the first, nor the last, time that the true teachings were altered—nay, perverted—for purely personal or political motives.

"After the Council of Constantinople the true teaching survived only among the so-called 'heretical' sects, and the soul Sarah, over the ensuing centuries, invariably found herself allied with one of these. In the thirteenth century, in the south of France, in the region known as Languedoc—the land of the Troubadors—she was a leader of the Cathari, a sect of religious ascetics who lived such pure and virtuous lives that even orthodox Catholics revered them and looked to them for guidance. So revered were the Cathari that orthodox Catholics often sought to be buried in their cemeteries—so as to spend eternity among the 'good people.' At a time when the Church was corrupt and many of the clergy lived only for the treasures of this world, the Cathari stored up their treasure in Heaven, as the Master had taught. In the past millenium it would be difficult to find any 'Christians' in all of Christendom who followed the teachings of the Christ more closely than the Cathari. Included in their doctrines were the doctrine of clean diet—the non-eating of animal flesh—and the doctrine of rebirth—the teaching that the soul is perfected only after many sojourns in the Earth—two doctrines that have been taught for thousands of years by the Jains of India, among whom the soul Sarah had spent several earlier incarnations—one of these has already been mentioned—and by many great religious teachers in all ages, from Pythagoras, Plato, and Plotinus in the West to Krishna, Buddha, and Mahavira in the East. And, of course, they were part of the true teaching of the Master himself.

"The darkness, however, cannot stand the light, and so these 'heretical' doctrines could not be tolerated for long. In the year 1215 Pope Innocent the Third summoned the Fourth Lateran Council in Rome for the purpose of making much-needed reforms in the Church. One of the first actions taken by the Council was to condemn the many 'heresies' that had crept into the so-called 'true faith' and to order the punishment of all unrepentant heretics. The various Cathari sects were among those specifically cited by the Council. In the ensuing years the Cathari were ruthlessly suppressed and all those who did not repent were put to death. The soul Sarah was among the last to survive. She, along with several hundred of her fellow-believers, sought refuge in the mountaintop fortress of Montsegur. When the fortress fell to the royal army from the north of France, she and others of her persuasion were taken captive. She, along with two hundred others who refused to repent, were led down from the mountain in chains to a field below, where they were burned alive."

Sarah gasped. "Burned alive?"

"Yes. The suppression of heresy in the thirteenth century plunged the continent of Europe into one of the darkest moments in its history. Sadly, it is a history that has seen far too many dark moments. Many innocents were put to death during the crusades against heresy and later during the Inquisition. The inhabitants of some towns in the south of France were massacred indiscriminately. Their religious faith was not even questioned. At least you were a true Cathar and were able to take comfort in the knowledge that a single Earth life is as nothing in the long march of the soul toward perfection. You went into the fire calmly and without fear—and unrepentant to the end—secure in the knowledge that by adhering to the true teaching and by forgiving those who persecuted you, your soul would receive its just reward."

"Could you, by any chance, tell me my name during that lifetime?"

"During that particular sojourn you were known as Joseph Lesage."

"I was a man then?"

"Yes."

Sarah lapsed into thoughtful silence, and the old woman continued. "After the sojourn in southern France, you decided to take a rest, so to speak. Your next incarnation was in Tibet in the fourteenth century. You lived a long and peaceful life as a Buddhist monk and were much venerated by the people of your village.

"But in the seventeenth century, after two other rather uneventful incarnations, you were back in the thick of it, as the saying goes. You elected to be born into that part of Europe that is now known as Germany. By this time the Church that had been founded in the Master's name had a great deal more to worry about than a few hundred heretics. The Protestant Reformation set in motion by Martin Luther a hundred years earlier now had the Church divided against itself. In the first half of the seventeenth century, the increasing hostility between Catholics and Protestants culminated in the Thirty Years' War. Although many of the countries of Europe were involved, most of the fighting took place on German soil—the very soil from which the Reformation had sprung. Germany was not then the single unified nation that it is today, but instead consisted of numerous small and independent states, each with its own autonomous political ruler. As many of these states were Catholic, and many others Protestant, the Thirty Years' War, in addition to being an international war fought on German soil, was also a German civil war.

"Against this background of religious and political factionalism and continuing warfare, the soul Sarah tried, as best she could, to live a peaceful life and to raise a family. Although once again interested in religious ideas, she chose not to become engaged in the dispute between Catholics and Protestants. As corrupt and misguided as she believed the Catholic Church to be, she did not feel that the Protestant reforms had even begun to address the fundamental problem, which was the false teaching that had been passed down through both Church and Scriptures from the first century. Therefore, she dismissed both Catholicism and Protestantism as irrelevant and kept her silence. It is not likely that her voice would have been heard in any case, as she was, during this incarnation, a woman. In fact, your life then was not too unlike your life now. You lived a normal life outwardly—the life of a simple peasant woman—but inwardly you were busily engaged once again in a search for the truth, a search for the kingdom of God within. Your name during that sojourn was Greta Bauer.

"It is quite possible that your life then would have been totally uneventful, despite the religious wars that raged throughout most of it, if it had not been for another hysteria sweeping Europe at the same time: the hysteria of witchcraft. Many reasons have been advanced to explain this phenomenon, which, over the course of three centuries, led to the execution of many tens of thousands of so-called 'witches': the upheaval in the Church, the breakdown of civil order, the Black Death—all of which contributed to a general feeling of insecurity—a sort of mass neurosis—and convinced people that God had forsaken the world and handed the reins of power over to the Devil. To be sure, some of those charged with witchcraft during this period of mass hysteria actually believed themselves *to be* witches—that is, believed themselves to be in a compact with the Devil—but for every one of these who was hunted down and executed, another thousand innocent men and women, whose only crime was unconventional behavior or unorthodoxy of belief, were accused of witchcraft and likewise executed, usually by hanging or burning. In the Duchy of Brunswick, where the soul Sarah—then Greta—

lived, the persecution was as ardent and ferocious as any in Europe. During the height of the frenzy, in the 1620s and -30s, the smell of burning flesh was seldom absent from the Brunswick air, as an almost steady procession of condemned witches–mostly women–were bound to the stake, beheaded, and burned. At the end of this reign of terror, there were so many charred stakes outside the city gates, it looked as though a forest had burned."

"Annie, please stop a moment," pleaded Sarah, burying her face in her hands. It was all coming so fast, she was having difficulty absorbing it all. And so much of it was so horrible! Beheaded and burned! Annie had said, beheaded and burned! She remembered the dream she had had as a child.

"Annie?" she asked tentatively, unsure as to whether she even wanted to know the answer, "was I–I mean, was Greta–among those who were beheaded and burned?"

Annie smiled. "Despite your decisions to be born, time and again, into the most dangerous of circumstances; despite your penchant for getting into trouble with the authorities; despite the fact that you seem to 'court' the stake virtually every time out–no, you were not among those executed in Brunswick. You were accused, but you were not executed. When the soldiers came for you, another offered herself in your place."

"Another?"

"Yes."

Sarah sat in stunned silence for a moment, absorbing this revelation. "It was Kati, wasn't it?"

"Yes, your old friend Kati, the soul with whom you had shared so many earlier experiences. It is from the sojourn in Germany that you know her as Kati. Her name was Katarina Bauer."

"You said *my* name was Greta Bauer. Were we sisters?"

"Sisters-in-law, to be precise. She was your husband's sister. She lived with you and your husband and helped you look after your four children. When the soldiers came for you, you were out in the fields. Katarina was in the house looking after the children. When the soldiers asked for Greta Bauer, Katarina said simply, 'Greta Bauer bin ich'–'I am Greta Bauer'–and handed herself over to them."

Sarah was quivering with emotion. "I saw it, Annie!" she cried, "I saw it all! I saw them tie her to the stake! I saw them sever her head! I saw them set her on fire!"

"Yes, you saw it all, but from the astral, not from the physical."

"From the what?"

"From the astral. The art of projecting the astral body, which you mastered during..."

"I'm sorry, Annie," interrupted Sarah, "I don't understand what you mean by the 'astral body.'"

"The astral body. Literally, the starry or star-like body. Also known as the second body or the double. That which you call the 'soul body.'"

"Oh yes."

"As I was saying, the art of projecting the astral body, which you mastered during your many earlier incarnations in India, was one that you carried with you into the German experience—as well as into the present experience. When you returned to the house and were informed by the oldest of your children that the soldiers had come and had taken Katarina, you were greatly distressed. You wanted to go to the authorities at once, to protest, to seek her release, but your husband, out of concern for your own safety, dissuaded you. This did not stop you, however, from searching for your beloved Kati, or Katchen, as you sometimes called her. You simply slipped out of the physical and did your searching from the astral. You found her, but, unfortunately, it was not until several days later, and then only in time to witness her execution."

Again Sarah buried her face in her hands as she recalled the gruesome execution from her dream. "She was very young, wasn't she?"

"Yes—and very old. At the time of her execution in Brunswick she was fourteen."

Sarah sighed. "But why did she do it, Annie? Why did she give herself in my place?"

"Why? Because you and your husband had four young children to look after. Because your work during that particular sojourn was not yet completed. Because you had not yet fulfilled your purpose."

"*My* work? *My* purpose? What about *her* work, *her* purpose?"

"Sacrificing herself for you *was* her work. That *was* her purpose."

"I don't understand."

"As previously stated, the soul you know as Kati is a very advanced soul, one who no longer needs to return to the Earth. You are a very old soul yourself, and your sojourn here is nearly completed as well. But the path to perfection that you have chosen is not the one that the soul Kati has chosen. You are, and have always been, a seeker after truth. You have chosen the path of knowledge. The soul you know as Kati has chosen another path to perfection, the path of devotional love. Again, it is a matter of emphasis, for no one who truly loves will be totally lacking in knowledge, and no one who seeks true knowledge will be totally lacking in love. It should not be so difficult for you to understand the concept of self-sacrificing love. If I am not mistaken, that scar on your right arm bears mute testimony to your own willingness to sacrifice self to save another."

Sarah looked at the scar to which Annie had alluded. "Yes, but I knew that Mr. Hicks' dogs would not hurt me."

"Just as Katarina knew that her executioners would not hurt her . . . Do you see what I mean?"

"I think so. You mean that even though they cut off her head and burned her body, they could not destroy her soul." Sarah could not help thinking about the violence that had just been done to her own body.

"Yes, even before her head fell, she had left her body and was singing with the angels in Heaven . . . Perhaps we should stop now. I think I've given you enough to think about for one night . . . Besides, Annie's not as young as she used to be–even though she thinks she is."

Suddenly the voice stopped. Sarah waited for Annie to move, but she did not. The old woman continued to sit quietly in the rocking chair with her chin resting on her bosom. Apparently she intended to spend the night right where she was. Sarah had not seen another bed in the house—only the one she had found herself in when she had first awakened—and she wondered now if Annie had been sleeping in the rocking chair for the past three, now four, nights. She stoked the fire, added another log, then checked to make sure that Annie was still breathing. Satisfied that the old woman had not expired, she went to the bed and lay down. The soft feather mattress felt wonderful to her bruised back and buttocks after the hard wooden bench.

As she lay in the bed watching the light from the fire flicker on the ceiling, her mind was racing. There had been many periods in her life when she had gone for many months without significant changes taking place, without any extraordinary event to interrupt the quiet passing of the seasons. Now, in the course of a few short days, events were following one upon another so fast, that before she had time to absorb and assess the impact of one, she was caught up in another. Otis was dead! She had not even begun to realize the full import of that yet. Then, as if in some surrealistic nightmare, she had been seized and raped and left for dead by two teenaged boys. She was not sure if her mind would ever be able to come to terms with that, to make sense of it, to fit it into the context of her life. In any event, she had not had time to think about it. One moment she had been inside a feedsack, pinned to a rock, struggling for breath; when she next woke, she had found herself lying in a feather bed being attended by a young man who couldn't speak and a strange old woman who made medicines from plants and "read souls."

Sarah cast a glance in Annie's direction. In the shadowy darkness of the cabin's interior she could see the old woman in her rocking chair silhouetted against the flickering light of the fireplace. Sarah could not stop thinking about the extraordinary "soul-reading" that Annie had just done for her. "We have before us a very old soul," Annie had said, "one that has made many sojourns in the Earth." She was saying that the soul incarnates not once, but many times in the Earth, that transmigration of the soul was indeed a fact. Throughout the reading, Sarah had sat perfectly motionless, frozen to the bench in wonder-filled astonishment. Now, as she lay in bed, she continued to be filled with wonder and incredulity. But what she had found so astonishing was not Annie's forthright assertion that "the soul Sarah" had lived before, many times–much to her surprise, she did not find that so very difficult to believe at all; it almost sounded "right" to her–but the fact that Annie had been able to "read" her soul in the first place. Though Sarah had watched the old woman closely, though she had used all the powers of reason and observation available to her, she had not begun to understand how Annie had done it. Sarah could not believe that Annie had simply invented, or made up, the past lives she had recounted for her, would not have believed it even if Annie had made no mention of the life in Germany in which she had witnessed the young girl being beheaded and burned. For many years Sarah had had a feeling that her childhood dream had had a basis in fact. She had also become all but certain that the young girl who had been so brutally executed was her friend Kati, and that it had happened a long time ago when Kati had lived on the Earth. Since reading Swedenborg, Sarah had been inclined to believe that it was Kati herself who, for some reason or other, had put the dream in her head. Now Annie was saying that *she*, Sarah herself, had witnessed the beheading and burning. If Annie had not read her soul, at the very least she had read her mind.

Sarah remembered the exploration of the soul that she and her mother had made many years before. They had agreed at the time, for the purpose of the discussion, that the words "soul" and "mind" were just two different names for the same thing. But clearly, if the soul was "very old" and had made "many sojourns in the Earth," then the soul and the mind were not the same thing at all. They were two very different things indeed. The mind, after all, had no memories of previous lives. She could not wait for morning to come, so she could begin to ask Annie more questions.

She was surprised to discover that Annie had not remembered *any* of the soul-reading! She hadn't even *heard* it!

"Not a word," said the old woman as she sat in her rocker sipping her ginseng tea. "The last thang I remember was me a-tellin' you t' be patient."

"Then who did the reading, Annie? Who was that talking inside you?" Sarah had again assumed her place on the bench.

"Hit was *me* a-talkin'. Hit was *me* who done the readin'. Only hit wasn't the same me who's a-talkin' to you now."

"Do you mean it was another part of your soul? Another part of your mind?"

"Listen, Miss Sarah, hit's like I told you yesterd'y. I don't know how I do it, I just do it . . . Do you understand how it is that you can get out of your body when nobody else can?"

"No," admitted Sarah, "but last night you said it was something I learned in India."

"Well, I'm sure I picked this up somewhar along the way too, but don't ax me how it's done. Once when Sophie was in her readin'-sleep, I axed her how she knowed all those thangs she knowed when she done her soul-readin's. She gave me a long answer, but I cain't say I ever understood it. Somethin' about ever'thang bein' recorded somewhar, out in the ether or somethin'. She said you could think of it this way: all souls is part of God, an' God knows ever'thang that's ever happened to ever' soul. Readin' souls is like readin' the mind of God."

Sarah found herself intrigued by this idea. It had started a whole train of thoughts in motion. "This past summer I read a book by a man—a psychologist—named Carl Jung. He talks about something called the Collective Unconscious. Have you heard of that, Annie?"

"Nope, I sure ain't."

"Well, I'll try to explain it as best I can, but I'm not sure I completely understand it myself. First of all, do you understand what is meant by the 'unconscious mind?' "

"You mean like yours was when we found you the other day?"

"Well, not exactly. When psychologists use the word 'unconscious,' they don't mean a condition of the conscious mind, they mean another part of the mind altogether. It helps me to think of the unconscious mind—or, simply, the unconscious—as being like a vast underground root cellar. During our alert, waking moments we live in our kitchens–that is, in our conscious minds–but during sleep we go down into our unconscious minds, into our root cellars. We've got all kinds of things stored away down there: our earliest childhood memories, our deepest yearnings, our deepest fears and anxieties . . . Now, some of the stuff stored away in our root cellar is stuff that we put there ourselves; it came out of our own kitchens. But there seems to be a lot of other stuff down there too–much older stuff–stuff which we didn't put there at all, but which seems to have *come with* the root cellar: stuff that we sort of inherited from earlier generations. If Jung is right–and if I'm understanding him correctly–then when you're reading souls, maybe that's what you're doing: maybe you're going down into this older part of the root cellar–into the Collective Unconscious–and looking at stuff that was stored away by generation after generation of our human race ancestors."

"Good gracious, child, hit was hard enough to understand when Sophie explained it. Have you been eatin' puffballs or somethin'?"

Sarah gave the old woman an uncomprehending look. This was hardly the response she had expected to her thoughts on the Collective Unconscious. "As a matter of fact, I *have* eaten a few puffballs this past month or so. I've been finding them under the apple trees after every rain. Why do you ask?"

"That explains it. Puffballs is brain food. Thar's nuthin' in all of creation that looks more like a human brain than a puffball–'ceptin' mebbe a cully-flower. The signature is plain as day."

Sarah smiled, but was anxious to change the subject. "I'm sorry you didn't get to hear the reading, Annie. You said some extraordinary things."

"Such as?"

"Well, for one, you said that Jesus was in India."

"That's true enough. Sophie said the same thang."

"And that he taught transmigration of the soul."

"What on earth is that?"

"Rebirth. The idea that each soul lives many lives on Earth."

"Yes, Jesus taught rebirth. Sophie said that too."

"And that the Church that was founded in his name has not been teaching his true teaching."

Annie nodded. "Let's put it this way: if Jesus showed up in church next Sund'y mornin' an' preached a sermon, most folks wouldn't understand a word he was a-sayin'."

"That wouldn't be surprising, Annie. Jesus didn't speak English."

"Wouldn't matter what he spoke. If Jesus *do* come back–like most folks around these parts think he's a-gwine to–he better either be a-trailin' clouds of glory or a-wearin' a big sign that says 'Jesus.' 'Cause if he ain't, folks ain't a-gwine t' know him. They ain't a-gwine t' know him from Edgar . . . Hmmm, mebbe Edgar *is* Jesus. Wouldn't that be somethin'?"

"Do you think he *will* come back?"

"Edgar or Jesus?"

"Jesus."

"He might. Hit's up to him. He's moved beyond the Earth plane, so's thar's no need for him t' come back. If I was him, I wouldn't."

"Why not?"

"Save hisself a lot of floggin'."

"Last night you said that a friend of mine whom I knew in past lifetimes has also moved beyond the Earth plane. By that I assume that you meant that she has gone to Heaven."

"Sophie never liked t' use the word 'Heaven' on account of the word's been so badly misunderstood. She talked about 'planes.' This is the Earth plane we're in now, also called the physical plane. Beyond this are other planes that are invisible to our Earth eyes: the astral plane, the mental plane . . . I cain't remember them all. Thar's seven altogether, countin' the Earth plane."

Here again was confirmation that there were more worlds or "planes" beyond this Earth than the single Heaven that most Christians seemed to believe in, though they differed in name and number. Sarah thought of telling Annie about her visit to some of the invisible worlds or "planes" with Kati, but decided against it.

She was much more interested in hearing what Annie had to say. "How many lives must we live on the Earth plane before we go to the other planes?"

"Depends."

"On?"

"On how strong we feel the Earth-pull inside us."

"What does that mean?"

"Let's put it this way. If a man lives only for this world—if he lives only t' satisfy the cravin's of his body, the lusts of his flesh—then he's sure enough gwine t' come back. When he dies, he'll go to the astral plane for a spell, but sooner or later he'll be back. The Earth will pull him back. An' he'll keep a-comin' back ag'in an' ag'in, til he overcomes his carnal lusts an' learns t' live for the pleasures of the soul.

"Hit's other thangs that bring us back too. Sometimes we come back to pay off a debt, or to make up for a wrong we done somebody in a past life. Sometimes we come back just t' suffer, t' reap what we sowed in the past. Sometimes I think the reason folks is born into these mountains is purely t' suffer, t' do repentance for all the sinnin' they done in the past."

"But, on average, Annie, how many lives does it take to get beyond the Earth plane for good? . . . Ten? . . . Twenty?" Annie laughed. "Fifty? . . . A hundred?" Sarah could see that Annie was greatly amused. "A *thousand?*"

"I done readin's for folks who done already lived over four hunnert thousand lives."

Sarah gasped. *"Four hundred thousand?"*

"That's why I nearly bust out laughin' whenever I hear folks talkin' about gwine to Heaven after just one lifetime. As if any of us is fit for Heaven after just one lifetime."

"Four hundred thousand!" repeated Sarah. She was still aghast.

"Over the past two billion years."

"Annie, that's not possible. People haven't been on the Earth that long."

"We been here a lot longer than most folks think—and I do mean *we*. An' these hunnerts of thousands of lives is just Earth lives, on this one planet. We came to Earth from somewhar else, an' before that, from somewhar else. As Sophie used t' say, 'the soul's march to perfection is not made in a day.' "

"It's hard to believe that anyone *ever* makes it, if it takes *that* long."

"Don't forget. We been at it a long time."

"How long ago did this all begin?"

"I reckon hit began when the world began."

"It sounds to me like it began long before the world began."

"When I say 'the world,' I don't mean this little clump of dirt we live on. I mean the *whole* world."

"The universe?"

"That's the one."

"And when will it end?"

"When the last soul has returned to God."

Sarah was still shaking her head in disbelief. "I don't imagine that will be any time soon."

Annie simply smiled as she took another sip of tea. Sarah lapsed into deep thought for several minutes as she tried to assimilate this flood of new ideas into the stream of her consciousness. Suddenly she jumped up from the bench and began pacing excitedly about the room.

"I just had the most incredible thought, Annie! In school I learned about something called the 'big-bang' theory. According to this theory, at the beginning of Creation, all the matter and energy in the universe was concentrated together in one heavy, dense ball. Suddenly it exploded, sending this great mass of matter flying out in all directions at a tremendous rate of speed. According to some astronomers, it is still moving out away from the center; the universe is still expanding. Some believe that eventually all the energy will be used up, and the universe will just run down like a clock and stop. Others believe that it works in a cycle, that after the universe has expanded as far as it can, it will begin to contract, and everything–all the stars and planets and moons; all the matter in the universe–will be pulled back into the center. Then it will explode again, and the whole process will begin all over again. It's an interesting idea, don't you think?

And it's not so hard to believe either, because everything in Nature seems to go in cycles.

"Let's suppose for a moment that this cycle theory is true. Let's also suppose that Swedenborg's Law of Correspondence is true. I was telling you about that yesterday, remember? Swedenborg said that everything in the natural world corresponds to something in the spiritual world, both in general and in detail. What if, in the Beginning, all the souls in the spiritual universe were sent out from God like in a big bang–in a silent big bang? Eventually they will all return to God–not all at once, of course, because some will have gone much further out than others. And then, after all those billions of years, when they've all returned to God, what if God explodes again in another big bang, and the whole process starts all over again? That way there would be no end to it; it would go on forever. We would be forever being sent away from God, then trying to find our way back again. And it would all work in perfect correspondence with the physical universe. Don't you think it's possible, Annie?"

Annie took another sip of tea and shook her head, not in disagreement, but in bewilderment–and a certain amount of awe. "I'll tell you what I think is possible, young Sarah Wicker. I think hit's possible that you done et entirely too many puffballs . . . You better lie down an' get some rest. You're gwine t' wear yourself out."

Sarah was on her way back to the bed when her attention was caught by a movement at the window. She looked and saw Edgar's smiling face pressed against the glass. Annie motioned for him to come in.

"Did you deliver Sarah's note?" she asked, as Edgar came through the curtain.

He nodded his head vigorously.

For the rest of the day Edgar sat next to Sarah's bed and watched her as she tried to sleep. Toward evening, just as she had fallen into a deep sleep, he took her hand and shook it. When she opened her eyes, he stood up and waved.

"Good night, Edgar," said Sarah, returning his smile. "Thank you for coming to visit me."

He bowed several times, then departed.

"I expect you'll be a-wantin' somethin' t' eat," said Annie, when the two of them were once again alone in the cabin. "I done made some 'tater an' onion soup."

"That sounds good," said Sarah, slowly getting up. "I'm starved."

"Hope you like lots of dill in it."

"Dill's fine. Just as long as there's no creosote in it."

As they sat in front of the fire slowly eating the hot, aromatic soup, Sarah found herself once again thinking about some of the extraordinary things Annie had told her the night before. She wished now that she had written everything down. "Annie, could I ask you some more questions?"

"These questions, would they be about the soul-readin' or about somethin' else?"

"About the soul-reading."

"Well, if hit's the soul-readin' you want t' know about, then hit's not *this* me you want to ax. Hit's that other me."

"Do you think it would be possible for me to talk to that other you again?"

"I don't see why not. You can talk to her tonight if you want. I think she'd take great pleasure in conversin' with somebody whose haid is filled with as many notions as yours seems t' be. But I must warn you, she likes t' talk. She'll talk all night if you let her . . . 'Course, you seem t' be able t' talk a purty good piece yourself once you get started."

Sarah blushed. "Yes, my cousin Otis once said that I could talk for days at a time without stopping."

Annie laughed. "Well, hit should be a real int'restin' conversation then. I only wish I could be thar."

Shortly after supper Annie once again assumed her position in the rocking chair and Sarah once again took her seat on the bench. Again Sarah watched in fascination as the old woman rocked gently back and forth with the light of the fire flickering on her face. Then, just as the night before, the rocking suddenly stopped and Annie's head fell forward. In the silence of the darkened cabin, Sarah waited for the voice to speak.

"Please state the purpose of this inquiry."

Sarah found the voice not as intimidating as the night before. "I'd like to ask you a few questions about the reading you did for me last night."

"What is your name, please?"

Sarah hesitated. "I don't understand. How is it that you know everything about me, but you don't know my name?"

"Asking your name is a mere formality. Your name is Sarah Wicker. Proceed with your questions, Sarah Wicker."

"My first question is a mere formality also. What is *your* name?"

Annie smiled. "The soul, as created, is without name."

"What shall I call you then?"

"You may simply speak to me without addressing me by name, as we are alone in the room—or you may continue to call me 'Annie.'"

"But you're not the same as Annie."

"No, not the same."

"Are you part of Annie's mind?"

"Rather, Annie is part of *my* mind. Annie is the personality, the incarnation; I am the principle that reincarnates. To put it another way, Annie is eighty-four years of age, I am ageless."

"Would it be correct to say that you are the soul and Annie is the mind?"

"That would depend entirely on how you define the terms."

"That's exactly what my mother would have said."

"A wise woman, your mother. You chose her well."

"I *chose* my mother?"

"Of course. Your father too."

Caught off guard by this totally unexpected and astonishing revelation, Sarah completely forgot her next question. The voice continued.

"Incidentally, I enjoyed your analogy of the kitchen and the underground root cellar. I have been called many things—Higher

Self, Transcendent Soul, Eternal Principle—but I have never been called 'Unconscious' before."

"I apologize."

"Apology accepted. Proceed with your questions."

"In the reading last night, you kept referring to Jesus as 'the Master.' Was Jesus the son of God as Christians believe?"

"We are *all* children of God to the extent that we manifest the Divinity within."

"Was Jesus God?"

"We are *all* God to the extent that we manifest the Divinity within."

Sarah was glad her Aunt Hester had not heard that. She was a little shocked herself. "But what I'm asking is, is Jesus the God of Heaven, as Swedenborg says?"

"For Christians, yes. Jesus was the personality through whom, for many, the Divine Ground finds expression. But Divinity is not limited in its expressions. Swedenborg said as much."

"Have you read Swedenborg?"

"I have read Emanuel Swedenborg *and* his writings."

Sarah was finding it necessary to pause after every answer in order to ponder its meaning. She had to do so again now, but she decided that the wiser course might be to press on with her questions, then contemplate the answers at a later time. "Did Swedenborg actually make visits to Heaven and speak with spirits and angels?"

"Emanuel Swedenborg was an advanced soul who *came* from one of the higher planes and was, during his life on the Earth plane, frequently in communication with beings from the higher planes—as you yourself have been."

"But in his book, *Heaven and Hell*, Swedenborg made no mention of the doctrine of rebirth. He said, when we die, we go to the spirit world—the one that Annie calls the astral plane. From there we go either to one of the heavens or to Hell. We don't come back to Earth."

"It should not be assumed that just because beings come to Earth from a higher plane that they have a full conscious understanding of who they are, or the mission they have chosen to undertake. They must, after all, operate within the framework of Earth bodies and Earth minds. The truth they transmit to us must therefore be filtered through the Earth consciousness—in the case of Swedenborg, through a very Christian Earth consciousness. He spoke as a Christian of his day *to* the Christians of his day, and he spoke the truth to the extent that he himself had been permitted to understand it—or, we should say, as he permitted *himself* to understand it, as the decision to limit his understanding was one that he himself had made before entering into the Earth plane as Emanuel Swedenborg."

"Wait, Annie, I don't understand. Are you saying that Swedenborg knew even more before he was born than he did during his lifetime on Earth?"

"Oh, quite so. The Higher Self always knows many things of which the incarnating personality has no conscious awareness or remembrance."

"But why? Why would Swedenborg or anyone else make a deliberate decision to limit his understanding before entering the Earth plane?"

"In the case of Swedenborg, ironically enough, in order to be understood. You must realize that the mission that Swedenborg undertook was a very difficult one. It was nothing short of the complete restoration of the true Christian religion, insofar as that was possible. As his success depended on his ability to be heard and understood by the Christians of his day, he found it necessary to speak to them in the condition in which he found them, and as that condition was one of almost total darkness, he chose to hide some of his own light under a bushel, as the saying goes. He wished to lead men out of the darkness, not to blind them. When men have lived in darkness and error all of their lives, their eyes must be allowed to adjust to the light a little at a time. Even that part of the truth that he did succeed in transmitting was far from being universally accepted. Had he attempted to transmit the whole truth, including such 'heretical' doctrines as the doctrine of rebirth, he would almost certainly have met with even more scorn and derision, and very likely would have succeeded in transmitting nothing at all. His mission would have been a complete failure."

"What is it about the idea of rebirth that upsets people so? Last night you said that the teaching of this idea has been suppressed throughout history by both church and political leaders. Why have so many people, including popes and emperors, been so opposed to the teaching of rebirth?"

"Those who attain power in this world are often corrupt and unregenerate souls. As such, they have no wish to believe a doctrine that would require them to return to Earth in some low and menial state, to do penance for their sins, to reap in some future life or lives the consequences of the evil they have done in this one . . . But even very advanced beings have had doubts about the advisability of teaching the doctrine of rebirth."

"Why is that?"

"Because the soul's march to perfection is such a long one, it is feared by advanced beings that the 'footsoldiers' would become discouraged if they had any idea as to the true scope of it. It is not uncommon for souls to make hundreds of thousands of sojourns in the Earth, as Annie told you. If a soul does not have a clear vision of the glory that lies at the end of this long march, it becomes very tempting to 'put off until tomorrow'—or worse, to give up in despair and quit altogether. For this reason, Jesus taught the doctrine of rebirth only to his closest disciples. For this reason also, Swedenborg elected not to bring it into the world, but to leave it on a higher plane of understanding. For this reason also, mercifully, we do not remember our past lives."

"Does that mean I shouldn't be asking questions about my past lives?"

"I think you are not one to 'put off until tomorrow,' Sarah Wicker, or to become discouraged. If you have questions concerning your previous sojourns in the Earth plane, do not hesitate to ask."

Sarah thought for a moment. Where to begin?

"I was surprised to learn last night that I had been a man in some of my previous lives—in most of them, as a matter of fact.

Why is it that we sometimes come into the world as a man, and at other times as a woman? And why have I so often been a man?"

"It depends on what is needed. If, over the course of many incarnations, the female principle becomes too dominant, then it becomes necessary to experience some lives as a man–and vice-versa–in order to re-establish the balance, so to speak. Over the past twenty incarnations, you have been a woman ten times and a man ten times. If the lives I have recounted for you have been mostly male lives, it is because we generally opt for the male form when we want to play an active role in the world. When we want to play a more receptive role, we choose the female. Both are essential for our development as souls. Your lives as women have been mostly spent raising children and developing the loving, nurturing side of your soul. This is absolutely essential, but it is not generally the kind of thing that comes to the fore in a soul reading.

"In you the male and female principles are in nearly perfect balance. You have the intellect of the male and the intuition of the female, the physical strength and agility of the male, and the gentleness and compassion–the softness–of the female. Because you are so complete unto yourself, it is quite possible that you will never marry in this lifetime. You *may* decide to marry, but it is not something you would *need* to do. Given the number of ascetic lives you have lived in the past, it should not be difficult for you to forego the 'pleasures of the flesh' if you should choose to do so."

Sarah could not help thinking that there had been nothing very pleasurable about her first experience with the "pleasures of the flesh" in her present life. "Have you ever been married, Annie?"

"Annie has not married during this present sojourn. As she grew up never knowing her father, she developed a strong bond with her mother, or, rather, renewed a bond which had existed before. Just as mother looked after daughter in the early years of the relationship, so did daughter look after mother in the later years. By the time of her mother's death, Annie was well beyond child-bearing years. She has lived alone ever since."

"I am interested in this idea that bonds can be renewed from lifetime to lifetime. *I've* always felt very close to *my* mother also. Have she and I been together before?"

"Oh yes, many times. In general, any soul for whom you feel an attraction, a closeness, an affinity, will be a soul you have known before. As for you and your mother, in your most recent incarnation previous to this one, you and she were together in England, in that part of the country known as the Lake District. This accounts, in part, for your mother's love of English poetry, especially for the poetry of Wordsworth. Wordsworth himself lived in the Lake District. He was Poet Laureate of England during the last years of his life, from 1843 until his death in 1850. Your mother was in her twenties then. You were mother and daughter in that experience as well, only *you* were the mother and *she* was the daughter. This was one of those 'uneventful' female lives I was telling you about earlier."

"What about my father?"

"Again, many times. The most recent was in Germany in the seventeenth century when you were Greta Bauer. The soul Daniel, who was your father in this present life, was one of your four children then. He was your son Rudolf...

"This seventeenth-century sojourn in Brunswick, Germany, while not your most recent, is the one that has the most bearing on your present life. Perhaps that is the reason you have had dreams of it. The relationship between you and your father is not the only one that has been carried over from the German experience. Your husband then—that is, Greta's husband—Johann Bauer—is the soul you now know as Jacob Wicker."

"Uncle Jacob!" cried Sarah in astonishment. As she allowed this extraordinary piece of information to settle into her consciousness, she smiled. The idea that she had once been married to her Uncle Jacob was not that difficult to believe.

"Also, the woman in that German experience who accused you of witchcraft—she was a neighbor; an unhappy, barren woman who envied you your four healthy children—is the soul you now know as Hester, once Wicker, now Andersson."

Sarah shook her head in disbelief. "No, no, that can't be true."

Annie continued, undeterred by Sarah's protestations. "One of the reasons that you, your father, and your Uncle Jacob decided to reincarnate together in this present sojourn—besides your strong mutual affection for one another—was to assist the soul Hester in becoming a more trusting, more loving soul."

"No, Annie, that can't be right. Aunt Hester *is* a loving soul. When my father and mother and I first moved here from Massachusetts, Aunt Hester allowed my mother and me to stay at her house during that first winter. Then, after my father died, she took my mother and me in again, and we've been living with her ever since—for the past two and a half years!"

"But you and your mother are family. The test of love is not whether we can love our own family. Even the least developed souls can do as much. The test of love is whether we can love and trust the stranger, the foreigner, the enemy, those who are different from ourselves."

Sarah capitulated. "I guess Aunt Hester does have trouble loving and trusting people outside the family—and people who are different. She even has trouble with me sometimes . . . But I know she would risk her own life to protect me. She has already done so."

"Yes, your Aunt Hester has made tremendous strides during this present lifetime. Her husband Nathan has been a positive influence on her as well."

"Was Uncle Nathan with us in Germany too?"

"No, his ties with the soul Hester are more recent. They were together in nineteenth-century Kansas. They were husband and wife during that experience also. Did you ever wonder why your Uncle Nathan was so drawn to these green, tree-covered mountains? After the flat, tree-less plains of Kansas these mountains seemed like Paradise."

"But I'm drawn to these mountains too."

"Yes, you like everything high. You have a need to see far. That is the seeker in you . . . There was one other soul from that German experience who has also left an imprint on this present sojourn. That was the soul Katarina, the young girl who died in your place when the soul Hester accused you of witchcraft. Katarina was Ruth Wicker."

Sarah was struck dumb. She could not have been more struck dumb if a beam from the ceiling had fallen and hit her on the head. "Kati... was... my... Aunt Ruth??"

"Yes. For reasons known only to herself, the soul Kati elected to be born again into the world, as your Aunt Hester's twin sister. Clearly, part of the reason was to show Hester the true meaning of love and forgiveness. Also, no doubt, she wanted to renew her acquaintance with the soul you know as Jacob. Like you and she, they too have shared many Earth experiences. They were brother and sister in Germany; they were brother and sister again in the present life. In fact, all three of you—you, the soul Kati, and the soul Jacob—have been together many times."

"I wish I had known my Aunt Ruth," lamented Sarah. "Why did she have to die so very young?"

"Annie knew your Aunt Ruth. Tomorrow morning, when she is rested, why don't you ask her about her... It is time for Annie to sleep now."

The next morning Sarah was awakened by a hand on her shoulder. She opened her eyes and looked into Annie's smiling face. "Do you think you're fit for travelin'?" asked the old woman.

Sarah saw that Annie had on her coat and was holding her "doctorin'" bag in her hand. "Where are you going, Annie?"

"Gwine t' catch me a babe. Allison McGill's babe is a-comin' this mornin'. In fact, her husband Caleb is on his way t' fetch me right this minute."

"How do you know?"

Annie shrugged. "Don't know how I know. When I woke up this mornin', the first thought in my haid was, 'Caleb's on his way.' I reckon mebbe I found it out when I was a-rummagin' around in that big old root cellar you was a-talkin' about yesterd'y."

670

Sarah sat up on the edge of the bed. "Yes, I think I can travel—provided it's not too far."

"Hit's only about a mile, an' hit's all downhill."

"Do you have anything I could wear? This dress I have on isn't very long."

Annie laughed. "That wasn't meant t' be a dress. That's just somethin' I made for you t' sleep in. Made it out of an old feedsack that Edgar must a-found in the woods that day he found you."

Sarah felt a shiver run up her spine. Annie walked to the fireplace and removed a dress hanging from a peg in the ceiling joist above it. "Here," she said, "try this one on. Hit should fit yuh. You can put it on right over top t'other if'n you want."

"I think I'll take this one off, if you don't mind."

"Suit yourself."

Sarah quickly divested herself of the feedsack and tried on the dress that Annie had handed her. "It fits perfectly!"

"Hit should. Hit's your dress. Hit's the one you was a-wearin' when we found you. I sewed up the tear. Couldn't wash the blood out, so I b'iled up some walnut hulls an' dyed it brown."

"I think I like it better now than before. Thank you, Annie."

Halfway down the mountain they met Caleb coming up. "Hurry, Granny, hurry! The baby hit's a-comin'!"

"Hold onto your britches, Caleb. I'm on my way. I even brung a helper with me."

Caleb cast a quick glance in Sarah's direction but did not take time to notice her. His mind was much too preoccupied with the impending birth of his child. Sarah noticed that Annie had not introduced her by name, probably quite intentionally, if it were true, as Annie had said, that people all over the mountains had been talking about her after the mill fire.

Even before the house came into view they could hear the screams. "Hurry, Annie, she's a-gwine t' die."

"Now, calm down, Caleb. I'm hurryin' as fast as I can."

They entered the house and followed the screams to a back room. Caleb appeared to be a man in his mid- to late-forties, so it came as a bit of a surprise to Sarah when she found that Caleb's wife Allison was a young girl approximately the same age as herself. She was lying on her back in the bed with her legs drawn up. It was evident from the huge bulge in her mid-section that the new life inside her had grown about as much as it was going to within the confines of her womb, and was seeking new space into which to expand. Annie examined the expectant mother, then turned to the anxious husband. "Caleb, get an ax an' be quick about it!"

Obediently Caleb ran outside as Sarah looked at Annie in disbelief. A moment later Caleb returned with the ax. "Now sink it into the floor under the bed."

Caleb got down on his hands and knees and did as instructed.

"Hush now, child," said Annie, mopping the sweat from the young girl's face. "Hit's a-gwine t' be all right. Your husband's stuck the ax in the floor under the bed. That'll take away the pain." She turned to Caleb. "You got the hot water ready?"

"Just like you told me, Granny."

"Good. First thang we'll do is make some birthin' tea."

"Birthing tea?" inquired Sarah. "What's that?"

"Oh, just a li'l of this an' a li'l of that," replied Annie as she removed several tins from her bag and opened each in turn. "First a few squaw vine leaves." These she crushed between her fingers and dropped into the kettle of water. "Then some powdered spikenard root." This too she added to the kettle. "An' then some black snakeroot—that's black cohosh."

"Yes," said Sarah, "I remember."

After allowing the tea to steep for a few minutes, Annie asked Caleb for a cup. "Hit should steep a bit longer," said Annie, "but I ain't sure we got time t' wait." She poured some of the tea into the cup and handed it to Sarah. "Here, see that she drinks it."

Sitting down on the edge of the bed, Sarah held the cup of tea as Allison sipped it. From the moment she had entered the room Sarah had felt her heart go out to this young teenaged girl who seemed to be suffering so terribly. She was glad now to see the young mother-to-be becoming calmer. At least she was no longer screaming and writhing in the bed. Either the pain was no longer as severe, or she was no longer feeling it. Either the ax or the tea had done the trick.

"Hold her still now," instructed Annie. "The babe's a-comin'."

Sarah positioned herself behind Allison's head and took hold of her hands. She felt Allison's fingernails dig into her palms.

"Ever seen a babe bein' birthed?" asked Annie of her young assistant.

"I've seen baby cows and pigs being born," replied Sarah distractedly, as she watched in fascination as Annie began feeling for the infant's head inside the womb, "and baby deer . . . and foxes . . . and bobcats . . . but I've never seen a human baby being born before."

Caleb shot her a quick questioning glance, but his attention was soon redirected to the drama transpiring on the bed. The infant's head was clearly visible now.

"Keep pushin', girl," encouraged Annie. "The haid's a-comin'."

Over the course of the next twenty to thirty minutes Sarah watched from her vantage point at the head of the bed as young Allison's belly slowly collapsed before her eyes and as the new being emerged, anxious inch by anxious inch, into the world.

"He's out," said Annie at last. "Now we gotta get him breathin'." Bending down over the bed she pressed her own mouth over the nose and mouth of the newborn infant and began sucking out mucus and spitting it into her hand. Then, quickly wiping her hands, she picked the still motionless infant up off the bed by its ankles and slapped the bottoms of its feet.

There was no response. Sarah and the others watched anxiously as Annie slapped the infant's feet a second time, even harder. Surely, thought Sarah as she watched Annie prepare to strike the poor, dangling, inverted creature a third time, this was no way to welcome a new soul into the world. But as the first cry of the newborn pierced the anxious silence of the room, she felt a sensation of great joy and elation rush through her.

"Congratulations, Caleb," said Annie, offering a smile of comfort to the nervous husband, "you got yourself another son."

She laid the baby on the bed, tied off the cord and cut it, then using the warm water Caleb had brought her, she bathed the small, cherub-like creature, bundled it in a blanket, and returned it to its smiling mother.

It was the middle of the afternoon before Annie and Sarah left the McGill house and began making their way slowly back up the mountain. Sarah found the return part of the journey much more exhausting than the earlier downhill portion. She was not nearly fully recovered from her own recent physical ordeal, and she found it necessary to stop frequently to rest. She used the rest stops as occasions to question Annie about some things she had not understood back at the McGill house.

"Annie, you congratulated Mr. McGill on the birth of 'another son.' How many other sons does he have?"

"Four other sons . . . an' three daughters."

"How is that possible, Annie? Allison couldn't be more than eighteen years old."

"She's only sixteen. But the other seven children weren't hers. Caleb had them by his first wife, Nora. Nora died two years ago. Caleb just married Allison this past spring."

"So this is only the first child they've had together?"

"Hit's Allison's first all right. Ain't so sure hit's Caleb's at all."

"What do you mean?"

"Takes nine months for a babe t' ripen. That means the seed was planted back in January. I don't think Caleb an' Allison was ever close enough t' hold a conversation afore they was married in June."

"Then that means that someone else must have been the father?"

"Good gracious, girl. For somebody who's so smart about some thangs, you sure are dumb about others. 'Course that's what it means."

"But why didn't she marry the baby's father?"

"Mebbe she didn't *want* t' marry him. Mebbe *he* didn't want t' marry her. Mebbe he was already married. I don't know, child. That's no concern of ours."

"But why did she marry Mr. McGill? He must be thirty years older than she is."

Annie shrugged. "She needed a father for her young'un. He needed a wife an' a mother for his other seven."

Sarah was not sure that Annie's explanation was entirely satisfactory, but she decided to let it pass.

"What about the ax, Annie? Why did you ask Mr. McGill to stick his ax into the floor under the bed?"

"Like I said: t' stop the pain." Annie could see that Sarah was skeptical. "Well, hit worked, didn't it?"

"She did seem to get calmer. But how does it work? How does driving an ax into the floor under the bed take away pain?"

"I'll let you in on a li'l secret: hit don't. Hit only works if'n the one sufferin' the pain *thinks* hit works. Pain's mostly in the mind, you know."

They proceeded slowly up the mountain. It was late in the afternoon when they finally reached the house.

"Looks like Edgar's left you a present," said Annie.

Sarah looked down and saw on the doorstep the "present" to which Annie had alluded. She bent down and picked it up. It was a necklace woven of wild grapevines and adorned with pine cones and bird feathers.

"He's a sweet . . . boy," said Sarah affectionately. She had hesitated to call Edgar a "boy," as he was five years older than herself, but he was so much like a child that she had not been able to bring herself to call him a man. She placed the necklace around her neck. "I'm sorry we missed him."

"Likely he'll be back tomorruh," Annie assured her. "Tomorruh's Saturd'y. He almost always comes around on Saturd'y."

Both gathered an armload of firewood before entering the house. "You rest yourself, child," said the old woman, once they were inside. "I'll make us a fire an' start supper."

Sarah took a seat on the wooden bench next to the fireplace. Even the hard bench felt good now. She watched as Annie laid the fire. Finally she had the opportunity to ask her something she had been wanting to ask her all day. "Annie, last night when you were asleep, you said that you knew my Aunt Ruth, and that I should ask you about her when you woke up." Sarah winced. She hoped Annie would take her meaning, as the series of words she had just strung together had come out sounding like nonsense to her own ears.

Annie smiled and nodded. "Yes, I knew your Aunt Ruth."

Sarah waited for Annie to continue, but the old woman seemed to be more absorbed in the task of getting the fire started. At the moment she was blowing on the still-tentative flames.

"You said the most surprising thing last night, Annie. You said that my friend Kati, who came from the White Light World—the White Light Plane—and who gave her life to save me when we lived in Germany back in the 1600s, was my Aunt Ruth. They were the same soul."

Again the old woman smiled and nodded. Satisfied now that the fire was going to catch without further assistance, she stood up and walked to the window.

"It seems so very sad, Annie. Katarina died when she was only fourteen; Ruth died when she was only eleven. Why did they have to die so young?"

Annie was staring out the window now. A winter wren flew up from its perch on the garden fence post, crossed her field of vision, and lit in a witch-hazel tree just outside the window, but she didn't see it. Her gaze was fixed far beyond. She began to speak slowly, vacantly, as if from a distance. Sarah wondered if she had fallen into another trance.

"Yes, why do they haf t' die so young? . . . When they come here straight from the Light, they don't always come t' stay. They come for a purpose, an' when that purpose is accomplished, they leave us. They wouldn't haf t' come at all—this Earth is no longer their home; their journey here is completed—but they come out of compassion for the rest of us. They have always come when they were needed, an' they will continue to come, til this world is redeemed, til ever' last soul has been set on the path to perfection."

Sarah watched Annie's face as she stared out the window. The sun was setting and the old woman's face was suddenly bathed in an amber light. She was smiling and her eyes were glistening with tears.

"No, Miss Sarah, they don't always come t' stay, but, my glory, how they do shine while they're here! They light up this dark, woeful world like a barn burnin' in the night! Ruthie was like that. She was a barn burnin' in the night! That child was filled with so much love, hit was like God hisself had touched the Earth with his finger. Ever'body noticed it. You couldn't help but notice it. Folks would say, this is what Jesus must a-been like, this is the way God wants us all t' be . . .

"I was with her the mornin' she died. None of my doctorin' could help her. Durin' that last week of her life when she was so awful sick, she never complained. She never cried, not even once, though the poor li'l thang must a-suffered somethin' terrible. And if'n she was afeared of dyin', she never showed it. Right up until the end she kept on a-talkin'–whenever she had the strength– about all the wonderful thangs in her life: about all the beautiful flowers an' trees an' birds an' animals that had been her 'brothers an' sisters'–she always called them her 'brothers an' sisters'–and about all the people she had come to love, an' who had loved her. In all her life she had never said an unkind word about anybody or anythang. She could find no fault with anyone, not even with her sister Hester, who had been less than kind to her. Right up until the end she prayed for Hester t' get well, but she never prayed for herself. When she died . . . I will never forget it as long as I live, that lovely smile on her face when she died. She was completely at peace with death. Just as she taught us how t' live, she taught us how t' die.

"At her funeral, folks who hadn't come down out of the mountains for years, came t' pay their respects. Complete strangers put flowers on her grave an' wept. They all knew–*we* all knew–that we had been blessed. For those few short years one of God's holy ones had walked among us, an' none of us, though we lived t' be a hunnert, was likely ever t' see such a one ag'in . . . No, they don't always come t' stay, but the light they bring with them, they leave here for the rest of us. Hit's been almost forty years now since Ruthie died, but I can tell you this for a fact, Miss

Sarah, nobody who ever knew her, has forgot her. She has lived in our hearts an' memories all these years. She changed ever' life she ever touched. Deep inside me, I can still feel her warmth."

Sarah watched Annie's face as the old woman fell into silent communion with her memories. In the old woman's bright, tear-filled eyes, in the sweet smile on her lips, Sarah could see the outward manifestation of the warmth of which Annie had spoken. Sarah smiled. She too had felt that warmth.

20

WORDS OF PARTING

The next morning Sarah prepared to take her leave.

"Annie, before I go, I'd like to ask your permission to tell one other person about some of the things you've told me these past three days. I think my Uncle Jacob would be very interested in hearing what you've said about souls being reborn, and especially about his sister Ruth coming from the White Light World."

Annie, who was huddled over her cup of ginseng tea, looked up. It was a damp, chilly morning and both the old woman and her young houseguest had sought out the warmth of the fireplace. Annie had taken the seat on the bench; Sarah had remained standing.

"I trust you, an' I trust your Uncle Jacob," replied the old woman, "but I'd be careful hit don't go no fu'ther than that."

"I promise you, it won't."

"That's good enough for me."

Just then Edgar's smiling face appeared at the window. Annie motioned for him to come in. "I told yuh he'd be around bright an' early this mornin'."

Edgar entered and without even looking at Annie hurried straight to Sarah. He would undoubtedly have thrown his arms around her in an act of spontaneous affection had he not reconsidered at the very last moment and stopped an arm's length short of her. The smile of childish delight on his face, however, left little doubt that he was overjoyed to see her again.

"Good morning, Edgar," said Sarah, returning his smile.

"Edgar," said Annie, "Sarah's gwine t' be a-leavin' us this mornin'. How would you like t' walk her over to Rushin' Creek?"

Edgar's smile vanished instantly. He shook his head in vigorous disapproval.

"That's all right, Annie," said Sarah. "I'm sure if you give me a few directions I'll be able to find my own way."

"Don't mind Edgar," said Annie, sipping her tea. "He'll be glad t' take yuh. Hit's just that he don't want t' see yuh leave." She turned to Edgar. "She's *got* t' go, Edgar. She's got family who's gwine t' start worryin' if we keep her too much longer . . . But mebbe she'll come back an' visit us ag'in sometime."

Edgar, who had taken his eyes off Sarah for just a moment in order to register his protest to Annie, now looked back at Sarah, an expression of entreaty and expectation on his face.

"Yes, I'd like that," said Sarah, "I'd like that very much."

Edgar nodded his head and smiled, but more in quiet resignation than in unabashed delight. Sarah put on her coat and buttoned it, then went to the window sill by the bed and picked up the necklace of grapevines and pine cones and bird feathers that Edgar had made for her. "Thank you for the gift, Edgar," she said as she placed the necklace over her head and around her neck.

This simple act seemed to have a transfiguring effect upon Edgar. Suddenly, like the sun emerging from behind a dark cloud, the expression of childish delight which had illunined his face when he had first entered the room, reappeared.

"Edgar," said Annie, "could you wait outside a minute? I'd like t' talk to Sarah alone."

Edgar bowed politely and did as he was bidden.

Finishing her cup of tea, Annie rose from her seat on the bench and walked to the curtain dividing the two rooms and looked through. Satisfied that she and Sarah were once again alone in the house, she drew her young companion aside. "Listen," she began in a low voice so as not to be overheard in the event that Edgar were listening just outside the window, "I ain't said nuthin' about what happened to you last Sund'y. I figgered if you wanted t' talk about it, you would. But you didn't, so I didn't ax. But hit was plain t' see from lookin' at the state of your clothin' an' the nature of your injuries that some feller roughed you up purty good an' took some liberties with your virtues . . . I just wanted you t' know that I know that, an' I think you're a mighty brave girl for bearin' up as well as you have."

"Thanks, Annie," replied Sarah uneasily.

"You ain't afraid of Edgar, are yuh?"

Sarah smiled. "No."

" 'Cause he won't hurt yuh."

"I know. He saved my life. You both did. I don't know how I'll ever be able to repay you."

"Just come back an' visit sometime. I expect I'll be here for another ten or twenny years or so."

"Yes," said Sarah, studying her closely, "I think you probably will."

She smiled, gave Annie a parting embrace, and let herself out.

It was a cold, overcast day and as she followed Edgar through the still, hushed forest, her thoughts turned inward. How would she explain her misadventure to her Uncle Nathan and Aunt Hester? In her note to her Uncle Nathan she had said only that she was at Annie Whitehead's and that she would be home in a few days. She had not said *why* she was at Annie Whitehead's. Did she dare tell them the truth? Did she dare tell them that she had been assaulted and raped by the two Hicks boys? What purpose would that serve? But they would want to know and she would have to tell them something. She had been gone for nearly a week. She felt that she owed them some sort of explanation.

But it was impossible for her to keep her mind focused on this problem. It seemed self-indulgent, frivolous even, to be thinking about her own small mishap and how to explain it when confronted with the almost certain knowledge that Otis was dead. That was the *real* tragedy. She had already decided to say nothing to her Uncle Nathan and Aunt Hester about Otis, but that did not stop her from thinking about him.

She had also decided that when she got back to Rushing Creek she would first go to see her Uncle Jacob. Not only would that defer the moment when she would have to face her Uncle Nathan and Aunt Hester, but it would also allow her to share the exciting news about Ruth with her Uncle Jacob.

As they descended the north side of the mountain, Edgar continued to cast frequent glances back at Sarah, just as he had done ever since leaving Annie's, to make sure that she was still following him and that he was not going too fast for her. Shortly after noon the bridge at Bryson's mill came into view through the trees.

"Thank you, Edgar," said Sarah when they reached the road, "I can find my own way from here."

Instead of stopping, Edgar continued on over the bridge. At Lehman's store he was about to turn left when Sarah called to him again. "No, Edgar, I'm not going that way. I'm going *this* way." She pointed to the right.

Edgar shook his head and pointed left.

"I'm not going to my Uncle Nathan's just now. I want to visit my Uncle Jacob first."

Immediately Edgar changed his course and headed down the road that Sarah had indicated. Sarah was about to repeat what she had said about being able to find her own way, but then thought better of it. It was becoming apparent that Edgar was determined to see her safely to her door—if not to her Uncle Nathan's door, then to some other—and it was equally apparent that he derived great satisfaction in being able to serve her in this way. She decided she had no right to deny him this small pleasure.

When they reached the lane leading into the Wicker farm, Sarah tried once again to bid her companion farewell. Again she was unsuccessful. With his long strides Edgar headed down the lane. Not even when Isaac's house and the barn came into view did he give any indication that he was prepared to consider his service fully rendered. Uncertain of his way, he dropped in behind her and followed her around the barn to her Uncle Jacob's house. When she stepped onto the porch, he did likewise. When she reached the door, she turned to face him.

"Good-by, Edgar," she said tenderly, as she might address a child. "Thank you. Thank you for everything."

Edgar bowed three times to acknowledge her words of gratitude, but the light had once again gone out of his face. Moved by the sadness that she now saw in his eyes, Sarah placed her hands on his shoulders, and lifting herself to her toes, kissed him lightly on the cheek. Whereas any further words of gratitude she might have spoken would have failed, this small act of affection was all that was needed to once again restore the childlike smile to Edgar's face.

She opened the door and let herself in. Closing the door behind her she went to the nearest window to watch Edgar make his way down off the porch and out along the walk to the driveway.

"Uncle Jacob," she called.

There was no response. She had not really expected to find her Uncle Jacob in the house this time of day. She went to another window and was able to catch one last glimpse of Edgar as he was heading out the lane. She felt ashamed of herself for wanting to be rid of Edgar–to be rid of someone so childlike and affectionate, someone so totally devoted to her, someone who had saved her life–but there were just too many other things on her mind just now.

As soon as she was certain that there was no chance of Edgar's hearing her, even with his remarkable ears, she opened the door and stepped back outside. Seeing no one about, she made her way out to the barn. Finding no one therein either, she began checking, one by one, the other outbuildings. At the tractor shed she found Isaac's tractor, but no Isaac, no Jacob. Scanning the fields for signs of activity, her eyes fixed on, not her Uncle Jacob, but another old friend, who was already cantering in her direction.

"Hello, Jesse!" she said, meeting the mule at the pasture fence. As she rubbed the mule's ears and neck, several cows also ambled over to the fence, then several more. As she greeted each animal in turn, her eyes continued to cast about for signs of activity of a more human kind.

Still seeing no one, she concluded that her uncles must be taking a late mid-day meal at the old house. She had just begun making her way in that direction when she heard Isaac's truck coming in the lane. As she rounded the barn, she saw her eldest uncle emerge from his truck and hurry toward the house.

"Uncle Isaac," she called after him, "have you seen Uncle Jacob?"

"Sarah!" he cried, wheeling about. "My Gawd, you're alive! Whar in tarnation have you been?"

"I've been at Annie Whitehead's house," replied Sarah, a little startled by her Uncle Isaac's reaction. "Didn't Uncle Nathan tell you?"

"Nathan has no idea whar you are! He's been out a-lookin' for you all week! We *all* been out a-lookin' for you! The whole town's been out a-lookin' for you! Nathan an' Jacob an' your Ma are still out a-lookin'! Most folks've given you up for daid!"

"Didn't Uncle Nathan get my note?" asked Sarah, becoming more and more bewildered.

"Note? What note?"

"I sent a note with Edgar."

"Who's Edgar?"

"Edgar? He's . . . Well, Edgar is a little hard to explain. He's a man who . . . Well, really he's more like a child . . . He can't talk." She was finding it difficult to talk herself.

"Cain't talk? You mean the Johnson boy from over the mountain? The boy I just passed on the road? You trusted the Johnson boy t' deliver a note? You must be out of your mind! That boy's a half-wit!"

Sarah bit her lower lip in an attempt to cut off the surge of emotions she now felt coursing through her mind and body. The anger in her Uncle Isaac's voice and the harshness of his words had hurt her deeply. Especially hurtful was the contemptuous manner in which he had spoken about Edgar. But if she was hurt, she was also confused. Why hadn't Edgar delivered her note? She turned to leave.

"Hey, whar you gwine?"

"To Uncle Nathan's."

"Get in the truck. I'll drive yuh thar. Just give me one second t' let Martha know you're all right." He hurried into the house, but re-emerged almost immediately with Martha right behind him.

"Sarah!" cried Martha, "you're alive! Whar've you been?"

"No time for blabberin'," shot Isaac to his wife as he cranked the engine. "I got t' get her over to Nathan's."

Martha waved after them as they roared out the lane.

When they reached the hard road Isaac slowed down only enough to allow him to negotiate the turn, but not enough to prevent his rear tires from skidding all the way across to the far shoulder. As they sped toward town they spied a solitary figure in the distance walking along the side of the road.

"It's Edgar," said Sarah as they approached. "Maybe we could give him a ride into town."

Isaac rolled down his window, but instead of slowing down, he accelerated and steered a course directly for the swiftly striding figure. Sarah could see the startled look on Edgar's face as he turned to see Isaac's truck bearing down on him. At the last instant Isaac swerved away.

"You half-wit!" Isaac yelled out the window as they roared past.

Sarah looked back in shock and alarm. The near miss had sent Edgar sprawling into the roadside brambles and had left him covered with dust. She herself had fared only slightly better. Isaac's sudden swerving had caused her head to be slammed against the side of the cab. The impact had re-opened the cut that she had received a few months earlier when she had been struck by the stone. The injury was not nearly as severe this time, but there was blood. A drop of it had fallen onto the necklace that Edgar had given her. Isaac seemed to be unaware that she had hit the side of the cab, as he was not looking at her, but rather craning his head out the window and looking back in the direction of Edgar in order to assess the extent of damage and humiliation his little prank had inflicted. Sarah vowed to say nothing about her injury or anything else for the remainder of the trip, which she was now wishing to be over as soon as possible.

Isaac turned his attention back to the road, but whatever satisfaction he had derived from running Edgar into the brambles, apparently it was not nearly enough. "Jesus, girl!" he cursed, pounding on the steering wheel, "how could yuh trust a half-wit like that t' deliver a note? You know how much trouble you caused us? Jesus!"

He came to a screeching stop outside of Lehman's store and jumped out. Bounding up the steps he crossed the porch and thrust open the door. "I got her!" he yelled to the storekeeper and to all others within earshot. "She was over at Annie Whitehead's."

Before anyone had a chance to respond or approach the truck, Isaac had already jumped back in and was speeding out of town to the west. As they careened around bends in the road Sarah braced herself so as to avoid further injury. When they reached Nathan's lane she placed both hands on the dashboard, but even this precaution did not prevent her from being tossed around as they rattled and bounced down through the woods. She was relieved when they finally came to a skidding stop in Nathan and Hester's driveway.

No sooner had she stepped out of the truck than she was seized by Hester. "Lord be praised! You're alive! You had us all worried to death. Whar you been, child?"

"She's been over at Annie Whitehead's," scowled Isaac.

"You're hurt," cried Hester, examining the cut over Sarah's right eye.

"It's nothing, Aunt Hester."

"How'd it happen?"

"I hit my head on the side of the truck on the way over from Uncle Isaac's."

Hester gave Isaac a scornful look. Isaac shrugged.

"Your Ma's gwine t' be glad t' see you!" exclaimed Hester, turning her attention back to Sarah. "She remembers ever'thang now! She remembers all about them years you all lived up in the mountains! . . . I better get the shotgun. I'm s'posed t' fire a shot as a signal that you come back, or else they'll be out a-lookin' for you til dark."

She went into the house and re-emerged with the shotgun. "I'll fire three shots," she said, walking around to the back of the house. "Three shots means good news." She fired the three shots. "They may be too far away t' hear, but they should be back soon anyway. Thar's only about three hours of daylight left."

Just before dark Nathan, Jacob, and Elizabeth came struggling up the hill from the direction of the creek. It was evident from their bowed heads and their slow, trudging gaits that they had not heard Hester's three shots. Sarah, who had been watching from the top of the hill, was the first to see them.

"Mother!" she cried, as she ran down the hillside between the hayfield and the cornfield in the twilight darkness.

Startled, Elizabeth looked up and peered anxiously and unbelievingly at the figure rushing toward her through the dusk. Suddenly Sarah was in her arms. "Oh, thank God!" cried Elizabeth, deliriously embracing her daughter. "Thank God! Thank God!"

Nathan all but tore Sarah away from Elizabeth and crushed her to his own chest. Jacob patiently waited his turn.

They returned to the house where they were joined by Isaac and Hester, but the emotions did not subside there. For the next thirty minutes so many tears were shed, so many prayers of thanks offered up, that it seemed as though a dam had burst. All of the anguish of the past week–all of the fears, all of the terrible dread–that had built up as hour after hour and day after day had gone by without a trace of Sarah, had suddenly been released in one overwhelming instant, sweeping all before it away in a flood of emotion.

Not until a full half hour had passed, not until the flood waters had begun to recede, did anyone think to ask Sarah to give an accounting of the week just past. Isaac's explanation that she had been at Annie Whitehead's did not satisfy everyone.

"Who is this Annie Whitehead anyway?" inquired Nathan. Nathan, Hester, Elizabeth, and Sarah had taken their seats at the table. Isaac and Jacob had elected to remain standing.

"She's a granny woman," explained Hester. "Three of us right here in this room was birthed by her. She used t' live with her Ma up on the mountain above Charlie Cole's. When her Ma died, Annie moved away. That was back durin' the war–the first war. She was an old woman even then. She must be in her eighties by now."

"She's eighty-four," confirmed Sarah.

"An' where does she live now?" asked Nathan.

"About five miles south of Bryson's mill," replied Sarah, "on the other side of the mountain."

"An' how'd *you* get there?"

Sarah paused to gather her thoughts. The moment of truth had come. She would have to decide, and decide very quickly, what to tell and how to tell it. She had already decided that under no circumstances would she tell the whole truth. "A man named Edgar carried me to Annie's house," she began, honestly enough. "Edgar is a friend of Annie's who can't talk. He and Annie were up on the mountain on the other side of Rushing Creek digging ginseng roots last Sunday afternoon when Edgar found me. I had had . . . an accident. I had fallen and hit my head on a rock. I was unconscious when Edgar found me. He carried me the whole five miles to Annie's house, up and over the mountains. He saved my life, he and Annie."

"This 'accident' . . ." interrupted Nathan.

"I never even regained consciousness until Wednesday morning," continued Sarah, deliberately cutting off Nathan's question. "I knew that you'd be worried about me, so I wrote a note. Annie gave it to Edgar to bring to you . . . but I guess he never did . . ."

"No, he never did," confirmed Nathan. "About this 'accident' . . ."

"Uncle Isaac says he's a half-wit. I don't know if that's true or not. It's hard to tell what he knows and what he doesn't know since he never talks. But he's a very sweet and gentle soul. He made me this necklace." She touched her fingers to the necklace, then looked directly at Isaac. "One day Annie and I were talking about the possibility of Jesus coming again. Annie said that if Jesus *does* come back, he might not be what people expect. She said that he might even come back as someone like Edgar."

Isaac lowered his eyes. "Aw, hell, I didn't mean nuthin' by it. I didn't know about you bein' hurt."

Nathan took advantage of the momentary silence to try to once again interpose his question. "Sarah, we found Frank Hicks' body in the creek. Did he by any chance have anything t' do with this 'accident' of yours?"

Now it was Sarah who lowered her eyes. For a long moment she stared at the grain in the oak table top in front of her, then slowly nodded her head. A blanket of silence fell over the room as everyone held their breath. Sarah had just confirmed their worst fears.

"My Gawd!" cried Isaac.

"Did he . . . hurt you?" asked Nathan cautiously, tenderly.

Again she nodded her head.

"How? How did he hurt you?"

"He came up behind me when I was sitting by a waterfall," she began in a deliberate monotone, so as to remain as detached and unemotional as possible. "He grabbed me and pushed me under the water. He held my head under water. I thought I was going to drown. I had swallowed a lot of water . . . But then he pulled me out. He carried me and dragged me . . . I kept trying to get away but I couldn't. He carried me and dragged me, then he picked me up and threw me down against a rock. He threw me down hard. It knocked the wind out of me . . . I couldn't breathe . . . I was choking . . ."

"We found a rope," interjected Nathan. "Was he chokin' you with a rope?"

Sarah felt a tremor go through her body. They had found the rope! She had hoped that she could avoid mentioning the rope. She had no choice now but to nod her head in affirmation.

"Oh my Gawd!" cried Isaac. "Hit's a good thang that son of a bitch is daid or I'd kill him myself!"

As anguishing and as emotionally wrenching as the past week had been, everyone found that they were being traumatized all over again by Sarah's recounting of her "accident." They had all heard enough, had no wish to hear another word, but there was one more question which had to be asked. It fell to Nathan to ask it.

"Sarah, there's just one thing I haf t' know. Did Frank Hicks . . . ? Did he . . . ?"

This was it, thought Sarah. This was one of the questions she had dreaded most. She knew perfectly well what the question was going to be, but she wasn't about to give her Uncle Nathan any help in asking it. "Did he what, Uncle Nathan?"

"Never mind," said Nathan, breaking off his interrogation. "We're all just glad you're home safe."

Later that night, after Isaac and Jacob had left and after a late supper, Sarah was confronted again, this time by her mother, and this time in the privacy of their room. As Elizabeth held her daughter in her arms, weeping tears of nervous joy, she asked the question that Nathan had been unable to ask.

"Sarah, I want to know something and I want you to tell me the truth, no matter how much it hurts. You've always told the truth before . . . Did Frank Hicks have intercourse with you? Did he penetrate you?"

Sarah gasped. This was the question she had been expecting, but she had not expected it to be asked so directly. But then, she had not expected that it would be her mother who would be asking it. "No, Mother," she answered without further hesitation, "he did not." It was true. Frank had not. Jemmy had, but Frank had not.

"Thank God, thank God!" cried Elizabeth.

Sarah too had reason to be thankful. Thus far she had been able to give an accounting of her terrible ordeal without implicating Frank's younger brother Jemmy. The last thing she wanted to do was to bring the wrath of the whole town down on Jemmy's head. If Isaac had threatened to kill Frank, it was not likely that he would have hesitated to kill Jemmy. If she had been asked if anyone besides Frank had been involved, she almost certainly would have lied. She was glad that she had not been asked.

Mother and daughter sat down together on the edge of the bed, their hands locked in Elizabeth's lap. They sat quietly for several minutes without looking each other in the face. Finally Elizabeth spoke.

"Sarah, I'm terribly sorry about your father. I feel that, in a way, I'm responsible for his death. When the bear attacked him, he called for me to get the gun. I tried. I really tried . . ." She broke into sobs.

Sarah put her arms around her. "It's all right, Mother."

"But I was too frightened. I dropped the gun . . ."

"I know, I know."

"I didn't know what to do. I ran up the hill screaming like a madwoman. I guess I was hoping to scare the bear away. But before I could get close, your father yelled at me to get back. 'Get back to the house,' he yelled, 'for God's sake, get back to the house.' . . . Those were his last words."

Elizabeth struggled to contain her emotions. When she had regained a degree of composure, she continued. "Yesterday your Uncle Nathan asked me what I planned to do with the old Puckett place. He's been paying the taxes on it since your father died. He wondered if he should continue paying the taxes, or whether he should try to sell it. I told him that *I* would never be able to live up there again, but that I wouldn't feel right about agreeing to his trying to sell it without talking to you first. At the time neither of us was sure we'd ever see you again."

"What *are* we going to do, Mother? Are we going to stay here with Uncle Nathan and Aunt Hester?"

"No, Sarah. I think we've imposed on these good people long enough. I think we should go back to Massachusetts . . . There's nothing for me here without your father."

The exterior calmness with which Sarah received this unexpected pronouncement gave no clue to the shock waves it had sent through her brain. Leave Rushing Creek? Go back to Massachusetts? The idea had never entered her mind even as a possibility. She could understand how, from her mother's point of view, it made perfectly good sense to move back to Massachusetts. Massachusetts was her home. Most of her life had been lived there. But Sarah hardly remembered Massachusetts. Most of her life had been lived here, in the mountains of western North Carolina. "When would we be leaving, Mother?"

"I have no definite plans. Perhaps in a week or two. I don't think we should wait much longer than that. With winter coming on, the sooner we get moved and settled the better."

The next morning was Sunday, and it came as a surprise to everyone, and to none more so than Hester, when Elizabeth announced her desire to go to church. She had her own reasons for wishing to do so. She felt that her prayers of the past week had been answered, and even though she had been thanking God almost without ceasing during every waking moment since Sarah's safe return, she decided it would do no harm to thank Him–or, as she would have preferred, That–from the inside of a church as well. In fact, she and Sarah did not even wait for Nathan and the wagon. As the morning air was crisp and clear and the sun was shining, they decided to walk.

Once inside the church, instead of taking her accustomed seat with the other teenaged girls directly in front of the pulpit, Sarah elected to sit with her mother and Aunt Hester in the section of benches reserved for the women. She hoped that no one would misconstrue this sudden departure from the norm. She wanted everyone to understand that she merely wished to be with her mother and not attribute this move to a belief on her part that she had suddenly, in a week's time, attained to womanhood, even though had anyone besides herself and possibly one other person in the congregation–one teenaged boy whose identity she was not about to reveal–known the whole truth of the matter, they might have had reason to do so.

The presence of Elizabeth and Sarah generated considerable interest amongst the congregation, as attested by the heavy drone of murmuring before the start of the service. In the course of the past week, everyone without exception had learned of Sarah's disappearance. Many of the men had even joined in the search parties. Nearly everyone had given her up for dead. Her sudden reappearance was greeted with surprise by all, with gladness by many, and with positive jubilation by the few who knew her well. The Reverend Eby was one of those in the last category. He caught sight of her as he rose from his chair on the platform to lead the congregation in the singing of the first hymn of the morning. Undoubtedly he would have learned of her presence earlier had she been sitting in her accustomed seat. Without regard for appearance or protocol, he immediately stepped down off the platform, drew her out of her seat, and embraced her as the organ played.

As for Elizabeth, all had known of her existence. Most had seen her at Emily Wicker's funeral. But few had ever expected to see her in church. Most had, years ago, given her up as a lost soul. Among those especially surprised and delighted by her presence was her brother-in-law Jacob.

After the service Elizabeth and Sarah found themselves the centers of attention. Many members of the congregation, most of them total strangers to Elizabeth, came forward with smiles on their faces and hands extended to welcome her to the church. To Sarah they expressed their genuine gladness that the Good Lord had seen fit to deliver her from her ordeal. Sarah was surprised by the rapidity with which the news of her "ordeal" had spread. Everyone seemed to know that she had met with foul play at the hands of Frank Hicks, even though she had not said a word about it herself. Elizabeth thanked everyone for their greetings, Sarah for their concern and prayers. Both left the church elated, and to allay any fears Hester might have about their being late for Sunday dinner, decided to ride home with Nathan and Hester in the wagon instead of walking.

After dinner Sarah excused herself and walked down to the creek. She needed time–time to organize her thoughts, time to order her priorities–and with the move to Massachusetts pending, time was running out. She also had to find time to talk to her Uncle Jacob. But there was another person with whom she wished to speak even more urgently: Jemmy Hicks. Since the death of his mother, Jemmy had been the only member of the Hicks family who had continued coming to church. But he had not come this morning. When Sarah reached the creek, she set her course for upstream. She knew that if either her Uncle Nathan or Aunt Hester had had any idea when she left the house that she was planning to pay a visit to the Hicks farm, they would have pronounced her crazy and done everything in their power to stop her–for which very reason she had purposely neglected to tell them.

She had never been to the Hicks farm, but she had a general idea as to its whereabouts. She knew that it was situated right along the creek, about a mile upstream from her Uncle Nathan's. Undoubtedly the easiest way to get there, and the one that anyone else would have chosen, was by road—out to the hard road, then left, then left again on Whiskey Run Road—but she calculated that the distance must be at least twice as far by road. The most direct route, and the most interesting—if not the smoothest or the least hazardous or even the fastest—was up along the creek, and as this was a section of creek she had never properly explored—she had never followed the creek for more than about two hundred yards *upstream* from her Uncle Nathan's farm—the option of going by road was one to which she had given no serious consideration at all.

She soon discovered that the upper section of creek was not nearly so difficult to negotiate as the lower. The banks were steep and the vegetation thick—in those places where vegetation was able to find any kind of roothold at all amongst the rocks—but as the stream narrowed and the rocks proliferated, she found that it was hardly necessary to resort to the banks at all. By simply jumping from rock to rock in the streambed itself, she was able to make good progress, as well as experience a sense of exhilaration which she never would have experienced had she taken the roads.

The first indication she had that she was nearing human habitation was the smell of woodsmoke. She began to proceed more cautiously, keeping her eyes fixed on the bank ahead. When the farmstead came into view, she paused to scan the landscape for any sign of movement. Seeing nothing but a few chickens, she climbed the bank and made directly for the cluster of ramshackle buildings. She listened closely for any sounds. The air was very still and up to this moment the only sound she had heard was the clucking of the chickens, but now as she approached one of the sheds—and she was approaching everything from the rear—she could hear the muffled grunting of hogs. Suddenly, without warning, two large hounds appeared and came rushing toward her. Smiling, she knelt down to receive them. Too late she realized her mistake. The charging hounds struck her with so much force that she was knocked off her feet, and once they had her down they were absolutely merciless in their affection. As they lapped liberal doses of saliva onto her nose and cheeks, into her ears, and even into her mouth whenever she dared to open it, she tried to reciprocate their greeting by vigorously rubbing the fur on their necks and chests. When their exuberance had spent itself, she picked herself up, shook the dust out of her dress, then retreated to the creek to wash her face, with the two dogs, their tails wagging, following her every step.

With the dogs at her heels she once again made her way up the bank and toward the house. As the dogs had not barked, she had no reason to believe that anyone was any more aware of her presence now than they had been before. She had still seen or heard no one. She had hoped to be able to find Jemmy without running into Wesley, but as there appeared to be no one about outside the house, she decided that she had no choice but to go knock on the door and take her chances. As she walked around to the front of the house she discovered that part of the porch roof had collapsed and that several braces had been shoved under the part still standing in order to keep it from falling as well. With a dog on either side of her she stepped tentatively onto the porch and knocked on the door.

From inside the house she could hear the scuffing of feet. At the last instant before the door opened, she lowered her gaze, remembering how fearful both Jemmy and his father had been about looking her in the eyes. Consequently, when the door swung open, all she could see was a pair of faded denim jeans and worn shoes, but whether they belonged to Wesley or to Jemmy, she could not be sure. She waited nervously for a voice to speak—an exclamation of surprise, a grunt, a scowl, a curse, anything—but there was nothing, not even breathing. The legs and shoes remained absolutely motionless, frozen to the spot. She was about to look up when she heard Wesley's voice.

"Who's thar?"

The voice had not come from directly in front of her, but from further inside the house. She looked up to find Jemmy staring at her with eyes so wide she could see a quarter of an inch of white all around the blue irises.

"Uh, n-nobody, Pa."

"Well, if thar's nobody thar, shut the gaw-dam door! You're lettin' all the heat out!"

Looking over Jemmy's shoulder, Sarah could see Wesley's prostrate form on the sofa. He looked pale and deathly ill. "Jemmy, I've got to talk to you," she whispered.

Jemmy continued to stare at her with eyes wide and mouth agape.

"Shut the gaw-dam door, dammit!"

Trembling, Jemmy stepped out onto the porch and closed the door behind him. "Is yo . . . is yo a ghost?"

She smiled. "No, I'm not a ghost."

"But yo's daid!"

"Jemmy, can we go someplace where we don't have to whisper?"

Jemmy looked around. "We can go anywhar, I reckon."

"Good. How about behind the barn?"

"Yo . . . yo wanna go out b'hind the barn?"

"Yes, or someplace else out of sight from the house. I'd rather your father not know I'm here."

"If'n yo wanna go out b'hind the barn, I reckon that's okay by me."

They walked out around the barn. Sarah led the way, followed closely by the two dogs. Jemmy, his head bowed and his eyes fixed on the ground, brought up the rear. When they were out of sight from the house, Sarah turned to face him.

"Jemmy, have you told anyone about what happened last Sunday?"

He shook his head without raising it.

"Good. I want you to promise me that you won't."

He looked up. "Yo want me t' promise *not* t' tell?" He could not possibly have heard her right.

"Yes. I don't want anyone to know you were there."

He breathed a sigh of relief so immense he nearly fainted from lack of air. "If'n yo want me t' promise not t' tell," he stammered,

696

"then I promise. I won't tell a livin' soul . . . But I don't unnerstand. How can yo be alive? I saw yo daid on the rock. I saw yo'r soul a-gwine up t' Heaven."

"It's true, I was out of my body. As a matter of fact, I was out for three days. But, as you can see, I'm back in it now."

"Yo can get out of yo body, then get back in ag'in?" he asked in astonishment.

"Yes. I don't always go out by choice, but whenever I've been out, I've been able to get back in—at least, so far."

"Then yo *must* be a witch!"

"Maybe I am. I'm not sure I understand exactly what a witch is. But I'm not wicked. I don't have a pact with the Devil. I don't cast evil spells on people. And I had nothing to do with your mother's death."

"I know, I know yo didn't," he said morosely. "She was sick for a real long time. She would a-died anyways, even if she never even hadn't a-seed yo at the mill that day."

Sarah had never heard the English language used in quite this way before, but she thought she understood what he meant. She was glad that he no longer thought of her as evil—if he ever had. Still, he did not seem altogether comfortable in her presence. "You're not afraid of me now, are you?"

"N-no," he replied nervously after a moment's hesitation. "Yo smiled at me. When I was about t' jump off the waterfall, yo looked right at me an' smiled . . . Was that yo'r soul I saw a-floatin' in the air?"

"It was *me*. I *am* my soul."

"But yo looked differ'nt. Yo was all bright an' shiny."

"Yes, I was in my other body. The soul has its own body. Normally people in Earth bodies can't see soul bodies, but I *made* you see mine. I had to. I had to stop you from jumping."

"Yo didn't want me t' jump?"

"No, of course not . . . But I couldn't save Frank. I couldn't make *him* see me. *Or* hear me. He fell off the log when he tried to cross the gorge."

"I'se glad yo didn't save Frank. I'se glad he's daid . . . I hated him!"

"No, you didn't. He was your brother."

"Don't yo hate him too? Don't yo hate the both of us for what we done to yuh?"

A pained expression came over Sarah's face as she recalled her harrowing ordeal of the previous week. It had been almost one week ago to the hour. "I can truthfully say," she said solemnly, "it was an experience I would prefer never to have to go through again. I've never been so frightened in all my life—or so physically distressed. There were moments when I thought I was going to have to leave this body for good . . . But, as you can see, I'm all right now . . . No, I don't hate either of you. I certainly don't hate you Jemmy." She smiled. "How could I, after all those nice things you said to me when you thought I was dead?"

Jemmy's mouth dropped open. "Yo *heared* what I said?"

"Every word. I was right above your head."

Jemmy buried his face in his hands. All he wanted to do at the moment was find a hole big enough to crawl into and die.

Sensitive to the fact that Jemmy was deeply embarrassed by his feelings toward her, Sarah decided to change the subject. "You weren't in church this morning."

He shook his head. "Pa was real bad sick this mornin'. He didn't want me t' leave him."

Sarah had seen with her own eyes the debilitated state of Wesley's health, but she did not think that this was the real reason, or at least not the only reason, for Jemmy's not being in church. "Do you think you will come next Sunday?"

He shrugged.

"I think you ought to. If you don't, people may start to get suspicious. They may think you have something to hide."

"Will yo be thar?" he asked hopefully.

"Yes, I expect I'll be there next Sunday. I'm not sure about the Sunday after that however. My mother and I are going to be leaving Rushing Creek soon."

"Yo's a-leavin' Rushin' Creek?" The shock and sadness in his voice and eyes were unmistakable. It was hardly less than the shock and sadness that Sarah herself had felt when she had first learned this news.

"Yes," she replied, nodding sadly.

On this solemn note she departed. As she followed the creek back to her Uncle Nathan's, she reflected on how one burden had been lifted from her, only to be replaced by another. For two and a half years she had worried about the state of her mother's mind. Now that mind had been restored, along with its full store of memories. Her mother now remembered everything about those eight years that they had lived in the mountains, down to the last painful detail. But it was those same memories–and the knowing that the joyous ones could never be repeated and the painful ones could never be forgotten–that were now forcing her to leave Rushing Creek and return to Massachusetts. Sarah also suspected that the experience of the past week had done little to make her mother want to stay. Her own ordeal had lasted less than an hour; her mother's had lasted six full days. Sarah could understand her mother's decision to return to Massachusetts, but it was a decision she found weighing heavily on her own soul.

"I'll be goin' up to Wesley Hicks' today," announced Nathan the following morning at breakfast. "I had a run-in with his porch last week, an' I promised him I'd come back an' fix it."

"Will you be needing any help, Uncle Nathan?" asked Sarah.

Nathan looked at her, a bemused expression on his face. "Now, who exactly would you have in mind?"

"Me."

He smiled. "If Otis was here, you know what *he'd* say, don't yuh? He'd say, 'Very funny!' . . . You're the *last* person I'd take up to Wesley Hicks' . . . I *should* take Isaac. It was his truck that done all the damage."

"I'd sure like to a-seen that," interjected Hester, laughing. It was the first time she had laughed in a long, long time.

Nathan laughed too. "Yeah, you should a-seen the look on Wesley's face when he came out of the house an' discovered Isaac's truck parked on his porch an' his porch roof on top of it." Then, turning to Sarah, he added, "I expect if I need any help, I'll be able t' get Wesley t' give me a hand. If *you* feel up t' workin' today, you can help out around here. You can give your Aunt Hester a hand with the milkin' this evenin' if I don't get back in time . . . But if you wanna take the day off, I can understand that too."

Sarah helped Nathan load his tools into the wagon, then returned to the house. She spent the rest of the day working around the farm with her mother and Hester. It was almost dark when Nathan returned.

"I'm tired and I'm hungry," he grumbled as he entered the kitchen. "I hope you saved some supper for me."

" 'Course we saved some supper for yuh," retorted Hester. "Did yuh think we was gwine t' let yuh starve?"

He sat down at the table. "What a job! It would a-been easier to a-tore down the whole house an' started from the ground up. Wesley was no help at all. The man's so sick he can scarcely get out of bed. He looks like death itself . . . 'Course, like you said, he'll prob'bly outlive us all."

He paused to shovel in several forkfuls of food. "So there we were, just the two of us—me with my bad back, an' Wesley who can hardly stand up—tryin' t' put this porch roof back up . . . Fortunately Jemmy came home from school when he did. He helped me the last couple hours, or I'd never a-got the job finished today . . . I think Jemmy's gonna be all right. He just might turn out t' be the one good apple in the whole rotten barrel . . . 'Course, he's skittish as all get-out. At first I wasn't sure if he was gonna be any help at all on the porch—he kept droppin' everything he tried t' pick up—but after he got used t' bein' around me, he did all right. He turned out t' be a purty good worker actually . . . An' by the time I left, he was even talkin' to me."

Sarah, who had come into the kitchen upon Nathan's return, smiled. She was glad for the kind things he had said about Jemmy. She too thought Jemmy was going to be "all right." But she could not agree with something else her Uncle Nathan had said. She knew for a fact that Wesley Hicks was *not* going to outlive them all.

By the time she awoke the following morning Sarah had reached a decision. "Mother, are you awake?" It was still very early, not yet light.

"Yes," came a very near voice from out of the darkness.

"Mother, before we leave here, I must go back up to the mountain one more time. We left a lot of our things up there which I really should bring back down."

"What kinds of things?" asked Elizabeth in a tone of voice which suggested that she was, if not disapproving of, at least very uneasy about Sarah's plan.

"Your books, your sewing machine, Daddy's tools . . ."

"We have no use for those things now, Sarah. Perhaps we could ask Nathan to go up and get them when he has some free time this winter. He may be able to make use of some of your father's tools. Some of my books too, for that matter. That is, if anything is still left up there after all this time."

"Do you think they might have been stolen?"

"Your father's tools may have been stolen. I doubt if anyone around here would have thought my books worth stealing. Worth burning maybe, but not worth stealing."

Sarah lapsed into thoughtful silence as she considered the possibility that their cabin in the mountains had been sacked and plundered in their absence, perhaps even burnt to the ground.

"I must go back up, Mother, " she said at last, with resolve. "Even if there's nothing left up there, I still must go back up. I can't leave here without seeing it again at least one more time."

"Maybe you could ask your Uncle Nathan to go with you."

"Uncle Nathan is so busy now. I hate to even *leave* him. I couldn't possibly ask him to go with me . . . Besides, I'd really like to go alone."

Perceiving that her daughter's mind was already made up, Elizabeth decided to keep to herself any reservations she had about Sarah's making such a long journey alone. "When would you go? Today?"

"I thought tomorrow. I thought I would go over to Uncle Jacob's this afternoon, spend the night, then borrow Jesse and go up to the mountain tomorrow."

"That's a good idea, Sarah, your visiting with your Uncle Jacob, I mean. He really cares a lot for you. Of all the people who were out there in the woods looking for you last week, it was your Uncle Nathan and your Uncle Jacob who never stopped looking, who never gave up."

"And you, Mother," added Sarah, reaching her arm across her and giving her an affectionate squeeze.

"Well, me, of course, but I'm your mother. What kind of mother would I be if I didn't look for a child who was lost? . . . But if something had happened to you . . . something even more terrible than what *did* happen . . . If we had found you . . ." She hesitated.

"Dead?"

"Yes, I didn't want to say that, but yes, if we had found you dead, I think your Uncle Jacob's grief would have been every bit as great as my own . . . He's going to miss you when we leave."

Sarah nodded. "And I'm going to miss him."

As Sarah walked down the long lane to the Wicker farm, the same lane that she and Edgar had trod just three days before, she thought about the very special relationship that she had with her Uncle Jacob.

She knew that her Uncle Jacob had a great amount of affection for her—and she for him—and it had always been so, right from the beginning, right from the moment they had first looked into each other's eyes when she was only six years old. Yet in spite of this affection, this closeness, they very seldom saw each other. In the eleven years of their acquaintanceship, aside from Thanksgiving gatherings and Sunday morning church services, they probably had not seen each other on more than half a dozen other occasions. It seemed always to be her intention to visit him more often, but weeks, months, and even years sometimes passed without her acting on her intention. And now again almost a year had passed since her last visit, since last December when her

Uncle Nathan had sent her away during hog-butchering time. Yet—and this was the strange part—no matter how infrequent her visits, whenever she and her Uncle Jacob were together, it always seemed as though they had never been apart at all. It was as if at some level of their beings they were always connected—the same level of their beings from which they had recognized each other in the first place. Sarah could readily believe that she and her Uncle Jacob had known each other before, in another lifetime, as Annie had said. Even if the conscious mind—the kitchen mind—had no recollection of it, the soul remembered. Somewhere in that vast underground root cellar the memory survived. And even if she left Rushing Creek, never to return, the connection would still be there, the memory would still survive, the soul would not forget. Then perhaps in some other time—perhaps two or three hundred years hence—and in some other place, they would meet again. She found comfort in that thought, but she doubted very much if it would be enough to see her through the pain of the imminent separation, or to take away the sense of loss she would feel for the rest of *this* life.

As planned, she arrived in time to help Jacob with the evening milking. She had looked forward to this, as well as to preparing his supper afterwards. During that week she had spent with her Uncle Jacob the previous winter, she had enjoyed coming in each evening after the milking to fix supper. Only at her Uncle Jacob's did she have an opportunity to prepare meals entirely on her own. When she had lived up in the mountains, she had sometimes helped in the kitchen, but her mother had done most of the cooking and baking. At Hester's she seldom had a chance to even get near the stove as Hester tended to guard her stove jealously, almost as if it were an appendage of her own body. Despite her inexperience and her unwillingness to prepare any meat dishes, Jacob never failed to compliment her on her cooking. Sitting down to meals with Jacob in the quiet of the kitchen—just the two of them—seemed the most natural thing in the world, as did retiring with him to the parlor to sit by the stove afterwards. It had been so the last time she had come to visit, and she found it so again. There would be no idle conversation this evening however. There was much that Sarah wanted to tell her Uncle Jacob and she could not be sure that she would have another opportunity to speak to him alone before her departure. As soon as they had settled themselves into their chairs, Sarah began.

"Uncle Jacob, do you remember when I was here last December, we talked about the transmigration of souls?"

"If you say we did, then I'm sure we did."

"Remember? You asked me if I thought it was possible for a soul to be reborn into the Earth?"

"Yes, I remember that. Is that what you axed me the first time?"

"Yes, the idea that each soul is born into the Earth many times is called transmigration of the soul or rebirth. I told you that I hadn't thought much about it, but that in order to believe it, I'd have to have some evidence."

"I *do* remember *that*," he replied, smiling. As far as Jacob was concerned, all the evidence for the transmigration of the soul that *he* needed was sitting right in front of him.

"Uncle Jacob, there's something I must tell you, but first I have to make you promise that you'll never tell another soul as long as you live."

"Hit sounds like you have a mighty big secret," laughed Jacob. "I ain't so sure I want the responsibility of keepin' a secret that big."

"I *must* tell you, Uncle Jacob, so you *must* promise."

"Well, if I must, then I reckon I must."

"Do you promise then?"

"I reckon I do."

"Did you ever hear of soul-reading?"

"Soul-readin'?"

"Yes."

"Nope, cain't say that I have. But then thar's lots of thangs I never heared of."

"When I was at Annie Whitehead's last week recovering from my injuries, Annie did a soul-reading for me. At least that's what *she* called it. Annie's a very unusual person, Uncle Jacob. She's more than just a granny woman. She has this ability to sit in her rocking chair and rock herself to sleep..."

"That ain't so hard t' do, Sarah. I done it many a time myself."

"Yes, so did my Daddy. But when Annie rocks herself to sleep, something very strange happens. She *talks* in her sleep. I know that's not so very unusual either, but when Annie talks in her sleep, it *is* unusual because the voice that speaks through her is not *her* voice! It's almost like Annie has left her body and somebody else has come in. It's sort of scary. But this other voice knows *everything*. It says that we have all lived many lifetimes on the Earth, both as men and as women. Some of us have lived *hundreds of thousands* of lifetimes. When Annie reads your soul, she tells you about some of the other lifetimes you've lived.

"Do you remember when I told you about my friend Kati who took me to the other worlds, to Heaven?"

"Hit would be hard t' forget somethin' like that."

"Well, Annie told me about Kati too. She said that Kati is a very advanced soul who lived many lives on the Earth but is now beyond the Earth plane. She has no need ever to return again. But before Kati moved beyond the Earth plane, she and I were very close. We shared many lifetimes together. The last one was in Germany in the seventeenth century. Her name was Katarina then, mine was Greta. She was beyond the Earth plane even then but she had come back anyway. Annie says souls from higher planes sometimes come back to Earth even though they don't need to in order to help the people who are still here. In Germany she gave up her life to save me. I was accused of witchcraft but Kati allowed herself to be executed in my place. And she was only fourteen years old! . . . And she came back again, Uncle Jacob! And you knew her! Katarina was your sister Ruth—my Aunt Ruth! They were the same soul! Ever since you told me about Aunt Ruth when I was a little girl, I have always wished that I had known her. But I *did* know her! Not as Ruth Wicker, but as Katarina Bauer—and by many other names as well. And I've known *you* before too, Uncle Jacob! In fact, Annie said that all three of us—Ruth, you, and I—have been together many times in the past. That is why we are so drawn to one another, why we keep finding each other lifetime after lifetime."

Sarah paused to give her Uncle Jacob time to absorb this, what to her mind was an extraordinary revelation, and to measure his reaction. He seemed to be enthralled, but confused.

"Don't you think it's an exciting idea, Uncle Jacob, this idea that we live many lives on the Earth, and that the people we love we never really lose, but keep meeting them over and over again? I find that a *very* exciting idea. But do you know what, Uncle Jacob? I have absolutely no idea if it's true. It *seems* so right to me. It's the only idea I've ever heard that makes any sense out of the world. It explains so many things. It explains *everything*. But is it true?

"Since leaving Annie's I've thought about that a lot. When I was *at* Annie's and sitting by the fire at night listening to that strange voice tell me about all my past lives, it was almost impossible not to believe it. I mean, it was all so extraordinary. If it wasn't true, then where was all that stuff coming from? I can't believe that Annie was making it up.

"But thinking back on it, I realize that, even with everything Annie told me, I still have very little real evidence for the theory of rebirth. I can't count the past lives that Annie told me about as evidence because I have no memory of being any of those people in the past. I don't think she did, but had she just made them all up out of her head, I would not have known the difference. I *know* that Annie is no ordinary person. She definitely knows things that she has no ordinary means of knowing. For one, she knew that my mother liked Wordsworth. How did she know that? She couldn't have made that up. And she knew about the dream I used to have when I was younger."

"The dream that was too horrible to talk about?"

"Yes. It was a dream about a girl being bound to a stake and burned." She decided to omit the detail of the severed head. "Not only did Annie tell me about a past life in which this had actually happened—the life in seventeenth-century Germany—but she also knew that I had had dreams about it. If Annie *isn't* reading souls as she says she is, then I don't know how she knew those things—

unless she was reading thoughts and memories right out of my mind."

"Didn't you say you was at Granny's house for three days afore you even woke up?"

"Yes."

"Mebbe *you* was talkin' in *your* sleep."

Sarah laughed. "I must admit, I hadn't considered *that* possibility . . . But I have no difficulty believing that Annie has means of acquiring knowledge that are out of the ordinary. After all, the same might be said of me."

"Like when you knowed the mill was on fire."

"Yes . . . Maybe Annie's soul is in this room at this very moment listening to every word we say."

Jacob looked nervously about the room.

"But even if there *is* evidence that Annie has means of knowing things which she has no natural way of knowing–or at least no *usual* way of knowing–and I think there is –unless she overheard me talking in my sleep as you suggested–it does not follow that everything she says about rebirth and past lives is true. Despite everything Annie told me, despite that extraordinary soul-reading she did for me, I still have seen no real evidence to support the theory of rebirth."

"So you don't believe in it?"

"Oh, I do! I think it's more likely than not that our souls are born into the world many times, just like Annie says. It's just that I have no proof–at least no proof that would convince anyone else."

"What about the doll?"

Sarah gave him a puzzled look. "What doll?"

"When I showed you Ruthie's thangs last time you was here, the first thang you did was pick up Ruthie's doll an' say 'Hit's my doll!'"

"Oh yes, I remember. I was struck by how similar it was to a doll that I had when I was little. I lost mine somewhere between here and Massachusetts. I must have left it on one of the trains."

Sarah knew how difficult it was for her Uncle Jacob to talk about his sister Ruth. Even now she could see an expression of sadness come over his face. When she had first learned from Annie that Kati and Ruth were the same soul, she could not wait to tell her Uncle Jacob. She was certain that the news that Ruth was a very advanced soul who had come from the White Light World would be a source of great comfort and joy for him. But as she was telling him about Annie and her soul readings she could not help but notice that Jacob often appeared to be as much confused as comforted, as much distressed as elated. And it was no wonder! Upon reflection she realized now that what she had said must have sounded very confusing to a simple man like Jacob. She had begun by telling him what Annie had said about Kati and Ruth being the same soul. Then she had gone on to say that maybe none of this was true after all, as there was no real evidence. Finally, she had concluded by saying that even without proof she believed it anyway. Most mountain roads didn't have that many twists and turns! She herself was accustomed to convoluted intellectual journeys of this kind. When she was younger, her mother had led her on many just like it. Like her mother she could get so excited by ideas that she would follow them anywhere, even off the main roads and into the thickets. She had thought the idea that Kati and Ruth were the same soul to be an exciting one, as was the idea of rebirth in general, but the question "Was it true?"–though not one she had planned to discuss with her Uncle Jacob beforehand–was one that had just naturally presented itself to her mind. But she realized now that while she had been weighing the merits of an idea with almost philosophical detachment, her Uncle Jacob had been remembering a real flesh-and-blood sister. She hoped that she had not caused him too much pain by her lack of sensitivity because it was that flesh-and-blood sister that she wished to talk about next.

"Uncle Jacob, do you mind if we talk about Aunt Ruth?"

He smiled. "I'd like nuthin' better."

This was hardly the answer Sarah had expected. "Annie told me a little about her. She said she had never seen anyone so filled with goodness and light. She called her a barn burning in the night."

Jacob laughed. "I reckon she was that all right."

"But she said something else that I didn't quite understand. Something about Aunt Hester. Was Aunt Hester sometimes unkind to Aunt Ruth?"

Sarah watched as Jacob's face settled into a deep frown. "Now hit's your turn t' keep a secret," he said, his voice very grave. "I'm a-gwine t' haf t' make yuh promise not t' tell anyone what I'm about t' tell yuh."

"I promise."

A long silence followed. Sarah wondered if her Uncle Jacob might be reconsidering his decision to share his secret with her.

"Sayin' that your Aunt Hester was unkind to Ruth," he began at last, "is like sayin' a hound dog is unkind to a rabbit, or a fox is unkind to a chicken. I wouldn't want t' say that Hester *hated* Ruth, but bein' an uneducated feller, I don't know any other word t' use. Even from the time they was wee young'uns, Hester was always a-pickin' on Ruth, a-lookin' for new ways t' hurt her . . . Ruthie was always such a gentle little thang. Like you, she had a special feelin' for animals. Knowin' how much Ruthie liked animals, Hester would sometimes kill a little bird or rabbit or chipmunk an' put it under the covers of Ruthie's bed. She was always a-doin' mean thangs like that."

"Why did she do that?" asked Sarah, horrified.

"Jealous, I reckon. Ever'body loved Ruthie. They was always a-makin' a big fuss over her. She was just the sweetest thang you can imagine. No matter how cruel Hester was to her, Ruthie never got angry, never fought back. She always did what the Bible says: turned the other cheek. 'Course that just made Hester all the madder . . . Did Annie tell you that Ruthie was crippled?"

"No!" cried Sarah, shocked.

"She wasn't born crippled. She was only crippled the last year of her life. She fell out of the barn loft–by accident, she said. Hester and I are the only livin' souls who know the truth about what happened the day of Ruthie's 'accident.' I can tell you for a fact hit was no accident–no more than the 'accident' you had last week. Hester had gone up into the hayloft t' kill pigeons. More'n likely she planned to put one of them in Ruthie's bed. When Ruthie discovered what she was a-doin', she climbed up after her t' try an' stop her. Hester pushed her an' Ruthie fell. I was the first one to her. She couldn't move. Her back was broke. She made me promise not t' tell anyone that Hester had pushed her . . . And I kept that promise to this very minute . . . D'you remember all those drawin's of birds an' animals in Ruthie's chest of thangs?"

"Yes."

"Well, Ruthie made all those drawin's durin' the last year of her life when she was crippled. She had always loved t' be out in the woods, so ever' day when the weather was fair, I'd carry her out an' set her in the woods—just lean her up ag'in a tree—an' she'd stay thar all day. Birds an' animals would come right up to her an' she'd draw them. Hit was almost like they was posin'."

"Uncle Jacob, would it be possible for me to see those drawings again?"

"I reckon hit would. They're right here." He reached under the table next to his chair and pulled out the small black metal chest with the brass clasps. "I bet you thought I'd haf t' go all the way up to the attic for it, didn't yuh?"

"Yes, I guess I did," answered Sarah, a little surprised.

"Well, the truth is," he said, placing the chest on the floor between them, "I brung this chest down here the day after you left here last winter, an' I've looked through it almost ever' day since."

Just as before, Sarah watched expectantly as Jacob opened the lid to the chest. Just as before, the first thing to meet her eyes was the smiling face of the once-gaily-colored rag doll, now faded with age.

"Here's 'your' doll," said Jacob, removing the rag doll from the chest and handing it to her.

"It *is* very much like the one I used to have," said Sarah, examining the doll more closely. "The colors are a little different but that's about all."

"Thar's a story behind that doll. This one was Ruthie's, but Hester had one just like it. They was birthday presents from their Gran'ma. If you ever have twins, Sarah, you'll understand that you haf t' give your presents in two's. Hit won't do t' give somethin' to the one an' not to the other. Hester dragged hers around with her ever'whar, but Ruthie always kept hers in her bed. After a while Hester wore hers out, so Ma threw it in the stove. Hester bein' Hester, she just naturally went an' took Ruthie's. Took it right off her bed. When Ma found out, she made Hester put it back. Ruth wanted t' let Hester keep it, but Ma made her put it back . . . Here's Ruthie's drawin's."

Jacob handed Sarah the bundle of postcard-sized drawings. She carefully removed the string and began looking through them. Just as before, she studied each one closely, handling each one with care, almost with reverence, noting once again the circle of light around the head of each bird and animal. Knowing that the little girl who had drawn these was crippled seemed to add even more poignancy to an already poignant experience. When she had finished, she retied the bundle.

"Where's the letter, Uncle Jacob?"

"Right here."

Sarah took the letter and opened it. "Would you like me to read it aloud again?"

A wonderful smile had come over Jacob's face. "I'd like that. I already know it by heart, but hit's differ'nt when you read it. Hit's almost like Ruthie herself is sayin' the words."

Once again Sarah read aloud her Aunt Ruth's parting words to her brother Jacob.

" 'Dear Jacob,

'I have seen the angels, my brother. Sometimes in the early morning I can see them gathering in the shadows around me. I know I will be going with them very soon now.

'I am not sad for myself. I know that death is not an ending but a glorious new beginning. I am only sad for all the dear ones I must leave behind, especially for you, my brother. No one could have loved me more than you. It is the thought that my death will cause you great sorrow that is the hardest for me to bear. Please do not be sad, dear brother. We will be together again, I promise. Our life on Earth is so short compared to the Eternity beyond.

'Good-by, dear Jacob. I will never forget you. I love you, I love you, I love you forever.

Ruthie' "

When she had finished she turned to her Uncle Jacob and smiled. "The first time I read it, it made me so terribly sad. But it was different this time. It almost made me feel happy inside. 'Death is not an ending, but a glorious new beginning.' What a wonderful thought!"

Jacob nodded in agreement.

Sarah read through the letter again, this time to herself. Suddenly she stopped short. "Uncle Jacob, what's this word? Is it 'our' or it is 'one'? It's hard to tell because it's smudged. It looks like a drop of water fell on it."

"More'n likely a tear," replied Jacob in a voice almost too soft to be heard. He leaned over to see to which word Sarah was alluding. "I don't know. Hit could be either."

"When I read it aloud, I read it as 'our': *Our* life on Earth is so short compared to the Eternity beyond.' But if it's 'one,' then the sentence becomes '*One* life on Earth is so short compared to the Eternity beyond.' "

Jacob shook his head. "Don't know," he repeated. "Could be either."

"But don't you see? If the word is 'one,' it makes a big difference to the meaning of the sentence. Why would she say '*one* life on Earth' unless she knew that we live *more* than one life on Earth?"

"Seems to me hit don't make no differ'nce."

Sarah gave him an uncomprehending look. "What do you mean?"

"Don't you remember what you said the last time you was here?"

"About what?"

"About how it don't make no differ'nce how many lives we live on this Earth."

"I said that?"

"You sure did."

"I don't remember. I don't remember *everything* I say. Which is just as well, I suppose."

"Well, hit's somethin' I'll never forget. We was talkin' about the idea of souls comin' back to Earth. You said you didn't think it made no differ'nce whether they did or they didn't. You said it don't matter if we live just one life on Earth or many, 'cause we're still here for just one purpose, an' that's to seek the kingdom of God."

"Oh yes," replied Sarah, smiling, "I remember. And I still believe that. But since then I've come to understand that there are different ways of seeking the kingdom of God. It's something Annie explained to me. She was comparing me with Kati, that is, with Ruth. She said that we were both advanced souls—Kati has already finished her journey on the Earth plane, and I am about to finish mine—but we had chosen very different paths. Kati, or Ruth, had chosen the path of devotional love, but I had chosen the path of knowledge. I guess that is why I am always asking so many questions: I *have* to know. Asking questions *about* the kingdom of God—trying to understand what it is and how one goes about attaining it—is *my* way of *seeking* the kingdom of God. Kati, or Ruth, had a very different way."

"Not so differ'nt as you might think, Sarah."

"Well, Annie did say that all paths do tend to converge near the end, as they all lead to the same place. Swedenborg, in his own way, says very much the same thing. He says that since the source of both goodness and truth is Heaven's sun—its warmth being goodness, its light being truth—then the nearer we come to Heaven—the more of Heaven we allow to flow into us—the more we are able to intend what is good and to discern what is true. But Swedenborg would not agree with Annie that all paths lead to the same place—at least not to *exactly* the same place. According to Swedenborg, not even in Heaven do all angels experience Heaven's sun in the same way. Some experience it more as light, others more as warmth. Both the path of truth and the path of goodness lead to Heaven, but to *different* heavens... Swedenborg says the most perfect angels are those who accept divine truth and divine goodness to the same degree."

"The most perfect angels?"

"Yes."

Jacob smiled. Once again Sarah had given him a thought to take to bed with him.

It was getting late. Both uncle and niece sensed that the evening's conversation had nearly run its course. But before they retired for the night, Jacob felt that there was something more that had to be said.

"Sarah, I don't want anythang I said here tonight t' cause you t' change your feelin's towards your Aunt Hester. This was a long time ago we was a'talkin' about. The differ'nce between Hester the child an' Hester the growed woman is the differ'nce between sour milk an' sweet. When Ruthie died, somethin' in Hester changed. Ruthie died of the smallpox, you know. But it was Hester who come down with the smallpox first. Ruthie caught it from her. An' hit weren't no wonder. The whole time Hester was sick, Ruthie stayed with her day an' night, prayin' for her. When Ruthie got sick herself, she just kept right on a-prayin' for Hester t' get well—never for herself, always for Hester. After Ruthie's death Hester was a changed person. I think she finally began feelin' sorry for the way she mistreated her all those years.

"An', Lord knows, Hester herself has seen her share of sufferin' in the years since. When she was about your age, the thang she wanted more'n anythang else in the world was t' get married an' raise a family. She used t' say she wanted a dozen kids, and if she couldn't have a dozen, she'd settle for ten. 'Course, as it turned out, she had t' settle for just one. She never even got married til she was nearly thirty. Then her first two babies was born daid. Finally Otis came along, but after him she couldn't have no more. Otis is her life, Sarah. Hit nearly broke her heart when he got sent overseas. If anythang should happen to that boy, I think it would kill her.

"Hester ain't t' be blamed, Sarah. She's t' be loved an' pitied. So don't you be holdin' anythang ag'in' her on account of what I told you here tonight. All that happened forty years ago. That's all in the past now."

"I won't, Uncle Jacob."

"I know you won't. Hit wouldn't be like you . . . Well, hit's time for me t' get to bed. I expect you'll be a-wantin' t' stay up an' read for a spell."

"No, I'm going to bed too. I want to get an early start in the morning."

They turned out the lights and went upstairs. After exchanging good-nights in the hallway, they went to their respective rooms, Jacob to the master bedroom, Sarah to the smaller room down the hall that Jacob had reserved for her many years before. Not until she was alone in her room did Sarah allow the great emotional storm that had been building inside her to release itself. As soon as she had changed into her nightgown she threw herself down on the bed and burst into tears. Once again she was left alone with the terrible knowledge that Otis was dead. But as always the tears were as much for her Uncle Nathan and Aunt Hester as for herself–perhaps even more for her Aunt Hester this time. Hester was to be loved and pitied, Jacob had said, but even he did not know how much. For a brief moment she had thought of telling her Uncle Jacob about Otis. Perhaps she should have. She did not know how much longer she could carry the unbearable weight of this terrible knowledge alone. She needed to share it with someone–someone other than her Uncle Nathan and Aunt Hester. They would learn soon enough, and she preferred it not be from her. Had her Uncle Jacob known that she was harboring such a secret, she knew that he would have insisted that she divulge it to him at once, in order that he might lift some of the burden of grief from her and take it upon himself, in order that he might draw her to his bosom and envelop her in all the love and sympathy his great and gentle heart was capable of pouring forth.

After saying his prayers Jacob crawled into bed and pulled up the covers. As he lay alone in his bed, peering into the empty darkness, he searched the shadows for any angels that might be gathering. If his sister Ruth had seen angels, perhaps one day he would also. Perhaps he might even see one of God's "most perfect angels." He smiled at the thought. But the smile quickly faded. He realized that it was only the terrible sadness and loneliness of his present life that obliged him to seek the company of angels and to dream of a world beyond this one.

If Hester was to be pitied, he thought, perhaps *he* was to be pitied even more. At least Hester had been blessed with one child, a strong and healthy boy. He and Emily had not been blessed with any. And now he didn't even have Emily. The empty pillow beside his head was an ever-present reminder of the vast and aching emptiness her death had left in his life. Again he found himself grieving, not only for the children he had never had–the children he would have loved so dearly–but for all those dear and gentle souls whom he had loved and lost: for his sister Ruth, for his mother Hannah, for his wife Emily. All these losses he had borne stoically–never once despairing, never once blaming God, never once doubting the ultimate goodness of the Universe– but it had not been easy. And now his niece Sarah was about to be taken from him as well. Not taken from him in the final sense, not in the sense that he had feared she had been taken from him only a few days before, but taken from him all the same. Once she moved back to Massachusetts he knew that he would very likely never see her again. He had once comforted himself with the notion that Sarah was his sister Ruth reborn, returned to Earth in another body, perhaps as compensation for some divine error. He was far less certain of that now. But it made no difference. If Sarah wasn't Ruth, she was still Sarah, and for the past eleven years she had simultaneously taken the place of the beloved sister he had lost and the daughter he had never had. The loss of her now–even of her physical presence–would be a heavy one to bear, but he knew that somehow he would find the strength to bear it, just as he had found the strength to bear all the others.

His thoughts were suddenly interrupted by the clicking of the doorlatch and the sound of the door swinging slowly on its hinges.

Raising his head he peered through the darkness toward the door. Through squinted eyes he was barely able to make out a shimmering white form standing in the doorway.

"Uncle Jacob?"

"Sarah, is that you?"

He watched transfixed as the white form floated toward the bed.

"Uncle Jacob, I need you to hold me, just hold me."

"Sarah, what is it? What's wrong?"

She was right next to the bed now, sobbing, scarcely able to speak. Jacob was about to get up when he felt her hands groping for the covers. She was getting into bed with him!

"No, Sarah, no! Hit wouldn't be right!"

"Otis is dead, Uncle Jacob! Otis is dead!"

For a brief moment Jacob's life stopped. His heart did not beat, his lungs did not breathe, his brain did not function. Then in a sudden outpouring of love and sympathetic affection, he put his arms around her shoulders and drew her gently beneath the covers.

21

NEW BEGINNINGS

By early afternoon of the following day Sarah was already deep into the mountains and nearing her destination. She had started at first light and by the time the sun had emerged from behind the mountains to the southeast, she had already left the hard roads and had begun making her way across country. Except for the oaks nearly all of the trees had shed their leaves now—it being late October—and the fresh blanket of red and gold and brown on the forest floor helped to obscure an already obscure trail. But Sarah knew the trail from memory, as did the mule, so they had, thus far, made their way easily and without false turn. Under normal circumstances Sarah would have walked herself, but as she was still not fully recovered from her recent injuries—it having been only a week ago this morning that she had awakened and found herself at Annie's—and as she had already done more walking over the course of the past five days than the present state of her health should have permitted, she had elected this morning to ride. Jesse did not seem to mind.

From the very outset of the journey Sarah had realized that she was going to have to make a conscious effort to maintain control over her own mind. Painfully aware that she would soon be leaving this enchanted land of mountains, forests, and rushing streams which had been her home for the past eleven years, she had resolved to remain as alert as possible, to put all of her energy into receiving and processing the vast array of external stimuli that would be presenting itself to her senses throughout the course of the day's journey, not to allow a single sight or sound or smell to escape her. She understood full well that the time to enjoy and appreciate these sights and sounds and smells—these stimuli—was *now*, that no memory she would carry away with her would ever be more than a poor substitute for the moment-to-moment experiences of this day. She was also aware that the moment she relaxed her resolve, the moment she allowed her attention to lapse, a multitude of thoughts was ready to rush in and occupy her mind. Once that happened, all communication with the world outside her mind would be broken. The sights and sounds of the forest would become nothing more than a blur of scenery and background noise.

The mountains were perhaps not as exciting to the senses in the late fall as they were in the early spring–the colors were more muted, there were fewer sounds–but there were compensations. Visibility increased. There was perhaps not as much to see, but it was possible to see further. Not only was the air clearer, but the view was less obstructed. Neighboring mountain slopes and peaks, the existence of which might not have been known or even suspected during the spring and summer, now became clearly visible through the nearly leafless treetops. Without the distraction of more delicate beauty, beauty of a more awesome kind could now be found in the spectacular topography of the land itself. In the absence of wildflowers and new green buds it was the massive mountains themselves that now asserted themselves, that now thrust themselves upon one's senses. Sounds too, though fewer, carried further in the clearer, less obstructed air. Sounds which could be heard in the forest year round, like the cry of the raven or the drumming of the pileated woodpecker, had a different quality now. They were clearer, sharper, more piercing, more urgent.

As Sarah coaxed the mule up the last steep section of trail, she found it difficult, if not impossible, to keep her mind focused on the present moment. It was the *next* moment that was now usurping all of her attention. The clear mountain air had suddenly become thick with excitement and expectation, just as it had been on that morning in the spring of 1933 when, as a child of six, she had first made this journey with her father and mother. When the cabin finally came into view, the sense of delight that rushed through her was the same sense of delight that had rushed through her then, only perhaps this time it was even more intense. At first glance everything appeared to be just as she had left it on that day in May two and a half years before.

When she reached the clearing, she reined in the mule and dismounted. As she removed the bridle and fed her deserving companion a handful of oats from the saddlebag, she kept her eyes fixed on the house. She was about to climb the steps when she noticed a deer standing just outside the garden fence, in the small orchard that her Uncle Nathan had helped to plant many years before. The trees had grown considerably since she had last seen them.

The animal had been casually grazing when she first saw it, but it was now staring at her with head lifted and ears erect. Cautiously, without making any sudden movement, she circled out around the garden fence and walked up the hill toward the spot where the deer was standing. When she was within eight to ten feet of it, the animal lowered its ears and commenced feeding. The sharp crunching sound told Sarah that it was not the grass under the trees that the deer was eating, but apples. She knelt down and discovered that under the leaves lay a whole carpet of apples—of Stayman Winesaps, her very favorite! She polished one on her coat and bit into it. Upon looking around, she discovered apples under other trees as well—Yellow Pippins, Black Twigs ... These trees, which had not yet produced so much as a single apple, and nary even a blossom, during the years that she and her family had lived up here, were now producing abundantly. With her apple in one hand, she stroked the deer's neck with the other, then walked back down the hill toward the house.

When she had first passed the garden, she had noticed, out of the corner of her eye, the sunflowers growing therein. These she now stopped to admire more closely. There were dozens of them scattered throughout the garden and even out beyond the garden fence. Apparently they had continued to reseed themselves year after year. Their heavy heads were bowed, and many of the seeds had already been plucked out by birds or had dropped to the ground. The birds and squirrels would get most of those on the ground as well, but doubtless some would escape, to insure a crop for yet another year.

She stepped onto the porch of the house. Still, everything seemed to be in proper order. The door was closed. The windows were not broken. She stood at the door for just a moment, then took a deep breath and pushed it open. Craning her neck, she peered inside. Still, everything appeared to be in order. Even her father's shotgun and rifle were still in their rack on the back wall. If *they* had not been stolen, then it was not likely that anything else had been stolen either. Crossing the threshold she entered the house.

There was evidence that *someone* had been there. Cooking and eating utensils lay in disarray on the table and sinkboard. *She* had not left them like that. She guessed that some hunters had taken a meal there, perhaps had even spent the night. But nothing appeared to be missing. Her mother's books were in the bookcase in the back room just as she had left them. Her sewing machine also had not been touched.

Not only did nothing appear to be missing, but, as she discovered upon climbing the ladder up to the loft, a considerable amount had been *added.* The top of her bed, as well as a good portion of the loft floor, were covered with an assortment of nuts–black walnuts, butter nuts, hickory nuts–piled two and three deep in some places. It was apparent that the squirrels had been quite industrious in her absence! She could see the small hole in the wall near her bed where they had gained access. Smart enough not to have tried to gnaw their way through the ten-inch-thick chestnut-log walls below, they had instead chewed through the inch-thick pineboard wall in the gable end of the loft. Sarah had planned to spend one night in the house before heading back down the mountain the next morning. She now decided that it might be easier just to spend it in her parents' bed downstairs. But she was glad to know that her old room was being put to good use.

Descending the ladder, she crossed the thick puncheon slab floor and went back outside. She next set her course for the barn, more specifically for her father's workshop in the southwest corner of the barn. Upon entering the workshop she found herself overcome with a succession of emotions. The most immediate emotion was one of relief, when she discovered that her father's woodworking tools had not been disturbed. But this was soon supplanted by a feeling of deep sadness. As she looked about the shop, with its piles of wood shavings on the floor and the unfinished whirligig on the work bench, she could easily have imagined that her father had been working there that very morning and had only recently stepped out. She could easily have imagined it, that is, if it had not been for the thick layer of dust that had settled over everything.

She stepped to the work bench and examined the unfinished whirligig. Picking up the main figure, an eight-inch-tall wooden "farmer," she studied its carefully carved features. As yet no arms had been attached. The two arms, a hoe, and several unfinished cornstalks, all carved from wood and all made to precise proportion, also lay on the work bench. It saddened her to think that her father's little "farmer" would never get a chance to hoe his corn.

Emerging once again into the sunlight, she walked up the steep hillside behind the house, the hillside which had once been their cornfield. No plow had crossed this field in nearly three years now, and once again the forest was attempting to reclaim it. Tulip poplar saplings had sprung up everywhere, as had several species of scrub pine. Not quite everywhere. There was a circular area in the middle of the field where nothing grew, not even a weed. With great sadness Sarah walked past this barren and lifeless patch of earth, giving it a wide berth. She was not able to look at it directly, but only to cast quick, uneasy, sideward glances at it as she passed. Most of the ashes had long since been washed by the rain down the hillside, but still nothing grew.

When she reached the upper boundary of the field, she turned and looked out across the mountains, just as she had seen her father do on many an occasion—just as *she herself* had done on many an occasion. If only she had thought to bring a hoe to lean on. As her eyes traced the line of mountains from east to west, they came to rest on the high rock-ridged peak to the south—the "holy mountain" of her childhood—from whose high rocks she had watched so many summer thunderstorms gather and break, amongst whose same rocks she had sought sanctuary when her father had killed the deer, from whose very summit she had, on that never-to-be- forgotten day in May of 1938, "fallen" out of her body and entered into other worlds.

She sat down on the hillside with her legs crossed in front of her and for the first time in the day relaxed her vigil and allowed the floodgates to open. All those thoughts she had struggled so desperately to hold back now came rushing forth. And along with them, with equal force and intensity, came all the thousands of memories which had been stored by her mind over the course of the past eleven years. For the rest of the day the world outside her mind did not exist. Not until the sun had nearly set, and darkness, like a pool of rising ink, had begun filling up the hollows between the mountains, did she get to her feet and walk back down the hill to the house.

The next morning she began gathering together those things she would be taking with her: her mother's drawings, many of which dated back to Springfield; her mother's books . . . Realizing that she would not be able to carry all the books with her, she selected only those which she knew to be her mother's favorites, among them the most finger-worn volumes of poetry– Wordsworth, Coleridge, Shelley, Keats, Lord Byron . . . Her mother had always had a special fondness for the English poets.

Then, finding several baskets in the barn, she went to the apple trees above the garden and began gathering up the firmest and least damaged of the fallen apples. These she carried to the barn and repacked into crates, using the sawdust and woodshavings from the workshop floor as insulation between the individual fruits. These she would not be taking with her. These she would be leaving here.

Over the course of the past eighteen hours a tremendous war of emotions had raged within her, a war that had deprived her of sleep and that had left her totally exhausted. But in the process she had come to a decision, perhaps the most momentous decision of her life. It was a decision that had brought with it both a feeling of intense relief and joy, and of deep heart-rending sadness. She would *not* be moving back to Massachusetts with her mother. She would be moving back *here*, back to her home in the mountains, back to the old Puckett place! She carried the two crates of apples to the house and stored them in the root cellar beneath the kitchen floor.

As she led Jesse down the side of the mountain, she wondered what her mother's reaction would be to her decision. At the very least her mother would be disappointed. Her decision to stay might even force her mother to reconsider *her* decision to leave. Sarah could not help but feel a little guilty when she contemplated the disruption her decision would cause in her mother's plans. As much as she dreaded the thought of being separated from her mother, she dreaded even more the thought that her decision might force her mother to change *her* mind and stay–stay on account of *her*–and be unhappy for the rest of her life. She wondered if she even had the right to make such a decision, or whether it was her duty as a daughter to abide by the decision her mother had already made, to sacrifice her own happiness for the sake of her mother's. It was a problem to which no happy resolution seemed possible.

She returned to Nathan's by late afternoon, her decision still weighing heavily on her mind. She ate more than usual at supper, which pleased Hester, but spoke less. It was not until later in the evening, in the privacy of their room, that she informed her mother of her decision. To her surprise her mother seemed to take it quite calmly, almost as if she had been expecting it. The look in her eyes was one of quiet resignation, not one of shock or anguish.

"When you left on Tuesday to go over to your Uncle Jacob's," began Elizabeth, her tone sad but philosophical, "Nathan told me that I should be prepared for this. I think he's come to know you even better than I do . . . I guess I shouldn't be too surprised at that. He's been with you these past two and a half years, and I haven't, not really . . . So, for the past two days I've been trying to decide what I'd do if you decided to stay . . ."

Her eyes were beginning to tear up. "It hasn't been easy. For the past sixteen years, almost seventeen years now, you've been my baby, my little girl. I guess I had always cherished this silly hope that you'd always be with me, that you'd be my little girl forever, but I knew it couldn't be. I knew that one day you'd grow up and I would lose you. It's something your father and I used to talk about: how one day you'd leave us to get married and we'd be left all alone up there on the mountain . . . Of course, we always thought that *you'd* be leaving *us*. Neither of us ever imagined that *we'd* be leaving *you*."

"I wouldn't be spending *all* my time up there, Mother," interjected Sarah, in an attempt to allay any fears that her mother might have. "I'd still be coming down here to work for Uncle Nathan, probably even more than Daddy did—and to visit Uncle Jacob. I *must* spend more time with Uncle Jacob."

Elizabeth nodded her head in approval. "That's good, Sarah. It's a comfort to me to know that there are people here who care for you and who will look out for you. In fact, I think if I took you away from here, it would break your Uncle Nathan's heart, to say nothing of your Uncle Jacob's. I know I will be leaving you in good hands."

"So you have decided to leave?" asked Sarah tentatively.

Elizabeth nodded. "Nathan told me that one of the most difficult things he had to do as a father was to learn to let go. And one of the most difficult things he had to do as a husband was to help Hester understand the need for letting go. He's helped me to understand too.

"You have a right to your own life, Sarah. I missed about two and a half years of that life, but that was my fault, not yours. You'll be seventeen in two weeks, almost a full-grown woman. As much as I'm going to miss you, I have no right to hold onto you any longer. Nathan says I have every right to be proud of you, and of course I am. I mean, just look at you! You're so bright and so beautiful, so gentle and so caring." She stroked Sarah's hair. "You're everything I had ever hoped for in a daughter and more. I just wish your Daddy could see you now. He always thought you were an angel anyway . . .

"So this is what I've decided: I'm going to wait until after your seventeenth birthday and then I'm going to leave. But I think it would be easier for both of us if we didn't think of our decisions as final. I am going to leave *for now*, with the understanding that one day I may come back. Do you think you can think of your decision in that way as well? Could you decide to stay *for now*, with the understanding that one day you may come join me? Our separation would not sound so final that way."

Unable to speak and her eyes now filled with tears, Sarah nodded her head and fell into her mother's arms.

"And, of course, we'll write," added Elizabeth as she clutched her daughter in an emotional embrace. "Nathan tells me you're quite a letter writer."

She could feel Sarah's head nodding against her cheek.

The next morning Sarah returned the mule to her Uncle Jacob's. She stayed only for a few minutes, just long enough to inform her uncle of her decision to stay and to move back up to the old Puckett place. For the next two weeks she continued to help Nathan around the farm, with the making of cider and the harvesting of feed corn, in addition to the normal day-to-day chores. On the twelfth of November she turned seventeen, and though Nathan and Hester threw a small birthday party for her after supper, the gaiety of the occasion was tempered by the knowledge that her mother would soon be leaving.

The following Monday Isaac came by in the truck. Elizabeth had requested only a ride to Haynesville, nine miles away, where she could catch a bus to the train station in Asheville, but Isaac insisted on driving her the full forty miles to Asheville himself. While he waited for Elizabeth to say her final good-bys to Nathan and Hester, he loaded her two suitcases into the back of the truck. Once his two passengers were on board—Sarah would be accompanying her mother as far as the train station—Isaac climbed in himself. As he drove slowly out the lane he allowed himself a broad grin and congratulated himself on his great good fortune. He would be driving all the way to Asheville with the two most beautiful ladies he had ever rested eyes on, and as he did not wish to cause either of them fright or injury, he was determined, in a break from habit, to drive as slowly and carefully as possible.

It was late in the day that he returned a very subdued Sarah to Nathan and Hester's. Without getting out of the truck himself, he dropped her off in the driveway, then turned around and sped off out the lane even more recklessly than usual, apparently anxious to make up for lost time. Upon entering the house, Sarah was surprised to find no one in the kitchen. As it was near to suppertime, she had expected to find her Aunt Hester busy at the stove as she usually was this time of day. But supper had not even been started. A sudden piercing wail from upstairs caused Sarah to freeze in alarm. She listened. Another scream pierced the air. It was Hester's voice. The terrible screams were coming in bursts, the shrill mournful wails rising and falling in pitch. She could also hear Nathan's deeper, softer voice, trying to comfort, but also struggling, also breaking. She knew that it was not her mother's departure that had caused such emotional trauma. Only one thing could have caused a crisis of this magnitude. While she had been away in Asheville, seeing her mother off on the train, Nathan and Hester had finally received the news with which she herself had been struggling to come to terms for the past four weeks: Otis was dead, killed in the war!

For the next two weeks it seemed to Sarah as though she were reliving the two weeks immediately following her father's death. No one spoke. No one smiled. Life continued, but only in its mechanical aspects. Everyone went through the motions. The work, after all, still had to be done. Sarah had planned to stay at Nathan and Hester's through Thanksgiving, to help Nathan lay in the winter's wood supply, before departing for the old Puckett place. She saw no reason now to change her plan. While her presence did not in any way seem to alleviate the terrible anguish that her aunt and uncle were suffering, neither did it seem to aggravate it. So intense was her Aunt Hester's grief, in fact, she did not even seem to be aware of her presence most of the time. Sarah could not help but feel pity for her aunt. Hester was, as Jacob had said, a woman not to be blamed, but to be loved and pitied. Sarah wished it was within her power to do something to relieve her aunt's awful suffering, but she knew it was not. Only another telegram saying there had been a terrible mistake, that her beloved son was not dead after all, could do that. But while Sarah's presence was having no effect upon Hester, Sarah found that being in Hester's presence was having an effect upon *her*. She found that the pity she felt for her aunt was only adding to the already considerable burden of grief that she herself had to bear. It seemed to her that some law of nature should require that as her own suffering increased, someone else's should decrease, but she could find no evidence that such was the case.

It was ten days after Elizabeth's departure that Sarah received her first communication from her in the mail, a postcard. On the front was a picture of Forest Park; on the back, in her mother's nearly perfect handwriting, the following brief inscription:

"Dear Sarah,
"Arrived safely in Springfield and after a few inquiries succeeded in finding my mother. For the past six years she has been living with Mrs. Cadbury, a widow like herself and one of her oldest and dearest friends. Am contemplating move to Boston. Will send you an address when I get one.

Love,

Mother"

Sarah had been waiting for an address at which to write her mother. Now it appeared as though she would have to wait a while longer.

The annual Thanksgiving gathering was another solemn affair, even more so than the one of two years before. Two members of the family had been lost on that previous occasion, but their deaths had occurred early in the year, Emily's in February, Daniel's in April. The survivors had had a few months to absorb their losses before the Thanksgiving gathering. This time the news of Otis' death had come less than two weeks before the holiday, and even the lively presence of Isaac and Martha's four grandchildren could do little to dispel the heavy gloom that hung over the table. Sarah did not go home with Nathan and Hester after the gathering, but remained instead with her Uncle Jacob.

She had already discussed her plan with Jacob–they had talked the previous Sunday after church–and he had agreed. She would borrow Jesse for one month. She would take him the day after Thanksgiving and return him the day before Christmas. She required the services of the mule to help pack a three-months' supply of food up the mountain–most of which would be coming from Nathan and Hester's abundant storehouses–and to help her lay in a supply of firewood for the winter. She had already helped Nathan lay in his winter's wood supply; now she would have to lay in one for herself. At the end of the agreed-upon month she would return the mule, and as the day of her return would fall on Christmas Eve she would then spend the Christmas holidays with her Uncle Jacob, in keeping with her resolution to visit him more often in the future than she had in the past. After the holidays she would then return to the mountain, but without the mule. Jacob was perfectly willing to let her keep the mule permanently, as he had already given it to her father, but as she had nothing on the mountain with which to feed the mule, she thought it best that Jesse spend this winter at least at Jacob's. As it was, she would have to carry with her enough corn and oats to feed the animal for the month between Thanksgiving and Christmas that she and Jacob had agreed upon. Jacob, in addition to loaning her the mule, had agreed to provide this as well.

The next day Sarah put the first phase of her plan into action. She left Jacob's, and after stopping at Nathan and Hester's for provisions, began her long journey. As she ascended into the mountains on foot, with pack mule in tow, her spirits seemed to ascend as well. If she had previously had any doubts about the wisdom of her decision to stay, those doubts were now forgotten. She felt exhilarated!–liberated!–as if she had just been plucked from the gloom of the Underworld and delivered into the brightness and splendor of the Elysian Fields or the middle heaven. She felt as the goddess Persephone must feel each spring when she is released from the World of the Dead and allowed to breathe once again the clear fresh air of Earth and to feel the sun on her face. Sarah had no doubt that part of the reason for her dramatic change of mood was the fact that she was no longer in the presence of her Aunt Hester. But another part of the reason, perhaps the greater part, was that she was back in the mountains again, not just to visit, not just to say farewell, not just to gather a few last memories, but to stay! Not since before her father's death had she felt so free, so excited, so full of hope for the morrow. Surely all of life's sadness was behind her now. She had been allowed to suffer her allotted portion of tragedy early in life, and she had survived it. It was now behind her. There would be no more sadness, no more sorrow, no more "accidents." The rest of her life would be filled with ever-increasing happiness.

This feeling of euphoria was not soon dissipated. It remained ever with her during the days and weeks that followed. The many hours of physical exertion that she had to expend in sawing, splitting, hauling, and stacking enough firewood for the winter did nothing to diminish it. She liked to work. Nor was it dampened by the first cold, rainy day. She liked rain. If conditions outside were not suitable for working, she simply moved inside, stoked up the fire, and made herself comfortable by the stove. From there she moved inside again–into her head–and once she stoked the fires of her mind, she could remain lost in contemplation for many agreeable hours. When she had first made the decision to move back to the old Puckett place, she was not sure whether she would be happy living alone, or whether she could even do it. After all, she had never done it before. But now, after her first month of living without human companionship, she wondered if she would ever be happy living *with* people again. She thought she could be quite happy to spend the rest of her life with no other company than that of the birds and deer and squirrels. The life of the mountain hermit seemed to come quite natural to her. She was, however, looking forward to seeing her Uncle Jacob at Christmas.

As she descended the mountain, her spirits remained high, dispelling any fanciful theoretical notions she might have entertained concerning the correlation between altitude and emotional well-being. She did not even allow the fact that it was Christmas Eve and not snowing put a damper on her festive spirit. Christmases without snow were something she had come to expect. If one did not expect snow on Christmas, then on the occasional Christmas that it *did* snow, it was all the more thrilling. She was determined that her enjoyment of the holidays at her Uncle Jacob's would not be dependent on precipitation. If it did not snow on Christmas, she would simply go back up to the mountain after the holidays and sit and wait until it *did* snow. Seldom did a winter go by when it did not snow at all. It *had* happened–she remembered the awful non-winter of 1937–but fortunately it had not happened often.

To test her new-found optimism she decided to visit her Uncle Nathan and Aunt Hester before going on to Jacob's. She found them very much as she had left them. Nathan seemed to have recovered himself a little, but Hester, if anything, appeared to have slipped even further into despondency. Her cheeks were ashen and hollow, her eyes brooding and devoid of life. She appeared to have lost weight. Sarah could not help but be reminded of the physical deterioration that both she and her mother had undergone as a result of the emotional shock and suffering–and in her mother's case, complete withdrawal–that had been caused by her father's death. Sarah had always thought her Aunt Hester to be made of a different alloy, richer in steel, than either she or her mother. She had always thought of her as someone who could meet tragedy head on and not give an inch, as someone who could take a sword in the breast and remain standing, remain fighting. It both shocked and saddened her to see that her Aunt Hester did not appear to be fighting now. She was still standing, but she did not appear to be fighting.

The main reason Sarah had wanted to stop at Nathan and Hester's was to see if she had received any mail from her mother during the month she had been away.

"She's in Boston," said Nathan with as much cheer as he could muster, as he handed her a still-sealed envelope.

Sarah took the letter and looked at the return address. It had, as Nathan had said, come from Boston. Borrowing a knife from the sinkboard, she slit open the envelope and removed the letter.

"Dear Sarah,

"Exciting news! I have made the move to Boston! Not only that, but I have a job!–my first job ever! What do they say? Life begins at forty? I guess it's true in my case–or would be with a couple of minor modifications. I'm forty-one, not forty; and life is not beginning, but beginning *again*.

"I must admit, coming to Boston to look for a job was a little intimidating. For the first time I was able to realize the anxieties your father must have experienced when he left Rushing Creek to look for work in the north. And he was only twenty! Until now I never really appreciated how much courage that took.

"Let me tell you about my job. This job reminds me of something you once said about Heaven. You said that in one of the heavens you visited, people create their own environment by simply imagining it. I remember your father saying that when he got to Heaven the first thing he would do would be to imagine himself in a cornfield so he could begin hoeing at once. Well, I would probably be rearranging my heavens every few days, but one of my heavens would certainly look something like the place I'm working now. It's a place called _____. It's one of the oldest and finest used book shops in Boston. I wish you could see it. You wouldn't believe it! If you can imagine Walter Lehman's General Store completely filled with books from floor to ceiling with only a few narrow pathways winding through, then you'll have the general idea. My job is to know what books we have, where to find them, and to be able to produce any given book on quick notice. Not only is it exciting to be around so many old books, but so many of the customers are so interesting! Some come in the shop and browse for *hours*! I have even *talked* to some of them for hours!

"Sarah, I'm happy! I hope you are happy as well. I miss you–I will always miss you–but I understand why you could not come with me. I am anxious to hear from you, to hear if you've followed through on your decision to move back to the old Puckett place. Life beings at seventeen! I certainly admire your courage. You must have gotten that from your father. If you want any books, just let me know. Between Susan Kinney and myself you will be the most literate teenage recluse in all of Appalachia!

> Love,
>
> Mother"

If seeing Hester had had a gravitational effect on Sarah's spirits–despite her resolve not to let it happen–then reading her mother's letter had caused them to soar again. She shared the letter with Nathan and Hester, wished them both a happy Christmas, and took her leave.

As she rode the mule out the lane, she was once again as high as the trees. She decided not to be overly concerned about her Aunt Hester. She knew from personal experience that people *do* recover from adversity. Both she and her mother had survived her father's death, even though the prospect for either one of them had not looked good at one time. It had taken two and a half years in her mother's case, but she *had* survived, she *had* come back, and now her life was beginning anew. Hester too would survive. She too would come back. She had done it before; she would do so again.

When she arrived at Jacob's the first thing she did was share with him her mother's letter. At the conclusion of it, Jacob smiled. "I reckon someone as smart as your mother can do just about anythang they have a mind to in this world," he said.

Sarah refolded the letter and put it back in its envelope. "I've brought you a present, Uncle Jacob," she said eagerly.

Jacob watched as she reached into the cumbersome pouch that she had brought into the house with her. "Why, hit's one of your Daddy's whirly-thangs."

"Yes, a whirligig. I finished it myself, so it's not as good as if Daddy had made the whole thing himself."

"Hit looks just fine to me," Jacob assured her, as he accepted the present. He turned the windmill with his finger and chuckled in amusement. "We'll stick it up on one of the garden fenceposts first thang in the mornin'." He set the whirligig on the table. "I was a-gwine t' wait til tomorruh t' give you your present, but seein' as how we seem t' be exchangin' presents now, I reckon thar's no sense a-waitin'."

He went to the pantry and returned with a peck basket of deep-orange-colored fruits.

"Tangerines!" exclaimed Sarah. "I haven't had a tangerine in years! I love tangerines!"

"All the way from Florida," said Jacob, tickled by her reaction. "Wait. Thar's more."

He made a second visit to the pantry and returned with a small but bulging burlap sack. She loosened the tie-strings and looked inside.

"Pecans!"

"All the way from Georgia. 'Course I didn't go all the way to Florida and Georgia myself. I didn't haf t' go no further than Walter Lehman's General Store. Walter's always got his store well-stocked at Christmas time."

"Thank you, Uncle Jacob," she exclaimed, embracing him. "Thank you very much."

"Have you et?"

"No."

"Good, 'cause supper's almost ready. I hope you can stand my cookin'. I didn't use no meat."

"I'm sure I'll love it."

After supper, while Sarah did the dishes, Jacob built a roaring fire in the parlor stove. By the time Sarah had finished in the kitchen, the room was toasty warm.

"Mind if I ax you a favor?" ventured Jacob, when the two had settled themselves near the stove.

"What is it?" She could see that Jacob was holding his open Bible in his lap.

"Would you read the first few pages here in the Gospel of Luke? You read so much better'n I do."

"The story of the Nativity?"

Jacob nodded.

Sarah smiled. "Of course." She took the Bible. "If you hadn't suggested it, I probably would have. I've been reading this every Christmas myself since I was twelve years old. My Daddy used to ask me to read it to him."

For the next quarter hour, as the fire in the stove popped and crackled, Sarah read from the first two chapters of Luke. When she had finished, she looked up at her Uncle Jacob. He had that wonderfully sweet smile on his face that she had come to love so well. His blue eyes were twinkling with joy.

"That's a wonderful story," he sighed.

"I agree," replied Sarah. Even if it was *only* a story, she thought to herself, it was still a wonderful story. Whether this or any other story in the Bible was true, she had no idea, but she was not about to express any doubts she might have had concerning the literal truth of the Nativity story to her Uncle Jacob, not on Christmas Eve.

"D'you reckon it really happened like the Bible says?" asked Jacob.

Sarah stared at her uncle. This was the very question she had wished to avoid. "What do you mean, Uncle Jacob?"

"I mean, d'you reckon angels really appeared to folks as often in the olden days as the Bible says? In just those coupla pages thar that you read, an angel appeared to Zechariah, the husband of Elizabeth, an' spoke to *him*; then an angel appeared to Mary an' spoke to *her*; then an angel appeared to the shepherds in the fields an' spoke to *them*. In fact, a whole band of angels appeared to the shepherds. Hit sure seems like thar was a lot more angels around t' be seen in those days than thar are now."

"Well, I do know this, Uncle Jacob. Angels *do* appear to people and they *do* speak, in their own way. My friend Kati used to appear to me and speak to me, and I'm sure that she's what the gospel writers would have called an angel. Usually she appeared to me in the early mornings, but once she appeared to me on

Christmas Eve. I don't think I've ever told you that story, Uncle Jacob. It happened eight years ago, eight years ago this very night. My Daddy had taken me out hunting with him that day. It was the one and only time he ever took me hunting. He had wanted to shoot a turkey for Christmas dinner. We were out in the woods all day, but we didn't see any turkeys. Then, after we got back home, a deer walked into the clearing in front of the house and Daddy shot it. I was only nine years old at the time, and I was *very* upset. I ran away. It was almost dark, and I didn't even have a coat on, but I just kept running. I ran all the way down off Puckett Mountain and all the way up the side of the next mountain. By the time I reached the top, it was completely dark. I just crawled under some rocks and cried. I remember crying for a long time. Then I got very cold, and I remember thinking that I was going to die. But then I thought it would be all right if I died, because then I could go to Heaven and be with Aunt Ruth. I remembered your telling me that Aunt Ruth had liked animals too." She smiled. "What I didn't know then was that it was *Aunt Ruth* who came to *me*—that is, if Annie Whitehead is right about Kati and Aunt Ruth being the same soul. I had always known her as Kati. But there she was. When I tried to find my way home through the woods in the dark, there she was, bright and shining and beautiful. It's a good thing she came when she did. When she found me, I was all scratched up from running into brambles, and all scraped and bruised from stumbling over rocks. I was completely lost and shivering with cold. She led me all the way to the house. If it hadn't been for her, I probably would have died that night."

Jacob made no vocal response, but Sarah could tell from the expression of wonder and amazement on his face, that she had his complete attention. "I suppose it's because of that experience that I get a thrill whenever I read the part of the Nativity story where the angels appear to the shepherds at night. I like to imagine that the shepherds were high on a hill, like I was that night that Kati appeared to me."

"I never seen an angel myself," confessed Jacob, "at least not the bright, shinin' kind. I reckon a person's got t' be an angel hisself before he can see other angels."

"What do you mean, Uncle Jacob?"

"I mean, the only two people I ever knowed who could see angels was Ruthie an' you. You told me yourself that Ruthie was an angel . . ."

"Well, if everything that Annie told me is true, then yes, Ruth was—*is*—an angel."

"An' to my way of thinkin' *you're* an angel."

Sarah blushed in embarrassment. "I prefer to think of myself as an angel-in-the-making," she said, almost reluctantly. "We are *all* angels-in-the-making. We *all* have Heaven inside us. To me, that's the true meaning of Christmas. The story of Jesus' birth is the story of Heaven entering into Earth, of holy spirit entering into a body of flesh. To me that's symbolic of the fact that we are *all* souls in bodies—not bodies *with souls*, but souls *in bodies*. Our bodies are of the Earth; we are only in them for a little while before they return to the Earth. But our true selves—our souls— are eternal; they are of Heaven. We have God, Heaven, Divinity— whatever you want to call it—within us. We are angels in the making. That is why Jesus came to Earth in the first place: to remind us who we truly are. And I think that is why we celebrate Christmas: to remind *ourselves* who we truly are—who and *what* we truly are."

Sarah broke off. She did not wish to offend her Uncle Jacob. She had come dangerously close to saying that the story of the Nativity was to be understood symbolically, not literally. She had not done so. She had said that it *could* be understood symbolically, not that it had to be. Even something literally true could have a symbolic meaning as well.

"An' the reason we haf t' keep remindin' ourselves who an' what we truly are," added Jacob, picking up where she had left off, "is because if we don't know who an' what we are, we won't know the reason for our bein' here in the first place."

"Right!" exclaimed Sarah, pleased that her Uncle Jacob had not only not taken offense, but actually seemed to have understood and appreciated her interpretation of the Christmas message.

"An' the reason for our bein' here in the first place," he continued, "is t' seek the kingdom of God."

"Right! To seek the kingdom of God, to find the Heaven within us, to let Heaven's light shine through us, to become barns burning in the night, to become angels. At least, that's how I understand it."

Jacob laughed. "I reckon if I hang around you long enough, one day I'll be able t' understand about half of what you're sayin' . . . Come t' think of it, mebbe that's the secret: if we want angels t' come visit us, we've got t' learn t' talk their language."

"Angels don't talk in a human voice, Uncle Jacob. They put their thoughts inside our heads. What we have to learn to do is listen."

Jacob nodded and smiled. The rest of the evening passed quietly, with few words exchanged. But at some deeper level of their beings, communication continued.

Christmas morning broke bright and clear. It had not snowed during the night, nor was there any snow in the air. Christmas morning or no, there were still animals to be fed and cows to be milked. Working together, however, Jacob and Sarah were able to dispatch the necessary chores in short order. They then set about to mount the whirligig on the garden fencepost nearest the kitchen window. That completed, they spent the rest of the morning visiting with Isaac and Martha, who had houseguests of their own. Their son Benjamin and wife and son were visiting from Raleigh. Sarah quickly befriended Benjamin's son, two-year-old Jonathan, and passed most of the time at Isaac's playing with and being entertained by him.

In the afternoon Harriet Ogle came to visit, bearing gifts for Jacob. These consisted of a pair of hand-knitted woolen mittens and a spicy apple cake. Although both Jacob and Harriet insisted it wasn't necessary, Sarah excused herself after an hour or so, to allow the widow and widower to have some time to themselves. She spent the rest of the daylight hours walking in the woods. In the evening she wrote a letter to her mother.

The next morning being Sunday, all members of both Wicker houses, permanent residents and guests alike, went to church. Sarah was pleased to see Jemmy Hicks in church. They exchanged brief smiles but did not speak.

After the service the Reverend Eby wheedled an invitation to Jacob's for dinner. As the greater part of the burden of preparing the meal fell to Sarah, and as she had not been forewarned, the dinner was rather modest. The preacher did not seem to mind. In fact, he had expected nothing more. He knew when he placed himself in the hands of a widower who could hardly cook at all and a teenaged girl who refused to cook with meat, that he was not likely to get the kind of dinner that he got when he went to Mary Bryson's or Harriet Ogle's or Hester Andersson's.

It was the opportunity to visit with both Jacob and Sarah at the same time that he had found impossible to pass up. So, while the dinner itself was rather limited in its variety, the dinner conversation ranged far and wide, with the Reverend Eby expressing his concern for Hester one minute and his interest in Sarah's return to the old Puckett place the next. Some subjects, however, were not discussed, among them the symbolic meaning of Christmas and the declining frequency of communications from angels. Perhaps they would have been had the Reverend Eby stayed longer. But soon after he had finished his second helping of apple spice cake–Harriet Ogle's gift to Jacob, a royal conclusion to an otherwise plebeian dinner–and his third cup of coffee, he got up to leave.

"Jemmy Hicks asked me to stop over and see his father today," he explained as he put on his coat. "Apparently Wesley has taken a turn for the worse."

"I know hit's an unchristian thang t' say," said Jacob, also getting up from the table, "but if you ax me, Wesley Hicks took a turn for the worse when Granny first pulled him from his mother's womb."

"It's not unchristian to speak the truth, Jacob. If there's a sin known to man, Wesley Hicks has committed it. Still, even the worst sinners deserve our prayers. Jesus taught us to forgive–not once, not seven times, but seventy times seven. By my reckonin' Wesley Hicks still has one or two forgivenesses comin'.

"But just between you and me–and Sarah here–I'm doin' this more for Jemmy than for Wesley. Today after church was the first time that boy ever even spoke to me in a complete sentence. He's always been so shy. But I reckon most boys his age are. I remember Otis–Lord rest his soul . . .

"I feel kind of sorry for Jemmy. Not only did he have Wesley for a father, but he had six brothers who were just as bad. Folks are just naturally gonna tend to judge him by what his father and brothers done before him. But it wouldn't be fair. I think Jemmy's different. They say the fruit never falls far from the tree, and in the case of the other six Hicks boys, I'd say it's true. But in Jemmy's case it seems like the fruit might've rolled down the hill a piece."

"He does seem t' be differ'nt," agreed Jacob.

"Did you know he's been lookin' after the farm, lookin' after Wesley, and still keepin' up his school studies? That's a heavy load for a sixteen-year-old."

"What's likely t' become of him if Wesley dies?" asked Jacob.

"Hard to tell. I'd like to see some good Christian family take him in. He certainly deserves better than what he's had."

At this point Sarah could no longer remain silent. "Maybe my Uncle Nathan and Aunt Hester could take him in. Uncle Nathan was over at Mr. Hicks' a couple of months ago to fix Mr. Hicks' porch roof. He said that Jemmy helped him and that he was a good worker and that they got along well."

It was clear from the reaction on the preacher's face that Sarah's idea had fallen upon fertile soil. "You know, Sarah, that's not a bad idea. Not only would it be good for Jemmy Hicks, but it might be good for Nathan and Hester as well. They seem to be needin' some new purpose in their lives just now. If Wesley Hicks should decide to do us all a favor and leave this world anytime soon, maybe I'll just suggest that to your Uncle Nathan."

Sarah remained at her Uncle Jacob's another four days. Then, on the morning of December 31st, she filled a knapsack with the tangerines and pecans that Jacob had given her—with those she had not already eaten—and said good-by to her friend and uncle.

"When will I see you ag'in?" asked Jacob as he escorted her out the walk.

"I'll come back in the spring to get Jesse," she replied. "I'll be needing him for the plowing."

They stopped and remained silent for a moment as they studied each other's face. The peacefulness of their expressions, the joy in their smiles, the love in their eyes made further communication unnecessary.

"Tell yuh what," suggested Jacob. "I been a-meanin' t' get up to the old Puckett place for a visit for quite a few years now. Instead of you a-comin' down for Jesse, why don't I bring him up to yuh?"

"I don't mind coming down, but yes, if you're not too busy, I'd love for you to come visit."

"Hit *is* a busy time of year with the new calfs a-comin' and all, but shucks, I reckon Isaac can look after the place by hisself for a coupla days."

Whatever misapprehensions Sarah might have had about Isaac's looking after the farm himself, she kept to herself. She did not wish to discourage her Uncle Jacob from coming to visit her in the mountains. She turned to leave but had not gone two steps when she suddenly stopped and pivoted one hundred eighty degrees.

"Oh! I almost forgot. When you come up in the spring, could you stop by Uncle Nathan's to see if any mail has come for me from my mother?"

"I'll do that," Jacob assured her.

She turned again and, with a song in her heart, departed. Her spirits could not have been higher. It had been a wonderful visit, for both of them. She could easily have stayed longer–and she knew that nothing would have pleased her Uncle Jacob more–but she had a reason for deciding to leave on this, the last day of December. She wished to wake up New Year's morning at the old Puckett place, to begin the new year, 1944, in the mountains.

It was in the second week of March, after the last remaining pockets of winter snow had melted and the gradually warming sun had begun to coax reluctant trees into bud and to lure the least timid of the wildflowers out from beneath their protective blanket of leaves, that Jacob came to visit. It was the excited braying of the mule that alerted Sarah to his arrival. She had been working in the cornfield above the house, digging out tulip poplar saplings with a mattock, when the musical twittering of the birds was suddenly interrupted by Jesse's raucous greeting. She looked down toward the house, only to find the mule, under heavy load, friskily galloping up the hill in her direction, exhibiting a level of energy that one might expect to find in an animal one-half or even one-quarter of his fourteen years. After the mandatory rubbing and stroking of nose and neck, Sarah led the mule down the hill to the barn where she began to unpack him.

After removing a sack of corn and a sack of oats, she discovered that the two remaining bundles contained provisions not for the mule, but for herself: corn meal, flour, dried beans, canned goods, dried apples and peaches, even garden seed. She was especially glad for the garden seeds, as the only seed she had on hand was now three years old. She had forgotten to mention to her Uncle Jacob that she'd be needing seed. Fortunately he had had the foresight to pack some anyway. Or *someone* had. Possibly Hester. Sarah guessed that some, if not all, of the foodstuffs had come from Hester's. Perhaps she had sent the seed as well. Sarah led the mule to the house, to finish the unpacking there. Still there was no sign of Jacob.

A quarter of an hour later he came struggling up the trail. "I couldn't hold him back," he explained, out of breath. "If I hadn't a-let him go, he'd a-run right over me. I never seen him so excited."

"Hello, Uncle Jacob," said Sarah, smiling.

He returned her smile and looked about. "My, your Daddy sure did a fine job on this place, didn't he? Hit sure has come a long way since that winter I was up here a-helpin' him saw boards out of whole trees by hand. What a job that was!"

He redirected his attention to Sarah, who was still standing at the porch unpacking the mule. "I see you found the eatables your Aunt Hester sent along for you."

She smiled. "Yes, I thought it was probably Aunt Hester who sent me all this food. She's convinced that if she doesn't keep after me, I'll starve myself to death."

"You look fit an' dandy to me. I think mebbe you even put on a few pounds since I last saw you."

"Yes, I've spent a very lazy winter. I've only recently started working again . . . By the way, how *is* Aunt Hester?"

"Much better. Nathan too. An' you're responsible."

"Me? How? You mean, by my leaving?"

Jacob laughed. "No, not by your leavin'. By your puttin' that idea into Reverend Eby's haid about Nathan an' Hester bein' the best people to look after Jemmy Hicks . . . Wesley died back in January, not long after you left. Reverend Eby spoke to Nathan at the funeral. He kind of mentioned to him how he hoped that some good Christian family might take pity on Wesley's youngest son an' give him a home. Nathan took the hint. He had t' do a little talkin' to convince Hester, but in the end she came around. Jemmy's been a-livin' with them these past two months. An' they all seem t' be a-doin' just fine."

"That's wonderful news, Uncle Jacob."

"Speakin' of news, this here letter came from your mother." He reached into his hip pocket and brought forth a letter.

Taking it, Sarah looked at the return address. It was the same as the address on the previous letter. "I'll save it until later," she said, stuffing it into the pocket of her work apron. She finished transferring Hester's shipment of food into the kitchen, then turned again to Jacob, who was still admiring the restoration work that his younger brother had done on the house. "Would you like to take a walk to the top of the hill? There's a wonderful view from up there."

"Well, I made it this far," joked Jacob, "I reckon I could make it up one more hill."

They walked up the hill to the spot where Sarah had been digging when Jesse's braying had interrupted her.

"At least hit's not as overgrowed as when your Daddy first started," said Jacob, noting the hundreds of saplings that had sprung up on the hillside which only three years before had been cultivated land.

"No, not at all," agreed Sarah. "In another two days I can have all these dug out. Then I'll be ready to plow."

Jacob shook his head. "I sure do haf to admire you, tryin' t' work this place all by yourself."

"Well, I'm not planning to do as much as my Daddy did. I'm not going to keep a cow or chickens, so I won't have to raise as much corn. It occurred to me that if I didn't keep Jesse, I wouldn't need a cornfield at all. All the food I'd need for myself I could grow in the garden . . . But I wouldn't want to do without Jesse . . ."

"An' from what *I* seen, *he* wouldn't want t' do without *you*.."

"Yes, we get along fine. Besides, I *like* to plow, and I *like* to plant, and I *like* to hoe corn. I'll probably always grow a cornfield, even if it's *just* to feed Jesse. But I would always hope to grow a little more than we'd need, so we could share with the deer and the raccoons . . . Who knows? If I didn't have Jesse, maybe I'd dig this whole hillside by hand and plant a cornfield *just* for the deer and the raccoons."

"The way you have with animals," mused Jacob, "hit wouldn't surprise me if'n mebbe you couldn't get one of them deer t' pull the plow for yuh."

"May be," laughed Sarah, "may be."

She walked further up the hill and Jacob followed her. When they reached the point where the field met the trees of the forest, she turned and looked out across the mountains. Jacob did likewise.

"I love it in the early spring," she said wistfully, "when the buds first start to open. Everything looks so soft and green, almost too fragile to touch. Every day from now on, right up until the time the leaves fall in October and November, it will keep changing. Every day will be different. The mountains will be different. The sky will be different . . . In the summers my Daddy and I used to come up here and hoe. We'd come up in the early morning when it was still wet and watch the mist rise out of the hollows . . . "

"Hit sure is purty," admitted Jacob, "but I'd think hit would get a little lonesome a-livin' up here all by yourself."

"It's funny, Uncle Jacob," she said, still gazing out across the mountains, "but since I've moved back up here, I haven't felt lonely at all. I haven't really felt that I've been alone."

"Sounds to me like once you get yourself settled in up here you may never want t' come visit us poor folk down in the holler ag'in."

She laughed. "I definitely plan to come down from time to time to visit. I've already made arrangements with Uncle Nathan to work for him. He's agreed to continue paying the taxes on this place in exchange for my labor. I plan to go down to his place for two or three days every couple of weeks during the summer–just like my Daddy did. Then I'll be there for *most* of September and October to help pick the apples. I could come visit you Sundays after church during that time. And I'd love to come stay with you again next Christmas."

Jacob smiled. "Yes, I'd like that too."

It was not until after supper that Sarah opened the letter from her mother. It was dated February 20, 1944. "She wrote it just over two weeks ago," said Sarah. She read the letter aloud.

" 'Dear Sarah,

" 'More exciting news! This past week I met a woman who writes children's books. Her name is Miriam Hennessy. I had seen her before—she comes into the book shop often—but until this past week we had never really spoken. When I learned from the owner of the shop that she was a writer of children's books, I made it a special point to speak with her the next time she came in, as that is something I had always thought I might like to do myself.

" 'On the day we met, we spoke for three hours, almost without stopping. When one of us would pause for breath, the other would jump in. We found that we have so many interests in common. Since then we have had lunch together twice and she has invited me to her home. She lives alone with her husband now, their five children having all grown and left home. It was when her children were young that the idea to write children's stories first came to her. To satisfy her own children's insatiable appetite for bedtime stories, and after reading all the traditional ones, she began making up her own. But it was only three years ago, after her children were grown and had left home, that she decided to try writing any of them down. Her first two books have been moderately successful.

" 'But here's the exciting part: we are going to *collaborate* on her next book. She is going to write the stories; I am going to do the illustrations. If that one is successful, we may do another. Between the two of us, I think we have enough ideas for stories to keep us busy for the rest of our lives. In the meantime, however, I have no plans to give up my job at the book shop.' "

The letter went on for four pages. After sharing her own good news, Elizabeth turned her attention to responding to the letter she had received from Sarah. She was glad that Sarah was so enjoying living in the mountains again, was glad that she had had the opportunity to spend the Christmas holidays with her Uncle Jacob, and was shocked and saddened by the news of Otis' death.

She had already written a letter to Nathan and Hester expressing her condolences. She concluded on a more personal note:

" 'I miss and think of you often. My happiness would be complete if only you were here with me. I can only hope that some day, somehow, we will be together again.

Love,

Mother' "

For the next few moments Sarah sat quietly with the letter in her lap, then laid it on the table and turned to Jacob. "I expect you'll be wanting to get an early start in the morning?"

Jacob nodded. "Hit seems a shame t' come all this way for such a short visit, but I got t' be a-gettin' back. Thar's work t' be done."

"You can sleep downstairs," suggested Sarah. "I'll sleep in the loft."

They talked for a little while longer, then Jacob retired. Sarah sat up for another hour, writing a letter to her mother, then she too turned in for the night. In the morning she gave the letter to Jacob to mail. He placed it in his pocket, and after a breakfast of apples, hickory nuts, and corn-and-wheat cakes, he set out on foot to retrace his long journey of the day before.

Over the course of the next few weeks, spring came gently to the mountains. The first faint green tips of March exploded slowly into a full canopy of leaves, the swollen buds into full-blown blossoms. A steady procession of wildflowers graced the woodland floor with their delicate beauty. Birds and insects filled the air; new life emerged from every crack and cranny. It was during this period that Sarah first knew for certain that new life was emerging within herself as well. She had suspected it for some weeks. It was not the cessation of the monthly flow of blood that had first caused her to think she might be pregnant. She had never had the normal menstrual cramping and bleeding that her mother had led her to believe were the lot of all womankind. She never had pain, and if she bled at all, it was only a few drops. Therefore, when she went four months, then five, without a flow of blood, she thought it not unusual.

Instead, it was the weakness, the dizziness, and the nausea she had experienced during the winter that had first led her to suspect that something unusual was happening inside her body. That, and the gradual increase in weight. During the winter she could attribute her gain in weight to her relative inactivity, but as she continued to gain weight throughout the spring, and as the weight began to concentrate itself more and more in the region of her belly, it became increasingly clear to her that a new life was being created within her.

Any lingering doubts she might have had were removed one morning in late March, when, while plowing in the field above the house, she distinctly felt something move inside her. The realization that she was with child filled her with both joy and concern. As she witnessed new life being created all around her, it was exciting to think that she too was participating in the process. As from the Earth, as from the myriad life forms that inhabited the fields and forests around her, so too from her, new life would spring. She would have the opportunity to experience firsthand the miracle of birth which heretofore she had only observed. Surely that was cause for great joy and celebration.

But there were reasons for concern as well. Would she be able to endure the terrible pain that child-bearing seemed to entail? And if, by chance, both she and the baby survived the birth, would she know how to look after a baby? Would it come naturally, as it seemed to come to the creatures of the wild, or would she have to read books to learn it? Of even more immediate concern, what would be the reaction of her family and friends—of her mother, her Uncle Jacob, her Uncle Nathan, her Aunt Hester, the Reverend Eby—when they learned that she was pregnant? They would be shocked! They would want to know who the father was. Was it Frank Hicks? If so, why had she said that he had not violated her when he had? If not Frank Hicks, then who? She thought that she had already laid this matter to rest, and if she had not become pregnant, she felt confident that no one would have ever again questioned her about the events that took place on that Sunday afternoon in October. But the fact that she *had* become pregnant now changed all that. The questioning would begin all over again. If she were capable of lying, her problem would be solved. She could simply blame Frank Hicks. She could say that he had apparently taken advantage of her without her knowledge after she had lost consciousness. Of all her concerns, this was the one that filled her with the most anxiety: that she would be forced to lie to protect Jemmy Hicks.

There was also another small matter to consider: she was not married. She had never understood why women who bore children out of wedlock should be held in such scorn and contempt, but she knew that they were. She knew it from gossip she had heard on Sundays after church and from things she had overheard her Aunt Hester say. Furthermore, it seemed to make no difference whether the woman had entered into the act of intercourse voluntarily or had been forced: in either case it was the woman who was charged with the responsibility and left to carry the burden of shame. She remembered Allison McGill, the young teenaged girl whose baby she had helped to deliver. Allison had apparently become pregnant out of wedlock and had chosen—or had been forced by her parents—to marry before the baby was born. Sarah wondered if she too should be thinking of marrying. She had no desire to marry the baby's natural father. She would prefer to live with the shame than to marry Jemmy Hicks. Whatever his feelings might have been for her, she had no such feelings for him. She was prepared to commit a sin against her own soul by lying to protect him from the wrath of the community, but she was not prepared to marry him. No, that was out of the question.

Again she thought of young Allison. Allison had not married her baby's natural father, but instead had married Caleb McGill, a good and responsible man some thirty years her senior. Presumably, by so doing, she had escaped much, if not all, of the scorn that would have befallen her had she borne the child out of wedlock. Also, by so doing, she had given her child a name, made him "legitimate." Sarah could not begin to comprehend how a child born out of wedlock could be any less "legitimate"–any less valid, any less real–than a child born to wed parents, but she knew that a child so born could be stigmatized for life, and not for any fault of its own, but for a "sin" committed by its mother. The idea of marrying did not come naturally to her. Therefore, when she thought of it at all, it was not for her own sake, but for the sake of the unborn child within her. And when she thought of prospective husbands, there was only one person who came to mind: someone for whom she already felt a strong love and affection, someone with whom she was already very comfortable, someone who would be a gentle and loving father. Like young Allison, she would choose not to marry someone her own age, but someone over thirty years her senior, someone old enough to be her father–or her father's brother.

The idea of marrying her Uncle Jacob certainly had its merits, not the least of which being that by marrying him she would be doing the "right thing" by her child. It would be the sensible thing to do, the "responsible" thing. Yet she had no right to assume that her Uncle Jacob would consent to marry *her*. He was, after all, one of the most respected men in all of Rushing Creek, a stalwart of the community. What would become of his good name should he suddenly marry his own niece, a teenaged girl over thirty years younger than himself? He could very well become the subject of malicious gossip and ridicule, especially when his young wife gave birth to a child only a few weeks after the wedding. Even if he *were* willing to marry her, Sarah was not sure that she would allow him to sacrifice his own honor in order to save hers, or even her child's. Moreover, he might have other plans as far as matrimony was concerned. He had, after all, been keeping company with Harriet Ogle for the past three years.

These were the kinds of thoughts that drifted in and out of Sarah's mind during the months of April and May, but like the bees and other pollinating insects that drifted from blossom to blossom, none of them lingered for long. The world was too beautiful for her to dwell long on anxious thoughts, the life force within her too irrepressible, her joy too deep. Alone in her mountain abode, it was easy to imagine that the rest of the world did not exist at all.

Early in June came a reminder that the rest of the world *did* exist. She was working in the garden when she heard the clopping of hooves coming up the rocky trail toward the house. Slowly, carefully, and with effort, she got to her feet and walked to the fence. It had been three months since she had seen another human being, and she knew that it was just a matter of time before someone would be coming to check on her. It was not a moment to which she had been looking forward. She knew that no one now could possibly mistake her condition for a simple gain in weight. This time she would be obliged to give a very clear and thorough explanation.

She had hoped that the person to whom she would first give that explanation would be her Uncle Jacob, but when she saw the head and chest of a large black horse emerge from behind the trees, she realized that it was not her Uncle Jacob, but her Uncle Nathan, to whom she would have to break the news. She was both surprised and relieved when the horse's rider came into view. It was not her Uncle Nathan after all. It was Jemmy Hicks.

From her position of partial concealment behind the garden fence, she watched with curiosity and some amusement as Jemmy rode into the clearing, reined in the horse, and attempted to dismount. It was apparent that he was not accustomed to being on a horse, as, in order to bring his mount to a stop, he had pulled on the reins too abruptly, causing the animal to rear up, and now, in his attempt to get off, he was holding the left rein too taut, causing the animal to turn in circles. Finally he succeeded in half-dismounting, half-falling out of the saddle and onto the ground. Picking himself up, he led the horse to a young tree at the edge of the clearing, and, after dropping the reins several times, finally succeeded in securing them around the trunk.

Sarah continued to watch as he then made his way nervously toward the house on foot, his eyes wide and fixed on the door. As of yet he had not seen her.

"Jemmy?"

Startled, he looked about.

"I'm here, in the garden."

"Oh!" he cried, suddenly seeing her. He redirected his course in her direction. "Mr. Nathan sent me up t' give yo this." He pulled a letter out of his pocket.

Sarah took the letter over the fence. She saw that is was from her mother. "How did you ever find your way up here?"

"I been up here b'fore. Me an' Frank was up this way a-huntin' a coupla years ago. Thar weren't nobody here then."

She shoved the letter into the pocket of her apron. "I don't suppose you've had any dinner, have you?"

"Nope. I been a-ridin' since early this mornin'."

"I was about to stop for dinner. Would you like to join me?"

"Okay, but I cain't stay long. Mr. Nathan wants me back b'fore dark."

Sarah quickly gathered a couple handfuls of lettuce and peas from the garden, then went to the gate and let herself out. When she came around the corner of the fence, Jemmy's eyes nearly popped from their sockets. His mouth dropped open. "Wh-what happened t' yo?"

"I had an accident," she replied calmly.

Jemmy followed her into the house. "Is . . . is yo gwine t' have a baby?" he asked anxiously.

"Yes . . . I was sorry to hear your father died."

He stared at her, uncomprehending.

"I understand you've been living with my Uncle Nathan and Aunt Hester."

He nodded nervously. 'Yeah, they been real good t' me . . . Who . . . who's baby is it?"

"It's *my* baby . . . How do you like working with my Uncle Nathan?"

"Uh, hit's okay. He tells funny stories."

Sarah was glad to hear that her Uncle Nathan was telling stories again. "Have you begun picking strawberries yet?"

"I only just got out of school yesterday. Miss Hester's been a-pickin' most of the strawburries so far . . . I expect I'll be a-helpin' t'morruh though. Mr. Nathan said *yo* might want t' come down an' help pick strawburries too."

She smiled. "Would you tell my Uncle Nathan that I won't be able to pick strawberries this year? But tell him I'm definitely planning to come down in the fall to help him pick apples."

Sarah was aware that Jemmy had not stopped staring at her protruding belly since she had stepped out from behind the garden fence.

"Jemmy, could I trust you not to tell anyone about this?"

"What should I tell Mr. Nathan? One of the reasons he sent me up here, besides t' bring yo yo'r letter, was t' see if yo was all right."

"Tell him I'm fine. Just don't tell him that I'm going to have a baby. Okay?"

"O-okay, if that's what yo want."

"It is. Now, why don't we sit down at the table and have some dinner?"

Jemmy pulled out a chair and sat down. "This is dinner?" he asked, looking about him. There was nothing on the table but a pan of cornbread, a plate of lettuce and raw carrots, and a bowl of unshelled, uncooked peas. "Ain't yo even gwine t' cook the peas?"

"I prefer them raw, but if you want me to cook some for you, I will. It would take some time though. I'd have to build a fire."

"No, no need t' do that. I'll try them like this."

Before she realized what he was doing, he had picked up one of the pea-pods and had pushed it into his mouth. She watched with considerable interest as he tried to masticate the tough, fibrous pod. Finally, after a heroic but unsuccessful effort, he simply swallowed it.

"I suggest we just eat the peas inside," said Sarah, trying not to sound like his mother lest she embarrass him, "and save the shucks for your horse."

"I think mebbe that's a good idea," he replied, gasping for air.

753

When they had finished their simple repast, Sarah carried the bowl of empty pea shells and carrot tops and a bucket of water out to the horse. After the animal had eaten the kitchen scraps and drunk its fill, she held the reins as Jemmy climbed into the saddle.

"It's a good thing you have Blackie," she said. "Uncle Nathan says that no matter where he is, he can always find his way home, even in the dark."

"Yeah, he told me the same thang."

"Remember," she said, placing her hands on her swollen belly, "this is our secret. Okay?"

"Okay."

He turned the horse and rode off down the trail. As Sarah watched him disappear from sight, she wondered if it had been just an accident or an act of Providence that it had been Jemmy, and not her Uncle Nathan or her Uncle Jacob, who had come to deliver her letter and to inquire of her well-being. With the birth of her baby now only six weeks away–the nine-month gestation period would terminate the third week in July–it was quite possible that she would have the baby before anyone, besides Jemmy Hicks and herself, even knew she was pregnant. It would be no easier to explain a baby than it would be to explain a pregnancy, but not telling anyone beforehand did have one very distinct advantage: if she should by chance *lose* the baby, then she would have nothing to explain at all. She and Jemmy could take their secret with them to their graves. On the other hand, not telling anyone would mean that there would be no possibility of her getting married before the baby was born. The child, if it survived, would, in the eyes of the world, be "illegitimate," a "bastard." If only there was some way of knowing *now* whether the baby would live or die. But without benefit of such knowledge, she realized that the only way to assure her child of a "legitimate" birth would be to *act*, and to act very quickly. Time was running out.

She thrust her hand into the pocket of her apron and pulled out the letter from her mother. She had seen no sense in opening it earlier as she would not have had time to send an answer back with Jemmy anyway. She tore open the envelope and removed the neatly folded letter. It was dated May 22nd.

"Dear Sarah,
"I have received a rather surprising proposal of marriage, which I am giving serious consideration. Because you were so close to your father I do not know how you will feel about my marrying again, and therefore I have decided not to give an answer until I have heard your thoughts on the matter.
"I think you may be as surprised as I was to learn that the proposal of marriage has come from your Uncle Jacob . . ."

Sarah's fingers clutched the letter so tightly that she crumpled it. She could not believe what she had just read. She read it again.

"I think you may be as surprised as I was to learn that the proposal of marriage has come from your Uncle Jacob. It is clear from his letter that he is as much interested in *you and I* being together as he is in *he and I* being together, and since he is convinced that you will never come to Boston, he decided he had to provide me with a reason to return to Rushing Creek. He pointed out–quite correctly, I might add–that I could 'write stories and draw pictures' just as well in Rushing Creek as I can in Boston. My friend Miriam and I could even collaborate by mail. I would have to give up my job at the book shop, of course, but if I continue to spend as much time on stories and illustrations as I have these past months, I might have to do that in any case.
"I have always liked your Uncle Jacob, Sarah. He is perhaps the sweetest man I've ever met. I could very easily accept his proposal. But if you do not approve, I will not do so. Nor do I think Jacob would want me to. Think it over. Take your time. There's no hurry. Even if I do decide to return to Rushing Creek, it would not be before the end of the year.
"I took a walk through the Common yesterday (Sunday). I was reminded of the walks that you and I used to take on Sunday

mornings. The Common is very green now. Spring comes even to the city.

"Take care, my darling daughter, until we meet again.

Love,

Mother"

For the next few minutes Sarah stood absolutely motionless, but inside her brain, thoughts were being generated at a furious rate. Her mother returning to Rushing Creek! Her mother marrying her Uncle Jacob! It was almost too incredible to believe! Did she approve? Of course she approved! It was the nearly perfect solution! She would have her mother back. Her Uncle Jacob would have someone with whom to share his big empty house and his lonely life. Her child would have loving grandparents to dote on it. The only respect in which this solution, this arrangement, fell short of perfection was that it did not provide a father for her child. Barring some unforeseen miracle, her baby now would almost certainly be born out of wedlock. But it was becoming increasingly clear to her that that was the way Providence wanted it. Perhaps it was just as well that she did not marry. She remembered the promise that she had made to her cousin Otis: not to marry before he returned. When she had made that promise, she had not dared to think that the worst might happen, that he might be killed—blown to pieces— and never return. By not marrying, regardless of what consequences that might have for herself or for her unborn child, she would at least be keeping her promise to her cousin Otis.

The heat was crushing. Not a breath of air was stirring. It was as though a large, smothering hand had been pressed down over the mountains, cutting off all circulation of air, trapping the heat beneath it, and causing the Earth and all it inhabitants to swelter in their own exudations and to pant for breath. The month of July, only a few hours old, had begun exactly as the month of June had ended. No storm had come during the night to clear the air. As Sarah wiped the perspiration from her eyes and from her brow, she vowed that if she ever became pregnant again, she would arrange it in such a way that her baby would not come due in the middle of the summer. She found it next to impossible to hoe her corn. She could scarcely bend over. Even simple movement had become difficult. Even *breathing* had become difficult. So great in size had become the new being who had taken up residence in her womb that some of her own vital organs–her lungs and her bladder, among them–now had no room in which to expand. In addition to being crushed by the heavy, unbreathable air from without, she was also being crushed by her own child from within. Yet somehow she had to find the patience and the will to endure another two weeks of this. She was not looking forward to the pain of childbirth, but at least when it was over, she would have her own body back, she would be able to function in a normal manner again. Several hours of excruciating pain could hardly be any more difficult to bear than prolonged *weeks* of impeded movement and labored breathing.

She realized that her thoughts were turning negative. Straightening herself up, she caressed her full-blown belly to assure the new life inside her that she was not harboring any ill feelings toward it. She looked down the rows of belly-button-high corn. Although it was only mid-morning she was already feeling tired. In three hours she had hoed less than a dozen rows. Needing inspiration, she raised her eyes and allowed her gaze to sweep slowly across the panorama. Through the heavy blue haze, gaseous images of mountains shimmered in the distance. Again she wiped the sweat from her eyes, but the visibility did not improve. She focused her gaze on the high peak to the south. It hardly seemed possible to her now that there had been a time when she could run, without stopping, from the spot on which she was now standing to the top of that peak–could traverse all that distance–in just over two hours! She doubted now that she could make it in a day—*if* she could make it at all. It would be folly, of course, to even try.

Or would it? Clearly she needed a diversion. It was apparent that she was not making much progress in her hoeing. She looked to the west, hoping to see thunderheads building on the horizon. But it was too early in the day. Rain, if it came at all, would not come until late afternoon. Again she turned her gaze to the high peak to the south. If she took it slowly enough, she thought, she could probably make it. She would not be able to make it over and back in one day, but she should be able to make it over. She could take food and a blanket and spend the night. Then, in the event of a late-afternoon or evening thunderstorm, or even a storm during the night, she would have the best vantage point in the mountains from which to watch it. Perhaps not quite the best. In her present condition she would never be able to climb all the way to the top of the highest rocks. She would have to settle for something less than that, but still, even if she could only make it to the base of the rocks, the view would be worth the climb. Even if the storm did not materialize, the long laborious climb would not be without its reward: there would still be the sunrise the following morning. And as the following morning would be Sunday, somehow that seemed especially appropriate. She remembered the one other time that she had spent the night on her "holy mountain." After her extraordinary visit to the worlds of Heaven, she had awakened that morning to see the sun rising in the east. She had promised herself then that one day she would return to watch another sunrise. What better time than the present?

Foolhardy or no, the decision was made. With her hoe in hand, she headed down the hill toward the house. Leaving the hoe on the porch, she entered the house and removed the blanket from her bed. After briefly reclaiming her loft from the squirrels in the late winter, she had been forced once again to retreat to the bed downstairs, as her increasing bulk had made climbing the ladder too difficult. She decided to take no food for the journey. Fresh greens would not keep, and it was too hot for anything baked. For the past month she had been living largely on berries that she had found in the woods anyway.

The service berries were now past, but there were still raspberries to be found, and the blueberries were just beginning to ripen. If she got hungry she could always find something to eat in the wild, just as her fellow creatures did every waking day of their lives. She rolled up her blanket, secured it at both ends with a rope, and slung it onto her back. Bulging both fore and aft, she set off down the mountain.

When after a slow, careful descent she reached the small stream at the bottom, she paused to drink and to refresh herself. She lingered for the better part of an hour along the shaded stream, splashing the cool water onto her arms and legs, and submerging her face in it. As she started to ascend the mountain to the south, she could feel an ever-so-slight breeze beginning to blow against her still-wet face. Finally the hot, humid mass of air had begun to move. It might rain yet!

Her ascent of the mountain was excruciatingly slow. She found in many places that it was easier to turn and walk backwards, or even to sit down and push off her legs, almost as though she were rowing a boat up the steep incline, than it was to attack the mountain head-on. She stopped frequently to rest. She saw no reason to hurry. Even if her fool's journey took her ten or eleven hours, instead of the six or eight she had estimated, she would still have enough time to make the top before dark.

About halfway up, she stopped again to rest and to catch her breath. She was about to resume her journey when suddenly she felt a sharp contraction in her belly. She had had mild contractions before, over the course of the past several weeks, but this one seemed a bit stronger than anything she had experienced heretofore. It passed rather quickly, and after another few minutes, she continued on her way.

By mid-afternoon she had completed about three-quarters of her ascent of the mountain, but the most difficult part still lay ahead. The course from here to the top was as much vertical as horizontal and would require her to clamber over rocks and to fight her way through thickets of mountain laurel. She was about to enter into the laurel when she heard the first rumbling of thunder in the distance. The sky to the west had become increasingly dark over the course of the past hour, and she realized that she might be in a race against the approaching storm. She knew that she could find shelter amongst the rocks at the top if she could just make it in time. Also, over the course of the past hour, she had become aware that she might be in a race of another kind: since her first contraction, she had had two more. After the second she had thought briefly of returning home, but as home at the time was close to six hours away and the shelter of the rocks less than two, she had decided to push on.

The race on her part would be a very slow one. She was not about to risk slipping and falling or doing anything else that might injure the young life that she had been carrying within her for the past eight and a half months. She was quite prepared to take a drenching if need be. She had been caught in the rain before. But it shouldn't come to that. She figured that even if she could do no better than maintain her present slow but deliberate pace, she would still be able to reach shelter in time. Over the years she had seen enough storms come over the mountains to be able to judge, within minutes, the time of their arrival, and she estimated this one to be still three-quarters of an hour away.

What she had not counted on, however, was that which happened next. Her progress was suddenly interrupted by yet another contraction, the strongest and most prolonged one thus far, and this one was accompanied by a sudden rush of water from her womb. Convinced that the birth of her baby was now imminent, she lowered herself to the ground and made herself as comfortable as possible amongst the rocks and clumps of mountain laurel. But when after ten full minutes nothing further happened, she struggled to her feet and resumed her journey.

But the ten-minute delay had cost her the race against the storm. Before she was able to reach the shelter of the rocks, the clouds burst. Immediately she removed the blanket from her back and clutched it to her bosom in an attempt to keep it dry. What was already a difficult climb became even more difficult as she was now left with only one free hand with which to grab onto roots and bushes to pull herself up and over rocks, all of which–roots, bushes, and rocks–were fast becoming slickened by the rain. The last remaining section of the climb, which would have taken only ten minutes before the storm, took a full twenty. With the rain beating on her back, she virtually crawled the last forty yards. By the time she reached shelter beneath the protruding bow of one of the great stone ships that straddled the ridge of the mountain, she was exhausted and soaking wet. Immediately she divested herself of her wet clothing and wrapped herself in the blanket, which, as a result of her efforts, had remained almost completely dry. She made a quick survey of her shelter. It could hardly be called a cave, she thought, as it had not been carved out by water, nor was it underground. It was more like a massive rock lean-to with one end open. At the moment a curtain of rain had been drawn across the open end. Retreating as far back under the low-pitched roof as she could comfortably fit, she settled herself in the bed of dried leaves that had blown in, and turned her full attention to the storm. It was, after all, for the purpose of possibly witnessing the first bona fide thunderstorm of the summer, that she had undertaken this foolhardy journey in the first place. As thunder rolled across the tops of the mountains and flashes of lightning illuminated the darkening sky, she felt the muscles of her uterus contract again. Despite her discomfort, she all but laughed outloud. All she had sought was a little diversion, she mused to herself. At the moment she was being dealt just about all the diversion her mind and body could reasonably accommodate!

The storm abated just before nightfall, but her labor did not. As she huddled in the dark under the rock with her blanket wrapped around her, her contractions continued, each succeeding one more intense and more prolonged than the one before. But even through the contractions were now more frequent–coming about ten minutes apart–and were lasting about a minute each, there was still very little pain. Discomfort, but not pain.

The real pain was yet to come. By midnight the contractions had increased in frequency to one every two or three minutes and were lasting in duration up to a minute and a half. She could now feel the baby coming, forcing its head into the birth canal. She had been lying in the bed of dried leaves, but in an effort to seek relief from the pain, she struggled to a squatting position, and with her hands clutching her knees, and her neck and shoulders pressing against the rock above her, she began to take deep breaths and to push downward with her abdominal muscles in an effort to expel the baby inside her as quickly as possible. The pain was now unbearable, and there was no relief from it. For the first time she understood what young Allison had gone through. And *she* did not have Annie to help her, had no one to drive an ax under the bed–had no bed!–had no one to brew her "birthin' tea" to numb the pain–the ever-present, never-ending, unremitting pain. She felt as though she were being ripped apart, split open with an ax. She continued to breathe and push, breathe and push. Finally, after what must have been an hour and a half, she could feel the top of the head emerge. She increased her efforts. Suddenly the whole head was out. The worst was now past. She placed her hands under the baby's head to cradle it, and in a matter of minutes the shoulders emerged, followed quickly by the rest of the body.

A great feeling of relief rushed through her. The terrible ordeal was over. Her baby was born, and it was alive! She could hear it breathing! She could feel it moving! Drawing the infant to her breast she pulled the blanket around the both of them, then fell exhausted onto the bed of leaves.

Not until the first glimmer of morning light was she able to see the miracle that had been wrought during the night. With great anticipation, she lifted the blanket and looked upon the small face that lay sleeping against her breast with its slightly parted mouth still touching her moist nipple. Rolling gently onto her side, she eased the baby off of her and onto its back. Two arms, two legs, two hands, two feet, tiny fingers and toes, all covered with blood but all accounted for. Nothing seemed to be missing. Even the umbilical cord and placenta were still attached. When the baby awoke she would have to find a means of tying off the cord and cutting it. She could see now that she had had a little girl.

She removed herself from the blanket and was about to wrap the infant in it when she noticed something very curious. An unusual light was emanating from the child. It was a light she had seen before. She remembered what Annie had said about souls-waiting-to-be-born choosing their own parents. Annie had said that *she*, Sarah herself, had chosen both her mother *and* her father. She had wondered about that at the time, but had later forgotten to ask Annie to explain what it meant. Did it mean that as a soul-yet-to-be-born she had somehow arranged for her parents to meet and marry? If *that's* what it meant, then her pre-Earth-life matchmaking skills must have been extraordinary. Her father had been born in North Carolina, her mother in Massachusetts. Just getting them together in the first place must have been a prodigious task. How had she accomplished it? But perhaps Annie had meant something else. The next time she went to visit Annie, she would have to ask. Now that she had decided not to leave the mountains, she expected to have many opportunities for such visits.

But Annie had clearly said that she had chosen her mother. What ever ambivalence there might have been about her being responsible for her parents meeting and marrying, there was no ambivalence about that: she had *chosen* her mother. And this had led her to speculate on the possibility that some soul that she had known in this or in some previous life might choose *her* as a mother, might choose to re-enter the world as *her* child. She had thought that possibly her father might choose to return through her, especially now that she had moved back to the old Puckett place . . . But this was not her father. It was not his light . . . She had also considered the possibility that her cousin Otis, whose life had been cut so short, might seek to re-enter the Earth plane, to return to his family, as her son or daughter (most likely her son; she could not imagine Otis as a girl) . . . But this was not Otis . . . No. This was a light that had first appeared to her in the pre-dawn hours of the morning back in Springfield when she was just a little girl, and which had paid her many a subsequent early-morning visit throughout her childhood as she lay in bed in the dark. This was the light that had appeared to her that terrible

Christmas Eve when her father had shot the deer, when she was so distraught, so frightened, so lost in the forest. This was the light that had led her safely home. This was the light that had appeared to her another time, on this very mountain, and which she had followed to the top of the high rocks, and beyond—out of her body and into other worlds. This was light *from* another world. This was Kati!

She covered the sleeping infant with the blanket and got to her feet. Picking up her wet clothing, she emerged from her shelter beneath the rock and took a deep breath of the early morning air. It smelled of wet pine! Draping her clothing over a nearby laurel bush to dry, she set her course for the high rocks. As she made her way through the graveyard of great stone ships in the morning twilight, her head was reeling, partly from weakness and hunger, partly from excitement and anticipation. She was scarcely less excited than she had been as a child of eight when she had first discovered her "holy mountain." What could it mean? Why had this soul which was beyond the Earth plane chosen once again to re-enter the Earth? And why through *her*? She had no idea, but just to consider the possibilities filled her with dizzying exhilaration and joy.

When she reached the top of the highest rocks, she felt again as though her soul might leap right out of her body! She was above the clouds! Mist, like fluffs of cotton batting, had settled into all the hollows, but above the mist where she was, the air was clear all the way to the far horizons. The storm had worked its cleansing magic. Standing on the bow of her great stone ship, she turned in all directions, surveying the great green ocean rolling and cresting and foaming beneath her, lapping at the hull of her ship. Then, raising her arms and extending them out from her sides, as if to embrace it all, she turned to the east to watch the sunrise.

END